PATRIC'S SAGA

PATRIC'S SAGA

The story of Ireland's high king, Brian Boru
and his mystical wife, Kormlada

A Novel By Leticia Remauro

iUniverse, Inc.
New York Lincoln Shanghai

PATRIC'S SAGA

The story of Ireland's high king, Brian Boru and his mystical wife, Kormlada

iUniverse books may be ordered through booksellers or by contacting:

iUniverse
2021 Pine Lake Road, Suite 100
Lincoln, NE 68512
www.iuniverse.com
1-800-Authors (1-800-288-4677)

ISBN-13: 978-0-595-36512-8 (pbk)
ISBN-13: 978-0-595-80945-5 (ebk)
ISBN-10: 0-595-36512-4 (pbk)
ISBN-10: 0-595-80945-6 (ebk)

Printed in the United States of America

This book is dedicated to my husband, Bob who encouraged me to keep on going until I got the job done.
To my father, Tony who was proud of everything I did.
And to my grandson, Ty who inspires me toward life.

Acknowledgements

I want to offer my sincere thanks to all those who encouraged me through the twelve years it took to finally finish this book:

My friend, Joe who read more drafts than any editor has had to endure. My sister-in-law, Colleen who was second only to Joe. My colleague, Sidney who was second to Colleen. My mother, Jo and my daughter, Jennifer who kept egging me on even while I was hogging the computer. My son, Robert who ate pizza far too often because I was wrapped up in my writing. My friend and boss, Timothy Carey who was the only one to be really tough on me. His son, Sean who helped me organize my thoughts. My friend, Chris who set a great example for me. My friends, Marge, Pat and Kathy who were always eager to accompany me on my many trips to Ireland. Donna, who almost joined us. Adrian Flannelly and John O'Neill who got me to Beal Boru safely. Dairmud and Doreen Drennan of Kincora House Hotel in Lisdoonvarna for their patience and hospitality as I searched for still more facts. Mary and Frank McCormac of Boston Tubber, who stayed up late at night to discuss Irish culture. The Irish Tourist Board. And finally, my friends in the Irish-American community, too numerous to mention, who encouraged this full-blooded Italian to reach back in time to find her Celtic roots.

I used the following internet resources to check facts contained in this book:

rootsweb.com—Ireland's History in Maps

searchagrgon.com

royaltynu.com—The Royal History of Ireland

okelly.net

obrienclan.com   bmgen.com

fanaticus.org   alia.ie

irishclans.com   behindthename.com

iol.ie   en.wikipedia.org

roman-emperors.org   doyle.com

indigo.ie   rte.ie

sbaldw.home.mindspring.com   fortunecity.com

newadvent.org—Catholic Encyclopedia

The following manuscripts provided additional resources:
Accessed through Berkeley Digital Library: *Heimskringla—Saga of Olaf Harald-son* and *The Story of Burnt Njal (Njal's Saga)*
Accessed through tripod.com—*Kincora* attributed to MacLiag (c.1015)
Accessed through goonan.net—*Annals of the Four Masters*
Accessed through aol.com—*Annals of Munster* and *Annals of Innishfallen*

The following reference books provided additional resources:
Compton's Encyclopedia
The Encyclopedia Americana

I also read the following books related to the topic:
How the Irish Saved Civilization by Thomas Cahill
Lion of Ireland by Morgan Llywelyn
The Princes of Ireland—The Dublin Saga by Edward Rutherfurd

This book is a work of fiction. No parts of it are copied or reproduced. Any resemblance of its characters to living people is wholly unintentional. I have done my best to acknowledge the resources used to check historical facts used in this book. Any mistakes are solely my own and any oversight is sincerely unintentional.

11TH CENTURY IRELAND

PROLOGUE
THE BEGINNING

▼

Darmaid was not the type of man to be described as worrisome. In fact, it was his job to keep the calm in his tiny village. He was the chief, better known as Ri Tuath in the Gaelic tongue of his time. He was tall and thin, with the ruddy coloring shared by many of his Dal Cais kin. A quiet man who would be described by anyone as the least likely to get involved in the troubles, but somehow the troubles found him.

He walked along the towering wooden stanchions surveying his lands. The day had been warm and still but now the wind was rising. It was blowing from the east, carrying with it a light spray of mist from the River Shannon that settled upon the budding trees of the surrounding forest. The sweet scent of moss and river grass swirled through the air. He leaned forward against the railing, praying that the fog wouldn't grow much thicker. At any other time he would have welcomed the rains. He had a freshly planted field that could stand a good soaking. But tonight he feared that a storm might provide his enemies the cover they needed to take everything he had.

The air was charged and he unconsciously rubbed his sword arm to settle the hairs standing on end as he watched a wispy cloud sail past the hazy full moon. They were gathering in the west—lying low over the mountains in a dark mass. If this storm let loose it would be powerful—the type that bent trees and raised rivers, covering any human sound with its own howling voice. If God were with him it would come quickly and be over just as soon.

He returned his gaze to the River Shannon. The mist was growing thicker— seeping through the trees that stood both north and south until it hid the reflection of the mountains that stood to the west. For all his life Darmaid had shared a relationship of love with the lively tributary—eating from it, bathing in it and transporting his goods through it. It was always there to be used in whatever way he needed but now he wondered just when it would betray him.

The wind kicked up again and he drew his woolen cloak around his ears before he moved his gaze west in the direction of Thomond where the troubles first began. Stretching northward to Connacht and west to the North Atlantic, Thomond was more than a *tuath* (ringed village) it was a vast expanse of fertile soil, mountains and estuaries sought after by every leader in the southern territory. His cousin, Cennitig, was the Ri Tuath. Perhaps more importantly, he was the leader of the Dal Cais Clan, an ancient sect descended from the invincible warrior king, Cormac Cas who was among Ireland's most revered rulers.

For as long as anyone could remember Irish chiefs were chosen for their ability to wage war. Only skilled warriors were worthy of the homage bestowed on them by the lesser men. But centuries ago in their southern territory of Munster, an edict was issued that changed the face of Irish culture for all time.

The edict came under the ancient King Oillil Olom. Both strong and cunning Oillil's people followed him without question. He raised his sons, Cormac Cas and Eagahon Mor to be as fierce as he was. But as the king grew old a competition formed between them—each vying to demonstrate that they were worthy of taking their father's place.

Over time the enmity between the men and their clans became so bitter that they were more at war with each other than against their common enemies. Eagahon Mor was Oillil's favorite, but when he died on foreign soil at the hand of an enemy the old king had no other choice than to give the throne over to Cormac Cas. Before he did Oillil issued an edict that whenever the time came that Cormac should vacate the throne it would then be passed to the Eagahonacts—the clan of Eagahon Mor. Following that the Eagahonacts would pass it to the Dal Cais—the clan of Cormac Cas. This alternation of the crown was designed to halt the hostility that existed between the clans and to ease Oillil's own grief. When it was applied it resulted in an unstable political landscape that allowed foreigners to invade.

While the Dal Cais remained battle skilled and capable of protecting the territory during their reign, a transformation took place among the Eagahonacts. Forced to beg scraps from the Dal Cais they withdrew into the church, learning to negotiate for their lot until their battle skills were all but lost. It was under Eagahonact rule that the Vikings invaded Munster and founded a city of their own which they called Limerick.

Located just south of Thomond at the base of the Shannon River, Limerick became a Viking empire. It was a thriving trading port that offered goods and services from around the world as well as a home to foreigners who quickly recognized the weakness of the Eagahonacts and preyed upon it. Together with Obdub O'Neill, the leader of a fast growing northern Gaelic sect known as the O'Neill Clan, the Vikings began plundering Munster. The powerful force of Viking and O'Neill ran rough shod over the Eagahonacts and soon all men were at their mercy. Any resistance was quickly cut down and eventually the O'Neills became the most powerful clan in all of Ireland.

They installed a high ruler who they called, Ard Ri and lesser rulers for the counties of Munster, Connacht, Leinster, Ulster and Meath who they dubbed Ri Tuath Ruire. Ri Tuaths of other clans such as the Dal Cais, were only allowed to keep their villages so long as they submitted to the superior role of the O'Neills. That's when the troubles began.

It was during the last harvest that the new Ri Tuath Ruire of Munster, Donchad macCellachain, gave his sanction to the Viking earl, Imar of Limerick, to raid Thomond. Cennitig was in his bed awaiting his wife's return from her bath. When she didn't come back he went out to investigate and found her dead—pinned to the old oak by the ax in her head. It was then that the Vikings revealed themselves, jumping out from behind trees and huts to wreak havoc on the tuath. By the grace of God, Cennitig survived that raid—so did his sons, Madamion and Brian, but he would never forgive it. Together with Darmaid and several other leaders of the Dal Cais clan, Cennitig embarked on a mission to remove Viking, O'Neill and Eagahonact from Munster once and for all.

They began by raiding the Eagahonacts, claiming their lands and taking their people as slaves. Then they moved on to Limerick, capturing the city but not its earl, Imar, who escaped to Scattery Island. Finally they moved east to the fort of Cashel, the home of the kings of Munster since the days of Oilill Olom. Although they lost most of their army in Cashel, Cennitig managed to kill Donchad macCellachain and the Dal Cais recaptured the crown of Munster for the first time in two centuries.

The wind caught Darmaid's woolen cape and it swirled around his neck. He expressed his breath as he turned into it, shielding his eyes with his hand while he wondered how he ever got himself involved in such a mess. His gaze fell on his sleeping tuath and his stomach gripped. Nearly eighty acres round it carried great wealth by way of its beasts. Not the dozens of horses he managed to acquire or the hundreds of chickens his daughter, Grace tended, or the endless number of goats and sheep scattered across the field. But the two hundred head of cattle now penned up against the southern wall where the surrounding forest hung low to disguise them. They were a gift from Cennitig for his loyalty and support during the troubles. Having them could well get him killed.

His eyes continued to scan the village, moving north from the pen then up over the path past the lean-to barns and thatched herder's huts until they rested on the large building that stood at the center just beyond the gates and stanchion. Built taller than those of most other tuaths to accommodate his height, it was solidly constructed of mud, stone and thatch. On occasion it had housed hundreds of people attending his feasts. Tonight, as on any other, it housed his most prized possession—his family.

He watched the white ribbons of smoke escape through the thatch hole from the center hearth within. His wife wouldn't put the fire out until he came to bed.

To the northwest of the hall stood the stone barracks housing ninety men, mostly second and third sons of his clan who had no future in Gaelic society except as warriors. Southeast in the village were scattered no less than fifty waddle huts, mostly occupied by elder kin. Just west of the river were the numerous tents and lean-tos of his *ceiles* and *fudirs* (tenants and slaves), and by the rivers edge stood the stone structure belonging to his blacksmith.

Cavenlow was a thriving village, noted for its marketplace and the extraordinary craftsmen who sold their wares there. Darmaid pulled his cloak closer around him as he continued to worry whether or not he could protect his people in these unstable times.

He gazed once more toward the river before looking to his sentries who were now standing beside him. They were capable and loyal and it showed in the way they looked at him—assuring him they wouldn't allow his family to be harmed.

The winds seemed to be driving the storm past them. If it did let loose, Darmaid was now certain that it would only last a short while. He nodded to his sentries to give them control of his tuath then turned to depart in silence.

In the distance a hawk cried. Darmaid looked up, curious that the beast would fly in such weather. He followed its path for a moment as it soared into a cloud passing the moon then he descended the split rail ladder so he could join his wife in bed.

He crossed the field with the wind howling around him and his cape flapping wildly. He heard a dog barking and he turned up his ear trying to mark its location. It was somewhere in the forest just south of where he stood, barking and growling so intensely that he decided to investigate.

He released his long sword from its holster at his back before moving forward. His heart hammered in his chest as he struggled to see beyond the mist and darkness into the woods where the sound was coming from. He felt the hairs on his neck rise as a presence came toward him, moving swiftly enough to cause a rush of air against his cheek. He jumped back.

Out of the trees popped a bleating sheep. It stumbled through the bracken as it beat a furious escape.

"Yah!" he yelled, tapping her hindquarter with the flat of his blade to hurry her along then he expressed his lungs and chuckled to himself that the animal could put him in such a state.

He was smiling when he turned back toward the woods waiting for the dog to follow. The familiar scent of the forest filled his lungs. He heard the rustle of bracken and the metal singing through the air but he never saw the Viking ax coming.

CHAPTER 1

▼

Cavenlow, Ireland: In the courtyard behind the great hall of Lorca macDunnough—Early morning—4, May 966 A.D.—The sound of footsteps echoed through the courtyard sounding more like an army marching than a lone man pacing anxiously. Lorca had begun the familiar vigil sometime the afternoon before when Grace first told him she was ready. He'd been walking ever since. It brought him luck the other nine times and he wasn't about to tempt fate by quitting now. Besides, the weather was fair and the courtyard air was sweet with the scent of cherry blossom from the tree he and Grace planted when they were first married.

The courtyard wasn't planned but evolved over the years as six sleeping huts were added, three north and three south, perpendicular to the walls of the great hall. A long kitchen to the east completed the rectangle that served as a family sanctuary from the busy village surrounding them.

Brian leaned against the doorway of the great hall, watching as the ray of sunlight streaming over the kitchens touched Lorca's face to cast deep angled shadows under his crystal blue eyes. The man looked a sight.

"Don't tell me that ye've been walking all night?" he cried as he rubbed the chill from his bare arms.

"Hush," Lorca replied brushing back a strand of golden hair from his brow. "I think I hear something. Did ye hear it?"

Brian chuckled and his dark blue eyes sparkled in the sunlight as he moved forward to appease his old friend. He pressed his ear against Grace's door but the only sound he heard from within was his sister's gentle whimper as she suffered through her labor. He shook his head in response to the question then took his old friend by the shoulder sighing, "Come inside and sit with me, Lorca. Take something to eat. Ye'll do her nay good by making yerself sick."

Lorca shrugged his shoulders causing Brian's hand to slip from its resting place. Not even the captain's soothing touch could ease his concern for his wife. "I worry for her, Brian," he whispered. "Grace isn't a young woman. The midwife fears there may be trouble after the last one." The last one being Kevin, a premature breech birth which left more blood on the bed sheets than coursing through Grace's veins.

Brian took a moment to untangle a wayward strand of red hair from his left earring before stepping closer to Lorca. Though Lorca was tall, Brian was even taller, nearly dwarfing the other man as they stood facing each other.

"But Grace came through it last time as she will this. There's nay a thing to worry over, man. Ye know my sister's as healthy as my warhorse and twice as stubborn as my mule. She won't let the likes of a babe take her down."

He gave a tug at Lorca's arm to direct him into the feasting hall but the man refused to follow. Instead he trimmed his fingernails with his teeth then spit the bits against the door of the hut.

Brian and Lorca were warriors but more importantly, they were friends. The two had been together as long as anyone could remember, battling in protection of the Dal Cais, battling to avenge the murder of Brian's father, Cennitig, battling to win the Munster crown for his brother, Madamion to wear. They were champions, each of them, but for all his bravery on the battlefield these were the times that brought true fear to Lorca's heart—the times when Grace suffered and he could do nothing to help her.

His emotions raged between worry and frustration causing his golden brows to knit together as he paced the courtyard balling his fists as he went. "Why doesn't she hurry it?" he blurted. "She knows how I hate to wait! And to keep *ye* waiting," he rolled his eyes, "that's unforgivable."

He stopped suddenly, looking to the door then to Brian as if to add something further but just as the captain raised an eyebrow to inquire, Lorca pivoted on the flagstone tiles to take up his pacing once again.

Brian shook his head then laughed. He'd been through this nine other times but he was never able to find the right words to comfort his friend. Finally he gave up, mumbling and muttering to himself as he made his way back into the hall to join the rest of his men.

"She still at it?" Connor questioned groggily while rubbing a meaty hand through his close cropped red hair. He yawned then stretched the stiffness from his back.

"Aye," Brian responded. He tugged at his crotch then grunted before settling himself on the bench next to Connor. He squirmed a bit and Connor nodded sympathetically. Though he was accustomed to wearing breeches, Brian had always preferred to wear the long flowing *lein* (gown) and overcoat that marked him as a noble.

Having been raised in Cennitig's house after his mother died in childbirth, there wasn't much that Connor didn't know about Brian. Likewise, there wasn't much that Brian didn't know about him. In fact, the only secret between them would be the one that Connor took to his grave.

Connor scooted further down the bench to give his captain more room. "Well if she doesn't hurry it up we'll have to leave him behind, aye."

Brian nodded his thanks to the servant who suddenly appeared before them setting wooden plates of brown bread, cheese and fruit on the table. He ripped a hunk from the loaf then sighed before taking a bite. "She'll give it up soon enough. Most likely she knows I'm waiting and will be thinking she can keep her husband from me if she holds on—but this is her tenth child and nature waits for nary a woman."

Connor grunted. Like him, Grace was raised in Cennitig's house after her family was killed in the raids but unlike him, Grace hated Brian thoroughly. From the first day she had come to live with them, Grace and Brian began competing for the little attention Cennitig could offer them. Connor was fortunate not to have such concerns. His father was Cennitig's brother—maimed in battle and unable to travel the countryside with the rest of the Dal Cais army.

"If ye can call her a woman," Connor spit. "More like a shrew if ye ask me."

Brian nudged him with his elbow. "Hush now," he offered through a crooked smile then cocked his chin toward Lorca who was walking toward them. "Any news?"

"Nay," Lorca sighed before taking up his pacing in the long aisle between the dozens of tables lining the hall. His movement stirred the other warriors who were sprawled atop them or on the benches beneath them and suddenly the hall was a symphony of grumbles, groans and farts.

"Tis a lively lot we have this time," he observed, wrinkling his nose without halting his pacing. "If we can't cut Imar down with our swords perhaps we can overwhelm him with our stench."

Brian chuckled but as he was about to respond he noticed Mora standing in the southern doorway closest to Lorca's great silver chair. He cocked his chin in her direction. "Ri Tuath, it seems ye have company."

Lorca looked at him then followed his gaze to the rotund woman who filled the portal. His worried frown quickly turned to a grin, splitting his golden beard straight through the center to allow a glimpse of his yellowing teeth.

"She did it!" he cried. "That makes ten."

He rushed forward with the warriors quick on his heels, all eager to know whether it was a son or a daughter born to the Ri Tuath. As always, there had been wages placed on it.

"Well?" Brian inquired of the new father as he made his way to the front of the crowd, "What is it ye have for us?"

Lorca turned, looking to the captain with eyes filled with love. He didn't take the child from Mora but instead leapt into Brian's arms, planting a sloppy wet kiss against his forehead. "Ye're a good friend to be keeping these men waiting for me."

Startled by the action, Brian chuckled then hugged him back. "Ease up there, brother. Ye'll have me suffocated before we get to battle."

"Ye better leave off, Lorca," Connor crooned, waving a fresh cup of ale under the man's nose. "Madamion has waited a long time for this battle. He'll be mighty sore if ye take the captain down before he has a chance to win it for him, aye."

"Och," Lorca issued before leaping to the ground, snatching the cup from Connor as he went. He tipped back his head to draw on it then wiped his mouth on his sleeve. "Bring them Vikings to me and I'll take them down on my own. It's the strength of ten men that I'm carrying with me today."

"So ye're sure it's another son then?" Brian questioned giving Lorca a jovial shove that sent him stumbling backward. "Ye know it could be a lassie that she gave ye this time."

"Hmph," Lorca responded.

He finished off the last of the ale then gyrated his hips to underscore his point. "I know it's a lad cause that's the only seed I carry."

"Get on with yerself," Brian bellowed with a slap to the air. "The way ye're going on ye'd think ye passed the child yerself."

Lorca raised a sly eyebrow as if to say that he could perpetrate the deed when Mora cleared her throat loudly to remind them that she was there.

Mora had been in Cavenlow since the first day Lorca took it. She was the one responsible for bringing each of his sons into the world. Knowing her master as she did, she was certain he had wages on the child's sex so she held it close to her ample chest scowling at the other warriors who were all trying to get a glimpse of it. She handed Lorca the bundle, careful not to let the blanket come undone when she did then smiled happily as she announced, "Both mother and child came through it just fine, *Ri Tuath.*"

Lorca winked knowingly as he took the child from her. It was plump and red and wailed like a banshee in his arms.

"Maybe ye should let the woman uncover it," Connor said with a tickle to the babe's chin to hush it. "We've got wages on what it is, aye. We don't want any funny business here, Lorca."

All at once there was silence in the hall as the warriors turned to Connor in disbelief. Before he realized the stupidity of his statement an unidentified hand pushed him over. "Careful there, man," Brian chuckled as he caught him. He patted his rump sympathetically. "We wouldn't want ye to damage that good brain of yers, aye."

"Aye, aye," Connor mumbled. His cheeks flushed. "I take yer meaning. Let's just have the bet settled now and be done with it. It's the only excitement we've had in days."

Strip by strip Lorca began the unveiling, slowly pulling back each corner of the blanket to reveal the babe's hands and feet. He touched each digit until he was satisfied they were there then smirked at the eager warriors as his hand hovered over the swaddling. "Are ye ready?" he asked.

The air was thick with suspense. Even Mora huffed as she shifted her weight from one foot to the other. "Get on with it, man," she finally urged, then, unable to control herself, she gave a tug to the bit of cloth.

"Easy, woman," Lorca snapped grabbing her hand. "Ye act as if ye don't already know what it is. Have ye got something on it then?"

Her face flushed red but soon enough she smiled as Lorca revealed his tenth son for all to see.

"It's a lad for certain," he sighed before ducking to avoid the squirting proof of it.

"And a healthy one at that," Brian chuckled. He patted Lorca's back before turning to get his purse.

The other men followed, mumbling to each other as they settled up their bets. Lorca called after them, "Ye should know better than to doubt me, aye." Again he gyrated his hips. "'Tis the only seed I carry."

He turned to Mora who confronted him with a twisted scowl. "The way ye go on ye'd think it was yerself that did all the work," she scolded, shoving him out the door and through the courtyard until they arrived at Grace's hut. "Go on then and see yer wife. It's her that's responsible for bringing forth that mighty seed of yers, aye."

She held the door open forcing Lorca to wriggle around her girth to gain entrance but if he was annoyed with her he didn't show it. He took a moment to allow his eyes to adjust to the dim interior light then moved forward toward the wooden palette and straw mattress that served as their marriage bed.

Grace's age was written on her face and beyond. The tiny lines at the corner of her hazel eyes deepened as they squinted against the pain of her tightening muscles. Her once rosy cheeks were drained of all color and the skin around her mouth was puckered. She reached up to take the child from him and her cracked lips parted to emit a sigh. "He's a fine babe, Lorca, but if his birth was any indication of his personality I fear this one will be the most troublesome yet. He's willful and strong, and I dare say I thought he'd cause my death."

Lorca smiled then tenderly brushed the fading auburn hair from her perspiration soaked face. "As if a babe could take down the likes of ye, woman." He slipped his index finger into the infant's hand, stroking the tiny fingers that instantly clamped around it. "But if he really is the trouble ye profess him to be we shall call him Gilla Patric for the warrior bishop of Eire. Let's see if he has the same tenacity as our great saint."

Grace nodded her agreement. Though the lower class of Ireland still held fast to the pagan rituals of the druids the *Ri Tuaths* of the petty kingdoms, the *Ri Tuath Ruires* of the five counties, the *Ri Ciocid* (territory king) of the north and south and the *Ard ri* himself, had begun to accept the bastardized form of Christianity taught by Saint Patrick nearly five hundred years earlier when he was taken into slavery by the Viking earl, Niall of the Nine Hostages.

The babe wailed as if he understood the expectations that came with such a name and she chuckled, "I've nay doubt that this one will easily prove his mettle, husband."

Patric fussed and cried until she offered her breast and Lorca looked on in awe. The new life reminded him of his purpose. It was them he fought for—them and the thousands of others who deserved to live without fear of being plundered or raped, or kidnapped to be slaves. They were the children of Ireland and he would gladly die at the end of an ax rather than sit by idle as the Vikings invaded them.

It was Brian's voice that shattered his mood, breaching the wooden door as if he'd been standing within. He was informing Connor that they would be leaving immediately to join the others he had sent ahead to Thomond. Once there, they would ferry across the Shannon Bay to the holy island of Scattery where they would march on Imar of Limerick.

"I'll be off now, wife," Lorca offered, praying that they wouldn't have an argument but knowing better. He leaned over to stroke her hair from her face then kissed her forehead. "Brian awaits me but I couldn't leave until I knew all was well with ye."

Her body stiffened with his words. It was none other than Brian's name that could swell such hatred within her. To know her husband would leave her for her mischievous brother was too much for her to bear.

She shook off his hand then muttered, "And whom do ye march on this time, Lorca? What battle's so important that ye'd leave me on the day I bore yer son?"

He set his jaw as he cursed his tongue. He knew better than to speak of Brian but facts were facts and he wouldn't hide them. He forced a smile as he willed his voice to be soothing, "Don't make me do battle with ye too, Grace. Ye know I'm sworn to Brian as well as Madamion."

He tenderly touched her cheek hoping his words would penetrate her hatred, but again she recoiled. His voice turned desperate. "Ye know Madamion isn't a violent man but in this he has nay choice. 'Twas Imar who commissioned Cennitig's murder. We must seek retribution or we'll have the lot of them thinking that we're weak. Ye must support me in this, Grace, if not for the pride of the Dal Cais than for yer own."

She ripped her eyes from his. She knew he must go but resented the hold Brian had over him. It was true that her brother, Madamion, was a peaceful man but their younger brother, Brian, lived for war. He had a blood lust that could never be satisfied.

She snapped her head around suddenly, leveling her narrow eyes against his as she barked, "Don't ye preach to me about Vikings and pride! I lost two fathers to those pagan rots but ye're fooling yerself if ye believe Brian can do anything to stop them. The Vikings have been here for longer than anyone can remember and neither yer precious Brian nor anyone else has the ability to rid us of them. Why don't ye live in peace and negotiate like the Eagahonacts and O'Neills instead of marching around with that fool brother of mine?"

His body stiffened with her traitorous words. The O'Neill price for peace was the sacrifice of their freedom and neither he, nor Brian, were willing to pay that. Not even when they were named outlaws, forced to live in caves and steal food in order to support their men did they give up their fight. At that time even Madamion thought their rebellion folly but once they began winning their wars he joined them. Now he was Ri Tuath Ruire. Yet for all their success there were still those who remained skeptical that they could keep their prize.

His face twisted as he hissed through clenched teeth, "It's negotiation that got us the Vikings in the first place. For that ye may thank yer precious Eagahonacts and O'Neills. But ye mark my words, wife—the Dal Cais will bring down the Viking earls. We'll break the stronghold they have in our territory and finally show them that the treasure of Eire isn't theirs for the taking! Two hundred years of Viking occupation will end with the reign of the Dal Cais."

His ire was fully piqued but she laughed smugly despite it. "And ye think Brian is the one to do it do ye? Well let me tell ye a thing or two about my brother," she offered as her index finger shot out to underscore her point. "He's a fraud—a user who pits people against each other to gain his glory. He did it with his own brother and now he does it with ye!"

Lorca leaned forward until his hot breath touched her skin. He willed his sharp eyes to focus through his anger. "Brian is a man of God! He leads his people when others cannot! He's our only hope to live in peace, Grace. I won't have ye speak ill of him!"

With that he slapped her finger aside then turned on his heel to march toward the door.

If he was angry, she was furious. Who was he to tell her about Brian macCennitig? It was she who was raised in his father's house and it was she who watched as his ill gotten schemes found even Cennitig slain by a Viking broad ax. Even Madamion tried to distance himself from their brother's wars. Though Lorca refused to admit it, he knew nothing about Brian but she knew everything.

She grimaced as she bolted from the bed, placing herself before him and leaving him no exit but to go through her. "Brian macCennitig a man of God—ha! Is that why he's preparing to battle on holy ground? I warn ye, Lorca, if ye don't leave him right now ye'll be dead for his antics!"

She gripped him by his forearms, desperate to win him over. "Madamion only gives in to Brian because he fears what he'll do if he didn't. He's mad I tell ye! Ye must leave him!"

Like the blinding white light of the sun in his eyes Lorca's anger exploded in his brain. He no longer needed to see her, he could smell her—smell her presence as he smelled his enemies on the battlefield. It was a stench—a putrid stink of hopelessness and doubt that had blanketed his country for too long. Now she carried it.

He ripped his arm from her grasp and she followed his knotted fist with her eyes as it came directly for her, but she didn't flinch. She could bare the pain of his blow easily enough but his following Brian into folly—never! She straightened her shoulders daring him to hit her.

In a split second Lorca regained his control, yanking back the blow before it was delivered. He looked at her long and steady. They had spent a dozen years together and each time they had words it was over Brian. She hated her brother—convinced that his single-minded ambition to control Munster was the reason for all their troubles. The mere mention of his name set her off but the irony was that she was most like him. She was both fierce and fearless and would easily face an army in protection of her family. It was that which made Lorca love her, as it was that which made him love Brian. She was the only woman in his bed and in his heart. He took a deep breath to allow that love to fill him as he dropped his open hand onto her shoulder.

"I know ye speak harshly because ye fear for my life," he whispered, his voice cracking under the anger he was forced to swallow, "but I promise I'll return to ye."

She pulled away as he bent to kiss her forehead but before she could escape he had her crushed against his chest with his embrace. She wriggled and squirmed as her baby cried from its place on the bed where she left him but Lorca continued to hold her close, only loosening his grip once she relaxed into submission.

"Go now," he finally whispered before releasing her. "Tend the child, Grace. Tell him his father will soon return. Tell him ye're proud to be my wife because I fight for our freedom."

They both knew the cause of the red tinge creeping up her neck. Lorca had the power to make her yield to him and he was using it now. She shook her head fiercely, struggling to keep her anger burning so that she could win the argument then forced the hatred back into her throat as she spit, "I'll tell the child that ye're a coward who couldn't bear the responsibility of another son so ye went off to give yer life to the Vikings. I'll tell him how much I hate ye and yer precious Brian!"

The words were biting and he tightened his grip on her shoulder until he felt her knees buckle from the pain but she only smiled at him, goading him to keep him with her—to keep him home safe from harm and the wrenching grip Brian had on his heart—the only grip tighter than her own.

Recognizing her ploy, Lorca stood silent as he weighed his next move. It wasn't like him to let her have the last word but in this it seemed he had little choice. He bit his lip until he tasted his own blood then released her. Without another word he turned then left the hut.

"Ye alright?" Mora questioned, stepping aside to allow him to pass. He didn't acknowledge her. He was somewhere deep in the reaches of his soul trying to understand how the two people he loved most in the world could hate each other so viciously.

He made his way to the cheery blossom tree then stood against it, rubbing his tired eyes. Brian moved to stand beside him. "She doesn't understand what we do therefore ye must make it up with her before we go," the captain offered. "If yer head isn't on the battle ye may well lose it."

Lorca looked up and smiled. Brian was gifted with the ability to understand what was in a man's heart by the movement of his body. He made a study of people, watching them for any tell tale sign that would gain him entrance into their soul. If he would lead them he must first understand them.

"Have nay worry," Lorca jeered as he nodded toward the hut. "It's my battles with her that keep me successful against my enemies."

Grace listened as the footfall in the courtyard grew more distant. Her brother's voice was calling out orders and she pictured Lorca snapping to his every command. If she was asked to name her husband's shortcoming it would have to be his utter devotion to her brothers—a devotion that should have been reserved for her.

She grumbled at the thought of it then turned onto her side to find a more comfortable position. As she looked down at Patric slumbering next to her heart she whispered, "If I have to sacrifice my whole life in doing it, ye can be certain that ye'll never be marching off to war with that fool brother of mine."

CHAPTER 2

▼

ELEVEN YEARS LATER

Cavenlow, Ireland: The Lookout—Four hours to midnight, 29, April 977 A.D.—Lorca stood upon the stanchions looking west toward the road. One hundred armed men being led by the Viking, Thorien of Limerick, were marching in three neat rows directly toward him. Thorien's powerful form was almost as impressive as that of the brown stallion he was riding. His golden hair streamed out behind him from beneath his conical helmet and the silver band that he wore on his bicep shimmered in the moonlight.

"It's them!" the guard shouted, not realizing that Lorca had already spotted them then he turned on his heel to alert the others.

Many years had passed since Lorca and Brian marched to Scattery Island to take their revenge on Imar for the death of Cennitig. The battle, if it could be called that, lasted less than an hour. They had stormed the island of churches with little resistance and found Imar and his sons hiding in the Tower of Saint Sean. Brian made quick work of disposing of them and for a time the Vikings had conceded. But now they were preparing to avenge the murder of a yet another Dal Cais king and Lorca hung his head in sadness that times of peace were fleeting.

Thorien halted his horse just short of the gate. His army drew up beside him. He leveled his gaze at Lorca who was visible atop the stanchion. A smile touched his lips. "Hail, Lorca, great chief of Cavenlow," he called as he lifted his arm in greeting. When he realized that his was the lone voice calling out he turned in his saddle to offer a glower to the rest of his men.

Soon they all sang out, "Hail, Lorca of Cavenlow."

Lorca returned the smile then raised his own arm in response. "Hail to ye, Thorien, friend and ally."

Thorien kicked his horse forward and Lorca descended the split rail ladder to make certain that his hall was ready to receive his honored guests. It was strange how life worked, he thought to himself as he crossed the field. Thorien was a Viking from across the sea but instead of being an enemy of the Dal Cais he decided to join Brian's cause. That was nearly fifteen years ago and the relationship between the men had now blossomed to near kinship.

Lorca reached the hall with spirits elevated but when he opened the door they plummeted. There seemed to be a battle raging but the participants were hidden from sight.

"Brian will be yer king and ye'll swear to him, Kevin! Swear to him or I won't let ye up," young Patric exclaimed as he straddled his older brother. A lock of his golden red hair fell over his crystal blue eye and he let go one hand to reach up and push it away.

Kevin used the opportunity to fight for his freedom but his fragile form was little match for his brother's thick body. He wriggled and bucked but soon Patric had both his shoulders pinned solidly to the ground.

"Get off me ye little rot," he gasped, short of breath from the wooden sword being pressed against his throat. His murky gray eyes bulged and his albino hair was plastered to his head with sweat from his struggle.

"I'll tell mother of this!" he croaked. "Ye'll be whipped for sure!"

Patric forced the stick harder. "Swear to Brian, Kevin! Swear to him right now or I'll run ye through!"

The glaring hatred in Patric's eyes left little doubt that he would follow through on the threat. Concession was fast on Kevin's lips when he suddenly caught sight of Lorca. "Father!" he screeched, "Get this rot off me before he kills me."

The cry rang out through the empty hall as if murder was being committed and Lorca drew his short sword, peering over tables and benches in search of Kevin and his attacker. He found them behind the head table between his throne and the rear door. When he realized that it was his youngest perpetrating the attack he stopped dead in his tracks, biting his lip to halt his grin.

Kevin was the runt of his litter, thin and frail from the sicknesses he suffered early in childhood. Though he'd outgrown his ailments long ago he never did outgrow his mother's doting and when Lorca offered him battle training to make up for his deficiencies, Kevin hid behind her skirts to avoid it. It was that lack of training that allowed his younger brother to best him.

"Patric!" bellowed Lorca without any real feeling for the reprimand. "Release yer brother immediately!"

Patric looked up at his father without releasing his victim. "He refuses to swear to Brian as Ri Tuath Ruire. He betrays our family!"

While the scene had been amusing for a time, Lorca wasn't a man to let his orders go unheeded. He stomped forward, grabbing Patric by the shoulders then hoisting him to his feet as he growled, "It's me who'll name the traitors of this clan, not ye. Yer brother will swear to Brian when he's old enough to do battle. When he's sixteen he'll take up arms for the Dal Cais just as I did and my father before me. Ye needn't threaten him with violence. Do ye understand me, son?"

Kevin grit his teeth as he stood dusting the dirt from his glorious lien and coat. He made no effort to hide his distaste for his father's statement. To Lorca battle meant honor but to him it was a useless exercise demanding a high price for little gain. He'd much rather live his life in peace, studying his scripts and basking in the love his mother so readily offered.

Lorca was bent low with his reprimand of Patric and Kevin used the opportunity to goad his youngest brother. He crossed his eyes and wagged his tongue at him from his position of safety behind their father's back. Patric had been a thorn in his side since he first arrived, always hanging on Lorca's heels as if his homage to the Ri Tuath could earn him something more than the soldier's life which was the destiny for any son other than the one born first to the chief. There were nine macLorca sons between Patric and the throne of Cavenlow. Kevin's only solace was that the coveted seat would be his before it ever reached Patric. He jumped back when Patric lunged at him then made an easy escape through the door.

Lorca grabbed Patric's shoulders to give him a harsh shake. "Did ye hear what I just said to ye, lad?" the Ri Tuath roared, this time with feeling.

Patric heard the question but he never took his eyes off his retreating brother. He wrinkled his nose in disgust. His chest heaved in anger. Kevin was a traitor— a weakling who didn't understand the importance of loyalty. He tried to spit after him but Lorca had a tight grip on his face. Their eyes locked and just as Lorca was about to offer his lecture, Patric forced his participation with a challenge between puckered lips. "Ye were the one who told me that anyone who didn't stand with Brian was a traitor to our clan. Kevin refuses to swear therefore I must force him to be loyal just as Brian does in his battles."

There was little doubt that Lorca was angry, it showed in the way the skin around his blue eyes bunched together, but he was also proud. Proud that his son would have the courage to state his position even when he knew he was out-matched. Long ago he recognized Patric's natural ability as a leader and had taken every opportunity to train the lad so that someday he might rise through the ranks to become captain of an army, or God willing, capable enough to conquer the *tuath* of an enemy to become chief of his own village.

He took a moment to consider how best to handle the situation. When he was finally decided he lifted the lad to his feet and shouted, "Sit there!"

Patric sighed when he realized that Lorca was pointing to the chair of authority, instead of the bench. *His father only made him sit on the bench when he was planning to beat him.* He hoisted himself into the hammered silver chair where he sat nearly a hundred times before then let his fingers play in the lion head carvings, stroking each crevice until the picture was formed through his hand. He was proud of his father and the power that came with owning such a chair. He smiled, hoping that if he played along he might even get a good story out of it.

Lorca looked down on him, narrowing his eyes in an effort to convey the anger he should be feeling at the lad's disrespect. "Do ye know why we battle, son?"

Patric's blue eyes sparkled with excitement. He leaned forward as he blurted, "So Brian can be Ri Tuath Ruire!"

Lorca's eyes narrowed further. There was growing talk that Brian was waging war to serve himself instead of his people and he wanted to be sure that his son didn't hold that same opinion. "Do ye know why that's important, lad?" he quizzed.

Patric shook his head then looked to the ground as he noticed the disappointment in his father's eyes. Lorca lifted his chin with his open palm. "Ye're getting older now, Patric," he offered, "and ye may hear things about Brian that may make ye question his motives. I want ye to remember that he's a good man—a man of God who wants nay a thing more for his people than freedom and peace. But sometimes peace is hard won. Sometimes we're forced to battle to gain our peace. Tonight I prepare to march with Brian on the O'Neill prince, Donovan and his Eagahonact ally, Malmua of Desmumu."

Patric's eyes widened and Lorca continued, "Do ye remember last season when I told ye that Madamion was called to a meeting with the two?"

Patric nodded.

"It was to have been a peaceful discussion about Imar's nephew, Volkren and whether or not Madamion would allow him to take control of Limerick. Neither

Brian, nor I were comfortable with the thought of having Imar's blood back in the territory and we told Madamion so, but Malmua convinced the Ri Tuath Ruire that Volkren was the only one capable of restoring the shipping trade in the city. Madamion's greed and ego overtook his good senses. Not only did he refuse to let us take part in the meeting he also refused us as escort."

Suddenly overcome with frustration, Lorca wrung his hands to stop their trembling. Patric noticed and squirmed to the edge of his seat awaiting his father's next words. "Well, Patric," Lorca finally sighed, "that meeting was a trap. Malmua murdered Madamion then convinced the Ard Ri's council of elders to make Donovan Ri Tuath Ruire."

Patric's mouth gaped and Lorca spit the bile from his throat onto the mud floor as he clasped his hands more tightly. "Those fool elders are planning to give our crown to that rot, Donovan so he can give the Vikings access to our river. Once that happens none of us will be safe from their plundering."

He brought his hand down hard on the arm of the silver chair causing Patric to start then he leaned in to hiss, "Well I'll tell ye right now that Brian won't have any of it! Tomorrow we'll march to Sulcoit and by the new moon we'll battle the O'Neills to take back the crown for the Dal Cais once and for all."

Confusion mingled with fear as Patric struggled to understand the complicated politics of his country. "But if the elders want an O'Neill on the throne how will ye stop them from giving it to another even after ye win yer war?"

It was a good question—one that had been asked over and again by members of the clan who preferred to keep what little they had rather than risk it by fighting again. Long ago the Ard Ri had given the council of elders the ability to appoint whomever they saw fit to the Munster throne no matter who won the battle. Lorca stepped back, resting himself against the table as he prepared to share with his son something he would never share with anyone other than those who were involved in it.

"Brian will be Ri Tuath Ruire because when we're done battling Donovan's army there won't be any elders left to stop us."

Patric's mouth fell open. It was one thing for warriors to battle for a crown but quite another to send assassins after the elders, which seemed to be what his father was implying. If they failed and were found out, the Dal Cais would be stricken from the territory.

Lorca searched Patric's eyes sensing his winnow and smiling for it. He reached out a scarred, calloused hand to take that of his son's, stroking it tenderly as he offered, "What I've told ye must be kept between us. Ye mustn't breathe a word of it to anyone. Nay yer mother, nay yer brothers, nay a soul lest we fail. Ye must swear yer silence to me. An oath between warriors, aye."

Patric looked deep into Lorca's crystal blue eyes. In them he saw something he had never seen before. It was more than tenderness and even more than love—it was trust. "I swear," he finally stated turning his hand inside his father's to grasp it fully then he raised his left hand, balling it into a fist before pounding it against his heart. "An oath between warriors."

The smile on Lorca's face touched his eyes causing them to twinkle. Feeling quite the warrior, Patric continued, "So once Brian is Ri Tuath Ruire we'll force everyone to follow the Dal Cais!"

The light in Lorca's eyes quickly faded as he realized his son still had much to learn. He had lost himself in the moment, revealing more information than perhaps he should have. "We can't force people to follow us, Patric," he said as he pulled the lad closer hoping he hadn't made a dreadful mistake by trusting him. "They must do it freely out of love and respect, nay from fear for their lives. A man fights best when he fights with his heart. To be a successful leader ye must have a courageous army. People fight for Brian because they know he protects them. They believe in what he's trying to do and follow him freely. Once Brian takes his crown our round fort will come under his protection as will every other round fort within the kingdom of Munster. All the southern *Ri Tuaths* will unite under the banner of the Dal Cais to keep peace in our territory."

"But will the O'Neills and Eogahnacts follow, father?" Patric whispered anxiously.

Will they indeed?

Lorca's eyes flashed with the mention of the nemesis clans. His hope was that most of them would be slaughtered on the battlefield but the reality was that many would run and hide so they would be free to fight another day. He nodded slowly. "Those who survive and continue to hold tuaths in Munster will live under Brian's law if they want to live in peace. But if they thwart his efforts they'll be called to battle."

Pride replaced anger in Lorca's eyes as he imagined the Dal Cais putting down the powerful reign of the O'Neills. He smiled then absentmindedly stroked Patric's head. He laughed, "I can assure ye that if Brian does have occasion to call them to battle, they won't win. Both the Eogahnacts and the O'Neills are weak, Patric. They're more capable at treachery than skilled in war."

It was then that the sound of his guests approaching caught Lorca's attention. He rose from his resting place to search for a servant but Patric detained him with a well-worn request that he was sure Lorca would oblige. "Tell me how ye came to know Brian, father."

As always, Lorca was only too happy to repeat the story. Without a thought for the approaching warriors he smiled as he resettled himself against the edge of the table.

"Brian and I are very old friends, aye?" He nodded his head and Patric responded in kind. "I came across him on Innis Fallen. We were a wee bit younger than ye are now. As I recall it, he was in the midst of a tussle with a lad twice his size. They were rolling around in the mud because the lad made some foul comment about yer mother who went to live in Cennitig's house after her parents were killed in the raid. At any rate, Brian was winning the battle but then another lad stepped up to hold him down and the first began pummeling him about the face. Mind ye," he said, wagging his finger under Patric's nose to underscore his point, "we had all been warned by the brothers not to be pulled into Brian's mischief but I couldn't stand by while he took the beating. I ran to him and soon we were a tangled mass of legs and arms thrashing in the mud as we delivered our blows upon one another."

He began to walk away but Patric drew him back with another question. "Did ye win the fight, father?"

Lorca turned then shook his head. "Ye know as well as I that we got our arses reddened that day. Not only by the lads but also by the brothers afterwards. They were flaming when they got hold of us." He chuckled before attempting another retreat, "As I recall, I even lost a tooth in it."

This new information excited Patric and he leapt from the chair. "Can I see?"

"See what?" Lorca asked, turning to look down on his son.

"The place where ye lost the tooth. Can I see it?"

"Och, lad!" Lorca grumbled, slapping away his son's hand that was creeping toward his mouth. "It was a wee tooth. A new one grew in its place."

Patric's embarrassment only lasted a moment before he urged his father's return to the story. "So was that when Brian and ye became brothers?"

Lorca huffed then turned again, making his way back to the platform with Patric fast on his heels. It was clear the lad wouldn't release him until the whole story was retold. "Aye," he nodded, "We were thick as thieves after that, and nearly as mischievous." He scratched his beard as his eyes looked into his memory. "I don't think either of us faced a battle without the other at his side ever since."

Patric brushed the golden hair of his father's meaty hand as he shared the concern that had been weighing heavy on his heart for weeks. "Some of the lads in the monastery school call Brian a usurper. Is that bad, father?"

Lorca screwed up his face. "Usurper is a word used to describe someone who takes what they don't deserve, lad. Brian's never taken anything that he didn't have a legitimate claim too. The throne of Munster's nay different. Ye tell those lads that Brian macCennitig has every right to that throne. Unlike the O'Neills who held it, he won't be selling our children into Viking bondage."

Patric reacted to his father's anger, expressing it in the only way he knew how. He used Lorca's shoulder as a handhold to stand upon the seat of the chair then thrust his wooden sword into the air as he shouted, "I hate the Vikings. I'll fight against them as Brian does."

Lorca clapped for the bravado but his smile soon faded. He grabbed Patric's sword hand before offering a piece of valuable information, "Ye better mind where ye point that thing, son. Ye might just be taking the head of a friend. Brian's taught me that ye can make a friend of a Viking. There are some Vikings dwelling in Munster who want nay a thing other than peace. We call them Galls because they've accepted Christianity and are our allies. They suffer the same fate as the Gaels at the hands of their foreign kin. They fight for the Dal Cais and have grown to love Brian because he protects them. We don't fight against all Vikings, only the savage ones from across the sea."

Patric looked down at his father in wonder, struggling to grasp the notion. "There are Vikings who fight for Brian? How can ye tell the difference between a Gall and a Viking, father? I thought they were one in the same."

Lorca pulled down on the soft skin of his left cheek to reveal even more of his crystal blue orb. "Ye'll know yer enemies by the look in their eyes, lad. Brian's Galls are peaceful. They're mostly ceiles looking for a quiet place to settle. But those who come from across the sea are scavengers. They have a wild look about them like that of a beast, always probing about in search of prey. They cross the seas in long boats docking in the shallowest rivers then they come ashore to take our women and children back to their country as slaves. They burn our monasteries to get at our treasure but they would rather fight an unarmed woman in her bed than face an army on the battlefield."

The image of savages wallowing in the blood of his people flooded Patric's mind until the heat swelled within him. He wrenched himself from his father's grasp and again waved his sword in the air. "I'll fight savage Vikings and won't stop until Eire is rid of them all!"

Lorca gave a tiny pat to Patric's rump before bringing him down from his perch. He'd spent far longer than he intended giving the lad his stories and now his guests would be arriving without hospitality. He set his jaw in preparation for the struggle he was certain would come. "That's enough now, lad. Ye'll go to war when ye're sixteen and nay a moment sooner. Off to bed with ye now. I expect Brian at any moment and I don't need ye scurrying about under foot. We have a battle to prepare for!"

"But father," Patric pleaded. "I want to stay and tell Brian that I too will fight with him. I too am his loyal soldier."

Lorca offered a firmer pat than the one previous. "I'll tell him that for ye, aye? Now be off! If ye force me to repeat it again ye'll be sorely sorry for it."

Patric gave a slight rub to his quickly reddening buttocks before thrusting his arm forward. He flexed it upward until his muscle formed beneath the skin. "But I'm strong and I want to show Brian I can fight. I'm stronger than any other lad in the monastery school. I'm a good warrior! Ye've said so a hundred times."

Their eyes were locked in a war of wills, neither relenting, and neither aware of the movement at the far end of the hall. They turned when Brian's laughter reached their ears. "I should say he is a warrior, Lorca," the would-be king thundered from the doorway. "The good brothers of the monastery tell me they haven't experienced so much turmoil within their classrooms since our own time studying there."

Brian's easy gait brought him quickly to the front of the hall, his red hair flowing behind him as the glow of the lamplight caused his deep blue eyes and chain mail vest to sparkle. His presence was all consuming and Patric's heart beat wildly as he rushed forward to greet the captain.

At six feet six inches, Brian was the tallest man Patric had ever seen. He was every bit the warrior with sharp facial features and a square jaw line covered by a close cropped beard. His long hair was brushed back from his face to reveal his high forehead and his thick brow below. Patric dropped to his knees, taking another moment to gaze at the man before bowing his head in homage. "I-I'm a good soldier, captain," he stammered. "I pray ye to let me join yer army."

With a stealthy stretch of the arm and a deep belly laugh for the scene, Brian reached down to pull the lad to his feet. "I think I'll surely be victorious in any battle where ye fight at my back, Patric," he offered as he stretched a long finger toward Lorca's chair, urging the lad to take it. "But if ye don't mind, I'd like to use yer brain before I use yer brawn. Sit with us while we discuss our strategy. Give us the benefit of yer wisdom for I fear our minds are too old and may be riddled with cob webs."

With Brian's invitation the lad would never get to bed. Lorca shook his head in defeat before mumbling, "Welcome, captain. 'Tis truly good to have ye in my home again."

Brian lifted a quizzical eyebrow. "And when did we become so unfamiliar that ye address me formally in yer own home, Lorca? Or perhaps I've done something to offend ye."

Lorca huffed then rolled his eyes. "'Tis bad enough that ye offered the lad a seat when I only just told him that he must go to bed, will ye also go against me when I try to teach him the respect of addressing ye properly?" He looked down at the hand Brian was offering him and when he took it he was pulled into a hug. "I swear ye're as incorrigible as the child," he chuckled against the captain's chest.

"Och," Brian issued with a clap to his back. "If ye want to teach the lad something, teach him that among his kin there's nay greater show of respect than love of Munster and loyalty to his people." He broke the embrace then leaned down close to Patric, looking deeply into his eyes to stress his point. "Even when I'm *Ri Tuath Ruire,* to ye I'll always be known as Brian. Though we don't share the same father, Lorca and I share the same soul. We hold nay greater love than Eire and her people. Any man who shares that love and swears to protect her shores will be as much my own brother as Madamion was. Do ye understand me, lad?"

Even when he whispered, Brian's voice was commanding. Patric was awestruck and barely managed to nod his understanding.

Brian gave a hearty laugh then brushed the hair from Patric's eyes. "I like men of few words, laddie. They're the great thinkers of our world. Be ever cautious of yer tongue lest it speak words which are better left unsaid."

Lorca edged between them, determined to keep his son on his best behavior. "Ye may remain with us through our consultation if ye promise to keep yer tongue as still as it is right now, but if yer mother should find her way into this hall ye had better hide yerself quickly. I won't have her wagging her tongue at me in front of her brother, aye."

Patric nodded his understanding then squared his shoulders as he prepared to become a soldier in Brian macCennitig's army.

Slowly the hall began to fill. At first there were a few men adorned with chain mail vests and sporting helmets of various origins. Some carried axes, some had long swords; all had short blades tucked into their belts. They looked very official and capable at war. Then came the ceiles and fuidirs who would fight with the hopes of gaining lands of their own—or at the very least—freedom from the raids. There were massive numbers of them until the walls of the great hall seemed they would burst. Some were Gael but most were Gall, all dressed in breeches and homespun woolen liens of the under class. They sported clubs and slingshots. Some were lucky enough to possess spears or swords they had taken from a slain enemy. There was an endless stream of them stretched out through the massive doors of the hall and across the field beyond.

Patric's heart beat furiously within his chest as the excitement of the impending battle blanketed the room. He reached out to touch his father's arm just to remind him that he was still there and the Ri Tuath offered a reassuring rub to his head before returning his attention to Thorien and the various maps covering the table.

Patric looked the Viking over, trying to understand the difference between him and the savages from across the sea. He was a handsome man with a blade straight nose and deep green eyes. A little scar ran from the corner of his right one. His hair looked like spun gold as it glistened in the lamplight and his skin was dark from the sun. But the thing that fascinated Patric most was the missing digit on Thorien's left hand. "What happened to ye?" he asked.

Thorien looked at the lad then followed his gaze to his missing pinky. "Ah, that," he sighed with a lilt of an accent Patric hadn't heard before. He leaned back on the bench to get a better look at the lad then flattened his hand on the table so Patric could better see his hand. "'Twas a battle, sure enough, between me and another lad named Throdier. We were just about yer age when Throdier called my sister a name…not a kind one mind ye. We tussled over it and he bit off my finger."

Patric's eyes widened. "He bit it off?"

"Aye."

"And what did ye do to him?"

Thorien laughed, "Well what could I do lad, other than run home to my ma and have her tend to it for me?"

That statement caused Patric's eyes to widen further. Thorien was just as tall as Brian but he outweighed him by a few stone. He couldn't imagine that a man of Thorien's size could have been much smaller as a lad.

As if the Viking read his mind, he leaned over to whisper, "The sign of a true man is knowing when he's licked. 'Tis nay a shame to concede a battle when there's nothing to gain from it. The true test of a man's mettle is when he fights for something, aye."

Patric nodded and Lorca rubbed his head, hoping his son had understood the message then the two men returned to their map.

Time seemed to drag as the separate conversations being waged around the hall gave Patric the impression that battles were more noise than action. He covered his ears with his hands then rested his chin on the table as his eyes fixed on the banner hanging from the nine-foot high ceiling beam in the center of the hall. The halls irregular shape, almost a rectangle with rounded corners, was reflected in the underbelly of its thatch roof. There were escape holes for the smoke over the northern and southern fireplaces. Fires burned in both, and as the cold night air mingled with the warm air from the fires, a breeze caught hold of the colorful Dal Cais banner causing it to twist magically. Patric blew on it to see if it would react and became excited when it did, but moments later the game lost its luster. He began to squirm.

"Settle down there, lad!" Lorca snapped when Patric's dangling foot clipped his shin. Patric's head shot up with the attention but it was fleeting and his father returned to the conversation he was now having with Connor. Patric looked to the northern hearth then heaved a deep sigh. The air smelled sweet from the peat fire and at the same time sharp from the musky smell of ale and men. He rested his head on his arm as he searched the glowing embers for the many colors of their fire. His eyes grew heavy. He blinked a few times in an effort to keep his focus but his lids betrayed him, shutting tight against the waking world.

He dreamed of battle. He was sneaking up behind a Viking who was carrying Kevin off to be his slave but suddenly his attention turned as Lorca and Brian called to him from their prison, reaching their arms through the wooden bars to draw him near. Patric lifted his sword to strike at the guard but his attention turned again as the chant of his name stopped him before he could deliver his blow.

"Patric. Patric!" Acard shook the lad gently. "Awake, Patric. Awake and see us off."

Patric knuckled the sleep from his eyes to see his eldest brother standing before him. He was a beautiful man with round, rosy cheeks that nearly matched the color of his hair which he wore long and loose except for the warrior braid hanging down his left shoulder. His green-blue eyes twinkled and a smile always seemed to play on his lips as if he had some wonderful secret to share. He carried Lorca's form, tall and broad of shoulder with well-muscled arms that served for both battling and planting. His golden, hoop earrings shimmered in the lamp-light as he shook Patric's shoulder more aggressively. "Do ye hear me, lad? Wake up and see us off."

Acard was Patric's favorite brother. Although he was married with daughters of his own he always had a moment to spare for his youngest brother.

"Aye, I hear ye." Patric grumbled. Though he was glad that his brother thought to wake him before they left he was sore that he wasn't invited to go with them.

"Well ye best be off to bed there, laddie," Acard continued, "Ma's already given Da grief over allowing ye to sleep in the hall."

Patric screwed up his face. His mother was always trying to keep him tied to her apron and away from the fun. He looked around the room and his eyes rested on his other brothers, Randa, Malora, and Lorcain who were huddled in the corner speaking with Connor. The vision reminded him of his dream. He blurted, "I was trying to save Da. A Viking took him and Brian prisoner. They were calling to me for help. I was just about to run the rot through when ye woke me."

Acard chuckled as he bent his knee so their eyes would be level. "Well go to yer bed so ye can finish him off, aye. Vikings are an anxious lot. They won't wait around forever for ye to take their heads. And while ye battle in yer dreams, we'll battle to reclaim the Dal Cais crown. When we return Brian will be *Ri Tuath Ruire*." He pulled Patric to his feet then pointed him toward the doorway with a pat to the rump. "Go now and take yer rest in yer chamber."

At first Patric complied, padding slowly toward the single southern door located just beside his father's chair. He yawned and scratched his head but suddenly a plan formed in his mind. He whirled around to blurt, "I think I'll come with ye, Acard. I'll act as yer weapons man and bring ye water when it's needed."

Acard looked to the front of the hall to see Lorca and Brian fast approaching. They'd passed a long night with little rest and there were dark smudges beneath Lorca's eyes marking his weariness. If he didn't get Patric off to bed quickly there was little doubt that the Ri Tuath would unleash on him. "I'd love to have ye with me, Patric," Acard cooed as he turned the lad back in the direction of the door, "but this battle will be a fierce one and I won't have time to watch after ye. Now shut up your mouth and go to bed before Da has at ye."

He jutted his chin in Lorca's direction, hoping the child would see the danger and relent, but Patric ignored him. Instead he stomped his foot as he threw back his shoulders in defiance. "There's nay need for *ye* to protect me, Acard! I'm a fierce warrior. Ye see I can best Kevin as I've bested ye. I'm just as ready for real warriors as the ones in my dreams."

The bravado brought a smirk from Acard, which he promptly covered with a cough into his rounded hand. The game played by the older Cavenlow sons of making Patric feel important by letting him best them was about to get the lad into more trouble than he could handle. He stroked Patric's hair, trying one last time to gain his submission.

"I pray ye to heed my words brave warrior," he whispered so that Lorca wouldn't overhear. "It's obvious that yer skills are great but I'd like to remind ye that ye're needed more here to protect our home than on the crowded battlefield. Ye must stay behind so that the soil of Cavenlow will be protected from a Viking scourge. If ye come into battle with us who will be left to protect Mahain, Breen and Kevin? Not to mention our own mother. Ye must stay behind for the sake of our family."

Acard made a good point. If Patric went, their tuath would be left in the hands of his other brothers and they were nearly useless. Patric tapped his chin with his finger as he pondered the statement then suddenly a thought occurred to him.

"Since all the savage Vikings fight on the side of the O'Neill the danger will be in Sulcoit not in Cavenlow," he stated proudly. "Therefore I must go to protect *ye.*"

The confidence with which Patric offered the words caused both his brother and Brian, who was now standing behind him, to chuckle, but Lorca wasn't amused. He grabbed the lad by the shoulders then shoved him toward the door as he firmly stated, "Enough of this chatter, Patric! There'll be time for yer soldiering when ye're older but for now ye must rest and grow yer muscles. Listen to Acard and stay to protect our family. We'll return shortly and tell ye all about the battle."

Patric was about to protest but was cut short by Brian who was now stroking his hair. "Remember lad," he cooed, "a good soldier obeys the orders of his superior officer. In this case, that would be yer father. But with his permission I wish to give ye a job that I consider most important. Are ye up to it, young soldier?"

At first Lorca's jaw twisted in frustration but when he realized that Brian was only trying to help he nodded his consent and Patric stammered, "I-I a-am up to it, B-Brian."

Brian pulled his short sword from his waist then offered it to Patric. "It's very important to me that nay harm come to this blade. It's very special and I need someone to polish it and keep it safe while I'm away. I believe ye're just the soldier I've been searching for to accept this duty. Will ye do it, lad?"

Patric watched as the lamplight danced off the polished metal of the knife. Its golden hilt was adorned with a rope of silver that wound its way down onto the silver blade. His heart beat wildly with anticipation as he reached out to accept it.

"Aye, Brian. I'll keep it safe for ye. I'll prove I'm a good soldier."

"Good, lad." Brian smiled. "Now take it and don't use it for mischief. I want to see both ye and the blade in fine condition upon my return."

Lorca sighed relief. Perhaps now the lad would finally go to bed. He gripped Patric's shoulders firmly as he again pointed him toward the door. "Off with ye now, lad," he growled as he issued a stiff pat to the rump, "and mind what Brian told ye about the blade."

Patric happily obeyed, hurrying toward the door while turning the gleaming weapon in his hands so the lamplight danced upon it. He was so focused on protecting it that he didn't turn when his other brothers began to taunt him.

"Be careful now, Patric," called Randa. "Ye wouldn't want to drop Brian's blade."

"Be sure not to cut yerself with it," offered Malora. "We wouldn't want yer wretched blood to stain such a good looking knife."

Patric curled his lip but dared not turn to retort for fear he would drop the blade. When he was part way through the door he felt, rather than saw, Brian staring at him. He turned his head and his heart began to flutter. Suddenly he couldn't contain himself. He carefully set the blade down on the head table then ran into Brian's waiting arms. "I love ye, Brian," he whispered into the captain's ear.

"And I ye, lad. But ye had better be off to bed before yer mother catches ye out here. She'll do more damage than ten Vikings if she sees us together. Believe me, I know her wrath."

Patric knew that his mother and Brian didn't get on well but he gave it little mind, instead he buried his face deep into Brian's strong neck, catching a whiff of his musky scent as he asked, "Will ye promise to take care of my family, Brian?"

Brian whispered back, "That's a promise ye can depend on, lad."

Kevin entered the hall to break his fast but was brought up short by the sight of the warriors still in it. He looked from Brian to Patric then back to Brian again, making no attempt to hide his hatred for the man. Brian met his gaze but before he could say a word Kevin turned then left the building.

CHAPTER 3

▼

Limerick Road—South of Cavenlow: Three hours past dawn—1, May 977 A.D.—The journey to Sulcoit was a long one but it was that much longer for the warriors who made their way on foot. Lorca looked back at Acard. He was walking his horse slowly to allow his brother, Malora, a more comfortable gait as they chatted. Just a year separated them but while Acard was broad and firm, Malora was narrower of back and chest. "The image of his mother," is how many described him but in Lorca's mind it was Kevin who was most womanly among his sons.

It was true that Malora carried Grace's coloring, red hair and light skin with blue green eyes. He also had her upturned nose and high cheekbones, but while Malora was only an inch or two shorter than most of his brothers, Kevin stood just an inch or two taller than Grace.

Kevin had none of Lorca's features. His form was tall and narrow and his coloring was most peculiar. His hair was so fair that it was almost white and his skin was nearly translucent. His eyes were a cold, murky gray, seemingly incapable of shining; his personality was no different. He was perpetually unhappy, never participating in the weapons games or challenges offered by his brothers but instead burying his nose in ancient manuscripts, lamenting the loss of the ancient kings who he insisted were the great thinkers among men. There was little doubt that Kevin was the most intelligent of his ten sons, a fact that made Lorca quite uncomfortable.

"Monastery material," he thought to himself then shook his head in hopelessness. It seemed a pity to waste a brilliant mind on transcribing text and memorizing prayers when it could be better used in laying out battle strategy.

His thoughts were interrupted as Lorcain came tearing out from behind the hedgerow with Gunra, Calcot and Randa in obvious pursuit. He smiled as his sons began shoving each other jovially then nodded his head in approval as Acard tried to put an end to the melee with a few smacks at each of them with the flat of his broad sword. They were a good lot and when you added Mahain, Breen and Patric to the group, Lorca had sired a little army of his own.

"Give it up there, lads," he called back in a tone more harsh than he had intended. "Ye'll have enough to do trying to beat back Malmua, don't be wasting all yer spirit on each other."

"Pardon, *Ri Tuath*," Randa replied, jutting his chin in the direction of Lorcain, "but yer fine son here was going after a camp follower. I caught him with her behind the bushes. I nearly wasn't in time to stop them."

Lorcain's face flushed bright red until it nearly matched his hair. At just seventeen he was anything but worldly in the ways of women but if it was possible that he would lose his life in a couple of days he wanted to be sure that his last memories were good ones. He cupped his meaty hands around his mouth as he called out to his father who was offering one of his penetrating glares, "She had a lash in her eye. I was just trying to relieve her of it."

Malora jabbed his elbow into Lorcain's rib as he spoke loud enough to breech the distance between him and his father, "The way Randa tells it, it was more than the lash he was trying to free her from."

By now Lorca had stopped his horse. He covered his smile by rubbing his calloused hand across his chin then composed himself enough to feign seriousness. "I told ye before, lad, to lay off those women. Lord knows what else they'll be carrying between their thighs besides the sweet stuff. I don't want ye scratching at yer balls on the battlefield while ye should be swinging yer blade, aye."

Embarrassed by the encounter, Lorcain nodded obediently then waited until Lorca urged his horse forward to offer Malora a solid blow to the stomach. It was returned most viciously and soon both of them were rolling around in the road. Nearby foot soldiers began cheering and wagering, awaiting the outcome of the skirmish.

Lorca gave a quick glance over his shoulder, dismissing the matter with a chuckle before pressing his horse into a trot to join Brian at the front of the precession.

"So ye're sure they'll show then?" he asked as he reined his horse into step with Brian's.

"They'll show," Brian nodded, "though they won't be happy about it. Ye know as well as I that Donovan's not a fighter but I hear his brother has come down from Ulster to be sure he's in it. There's bad blood between the two. Donovan won't risk having his name marred throughout the north by running from a fight."

Lorca nodded agreement as Connor joined the conversation, "Their full of themselves because they got the Ard Ri on their side. My spies tell me that Donovan's so certain of his victory that he's already ordered new clothes and a celebration feast for his return to Cashel."

Brian offered a, "hmph," as if to dismiss the information but Lorca recognized the concern in his eyes. He leaned forward to better see Connor who was riding on Brian's left then let his eyes glow solemn as he spoke.

"Those filthy murderers don't know what they're dealing with." He turned slightly in the saddle, nodding his chin at the steady stream of warriors marching behind them. "When they see the Munster men coming they'll realize that Donovan's feasting clothes will more likely be used at his funeral."

This brought a smile and nod from Brian but the would-be *Ri Tuath Ruire* remained silent. Lorca continued, "We fought too hard to regain this crown and I can tell ye right now that the hatred that burns in me is only half as bright as what these men carry." Again he cocked his head in the direction of the warriors. "They'll not be going home with anything less than Donovan's head."

With that Brian lifted his eyes toward the sky. There had been a storm brewing in the west all morning and now the heavy clouds were lying so low that they covered the tops of the mountains. A sudden gust of wind caused his cape to whip up around his shoulders. He fumbled for the ends of it, tucking them under his saddle as he turned to Lorca.

"Hatred or nay, both sides are going to have a tough way of it if this storm lets loose."

Both Lorca and Connor nodded their agreement then reined their horses behind Brian as he stepped up their pace.

✳   ✳   ✳   ✳

Cavenlow: The kitchens—One hour past noon—8, May 977 A.D.—The black clouds hovered close over Cavenlow sending heavy droplets of rain crashing to the ground in a fury that bent the fields beneath their weight. Sheep huddled against the southern wall where the forest overhung it, pressing their bodies together to form a tinged snow-like blanket across the grass. In the mountains, the wolf cried causing the cattle to bunch up in the gated pasture.

Patric watched from the doorway as he twirled Brian's short sword in his hand. For two days his youthful energy had been imprisoned within the mud walls of the huts. He picked at the wood with the blade wondering if the rain would ever cease.

"Go away from here, Patric," Grace scolded with the shooing of her hands. She took a moment to straighten the brooch at her right shoulder that attached the toga fashioned material making up her apron then took another moment to be sure the left one was secure before wiping her hair from her face with her forearm.

"Yer father'll be home when he comes and nay sooner. Moping about as ye've been only serves to have me tripping over ye."

"Do ye think the rain will hinder them?" he asked as he tried to picture the battlefield of Sulcoit in his mind.

"Och," she issued then came to stand behind him, following his gaze to the empty fields. "As if a bit of rain could stop the likes of yer father. Once the man gets a thought in his head he's possessed by it. He'll fight. Have nay worry for it."

She remembered the sight of Lorca riding up to the keep in Thomond back in the days when he was an outlaw. He'd ridden through the night and half the day to bring Madamion word that they'd secured the round fort at Raithlind. He was bleeding from a wound on his shoulder and was so thin that she was certain a good wind would blow him off his horse, but still he rode. She couldn't believe that after all these years the man was still forced to battle. "Aye, he'll fight. 'Tis all he knows."

"He's a good fighter, isn't he, mother?"

"The best," she mumbled, still daydreaming about the handsome man who had stolen her heart.

Where had the time gone?

"When I grow up I want to be just like him."

Those words ripped Grace from her memories and she reached down to grab him by the shoulders. "Never, Patric!" she snapped, her eyes suddenly furious. "Never will ye march with that fool brother of mine!"

*   *   *   *

Sulcoit, Ireland: One hour before dawn—9, May 977 A.D.—In the far reaches of the southern territory the sodden field of Sulcoit churned under the feet of a thousand warriors. The storm had let loose with an unpredictable fury causing tents to collapse under the constant barrage of wind and rain. Being

familiar with the area, Brian sheltered his army in a hidden cave where he and
Lorca had once resided during their time as outlaws. On the other side, the army
of Donovan and Malmua struggled against the rage of nature.

Connor had suggested that they put off the battle until a time when the mud
and rain wouldn't hinder them but Brian and Lorca refused. Though it would be
difficult for their army to fight under such conditions they would be more capable at navigating the soggy field than the O'Neill's army would. After all, Brian's
soldiers were mostly farmers, accustomed to herding and working the fields no
matter what the weather. They would have the advantage over the O'Neill army
whose soldiering skills were most effective under favorable conditions.

Assignments were given out in the damp, darkness of the cave and as usual,
Lorca would oversee the Galls who were being led by Thorien of Limerick. He
had a great respect for Brian's Galls and a greater respect for Thorien. It couldn't
have been easy for him to give up his lifestyle and his religious beliefs to accept
Gaelic customs but he did it willingly and had been a loyal soldier to Brian ever
since.

Lorca looked up from his resting place as the Viking approached, a look of
apprehension clearly marking his face. "May we speak, Lorca?" came Thorien's
deep baritone, the sound of it echoing off the walls of the cave.

Lorca rose, sweeping his cape wide before settling it around his shoulders. He
sensed the news was bad and didn't want the others to overhear. "Outside," he
whispered.

They stood at the mouth of the cave leaning back against the mountain so that
the jutting rocks above would give them some cover from the rain. The Viking
leaned in close to be heard over the wind. "Volkren won't be bringing his army.
My man just told me that the earl is tucked safely in his hall drinking and feasting."

"Damn," Lorca hissed as he wiped the rain from his face. "Does he think he
can remain in Limerick without taking a position in this battle? If he does, he's
more of an idiot than his reputation professes."

"Ye know that's for certain," Thorien exclaimed with a chuckle. "The man
hasn't got the good sense to know when to get in out of the rain."

Lorca raised an eyebrow as the droplets of water spattered both their faces
causing Thorien to huff, "Ye know what I mean, man. He's a dolt. And the best
of it is that he hates anyone who has more sense about them than he does so he
surrounds himself with incompetents."

Thorien knew a thing or two about Volkren. For the last two years it had been his job to spy on the Viking who had been exiled to Limerick from Orkney by earl Halfden Long Leg as punishment for the murder of Dorfarv the Fair.

"That makes nay sense," Lorca replied, knitting his brows in confusion. "How can an idiot manage to keep Limerick for himself?"

"He's a grand swordsman, for sure," Thorien replied with a shrug. "Though I like the brains in my head just fine, it wouldn't matter if I lost them so long as I had my brawn. Men follow a champion."

Lorca smiled wryly. "So then once we win this battle it shouldn't be hard for us to rid ourselves of the earl. Just think how happy Volkren's men will be to know that their new Ri Tuath Ruire has both brawn and brains."

"Amen to that," Thorien responded. He was about to walk away when Lorca grabbed his hand to stop him.

"What of the council?" he whispered as he leaned in close. "Is everything set?"

"Aye," Thorien responded in the same somber tone being offered him. "Twelve raiding parties have been sent forward, each sporting war paint and carrying foreign weapons. Every member of the council will be slain but if any escape they'll have nay choice but to attest that it was Vikings what did it."

The sight of Brian's tall form emerging from the mouth of the cave drew Lorca's attention. He held his finger to his lips. "Speak nothing further of it. 'Tis best that Brian be left unaware so that if he's questioned about it later he'll be truthful in his answer."

He moved forward, blessing himself with the sign of the cross and asking God's forgiveness for his sin as he prepared for yet another battle.

CHAPTER 4

▼

Sulcoit, Ireland: On the Battlefield—Noon—9, May 977 A.D. The pungent scent of blood caught in Brian's nose forcing him to turn his head away from his enemy's open wound. He gave one last twist of his blade before withdrawing it to leave the O'Neill in a crumpled heap upon the muddy pasture. His dark blue eyes swept the expanse of the clearing in a methodical rhythm, marking his enemies and sending the information up through his brain so that his arms reacted with lightening speed. He carried a sword of forged metal measuring nearly five feet long and possessing such great weight that it required two hands to wield it. He rested it against his shoulder as he heaved a deep sigh.

Lorca fought to his right, ever mindful of the captain's vulnerability for being left hand dominant. Brian watched as his friend opened a neat slice in Malmua of Desmumu's throat then jabbed his short sword into the Eaghonact's heart to be sure he was dead.

"One down and one to go," the captain cried, adding his own damage by kicking Malmua in the ribs.

Lorca leaned over to catch his breath. "Aye, and then we deal with Volkren," he gasped.

"Aye," Brian agreed. "I worry more over him than the others. Where does he..." The oncoming blade halted him in mid-sentence but it only took a moment for him to lift his sword in a high arc to send it slicing through his enemy at the juncture between hip and waist. It happened so quickly that neither Lorca, nor Donovan's now very dead soldier, had time enough to react.

Lorca smiled wryly. "That's a good knife," he muttered when his shock subsided.

"That it is." Brian wiped the blade against the leg of his breeches before returning his attention toward the southern portion of the field. "Where does Volkren fight?"

"He doesn't," Lorca replied then swept the field with his eyes to be certain there wouldn't be another attack. "We'll have to deal with him once we've won the battle and that will be soon enough." He gave another sweep of the field. "Where does Acard fight? I haven't seen him."

Brian jutted his chin westward. "He was flanking the woods last I saw him. He's doing well, Lorca. Ye should be proud."

Lorca smiled before surveying the field once more. With no enemies in sight it would be safe for him to leave Brian so he could assist Acard.

While Malmua's men fought capably, Donovan's men fell back as they were mired in the muck of the field. Soon the red liquid of blood ran as abundantly as the clear rain on the field with Brian's army continuing to push the O'Neill back towards the woods.

Panicked by the annihilation of his army, Donovan leapt upon his horse to take cover in the trees but just as he entered he noticed his brother locked in a fierce battle with a Munster man. At first he thought to turn back, not wanting his brother to know he was fleeing, but then he realized he had the advantage of his horse. He smiled to know his brother would be obliged to him for saving his life then quickly pushed his sword neatly into the back of the Dal Cais warrior.

As the young captain fell to his knees a heart-wrenching scream from somewhere up field echoed off the mountaintops. "ACARD!"

✶   ✶   ✶   ✶

Cavenlow: Two hours before noon—16, May 977 A.D.—The sunlight sparkled off the dew covered pasture giving it an emerald glow. The air was thick with the fragrance of cherry blossom and bells and a cool breeze blew from the Shannon where swans were gliding effortlessly through the water. For anyone else, the sight would have been breathtaking but for the eleven-year-old warrior who'd been imprisoned by the rains, it meant nothing more than his freedom.

He tore through the courtyard with Brian's short sword in hand then raced up the aisle of the great hall to burst through the open doors. He would begin his sentry at the gate like any good warrior then continue on through the rest of the village until he was certain it was safe.

He gave a quick nod to the guards atop the stanchion before stepping out into the road. They smiled after him but soon began to chuckle as the lad walked directly into a cloud of dust left by the passing merchant wagon.

With dignity drawn from the deepest crevices of his soul, Patric waited for the dust to settle then calmly patted it from his clothes, giving a tiny cough then a prideful nod to the guards as he stepped back through the gates.

The guards quickly returned his silent salutations before chuckling to one another behind their hands. Seeing the exchange, Patric uncovered Brian's short sword then touched it to his forehead in salute, eyes glaring. His meaning was clear and the guards looked away. A confrontation with the youngest son of the *Ri Tuath* was more trouble than they needed.

Victorious, Patric continued his rounds, picking up a stick and letting it play along the bumps and cracks of the uneven stonewall that made up the round fort's enclosure. It was market day and merchants were busy setting out their wares and connecting the leather covers of their booths in preparation for the midday sun. Soon Cavenlow would be alive with movement as travelers and villagers negotiated for its merchandise.

Patric straightened his shoulders before nodding to a rotund woman arranging her herbs on a table. She took a moment to adjust the scarf covering her hair that marked her as a married woman before offering him a friendly smile.

The sun was throwing off an incredible heat by the time Patric reached the end of the fort's southern wall where it met the River Shannon. He had thought to take his lunch there but the rank odor of emptied chamber pots and refuse deposited at the river's edge offended his senses forcing him to move along to a more welcoming spot on the grassy rise down wind.

He took his lunch of cheese and fish under the shade of a standing willow as he watched the cattle grazing on the lush green pasture grass, flicking their ears and lifting their heads toward the call of the eagle ringing out from the mountains.

When lunch was finished he walked past the mill and through the orchards, snatching a jewel colored apple from a low-lying branch. The juice ran down his chin when he bit it and he wiped at it with his sleeve as he turned Brian's short sword in his hand. He watched the sunlight dance off the blade and repeated Acard's words out loud: "Ye must protect our village from a Viking scourge."

He smiled.

It was the laughter of children that turned his head and for a moment his stomach burned as he thought it was meant for him, but as he spied them in the distance pawing and scraping at the earth behind the old barns, he realized their laughter was for whatever childish game they were playing. Blade in hand, he stiffened his spine then marched over to them as if he were part of an unseen army. He squared his shoulders and held his chin high, casting a scrutinizing look toward them.

Eagan, a speckled faced red head only a year older than him turned to call out. "Come play with us, Patric. We've found some old bones buried in the side of this hill. Come see them."

Patric looked down his nose. Games were for children. He was a soldier now and didn't have time for such nonsense.

"Nay, I cannot," he called in his most authoritative voice. "I've important work to do. I'm holding Brian's short sword and must protect Cavenlow until the new *Ri Tuath Ruire* and my father return."

Eagan ran to him, eager to know if he told the truth about holding Brian's blade. He watched as Patric turned the knife for him to see. "That's not Brian's short sword," he chuckled. "The great warrior would never go into battle without taking his weapon."

Patric flashed at the accusation. "It's *his* short sword I tell ye!" He took a step forward as the heat began to rise in his blood. "Brian gave it to me and asked me to keep it for him. It's his and I use it to protect *ye* from the Vikings!" He touched the tip of the blade to the boy's chest to emphasize his point.

Eagan laughed as he brushed it aside then called to his comrades, "Patric says he holds Brian's short sword and that he's charged with protecting Cavenlow. Can ye believe such a foolish story?"

"It's his short sword and I'm his soldier!" Patric shouted, holding the blade above his head for all to see.

Amin was twelve years old. His thick body moved with the speed of a turtle but there was no denying he was coming as the ground beneath his feet trembled from his weight. He pushed his brown sweat matted hair from his eyes as he marched up to Patric, yanking the blade from his hand with the menacing growl he used to gain submission from the other children. "Let me have a look at that!"

Patric stood silent while Amin checked out the blade but he never let his gaze slip from the lad's bloated face. The other children watched them, certain that the larger boy would take the blade for himself.

The seconds ticked by in a drag of time, doubled by the beat of Patric's own heart. There was a deep pressure stirring within him, starting about his feet and pushing itself further up his form as it rumbled like thunder along his spine. His meaty hands opened and closed; opened and closed; open and closed until his fingers were pressed so tightly against his palms that his nails cut the skin. It was a red-hot heat churning in his stomach until it flew right up through his head to explode in a fury.

Suddenly Amin was on his back, his chubby hands flailing about his face in an effort to block the punches that were seemingly delivered by a dozen or more hands. Each of them connected, some on Amin's chin, some about his forehead, one square in the nose to cause a geyser of blood to pump up in furious escape. Some time later the throb of Patric's own hand put an end to his assault. Without really seeing him, he looked down at Amin then slowly slipped from his unconscious body to root in the mud in search of Brian's blade. He took hold of it, shaking his head hopelessly for the mire that covered the previously gleaming weapon.

"Ye killed him, Patric!" Eagan gasped as he and the other children backed away in fear.

Patric's head snapped around. He was so intent on Brian's blade that he almost forgot about the chubby child who was now a gnarled and bloody heap at his feet. "Quick—get some water!" he shouted.

One of the girls ran to the mill to bring back a bucket. She placed it just beyond Patric's grasp, jumping back as he reached for it.

He picked it up then dumped the contents over Amin's head. The boy didn't stir. He gave a nervous tug to Amin's shoulder silently praying he hadn't killed the lad. *That would get him into more trouble than even he could talk his way out of.* He shook more furiously and finally Amin groaned, slowly opening the one eye that he could.

Patric sighed with relief as he helped the boy sit upright. "Ye should never touch a warrior's weapon, Amin!"

Amin rubbed his head with one bloated hand while the other rooted around his mouth to come up with a bit of broken tooth. His voice whistled as he shoved Patric back and cried, "Wait 'til my mother sees what ye've done. This time ye'll be in trouble for sure!"

Amin used Eagan's kilt as a handhold to help himself up, popping the brooch and leaving the smaller boy's shirttail flapping. He steadied himself against the heads of two other boys then with one under each arm, slowly staggered back toward his own hut.

Eagan refastened the brooch of his kilt then brushed the soot away from the material that hung to his knees. "Ye're in for it now, Patric," he sighed as his eyes expressed his sympathy.

Patric shook his head slowly. He never liked Amin much, no one did, but at least he wasn't afraid of him. He slapped the air after him then returned his attention to the mud covering Brian's blade.

As he struggled to bring the shine from the metal he heard the cry from the front gate. He shielded his eyes against the glare of the sun, squinting to make out the shadows of two riders followed by an endless procession of foot soldiers, horses and carriages. He looked to Eagan who saw it too and together they burst into a youthful sprint that carried them above the grass as their spry muscles propelled them forward. They jogged alongside Lorca's horse eagerly probing the man's expression for news of their victory but the *Ri Tuath's* face was sullen.

Patric gulped hard. "Did we lose, father?"

The misery on Lorca's face was unmistakable. His crystal blue eyes never moved, never blinked, they only stared ahead to the hall as they rested on the darkened circles of his cheeks below. The sight of it caused Patric to panic. His breaths came too quickly. He asked again, "Did we lose, father?"

It was Brian who responded with a finger against his crimson beard to hush the lad.

Suddenly Patric's legs lost all strength. Like a newborn colt they warbled beneath him, forcing him to steady himself against the old oak just before the hall. How could they lose? How could the crown be left for those evil O'Neills? How soon would it be before the Vikings came to them? The questions raged inside his brain without answers causing him to gasp with anxiety.

The wagon carrying the dead passed him by and as he struggled to catch his breath he noticed the glimmering ray of light cast off by a ring on the finger of one of the dead soldiers. It was familiar to him—not just the ring but the whole hand. He moved closer, searching his memory to identify where he had seen it before.

The return of warriors was always a spectacle. If they returned victorious there was a feast, defeated, there was a mass, but win or lose the process of returning dead warriors was a daunting one.

They gathered outside the hall, mostly women and children but also a smattering of men who could no longer fight. They crawled over one and other as they searched the lines for their kin. Names were shouted between the masses bringing cries of jubilation when the warrior was brought home whole, but when the call was left hanging on the air without a response, the wails of grief could penetrate the skull of a wild boar.

The kerchief on Grace's head slipped back to expose her flaming red hair as she clawed her way to the front of the procession. She yanked on Lorca's ankle to draw his attention down to her. "Are ye unharmed, husband? Where are my children?"

In a slow, painful motion, Lorca dismounted his cherry mare, lowering himself to stand within inches of his wife but never touching her. Randa, Malora, Gunra, Calcot and Lorcain surrounded him. His silence was heard with a penetrating ring that halted all movement around them.

Grace stared into his eyes, the grief in them speaking as clearly as if he uttered the words but still she pressed him. She needed to hear it from his own mouth. It wouldn't be real until he told her of it. "Where's Acard, Lorca? Where's my son? Does he stay behind to break camp again?"

It was then that Patric came, nearly colliding with Acard's wife, Eabha, and her daughters as he thrust himself into Grace's skirts to find comfort for the incomprehensible sorrow he now felt. He took up his father's limp hand to stroke the blonde hair on it but the weight was too heavy to hold and it tumbled back to Lorca's side as he continued to stand silent.

"Lorca!" Grace shouted, "I ask ye again, where's Acard?"

"Please, father," Eabha croaked, the tears streaming down her face belying the fact that she already knew the answer.

There were no words in Lorca's throat—only the lump left there at the moment the long sword entered his son's back. He'd seen death before, slept with it, ate with it, wallowed in it caused by his own hand, but this death was all consuming and he'd not uttered a word since the final rattle of it.

Grace took him by the shoulders—a grip of desperation as her eyes flicked back and forth drawing both tears and words from him.

"He was a good captain, wife," Lorca finally croaked. "He gave his life in defense of one of his men. Ye would have been proud to see how well he fought."

Eabha burst into hysterics before fleeing through the crowd. Grace watched her. There was nothing she could do to comfort the young widow. It would be no different for her. She turned back toward her husband, gripping his coat and clinging to him in dolor as the vortex of her grief tugged her further away. The words played over in her head as she careened ever downward, the cracking of her heart almost audible to those around her. Patric felt her knees caving and struggled to hold her up.

"Mama!"

It was that simple cry, the cry of her youngest calling out in despair that brought her strength back to her. There were still others to protect and she must be the one to do it or her husband would have them all dead fighting for Brian.

She willed the stiffness back into her body, reaching out with a strong hand to force Patric behind her. With prideful disdain she hoisted her shoulders, straightening her spine until her glance was leveled at Lorca.

"He was a good warrior but he's dead now! My first born son is dead for yer precious Brian!"

Brian had expected as much but still the words griped his heart like a cold hand causing it to skip a beat. Grace was looking to him now, that cold, calculated gaze that he'd seen so often penetrated him to expose his soul for the world to see.

He dismounted slowly, dangling from the saddle as his mind dutifully scrambled for the words that would bring acceptance of the tragedy. "I'll raise a memorial to him, Grace. All will know yer son was a good and loyal warrior. They'll revere him for all time."

From his place in the shadows of the doorway, Kevin saw the rip of pain as it slashed through his mother's body. He rushed toward her. Only a mindless warrior like Brian macCennitig could bring such grief upon his family. He was a barbarian, preferring to use brawn and intimidation to get his way rather than following the teachings of the ancient ones. He was a disgrace to his lineage.

Grace didn't acknowledge Kevin or her other sons who now surrounded her, instead she stood tall, rocking herself up on her toes to bring her eyes level with Brian's. "Are ye *Ri Tuath Ruire* now, brother? Do ye own the precious crown ye sacrificed so many lives to win?"

It was a war of wills as brother and sister squared off to gain the adoration of the gathered crowd. They had played the game many times before with Cennitig. Grace had always been the winner then—she had an unnatural hold on his father which she exploited thoroughly whenever they disagreed, but Cennitig was dead now and it was Brian's turn to claim victory.

He straightened his shoulders. "Aye, Grace. I'm *Ri Tuath Ruire*. Both Donovan and Malmua are dead."

Kevin said a silent prayer for the last Eagahonact prince. It was a sorrowful thing to see a clan of thinking men destroyed. As always, there was Brian to blame for it.

Grace nodded her head before rocking up on her toes again. "Then yer crown shall be forever stained with the blood of my son," she issued then, with a growl from deep in the pit of her stomach, she spit in Brian's eye.

The gasp of the crowd caused a gentle breeze at Brian's back and for a moment he was uncertain of them. Many of their own lay dead in the carriage for his crown. He tried to feel them through his skin—to know what was in their minds before choosing a response to her action but suddenly Lorca lurched forward halting the necessity for a response.

He grabbed Grace's arm, scattering his children like frightened geese as he pushed past them. He was surprised to see Kevin remaining but paid him little mind as he yanked his wife's arm to force her to face him.

"The lad died an honorable death, Grace! Ye've nay cause to treat the *Ri Tuath Ruire* harshly!"

Now the crowd was pushing at Brian's back. A low pandemonium broke out among them as they took their sides in the altercation. Horses were removed from the scene so that the people could have a better view and the dead continued to cool in the wagon, but all eyes remained on the new *Ri Tuath Ruire* and his sister.

Brian raised his hand high as his voice thundered on the wind. "Don't be angry with her, Lorca. She speaks the truth! My crown *is* stained with the blood of yer son and all those felled in this battle."

Realizing that he had usurped Brian's right to deal with the situation, Lorca gave his wife a tiny shove so she'd again be standing before him, but it was the crowd that Brian was addressing not her. "I'd rather wear a crown stained with the blood of those who fight for Eire than one stained with the blood of those murdered by the foreigners for the sake of greed! Acard wanted nay less and I'll give my last breath to assure ye'll never lose yer children to a Viking raid again. Eire is yers! I'll not tolerate foreign occupation!"

It was his patent speech, one Grace had heard many times before but wide eyes marked her surprise for the impact it had on the crowd that was now demanding her homage to their savior.

Half smiling, Brian turned to take her by the shoulders. She recoiled and Kevin quickly made himself a barrier between them. Brian nodded then backed away. He would be forced to perform his monologue with different visuals.

He pulled the silver head ring out from the folds of his coat, holding it high for all to see. "This crown is as much Acard's as it is mine. Ye can be sure I'll use it to protect his people instead of selling them into Viking slavery like the Eagahonacts and O'Neills."

Grace's lips quivered in defeat and despair causing her words to be a hiss of breath as she scrambled around Kevin to face him, "I hate ye, Brian! I hate ye and yer wars!" Again the vortex of grief gripped her, pulling her into the darkness as her body sailed ever downward.

To Kevin's chagrin, it was Brian who caught her, crushing her against his chest as he buried his moistened face into her hair. With the love of a brother he whispered, "I'll make this up to ye, Grace. I promise I will."

In a moment of weakness Grace threw her arms around Brian's neck, sobbing into his chest as he hushed her with the clucking of his tongue.

Kevin's eyes went wide before he realized that his mother must have been confused. Surely she didn't believe that Brian could save her from the Vikings who raped her as a child and left her for dead in her own hall. Nay, it would take a leader of greater intelligence than Brian's to negotiate with the Vikings and stop their raiding.

He looked at the warriors milling around the field and thought to himself, "*I can be that leader.*"

CHAPTER 5

▼

Cavenlow, Ireland: The Great Hall—Just Past Midnight—17, May 977 A.D.
Night had fallen heavily upon Lorca's village. Some families retired to the chapel to prepare their dead for burial while unwounded husbands returned to their huts to assure their wives they were whole. For everyone else it was time for rest, the time when the hush of the world was only broken by the deep rattles of sleep bouncing off the mud walls. It was a time of silence, but in the great hall of Cavenlow the struggle of a new king's heart could be heard in the gentle whisper of the night.

Brian knelt upon his pad, running his hands over his face as his conscience struggled within. The day's battle had been won with Grace but it wouldn't be long before he would have to face many similar scenes within the unrest of his people.

They would come to *him* now, begging him to make easy their struggling lives, to decide in conflicts over cattle ownership or encroachment, or worse yet, to decide the fate of children left over from the raids. And there would be raids—there were always raids. Even in the time of Madamion the savage Vikings couldn't be kept completely down. Now it would be up to him to stop them once and for all or be made a mockery for his lifetime of promises.

He looked to the thatched roof but beyond to the Lord, considering a prayer for assistance. He half mumbled something inaudible even to himself as his mind drifted away from his spirituality and again into the world of men.

His prostration to the Lord abandoned, he crossed his legs to sit upon his pallet.

He sighed deeply as his mind took him to that terrible place of self-doubt and failure he so dreaded.

The wipe of his face with his hands was a habit, done without forethought as he struggled for a plan that would win him the loyalty of his people but to Patric, who was spying from the doorway, it resembled sobbing. He raced across the hall to offer comfort to the *Ri Tuath Ruire*.

Brian turned a quick eye to glimpse the lad's hand on his shoulder, his brain easily establishing its owner and the thought behind the touch.

Through the children they would come to him.

With a will mastered long ago, Brian summoned his tears—not full sobbing but a glazing that let them slowly roll down his cheeks. He turned to look at Patric. "Do ye hate me for the loss of yer brother, lad?"

Patric gazed deep into the watery dark eyes of his leader and gasped, "Nay! I could never hate ye, Brian. I love ye. Ye're *Ri Tuath Ruire*!"

"Do ye love me, Gilla Patric?" Brian urged, needing to hear the lad say it again—needing the total loyalty. "Do ye love me even after I broke my promise to keep yer brother safe?"

Patric's eyes were wide, seeing the *Ri Tuath Ruire* but not the tortured soul beneath. "Of course I love ye, Brian—everyone does."

Brian took him by the shoulders, demanding, probing, begging, "Why do ye love me, lad? Why?"

The answer was there right on the tip of Patric's tongue. He had always loved him—his father made him love him—it was bred into every fiber of his being.

"My father loves ye more than any other man, Brian."

Frustration took over and Brian shook the lad with strength enough to rattle his teeth. "I didn't ask after yer father, I asked after ye. Why do ye love me?" He was desperate. "Tell me—tell me now!"

Patric's probing, puerile eyes darted furiously as his brain scrambled for the answer Brian sought. He didn't know why he loved him, he just did. He began to shake. Every muscle in his body contracting and loosening until the tremble was enough to make him nearly drop the blade in his hand—Brian's blade—the one he asked him to look after and the reason for him being in the hall. He held it out, hoping Brian would forgive him not answering if he saw the great care he had given to the weapon.

"I kept it safe as ye asked, Brian."

Indeed.

Brian sighed as the light of the oil lamp danced off the polished metal. It was obvious the lad took great pains to keep the weapon safe. Half smiling, he placed the blade into Patric's waist belt as a gift. If the lad could still love him after losing his brother then there was hope that his people would follow.

*　　　*　　　*　　　*

Kings never did such things—it was far beneath their station. They were to be lauded over the people as a power beyond their grasp—an all knowing, all wise being who couldn't possibly be found amongst the common man. But it was Brian's habit to be among his people, that's why he slept in the hall rather than the private quarters Lorca had offered him last night. He was doing it again now, kneeling over his great two-handed sword beside the body of the young captain, Acard, and amongst the rest of the dead of Cavenlow. His head remained bowed even when the whispers from the crowd reached his ears. If they would follow him he must first show them that *their* losses were *his* also.

The chapel stood in the northern section of the round fort, beyond the barracks on a path branching off from the main road. Tufts of pink heather and lavender surrounded it. Beside it stood two gnarled yew trees with low lying branches. It was built on timbers to allow a small creek to run beneath it in the wet weather making it necessary to climb three steps to gain entrance.

Brian stood beside the abbot on the wooden deck with the bodies of his fallen warriors lying in neat rows beside him. After finishing his Latin incantations the abbot turned to the new *Ri Tuath Ruire,* coughing to clear his lungs of the incense smoke before asking, "Will ye address yer people, Brian?"

Brian looked up at him, eyes again glazed by his own will. He nodded his head as he got to his feet then stepped to the edge of the platform. He searched the crowd below him and his heart pounded deep within his chest. The fear of their rejection dried his throat but he took a deep breath, cleared it then spoke in thunderous tones.

"Who has the power to stop death?"

The crowd stared at him blankly, waiting for him to answer the question by invoking the name of the Lord.

"Ye do!" he shouted at them.

The abbot quickly crossed himself against the blasphemy. The crowd soon followed as they mumbled amongst themselves that the *Ri Tuath Ruire* had obviously gone mad with grief.

Brian smiled wryly then stepped forward a bit. "And who has the power to give life?"

This time their stares were full of fear for his answer.

"Ye do!" he shouted again, lifting his sword above his head as he did.

The abbot stepped forward hoping to waylay the *Ri Tuath Ruire* before it was too late but Brian only brushed him aside, bringing an audible gasp from the crowd for the harsh treatment of the holy man. He was in the full swing of it now and it wouldn't do for him to turn back. He stepped still closer, eyes wild with intent as he howled, "Every time a Viking long boat comes ashore on our island with the sanction of the O'Neills they bring death to us. We can stop it! We can give life to those who would have fallen to the Viking ax if only we unite! If only we show them that we will fight *together* in protection of what's ours!"

The crowd began to come around. There were a few nods and fewer mumbles as he continued, "We have the power of life and death in *our* hands but for too many years we've set it aside. We've been divided amongst ourselves, always begging for scraps in petty skirmishes, selling each other out for the leftovers of a foreigner. It ends now, with us, with the people of Munster!"

"I lost my son in yer battle, Brian," came the call from the back of the crowd, "I'll not lose another. We've enough of war, we want the peace ye promised us."

Brian probed the masses to identify the middle-aged woman who made the comment. He locked onto her, eyes burning into her soul as he retorted, "Many here have lost loved ones, but I wonder if ye'd prefer yer son to have died in a Viking raid rather than fighting like a hero on that battlefield as he did."

The woman hung her head with the truth and Brian continued, "We must battle to show our strength—to make *them* fear us so that we may give life to our children and theirs who come up after. When foreigners hear of Munster they should tremble with fear of us instead of laughing as they lay fire to our homes and take our treasure. Ye have that power and I pray ye to use it. Follow me and I will lead ye, arm and arm, brother to brother until the Lord's hand separates us."

The abbot gave a gentle sigh as the *Ri Tuath Ruire* finally invoked God into his monologue.

"Will ye fight with me?" Brian challenged, again waving his sword above his head.

It was the woman herself who called out, "Long live Brian macCennitig, *Ri Tuath Ruire!* May his mighty sword protect us always!"

The woman's words sparked a frenzy and soon the crowd was cheering—clapping frantically as they repeated his name over and again. Broken warriors found the arm of a comrade, jostling each other in a playful fashion, reliving the glory of the battle a few days previous. There was a light in them, the light of victory, the light of bravery, the light of pride. It was a success, minor though it was, the first step in many such to follow.

But there was one in the crowd who didn't celebrate, or smile, or love him loyally. There was one who hated him, wishing him dead from her place behind her hands. Brian saw her and leapt from the platform to put himself before her.

"I pray ye to forgive me, Grace."

She turned her head away.

He dropped to his stomach to kiss both her feet causing the crowd to suddenly gasp. To add drama to the scene he thrust the hilt of his blade up at her. "If ye want my head then take it but I can't go on without yer forgiveness. Either give me forgiveness or strike me, Grace."

The crowd pushed at her back, identifying the one weed that could spread doubt among them. They grumbled at her, preferring to pluck her out than allow her to pull them apart with her skepticism.

Grace closed her eyes as she silently prayed for Brian to stand but he knew he was winning and wouldn't allow her to escape so easily. He remained prone before her, waiting for her concession—or demise.

"Who are ye to deny the Ri Tuath Ruire forgiveness?" another woman who stood nearby shouted. "It should be ye prone at his feet in thanks giving for saving us from the Vikings."

There was anger in them now, a deep throbbing hatred for a common enemy. Brian mouthed the words on the arch of Grace's foot, knowing she'd understand them if not hear them. "They're mine, Grace."

Grace tried to tug her foot away but he held her by her ankles as the crowd surged against her back. She was defeated and she thought quickly, forming a plan to gain back at least a bit of her power.

First she dropped the blade that he had thrust into her hands then, with her body trembling in hatred, she slowly sank to her knees. She lifted Brian's chin with her open palm so she could see his eyes before forcing a smile.

The action brought a half grumble of acceptance from the crowd and for a moment her eyes flamed as she stared right through him, hating him for making her debase herself, but as she glimpsed the childlike expression on his face her heart softened. She kissed his forehead.

Someone clapped, others soon followed and Brian flashed a fleeting smile for his victory.

She saw it and nodded as her face relaxed into a more natural smile. It was a masterful performance that beat her and her kiss on his lips was her tribute to it. Her people were now roaring for her and she gave them everything they demanded. She kissed his eyes then his cheeks and again his lips before rising to her feet, pulling him up with her. She spoke in a loud, sharp voice rivaling his own. "I forgive ye, *Ri Tuath Ruire*. I forgive ye and love ye loyally," she lied.

It was up to him to conclude the performance and as usual he did it grandly. He let his body collapse against her bosom then sobbed openly as a hundred hands tenderly stroked his head.

✳   ✳   ✳   ✳

As the sun rose in the sky on the morning of 16 June in the year of Our Lord 977, Brian Boru macCennitig stood upon the rock of Cashel before the nobles of the Dal Cais clan to receive the crown of *Ri Tuath Ruire of Munster*. Patric macLorca, prince of Cavenlow, felt the weight of his father's hands on his shoulders while he looked on.

CHAPTER 6

▼

THREE YEARS LATER

Meath, North Ireland: The stronghold of Malsakin O'Neill: five hours past noon—14, June 980 A.D.—Malsakin leveled his round blue eyes at his cousin, Fladbartoc knowing full well that his kinsmen would heed any direction the Ri Tuath of Ailech offered. It was widely known that Fladbartoc was both honest and protective of his clan, but the trait that brought him the most reverence was his reputation as a fierce and vicious warrior.

The shadowy hall grew noisy as the various O'Neill leaders debated the proper way to handle the invitation issued by the new Ard Ri. The past years had been riddled with usurping and bitter defeats for the O'Neills. Not only had Donovan been brutally murdered in Sulcoit leaving the crown of Munster to a Dal Cais, but also the high throne of Ard Ri, which had been held by the O'Neills for nearly two centuries, was lost to the Viking earl, Olaf Curran of Dublin. Not since the days before Obdub O'Neill had the clan been so weak. Now they gathered to discuss what to do about it.

There were those who proposed rejecting the Ard Ri's invitation believing that to heed it would further empower the Viking. Others thought it best to go to Tara to hear him out with the hope of gaining back some of what had been taken from them. But in the end it would be Fladbartoc who would decide—a fact that made Malsakin, their host for the evening and the only Ri Tuath not invited to Olaf's meeting, most uncomfortable.

The great enmity between Malsakin and Olaf began years ago after the Viking settled Dublin. Rather than be content with the fact that his city boasted the richest seaport in all of Ireland, Olaf insisted on expanding its boundaries by menacing its neighboring territories of Meath and Leinster. Though Meath was able to beat Olaf back, Malsakin suffered a loss in the form of a broken marriage contract when Madavan of Leinster, a descendant of the mystical Tuatha daDannan clan, was forced to give his daughter, Kormlada, to the Viking in exchange for peace.

It was said that Kormlada possessed the power of sight and that any man who lay with her would achieve greatness. It was one of the reasons Malsakin had sought a marriage with her in the first place—that and her overwhelming beauty. But now it was Olaf Curran who claimed those riches, a fact that caused Malskin to seethe.

"I feel we have little choice in the matter but to go to Olaf and hear him out," Fladbartoc issued as he tucked a wayward strand of chestnut hair behind his ear. The warrior's broad shoulders and well muscled arms stretched against his lein with each movement of his hand. He was taller than most of the O'Neills and often used his size to intimidate his enemies.

"This invitation may be our only chance for negotiation. If we let it pass there's nay telling what the foreigner will do next."

"He's a treacherous man," offered Assaroe, Ri Tuath of the northern village, which carried his name. He gave a scratch to his bulbous nose before sipping from his cup. "He's all but annihilated Leinster since Madavan's death and if he can…."

"Ye mean murder," Malsakin interrupted, drawing grumbles and nods from the other leaders. Though Malsakin's form wasn't as grand as Fladbartoc's his voice was commanding, gaining immediate heed whenever he spoke. His posture was straight as a board and his sharp eyes struck fear where his muscles couldn't.

"Ye know as well as anyone that Olaf murdered Madavan in cold blood even after the chief gave him Kormlada."

Fladbartoc shook his head for the folly that lost Madavan his life—it seemed such a waste. "There are those who would tell ye that Olaf had every right to kill the chief after the lass didn't prove to be as magical as her father portended."

"She was nay more than a babe when Madavan gave her over," Malsakin huffed defensively. "Ye can't expect a lass of twelve summers to be producing much of anything never the less magic."

"Well she did give him a son," Morgan of Dundalk replied, "though I'm surprised there weren't more." He plucked a loose thread from his perfectly tailored coat then tossed it aside with disdain. "They say the woman has as much an appetite for the bedchamber as she does for offering counsel to the high king." He issued an elbow to Malsakin's rib as he chuckled, "Grew into a real beauty that one did. Stands nearly six feet tall with golden hair that hangs down to her ankles. I'd say Olaf had nay right to grumble over the bargain."

"If ye ask me the bargain was kept," Ardmore of Airgialla broke in, the scowl on his gaunt face demonstrating his distaste for the turn the conversation had taken. "Madavan said that the lass would bring any man she laid with great power and now Olaf sits as Ard Ri."

Malsakin chaffed at the remark and Fladbartoc turned to look at him. Truth be told, if it hadn't been Olaf who took the lass from his cousin it would certainly have been him. Not for the magic that she was said to have possessed—being a logical man and a Christian, Fladbartoc didn't believe in such tales, but beauty was something she promised even as a wee lass and it had long since come to pass. "Since that magic was promised over twenty years ago and Olaf has only had the crown for these few," he droned, "I'd say the Viking had every right to believe that Madavan betrayed him."

"Well however he got the crown the fact is that he has it now," Malsakin issued, knowing full well the thoughts behind his cousin's statement. "Now let's get back to the matter at hand. We're here to decide what to do about Olaf and we best get on with it. If he treats the whole of Eire as he's treated Leinster we'll have more trouble than any of us can handle."

"Leinster's Boru's problem now. Let him deal with it," Assaroe interjected, clearly surprising the others.

They looked at him with wide eyes. "Don't tell me ye didn't know that Boru marched into Laigan on the new moon and took the territory for his own?"

Their querying looks told him he had a bit of juicy gossip and he offered it happily. "Since Olaf left the territory leaderless he had nay knowledge of Boru's presence. By the time he became aware of it the Dal Cais had mustered the Leinster Galls and swiftly beat back the Ard Ri's army. Brian Boru macCennitig has named himself leader of the south from Uisnech to Cork and from the North Atlantic to the Sea of Eire. All that's left to Olaf Curran is Dublin, Clontarf and whatever northern villages he can lay his hands on."

They sat silent for a moment, each man taking in the news. Brian had been dubbed *Boru* (tribute) because as an outlaw he demanded payment to stop his raiding. Now he was usurping both titles and lands giving the name a far more dangerous meaning.

At length it was Morgan who broke the silence. "Serves Olaf right," he replied with a shrug of his shoulders. "Any man who would take his wife's people into bondage and let her homeland rot without a leader deserves to be taken out. Makes me sick with worry that a man such as that now sits on our high throne."

Malsakin took hold of Fladbartoc's arm as a hopeful thought struck him. "Do ye think that Olaf gathers us to march on Boru?"

"Nay," Fladbartoc replied with a shake of his head. "Boru's been invited to the meeting as well."

That information made Malsakin even more uncomfortable than he had been before. Though they had never met, Malsakin feared Brian Boru macCennitig more than any other man. A shudder ran up his spine as he remembered the long ago prophecy delivered by his mother on her deathbed. She had told him that he would one day be Ard Ri but she also cautioned that if he wasn't careful, Brian Boru macCennitig would take everything away from him.

"So the time has come," he mumbled to himself, wondering exactly how the prophecy would play out.

"Are ye alright?" Fladbartoc inquired of his cousin, thinking that he was embarrassed by the fact that he wasn't called to the meeting. "I've already said that I'd take ye as my second. Ye needn't worry over it, Malsakin."

The other kings turned toward Malsakin, silently trying to guess the reason why he hadn't been invited to the meeting, but Malsakin didn't acknowledge them. His thoughts were still with Brian.

"So do ye think Boru will attend then?" he asked his cousin.

"Could be," Fladbartoc replied. "I'd say that with his taking of Leinster he now has the most at stake. He may well want an alliance with the Ard Ri."

"And what of Balder?" Ardmore inquired. "He's as fierce as ye are, Fladbartoc. With his Viking mother captain of Olaf's army, I'd say 'twould be good to have him with us. He's kin to ye, aye."

"Aye," Fladbartoc responded. "To both Malsakin and me through the blood of his father." He thought about it for a moment as he twisted his long, dark beard between his fingers. "If he came, I'd say 'twould be a good thing, if he doesn't, I'd say we should be worried."

"I think we should worry either way," Morgan replied. He smoothed a crease in his lein then wrinkled his brow as he gave his full attention to the other men. "I for one would cast my vote against going."

"So it's on the table then," Fladbartoc issued, seizing the opportunity to put them in a position to make a decision. "Do we go or nay?"

"I say we go," Malsakin blurted.

"Ye say?" Morgan questioned. "I thought Fladbartoc said that ye weren't invited."

"I just said he'll come as my second," Fladbartoc interrupted. "If Olaf doesn't like it let him lash out at me."

"Invitation or nay, I'll be there," Malsakin issued. "Olaf has taken more from me than anyone else and I plan on getting some of it back."

"I see," Assaroe chided knowingly. "So are ye planning to kidnap the woman right out from under Olaf's nose? If ye are, ye better bring a ladder, she's taller than ye, aye."

"Kormlada has little to do with it," Malsakin snapped back, though Assaroe wasn't far from the truth. "I go because my land is ever threatened by Olaf's aggressions. I'll not be kept from the meeting only to find out that ye rots struck a deal with the demon to take my lands and move me somewhere else."

"That's ancient history," Morgan growled in defense of himself. Long ago he was part of a group that tried to overthrow Malsakin's father, a fact Malsakin never failed to remind him of.

"It'll do us nay good to bicker amongst ourselves," Fladbartoc broke in. "We must decide if we're going and if we are, what we will demand from the Ard Ri."

"Then again," Morgan broke in, "we could wait for Boru to make a move."

The others looked askance of him. "Well, he's taken Leinster, mayhap he's thinking of taking the high kingship as well?"

"Over my dead body," Malsakin growled as the gooseflesh spread across his arms. "It's bad enough that we lost the throne to a Viking, I won't add insult to injury by letting a Dal Cais usurper have it."

They all nodded in agreement and suddenly Malsakin was overtaken by a thought. He got to his feet, stretching himself a bit before pouring another cup of wine.

"I say we go to Tara and bargain with Olaf for peace. If he wants to expand his holdings, let him expand south along the coast. Waterford and Wexford are strong Gallish kingdoms. Let him ally with his own people to take the land surrounding those cities."

"But that's Dal Cais territory now," Ardmore huffed. "Boru will certainly stop him if he makes a move there."

"He may try," Malsakin offered with a wry smile, "but if we swear allegiance to Olaf and lend him our armies it will keep the Ard Ri from raiding in the north and at the same time keep Boru too busy to think about making a grab for the high throne. In the end we'll all have what we want."

The room grew silent as Malsakin O'Neill demonstrated that brains could be as useful as brawn.

✳   ✳   ✳   ✳

Cenn Cora, Ireland: three hours past noon—11, July 980—More fort than village, Cenn Cora was founded by Brian after his falling out with Madamion years earlier. It was from within the wooden ringed fortress that Brian and Lorca first laid their plan to take down the O'Neill Ri Tuath Ruire, Dub daBairenn. When the plan failed they were named outlaws and forced into hiding but they always managed to find their way back to the village nestled amongst the trees and located so close to the River Shannon that the sound of running water was ever present.

The sun streamed through the long windows of the whitewashed structure that served as the great hall, playing off the colorful banners hanging from the rafters to give the room a serene atmosphere. Connor kept himself busy pacing the floor while Brian's uncle, Turlog, Ri Tuath of Thomond, rambled on. Though only two summers older than Brian, Turlog looked like a much older man with his long stringy hair hanging white on his head and his greasy beard hanging white on his face. His appearance was odd, as if there wasn't enough skin to cover his bones, and his eyes were small, set deep in their sockets. For as long as Connor had known him, Turlog was enamored by his own voice, unable to put anything plain but instead choosing to draw out his words as if he were a great thinker.

Connor huffed as he moved to stand beside Lorca who was gazing out the window surveying the lush surroundings of the hall, but Thorien of Limerick was intent on the speech. He leaned forward to be certain that he didn't miss a word since Gaelic wasn't his native tongue.

At last Turlog finished and Brian nodded agreement with his uncle's assessment of Olaf's intentions. He called to Lorca who was basking in the sunlight streaming on his face, "Olaf must have evil on his mind if he's gathering the leaders together in Tara. It puts me to mind of when Donovan called Madamion to their meeting."

Lorca jumped at the sound of Brian's voice. He hadn't been listening to Turlog but instead had been thinking about his sons. He'd paid a heavy toll for their victory in Laigain with the loss of Lorcain, Breen, Randa and Calcort. He said a silent prayer for the Lord to keep their souls then rubbed the sadness from his eyes before turning to respond, "Aye. It seems the Ard Ri has only invited those leaders with reputations as fierce warriors to the meeting. I hear that Malsakin wasn't asked to attend which leads me to believe that he wants only those capable of challenging him in one place at one time. What he'll do with them once they're there is a puzzlement for certain."

The intensity of the conversation drew Connor's attention. "But how can he take them all down at once? Even if he had dozens of the most capable assassins hidden all around the place there would be no guarantee that he could manage to strike them all down without risk to himself."

He went silent for a moment to ponder his own words then he shook his head. "Och, it can't be done."

He made a move to walk away but Lorca grabbed his arm. "Wait. Ye may be on to something." He turned to Brian. "Certainly Man boasts the most skilled assassins in the region. Olaf has strong ties in Man, aye. He could have hired as many as he needed then brought them over by boat without anyone being the wiser." He nodded his head certain that he'd solved the riddle. "I say that's exactly what he's planning."

"Well," Brian issued then slapped the table with his hand as he rose, a wry smile playing on his face. "I should think that the best way to find out would be to get as close to Tara as possible on the day of the meeting without being discovered. If it is as ye say and Olaf has the O'Neills murdered then we shall strike at Olaf and take the high kingship ourselves."

A chill of excitement ran up Thorien's spine as he expanded on Brian's plan. "Aye. We'll gather the Leinster Galls together in Clontarf, just outside of Tara. Together we'll lay in wait for Olaf to do his deed. Once it's done we'll storm the village and take the crown for the Dal Cais."

"Aye," Turlog agreed. "The Galls fought for ye once, they'll be happy to do it again. There's nay doubt this could work."

All in turn they looked to Connor who had been picking at a splinter of wood from the windowsill. Sensing their stares, he looked up at them, an impish grin slowly spreading on his face. The twinkle in his eyes spoke louder than words and he moved forward, extending his right hand and suspending it in front of Brian. Brian covered it with his, then Turlog, then Thorien and finally Lorca. It was an oath of loyalty to remain bound to each other in victory or in death.

CHAPTER 7

▼

Tara, Ireland: Two hours past noon—23, September, 980 A.D.—The road to Tara was eerily silent putting Fladbartoc's skin to crawling. It had been an uneventful ride but there was something about the sky and the way the clouds were rolling past the sun to cast strange shadows on the ground that made things feel unnatural.

An abundance of trees lined the road that stretched out ahead of them and in the distance they could see the gleaming white walls surrounding Tara. Even there the strange shadows seemed to appear, ringing the fort from the ground to quarter height of the walls.

Tara was an ancient city located just a days ride northwest of Dublin. It had been the sacred home of the druid sect, Tuatha daDannan, but was now used as the seat of Ireland's high king. It was a grand fortress, boasting a feasting hall as well as five lesser halls representing each of Irelands five counties. For four hundred years, it had been the setting for the Fair of Tailtan, a national assembly where Ireland's Ri Tuaths and most of her villagers would enjoy a fortnight of music, games and feasting before they appealed to the Ard Ri for settlement of their disputes. The tradition ceased when Olaf Curran took the throne.

They plodded on slowly until they could smell the roasting meat and the fire that cooked it wafting down the road, then they stopped. What Fladbartoc mistook as a shadow ringing the village was instead a contingent of men. He turned to his cousin whose surprise at the sight of the many guards was as evident as his. There were thousands of them lined outside the walls and up the path. He looked back at the few warriors they'd brought with them. They were no match for Olaf's guards.

"Do we turn back?" he inquired of Ardmore who had reined in next to him.

"Nay," Ardmore replied in hushed tones, never taking his eyes from the walled city. "If we turn back now he'll surely strike at us. I say we present ourselves and see what he's up to. When I die, I want to see the face of the one who kills me."

Though he smiled at his kinsman, Fladbartoc felt little joy. His warrior instinct told him that something was amiss yet there was little that he could do about it other than face it head on. "Let's do it then," he offered as he kicked his horse forward to address the lead guard.

"I'm Fladbartoc O'Neill of Ailech and these are my clansmen. We've been called by the Ard Ri for the purpose of a meeting."

The guard nodded then leaned over to whisper in the ear of the man to his left. They exchanged a few words in their native tongue then he returned his attention to Fladbartoc. "Ye may each take one man inside. All others can be kept at the ready just outside this gate. As ye can see, none of us is armed. Ye'll be safe enough inside."

Fladbartoc nodded his understanding then the guard issued a silent order for the gates to be opened for them. As each man passed they were asked to give their name and the territory from which they hailed. Fladbartoc led the way followed by Ardmore then Morgan but when Malsakin gave his name the guard halted him.

"I can not let ye pass, lord."

"What do ye mean ye can't let me pass?" Malsakin barked. "I'm the Ri Tuath of Meath and I've every right to be in attendance at this meeting."

"Forgive me, lord," the guard replied humbly, "but I've been given strict orders that only those who have been invited may pass. All others must wait outside."

"Ridiculous," Malsakin huffed as he urged his horse forward but the guard grabbed the steed's halter.

"I pray ye, lord to keep back," he said in a tone loud enough to draw attention. Soon several other guards, none wearing weapons but all large enough to do damage without them, joined him. "I pray ye, lord, heed my advice and remain outside."

Noticing the struggle, Fladbartoc doubled back to lend his assistance. He called down to the guard, "Malsakin is acting as my second. Ye've let the others pass with their men, I pray ye let him pass as well."

"I can not, lord," the guard replied in an apologetic tone. "I've been given strict instructions that only the leaders who've been invited may pass. Whether a second to ye or nay, this man has identified himself as a king and he wasn't invited to partake in the discussions. These orders were given to me by the lord Olaf Curran himself and I'm not fool enough to break with them."

Malsakin was about to protest but Fladbartoc placed his horse between his cousin and the guard. "Let me get inside and speak with Olaf myself. Once I tell him of his oversight I'm certain he'll invite ye to join us."

The heat of his anger caused Malsakin to shake but he steadied his hands by wrapping the reins around them before nodding agreement. "Do as ye will," he whispered. "I'll be out here waiting for ye."

Fladbartoc clapped him on the back then turned his horse. "I'll be back, aye."

Malsakin sat his horse, watching as the many chiefs passed through the gates. He nodded to each of them, hoping they would believe he was acting as sentry but in his heart he was certain that they knew he was excluded from the meeting. Moments later they were gone and the gates closed behind them. Malsakin continued to sit his horse for a time but when Fladbartoc didn't appear he became impatient.

He rode back through the gathered army, deciding that they needed guidance and organization. He shouted orders for them to keep a sharp eye and to remain at the ready but as night began to fall without the slightest sign that Fladbartoc would return he decided that he'd had enough.

"Radac, gather our men and let's make our way home," he called before hoisting himself into his saddle. "It's obvious they don't need us here."

Radac nodded then shouted to the other men from his contingent. When they were all seated Malsakin gave the order to pull out.

They made their way up the Leinster road taking their time owing to the falling darkness and Malsakin's grumbling over the way he'd been treated.

"It's Malsakin, for certain," Thorien whispered to Connor from their hiding place in the bushes. "I wonder where the rest of them have got to."

"Maybe they split up after the meeting," Connor replied, his voice a bit shaky as he struggled to keep it low so the army wouldn't hear him. "There's more roads than this one out of Tara."

"Nay," Thorien answered with a shake of his head. "If the meeting was over Fladbartoc and Assaroe would have been riding back this way as well. Something must have happened."

As they continued their debate a rider came barreling up the road with his horse kicking up dirt in its haste. "Olaf has taken them hostage!" he called out when he reined to a halt. "He calls for ye to forfeit yer lands if we're ever to see our leaders alive."

"Come on," Thorien whispered to Connor as he quietly retreated into the forest so they wouldn't be seen. "Brian needs to know about this."

Malsakin smiled when he realized what Olaf was up to. It wasn't that he was unimportant to the Ard Ri, quite the contrary, this elaborate ploy was staged just to get at him. "Where are the soldiers?" he snapped at the messenger, feeling that he had been vindicated. "Do they remain?"

"Aye. They backed out into the woods to take cover in the darkness. What shall we do?"

Malsakin thought for a moment then mentally ran through the leaders who had filed into the gate in Tara. Remembering that Balder wasn't among them, he turned to the messenger. "Can ye ride on?" The messenger nodded and he continued, "Ye must go to Caran Balder and request that the Ri Tuath join us in Tara. Tell him of Olaf's duplicity. Do anything ye can to gain his trust but ye must be quick about it."

The messenger nodded and began to rein his horse but Radac halted him. "Naill," he called to one of the young warriors, "bring some provisions so the lad can ride comfortable," then he turned to Malsakin. "Ye know as well as I that Balder won't get into this. His mother is more loyal to Olaf than any other human being. It was probably she who staged this whole scheme."

"I must try," Malsakin huffed. "My ancestors have managed to keep Meath from Olaf for all these years, I can't be the one to lose it to him now."

*   *   *   *

Brian sat crossed legged in his tent as he pondered the information Thorien had just given him. "What do ye think Malsakin will do?" he queried.

"By the look on his face, he's not planning to give up his lands," Thorien replied. "My guess is that he'll gather up whatever army he can lay his hands on and make a stand at Tara."

"I don't know," Connor interrupted. "There are at least a thousand men lining the gates, probably as many inside. My guess is that the hostages are already dead. If Malsakin shows up he'll be joining them for certain."

"And if he's victorious he'll gain the high crown," Lorca blurted.

"Aye," Brian replied, "that's exactly what I was thinking."

He unfolded his legs then rose to his feet, walking the short distance to the tent flap. He lifted it, letting in a wave of misty air that filled the tent with the scent of moss and fern. "There are two thousand men out there, rested and well fed. Our plan was to bring them to Tara to stand against Olaf and I see nay reason why we shouldn't keep with it."

"Ye mean to ally with Malsakin?" Turlog gasped.

"Aye," Brian replied. "'Tis our best chance to take the high crown from the Viking. I'd rather ally with Malsakin against Olaf and take my chances as to who will gain the high crown than to let him march in there alone and take it for himself should he find success."

"I'd say he'd have little chance of finding success alone," Connor grumbled. "Any success he finds will be due to ye."

"Brian's right," Lorca barked back at the captain. "I've sacrificed five sons to gain this crown. I'll be damned before I see Malsakin take it right out from under our noses. We must ally with him and when we find victory we'll take the crown for ourselves." He turned to Brian. "Malsakin's too weak to stand against ye. He'll make nay move to stop ye from declaring yerself Ard Ri once ye save his life. We must do it, Brian."

Brian nodded his agreement. After these long years of battling the prize was within his grasp, he need only reach out to take it.

＊   ＊   ＊   ＊

Tara, Ireland: In the hut of the Ard Ri: two hours past dawn—25, September 980 A.D.—Kormlada slid her fingers through the ends of her golden hair as she looked adoringly at her husband. Though considered old by most people, to her he was still a virile warrior. His hair had thinned and grayed but he wore it long with a warrior braid on the side. His beard was white and trimmed to the last hair showing off his pointed chin and straight jaw line. His eyes were blue as ice, the windows to the great mind that lurked behind them. Her cheeks flushed and she sighed for his beauty before touching his arm to draw his attention.

"What ye did was wrong," she stated, hoping that he wouldn't notice the fear in her voice. "The only way to save yerself now would be to release them."

Olaf turned to look into his wife's round green eyes, soft with the love she held for him. He never ceased to be amazed that this beautiful creature was truly his, both body and soul. He covered her hand with his then smiled. "That's behind us now, woman," he whispered. "If I free them they'll strike me."

"And if ye kill them ye'll be defeated!" she snapped. She bit her lip then continued more calmly. "I've seen it, Olaf."

"Nay, wife," he whispered again. He took her chin in his hand, forcing her to look deep into his eyes. "Trust me on this one, Kormlada. I cannot fall to them because they've no one left to save them. Balder would never stand against me so who's left?"

She pondered the question, running down the list of warriors who weren't among Olaf's captives. It was true that Balder would never stand against Olaf. He feared his mother far more than he hated the Ard Ri. Then there was Malsakin of Meath. He was certainly cunning but war was never his strong suit. Of those who were left, none had the reason or the ability to save the captured kings.

She was just about to concede the point when she heard the whisper on the wind, reminding her that there was one other who could cut her husband down.

"Boru!"

She shuddered as the name passed her lips.

Olaf chuckled then quickly recovered when he glimpsed the fear in her eyes. He leaned in to kiss her but she drew back. "Calm down, my love. Ye've got yerself tied up in knots and the visions are failing ye. Boru will nay more stand with the O'Neills than I would."

Her glare made him feel as though he had been stripped of his skin. He cleared his throat hoping that the information he was about to offer would put her at ease. "I'll admit that Boru is a menace but yer husband's nay so much a fool as ye may think."

She lifted her eyebrow and he winked at her. "I sent Brodir to Munster to take care of him," he stated with a sly smile. "So ye see, there's nay a thing to be concerned about."

He pushed out his stool then moved behind her to rub her shoulders but as she closed her eyes and leaned into his embrace a vision came clear to her. She opened her mouth to warn him but before she could the voice of their enemy came crashing through the walls.

"Check those huts there," Brian bellowed as he fought his way closer to their chamber. "I doubt he's gotten around to murdering them."

Kormlada's eyes flew open. In desperation she turned toward her husband. "'Tis him, Olaf. Ye must get away from here or ye'll fall to him."

Though he knew she was right he couldn't help asking, "But how? How did he manage to break through the guards?"

She could have told him that Brian drugged the water in the drinking barrel and that he now fought beside Malsakin, but relaying the information would take precious time—time they didn't have if Olaf was to escape.

She took him by the hand then began to make her way toward the door. "We must leave, Olaf. We can run to the forest and wait until it grows dark. After that we'll steal a ship and head for Man."

He stopped dead before pulling her to him. "Nay, wife. I won't run."

"But ye must," she cried.

There was a long silence as they stood facing each other, he knowing that he must go, she willing to do anything to make him remain. She buried her head in his chest and sobbed, "If ye go, I'll lose ye."

He lifted her chin with his finger then stroked back her hair. He smiled. "If I run ye'll lose me just the same. Ye know as well as I do that I must finish this. Now cease yer crying and let me go with a clear head."

When he bent to kiss her she wrapped her arms tight around his neck. She knew it would be the last kiss they ever shared and she wanted him to remember it.

He was breathless when he broke from her and he settled his gaze upon her face, drinking in her beauty. "Take cover, Kormlada and should the worst occur for me, keep our son safe."

She flashed a weak smile then sat silent while he strapped on his sword but when he turned to leave she couldn't control herself. She called out, "Stay with me, Olaf!"

He never looked back as he disappeared through the doorway.

Blood flowed freely on the soil of Tara and the wind howled through the ancient buildings as the light mist dampened the air. Brian had suffered a wound to his right arm and Lorca suffered one to his cheek but they continued to fight, propelled by a dream that was about to become a reality.

Brian turned in time to see Olaf approaching but before he could move toward him a brilliant black horse galloped into his path. His blade collided with that of the dismounting warrior. He was knocked backward.

To Brian's surprise, the warrior waited for him to regain his feet before closing in on him again. They parried several times and with each blocked blow Brian felt the power of the warrior tremor through the metal of his blade. He lunged but the warrior ducked and weaved as if the black armor he wore bore little weight.

Every one of Brian's advances was blocked. He delivered an upward thrust to no avail. He tried to use his height advantage to deliver a downward jab but that was blocked as well. Finally he saw an opportunity to deliver a straight forward stab but to his chagrin the warrior ducked then rolled backward coming to his feet several yards beyond his reach.

Brian was about to charge again but stopped short when he realized that he wasn't fighting a man at all.

Neila kicked her dropped helmet aside then shook her head to cause her shimmering blonde hair to cascade around her shoulders. Her black eyes burned in fury. "Lift yer blade, man!" she barked, her voice thick with her Manx accent. Seeing Brian's hesitation she cut the air with her blade. She was as much a warrior as any man and a good fight got her juices flowing.

Brian took his sword in hand as he eyed the woman circling around him. She wore metal cuffs and a breast plate but still she moved with ease.

"So, ye are the great Brian Boru," she sang as she switched her sword from right hand to left, matching him. "The outlaw king who wants to rid Eire of my people."

"Ye're a plague," he offered, his upper lip lifting in disdain.

"Are we now?" she laughed. "Well let's just see what ye can do about it." With that she lunged, catching him at the knee to open a neat slice that exposed the bone.

Realizing her skills, Brian quickly refocused then went on the attack. He raised his sword in a high arc to cleave her at the shoulder but she deflected it, then he swept down to catch her on the leg but she pulled a short sword from her waist with her right hand and deflected that blow as well.

Brian thought her inhuman as both her hands kept swinging until all he could do to protect himself was to step back out of their path.

When she took a moment to brush back a hair from her eye he lunged forward to jab her in the side. His blade bounced off her breastplate and she laughed at him.

He rushed her, pushing his forearm into her throat to stagger her back a step or two but she was strong, stronger than any man he had ever fought. She pushed his arm forward until he felt his muscles strain.

He was sweating profusely and his jaw was locked as he struggled against her resistance then all at once she lowered her head and he felt her teeth cut into his arm.

"Bitch!" he bellowed as he pulled his arm away then spun on his heel to put some distance between them.

"Aye," she replied, again brushing back the hair from her brow. "And the meanest one ye'll ever know."

Brian had thought that his first wife would forever hold that title but after meeting Neila he had begun to rethink that opinion.

He lunged again and this time he caught her in the face causing a trickle of blood to run down her cheek and into her mouth.

As if she drew pleasure from it, Neila leaned back her head then flicked her tongue out to catch the crimson fluid. While Brian watched, she struck him on the left shoulder. That blow was followed by another to his side then one to his hip. Soon he was backed against a wall. With no room to swing his arms, he held up his blade in a defensive posture. He thought about going for his dagger but she was moving with such speed that he was afraid to break his concentration.

From the corner of his eye he barely glimpsed the warrior riding toward them. His heartbeat hastened with the realization that if the soldier were one of Olaf's he would be dead for sure. He was just coming to terms with the thought when Neila suddenly became still.

Her eyes opened wide before she tilted forward into his arms. It was then that he saw the dagger protruding from her neck. She gasped for breath before crumbling into a ball at his feet.

Brian looked up to see Connor smiling down at him. It wasn't the first time that the burly captain had saved his life. He nodded his head in thanks before stepping around Olaf's fallen captain. For a short time they watched in silence as Neila squirmed like a worm in the sun. She looked to Brian as if asking for mercy and he gave it to her by way of a single blow that separated her head from her neck.

"'Tis the only way to stop a demon," he said to Connor.

Connor smiled but when he turned to look at the field it quickly faded. "Shit," he mumbled as a contingent of Olaf's guards broke through their barricade on the west side of the field. He offered Brian a hand up and in short order they were galloping straight toward them.

They rode into the thick of the battle where the Munster men were being pushed back from the land they had just gained. Malsakin's men fought closest to the great hall and when they opened the doors to take cover, they found Fladbartoc and the other leaders stowed there. Once they were freed it was quick work to secure the village. It was Malsakin who took Olaf as hostage. He bound the Ard Ri hand and foot then had him tied to the center post that held up the roof of the great hall. He gave the order to Radac to find Kormlada and bring her to him. She fought viciously but in the end she was captured then dragged behind his horse into the great hall just under Olaf's nose.

"Release her!" the Ard Ri bellowed as he struggled with his bindings.

Kormlada's eyes were pleading as she looked to him for help but it was Malsakin who saved her, lifting her to her feet then forcing her to take the seat beside him. "She belongs to me now, Olaf and as such, it will be me who decides what's to be done with her."

Olaf's eyes burned with anger but any voice he lent to those feelings was quickly muted by Brian's sudden appearance.

Brian's eyes swept the room crammed with no less than one hundred tables lined in rows as neat as pews in a chapel. Colorful tapestries clung to the walls and canopies of candles hung from the rafters above. Polished bowls of gold and silver rested on sideboards reflecting their flickering light. At the front of the hall sat Malsakin, in the chair of the *Ard Ri*, an ornate assembly of tanned animal hide and gold twisting into a decorative pattern at its crown. "What goes on here?" he growled in a tone so fierce it brought the room to a stand still. "This victory isn't yers alone, Malsakin."

"Aye," Lorca cried as he followed his king into the hall. "'Twouldn't be a victory at all if it wasn't for us. Ye've nay more right to that throne than Brian does and I demand that ye vacate it immediately."

Fladbartoc looked to his cousin, certain he would fall to Boru if the man decided to challenge him then he looked to his clansmen. It was a strange twist of fate that the least capable among them was seated in that coveted chair, but Malsakin was an O'Neill and his closest kin, he'd rather see him as Ard Ri than suffer the alternative of the Dal Cais. He stepped forward, bloody hand on his sword as he placed himself between Malsakin and Brian.

"Lorca's right," he bellowed so that all gathered could hear. "We must put this to a vote."

"Vote," Connor thundered, realizing most of the leaders present were O'Neills, "we're out numbered. 'Twould hardly be fair!"

"Fair enough," Morgan shot back, pushing a wayward strand of hair from his scraped and sooty face. He knew what Fladbartoc was after and he had little choice other than to support it. "Each leader here has a right to choose who will sit on this throne. I for one cast my vote for Malsakin."

"And I cast mine for Brian," Lorca growled, knowing full well it was futile.

"So then it's on the table," Fladbartoc called out. "We have two candidates and each has been presented. It'll be up to those holding titles to declare the Ard Ri. All those in favor of Brian signify by aye."

Of the hundreds gathered in the room less then a quarter went to Brian. Fladbartoc turned his gaze on him. "Need I continue?"

Brian's face was nearly as red as his hair as he struggled to keep control of his anger. He noticed Lorca fingering the hilt of his sword and he reached out to stop him. "Nay," he whispered, still leering at Fladbartoc. "There's nay need to go on. At least not now."

As he turned to leave he caught sight of Kormlada from the corner of his eye. Though obviously distressed by her captivity, she sat regally in her chair, her long blond hair cascading over the side of her face to cover one eye. Their gazes met and for a moment he was overcome by the desire to smile at her. It seemed she felt similarly because she sat full up, brushing back the hair from her face as if to see him better.

He caught himself on the balls of his feet then faced her full on. He bowed to her before spinning on his heel to exit the hall. A lifetime of dreams had been stolen from him by Malsakin but for some odd reason he had the feeling that all was not yet lost.

Kormlada's back stiffened as she noticed the blue light surrounding the Dal Cais king. Since childhood, she was able to see these lights surrounding certain people but the only one who ever carried one so vivid and bright was Olaf.

The door slammed shut and she ripped her vision from Brian to return her attention to Olaf who was now a crumpled heap on the floor of his own hall. The light had gone out around him. She wept for him.

CHAPTER 8

▼

TWO YEARS LATER

Limerick, Ireland: Four hours to midnight—18, April 982 A.D.—By day the mead hall of Limerick was awash in sunlight from the windows cut high on its walls but by night it glowed with the light of six-dozen torches hanging from their metal cages.

Stones of enormous proportions reflecting blue, gray and green laid snugly atop one and other to make up the outer walls that rose to thirty feet at the center peak. Atop them laid the heavy cross beams that formed the shell for the perfectly packed sod roof in which six holes were cut, three to the north and three to the south, to allow an escape for the smoke from the hearths below. Between each hearth hung a tapestry, the length of each falling nearly to the mud packed floor.

At the front of the sixty foot expanse, furthest away from the door but centered on its opening, stood a rough hewn table with twelve rounds of tree trunks as its legs. Behind it stood the earl's chair.

Volkren slipped his meaty hand from the armrest of his chair to pull a loose thread from the fringe of the stag hunt tapestry behind him as he watched the messenger approach. By the look on his face the news couldn't be good. He rolled the thread between his fingers to keep his hand busy. "Out with it!" he barked, startling the messenger as well as Gunner, his high counsel, who was dining across the table from him.

The messenger cast his eyes toward the ground in order to avoid Volkren's cold, green-eyed stare then backed up a few paces.

"Boru's ships block the Shannon. They won't allow any foreign ships through the barricade. Those captains foolish enough to take issue with the edict are being massacred and their ships confiscated. Boru now controls the Shannon and there's nay hope of a bargain."

Volkren's thick brows rushed together as he concentrated on the messenger's words then he laughed, showing an uneven set of stained and yellowed teeth. He looked to Gunner then back at the messenger. "Boru stops my ships? That can't be."

The messenger balled his hands into fists to stop his own fidgeting. "It's as I've told ye, lord. If ye don't believe me, just look outside the window and see for yerself. The city is in an uproar."

Volkren's anger exploded. He swept the trenchers they'd been eating from across the table then leaned down from his chair so he could better see Gunner's face. "I thought ye paid the tribute!"

"I did," Gunner replied forcing the fear from his eyes as he swallowed the bite of food he'd taken before the earl unleashed his tirade. "I gave him both gold and cattle but he said it wasn't enough."

Volkren was unmoving and the counselor straightened himself so that his form would seem less diminished on the low bench. "When I came to give ye the news before ye said ye were too busy to think about it and would seek me out when ye were ready to hear. Shall I presume ye're ready now?"

Volkren tipped his head. "Out with it, man. What does he want?"

Gunner cleared his throat. "He wants triple what ye paid him last year."

"Triple?" Volkren barked. "That would ruin me."

"He said if ye didn't pay him triple what ye gave him last year he would get it from yer ships. I guess he made good on the threat."

It took a moment for the words to sink in but when they did Volkren took little time in reacting. With one fluid movement he wrenched the eating knife from Gunner's hand then sunk it deep into the table precisely between the counselor's index finger and thumb. "Swine!" he spit. "'Tis true Boru has been growing more hungry but no man would ask so much. What did ye say to anger him?"

Gunner opened his mouth but Volkren continued before he had a chance to answer, "Why should he come after me this way? Wasn't it me who uncovered Brodir as his would be assassin? Haven't I always paid my tribute on time without question? Certainly he doesn't ask so much from the others to support his wars. Why would he turn on me unless ye did something to anger him?"

With that he flung himself from his chair, pacing back and forth like a caged animal. He could feel the other men in the hall watching him and was uncomfortable knowing what they were thinking. They thought he was weak and not clever enough to rule Limerick. It was no different in Orkney when he was being considered for the position of under lord. His father had paid off the council to ensure his ascension but that idiot, Dorfav the Fair, spoke out against him. Dorfarv said he was too feeble minded to carry such great responsibility. What choice did he have but to slice the man's throat in an effort to silence him? True, it would have been better done outside the hall without the whole council watching, but there wasn't the time. If he hadn't silenced Dorfarv then and there they would have voted against him for being a dolt instead of voting against him for being a murderer. His punishment for his crime was his exile to Ireland where he immediately assumed his uncle's responsibility as earl.

"Not bad for a dolt," he mumbled to himself then smiled to know he had outsmarted the smartest men in Orkney.

But Brian Boru macCennitig was a very difficult problem indeed. Ever since Malsakin defeated Olaf at Tara, Boru had become more demanding. He'd been waging endless wars across the territory and no amount of tribute seemed to satisfy him. Now it seemed that he was ready to take Limerick for himself.

His ire bubbled as he failed to come up with a plan to get the Ri Ciocid off his back. "I don't understand this," he mumbled then realizing he had said the words out loud he spoke up to save himself further embarrassment. "Boru can't believe that he would be better off without me."

He spun on his heel then threw himself into his chair to face his counselor. "Boru must be reasonable and ye must make it so, Gunner! What counsel do ye have man?"

Gunner gingerly slipped his hands from the table, securing them firmly in his lap to hide their shaking. He sat very still as he slowly spoke the words, more to ensure that the earl would follow his logic than for fear of what he might think of them, "Brian knows ye were Imar's choice as earl and since Imar killed Madamion he wants ye to suffer. It's obvious that he nay longer needs Limerick in order to control the river so therefore he would rather see ye out than have to do business with ye."

Volkren's eyes held the far off look of incomprehension that dogs get when you talk to them forcing Gunner to speak more plainly, "Brian is taking revenge against ye for yer uncle's actions. His systematic sanctions will leave Limerick barren and yer people will flee because they won't have any food. Perhaps it's time for ye to return to Orkney. Yer exile was only to have been five years. I'm sure the family of Dorfarv will agree that ye've paid yer debt for his murder. They won't move against ye if ye choose to return."

If the earl was angry before, now he was blind with fury. He grabbed Gunner by the straps of his vest and lifted him up from the bench in one fluid motion. He might not understand talks of sanctions and negotiation but he definitely understood the difference between cowardice and courage. If he had nothing else, he would always have his pride.

The spittle flew from his mouth as his emotion exploded, "Run? That's the counsel ye give me? Run back to Orkney and let Boru have Limerick. I won't do it! Limerick is mine and I won't be handing it off to a Gaelic pig. I'll meet him on the battlefield before I'll tuck tail and run."

He pulled his counselor closer, letting his hot breath brush across his face as he threatened, "And when we do go to battle, my dear Gunner, it will be ye carrying my banner. Let's see what good counsel ye give as ye're the first one to march into Boru's army."

Erik, Volkren's war captain, was a dark man, short of height but wide of breadth. He was anything but handsome with a sharp sloping forehead and thick bushy eyebrows. His dark brown eyes held a glint of humor as he slowly approached the earl. He alone had the plan that would put an end to Boru and he was eager to offer it. He cleared his throat to draw Volkren's attention. "With respect, lord, maybe we should show the great king that he's nay match for Volkren of Limerick. Instead of meeting Boru on the battlefield where we've little hope of winning, we should raid the home of his kin who provides him the greatest assistance."

"A raid?" The earl's fury was at full throttle. He released Gunner with a shove, sending him sailing over the bench until both it, and the table was toppled, then he rounded on Erik, his mouth foaming and his eyes bulging in astonishment that he could achieve what little success he had with nothing but idiots as his chief advisors.

"Ye're saying ye believe me fool enough to perpetrate a raid in Munster!" He uncovered his short sword. "Step away from me, man before I take yer head."

The captain swallowed his nervousness but continued on despite it. "I pray ye to hear me out, lord."

There was a long moment of silence before Volkren returned the blade to its sheath but he didn't let it go. Beads of sweat formed on Erik's forehead as he continued. It was the only way to get the earl to recognize his worth. "It's been some time since a raid's been deployed in Munster. Boru would never expect it and with the element of surprise on our side our chances would be better taken with a raid than against the king's army."

Volkren relaxed his grip as he urged, "Go on."

The captain smiled, certain that when Volkren heard the sense of his plan Gunner would be cast aside and he would take his rightful place as counselor.

"The key to our success relies on disabling Boru's retaliation. My spies tell me that without Lorca of Cavenlow, Brian's army would be useless."

Volkren stroked his bare chin. "Lorca is indeed important to Boru. His men make up a vast portion of the Ri Ciocid's army and Cavenlow itself is a vital round fort due to its place along the river."

He took a step closer, resting his hand on Erik's shoulder as he pondered the situation further. The captain didn't flinch.

"Aye," Volkren continued with a nod of his head. "Cavenlow is very valuable indeed. If I take it right out from under Boru's nose people will think me brilliant."

Not to be outdone by the lowly war captain, Gunner got to his feet as he prepared to offer his warning.

"If I may, lord. Lorca's army is always at the ready. They are many and each skilled warriors, both on the battlefield and against a raid."

Volkren didn't turn to acknowledge his counselor but his face did sour a bit. "It's true, captain. How do we handle the raid without being cut down ourselves?"

Erik straightened his shoulders as he prepared to deliver the final piece of his plan.

"I have a particular spy in Cavenlow who I've come to depend on. He tells me that over the years Lorca has lost eight of his sons in Boru's battles—the last having fallen two moons ago in Desmumu. Now he prepares for the celebration of the coming of age of his youngest. Boru is residing with them to partake in the feast to assuage any ill feelings for the loss. If we attack during the celebration, we'll not only take Cavenlow but could cut down Boru as a bonus."

A sly smirk played on Volkren's face urging Erik to continue. "Out of deference to his sister, Boru has ordered his guards to remain behind in Cenn Cora and nay doubt Lorca's soldiers will be drunk from the celebration. I believe this raid is yer only chance at keeping Limerick."

Volkren patted the captain's shoulder as he turned to look at Gunner, an evil grin playing on his face. "'Tis the counsel I was seeking from ye," he hissed.

*   *   *   *

Cavenlow, Ireland: The Ri Tuath's private chamber—One hour past midnight—5, May 982 A.D.—The chamber was dark except for the glow of the peat fire and the flickering light from the candle. Lorca hunched over the writ he was composing, carefully forming each letter with the tip of the quill and muttering to himself whenever the ink flowed unevenly on the paper. The art of writing had never come easy to him but this was a most important document so he labored to make each letter crisp and clear.

He jumped a bit with the knock on his door, causing a puddle of ink to form where he let the quill linger too long. He hissed between clenched teeth for his mistake then dipped the quill again to finish his signature. He was eager to have the writ finished so he could make his announcement to those gathered in the hall.

He had kept the information a secret, choosing to discuss it with only one other person before he made it public. Not even Brian knew that he was planning to break with the new tradition of succession and he wanted to keep it that way lest the Ri Ciocid try to convince him otherwise. True, Brian might be sore for being kept unawares but when Lorca made the announcement he was certain that his old friend would forgive him and agree wholeheartedly. Most likely he'd act as if he'd known all along.

The knock came again but this time Lorca was expecting it. He laid the quill aside then weighted down the ends of the vellum so the writ could dry. "Come," he finally called, satisfied with his work.

Kevin pushed the heavy wooden door open, peering around the edge to spy his father sitting behind his table. The tapestry that hung above Lorca's head carried the mark of Cavenlow. It was the same tapestry used by Darmaid during his reign—a single dancing lion carrying a sword and thistle on a red background. It was faded and threadbare in spots but in the low light of the chamber it still looked grand.

Kevin squelched his nervousness by reminding himself that his father was just a man, not anyone of magical powers who could cut him to the quick with a single glance, but still his hands shook for what he was about to do so he took the time to latch the door behind him, collecting the courage to see the deed through. "Yer guests are beginning to inquire over ye," he offered, stepping forward but keeping his eyes on his shoes so his father couldn't see the betrayal in his eyes. "Are ye planning to join us?"

Lorca looked at his son. Pale and thin, he looked ghostly as the candlelight cast shadows under his eyes and nose. It was sheer luck that brought the lad to him now.

"Kevin," he cooed, too comfortable to be true. "I was just about to call for ye."

Kevin lifted an eyebrow of inquiry and Lorca called him closer with a wave of his hand then pointed to a stool for him to sit on.

Kevin followed the silent instructions and when he was comfortably seated, Lorca came around the table, resting back against it and folding his arms over his chest as he looked down on his son. "I wanted to speak with ye about yer future. I've only just received word from the abbey in Clonmacnoise that they would be happy to have ye join them so that ye may continue yer studies. I was thinking that ye shouldn't dawdle in accepting the invitation so I've prepared a caravan to see ye safely there by the full moon."

Kevin's face twisted, making him appear more ghostly than he did before. "But ye can't send me away, father," he whined. "My home is here."

Lorca stiffened his back in preparation for the argument he knew would come. Kevin was anything but foolish—he could see right through words to the crux of the plan so Lorca chose his carefully to avoid any misunderstanding.

"I've made my decision and there's nay a thing ye can do for it. Ye refuse to marry as well as to be trained for battle. Ye've reached yer manhood more than four summers ago yet ye've set not one plan for yer future so I've set them for ye. Ye'll study in the abbey and Patric will lead…."

"My future is here!" Kevin interrupted as he leapt from the stool. He always knew it would come to this, which was the reason for his treachery. "Need I remind ye that the loss of yer elder sons leaves me next in line for the throne?"

The comment brought an audible growl from Lorca but Kevin refused to be intimidated, instead he took a step closer, shaking his head as his voice lilted with the accusation, "It's not my edict that makes it a fact, father, but Brian's. Neither was it my wars that caused things to fall out as they did. That was Brian too. I just happen to be the beneficiary of his ill begotten schemes and I won't be denied."

"*Ye* won't be denied?" Lorca spit as he balled his fists against his instinct to use physical force against his son. "Ye've done nay a thing for Cavenlow except sap it of its wealth. Hear me now, lad, ye will never sit on my throne, not while I live nor anytime after."

His eyes locked with Kevin's until the stress of hatred was almost tangible. "Ye're quite right," he hissed, "I *have* lost my sons in Brian's wars but their lives were given to ensure the safety of others not to put a rot like ye on the throne. Every one of my eight went to battle willingly so that Brian could someday be Ard Ri and ye can mark my words that when the day comes that I see him as such and finally take my rest it'll be Patric the warrior, nay ye the coward who takes my place!"

He moved still closer so that he towered over his son as he prepared to end the argument once and for all. "Ye, my fair lad, *will* go to Clonmacnoise where ye'll become an abbot and live in peace or else make yer own way as best ye can. The choice is yers, but I suggest ye make it now for I plan to make my intentions known this very night."

Kevin's chest heaved with rage as he struggled with the desire to kill the man who stood before him. From the moment he lost Gunra in the battle of Desmumu, Lorca had been making plans to give Cavenlow to Patric and now the hour was drawing near. He needed time and he scrambled for a plan to gain it.

He drew in a deep breath then willed the sorrow into his eyes. After a long silence he finally whispered, "Ye never hid the fact that ye loved Patric more than ye did me, father, but I never knew ye hated me so thoroughly."

The words were like a blow to Lorca's gut, taking him by surprise and causing him to step back. He could see the pain in Kevin's eyes and he reacted. "I-I don't hate ye," he mumbled, uncomfortable discussing such things, "but ye must admit that Patric is better suited to leadership than ye are."

"Aye, he is," Kevin agreed. "Everyone knows it. But to name him now, before I've had a chance to settle myself elsewhere, will only bring me embarrassment. Ye're in good health, father. What is it ye hope to gain by revealing yer intentions now besides my embarrassment?"

Lorca struggled with his answer because the truth would make him look bad. His decision to name Patric as his successor was nothing more than a tactic to keep his village thriving. Ever since Malsakin took the crown at Tara, Brian had been waging war on the O'Neills. When Gunra fell in Desmumu, Lorca's people became uncomfortable with the thought that a weakling like Kevin would be next to succeed him. They were beginning to flee. Naming Patric as his heir would return a feeling of security to Cavenlow and ensure its continued wealth.

He looked deep into Kevin's eyes, regretting that he was the cause of the pain he saw in them. If he had only taken more time with the lad perhaps things would have turned out differently. "There are many reasons for what I must do but I pray ye to know that none of them have anything to do with embarrassing ye."

He put his arm around his son's shoulder. "Ye know as well as I that Clonmacnoise is the right place for ye and there isn't one among the many in attendance tonight who'll think any less of ye for going."

He felt Kevin's shoulder relax and thinking that he'd won his battle, gave a tiny rub of his head. "Go now and enjoy the feast," he said before making his way back around the table to investigate the drying writ. He looked it over as he spoke, "Before I make the announcement, I'll first tell everyone of yer plans so they'll believe it was yer choice to leave the throne behind. There'll be nay embarrassment, only happiness that both my sons are getting what's best for them."

Kevin knew he must delay the announcement but for the life of him he couldn't think of what else to say. He stepped closer to the table, laying his hands upon it to stop their shaking when he spotted the writ. Lorca carefully folded the vellum then dripped candle wax on the seam to seal it. As he pressed his ring into the wax to give it his mark, his dirk worked its way out of his waistband and rolled onto the table.

Kevin looked to the blade that landed near his fingertip and a thought passed his mind.

"If ye think ye can do it then pick it up," Lorca growled as his penetrating stare bore down on him.

Kevin's eyes locked onto Lorca's. His breathing grew heavy with concentration causing the flame on the candle to flicker then die out. At length they stood in near darkness, the red glow of the peat fire dancing more in Lorca's eyes then in Kevin's since his back was turned against it.

Kevin fingered the edge of the dirk and with lightening speed Lorca smashed the heavy candlestick down on his hand, shattering every bone in it.

"Get out!" the Ri Tuath raged, his nostrils flaring and his face glowing red. "Get out and never let me spy yer miserable face in my village again!"

The pain in Kevin's hand was no match for the agony he felt for his failure. He cupped the limp and shattered appendage in his left hand, holding it against his chest as he exited the room praying that Volkren would manage what he had not.

*   *   *   *

Dublin, Ireland: The great hall—One hour past midnight—5, May 982 A.D.—Set high atop a rise on the coast of the Irish Sea, Dublin was an expanse of rolling hills surrounded by bog and woodlands split through it's center by the river Liffey. Olaf happened upon it years earlier when he sailed his boat through the bay and up the river to its lowest point. He marked his landing with a carved standing stone proclaiming his arrival then built up a quay around it to conduct his business of trading.

The port quickly took hold and soon ships from around the world filled its docks. Shops sprung up along the quay offering food, clothing and medicines to the many sailors taking respite in the city as well as the now burgeoning population residing there. An exterior wall standing twenty-two feet high, fortified the city. Atop it and on poles in the streets hung oil lamps that were lit at night to keep people safe from unexpected mischief.

Whether night or day, the quay was alive with movement—cargo being loaded or unloaded, young men seeking employment as deckhands or companions, spirit peddlers and whores strutting the wooden promenade hoping to attract customers—all this provided a cacophony of street music that wafted up into the air to penetrate the massive stone fortress sitting high above it all.

Malsakin the Great, Ireland's new Ard Ri, held his head in his hands as the noise outside his hall collided with the sounds within. He had been struggling all day with the decision over who should be named earl of Dublin City and the barrage of noise wasn't helping him to think clearly.

For the last two years the job of running Dublin had fallen to him. Though he was more than capable at leading men, ruling a port city filled with Vikings was a task he couldn't quite put his arms around. If he didn't appoint someone capable at running the port soon, Dublin's trades would surely move to the better functioning ports of Wexford, Waterford or Limerick.

He looked to Kormlada's brother, Maelmora, who sat beside him picking berries from a bowl. The only way to describe the man was "gorgeous." Maelmora was every woman's dream with hair like woven gold, curling slightly on the ends to frame his perfectly sized forehead and high cheekbones. His eyes were brilliant green, his nose straight and narrow and his lips full and pouting. But it would take more than good looks to be earl of Dublin and unfortunately, Maelmora's looks were the only thing he had going for him.

Beside Maelmora sat Sigtrygg, Kormlada's only son by Olaf Curran. Though he strongly resembled his uncle, Sigtrygg was merely handsome. Malsakin rubbed the weariness from his eyes before considering Sigtrygg. The lad had reached his majority more than a year ago but as of yet hadn't demonstrated the level of maturity necessary to rule the great city.

"Eat something, Sigtrygg," Maelmora huffed at his nephew who seemed more interested in the way his coat fit then the food on his plate. "Ye're mother will have at ye if she sees ye lanky and thin as ye are."

"Mind yer own plate, uncle," Sigtrygg snapped back at him. It seemed that whenever they were in the Ard Ri's presence his uncle would treat him as a child. Most likely he wanted to keep Malsakin believing that he was too young to rule the city. "I'm perfectly capable of determining whether or not I'm hungry."

"Stop this now, the both of ye!" Malsakin snapped as they continued to exchange barbs. "Must we go through the same thing at every meal? Ye're like women in the way ye pick at each other."

Maelmora nodded then sat back in his chair. The Ard Ri had been in ill humor all day. The last thing he wanted to do was have words with him. Sigtrygg, on the other hand, decided to seize the opportunity to unravel Malsakin's last nerve. "We only bicker because of yer indecision," he blurted. "If at last ye would name the man who will sit upon my father's throne ye would see that there would be nothing left for us to fight about." He flicked the edge of the azure coat he was wearing as if the material offended him then screwed up his face awaiting Malsakin's response.

Maelmora held his breath. Both he and Sigtrygg had been angling to get Malsakin to name them earl of the city. Now that the moment was at hand he could barely contain himself.

Malsakin's eyes narrowed. He had hoped that by now the lad would have learned that challenges were something he didn't take kindly to but as always Sigtrygg's arrogant nature kept him blinded to the truth. "If ye want the city, laddie, I would suggest that ye be more mindful of yer tongue. The last thing Dublin needs is an earl who is so enamored by the sound of his own voice that he doesn't consider the consequences of his words."

"With due respect, Ard Ri," Sigtrygg snapped back in that condescending tone he so liked to use when he spoke, "I should say that ye of all people would be least capable of knowing what it is that Dublin needs. My father taught me all there was to know about running this city. Why not put my poor uncle here out of his misery and name me to the throne right now so that we can all get on with the business at hand."

Seeing the opportunity to gain the Ard Ri's favor, Maelmora grabbed his nephew's arm. "Sigtrygg," he blurted. "I knew yer father as well as ye and one thing was for certain—he'd never spark a row that he wasn't sure he could win."

Malsakin sat silent and Sigtrygg smiled as he raked his gaze over him. The one thing he *was* certain of was that he could best the Ard Ri one on one. If it hadn't been for his mother's insistence that she had the situation well in hand he would have stricken the man long ago. He turned to his uncle with a sly smirk playing on his face. "Yer words are true, Maelmora but I don't see yer point."

Malsakin gripped the edge of his chair in his effort to control his anger. If it was anyone other than Kormlada's son issuing the insult he would have had him dragged then hanged. But he needed her if he were to remain as Ard Ri and so he swallowed his hatred. "Ye're tongue is sharp, laddie," he whispered through tight lips. "Be careful lest it be taken in yer sleep."

Maelmora saw the storm brewing behind Malsakin's eyes. Another taunt from Sigtrygg would destroy any chance the lad had of sitting as earl of Dublin. He remembered the conversation they had been having before Malsakin joined them then looked out over the crowd to be sure that the woman was still in the hall. He turned to his nephew. "Perhaps ye should find a better use for that tongue than trading barbs with the Ard Ri. Didn't ye say earlier that there was a particular lass who sparked yer interest?"

Sigtrygg ripped his gaze from Malsakin to level it at his uncle. Though he was fairly certain Maelmora was teasing with him he decided to show them both the extent of his courage. "Very well," he droned before rising from his seat. He looked around the room for the one woman he was certain would spark the Ard Ri's ire. When he found the sultry red head standing by the door, he leapt from the platform and headed right for her. His eyes briefly locked with Malsakin's before he tilted her head back to issue her a bruising kiss.

Malsakin bit his bottom lip as he watched the display. It was widely known that the lass belonged to him. Sigtrygg's transgression was one that wouldn't be easily dealt with.

✳   ✳   ✳   ✳

Cavenlow, Ireland: The great hall—One hour past midnight—5, May 982 A.D.—The all too familiar grief at the loss of Cavenlow's sons had been hanging in the air for all the seasons but no amount of grief was enough to suppress the raging hormones of a sixteen-year-old lad. Patric sat at the right hand of Brian, swaying happily to the music as he kept the young Freara, daughter of Ogden, always in his line of vision. His weaving in his seat brought a poke in the ribs from the Ri Ciocid.

"Ye act as a duck with yer head bobbing on yer shoulders. Don't just sit there ogling the lass—ask her to dance with ye." Brian's voice boomed off the walls.

"Shh," Patric responded with his own elbow to Brian's side. "She'll hear ye and then I'll die of embarrassment."

"Are ye telling me a lad of sixteen summers is yet too shy to ask a lass to dance?" Brian queried, his eyebrows rising in disbelief.

Patric hung his head drawing a tsk-tsk look from the Ri Ciocid.

"Really, lad, I thought so much more of ye than that. Have some confidence. She's a female nay a sword. She won't cut ye or make ye bleed."

"If only she was a weapon," Patric moaned, "I'd be more comfortable handling her. I've nay trouble dealing with the most dangerous of weapons but put me around a lass and I become all elbows and thumbs."

Brian laughed, "Ye're wise to be wary of them, Patric. They've a weapon in their touch that can bring down even the strongest of men. Their soft lips can do more damage than any dagger, and their soft thighs can cut ye down quicker than a Viking broad ax. But take it from an old one whose had his fill of them, they're well worth yer blood."

He offered a shove that nearly dislodged Patric from his bench. "Now go on and ask her to dance."

Patric caught himself on the edge of the table, eyes darting between Freara and Brian. "Do ye think she'll agree?" he asked, begging for affirmation.

Brian leaned in to whisper, "She hasn't taken her eyes off ye the entire evening. She'll agree to more than a dance, laddie."

Patric swallowed hard as Brian's nudge assisted him from the platform. The short distance between him and the dark haired maiden took an eternity to diminish as his confidence ebbed with each step. He turned to look back at Brian but the Ri Ciocid only offered an insistent wave toward the lass.

Freara was speaking with Margreg, Patric's cousin and a beauty in her own right. Several other maidens surrounded them and Patric cleared his throat loudly before touching Freara's shoulder to draw her attention. "Will ye be my partner in a dance?" he croaked.

The crack of his voice brought a giggle from Margreg but Freara issued a look to silence her before turning. She took a tiny breath to swell her bosom as her dark lashes lowered toward the ground. "Surely ye wouldn't waste yer birthday dance on me, Patric. There are others here ye fancy more."

"Och, nay," Margreg broke in, her dark chestnut hair swinging over her shoulder as she lifted her head to look down her upturned nose. "I think it's ye he wants. Just look at the way his hands are shaking. I just hope he doesn't crush yer foot for his clumsiness."

The lump in Patric's throat seemed to press against his skin as he desperately tried to moisten his lips with the last of his saliva. Margreg's dark beauty was little cover for her venomous tongue and he wondered how the lads hadn't yet throttled her for it.

The heat of his anger blushed his cheeks but before he could respond to his cousin's chiding, Freara had her arm linked through his and was escorting him to the dance floor.

"I'd love to be yer partner, Patric," she cooed as she scowled over her shoulder at Margreg.

Margreg and the other girls tittered as they walked away but Patric paid them little mind. A tingle rose across his skin from the touch of the young woman he had coveted for so long.

The bodhran pounded over the flute calling a dance demanding the constant switching of partners, but even Freara's limited time in his arms brought Patric's heart to a thunder and the pressure mounted against the walls of his skull until every beat could be felt in his brain. He watched as she spun away from him, wondering if her next partner would be similarly affected.

Her hips swayed seductively as she made her way back to him. He barely embraced her and she chuckled, "Ye can hold me tighter than that, Patric. I fear ye may lose me." She pressed her bosom against his chest to whisper, "I won't break if ye hold me close."

He felt the stir deep in his groin then the hardening of muscle against his lien. He tried to push her back but she'd have no part of it. She knew full well what she was doing to him and she continued happily, crushing her hips close to his until she sent his head reeling from his lust.

Though the sensation wasn't alien to him, it did surprise him that it could be brought on by her mere touch. Suddenly the blinding white ecstasy exploded in his brain as his blood pumped through his veins at a vicious rate. Every inch of his skin tingled, magnifying her softness to send a shiver up his spine. Without thinking, he crushed her tighter as the desire to be inside her sent his head spinning out of control.

It was the laughter that finally shattered his joy, fiercely pulling him back to reality so that he was forced to open his eyes. Freara's body stiffened against his spent erection and Brian's voice thundered over the noise of the crowd, "Ye're a wonderful dancer, young Patric but perhaps ye should wait for the musicians to return before ye continue."

Patric's face flushed as he quickly straightened his lien. He probed Freara's eyes, wondering if she knew what had happened but she cast them away from him, looking down at her worn leather shoes as she shuffled her feet on the mud floor.

He forced a smile before leading her to her seat in silence and she returned it with one of her own, but Margreg's laughter continued to drone on and his embarrassment soon turned to anger.

He balled his fists then turned on his heel to march back to his seat but again Brian's voice called over the crowd, "Stay where ye are, laddie. I wish to present ye a gift."

Patric looked to the Ri Ciocid in fury but Brian only nodded toward the double doors at the front of the hall until the lad followed his gaze.

Standing there in the brilliance of the streaming moonlight was the most beautiful chestnut mare Patric had ever laid eyes on. She snorted as she shook her head, sending her golden mane rippling about her long neck to shimmer in the lamplight. Her brown eyes were soft and playful, beckoning him to stroke her. He did and she reacted with a playful nudge that caused him to forget his anger.

"She's beautiful, Brian," he sighed, "How do ye call her?"

"She's yet unnamed, young Patric," the Ri Ciocid chided, "but perhaps ye'd like to name her for yer dancing partner. I'm sure she too is a comfortable ride."

No more than that was needed to replace Patric's joy with anger. It happened often and in an instant. A word, a look, a jovial touch given too forceful for his liking, they were all that was necessary to set him off. He turned on his heel, brewing and festering as he marched forward to the great table to sit with a mighty thud.

"I don't find this humorous, Brian," he offered through clenched teeth.

The Ri Ciocid set his jaw in dissatisfaction. "Learn to check that temper, son. Ye're too quick to become inflamed and may one day find yerself challenging an enemy ye don't wish to fight."

Brian's eyes told him that there was more than sage advice in his words, and he slumped in his chair as the fear rose in him. "Forgive me, Ri Ciocid."

Brian nodded acceptance of his apology then smiled as he rubbed Patric's head. "There's a time for battle and a time for humility and negotiation. Ye must keep yer mind clear so ye'll know which to engage at what time. Learn to laugh, even at yerself. Ye never know when such an action will save yer life."

Just then there was a stir from the crowd nearest the double doors where the mare had been led in only moments ago. Patric turned to see what was happening. He got to his feet, as did Brian, then each looked at the other as an obviously disgruntled Lorca began to make his way through the crowd.

The Ri Tuath stopped momentarily to admire the mare then stopped many times after to respond to the greetings his guests were offering. Though his face was fixed in a smile it was obvious to anyone who knew him that Lorca was in ill humor.

"Yer Ri Tuath doesn't seem in the mood for celebrating," Brian offered as he watched his old friend make his way through the crowd. "I wonder what's amiss."

"I couldn't say," Patric responded, then a thought came to him. "Ye don't think he saw my dance and was…."

"Och," Brian spewed with a wave of his hand. "Come now, laddie, that look on yer father's face comes from the weight of a deep problem, nay a little…um…let's call it, enthusiasm." Brian patted Patric on the shoulder but never took his eyes off Lorca. "We'll know soon enough what's eating at him."

Lorca offered his last false smile to a guest before making his way up the platform to take the seat beside Brian. He had been searching for Kevin to no avail—it was clear he wasn't in the hall either.

"I owe ye a great debt, Ri Ciocid," he grumbled. "It was good of ye to preside over the feast in my absence."

"Och," Brian spewed again, taking the time to rub Patric's head before continuing, "The lad's like my own son. 'Twas my pleasure to oversee things for him."

"I'm glad ye feel that way," Lorca whispered before ripping the cup from Brian's hand, "because I've an announcement to make."

The hair on Brian's neck rose in warning but before he could draw Lorca's attention the Ri Tuath was on his feet and the crowd was encouraging him to speak.

"We're gathered here to celebrate the ascension to manhood of Gilla Patric macLorca of Cavenlow," he began.

"Here, here," cried Brian as he wondered just what his friend was up to. Others in the hall did the same offering Patric their congratulations and wishes for long life and as the sweet smell of peat smoke, ale and wine wafted through the air, Lorca was suddenly reminded that this was a night of celebration. He drew a deep breath, calming his nerves before taking the time to look over the many faces in the room. Villagers sporting their best garments, warriors passing through on their way back home, several of Brian's soldiers—all there to celebrate Patric's ascension to manhood. He searched for Grace in the crowd but when he didn't find her he suspected that she was off somewhere soothing Kevin's wounds. Well, he would deal with them when he had completed his mission and not a moment sooner. He held up his hand to silence the crowd then cleared his throat in preparation for his speech.

"Patric's ascension into manhood isn't the only reason we gather," he offered before looking to the lad who was clearly confused.

Patric tugged on Brian's arm as if to inquire about his father's plans but the Ri Ciocid issued a look to silence him. He was as eager as the lad to know what was in Lorca's mind and he wouldn't miss it by having a side conversation.

They returned their attention to Lorca whose face now sported a curious expression. He slowly cocked his ear to one side. Brian opened his mouth to urge him on but then he noticed it too…so did Patric. They both leapt to their feet, turning toward the door at the north side of the hall as the roaring thunder set the ground to shaking.

Warriors grabbed for their swords then scrambled through the crowd to position themselves in front of the Ri Tuath's table but when the door finally opened they were surprised by what they saw.

The crowd burst through with fury enough to put out the flames of several oil lamps while others were sent crashing from their chains. Lorca's captain, Rouric, huddled the villagers into the hall, pushing at them as he frantically called, "All men to arms, it's a raid!"

Patric stood in awe as the myriad of people filled up the hall then, following the lead of his father and Brian, he leapt over the long table to surround the man.

Rouric's face was ashen as he struggled to find breath enough to relay the information to all those gathered around him. He whirled around frantically offering the story to Connor, then Brian and finally ending with Lorca, unwittingly pulling on the Ri Tuath's lien as he relayed, "I believe they're Volkren's boats. They came ashore at the southern clearing and immediately laid fire to the herder's huts. We tried to hold them back but there were just too many. We thought it best to bring the innocents here for safe keeping."

"How could he overtake the guards?" Brian asked of Connor who was the one in charge of setting up the river blockade.

Before the captain could answer Brian ripped the sword out of his hand then turned to Lorca. "Tend yer family, brother. I'll lead yer warriors."

Everything was moving too quickly. The rush of people into the hall tangled with the warriors making their way to the field. Patric found himself spinning around aimlessly as his heart beat against his chest. It was Lorca's steel grip that jarred him to his senses.

Patric opened his hand to accept the blade being thrust at him. "Find ye're mother, Patric," Lorca cried. "Be sure to protect her from the heathens. Keep her safe!"

Patric's mouth gaped as his eyes flew open. Confusion swelled his brain and he mumbled, "But, father, I want to fight with ye."

Lorca's head snapped around. "Ye do as I say! Find ye're mother and protect her! I'll allow nay harm to come to her and *ye* better be sure that it doesn't. I warn ye not to fail me, Patric."

There was something in Lorca's eyes that Patric had never seen—an earnest pleading for the life of his wife, an alien fear that they never held before. Patric shuddered as he responded, "Aye, father."

Lorca threw a strong arm around the lad's shoulder, pulling his head into the juncture of his neck to kiss his ear. He suddenly realized that his son was nearly as tall as him. He looked him over from the top of his golden red head to his square cut chin—every inch of him a Dal Cais, then he remembered that his announcement had gone undelivered. Nay matter—should anything happen to him there was always the writ.

He looked into Patric's crystal blue eyes before pulling him into another suffocating embrace. "I chose right," he sighed into his son's ear. "Ye'll be a grand leader and I'm proud of ye." Then he was gone, passing through the doors with the flood of warriors leaving Patric with his musky scent in his nostrils and his own words trailing on the wind.

"I love *ye*, father."

Before he could stop it, Patric was pulled backwards by the sea of people huddling together as if the closeness of their bodies would protect them from the Viking broad axes. They were a tangled mass, filling up the hall and spilling outside to the courtyard beyond until even the smallest child found difficulty passing them. When he finally managed to reach Grace's hut he opened the door to find her praying, her beads clasped tightly to her heart. She rose slowly.

"What's happening, Patric? Where's yer father?"

The cold hand of panic gripped him as his mother's eyes probed him for an answer. He didn't know what was happening. It was all moving too quickly for him. For years he dreamed of battling with his father but now the reality of it left him shaking and frustrated. He didn't know where his father was or if any of them would survive.

He raced to the window, unfastening the cover to gaze upon the total annihilation being waged just outside the mud walls. He swallowed back his tears then turned to her. "It's a raid. Father's out with Brian trying to hold them off."

"Damn that Brian!" Grace spit. "It's him who brings us such misery!" She sank to her knees, consumed by tears as she rocked back and forth calling to the Lord to assist in protecting her family from her brother's mischief.

Patric wanted to jump from his skin—to be anywhere other than in that tiny room with the sounds of battle blaring around him and his mother's blasphemy of the Ri Ciocid tearing at his heart. The heat swelled within him and before he realized what he was doing, he burst through the door then began marching back toward the hall, nearly running over Kevin who stepped into his path from the doorway of their father's hut.

"Where are ye going?" the elder brother inquired as he tucked the folded vellum into his lein.

Patric was about to answer but when he noticed Kevin's injured hand he panicked, "Were ye out there? What happened to ye? Is father alright—and Brian?"

Kevin followed Patric's gaze. "Aye, I was out there," he lied. "They struck me with a club. I can hardly fight as I am so I came back to have it tended. Where's mother?"

"She's in her chamber. She's safe," Patric responded. "Who is it?"

"It's Volkren," Kevin blurted, but just as he was moving toward Grace's door he stopped then turned. "Where's father? Has he gone to the field?" Patric nodded and he continued, "Did he say anything to ye before he went?"

"Aye," Patric replied. "He said I was to protect mother."

A fleeting smile drifted across Kevin's face for his good fortune but he quickly covered it. "So then what are ye doing out here?" he snapped then grabbed the sword from his brother with his good hand. "When ye're given an order, ye best heed it." He opened the door then held it so Patric could enter but when the lad didn't move he urged, "Go on."

Grace had gotten to her feet, her glance flicking between her two sons in askance. Patric looked at her then at Kevin. With his brother to keep his mother safe, he could join his father on the field without concern. "Ye stay with her while I go to assist father. My mind is made up, Kevin and there's nay a thing ye can do to stop me!"

Grace lunged at him protesting but Kevin pushed her back. "If that's yer wish," he said then slipped into the chamber taking the sword with him and bolting the door behind him.

Patric could hear his mother's cries but he paid them little mind. Though Kevin wasn't a fighter, he loved Grace above all things. He would keep her safe.

He spun on his heel to march straight into the hoard of people milling around the courtyard. He tried to push past them but there was little hope of getting through the chaos. "I want all of ye to disperse immediately," he barked. "Take cover in the hall! If there isn't room enough there, hide in the sleeping huts."

He spoke in a voice so commanding that it brought immediate heed. Soon his people were filing through the doors in an orderly fashion. When they were all inside he shouted, "Once I've left I want these doors bolted. Our senior men and older boys should take their positions at all the thresholds. Grab anything ye can which will act as a weapon. If they get us, they won't get all of us."

His eyes darted over the crowd. "Where's Eagan?"

The well-muscled boy stepped forward. "I'm here, Patric."

"Eagan, ye take up this torch," he commanded as he released the flaming stick from its holder. "Use it as a club to defend yerself. The rest of ye do the same."

As he exited the hall he spied two boys about seven or eight years old and a girl who was still a toddler huddled in the corner just outside the doors. Their faces were covered in soot and their clothes singed. "Where are yer parents," he whispered taking the youngest by the hand.

"Don't know, lord," the elder lad replied. "The hut was burning and I put Rada and Morin out the window then climbed out myself. We followed the people here. Forgive the trespass, lord."

Patric looked into the lad's round blue eyes. He didn't recall ever seeing him before and decided he must be the son of a fudir. He opened the door then scooted them through with a wave of his hand. "Go and stand by Eagan. Ye tell him that Patric sent ye to him. He's a good fighter. He'll protect ye."

The lad smiled then kissed Patric's hand before scurrying off behind his brother and sister. As Patric closed the door on them he said a silent prayer for their parents who he was certain were dead, then one also for his father and Brian.

He heard the bolt being thrown on the door then turned into an eerie darkness. His eyes swept over the stanchions—nary a man in sight. He slowly followed the road to the barracks—all empty. He traveled some distance before he finally heard the clash of metal then an order barked in a foreign tongue.

He ran past the chapel...burnt and ruined, the barns also. He could hear the sounds of cattle being led across planks then the splashing of men in water. A few more calls, these in Gaelic. Someone screamed. Everywhere it was dark, except for the glowing embers of what was once his village.

He made his way down the incline toward the water, his hand gripping the hilt of Brian's short sword. In the distance he saw the shadows of injured warriors helping each other up the slope and the outline of livestock wandering aimlessly through the field. He cursed himself for taking the long way around. His foot hit something and he stumbled forward, landing on a slippery soft mass but his head struck something hard. He rubbed at the fast rising bump with what was now his own bloody hand then struggled to get to his feet. He heard the release of breath then looked down to see the man with a broad axe protruding from his face. He took a step back but the man's hand shot out to grab his ankle.

"Find yer father, Patric," Amin croaked, his lips flapping around the Viking ax that was buried in his face.

Patric would never be able to describe the terror that gripped his heart as he heard the last rattle of breath escape Amin's body, or the absolute helplessness he experienced as he found his childhood friend, Turlach, reaching out to his brother, Mahon, in death, but he'd always remember the sight of Brian when he rose to his call.

"Father!" he screamed as he ran toward the river stumbling over the dead at his feet. "Father, where are ye?"

Tears glistened on the Ri Ciocid's cheek as he rose from his knees, struggling to find his voice. It cracked when he responded, "We're here, Patric."

In blindness Patric rushed forward, knowing all would be well once he stood between his father and Brian. He wiped his tears with the back of his sleeve. "Thank God I found ye," he sighed breathlessly as he threw himself into the Ri Ciocid's arms. "Are ye hurt, Brian? Where's my father?"

Brian crushed him to his chest before whispering, "Nay mortal wound could cause me the pain I'm in now, laddie." He sobbed tenderly. "I've found yer father."

It was a yanking similar to Amin's grasp but this one on Patric's heart, pulling him ever downward. His body trembled as he heeded its command then he slipped through Brian's arms to collapse onto his father's dead body. He was startled by the warmth of it and for a moment thought Lorca might still be alive, but when he saw the blank stare of death in his eyes he pressed his head to his father's heart and let the warm blood mingle with his tears as he breathe his scent one last time. Nothing would ever be the same again.

CHAPTER 9

▼

Dublin, Ireland: Outside the gates—Two hours to Noon—2, February 983 A.D.—"Halt," Kormlada called noticing that the carriage was about to turn onto the main Dublin road. The vehicle pitched and swayed as the driver obeyed her order, coming to a stop just outside the new city gates.

"Everything all right, lady?"

"Aye, 'tis fine. I just need some time is all," she responded. She dabbed away the perspiration that had formed on her upper lip despite the frigid temperature then peered through the window to gaze upon the city that she once called home. The last time she was in Dublin it was as the wife of the great Olaf Curran but now everything had changed.

The hall of the earl sat high atop a hill, long and glistening in the morning sun. It was built of granite with large windows providing an ample view of the city below as well as Dublin Bay. Inside, heavy tapestries hung upon the walls and colorful rushes covered the floors to offset the grand furnishings, all hand carved by artisans of superior talent.

She took a breath in preparation for her homecoming to her beloved city. She had stayed away from Dublin for these years trying to avoid the memories of her past life but when Malsakin intimated that he'd be handing over the throne to one of his kinsmen instead of her son, she decided that it was time that she returned.

Dublin was Olaf's creation, built by his own hands and thriving due to the great care he had given it. The Ard Ri's mismanagement had all but ruined the place and now she was there to offer him an ultimatum.

"Move out," she cried, rapping the ceiling with a force greater than she intended. Her knuckles immediately reddened but she wanted to get going again before she lost her nerve.

The carriage pitched and rocked as it clamored up the hill, only slowing once it came to the bridge that crossed the Liffey River. Kormlada found comfort in the plodding rhythm of the wheels rolling across the wooden boards and she looked to the south to see if Olaf's stone was still standing. She thrilled at the sight of the slab in the distance, standing erect at the exact spot where Olaf's boat had first come ashore decades ago. It glistened in the sunlight and for a moment she thought she might be able to read the rune carved on its face.

A tear escaped her eye as she thought of her husband, the great warrior, spending his last days alone as the slave of some foreign earl but she quickly pulled herself together. Her anger and pity would have to wait for a more appropriate time, for now she was on a mission and she meant to have it done.

They entered the interior gates leading to the hall and several of the guards flashed a smile of recognition for the high queen's return. Kormlada nodded back then prepared to disembark as the carriage rolled to a stop before the great doors. She floated from the carriage and all eyes turned toward her. Her amber cloak fanned out behind her creating a lush backdrop for her golden hair, which cascaded to her ankles. Both were decorated with rubies that glistened when she moved giving her the look of a fairy.

"Hail the high queen," came the guard's cry as he bent a knee for her. Others responded in kind and Kormlada smiled approvingly as she made her way past them and into the hall.

"Mother!" Sigtrygg called out when he spotted her. He opened his arms in greeting hoping that she would wait until they were alone to lambaste him for his poor behavior. "Ye're as beautiful as when I left ye in Tara."

She looked him over as he made his way toward her. He had filled out a bit and was a fine looking lad with bright green eyes and high cheekbones. Like hers, his nose turned up at the end but his square jaw and sandy hair he took from Olaf.

"What's this?" she questioned rubbing his downy chin. "Are ye thinking to sport a beard?"

"Aye," he responded shyly, thankful that his grooming seemed to be her only concern. "It gave Olaf character. I thought it might do the same for me."

She turned his face from side to side, scrutinizing him as only she could. "Perhaps ye should keep yer chin bare. Ye have a marvelous jaw line and besides, the style has gone away from facial hair these days."

He supposed he should be thankful for the delicate criticism, but if ever he thought to shave the thing off he was certain now that he should keep it. He didn't argue the point but instead placed her arm through his, straightening his back so his head was higher than hers. "We have plenty of time to discuss my grooming, mother," he replied gently. "For now, why don't ye settle in? I'm certain that ye're weary from yer trip."

"Nay," she replied, fixing herself against his gentle tug. His intentions were transparent. "I think that we should get right down to business. Where is Malsakin?"

His face dropped visibly as he searched for a plan that would keep his mother from the Ard Ri. "Wouldn't ye prefer to see yer brother first? When he heard ye were coming he decided to remain in Dublin."

Kormlada's heart jumped at the mention of Maelmora. Other than Sigtrygg, he was the only one of her blood kin that she could abide. "Where is he then?" she asked with glee. "I've as much to discuss with him as I have with ye."

"He's above in the Solarium," Sigtrygg replied. Though Maelmora's testimony regarding his actions could paint him in equally bad light as Malsakin's could, he was fairly certain that his uncle would go easy on him seeing that his intentions weren't exactly pure. "I'll take ye to him."

They made their way up the two levels of winding stairway leading to the solarium. When they reached the doorway, Kormlada drew breath. Maelmora was a thing of beauty, lounging back in his chair with the sunlight dancing off his face. His thick golden hair cascaded over his broad shoulders to rest at his perfectly tapered waist, which was cinched by a belt of gold. His boots were of the same skin as his trousers making it seem that his legs went on forever as they rested across a stool.

The sound of her entry woke him and his lids fluttered before they opened to expose his sea green eyes. He smiled as he got to his feet and the dimples on his clean shaven cheeks deepened. "Sister!" he cried, holding out a hand to her. He fell to his knees when she took it. "Ever the beauty ye are."

"I might say the same about ye," she cooed, looking down her nose at him to hide her emotions. She learned early in life that shows of emotion were often taken as weakness. Olaf was the only one she had truly opened up to. That mistake nearly found her dead of a broken heart. "Have ye left yer wife then?"

Maelmora shook his head before getting to his feet. "My, but ye are direct. Not even a question as to my well being or small talk about the weather."

"Well, since I've only just come from outside I can tell ye that the weather is brisk but that's expected at this time of year and as for yer well being…" she hesitated as she raked him with her eyes. "By the looks of ye I'd say ye're as fit as ever."

"And by the looks of ye," he cooed before raising her hand to his lips, "I should think ye're as much trouble as ever."

"Trouble?" Kormlada questioned coyly as she moved to take the seat he only just abandoned. "When have ye known me to cause anyone trouble?"

Maelmora and Sigtrygg exchanged knowing glances before the older man burst out with laughter. "My dear Kormlada," he thrilled, lowering himself onto the stool then lifting her foot to set it upon his lap, "the question should be, when haven't ye caused anyone trouble?"

She pulled her leg back but he kept a grip on it, massaging her foot through her slipper. "I resent that," she snapped. "Need I remind ye that ye're addressing the high queen, nay yer little sister?"

"Och," Maelmora chuckled, rubbing her foot still harder. "Ye needn't remind me. Anyone who looks on ye would know yer station."

She laughed along with him then sat forward to take him by the shoulders. "I've missed ye, brother," she offered before planting a cool kiss upon his cheek. "But we shall remedy that now since I plan on making this visit a long one."

"So ye've returned to Dublin?" Sigtrygg asked, wondering what she was planning to do with him. He knew his mother loved him and he loved her, but Kormlada had a way of getting into a man's life and controlling it without his ever knowing.

"Aye," she cooed before wriggling out of the heavy fur trimmed cloak she was wearing. She cast it to the floor then resettled herself back into the chair to allow the sun to warm her face. "There's much to do here and I mean to have it settled before I leave."

Sigtrygg looked to his uncle who shrugged his shoulders then he turned back to Kormlada. "What are ye planning, mother?"

She opened one eye to gaze upon him. "Ye know—ye really should shave that thing off. It makes ye look more childlike than manly."

"Mother," he huffed nervously. "Can we set aside my grooming and discuss the matter at hand?"

She rolled her eyes than straightened in her seat. "Very well. Let us discuss the matter at hand." Sigtrygg pulled up a stool and Maelmora leaned in close as the high queen prepared to reveal her plan.

"I was thinking that ye both need a place of yer own to rule and so I'll be insisting that Malsakin provide it for ye."

She paused for a moment to let her words settle on their brains then continued, "Sigtrygg—since yer father built this city it would only be fitting that ye rule it. Now, I know all about yer escapades and I'm willing to overlook them. I think ye will make a great earl as long as I'm here to assist ye."

Sigtrygg raised a brow. He had been hoping for such a thing but didn't expect that it would come at this price. He weighed the terms in his head then at length decided it would be worth it. "What makes ye think that the Ard Ri will agree?" he asked anxiously.

"He'll agree," Kormlada cooed as she swept a stray lock of hair behind her right ear. "He reveres my counsel. He'll do what I ask because he knows it would be best for him."

Maelmora smiled wryly. His sister had a splendid way of wrapping men around her finger. It was a fact he knew for certain because he was one of her victims.

"And for me?" he asked, dimples again displaying themselves. "What bit of land do ye think I should be ruler of?"

She leaned far forward, taking his hand in hers then stroking it. "Ye, my handsome brother, shall be southern Ri Ciocid."

"Indeed?" he replied, his heart falling with disappointment that her plan was unattainable. "And how do we manage that bit with Boru claiming the title for himself? Do ye expect me to be calling him to war?"

"Nay ye, fair Maelmora, but Malsakin."

"Malsakin," he blurted, unbelieving that the Ard Ri would buy into such a plan. "May I remind ye, sister, that yer husband has spent quite some time avoiding just such a thing. What makes ye believe that he'll do it for me."

"He won't be doing it for ye, brother, but for his enchanting wife. It's our birth right to control Leinster and I'll not continue to sit by idle as some usurper runs it into the ground."

She pushed herself from her chair then stomped around the room displaying her ire. "If I wasn't a woman, I would have had the territory myself long ago but instead I'm left begging for my husband's favor. I'm sick of it, I tell ye! Leinster is mine and I'll do whatever I have to in order to get it back."

The chill running up Maelmora's back wasn't an unusual occurrence. It had happened many times before—most often in his sister's presence. She was nothing if not determined leaving little doubt that she'd be successful.

✳   ✳   ✳   ✳

Cavenlow, Ireland: The Great Hall—Four hours past noon—23, March 983 A.D.—Kevin's knuckles were white from gripping the arms of the polished metal chair. He could feel the bumps of the carved lion heads biting his palms but still he gripped them tighter as he willed his hands to cease their shaking. He straightened his shoulders in an effort to make his five foot six inch form appear more substantial then gave a quick glance toward his younger brother who stood at least a head taller than him.

Any man who laid eyes on Patric would agree that he was an imposing figure and standing there in his warrior costume he appeared even more so, but for all his brawn Patric was never able to figure out the truth of the situation. That inability was exactly the reason why he shouldn't be Ri Tuath and exactly the reason why Kevin had no worry for his deception.

After Lorca's death, all the pieces of his plan fell into place. He had destroyed the writ and since no one else knew his father had intended to name Patric as his heir, he assumed the throne as a rite of succession with Brian himself presiding over the installation. Now all he had to do was keep himself there until he was ready to make his next move.

By Brian's own edict there were only two ways to remove a Dal Cais Ri Tuath from his throne without a battle. One was to prove his inability to protect his people and the other was to prove his treachery against Brian. So long as Rouric, Eagan and Patric remained in Cavenlow, Kevin was fairly certain that he wouldn't have any trouble protecting his people, and since he was far wiser than Brian could ever hope to be, he was also certain that his treachery wouldn't be exposed until he was ready to have it so. The tides had finally turned. The proof of it was what was about to happen.

He tightened his jaw as the messenger approached. He knew why Brian had sent him—so did Patric—but no amount of fear or cajoling would make him change his mind.

The messenger placed the box carrying Brian's offer on the ground in front of the Ri Tuath before preparing to bend his knee but Kevin halted him with his uplifted palm. A wave of anxiety caused his hand to shake again and he quickly returned it to the arm of the chair before shouting, "Ye may tell the Ri Ciocid that the days of Cavenlow's participation in his wars have ended with my father's death. He failed in his responsibility to protect us from Volkren that night and he has nay right to ask us to expose ourselves to additional harm now. Until he removes Volkren from Eire, I've nay obligation to stand with him."

The flinch of Patric's jaw drew Kevin's attention and he turned to offer his brother a glare of warning. The messenger noticed and turned also, hoping the younger brother would find the courage to speak out against his chief, but Patric continued to stare straight ahead.

Disappointed that Patric wouldn't be intervening, the messenger returned his gaze to the Ri Tuath. He stepped forward offering, "We've known each other since we were children, Kevin and though I always knew of yer distaste for battle I would never have imagined that ye could act dishonorably when it came to matters concerning yer clan."

Kevin's jaw twitched as his anger swelled within him. Ryan was his childhood friend, second youngest son of Turlog of Thomond. He had always been dim witted but his current insolence was something that Kevin would never forgive.

"Ye forget yerself, Ryan. Ye're not addressing a cousin but the Ri Tuath of Cavenlow. I'm sure Brian would have yer hide if he knew ye were being so familiar in a matter of such grave importance. I'm within my rights to deny my assistance without being shunned by my clan and I warn ye to deliver the message to Brian just as it was given without adding any of yer own sentiments to it."

"And if I don't?" Ryan goaded as he stepped closer to the Ri Tuath who looked more like a child than a king sitting in that huge chair with Lorca's brass ring upon his head. Kevin had no more right to that throne than he had a right to refuse Brian's request for assistance, but if the throne couldn't be taken from him perhaps he could be taken from the throne.

"What shall ye do to me if I don't obey yer command, Kevin?" Ryan continued, hoping to spark a row.

Again Kevin's eyes darted towards Patric but the younger brother remained unmoving, head up and back straight as if he heard nothing of the conversation being carried on around him.

A film of sweat glistened on Kevin's forehead as he tightened his grip on the chair. "Don't test me, Ryan," he hissed through clenched teeth. "Ye know not what I'm capable of. I warn ye again to hold yer tongue."

Ryan threw up his hands as he totally shed any pretense of respect. He laughed out loud, strolling the empty hall with arms opened wide. "And which one of yer many men present will ye use to bring me into submission, Kevin?"

He turned suddenly, rushing forward then hopping onto the platform until Kevin was pushed back against the chair. "Or maybe ye think ye can do it yerself."

The action drew Patric's attention. He turned his head to look and Kevin sighed with the knowledge that his younger brother would offer him protection.

When Ryan noticed the movement, he jumped down from the platform to challenge him. "So will ye be the one, Patric? Will ye join yer brother in his traitorous behavior and strike a member of yer own clan?"

Patric looked deep into Ryan's dark eyes. Unlike most of the Dal Cais who were fair of hair and skin, Ryan was dark, presenting a sallow look even though he was obviously well fed. As next in line to become captain of Cavenlow's army, it was Patric's duty to protect his brother whether he agreed with him or not. He stood silent as he calculated the moves necessary to drop his cousin. A grab of the neck by his left hand while unsheathing his short blade with his right then tug forward with the left as the blade in the right pierces the skin just under the ribs. A quick thrust into the heart and it would all be over. Five moves to fall the man. Five moves to take a life.

Ryan searched Patric's face, knowing full well the intentions lurking behind his eyes. "Ye sicken me," he cried before spinning on his heel to let his long legs carry him quickly to the doors. He looked back at the sight of the pathetic little king being protected by his less than loyal guard and he heaved a great sigh for the days when the hall of Cavenlow was the glory of every warrior in the southern territory. "This day shall mark the name macLorca as one in the same with traitor," he called before throwing open the door then passing through it.

Kevin leapt from his seat as the door swung on its hinges then raced to where Patric was standing. He laughed as he took hold of his brother's shoulder. "Did ye see the look on his face? It was precious."

Patric looked into Kevin's eyes, silently counting the moves to fall the Ri Tuath. In under two seconds he had completed the first few then let his hot breath play on his brother's face as the point of his blade pressed the soft flesh just under his ribs. "If ye ever force me to play witness to such a deed again ye'll feel the bite of this blade. Do I make myself clear?"

Kevin's heart pounded in his chest as he was forced to look into Patric's eyes. In them he saw death. He pulled away slightly, saying a silent prayer for his brother to break the embrace.

Patric let his hand slip from Kevin's neck but continued to stare at him when he recalled Grace's words. It was following Lorca's death that she told him about his father's plan to name him captain of the army. Lorca trusted him to protect his people and he would be dead by his own hand before he allowed harm to come to any of them—including Kevin.

Kevin stepped back a few paces to be sure he was out of Patric's reach before offering, "If ye continue to lash out before thinking, ye'll never be ready to fulfill our father's wish to have ye captain. Like it or nay, my decision to withhold our army from Brian is the absolute right one. Brian was the one responsible for our father's death and he knows that until he rids us of Volkren I have nay obligation to stand with him."

Patric lifted an eyebrow and Kevin strolled across the room to retrieve the box Ryan left behind. He opened it then removed several pieces of the gold contained within. He held them up. "Why do ye suppose Brian sends us this treasure?"

Patric remained silent and Kevin continued, "To ease his guilty conscience." He sucked his teeth and shook his head. "The Ri Ciocid knows he's the reason for the poverty of our village and he wants to ease his tortured soul by buying our forgiveness." He threw the gold back into the box then slammed the lid shut before making his way back to Patric. "He was my father too," he growled, "and as long as I live, I'll never forgive Brian for what he did to this family! Do ye understand me?"

Patric looked into Kevin's eyes hoping to see some of the grief he portended but there was none. He returned his short sword to its sheath then spit the bile from his throat. "We see things differently, Kevin," he mumbled before passing his brother by, "but so long as I live within these walls, ye have my word that I'll give my life in protection of the others who dwell here."

At that moment Grace entered the hall. The tension between her sons was so thick it nearly knocked her to her knees. She took a moment to assess the scene before grabbing Patric's arm as he brushed past her.

"What's happened, Patric? Ye look a sight. Are ye unwell?"

He patted her hand before prying her fingers from his arm. "I'm fine, mother," he offered then nodded his chin toward Kevin, "but perhaps ye should take a moment with the Ri Tuath. I think he needs yer counsel."

Her brows rushed together as she struggled for his meaning but he was gone before she could inquire. She turned toward Kevin, "What was that about?"

Kevin waved a hand of dismissal. "Nay a thing. He's just confused about Volkren."

"Volkren," Grace mumbled, the name catching in her throat. She rushed him. "What's this all about?"

The true concern in her eyes compelled him to make her aware of the situation. He took her by the hand to lead her to the bench beside him. "It seems yer brother will march on the Viking as vengeance for yer husband's death," he offered as he opened the box to reveal the precious metals and gems within. He lifted out a ruby and held it to the torchlight as he continued, "He wanted us in it but I refused."

Her eyebrows shot up as the frown marked her face and he answered it with a scowl of his own. He knew that the only battle she would condone was the one to avenge Lorca's death but he had every reason to stay out of it and he meant her to know it.

"Why should we risk our lives in this battle when it was yer brother who called the scourge down upon us? It should be left to him to protect us since he's the reason we've suffered so."

Her face was unchanging so he decided to use the only tool he had to gain her submission. He closed his hand around the ruby then turned to face her fully as he snapped, "Alright then, if ye think me wrong in this I'll call Patric back and tell him of Lorca's true desire for him to be Ri Tuath. There's nay a doubt in my mind that the lad would choose to fight with Brian. Why not give him the benefit of his true title as he rides to his own slaughter?"

"Nay," she panicked, grabbing his hand and lifting it to her cheek. "We both decided that it would be best for ye to take the throne to keep us out of the battles. We shouldn't rethink it now."

She rubbed her cheek over his knuckles and sighed as she realized she had no choice in the matter. "Ye're right of course," she offered with a nod of her head, "It should be Brian who avenges Lorca's death. Let it be his neck that's risked against yer father's murderer."

"Good then," he cooed before rising to his feet. He smiled. "Perhaps we'll be lucky enough to find the Ri Ciocid killed in the battle so that we can finally put an end to these troublesome conversations."

He bent to kiss her cheek but she grabbed his hand, turning to face him full on. "And ye'll make good on yer promise never to let Patric assume the position of captain?" She frowned as her concern for her lie was renewed. "I wish ye had never forced me to offer up the story."

He too frowned as he placed a hand on either side of her chair to pin her to her seat. "If ye hadn't he would have run to Brian to support him for this throne and one of us would have been lost in the ensuing battle!"

She pulled back from him and he straightened up, tossing the ruby in his right hand as his eyes narrowed. "Ye just leave Patric to me. I know how to handle him. I don't want yer meddling getting either one of us killed, aye, mother."

With that he turned to exit the hall leaving Grace with the haunting feeling that Lorca was breathing down her neck.

✳   ✳   ✳   ✳

Scattery Island: Three hours past dawn—28, March 983 A.D.—Patric pulled at the oars with all his weight, determined to reach the island as quickly as possible. It was nestled west off the Limerick coast at the mouth of the River Shannon.

The vessel he was using was rented from a fisherman. At first the man denied him the favor, explaining that he'd seen Brian and his army come ashore yesterday and that the fighting was long over, but once Patric offered him silver the man quickly ceded.

The old fisherman supposed Brian won the battle owing to the large number of warriors that returned with him but he wasn't certain that Volkren was among the dead—even though he deserved to be. "He's worse than his uncle, that one is," he offered in reference to Volkren. "Thought he could flee to the Isle of Saint Sean and rule his roost from there, collecting his taxes and raiding by night. If Boru did fall him, there's nay doubt in my mind that he fed him to the sea."

There were rumors that Volkren had returned to Orkney after raiding Cavenlow, but when he began to appear in the night at the farmsteads surrounding Limerick to demand his taxes it was determined that he had followed in the footsteps of Imar and set up camp on Scattery Island. It was said that he was using the church on the Hill of Angels as his hall and that his warriors were looting graves to get at their treasure. It was little wonder that Brian chose to besiege him, if not as vengeance for Lorca then for the sacrilege he was perpetrating on the most holy island.

Patric wanted more than assumptions about Volkren's death, he wanted proof of it. Everything that mattered to him rested on whether the Viking lived or died and if he had to comb the bay himself to find the earl's dead body he would do it.

He turned to look over his shoulder. The hundred foot round tower built by Saint Sean was growing larger with each pull of the oar and he quickened his rhythm. Moments later the boat hit the shingle beach. He wasted little time gathering up his sword and shield to climb the grassy hill leading to the Damliag.

Fallen warriors were strewn in heaps along the plain, easily mistaken for stones if it weren't for what was left of their garments. Brian was no fool—weapons cost dearly and he would have had every dead man stripped of mail, shield, sword and cloak before he receded back to the shores of the mainland. Patric called out as he made his way up the incline of the Hill of Angels but the only answer he got was the echo of his own voice as it bounced off the twelve churches dotting the island.

He looked westward across the plain and to the open sea beyond. It would take him a fair amount of the day to check the dead to see if Volkren was among them and he sank to the ground so that he could decide where to begin.

"Be still now, man," the raspy voice whispered.

Patric laid his hand on his sword hilt as he turned a cautious eye to see who had spoken. "Grab his arm now," the voice continued. "By the gods, man, ye almost had me dropping him."

Patric rose to his feet then walked quietly to the arched doorway of the church. From there he could see clear through the structure to its southern door, which was arched in the same fashion as the northern one. Beyond, on the field between the tower and the church, was what looked to be a Viking and an abbot struggling with a very large satchel. He heard a groan before the abbot whispered something to the Viking.

Patric uncovered his sword then stepped with care onto the gravel floor of the church. He tried to keep his footfalls easy but the stones shifted beneath the weight of his feet and soon the Viking turned in his direction.

"And who do ye belong to, laddie?" he called out, giving little mind to the fact that Patric was armed, then he returned his attention to the satchel.

Patric continued to move forward and soon he realized that what he thought was a satchel was instead another man. "Watch what yer doing!" the Viking snapped as the abbot's ministrations caused the fallen warrior to groan again. "Here, give that to me."

The "that," which the Viking referred to was a small keg. He unstopped it then bathe the strips of cloth he was holding with its contents before wiping them over the warrior's chest to expose a gaping wound. The man's face was bruised and swollen, distorting his features beyond recognition and his left arm and right leg were twisted in an unnatural position.

"What happened to him?" Patric asked, realizing that the man was also soaked through to the skin.

"The captain was tangling with one of Volkren's rots up there on the bluff." The Viking motioned with his chin in the direction of the cliffs. "When the blade caught him he was cast into the sea. I thought he was lost and nearly left without him, but thanks to the abbot here, there's hope he may pull through."

The abbot was little more than half the size of the other two men and Patric marveled that he was both brave and strong enough to lend his assistance. Just then, the warrior bucked and cursed, catching the abbot with an uppercut from his good arm. Patric leapt forward to hold the captain down while the Viking tried to pour some ale into his mouth.

"Drink it, damn ye," he demanded as the captain fought against him but when his orders went unheeded he decided to employ other measures to settle him down.

Reaching into his boot, he pulled out what looked to be a metal ring. He slipped his fingers through it then hit the patient square in the jaw to knock him unconscious. He smirked. "He's a tough one alright but I'll see him mended if I have to kill him to get it done."

Patric chuckled while he helped to secure the bandages around the captain's lean gut to stem the bleeding from a jagged cut then looked up startled when the Viking blurted, "Hey! Ye never did say who ye were."

"I'm Patric macLorca, prince of Cavenlow. I came to fight with Brian."

The statement was one worthy of the Viking's full attention. His worry for his captain abandoned, he rested back on his heels then looked to the abbot who was making a hasty sign of the cross. "Patric macLorca?" the Viking huffed. "Well, if ye wanted to fight, man, ye should've brought yer army. Many good men were lost here battling yer father's enemy."

As if to underscore the point the captain suddenly came around, thrashing and groaning fiercely. The Viking repeated the tactic he'd used earlier to keep him still causing the abbot to admonish, "Ye're going to kill him if ye keep that up, aye!"

"Would it be better for him to rip open the wound we only just bandaged?" the Viking snapped back before grabbing another strip of material from the abbots hand to wrap it around the unconscious man's head.

"Och," was the abbot's reply. He ripped the cloth from the Viking's hand. "Here, let me tend him while ye speak with the lad. Ye've got yerself in a lather and ye may as well cure it by getting his story."

Patric was certain they expected an explanation as to why Kevin had refused to participate in the battle but he had none to give. Instead he asked a question that seemed to anger the Viking further. "Can ye tell me if Brian succeeded?"

"Of course we succeeded!" the Viking barked. "Just look at that field. We routed them, nay thanks to ye and yers."

Patric eyes lit up with excitement. "So Volkren's dead? Brian killed him?"

The abbot looked up for a moment then turned back to his work as he shook his head pitifully. The Viking's answer came in a hiss. "The rot got away. Escaped in his boat with little more than twenty others but I doubt we'll see him back on this soil."

"With the help of God," the abbot mumbled.

Patric hung his head. It was the worst type of luck to have Volkren defeated but left still alive. Even if he didn't return to Ireland, Kevin would continue to have him as an excuse against standing with Brian.

"May God have mercy on us," he mumbled.

"Mercy on ye?" the Viking replied. "How about the forty we lost fighting this battle? May God have mercy on them and their families who'll have to make their own way." He took a swig from the barrel then spit it on the ground as he shook his head. "Ye should have come when ye were called."

A wave of nausea swept through Patric's gut. It was clear that Ryan made good on his threat—the macLorca's were marked as traitors. There was little hope that anyone, even the abbot, would believe differently until Kevin declared himself an ally to Brian.

He rose to his feet, the sorrow in his heart weighing heavy on his chest, then made his way to the door. He stopped before passing. "I presume ye'll need help getting yer fellow back to shore."

"Nay," the Viking mumbled without looking up. "He'll remain here until he's sufficiently healed. He's Brian's man. He'll be well tended." The abbot nodded agreement.

"Very well then," Patric offered as he began to walk away then he thought of something. He turned but neither the abbot nor the Viking looked up at him. "I've a horse on the other side. When yer man is healed, I want ye to collect it from the fisherman and present it as a gift to the warrior. Tell him it's from the Ri Tuath of Cavenlow in acknowledgment of his deeds on behalf of our village." He walked away.

The abbot and the Viking exchanged a lengthy glance then suddenly the Viking was on his feet. He gaped in disbelief as the lad marched through the church, head held high displaying all his nobility. He called after him. "I guess it's the least ye could do, aye?"

Patric didn't look back but at that moment the captain regained his consciousness. "Who is it, Havland?" he moaned then struggled to raise himself on his elbow so that he could see.

"Och," Havland issued, scurrying toward him to stop him from displacing the splint they had only just applied to his broken arm. "Careful with yerself, Thorien. 'Twas no one ye need worry over. Now lay ye back down so we can finish yer bandaging. When Brian hears that we found ye alive, there's nay doubt he'll be calling ye back to Limerick so that ye can oversee the territory for him."

CHAPTER 10

─────────────── ▼ ───────────────

Cashel, Ireland: Two hours to noon—1, September 983 A.D.—Cashel may have been home to the various kings of Munster but for Brian, it was little more than a place to conduct his business. He much preferred the natural warmth of Cenn Cora nestled amongst the trees and river to the cold formality of the ancient granite fortress that seemed devoid of life.

Cashel was a hodgepodge of stone structures set high atop a hill affording unobstructed views of Osirage to the south, Limerick to the west and Leinster to the east. Its abbey was the richest in territory, with arched doorways and stained glass windows that sparkled in the midday sun. An old Viking round tower stood east of the abbey and was now used as a keep for hostages. Along the western wall were the barracks and the weapons hold. To the south was the great hall.

The entire accumulation was surrounded by a thick wall of stone with gates both north and south but since the village lay so far below, down a steep and treacherous path, the fortress usually lacked the presence of people, save the soldiers and servants whose duties were within.

The northern upper bank of the fortress was reserved as a burial site for the many kings who once ruled the territory. Brian spent much of his time there, calling upon them to lend their wisdom when things were most difficult. Turlog spotted him sitting beside the burial mound of the dead king, Oillil Olom, father of Cormac Cas from whom the Dal Cais were descended.

"Thank heavens I found ye," the Ri Tuath of Thomond called. "We must speak, Brian."

Brian turned his head in acknowledgement of Turlog's presence but remained silent, nodding for his uncle to back away until his prayers were completed.

Turlog offered a tiny "hmph," as he obeyed then leaned against another mound contemplating his fingernails until Brian finally approached.

"Aye, what is it now?" the Ri Ciocid inquired. Being in Cashel usually put him in a foul mood—having Turlog interrupt his prayers didn't do much to elevate it.

Turlog sucked his teeth in dissatisfaction for being kept waiting but Brian ignored it. Instead he brushed past his uncle and began to walk the path back to the hall.

Turlog scrambled behind him, sidestepping the tiny rocks and rubble that seemed constantly present on the path. His lein caught on a gorse bush and he stepped back to untangle it, being careful not to prick his fingers on the thorny golden flowers.

"Damn weed! Can't ye do something about these abominable bushes?" he called to Brian who was many paces ahead of him. "They're taking over the countryside."

"I like them," Brian retorted over his shoulder. "They're the only bit of nature this stone prison holds."

Finally freed, Turlog stepped up his pace until he was walking a few paces behind the Ri Ciocid. His shortness of breath caused his speech to be halted. "Kevin's—becoming—a bit of a problem for ye—I think. There's talk—that he's been consorting with—Volkren."

While such a comment should have commanded Brian's total attention, he only waved his hand as he descended the steep path.

Since Lorca's death, rumors about Kevin's supposed treachery had been running rampant around Munster. They began in the barracks amongst soldiers who were angry about having to fight in defense of Cavenlow without assistance, but now they were spreading amongst the nobles as well.

"Volkren's gone," he huffed in frustration. "By now the rot's probably safe and sound in Orkney." He turned slightly. "I warn ye against buying into rumors, uncle. I've all I can handle trying to explain the situation to the troops. I don't need ye stirring up the cauldron."

They had reached the portal of the great hall and Brian leaned against the wooden door in order to allow Turlog a moment to catch his breath. Turlog placed his palm against the stone, pulling his white lein away from his chest to let the cool breeze refresh him. He gulped for air until his lungs found a comfortable rhythm. "Did ye ever stop to think that perhaps these rumors are true? Ye may need an overseer for Cavenlow, aye."

"Bah," Brian offered before opening the door. "How could ye even think the man would ally with the Viking who killed his father? 'Tis absurd."

"Not every child bears good will for his sire, Brian. I have it on very good authority that Kevin has spent his life revering the Eaghonacts. He may very well be working to help them take yer throne."

Brian raised an eyebrow at the possibility but when the whole of the statement settled on his brain he again waved a hand in dismissal then stepped into the shadows of the great hall. Turlog had been eager to get his hands on Cavenlow ever since Cennitig refused his offer to marry Grace. No doubt, this was just another attempt to gain what he wanted.

"Don't be so eager to dismiss me, Brian. At the very least, ye should let me oversee Cavenlow for ye so that Kevin doesn't have a chance to build up his army. If he does, it may only be a matter of time before he gathers yer enemies together. Then yer time on the throne will be short lived."

Brian flashed a smile at the serving maid who offered him a cup then walked the short distance to his chair, nodding his head in greeting to the few warriors taking a respite in the hall. He waved Turlog to the seat next to his then leaned over to speak lowly so the others wouldn't hear, "If ye're right about Kevin..." Turlog's eyes twinkled and Brian held up his hand to halt his victory, "which I don't believe ye are—then how is it that Patric wouldn't come to tell me of the scheme?"

Turlog gave his nephew a tsk-tsk look before taking a long draw from his cup. He wiped his mouth with the back of his sleeve. "The explanation is that he's as deep into the scheme as his brother is."

Brian rolled his eyes before waving him off but Turlog continued, "It makes sense Brian. Ye know as well as I that Grace has never been..." he hesitated a moment as he searched for the proper words, "err...Well let's just say she's nay quite fond of ye."

This statement caused Brian's lips to pucker but Turlog ignored him. "Everyone knows it's true. And where lies the mother's heart so lies the child's."

"That's nonsense," Brian retorted. "Ye've been in that house. Ye know those lads. They're the image of their father and they carry *his* heart."

"Ahh," Turlog cooed as he wagged his finger under Brian's nose, "maybe the other eight but they're all dead now. Ye know as well as I that Kevin was always more for the book than the sword."

"Nay Patric," Brian shot back, remembering the night when they prepared to march on Donovan and Malmua. "That lad's a warrior if ever there was one."

"Aye," Turlog nodded in agreement, "but that was before he found his father slain by the Vikings. To witness such a death is enough to turn even the heartiest warrior away in fear."

Brian took a sip from his cup, using the wide rim as a cover to the emotions that were playing on his face. As if it were happening right there before his very eyes, he remembered the look on Patric's face when he found his father lying dead on the ground. Though the lad barely uttered a word it was clear that he blamed Brian for his father's death. Not even when they lowered Lorca's shrouded body into the ground did he say anything, or for that matter, shed a tear. Now all this time had passed without word from him. Could it be his uncle was right?

He shook his head in an effort to clear the doubt that was settling there. "Forget about Cavenlow for now and tell me what news ye have about Malsakin."

Turlog sat bolt upright to relay his urgency, "I warn ye not to put this off, Brian. It'll be the end of ye for sure."

Brian's eyes grew sharp with the insolence. Again he leaned in close to his uncle as he spoke, "Are ye telling me that ye'd want to take part in another battle? Haven't ye had enough death, Turlog? Wasn't Ryan enough for ye to lose, must ye risk Joseph also?"

The reminder of Ryan's loss struck Turlog like a knife. "It was to avenge Lorca's death that I sacrificed my son to Volkren. I should think Kevin owes me something for that!"

Brian cringed as his own edict weighted the argument against him. He took a deep breath then covered his uncle's hand with his own. "Though it pains me to admit it, Kevin was within his rights to deny me, uncle. If I hadn't struck at Volkren then perhaps he wouldn't have raided Cavenlow in the first place. It was me who brought the scourge upon them so then it must be me who pays for it."

"So ye're telling me that ye'd allow a traitor to live amongst us unpunished?"

"That's not what I said," Brian huffed as his anger began to stir. "If ye bring me proof of Kevin's so called treachery, I'll act on it, but until that time I'll do whatever I can to support Cavenlow."

Turlog didn't bother to hide the scowl on his face but he knew that if he continued to speak about it his nephew would deny him just to prove his point. "Very well," he muttered before taking a sip from his cup. "Getting back to Malsakin. It seems he's beginning to weaken from yer tactics. Mind ye, he's nay willing to call ye out yet but there's talk that he's planning to travel the country bringing his court to the tuaths of his kin to prove that he can protect them."

"Ye don't say," Brian cooed through a crooked smile, happy to know that his plan was working. For the last several years he'd been systematically raiding key leaders of the O'Neill clan hoping that the Ard Ri would risk his crown by calling him out. "He could have saved everyone a lot of trouble if only he'd done the right thing in Tara."

"He plans to hold Christmas court in Ailech," Turlog added. "Fladbartoc's his champion so it makes sense that he'd choose his home to show himself off."

The two men sat silent for a time watching the comings and goings of the warriors and servants. Every so often Brian would nod or raise his hand in acknowledgement of someone who was offering their respects but all the while he was pondering the information Turlog had given to him. At length it was Turlog who spoke. "What if ye brought yer army to Ailech? Ye have as much a right to court as anyone else. Perhaps our mere presence will spark the war ye've been after."

Brian considered this statement for sometime before his eyes lit up in excitement. "Aye," he chuckled, "that should put the fear of God into the Ard Ri but if it doesn't I have an even better plan."

Turlog looked up at his nephew in askance.

"Surely ye've heard the talk about Malsakin and Kormlada. The Ard Ri has told everyone that his marriage to the woman and his ascension to the high throne was preordained by the gods. How do ye suppose he'd react if she suddenly disappeared?"

Turlog's eyes flew open as he began to see the plan forming in Brian's mind. "Kidnap?" he sighed.

"Why not?" Brian questioned with a wry smile spreading across his face. "The Ard Ri has so much as admitted that his possession of Kormlada brought him the throne."

"Och," Turlog spit. "Ye can't believe those rumors!"

"I don't," Brian issued, "but if the Ard Ri does, he'd be willing to wage war to get her back and then I'll have what I've been after."

Turlog thought about it then nodded. It might be just the thing to spark the war. Again they sat silent before he chuckled, "Ye could wind up with the throne either way."

Brian looked askance and he continued, "Perhaps the rumors are true."

Brian laughed so hard that he spit the wine he just sipped across the table. He mopped it up with a rough linen square. "All the same, I think we should lay a plan." He used the residue from the wine to trace a map with his finger. "We'll gather the largest army we can muster then split them up. Half will travel with ye and Connor on the eastern road to Ailech and the other half will travel with me on the western road. We'll wear our colors of course, but if anyone sees us they'll be hard pressed to say where we're headed."

Even if he didn't believe that the plan would work, riding with Connor was enough to have Turlog agree. For quite some time he'd been after the man to leave Brian and serve him instead. Perhaps the ride would give him a chance to convince him. Another thought struck him. "And when ye gain yer crown, what will happen to me?"

Brian lifted an eyebrow at his uncle's blatant grab for power. It wasn't unlike him to want to negotiate the spoils even before they were gained but that was something the Ri Ciocid never did. Situations often changed and a promise made in good faith today might not be best filled tomorrow. He placed a hand on his uncle's shoulder as he gave him the only thing he could. "When I gain my crown ye can be certain that all our troubles will be over."

* * * *

Clonmacnoise, Ireland: In the tavern run by Mangus Horn—14, September 983 A.D.—There was no more thoroughly Viking place in Ireland than a tavern hall and the one in Clonmacnoise was no exception. A three-day ride northeast from Cavenlow, it was located in the kingdom of Leinster and was surrounded by the Viking villages of Torshav and Athlone.

After he took the territory from Olaf Curran, Brian had empowered the Galls to rule themselves so long as they paid him tribute, a situation Kevin much appreciated. He let his eyes adjust to the darkness before closing the door behind him. When he realized the tavern was nearly empty he released his breath. Garvin touched his arm.

"There he is."

Kevin followed the man's gaze to the broad Viking sitting in the corner. Garvin usually made the monthly trip alone but this time Kevin needed to be there. Volkren spotted them immediately.

"So," he crooned, smiling to display a set of uneven teeth. "This must be my benefactor. Come, Ri Tuath. Sit and have a pint with me."

Kevin looked to Garvin who nodded his assurance that he wouldn't be harmed before leading the way and soon they were all seated around a rough hewn wooden table. The dark pouring maid brushed up against Kevin's arm as she handed him a pint but he recoiled. His father had always warned him against camp followers and whores—it was the only valuable information he imparted.

She bowed from the waist with the obvious rebuff then went around the table to offer her services to Volkren. "Later, lassie," the earl responded, patting her soft behind before sending her away. He looked to Kevin.

"I've heard that ye like to get straight down to business, Dal Cais, but this one's worth the time," he said as he nodded his chin in the woman's direction.

First meetings were always difficult for Kevin, especially when they were taken with men the size of Volkren. Respect that couldn't be gained by Kevin's appearance had to be earned with attitude. He offered a "hmph," then took a sip from his cup.

"I've nay the time just now, Volkren. I've come with a…."

"See there, laddie," Volkren interrupted, "that would be yer problem. There's not a man from here to Ulster who wouldn't find the time for the fair Freyja. She might look innocent but she certainly knows her way around, if ye know what I mean."

Volkren's stare was intense and Kevin fought back the urge to lower his eyes. "Maybe next time, aye," he offered with a smile then got straight to the point. "I've come with a proposition."

Volkren slowly leaned back in his chair then waved his hand to get the attention of Erik who was standing in the shadows. "Just let me get my man here."

Startled by Erik's presence, Kevin drew breath causing the captain to chuckle as he took the seat beside him. "Now there, Ri Tuath, what's eating at ye? Surely ye didn't expect the earl to take a meeting without me?"

"Of course I expected ye," Kevin replied before taking a sip from his cup to hide his growing nervousness, "I just wonder why ye would keep us waiting is all."

Erik opened his mouth to retort but Kevin stopped him with his upturned hand, demonstrating his superiority. "I want ye to carry out another raid."

Volkren laughed from deep in his belly. "And what am I now, a lap dog?"

Everything about Volkren was intimidating but if Kevin displayed even the slightest sign of fear all hope of making a deal would be lost. He stiffened his back then looked each of the Viking's over. "If ye're not up to the task then perhaps I should offer my proposition elsewhere." He got to his feet but suddenly Volkren's hand was covering his—a grip so tight it caused him pain.

"Who said I'm not up to it?" the Viking growled.

The fear Kevin felt was genuine and not without reason but he stood his ground. "So will ye hear me out?"

"I'll hear ye out," Volkren replied, eyes still burning with anger over the challenge that had been issued. As a rule, he didn't take meetings with learned men but the Dal Cais sent a message that he was willing to help him take back Limerick and he supposed he would need someone of intelligence on his side if he were to do it.

"Sit down and tell me what ye're thinking."

Kevin took his time returning to his seat, all the while keeping his eyes trained on Volkren. He took a long draw from his cup to settle his nerves then at length offered, "Brian's been as much a thorn to me as he has to ye but in order to stand against him I must first secure an army and for that I need assistance. Ye can buy me the time and cover I need to do it if ye raid Cavenlow and kill my younger brother."

"Raid Cavenlow?" Erik chuckled, disbelieving of what he just heard. "We did that once on yer say so and a lot of good it did us. We lost everything in the deal."

"Aye," Volkren growled, suddenly angered again. "How dare ye come to me now after ye cost me Limerick? I should take yer head right now!"

He uncovered his short sword and held it under Kevin's chin.

Kevin dared not move, or even swallow. He lifted his eyes to Volkren's without moving his head. "If ye think ye'll be better off without me then do it."

The display of bravery wasn't lost on Volkren. The truth was, that without Kevin's tribute each month he would have been forced to return to Orkney long ago. He returned the blade to its sheath before sitting down. "Let's put the past behind us and discuss the future," he grumbled. "Tell me how raiding Cavenlow will get me Limerick back."

Kevin explained that Patric's death would devastate Brian. He'd never think to ask Cavenlow to stand with him again after suffering such a loss. Once it happened, Kevin would make an alliance with the O'Neills and take the territory for himself. He would be Ri Tuath Ruire and Volkren would return as earl of Limerick.

"So—how will we know which one is yer brother?" Erik asked when they had all decided that the plan was a good one.

Kevin shrugged his shoulders. "Just level the field. Any who I want safe will be kept from it." He chuckled as the grin split his beard, "Ye'll catch my brother up, alright. Nay doubt, he'll be the first fool to run into the battle because he wants to see ye dead more than anything else."

Volkren frowned and Kevin continued just to give the Viking incentive, "Against my command the lad was with Brian on Scattery Island. He's willful that one. He won't be easy to defeat."

"We'll see about that," Erik blurted.

Volkren sat silent as he sized up the man who sat before him. Kevin was slight of build with hair so fair it looked white in the glow of the lamp—definitely not a warrior but a thinker for certain. Unlike the other educated men Volkren had known, Kevin was likeable. He was easy to talk to—never speaking in riddles or disguising his words so the thought was unclear. Instead he spoke plainly, a great relief to the Orkney man who always struggled with the Gaelic language.

"So," the earl finally offered as he placed both his palms down on the table. "show us what ye brought to inspire our success."

Kevin reached into his waist belt to pull out a pouch. He emptied the contents onto the table—a ruby, a sapphire and two ounces of pure silver.

"I think this will be fair."

Volkren picked up the ruby to hold it up to the light. Satisfied he placed it against his left eye, holding it there with his wink. "Seems fair enough," he chuckled, then a thought struck him. He dropped the gem from his eye into his open palm. "This treasure ye've been sending—where have ye been getting it?"

It wasn't hard to read Volkren's thoughts and Kevin answered quickly to ensure his own safety. "There aren't any riches in Cavenlow. Ye saw to that with yer last raid—burning the place up as ye did. The treasure I've been sending has come to me from Brian. He's using it to ease his guilt."

Volkren thought for a moment, remembering the price of his annual tribute to the Ri Ciocid. "So in reality, what ye've been giving me has been mine all along."

Kevin lifted an eyebrow in askance and Erik interjected, "Brian took ten times this amount from Volkren each year as tribute."

"Aye," Volkren grumbled, "and I mean to have it back."

"Ye'll get it back," Kevin stated confidently. "Once ye've killed Patric, Brian will send a hundred times more than this as restitution for his loss. Ye have my word that it'll be yers."

Volkren nodded then offered his hand. Kevin cautiously took it.

"Good then," he thrilled, getting to his feet and silently thanking the Lord that the deal was done. "I'll expect ye in Cavenlow by the new moon."

*   *   *   *

Cavenlow, Ireland: Dawn—25, September 983 A.D.—Patric turned the last shovel of dirt to reveal another half dozen potatoes. Though small, the garden was providing ample sustenance for the warriors housed in the barracks who would have starved if they were left to depend on the meager scraps Kevin sent from the house. He leaned forward against the shovel as he gazed upon what was left of his father's kingdom. The once thriving village had been reduced to ruins by Volkren's raid and Kevin was doing little to recover it.

"That's a grand crop yer bringing in," Rouric shouted as he approached. His blue eyes twinkled and his white hair blew free against his ruddy cheeks as his once powerful form labored up the incline.

Patric nodded in response but continued to gaze around the village. Even the great hall was beginning to fall into disrepair with loose patches of thatch slipping from their bindings to flap free with the breeze. He made a mental note to send a few men to make the repairs then turned toward Rouric. He smiled at the captain—the only man left from his father's army. He cherished every moment spent in his company.

"Aye, it is. We'll be eating good this winter nay thanks to my brother."

Rouric screwed up his face causing the tiny lines around his eyes to bunch up. "Now there, laddie. Yer brother does the best he can. Ye shouldn't be speaking ill of him."

Patric considered the captain for a moment. There were no binds to tie him to Kevin yet he remained in Cavenlow eager to serve a chief who clearly had little use for him. "Why do ye remain here, Rouric?" he questioned flatly.

Misunderstanding the thought behind the question, Rouric scrambled for an answer. "See here, laddie. Don't be thinkin that I'll be keepin ye from the position of captain. If that's what yer Da wanted for ye, I've nay a problem steppin aside whenever it suits ye. I've known ye since ye were a wee one and believe me when I tell ye that I'm just tryin to look after ye."

Seeing the genuine concern in Rouric's eyes, Patric stepped forward to set him straight. "I didn't ask because I was eager to assume the position, I only asked because..." He shifted from one foot to the other, unsure of how to proceed without causing further confusion. "I only asked because it seems that Kevin has nay use for any of us so I wonder why ye should remain loyal to a chief who looks at us as a bunch of rabble?"

"I see," Rouric said then rubbed his chin as he pondered the question. He'd always liked Patric and, truth be told, had sincerely hoped that Lorca would have seen the sense in naming him his heir instead of Kevin, but that wasn't to be and now they were left to deal with the situation as it stood.

"See here, laddie," he stated, leading Patric to a rock where they could both have a seat. "Whether Kevin wants us or nay, Cavenlow needs an army to protect it. I'll be dead at my own hand before I let another bit of harm come to this village. Yer father was a good man. One of the best. I served many years by his side and together we accomplished great things. Not many knew how truly brilliant Lorca was, but I did. So did Brian, that's why he named him his second. I figure that yer Da had his reasons for deciding that things should be as they are and so as long as that was his wish I'll see to it that it happens. It's for Lorca that I stay. Do ye understand, laddie?"

Patric did understand. He too remained for Lorca but for the life of him he couldn't believe that his father would be happy to know that Kevin had abandoned Brian.

"Do ye think my father would approve of the way my brother's handling the situation with the Ri Ciocid?" he asked as he searched Rouric's face.

Rouric's eyes shifted from side to side in consideration of the question. When it came to the matter of Brian, Lorca had always known Kevin's heart. Certainly he must have expected things to turn out poorly but still he let Kevin take his throne. He rose to his feet, shaking his head as he sighed, "Yer father set things on their course and now we'll have to wait to see how they turn out."

He held out his hand, beckoning Patric to join him. "Why don't we find Eagan and have ourselves a little gathering. I hear that some of the lads swiped a barrel of ale from the house. I've always said that if ye have to think, ye best not do it while ye're parched."

Patric chuckled as he joined the captain on the path leading to the barracks. Other than Brian, there wasn't another man alive who knew Lorca as well as Rouric did. He was eager to share a few pints that could lead to many grand stories.

By the time they reached the barracks it was clear that the drinking had already begun. A group of men were huddled together in the corner singing old songs and some others were playing dice against the wall. The festivities lasted well into the night.

Since Lorca's death, sleep hadn't come easy to Patric but that night it eluded him completely. He tossed in his cot, hoping the effects of the sour ale would finally put him to sleep but when he remained awake, he looked to the thatch roof, listening to the sounds coming from the river. A riot of noise was being carried on the wind but before he could identify what it was all about the door burst open and the guard's voice filled the room.

"Volkren's returned. We're under attack! All men to the field!"

Patric bolted from his bunk, needing no more than ten strides to put him squarely in front of Eagan who was issuing weapons at the door. Eagan hesitated forcing the command, "Give me a blade!"

Rouric grabbed Eagan's arm to stop him from handing over the weapon. "Take Patric to safety then join us."

"Aye," the young soldier responded.

Patric's face flashed red. "Nay! I won't hide!"

"Ye must," Rouric snapped. "I'll not lose another member of this family. I may have lost yer father and brother's but I'll not lose ye!"

"Nay! I'll stay and fight."

"Don't let him win ye over, Eagan," Rouric boomed as he took the sword meant for Patric then turned to leave. "Take him to safety immediately!"

Eagan doled out the last weapon to another warrior then held the door open for Patric. "Come," he commanded. "If Volkren has his way there'll be many other battles for ye to fight. Away with ye now."

"Give me a sword, Eagan!" Patric demanded. "I won't run from my fate!"

"Rouric will have my head," he huffed then ran his hand along the empty rack. "Besides, there aren't any blades left. I pray ye to heed the captain and be off to the house."

Patric looked to the corner. The old sword lying there was a bit rusty but it was still sharp. He grabbed it then raced through the open door.

Eagan shook his head as he ran after him. Truth be told, Patric was more capable in combat than any warrior in Cavenlow. They had spent a lifetime together and he knew full well that nothing in heaven or on earth could change Patric's mind once it was made up.

He jogged along side the prince, winking as he tossed him a shield. Patric caught it and smiled then he stretched his long legs until Eagan was left far behind him.

The Viking appeared from nowhere, opening his mouth to emit an inhuman howl as he hoisted his blood stained ax above his head. He brought it down so quickly that the rushing air made the metal sing. Muscle trembled, sweat poured, and bile rose up from Patric's stomach to burn his windpipe as he watched the weapon descend. Instinctively he lifted his shield and it shattered into splinters across the meadow as the ax bit through it.

He wanted to run, to be safe in the house once again hiding behind his mother's apron but even if he weren't frozen with terror a move to retreat would find him dead.

His eyes locked on the steely head of the ax—it was moving again, being propelled through the air by an arm larger than his own thigh. The Viking cackled—an ominous vibration that rippled down his body to tremor the ground beneath Patric's feet.

The meeting of their eyes before the blow was fleeting but the flash of the steel blue orbs of death was enough to remind Patric of his newest companion, the ever-present anger that had become as loyal to him as Eagan.

With eyes closed and total resolve to live another day, Patric held up his sword to let the momentum of the Viking's lowering appendage impale it at the joint then he gave a hearty jerk that sent the Viking's arm, still holding the ax, sailing into the thicket.

Again the Viking howled as he gripped the amputation to ebb the flow of blood. Unfortunately, Patric wasn't the only one to hear it.

The next shimmering leviathan stood forty paces beyond. His head snapped around and he caught sight of the young warrior who had fallen his comrade. No eyes could be seen beyond the nose guard of his conical helmet but death radiated around him as he balanced the long spear atop his shoulder. His mass should have presented a slow approach but his strong legs propelled him over the grass with speed enough to whip up the wind.

Patric's nostrils flared in preparation for the attack. He sprinted forward, sword out thrust and muscles straining as he dug his leathered feet into the mist covered pasture. Then suddenly he slipped, gliding across the glen with impunity.

Seeing the danger of the Gael sailing toward him with an open blade, the Viking tried to reverse but he too slipped in the moisture. He fell forward onto Patric's sword skewering himself like a pig on a spit. Patric gave the blade a forceful twist that sent a gurgle of blood up and over the Viking's lips.

Every muscle in Patric's body shook with relief as he withdrew the blade from the dead Viking. He closed his eyes then prostrated himself while thanking the Lord for saving his life. His homage was soon interrupted when the steady beat of metal on wood caught his attention. He was taken aback to see the Viking so close.

"Come to me, laddie and I'll show ye how to use that thing proper."

The Viking stood head and shoulders above any other on the field, eyes so pale they were almost unseen against their whites. His clean-shaven face wore a beard of blood from where he bit into his enemy's heart, presumably the man whose head now hung from his waist belt. His steps were broad and slow but it didn't matter since Patric was welded to the ground like a bit of iron.

"Our Father who art in heaven, hallowed be thy name…" Patric mumbled but for all his prayers he was certain there would be no escape this time. No great hand of God would sweep over him in protection.

The earth trembled as the colossus quickened his approach and Patric rose to his knees, bowing his head over his blade as he recited his prayer more intensely.

A stumble, bad aim or just the sweat of blood lust dripping into the Viking's eyes to mar his vision, any of these would have caused the blade to miss, and miss it did, barely catching Patric at the cheek before burying itself in the hard ground just over his shoulder. Unfortunately for the Viking, the force meant to split his victim in two wedged the blade deep into the limestone ledge causing him to curse furiously as he struggled to release it.

God had given him time and Patric used it wisely. He rolled onto his back then, drawing his sword in both hands, swept it through the back of the Viking's knees. The first leg severed completely but the second gripped the sword in its bone.

Trembling and sweating, Patric used all his weight to push the blade through. The leg gave way and the Viking tumbled, end over end, down the grassy hill, a barrage of curses pouring from his mouth before he came to rest against a tree stump. Then, in a moment that Patric would remember for the rest of his life, the Viking uncovered his short sword, held it up to the stars and, invoking the name of the war god Thor, pulled it across his own throat.

Patric gasped as the soft skin of the Viking's neck opened to release a flood of crimson fluid. There was a gurgle and a sputter as his already pale orbs drained to total whiteness.

Patric scurried down the hill, reaching out his hand to touch the cooling corpse and wondering if he could feel the moment when the Viking's soul left his body—or did such savages even have a soul? He felt nothing other than the cooling meat beneath his hand—then he cried—deep heaving sobs of both terror and relief.

Each step brought a bolt of blinding pain as the spear handle protruding from Eagan's thigh scrapped against the ground. He pulled the collar of his chain mail vest into his mouth, biting hard to keep his consciousness. He had to find Patric before he could succumb. He spotted the prince standing over a fallen Viking and stepped up his pace to reach him. "Thank the Lord ye've survived," he croaked as the blinding pain shot through him once again. "Get to the barracks and have yer wound tended."

He stumbled over the spear handle and Patric lunged forward, catching him before he hit the ground. "Jesus, Eagan," he mumbled, ripping the man's breeches to reveal the spearhead poking through the flesh at the front of his thigh.

"Never mind about me," Eagan groaned as his strength began to ebb. "Go and have yerself tended."

Patric called for assistance from three passing soldiers before running his finger across his own wound. It was a long, wide gash running from his eyebrow to his chin but it was nothing compared to what Eagan was suffering.

"My wound doesn't affect me. It's ye who needs tending, brother."

"Nay," Eagan protested as the soldiers hoisted him face forward onto a shield. "Get Patric to the barracks. Rouric'll have my head if he learns I gave him a sword."

Patric surveyed the field. No sign of Rouric but the Vikings had retreated. Cavenlow would live to see another day. He bent down close to Eagan's ear. "Tell me where Rouric was fighting and I'll smooth things over for ye, aye."

The only response he got was a grimace as Eagan slipped into unconsciousness. The rest of the journey was made in silence.

The shock of battle was mild compared to the aftermath. The blood of broken warriors left the ground sticky and the air fetid. Some were missing limbs and eyes—many had arrows protruding from their bodies. The collective groaning was like a low thunder that rocked the walls of the barracks. Warriors called out to the servants who were scampering about in a maniacal state. Those with mortal wounds were left to die without so much as a rag to bite on while complete attention was given to those who had a chance of survival. Patric thought of the Viking and his lips moved in silent prayer that he would be as brave in the face of his own mortality.

Amidst the chaos the boy rushed through the door to deliver his news. Forty-nine dead—among them Rouric.

Patric put his head in his hands causing a servant to rush forward to tend his wound. "Nay, not me," he protested as he shoved her hand aside then directed her toward Eagan. "Attend the soldier first."

The old woman turned toward the direction of the young warrior. Her eyes widened; she whispered, "But, master, I think the leg will have to come off."

Patric's head shot up and he drew her close by the neck of her apron. "Ye heal him. I don't care what it takes but ye'll save that leg. Do ye understand?"

She nodded nervously then took a moment to reassess the situation.

When he was certain Eagan would have proper care, Patric made his way into the hall, his bloody footprints leaving a trail on the mud floor. His eyes widened when he spotted several soldiers surrounding his brother, none appearing to have been touched by the battle. He stormed forward.

"Patric!" Grace cried, breaking from the circle. She hesitated long enough to offer Kevin a glower before rushing forward to take Patric's face in her hand. "My God, ye're wounded!"

She used the linen she'd been crying into to wipe the blood from his face but Patric pushed her hand aside then marched over to his brother whose face was as white as his hair. Kevin's throat went suddenly dry. He licked his lips to moisten them before croaking, "What's happened? Are ye all right, lad? Yer mother's been sick with worry."

Grace gripped Patric's face more firmly, turning him toward her so she could perform her ministrations. "Leave off," he shouted as he wrenched away from her. "It's my duty to protect our home!"

Anger and frustration raged inside him as his eyes locked onto his brother. "And where were ye while the Viking's were slaughtering our people?"

Kevin pushed himself from his chair. He was as angry as Patric was but his ire was for Volkren's failure. "And where is Rouric? I'll have his head for allowing ye to be harmed. How bad is the wound, mother?"

"Ye're too late!" Patric growled, ignoring his brother's concern. "Volkren already took it!"

Kevin's eyes widened in mock surprise. "Volkren?" he gasped then staggered backward. "Yet again he besieges us."

"Aye," Patric huffed, oblivious to his brother's collusion. "He's returned and killed yer war captain as well as forty eight others who were ill prepared for the attack." He stepped closer until the heat of his anger was tangible. "It's ye who's responsible for this, Kevin!"

Kevin raised an eyebrow as he searched for a response to the accusation. "How dare ye accuse me of such a thing?" he shouted, not certain how much his brother knew. "'Tis Brian who brings this misery on us—and ye for fighting beside him when I forbid ye to do it."

As if he were gut punched, Patric staggered backward. He had been certain that no one, other than Eagan, knew he was on Scattery but if his brother found him out Volkren could have also. The raid may well have been his revenge.

"Do ye deny that ye disobeyed me?" Kevin asked smugly after seeing the guilt in his eyes. He moved closer to him.

"Nay," Patric mumbled, hanging his head low.

"So *ye* brought this on us!" Kevin continued, "Ye and yer precious Brian."

"That may be partly true," Patric mumbled, ashamed for what he had done. But as he thought more about it he realized that this might be the opportunity he had been waiting for. "Now that it's happened we must fortify ourselves against further aggression. Volkren knows that we're weak—everyone does. I want ye to put me in charge of the army this very night. I know I can outsmart the Viking scum next time."

"Nay," Grace panicked. "Ye won't put yerself in such danger. I'll not hear of it."

"Wait, mother," Kevin interrupted with his upturned hand nearly pressing against her mouth. He turned to Patric. "So ye believe ye can defeat Volkren next time do ye?"

"Aye," Patric responded.

"Kevin!" Grace commanded. "What are ye doing?"

He looked at her long and hard. "Wasn't it ye who told Patric that Lorca wanted him to be captain of the army?"

"Aye—but…" He had bested her and she didn't know what else to say. If she revealed that she'd been lying she'd lose both her sons with a single action.

"Well then," Kevin thrilled, offering a tiny wink. "If Lorca wanted it so then that's how it shall be. The lad's already admitted that his disobedience brought this misery on us. 'Tis only fitting that he be the one to protect us from it next time."

He turned then, his eyes growing cold when they were leveled at Patric. "I warn ye brother, if ye ever disobey me again I'll use every power that I have to see ye punished for it."

Patric squirmed under his glare and Kevin continued, pointing his finger in the direction of the doors as he bellowed, "Go now! Do what ye must to protect us but never leave this fort without my approval again."

Patric nodded then cocked his head toward the other soldiers in a silent order for them to join him. They hesitated a moment as they looked to Kevin for instruction.

"Go with the captain!" the Ri Tuath barked, his eyes lingering on Garvin longer than was necessary.

Patric noticed and his stomach turned. While male on male companionship was acceptable among warriors it wasn't something he held with. He forced the thought from his mind before leading the men through the doors, ignoring the argument brewing between Grace and Kevin. He was about to fulfill the destiny his father laid out for him and nothing else mattered.

CHAPTER 11

▼

Dublin, Ireland: The bedchamber of the high queen—One hour past noon—27, September 983 A.D.—Kormlada pulled the brush through her hair but the golden tresses stretched far beyond her reach forcing her to gather them up in order to get at the ends. She recalled the conversation she had with her husband earlier in the day and immediately she tensed. It was true that Sigtrygg was a bit young and hot headed to rule Dublin on his own, but the mere fact that he was Olaf's son would bring him more respect from the Viking community than Malsakin could ever hope to gain.

She yanked her brush through a knot, yelping when the hair was torn from its root. "Damn ye, Malsakin," she mumbled then lifted her looking glass to see what damage she caused.

As if a fog had suddenly rolled in through the window, the glass grew hazy, covering her reflection. She squinted hard to see what lay behind the mist but saw nothing. She heard the sound of running water and her feet grew instantly cold. The air became thick with the musty smell of pine and rotting leaves until she thought she would choke...then the haze lifted and she saw him.

Bedecked in war armor and surrounded by a brilliant blue light, Brian Boru macCennitig sat his horse looking at her as if she were the last woman on earth. His long red hair cascaded over his shoulders, shimmering in the light of the moon.

At first she didn't know him but then she remembered him from Tara. A queer sense of joy stirred in her making her feel giddy. He was staring at her, warming her skin with the lust in his eyes. She reminded herself that he was among the men who took her husband from her but somehow she couldn't bring herself to hate him.

The vision was so real that she could hear the crickets in the distance—behind her there were voices. A cool breeze kicked up and she felt goose pimples rise on her skin. She blinked several times to see if she could break the spell but when she opened her eyes, Brian was still there, smiling at her with his neat white teeth and a deep dimple in his right cheek.

Every muscle in her body trembled as she fought back the urge to go to him. She could feel him drawing her deep in the pit of her stomach. She ripped her gaze from him, looking down to see that her feet were submerged in water. She wriggled her toes, feeling the wetness between them.

Where was she? What was she doing with Boru of all people?

She looked up at him and he reached out a hand to her. She wanted to oblige him—to feel his arms around her waist as they galloped away into the forest behind him but she knew she mustn't. She closed her eyes, hoping to break the spell before she weakened. Her skin was alive with excitement and her heart beat viciously in her chest. For a moment she thought she felt his breath on her neck. She opened her eyes with a start. He was still there, his dark blue eyes raking her from head to foot, so real she could see the glow of the moonlight glinting in them. At length he nodded then opened his mouth to speak.

"Perhaps another time, lady." His voice touched her soul. "But mark my words—ye will be mine."

Her mouth opened with the words fast on her lips. She wanted to call out that she would be his, that all he need do is take her and she would go willingly but a voice called out behind her and when she turned her head to see who it was, the vision dissolved.

She looked around her chamber, marking the familiar surroundings until her mind accepted her whereabouts then she returned her attention to the looking glass. She stared at her reflection for a long time, her heart pounding so furiously she could hear it in her ears. There was a presence surrounding her, his presence. She closed her eyes then took a breath, basking in the scent of him until that too faded. All at once she felt empty and alone. She looked into the mirror again, willing him to return to her. When he didn't, she thought she would cry.

Take hold of yerself woman!

She reminded herself of her station. She was Kormlada, the high queen of Ireland—the desire of every man, yet she was acting like some forlorn lass. She gave the mirror one last look before lifting it above her head to bring it down on the table's edge. It smashed into a thousand pieces and she laughed out loud. No man would ever possess her—least of all, Brian Boru macCennitig.

*   *   *   *

Cavenlow, Ireland: Two hours to noon—18, October 983 A.D.—The grassy slope above the smithy's cottage was one of Patric's favorite places in all of Cavenlow. As a child he would sit there for hours, watching the millers working the wheel or the farmers sowing their seed, but they were all gone now. The only thing left to watch was the three fuidirs who were hinging the wooden gates on the newly built stone wall that would protect the village from further attack. He heaved a great sigh before turning toward Eagan who was limping up the rise.

"Yer wall is looking well, captain," Eagan cooed as he struggled to lower himself to the ground next to Patric. His wound was mending but he would probably carry a limp for the rest of his life. "So why do ye look as if ye're disappointed?"

Patric smiled up at his friend. It seemed that Eagan had the ability to read his mind. "The wall may hold Volkren off for a time but if we want to defeat him we must do much more than that."

"'It's a grand expectation to lay waist to Volkren," Eagan chuckled. "What do ye have planned?"

Patric did have a plan—in fact he'd spent the better part of the morning devising it and he was eager to have someone else listen.

"If we erect a shack in the woods just outside the gate and cover it with shrubbery it will make an excellent hiding place for one of our soldiers. He can wait there for Volkren's ship to come ashore and when the Vikings disembark he can lay fire to it. Volkren will be trapped on shore where we'll extinguish him once and for all."

If it weren't for the newly acquired lines of stress marring his freckled face, Eagan may have been mistaken for a child. His brow furrowed as he pondered Patric's idea and the ability of the men left in Cavenlow to implement it.

"It's too risky for any of these soldiers. Ye can't sacrifice the life of one of yer men, Patric."

"He won't be sacrificed," Patric retorted as he grabbed his friend's hand. "He'll only have to take the oil and the torch and set the ship aflame."

"And what if he's found?" Eagan frowned. "He'll be alone against how many of the barbarians? He'll be slaughtered."

"It'll work I tell ye!" Patric persisted. "I'll find a volunteer for the duty. In fact, it wouldn't have to be a skilled soldier, a servant could carry out this simple task."

Eagan's round, blue eyes darted across Patric's face. The lad he once knew was turning into his father. He took a moment to study Patric's long straight nose and high cheekbones rising up to meet his crystal blue eyes—the color of Lorca's. His square jaw line, broad neck and shoulders, even the color of his hair, red with golden undertones, were exactly like Lorca's. He was a warrior indeed, and a stubborn one at that. When Patric macLorca became attached to an idea it usually meant it would work.

Eagan rubbed his downy chin as he asked the question he already had the answer to, "Ye truly believe ye'll have success?"

"Aye," Patric blurted, nodding his head with the hope that Eagan would agree. "It's a simple plan but it could end our troubles forever. Think about it, Eagan. We'll be nay worse off if it fails than we are right now."

At length Eagan sighed. "If ye believe it will work then I'll volunteer for the job. Just tell me when ye want me there and I'm yers."

Patric was so excited by the prospect that he nearly forgot about Eagan's injury. He looked to his leg, realizing that his friend couldn't possibly carry out the task. He smiled then placed his hand on Eagan's shoulder.

"Nay, brother. Ye're too valuable to use on such a menial task. I already know who must do it."

✳   ✳   ✳   ✳

Cenn Cora, Ireland: In the bed chamber of Brian Boru—Midnight—19, October, 983—Brian's eyes fluttered open causing the foggy mist of his dream to dissipate. He blinked several times before lifting himself up on one elbow to look around the room. It was his sleeping hut, the place where he had spent countless hours in slumber or in the throws of passion with a woman not his wife. He looked over to the woman he had chosen that night. His heart was pounding so heavily in his chest that he wondered if it would wake her.

He leaned over her, gently sweeping back the lock of brown hair resting across her face. Her eyes were closed and her breathing was deep. She was still sleeping.

Satisfied, he rested back against his pillow with his arm across his forehead as he struggled to control his breathing. The pleasure he'd taken with the servant girl was unusually intense but it wasn't that which caused his excitement. He closed his eyes again and the dream was immediately upon him. He didn't have them often and when he did they were usually fleeting but this one was pursuing him.

The woman hovered over him with her lips so close that he could swear he felt her breath on him. Her long golden hair blanketed his body. It was so soft that he could easily lose himself in it. He rubbed his head against her cheek, eager to turn her face toward him so that he could know her identity but the shadows played over her obscuring her features. He ran his tongue along her neck, flicking it against her pulse point. A moan escaped her lips heightening his desire for her. Finally he took her head in his hands, forcing her to face him so that he could kiss her lips. When he did, he instantly knew her.

Kormlada!

His brain muddled for a moment as he remembered the first time he laid eyes on her. She was every bit the beauty people professed her to be. Now she was in his arms, making love to him as if they were meant for each other.

Suddenly his eyes flew open. He looked around the room, once again confused as to his whereabouts. It was his chamber, stark and white except for the heavy wooden shelves lining the wall where his maps rested in a riot of cylinders. His horsehair stuffed chair stood in the corner against the window as always.

He leaned back against his pillow then chuckled to himself. *Perhaps she does possess mystical powers after all.*

When he closed his eyes again, he felt her hair against his hands, so soft and silky it seemed unreal.

It is unreal. It's a dream.

Her green eyes were glazed and her lids heavy with desire. Her warm skin smelled of cherry blossom. The blood rushed in his veins causing him to stir.

What the in hell was she doing to him?

It took every ounce of strength that he had to open his eyes. He was breathless when he sat bolt upright. He looked to the woman sleeping beside him. He thought about taking her again but when he did his desire ebbed. "Out!" he finally barked. "Get out and leave me in peace."

The servant groaned and he shook her until she sat up. She brushed her straight brown hair from her eyes before rubbing them then turned to him, her confusion clearly marking her face. "Master?" she questioned, wondering exactly what it was she had done wrong.

Brian hurled himself from the bed then scooped up her lein and shoes from the floor. "Go now and leave me be," he growled as he pressed them into her hands. "I need my rest."

"Of course," she mumbled without looking directly at him. She had no idea why he was so upset. Their time together seemed to have pleased him for he'd fallen asleep straight away, but now he seemed angry with her.

She quickly slipped the lein over her head then bound her hair with the leather strip he had tossed aside during their passion. It wasn't her place to question his whims, only to obey them. Her shoes were still in her hand when she slipped through the door.

Brian watched her leave then sighed to release the tension from his shoulders. There was an eerie presence enveloping him and he looked around the room again before taking the coverlet from the bed to wrap it around his shoulders. There was a chill in the air but that wasn't the cause of the gooseflesh prickling his skin. He sat in the chair, staring out the window toward the river. He tried to recall the dream but now it was a distant memory.

"Damn, woman!" he barked. "What are ye doing to me?"

His question went unanswered but he pondered it for sometime before falling asleep in his chair.

✳   ✳   ✳   ✳

Cavenlow, Ireland—In the guard shack beside the River Shannon—Two hours past midnight—28, October 983 A.D.—Patric rubbed his nose in his cloak. Even the smell of damp wool was better then the fetid air wafting up from the rivers edge. He moved on the stool to try to find a more comfortable position but then he heard the rustle of leaves and he was instantly on his feet.

He peered through the spy hole of the flimsy door, his heart pounding in his chest. He'd spent more nights then he cared to remember waiting for Volkren. The prospect of meeting him now was a welcomed one. He held his breath, closing one eye while the other searched the darkness before him. He released it when he spotted the deer in search of food.

"Damn," he muttered to himself before returning to the stool. Spending his nights in solitude awaiting a raid was the last thing he expected to be doing as the captain of his father's army, but it needed to be done and he leaned his head against the clapboard wall fully prepared to pass another long night.

He thought of Freara and wondered what had become of her after her father moved them to Cashel. Every one of his friends, save Eagan and his cousin, Margreg, was either dead or moved away to a safer place than Cavenlow. A fleeting thought crossed his mind that perhaps Kevin was right—perhaps Brian was the reason for their misery and now him as well. He sighed deeply before offering up his prayer.

"Father, give me the patience to see yer will done here on earth. Don't let me fall prey to envy nor become so enamored with myself that I am blinded to the wisdom of the plan which ye have put in motion."

He sat silent for a time, hoping to hear his father's answer in the whisper of the night but when it didn't come he concentrated on nature's song instead.

The draw of the river was soon after followed by a gentle whoosh as it came back to the shore. He made a game of it, predicting when the next wave would hit the banks, usually a few seconds after the draw and almost always on his count. Suddenly the crashes became chaotic as if something was forcing the Shannon more quickly, more sporadically.

He jumped from the stool, again peering through the tiny slit as he took a deep breath. The bow of the long boat came into view. Both his heart, and the Shannon's waves, beat ever faster.

The sound of the horn bellowed into the night as the watchmen of Cavenlow called her soldiers to arms. Patric swallowed his fear then took hold of the hilt of his sword.

Like swarming ants the Vikings threw themselves from the ship, crashing into the shallow water of the river, swords bared and shields at the ready as they made their way toward the round fort. They were brought up short when they reached the gate.

"They've surrounded themselves, lord," the scout shouted. "We can't get in."

Volkren stood the bow of the ship, his hands on his hips and his strong chin jutting out in defiance. He wore a conical helmet and breastplate that glimmered in the light from the guide torches. His short, white lein billowed around his bare legs.

"Filthy Irish pigs," he spit, "they surround themselves with a pen."

Patric watched in fury as the man who killed his father stretched a long finger in the direction of the hut. "Captain, fall a tree and break through their meager gate. We've a job to do and I won't be put off it."

Patric twisted his eye against the spy hole then jumped back slightly as he saw the captain who Volkren had just addressed only yards away from his hiding place. The Viking was half hidden in the shadows making him look almost ghostly as he nodded his head and responded, "Aye, lord," then turned to the Vikings who were poised on the shore awaiting his command.

"First section! Fall that tree and take it up against the gate!"

Patric struggled to follow the Vikings' movements. They made quick work of falling a tree, and except for the few unfamiliar words spoken by a man who Patric assumed to be the leader of the first section, they worked in total silence.

Within minutes, the first section had the tree poised and ready to strike. Patric watched as the leader looked to the captain and the captain looked to Volkren. With a nod of Volkren's head the signal relay began and the Vikings hoisted the tree onto their shoulders then made off running toward the gates.

With a thundering crash, the battering ram smashed against the wooden doors, creaking the heavy iron hinges as they strained against the assault. Patric twisted his body, pressing his eye against the slit in the door in an effort to glimpse the archers who by now should have been in position atop the stanchion.

"Come on," he whispered to himself. "Let loose. What are ye waiting for?"

His answer came in the hail of arrows that struck down the first section completely.

"Filthy, bastards!" Volkren cursed as the last of the first section fell wounded to the ground. He removed his helmet, wiping his hair back from a face twisted in fury. "Captain," he bellowed, pointing his finger over the port side of the ship. "Have *yer* men take up the tree!"

Gunner stepped out of the shadows to look up at Volkren. It was humiliating enough to have been reduced in rank, but to have his men slaughtered by the Gaelic archers was too much for him to accept without argument. "But lord," he muttered, "they'll be….."

"Have them take it up or it'll be ye I use as the battering ram!" Volkren snapped.

Gunner lowered his head in disgust before proving himself a loyal soldier. He nodded his assent then raised his voice so his men standing portside would hear, "Second section! Take up the tree!"

Both Patric and the archers watched as the second section scrambled around their fallen comrades to take up the battering ram. It only took a moment before the chaos of raining arrows and howling targets created the cover necessary for Patric's escape. He darted from the hut then stealthily boarded the ship. He could see Volkren standing the bow but there was no one else in sight as he moved aft to set his plan in motion.

The thick liquid burped and sputtered as it forced its way through the hole of the small oak barrel to spill upon the ship's deck. In a slow, creeping manner it fanned across the boards, glistening in the light of the guide torches and warbling the reflection of the moon. Patric gave the barrel a tiny shake to hasten the flow but suddenly it was out of his hands, crashing against the boards and rolling across the deck as the oil dribbled from the escape hole on the downward turns. He swallowed hard against the blade that had his neck forced back.

"So lad, what've ye here?" Volkren sang, his foul breath forcing Patric to turn away.

The movement caused the blade to bite deep into Patric's neck until a thin trickle of blood flowed onto his collar but he gave it little mind. Instead he used the practiced swiftness of his time spent in the barracks to draw Brian's short sword from his waist belt then bury it deep into Volkren's thigh.

Reflexively, Volkren dropped his sword to clutch at the blade that was imbedded so deep in his bone that no blood flowed from it. A barrage of curses escaped his mouth as he struggled with it allowing Patric ample opportunity to get to his feet. "Beg for mercy filthy Viking!"

Volkren looked at his thigh then at Patric who, by now, had both teeth and sword bared. It was obvious that this victory would go to the Gael and he clamped his mouth shut, refusing to allow the lad further satisfaction of his conquest.

He forced his spine straight and his eyes into a cold, blank stare as he erected his head and squared his shoulders. He'd been prepared for Valhalla from the day of his birth. He would meet his gods in the way of a warrior.

Patric's burning hatred only intensified with the display of courage. He kicked Volkren's dropped sword away from the earl causing it to glide through the oil until it rested against the sideboards.

"Ye've not asked for mercy, so I'll not give it." He drew back long, and with all the weight of his body backing the swing, severed the earl at his waist.

Volkren's torso sailed to the left as his legs fell forward, blood from his still pumping organs gushing to freedom to mingle with the glistening oil on the ships deck. Patric pressed a leathered foot to the Viking's chest, taking a moment to spit in his eye before sending the earl sailing in the direction of his sword. "Take up yer blade now, man!"

It was then that the ship rocked and pitched as Erik boarded with a compliment of soldiers. He took a moment to survey the gory scene before lurching forward in a fury but his footing was lost in the oil causing him to fumble and slip as he tried to keep himself upright.

Patric used the borrowed time to quickly release the aft torch then set it to the liquid. The blue white flame chased the oil across the deck like a heated apparition, quickly taking hold and billowing black smoke into the air as the salted oak was consumed. The warm kiss of the flames lapped at his legs before he leapt into the Shannon.

The flash of fire left Erik blind. Both sweat and oil spewed from his pores as the flames enveloped him completely. He scrambled—sliding across the blackened planks then slamming against the stern before a quick hoist sent him crashing into the river below. His skin hissed as the cold water forced under it, lifting it from its root to feed the river. His tears mingled with the Shannon as each movement caused him blinding pain. He sputtered towards death, begging for the unconsciousness that eluded him with each slap of the cold waves against his face. Then he spotted Patric.

The lad, who in a matter of minutes had taken everything from him, was just a few feet down river, cheering for his victory as he splashed the water all around him. Forgetting his pain, Erik swam forward to offer the last act of vengeance he'd take on this earth.

Patric noticed him coming. With long, reaching strokes he swam away from the charred monster stopping only when his arms began to cramp. He took a deep breath as he glanced over his shoulder—no sign of him. Once again the good Lord had intervened on his behalf. He began to offer his prayer of homage when something grabbed his ankles. Suddenly he was being dragged beneath the water, his struggle for freedom being met by a battery of blows delivered by an inhuman force. He could see the silver bubbles floating toward the surface as the last of his breath was released from his lungs and just as he wondered how long it would take for death to claim him, a powerful uppercut to his chin propelled him through the water. He broke the surface, gulping air hungrily.

All too quickly, a bubbling pool erupted behind him marking Erik's return. Patrick dove beneath the water to avoid him, his half filled lungs nearly bursting as he undid the strap of his shoe. He broke the surface just behind Erik then slipped the strap over the Viking's head, pulling it tight against his throat.

Erik's thrashing only served to cinch the strangling strip tighter as it cut through his cooked flesh with the sharpness of a knife. The darkness he had longed for moments ago began to descend on him and finally, with a bob of his head and a deep gurgle in his throat, he expressed his dying breath.

Patric released his grip and the Viking sank deep below the river in an explosion of bubbles that nearly took him with it. With his last ounce of strength, he pushed off toward the shore but by now Cavenlow was a mere speck on the horizon. He thrashed against the river's draw until his battle-fatigued muscles cramped then he too began to sink into the murky water of the Shannon.

He spotted the tree branch in the distance, bobbing on the river as the current dragged past. He kicked out, breaking through the water with a determined force until he hoisted himself across the log and nestled his head in the twisted branches at its end. He wiped both water and tears from his face as he floated further away from the horizon and the only life he'd ever known.

*   *   *   *

**Cenn Cora, Ireland: In the fortress of the southern Ri Ciocid—dawn—
29, October 983 A.D.**—Connor frowned at his reflection in the water then
rubbed a hand over his head causing his close cropped red hair to stand on end.
He abandoned his long tresses and warrior braid long ago, preferring not to give
his enemies a handhold in battle. He squinted his right eye as he ran his finger
along the half moon scar starting in the corner and draping down to his cheek—
he was lucky he hadn't been blinded in that battle but he did break his nose. He
moved that from side to side then ran the tip of his index finger along the
crooked, flattened bridge deciding that it made him look more ferocious. With a
growl, he thrust his head into the water shattering his reflection and plunging
himself deeper into his troubles.

He withdrew with a gasp, wiping his hands over his face to release the water
from his mustache then he dried them on his woolen lein and walked the few
paces up the riverbank to find a spot to sit. It was damp and he could smell the
forest from where he sat. No birds sang—there would be rain. He held up his
nose to smell it on the breeze.

None of it made sense to him. He had spent a lifetime beside Brian, torturing
himself with the love he felt for the man but never expressing it for fear he would
be cut down. He knew Brian could never abide love between men and he was
ever cautious to keep his feelings to himself. But now it seemed that the Ri Ciocid had found him out—the proof of it being their separation on the trip to
Ailech.

It was Turlog who brought him the news, shattering his world into a million
pieces as they conversed outside the stables. He had found him there after his ride
and called him over with a crook of his finger.

"We must speak," he said in that mysterious way he had whenever he was
eager to share information of the dangerous sort.

Turlog explained Brian's plan for Ailech and when Connor protested the
arrangements and threatened to take his case to Brian the Ri Tuath stopped him.

"Ye're becoming transparent," he cooed in that evil tone. "Ye've been hiding
yer secret for quite some time but lately ye've been lax."

At first Connor thought to wave Turlog off but it was clear that he had proof
of his accusation and he was certainly someone to use it.

"Ye never should have taken Falkden's son the way ye did, Connor. The lad
has been speaking about it to anyone who'll listen."

The lad in question was the son of the Ri Tuath of Desmumu taken by Brian to foster after his father was killed in battle. He'd come to Connor willingly but had now been using the affair to get all that he could from the captain.

Connor hung his head in despair and Turlog continued, "I needn't tell ye what Brian thinks of such things. True, he'd let it slip if we were on the march but to have yer way with a lad—a Ri Tuath's son at that—during peace time, well, that says a thing or two about ye doesn't it?"

Turlog's assessment couldn't have been truer leaving Connor little choice but to finally give in to what he had been after for quite some time—becoming captain of the Thomond army.

He pounded the earth on either side of him, his breaths quickening as he envisioned his life without Brian. How could he wake each day knowing that someone else was advising the Ri Ciocid—sharing his secrets—protecting him from harm? What would be left without Brian's smile and quick wit to put him at ease when things were at their worst? How could he live?

The questions whirled in his head and he chastised himself for being so careless. He'd sworn an oath long ago that he would be dead at his own hand before he let Brian know the truth about him. Only Brian's opinion of him mattered and now it had been debased.

He took the dagger from his waist then laid the blade on his thigh to let the sky reflect in the metal. In two swift moves he could have himself gutted and it would all be over—but he hadn't the courage for such a thing. Ending his life would mean never seeing Brian again. Never seeing him lead an army onto the field with his hair blowing back in the wind as he sat his horse in brilliance. Never again hearing his stirring words as they moved men to loyalty, love and even tears. Never again seeing him lift his mighty sword or laugh at a bad joke or flirt with a maiden. His stomach turned for his own cowardice but he'd rather live as captain of Turlog's army catching a glimpse of Brian whenever he could rather then face an eternity without him. And who knew—perhaps his marriage to Turlog's daughter, Lara, would renew Brian's belief that he was a whole man.

With a sigh heaved from deep in his chest, he nodded acceptance of the situation. He would lead Brian's army to Ailech and upon their return he would tell the Ri Ciocid of his plans.

He uncrossed his legs then hoisted his solid form from its sitting position to walk back to the rivers edge for one last look.

Nearly as tall and lean as Brian, he was a fearsome figure to behold. He tossed the stone he'd been fidgeting with into the river shattering his reflection and marking that moment as the last time he would think of Brian Boru macCennitig as anything other than his Ri Ciocid.

*   *   *   *

Limerick, Ireland: In an open field by the banks of the River Shannon— Sometime in the afternoon—29, October 983 A.D.—"Over here, lad," the raspy voice called.

Patric opened his eyes to a blur of white tufts floating against azure. He blinked a few times to bring the picture into focus but his vision warbled.

Was he dead?

He continued to stare as the spray from the rushing river moistened his face. He smelled grass, sweet pine and moss. The sun was warming his skin but still he shivered.

"Come to me, man," the voice called again. "I need ye."

Though the voice was harsh it was also soothing. He shivered again then closed his eyes, willing his body to draw all the warmth that it could from the light.

The last thing he remembered was crashing into a rock. He'd been so happy to be on firm ground again that he dragged himself over the stones and shrubs of the riverbank until he was clear of the water. He collapsed on the grass and had little memory of anything else until this moment.

"Over here, man," the voice called again.

This time Patric turned toward the call. He saw nothing but trees and the dark shadows of the forest beyond. It took every ounce of strength he had to lift himself up. Once he was steadied he staggered forward in the direction of the voice.

When the Lord calls, ye go no matter what yer condition!

His bare foot scraped against a half buried stone and he stumbled, hitting the ground with force. He lay still momentarily until he mustered the strength to lift himself again then stumbled forward into the forest and the shadows surrounding the strange voice.

The sudden darkness put him slightly blind and he blinked a few times before his eyes adjusted to the low light but when his vision cleared his mouth hung open for what he saw.

It was a man—naked as the day he was born dangling from a tree branch by the rope that ensnared his foot. The scene put Patric totally off guard and for a moment he wondered if he was in hell, but as he watched the man struggle against his snare and bounce with impunity against the thorns of a thistle bush, he thought it unlikely that the devil would be so humorous. He was alive and he let out a hearty laugh in celebration.

"What kind of rogue are ye who'd laugh at my obvious difficulty?" the man growled as he struggled ever harder. "Ye must be a half-wit of some sort."

Patric moved forward slowly, spirits quite elevated as he assessed the situation. He rubbed his chin then followed the line of the snare until he marked the end of the rope that released its slipknot.

"Easy there fellow," he commanded before taking hold of the rope. "If ye continue to thrash about as ye are ye'll be unable to father children." With that he gave a quick tug on the rope and the man was dropped right into the offending bush.

With a hearty howl and movements quick enough to make Patric reconsider whether it was indeed a human he was dealing with, the man scrambled away. "Ye could have at least seen me clear of the nature!" he scowled as he plucked at the thorns embedded in his skin.

Again Patric chuckled, but this time the Viking rounded on him. He was a large man by any account, bronze of both skin and hair—vaguely familiar. Patric took a step back as the man hissed, "While I thank ye for yer kindness, stranger, I'm sore my predicament amuses ye so."

The man's twitching muscles and unplaced familiarity caused Patric to become uncomfortable. He bit back his laughter before offering his cloak. "Ye must admit yer—um…" he chose his words wisely so as not to offend the man, "…predicament…is amusing. How is it ye find yerself strung up so?"

The Viking sniffed the wet cloak before donning it then waved a hand in the direction of the road. "Those rogue bastards caught me bathing. They made off with my clothes as well as my purse. As I chased after them they ensnared me in this animal trap."

The thought suddenly struck Patric that the Viking could be one of Volkren's men. If he landed there it was possible that any who escaped could have landed there also.

"They robbed ye huh?" he mumbled, nervous about how best to deal with the situation. "Well, what kind of men were these, brother? Were they soldiers, and if so how many? How about ye? Are ye one of the earl's men then?"

The Viking screwed up his face unnaturally as Patric offered his barrage of questions. It was obvious the lad didn't belong there—or even know what he was talking about—no doubt he was a Gael. The last thing he needed was to be caught up in someone else's mischief.

After a tiny scratch of his beard he decided to answer the questions cautiously. "Nay, I'm not one of the earl's men, although it might have been them what strung me up."

He marked Patric's flinch as good information to have then continued, "There were about fifteen of them. Nay, nay, more like twenty. Aye, twenty. It took every last one of them to disarm me and tie me up then they grabbed my purse and clothes and made off into the woods."

Patric raised his eyebrow at the queer comment. "Ye said ye were bathing. How could they disarm ye if ye had nay a weapon…or do ye bathe with yer sword?"

Suddenly uncomfortable, the Viking began to stammer, "D-d-did I say I was b-b-bathing? Nay, I meant I was just returning from my bath when they sprang on me from the trees. They were huge, each of them, and one has my short sword still in his shoulder."

Patric was young but he knew a thing or two about men and their need to exaggerate to make themselves seem more courageous. Fairly certain that this was the case he continued the game if for no other reason than the sheer amusement of it.

"So ye say they were Volkren's soldiers who did this to ye. How do ye know it was them?"

The Viking flailed his arms in exasperation too fierce to be true. "Because they bore the hawk on their garment."

"Volkren's mark is that of a wolf," Patric snapped back.

The man opened his stance then crossed his thick arms over his chest. Like a chiseled statue of a warrior god he towered over Patric. "Well, Imar's mark was the hawk and Volkren's his nephew, aye. They could have belonged to him."

Despite his size the man's face was quite charming, almost childlike. Perhaps he was an idiot. Patric decided he'd better not stay around to find out. He turned on his heel to search for help.

Unused to such treatment the Viking pursued him. "They were soldiers I tell ye! And it took every one of the thirty to tie me up and leave me stranded here."

Patric stepped up his pace as he threw the comment over his shoulder. "So now it's thirty? A moment ago it was twenty."

The man's large feet struggled over the rocks and bracken. He hopped a bit. "Thirty—twenty—I didn't exactly have time to count them, aye. They were on me like flies."

Amusement took the place of his fear and Patric stopped suddenly, reaching out his hands to keep the man from running into him. "What's yer name, stranger?"

The man smiled as he bowed from the waist leaving a good portion of his buttocks exposed as he did. "The name is Havland the Bold."

He searched Patric's face for a glimmer of recognition. He was disappointed when he saw none. "I'll have ye know that I'm a great warrior!"

"A great warrior was left hanging from a tree?" Patric sniffed. "I'd suggest ye keep that information to yerself to save ye from embarrassment, brother." Again he turned but in a moment he was flat on the ground.

With one swift movement, Havland flipped him onto his back then sat astride him forcing Patric's chin up with one hand while the other threatened him with a dead branch. He sneered, "While I'm not given to killing my saviors, I'll make an exception if ye continue on as ye've been."

Every inch of Havland's face glowed sacred and Patric knew he didn't have the strength, or the advantage, to win the fight. He recalled Brian's long ago advice then offered Havland a remorseful glance.

"Forgive my foolishness, brother," he gasped. "It won't happen again."

Havland slowly slid off his chest then cautiously offered him a hand up.

Realizing he had little choice in the matter, Patric took it. They stared at each other for a moment, the Viking fingering the silver brooch of his borrowed cloak before he finally asked, "Why are ye wet?"

Patric looked down at his sopping clothing, thankful that he'd been dressed in homespun instead of his lein and coat that carried his father's mark. He'd heard stories of princes being taken as hostages on the road so that their captors could bargain for their return.

"Will ye answer me or nay?" Havland demanded, his arms folded across his chest and a menacing look in his eye. "If ye're an outlaw, ye best tell me now."

"An outlaw?" Patric scoffed. "Do I look to be an outlaw?"

"Ye look to be wet and scared and I mean to know why. I won't be traveling with ye if there's a price on yer head lest I be accused of taking part in whatever mischief got ye into this condition."

"Now see here," Patric barked, but before he could continue the Viking was walking away.

"If ye won't answer then I'll be leaving ye here to make yer own way. I'll consider the cloak a gift for my taking ye this far."

"This far?" Patric bellowed as he struggled to catch the man up. "We've barely moved."

The Viking was pulling far ahead of him as Patric struggled with one shoe. He stopped to remove it. "Come back here! Need I remind ye that it was me who saved ye?"

The Viking ignored him until Patric was jogging along side him. He turned and looked the lad over. He reeked of nobility and from a familiar house at that. "Will ye give me yer name or should I just leave ye?"

Patric puzzled over how he was suddenly put into the inferior position but before he could gather his wits his ego got the best of him. "I'm Patric macLorca, prince of Cavenlow."

The Viking seemed impressed and Patric offered a cocky smile of victory but in a moment Havland was moving again, waving his hand over his shoulder as he called out, "Nay, 'tis too hot for me."

"Too hot?" Patric replied. "What do ye mean 'too hot?'"

"I've nay a need for ye're kind of trouble, Patric macLorca. If it's all the same to ye, I'll just be getting on home and leave ye to whatever business ye have in Limerick."

"Limerick?" Patric stopped dead. He was a long way from home and with nothing other than his brooch to trade he'd be hard pressed to get back—and his brooch was getting away.

"Brother!" he called out as he again caught the man up. "If ye won't explain yerself then at least return my belongings."

Havland looked at him as if he were considering it. "I suppose ye came to speak with Thorien then? 'Tis about time too. He's been waiting for ye since I let ye get away on Scattery. He nearly had my hide for not keeping ye there. He wanted to talk to ye about yer refusing the throne and not bringing yer army to Brian."

"Refusing the throne?" Patric reached out his hands to grab Havland's shoulders but he was instantly blocked. The Viking faced him, fists clenched and ready for battle.

"I pray ye, brother, to explain yerself," Patric requested with eyes full of askance. "Who is this Thorien ye speak of and what does he know about my father and the throne?"

"Who is this Thorien?" Havland growled in response. "Ye may look the fool but I doubt that Lorca's heir was raised as one. I don't know what yer game is, laddie, but I can tell ye right now that I want nay part of it. Be on yer way and leave me in peace."

There was no doubt the Viking was mad. If Patric wanted to get any information out of him he would have to be smart about it. "We'll make a bargain of it then," he offered. "I'll make ye a gift of the brooch if ye tell me what it is ye're speaking of." Havland stood silent and Patric pleaded, "I pray ye, brother, if there's any decency in ye at all, ye'll tell me what ye know. My life depends on it."

That brought a smirk to Havland's face. "Does it now?" he cooed as he fingered the brooch. The shape of the lion was formed under his finger and he laughed that he hadn't noticed it when he first put it on.

"Okay, laddie," he finally responded. "We'll go inside and I'll tell ye what I know."

Patric followed Havland's hand as it unlatched the fence gate. He'd been so engrossed in the conversation that he hadn't realized that they had been walking. The yard was littered with livestock and when he entered a kid came to nibble on the hem of his shirt. He pushed it away but before he could inquire as to their whereabouts, a band of children raced by singing a tune.

> "We caught Havland bathing,
>   now we have his clothing.
> The great warrior was left naked,
>   hanging from a tree."

The red blush started somewhere low on Havland's neck then swept up his face until it glowed. Patric noticed the throbbing vein at his temple as the Viking pushed past him, growling in fury. "Ye little rot," he cried as he chased one lad down then caught him by the hair. "I'll have yer head for this."

He ripped the bundle from the lad's hand with one movement then dangled him by his hair for his comrades to see. "Return my things or I'll whip the lot of ye," he threatened.

The other lads dropped what they carried in the road before tearing off with little care for what would become of their friend. Havland released the one he held with a shove. "Go away from me now and don't let me catch ye near here again."

As if by magic, the lad vanished, leaving Havland in the road to gather his things muttering, "I was too far away to see them. How could I know they were children?"

He brushed past Patric who remained near the gate, worrying that his host would be too embarrassed to make good on the deal. It wasn't until the Viking was at the door that he called out, "Well, are ye coming in or nay? I haven't got all day."

Patric moved forward in silence, deciding that it would be best to ignore the situation. He stepped through the threshold of the dark hut and was greeted by a pungent odor of rotting meat, smoke and male perspiration.

"Rest there while I dress," Havland called motioning to the pile of animal skins in the corner.

Patric filled his lungs with one last gasp of fresh air before entering. He kept his breathing shallow to adjust to the smell as he eyed the interior of the single room waddle hut.

The fire pit stood on the western wall, nothing more than a circle of stones on the mud floor with a hole cut in the thatch roof for the smoke to escape. Next to the fire pit was a rough hewn table littered with a trencher of half eaten food and a few leather cups. A single stool rested beneath it, crooked for the one leg shorter than the rest. On the walls hung several badly tanned animal hides, presumably the cause of the offensive odor, and in the corner stood what seemed to be a human skull.

The only items in the hut that seemed to receive any care at all were the gleaming sword, shield, breastplate and conical helmet that were the tools of Havland's trade.

"Ye must be a grand warrior to own such finery." Patric commented nodding toward the weapons.

"And ye best remember it," Havland grunted while he shrugged into his shirt.

Suddenly excited by all that had happened, Patric blurted, "And ye fight for Brian. Did ye know my father as well…Lorca of Cavenlow?"

"I know very well who yer father was, laddie."

Patric remembered their encounter on Scattery Island. At the time he presumed that the Viking's anger was due to Kevin but now there seemed to be some other reason. "I pray ye to tell me what ye know about my father's throne."

"Are ye telling me that after all his service to yer father the name of Thorien of Limerick is unfamiliar to his heir?" Havland asked as he opened the door to empty two cups.

The fresh air rushed in and Patric took a deep breath before Havland brought the cups back to the table to fill them with mead.

"Thorien's the earl of Limerick," Havland said when he handed Patric the cup. "He's Brian's Viking champion and was a trusted ally to Lorca. Ye gave me yer horse to take him back to Cenn Cora. He rides it still—waiting for ye to come back to Brian."

"Thorien," Patric sighed as the memory flooded back to him.

Thorien was in Cavenlow on the night his father left for Sulcoit. The man with the missing finger. He remembered that Lorca spoke of him and his loyalty but he didn't realize that the two were as close as Havland was professing.

Suddenly Patric was sobbing openly, a situation that caught Havland off guard. He refilled the lad's cup then waited for him to drink but when Patric seemed to have no want of it he took a long draw from his own. He waited for what he expected was the proper amount of time before asking, "Why did ye do it, laddie?"

Patric looked up puzzled then wiped his eyes with his sleeve. "Ye mean the horse? I th…"

"I mean the throne," Havland interrupted. "Why did ye give it to yer brother instead of taking it for yerself?"

Patric shook his head. "I don't take yer meaning. It wasn't mine to take."

"That's not the way Thorien tells it," the Viking replied. "He said yer father named ye as heir to Cavenlow. The two of them spoke about it."

"Ye're mistaken, man," Patric huffed as all at once hope rose then diminished. "Lorca made nay declaration about an heir so when he died his throne went to my brother. Brian installed Kevin himself under the rite of succession."

Havland scratched his beard in puzzlement. "I won't argue the point since I wasn't there. I'll only tell ye that for these past seasons Thorien has been waiting for ye to show yerself. Said ye were the true heir and that if he ever got his hands on ye he'd shake ye until ye remembered who yer father was. He nearly had my head when he learned that I let ye get away last time."

"Will ye bring me to him now?" Patric asked, still not convinced that the Viking had his story straight. Too often men told tales to make themselves look greater than they were, and even though that behavior would go against everything his father ever said about Thorien, he needed to speak with the man himself before he could believe the story was true.

"I will," Havland responded, "that is if he hasn't left already. Give me a bit of time to fix us something to eat. It wouldn't be right for us to show up on his…"

"Left?" Patric questioned anxiously.

"Aye," Havland replied as he fastened his breeches. "Boru's planning a march to Ailech. Thorien would never dream of missing it. As for me, I decided to sit this one out. Boru's been moving around quite a bit these last seasons and I've earned enough to live on 'til the next. 'Tis folly to be marching north in the winter months."

"But if Boru plans to march I should be with him," Patric blurted as Havland skittered around him to lay a fire. "If ye take me now, I'll be forever in yer debt."

Havland sat squat on the floor as he considered the lad's words. He tossed down the peat log he'd been holding then smacked the residue from his hands.

"So yer finally getting some sense in ye, aye. Alright."

He stood full up, smoothing the wrinkles from his shirt before walking to the corner where his weapons stood. He lifted his breastplate so that he could see his reflection as he ran his index finger over his teeth. When he was through, he pulled a bone comb from on top of the pile of skins to untangle his hair—this took a bit of time.

Patric sat anxiously on the stool waiting for the ritual to be done. When Havland approached he rose to leave.

"Ye're not planning to go calling looking like that, are ye?" the Viking barked. "I'll tell ye right now that I won't be walking beside ye if ye are."

Patric's anxiety caused a fleeting thought of protest but when he looked himself over he decided Havland was right. He performed the same ministrations as the Viking had then borrowed a pair of Havland's old shoes. A quarter hour later they were on their way to meet Thorien.

The main road of Limerick ran along the eastern edge of the River Shannon, tightly cobbled and wide enough for a carriage and two cows to pass in either direction. Wood planking lined either side of the road—the designated area for pedestrians. The boards bounced beneath their feet as scads of people eagerly passed them by. Even the river was alive with movement.

There were ships at every dock and sailors, mostly Vikings, unloading barrels, boxes and bags for trading in the market.

It seemed Havland was well known throughout the city and it didn't take Patric long to understand why he took such care with his grooming. Nearly every woman they met flirted with the warrior, batting their eyelids and giggling under dainty fingers when Havland returned their attention.

As they came to the market, Havland slipped inside a colorful merchant tent then closed the drape behind him. Patric could hear the whispers between the obviously married woman and his new friend and he busied himself fingering the fine jewelry and pig feed being offered by the merchant at the next booth so that it wouldn't appear that he was listening. A short while later, Havland emerged carrying two bundles. He handed one to Patric mumbling, "I assisted her husband a while back. 'Tis a gift."

Patric smiled knowingly but dared not comment. They pressed on.

As they walked along the road, Havland pointed out the homes of friends and neighbors as well as the standing stones marking the graves of historical warriors. Off the main road sprouted several minor roads lined with small thatched roof huts surrounded by wood rail fences. Most yards boasted pigs wallowing in mud or geese honking as they circled within but in the end all streets led back to the main Limerick road and one ominous, ever present building that stood at its end.

Patric's eyes widened as he stretched his neck to see the Mead Hall of Limerick. Covered in a smooth layer of mud, the structure jutted from the ground in an arch that stood more than thirty feet tall at its high point. A path of blood red stone led from the low exterior gate to two massive oak doors carrying the same arch as the building. They were hinged in heavy decorative iron that was polished to a glow.

Ten times the size of the great hall at Cavenlow, Havland explained that the massive size of the mead hall was necessary for the many Galls and Vikings who gathered for the *Althing*. All business was conducted during the conference from political meetings and celebrations to husband gathering.

"Husband gathering?" Patric questioned. "Do the Vikings think of themselves as cattle?"

"We're a virile bunch, Patric," Havland chuckled. "We make more children than we know what to do with and are forced to marry off our daughters as quickly as possible. The Althing is the perfect place for a Viking father to show off his women. He'll bring the unmarried ones to tend his booth and cook his meals between meetings. When an eligible bachelor becomes attracted by a woman's skills a bride price and dowry are negotiated before witnesses and the betrothal is sealed with a handshake."

Patric smirked. "Well at least the poor rot knows what he's getting in the woman he takes to wife. Most times the Gaels take their women sight unseen as a bargain for peace."

Havland laughed, "Unfortunately Vikings don't always know what they're getting in a woman. Sometimes fathers of less attractive daughters offer to share their drink to attract a bachelor. When a Viking's sufficiently drunk he'll agree to anything."

"Come on, man!" Patric slapped the air. "Do ye expect me to believe a man would take a wife because her father has good mead?"

"Aye," Havland retorted as his face turned suddenly serious. "It happened to a friend of mine. The poor rot went in to have himself a pint and tell a few sagas and came out promised to a woman who was uglier than my neighbor's pig. When he came to his senses the next morning he begged me to hack off his hand. He hoped the girl's father would see he couldn't support her and renege on the deal."

Patric's eyes widened. "Did ye do it, man?"

"Nay," Havland responded as he dismissed the idea with a wave of the hand. "I didn't like him that much."

Patric chuckled and Havland yanked his arm, directing him to the large hut located across the road. It was painted a vivid blue and the thatch was clean and tight.

"That's where Thorien lives," he announced. "He likes to be nearest the action, aye."

Patric felt his heart jump. It took every bit of control for him to stand back while Havland knocked on the door. Moments later a woman answered. She was tall and well rounded with a blush in her cheek. Her green eyes sparkled with adoration as she greeted the Viking.

"It's been a while since the likes of ye darkened this door, Havland," she scolded through her smile. "The most I've seen of ye lately is when ye come stumbling out of the Althing."

"I'll own the charge, Gayla," Havland replied as his eyes dropped to his shoes. "I'm sorry if it offends ye so much but I brought something to make it up to ye."

"Nay so much," she replied, taking the packages he offered before looking to Patric. "Who've ye brought with ye then?"

Patric straightened his shoulders in preparation for the presentation but Havland bent down to whisper in Gayla's ear. All at once the woman yelped, "By the gods it can not be."

Havland nodded his head to affirm what he had just told her and Patric stepped forward. "What? What did ye tell her, Havland?"

She dropped the packages on the step then pushed past Havland to take Patric's face in her hands. "Thorien said ye would come. 'Gayla,' he says to me, 'give the lad time and he'll do the right thing. He's his father's lad. He'd never turn his back against Brian. He'll come when the time is right and nay a moment sooner.' And by the gods, here ye are, looking every bit of yer father."

She looked him over and Patric had to fight back the urge to grab her up and hug her to him. It was the warmest welcome he'd received by anyone since Lorca's death.

"Is Thorien here, Gayla?" he asked with a hint of urgency in his voice. "Can I speak with him?"

Her eyes turned apologetic as she swung around to face Havland. "He rode out days ago to Cenn Cora. Took a hundred men with him. He wanted to be certain they'd be there in time to march with the Ri Ciocid." Then confusion marked her face. "He said ye wouldn't be joining him on the trip, Havland. Did ye know the lad was coming?"

Havland shook his head. "Nay—I don't think he knew himself."

"But I don't understand," she muttered.

Havland put a strong arm around her shoulders then shook her jovially. "Well, it seems we have some time to explain it to ye since we can't set off toward Cenn Cora until morning."

He began to escort her into the house when Patric grabbed his elbow. "Do ye mean to go with me then, man?"

"Aye," Havland responded with a nod. "I should think that if I deliver ye safely to yer king there may be a reward in it for me."

Patric smiled. For all his time spent praying to his father and the Lord it seemed that someone was finally answering.

CHAPTER 12

▼

Dublin, Ireland: The chambers of the high queen—Three hours past noon—30, October 983 A.D.—"Ye're acting like a spoiled child, Kormlada," Maelmora offered as he tried to calm his sister. He ducked his head when the next missile sailed past him. Apparently his efforts weren't working.

"How dare ye call me spoiled?" she seethed, picking up another bottle then taking aim with it.

He rushed her, grabbing her wrists and pulling her close to him. She beat him about the chest then nipped at his chin with her teeth in an effort to be free but he only chuckled as he ducked and bobbed to avoid damage. "Settle down there, lassie," he cooed with his mouth close to her ear. "Is this any way for a high queen to be acting?"

She drew back then, lifting her head and stiffening her back nobly. He still had hold of her wrists but she paid it no mind as she leveled her gaze at him. They were nearly equal in height, his head being just the slightest bit taller than hers. She stood on tiptoe. "Will ye release me or shall I call my guards?"

He laughed without humor, knowing full well she'd make good on the threat. At length he let her go. "The reason ye act as a child is because no one around here has the courage to keep ye from it," he grumbled, offering her a fatherly glower before backing away.

"Well I'm certainly sorry that ye feel that way since it was ye I was fighting for."

He held up his hands as he shook his head. "Don't do me any favors, sister. The last thing I need is for the Ard Ri to be angry with me."

"Leinster is ours and we should have it!" she exclaimed with a stomp of her foot. "Malsakin has nay right to deny yer request to march on Brian."

"Let's get a few things straight," he said as he made his way across the room then climbed the stair to the window. He opened the drapes and the light washed over him.

"It was yer request to Malsakin, nay mine. I'd do just as well without Leinster as I would with it."

"Coward," she spit as she crossed the room to sit opposite him on the sill. "Ye're afraid, aren't ye?"

"I'd prefer to use 'cautious' as a term."

She threw her head back with laughter and the sunlight caught in her eyes making them sparkle. "Coward, coward, coward," she sang, "Maelmora of— hmm, Maelmora of where? Certainly not Leinster." She curled her lip in distaste. "Ye're a man without a country."

He felt the anger warming his blood but he wouldn't give her the satisfaction of it, instead he smiled then descended the stair. "That may be so, dear sister, but I'm still a man which is more than I can say for ye. If I wanted a country, I could take one, but ye…well, 'tis a pity is all."

She flung herself from her seat then crossed the room with speed, cracking her hand across his cheek before he had a chance to stop her. "Bastard," she hissed.

He hurt her and he knew it. He was the only one who could cause her such pain because he knew all her secrets. She felt cursed that she was born a woman with little power and fewer rights. Truth be told, her mind was sharper than any man he'd known. It was a pity she hadn't been born in the time of Queen Maeve when women controlled both property and battlefield.

"Forgive me?" he pleaded as he took her hand in his. He kissed it.

She could feel the tears welling inside her but she choked them back. It wouldn't do to display such weakness in front of him, particularly since he was ready to give in. She turned her back on him.

"So will ye accompany me to Ailech or nay?" she questioned, already knowing that he would.

"I'll take ye," he replied, "but I don't see what difference it will make, ye traveling behind the Ard Ri. Why don't ye just remain here?"

"It will make a world of difference," she said as she rounded on him. "If I stay behind he can tell people that I wasn't up to traveling but that all is well between us. If I arrive after him and treat him harshly, people will talk about the trouble in the marriage. The last thing Malsakin wants is for people to think that I might leave him. He'll do anything I ask to avoid it."

"And what ye'll ask for is Leinster," Maelmora mumbled seeing the brilliance of her plan.

"Precisely," she cooed quite pleased with herself.

"So when do we leave?"

She flew to his side, eager to share her plan. "I've already made arrangements for the carriage and a few guards. I don't want much fanfare in the event that there's trouble on the road. Besides, when people see me riding up with such a small compliment they'll think Malsakin has been neglecting me and I'll earn their sympathy."

"And what will Malsakin think of all this? Does he know ye're coming?"

"Of course not," she snapped as if it was the silliest question ever asked. "When he denied my request for both ye and Sigtrygg I told him he was on his own, and ye should have seen his face when I did. At first I thought he would cry. He begged and pleaded with me to accompany him but when I continued to refuse I worried for a moment that he would use physical force against me."

"Perhaps he should have," Maelmora mumbled in a voice low enough that he was certain she couldn't hear. He was wrong.

"He'd never strike me!" she barked, straightening her head on her shoulders. "He'd do nay a thing to lose me because he knows how important I am to him."

"Kormlada," Maelmora huffed. "Ye have the gift, I'll give ye that, but I know ye don't believe that ye're the reason Malsakin has his crown."

She lifted a sly eyebrow. "Can ye dispute it?" she questioned smugly. "I've served as high queen to two Ard Ri's—I'd say that was proof enough."

He rolled his eyes and she settled herself in his lap, stroking his hair back from his brow. "I think ye should be kind to me, brother," she purred, "because if ye're not I might forget about making ye Ri Ciocid and make ye a toad instead."

*   *   *   *

Cenn Cora, Ireland: Just outside the round fort of Brian Boru—Six hours past noon—30, October 983 A.D.—Havland's shortcut from Limerick to Cenn Cora took them through the hills of Slieve Bernagh. It was more path than road with gorse and thistle jutting out from between jagged rocks. Every so often a patch of grass appeared along an expanse of flat land but there was no ease of going at these points since the travelers were forced to weave through grazing sheep and billy goats. It seemed as if the earth was rising up to meet them, blinding them to what lay ahead.

Half way up the rise, Patric stopped to wipe his sweating brow. A falcon's cry caught his attention. He watched it soar through the azure sky and through a wisp of cloud before it gave a final call then disappeared behind a distant mountain.

Havland was far ahead of him, his unassisted gait strong and easy as his well muscled calves made the journey yet another time. Patric sighed heavily then plunged the end of the yew branch he was carrying into the earth to pull himself up. He focused on the scabbard bouncing at Havland's back, using it to set a rhythm to climb by.

Havland cleared the rise with a final leap then stood hands on hips as he surveyed the territory. He turned east toward the Arra Mountains, smiling as their majestic beauty was reflected in Lough Derg. "'Tis indeed a sight to behold; well worth the effort."

Suddenly his golden hair and woolen cape caught on the wind, billowing out behind him in a most attractive fashion. His blue eyes were serene and confident and for a moment Patric thought him holy.

Excited by the scene, Patric pressed on, forcing his weight against the yew branch until it finally snapped. He cast it aside, leaving him searching for handholds to hoist himself up the remaining few feet.

Like a glimpse of heaven, Cenn Cora stood on the next rise, shimmering under the setting sun. Banners of yellow marked with three red lions waved freely from their posts above, lapping erect on the upward streams of air. Beneath, shimmering stones lay snugly upon one and other to form an impenetrable wall surrounding the vital village. Within, villagers moved about the market negotiating with merchants over the purchase of their wares, but nowhere was there any sign of Brian's army.

Havland raised a quizzical eyebrow. "We may be too late."

Patric's heartbeat doubled. "What shall we do now?"

Havland smiled then shrugged. "Just leave it up to me." With that he was gone, bouncing down the hill with Patric fast on his heels.

They passed through the gates of Cenn Cora with a hearty welcome from the sentries, none of whom expected to see Havland this trip. When he inquired as to when the army left and by which road they traveled, the sentries explained that the army led by Connor had departed three days earlier taking the Connacht road while the army led by the Ri Ciocid left just that day headed for the Leinster road. Havland thanked them then begged lodgings for the night.

"I don't understand," Patric puzzled as he followed Havland to the old hut with a threadbare blanket in his hands. "If we press on through the night we may be able to catch Brian up."

"Och," Havland replied. "That'd be grand, ye coming up on the Ri Ciocid after all this time with nay a soul to vouch for ye except me." He shook his head. "Nay. We'll take our rest and do our best to catch up with Connor's army. Nay doubt they'll be moving slowly owing to their burden. If I figure it right, we'll catch them up in Port daChainoc. It's there we'll find Thorien. He'll be the one to bring ye to Brian."

Though he was certain that he'd find little rest until they met up with Thorien, Patric assisted Havland in making a fire then threw down his blanket over a pile of straw and laid himself down. He woke to the smell of food.

"Ah, he wakes," Havland mumbled as he offered Patric a plate. "By the way ye were snoring I thought ye'd sleep through the day."

Patric stretched a bit before accepting the plate being offered. "I don't even remember closing my eyes." He waved it beneath his nose. "Smells great."

"Don't let the aroma fool ye," Havland smirked. "The actual taste is so much better than the smell."

Patric's mouth watered as he took a huge spoonful of the eggs. At first the taste was wonderful but suddenly his tongue began to burn. He grabbed the cup out of Havland's hand then drained it but the sensation didn't subside. He found another on the ground and began to drink from it but Havland stopped him.

"Ye don't want to drink that," he said screwing up his face. Instead he handed Patric a slice of bread. "Try this."

Patric shoved the whole of it into his mouth, chewing eagerly until the burning slowly subsided. "What in God's name is the trouble with these eggs?" he gasped.

"It's a special spice from across the sea," Havland offered between mouthfuls. "I got it from a Viking friend of mine. It's said the fire causes fierceness in battle and virility in bed. I eat this every morning."

Patric ripped another hunk from the loaf, shoving it wholly into his mouth. "I think I'd rather be dead and limp than suffer this sensation every morning."

"Ye grow accustomed to it after a while," Havland replied, scrapping his plate with his finger. "Are ye going to eat yours?"

Patric handed Havland his plate, continuing to chew the rye as he watched the Viking consume everything on it.

"Ah," the warrior sighed, stretching and patting his stomach before he got to his feet. "What say ye to lifting yer lazy sack out of bed so we can be on our way.

If ye thought the trip here was exhausting ye should know that what lays ahead is double so."

No more than that was necessary to get Patric moving. In short order, they had packed up the rations the sentries left for them and were headed north toward Port daChainoc.

The Connacht road was narrow and straight, bounded by forest on both sides. Just past Cavenlow it turned west and the trees fell away opening on to an expanse of white stones climbing high into Slieve Aughty. It was there that they took their rest for the night, sleeping under a clear sky dotted with stars that seemed close enough to touch. They used the rocks as their beds and Patric was pleasantly surprised to find them still warm from the sun beating down on them all day. The weather was fair and they slept comfortably but an hour into their next days journey the rains came.

They trudged slowly northward until a fierce storm forced them to take shelter in the shop of a local blacksmith. The weather was only slightly improved by morning but they pressed on anyway. They had thought to follow the River Shannon to their destination but it was swollen past its banks. Instead they traveled inland on the Uisnech road. It was there that they finally picked up the trail of discarded food and banked campfires left by Connor's army.

By nightfall the rains had stopped and just as Havland had promised, they found Thorien in the field at Port daChainoc seated on a large rock as he regaled his warriors with a saga.

Havland held a finger to his lips as he urged Patric through the gathering so they could get close to the fire. There was grumbling and grousing from the warriors who were being stepped over but when they recognized Havland they welcomed him with silent nods so they wouldn't interrupt their leader.

For reasons not limited to his extraordinary size, offending Thorien wasn't an option and Patric quietly took a seat next to Havland as the great man recited, "Madamion ruled Munster for six glorious years before Donovan of the O'Neills and Malmua of the Eaghonacts committed treachery against him. They summoned Madamion to a meeting of clan leaders under the guise of friendship and tribute. Madamion's own inflated ego led him to believe the O'Neill prince came to revere him and against Brian's advice, the Ri Tuath Ruire went alone to meet his would be assassin. It was Donovan who sent the message to Cenn Cora that Madamion didn't keep his appointment and that he feared for the man's safety. Brian was out of his mind with rage and together with Lorca of Cavenlow, the Dal Cais searched for their beloved king. They found him in these very woods, strangled by his own crucifix. Many assumed that robbers did the deed but Brian knew the truth. On that day he swore revenge for his brother's death. He took it two seasons hence.

"Brian argued with the elders that he should succeed his brother as king of Munster since they shared the same blood and since Madamion's reign was ended by treachery but the elders didn't agree. They wanted Donovan to have it and as God is my witness, they gave it to him. Brian wouldn't hear of it.

"Above the protests of some of his kin who still didn't believe he was a great leader, Brian of Cenn Cora marched on Donovan and Malmua with nay less than the kingdom of Munster as his prize. He'd move heaven and earth to avenge his brother's death and retake the crown from the traitorous O'Neills. We followed him because we knew he was the only prince willing to protect us from the raids so we could live our lives in peace.

"Together, Gael and Gall gathered from the fields and farms. The O'Neill's army outnumbered us three to one but Brian never wavered. He spent his time before the battle in Cavenlow, devising strategy with some of the great minds of Lorca's army. They came armed with maps, battle plans and weapons of strange origins. Lorca himself taught me the proper way to fight a man with my body pressed close so I couldn't be cut. This battle meant as much to him as it did to Brian and neither of them was too grand to get into it."

Havland offered Patric an elbow to the rib but neither took their attention from Thorien.

"Now, any man who still had doubts we would be victorious put his fears aside on the day of battle. Courage that couldn't be imparted by plans and weapons came in the way of Brian's words. The would-be king moved some of the greater warriors to tears with his language of peace and love and a united Eire.

"It was a dreary day, fraught with rain and the fields were so muddy our feet were sucked into the earth. The rain whipped at Donovan's banner, twisting it to hide his mark as if God was embarrassed by the man. Brian's banner, on the other hand, waved free and open so all could see the three lions upon it. We knew it was a sign from heaven that we'd be victorious."

To invoke drama, Thorien reached out to sip from the mead barrel. When gaping eyes and slack jaws assured the attention of all, he continued, "We charged in with angels at our backs. Suddenly it was as if our feet had wings and the mud hindered us nay longer. On the other side, Donovan's men were bogged down with the stuff, each moving as if they carried a great weight in tow. I cleaved three men before any of them were able to lift their swords. Likewise did my fellow Yon here…."

"Aye," Yon interrupted as he stood, wiping a lock of golden hair from his brow. His green eyes sparkled with pride and the light of the fire. "The angels lifted us one and all"

Thorien raised an eyebrow at the interruption but continued on in good nature as Yon returned to his seat.

"Lorca killed Malmua in the first hour then we moved ever closer to Donovan's banner, swiftly killing his guards to leave him unprotected. The O'Neill prince galloped his horse into the woods in an effort to escape his inevitable death but as he retreated he took the life of young Acard of Cavenlow, Lorca's first born son."

Thorien's eyes expressed his sorrow and his voice became low, "The new captain was winning his mortal combat against Donovan's own brother who tried to strike down one of his men. Donovan took the advantage of his horse to plunge his long sword into Acard's back. Seeing the abomination I gave chase, catching the reins of Donovan's horse and preparing to strike but I stopped. That would be the thing for Brian."

He shook his head in pity then heaved a long sigh with the memory of Lorca's grief. The action nearly moved Patric to tears.

"Brian looked like an angel upon his gray horse, untouched by battle even though he'd slain dozens. With tears in his eyes he looked to the fallen Acard then on Donovan. I could feel the hatred building between them as they stared at each other for what seemed an eternity but nary a word was uttered by either. The battle stopped around us and each of us looked, wondering what Brian would do. There was many a time when Brian would bid his enemy peace and only take his belongings—that's how he got the name "boru," it means tribute, aye."

The warriors nodded and he continued, "But if the pain of Madamion's loss wasn't fresh enough for him, the loss of young Acard renewed his hatred. He uncovered his long sword and held it high above his head. I watched as the muscles in his face constricted and for a moment it looked as if the devil were in him. With a single blow, Brian cleaved Donovan from his head to his groin. The O'Neill split like a melon—the two halves falling on either side of his horse. The beast was unharmed and Brian took it for his own. The animal bares the red mark of Donovan's blood to this day.

"We cheered as Brian's banner continued to wave against the rain then suddenly, as if a great hand moved over the sky to protect the new king from wetness, the rain stopped. The sun broke through the clouds and a ray of light shone only on Brian.

"When we returned home there were those who expected that the council would convene and deny Brian the crown yet another time, but there was nay a council to convene."

He smiled an evil grin then rinsed his mouth with a swig of mead. "Oddly enough they were all murdered by their Viking cohorts."

The warriors began to discuss the strange event when Thorien cleared his throat to regain their attention. "We were all invited to Cashel for the celebration. The stronghold of the Ri Tuath Ruire of Munster teamed with his allies as Brian took his oath. The historian read the names of Boru's people to prove he was of royal lineage then the king was crowned. That day he vowed to unite Eire once and for all and we knew we must stay with him through his battles until it was done."

Thorien stood, taking another swig from the barrel before bowing at the waist to offer, "And that, my brothers, is the story of Brian Boru."

Patric held his head in his hands as his tears flowed freely bringing a clap on the back from Havland. "So, do ye still question whether the captain knows the truth about ye?"

Patric shook his head then gathered his breath to answer but before he could, Thorien was calling out over the fire, "Havland the Bold, is that ye sitting there?"

"Aye, earl," Havland replied rising to greet his master. "And I brought reinforcements." He waved a hand toward Patric as he announced, "Brothers, I'd like ye to make the acquaintance of Patric macLorca, the true Ri Tuath of Cavenlow."

Thorien looked queer; one eyebrow jutted up in askance while his mouth fell open. Suspicion marked his face then he moved forward slowly, clearing his path to the lad with a wave of his hand. He stood towering over Patric as he raked him with his eyes.

Patric swallowed his nervousness, which only heightened the scrutiny then all at once the Viking named Yon broke in between them, waving his dirk at Patric. "I'll show ye what we think about Cavenlow men 'round these parts," he growled as he prepared to strike.

Patric defended himself. In three swift moves he had Yon's neck stretched and the dirk pressed against *his* throat. A trickle of blood marked a shallow cut to the skin.

"And this is what I think of those who'd accost me without first hearing me out," he replied.

Both Havland and Thorien drew short swords from their belts as a warning to any who would join in the mayhem. "Release him, laddie," Thorien offered calmly. "He was teasing is all. A test of yer mettle."

Patric looked up at the giant. His long golden hair and piecing eyes were the same as he remembered them. Suddenly regretful of his actions, he spewed a good belly laugh to ease the tension then released Yon with a gentle shove.

He brushed the dirt from his shirt before bowing to the gathering. "Well—though I'd much have preferred a simple greeting, I hope that I've proven that I'm capable enough to fight at yer backs."

Yon remained where he was until Thorien cocked his head in a silent order that he should step aside. He turned, ripping the blade from Patric's hand before finding his way into the throngs of his comrades to receive their sympathy. Thorien stepped forward.

"So, ye've finally come, laddie," he growled in a tone that made Patric wonder whether he'd been played. "I should say it took ye long enough." Then he turned toward Havland who still held his blade. "I might have figured it would be the likes of ye what brought him."

Havland grunted; a tiny smile marked his face as he thrust the blade back into his belt. Patric stepped forward, remorseful. "I pray ye forgive me, earl. I was only defending myself."

"Aye," Thorien replied, swinging around to face him fully. "Well—now that ye've disrupted our evening I think we should meet privately so that ye can explain yerself."

"Yon, bank the fires," he called over his shoulder as he headed toward the road. "Ye other rots better take yer rest because I expect we'll be pulling out at first light. Havland, bring the lad to me."

Patric's anxiety caused him to tremble. "Give him nay mind," Havland whispered as he directed him by the arm. "Ye'll see in a moment that all will be well."

✳   ✳   ✳   ✳

Athlone, Ireland—In the home of Ranfert macDonnough: Two hours to midnight—2, November 983 A.D.—Brian sat crossed legged on his mat replaying the conversation he had with Turlog just before they left Cenn Cora. Connor would be leaving him to take a wife. He knew he should be happy for the man but he couldn't help wondering why his old friend would keep such news a secret. He was pondering the situation when he heard the wagon wheels in the distance. He uncrossed his legs then got to his feet, pulling back the curtain so he could see outside. The moon was only half full making everything look shadowy.

"We'll make camp by the stream," the distant voice seemed to be saying.

Anthlone was open territory, bounded by Lough Ree to the north and nothing but streams and flatlands everywhere else. There was no fence surrounding the village since it was mostly farmland.

Brian listened for a moment, recognizing the sound of wagon wheels and perhaps a dozen horses. He passed a fleeting thought that fate had put the Ard Ri's caravan directly in his path then shook his head when he realized that Malsakin's contingent would be much larger. Whatever it was, it had stirred his curiosity and he'd find little rest if he didn't investigate.

He pulled on his breeches then began to walk out the door but he doubled back, deciding that if he were going to investigate he'd best be dressed for it. He donned his mail then strapped on his sword before making his way to the stables where his gray steed was resting. His guard snapped to attention upon his approach.

"Is there trouble, Ri Ciocid?"

Brian shook his head. "Just something I want to see down the road a way. Why don't ye saddle up a couple of horses for us, aye."

"Shall I call the others?"

At first Brian thought to respond, "aye," but his army had a rough way of it with the rains and he wanted them to rest. Besides, he hadn't acted as a spy since his time as an outlaw. The thought of it thrilled him.

"Nay," he replied, gripping the lad's shoulder. "We can handle this on our own."

The guard smiled proudly then saddled two horses. In short order, they were riding northwest through the trees in an attempt to catch up with the small caravan.

They came to a clearing at the rivers edge and watched in silence as several men made camp. Though they were dressed in homespun, Brian was certain they were O'Neill soldiers. They pitched two tents under a low lying tree nearest to the stream then built a fire in the center of the clearing.

A movement from the wagon parked at the edge of the clearing caught Brian's attention. His eyes opened wide as what appeared to be an angel descended from it. He drew breath at the sight of the moonlight shimmering in Kormlada's hair. She wore a lein of white with a cloak to match.

"She certainly is a beauty," the soldier mumbled in response to the Ri Ciocid's reaction.

"Do ye think so?" Brian flashed a crooked smile. "I don't much fancy the way her nose turns up at the end. Makes her look haughty."

The young man raised his eyebrow for a moment before he realized he was being played then all at once he gasped, "She's the high queen, aye. The one they call Kormlada."

"Shh," Brian issued with a finger to his beard. He understood the lad's excitement but he didn't want to be uncovered. "Aye, she's the high queen alright."

"Do ye mean to take her as hostage?" The lad's voice was barely audible.

Brian watched Kormlada disappear inside one of the tents then sat cross legged on the ground. "Perhaps."

For the better part of an hour, they watched in silence as Kormlada's guards settled themselves in for the night. Only when there was movement from Kormlada's tent did Brian speak again.

"See that guard?" he asked as he pointed through the trees. The lad nodded. "I want ye to ride around near the road loud enough to draw his attention. Can ye do it without letting him catch ye?"

Again the lad nodded then silently mounted, riding south through the forest until he came to a clearing that would lead him to the road. Brian mounted also but he rode north, circling around until he was even with Kormlada's tent. He exited the woods just before the stream then pulled back on the reins when he spotted her squatting over it.

The sound of his approach frightened her and she turned so quickly that she lost her footing on the slippery rocks. She fell back with a splash.

"By the gods!" she barked, struggling to catch her breath as she failed to come upright.

Her gown was sopping wet from the waist down, clinging to her and outlining her broad hips and long legs. Brian's breath hitched and a wave of apprehension washed over him. He was suddenly reminded of the dreams he'd been having. It was all he could do to keep his hand from shaking as he reached down to help her up.

She looked up at him with wide eyes but didn't take his hand. Instead she looked him over as if she were devouring him with her eyes. He reached his arm down further and just when he was sure she would take it, an outburst erupted from behind her tent. She looked toward the noise then back up at him.

"Go now," she whispered as if she were trying to protect him.

"Come with me," he replied.

She scrambled to her feet, draping her long wet hair over her arm like a cloak. For a moment he thought she would come to him but she continued to look over her shoulder as she responded, "I can not. Ye must go without me."

She was bathe in moonlight and when she turned back to look at him her eyes twinkled like gems. She looked every bit the queen that she was and for a moment Brian wondered if he would ever be able to rip his gaze from the glorious vision.

It was she who broke the visual embrace, turning to look over her shoulder as the distant voices came nearer. From his vantage point, Brian could see her guards coming closer. He began to turn his horse but before he did he called down, "Look at me."

She did as he asked and it took him a moment before he could find his voice. "Perhaps not this time, lady, but mark my words, ye will be mine."

He didn't know why he said it, he just did. Then he turned his horse and galloped away through the forest leaving her standing there soaked and breathless.

"Are ye alright, my queen?" came the guard's call from over her shoulder.

She turned to look at him, not really knowing the answer.

Brian rode through the woods at lightening speed, ducking his head under branches as his heart soared. He hadn't felt so alive since he and Lorca were cattle raiding. He caught up with his guard at the clearing and yelled out, "Come on! What are ye waiting for?"

The guard swung around to ride behind him, certain that the high queen's guards must be following, but when he looked over his shoulder no one was there. Brian had already dismounted by the time he reached the stables. "Is everything alright, Ri Ciocid?"

Brian threw back his head in laughter. He coughed a bit as he struggled to catch his breath. "Fine, laddie. Just fine."

"I'm sorry about the woman," the guard offered as he dismounted.

Brian looked west toward the forest as if he could see her from where he stood then he smiled and turned. "Nay need to be sorry, laddie. She'll be mine soon enough."

*   *   *   *

Port daChainoc, Ireland—In the tavern run by Six Finger Maeve: Two hours to midnight—2, November 983 A.D.—They walked in silence, Thorien leading the way and Havland following behind with Patric in tow. The air still smelled of rain and Thorien looked up to the clouds churning in the night sky.

"We may be here a while," he grumbled to no one in particular.

In the distance Patric could see a single light shinning from what appeared to be a tavern. As they drew closer, he smelled the sweet scent of peat smoke and heard the muffled clamor of voices. It was then that the rains came. Strong, driving drops that immediately soaked them through. Thorien stepped up his pace and was the first one through the door. Havland followed and behind him, Patric.

The tavern was nothing more than a huge sod hall with a great hearth along its northern wall and tables and stools strewn chaotically about the room. There were barrels of mead and ale set up toward the front; in the back was a wall of curtains, presumably the area where the serving maids plied their other trade.

"Well, come on, laddie," Thorien thundered. "Will ye come in and join us or will ye continue to stand in the way of the door so the place can flood?"

Patric pulled the door shut then swallowed hard to hide his nervousness before following the men to the table. He took a moment to look around and caught the eye of a red haired serving maid. She smiled at him and he smiled back as he clumsily took his seat.

"Don't tell me ye've never been in a tavern hall before?" Havland asked as he rubbed Patric's head.

The red flush creeping up the lad's neck gave him his answer and he chuckled, "Well, Thorien, it seems we should show the man what a pleasant place a tavern hall can be."

"He can have his fun when I'm through with him and nay a moment sooner," the Viking snapped back then he drew up his stool, resting his elbows on the table as he looked deep into Patric's eyes.

"Speak."

Patric glanced over to Havland who was busy ordering their drinks from the red head, an action that was taking far longer than necessary due to the abundance of flirting going on between the two, then he looked back at Thorien. The Viking's eyes were filled with determination.

"I don't know what it is ye'd like me to say."

Thorien drew a deep breath and his shoulders tensed. He wiped his mouth then nudged Havland as he barked, "Why don't ye let her do one job before ye engage her in another else we'll all die of thirst."

The woman offered a bow from the waist then turned to fill the order and Thorien returned his attention to Patric. "I'd like ye to tell me how ye could turn on yer da and yer king."

"I've turned on no one!" Patric snapped back, leveling his gaze directly at the Viking. "Why don't ye tell me what the fek ye're talking about?"

"Patric," Havland interjected but Thorien halted him by placing his hand on his arm. He rotated his head on his neck to relieve some of the tension and when he spoke again his voice was even.

"Yer father named ye heir to Cavenlow on yer sixteenth birthday so why is it that ye'd give the throne to yer brother and allow him to make such a mess of things?"

"There's yer first mistake," Patric replied anxiously. "My father never named me his heir."

This information wasn't received well by Thorien. He leaned away from the table to allow the pouring maid the room necessary to place the cup she had returned with in front of him then waited while she did the same for Patric and Havland before speaking again.

"Don't be taking me for a fool, laddie. Lorca spoke to me about it nay more than a fortnight before the celebration. Said he was planning to make a writ of it but I convinced him to name ye publicly in the event that fool brother of yers took it into his head to challenge the document."

Patric looked long at the Viking. There had been rumors of this sort running through Cavenlow immediately following Lorca's death but Patric attributed them to some disgruntled warriors who didn't care for the way Kevin was running things. When they finally left, the rumors went with them. He hadn't heard such things again until now.

"Ye say my father told ye this himself?" The Viking nodded and Patric's stomach twisted. "Well," he began but was forced to clear his throat of the bile rising in it. "If my father spoke to ye of such things he obviously changed his mind because he made nay announcement and he never made the writ."

Thorien looked at him in wonder. Either the lad was lying to him or something had gone terribly awry. "Do ye tell me that yer father didn't have the time to make the announcement?"

Patric remembered that night. Lorca had been absent for most of the feast leaving Brian to attend his guests. If he was planning to do what Thorien claimed he would have done it straight away—unless he was struggling with the decision. That thought made Patric even more uncomfortable and he shook his head preferring to believe that Thorien had misunderstood than to believe that his father didn't have the confidence in him.

"He had the time but I believe ye're mistaken about his intentions."

"Listen to me, laddie," Thorien snapped, convinced now that Patric was hiding something. "I knew yer da as good as anyone did! I fought beside him on the battlefield and did his biding when he needed it. The only mistake I made was to believe ye were anything like him. Ye're a coward and ye gave the throne to yer brother because ye were afraid to rule yerself! I should have let Yon have at ye while he had the chance."

Patric sat stock still as his eyes wandered over the table in search of a weapon but when he found none he decided that his fists would serve him just as well. He reached over the table, grabbing Thorien's lein in both hands to draw him close. "Don't ever accuse me of betraying my father or my king. I had Brian's blade with me when I killed Volkren but for ye my bare hands shall have to suffice."

Thorien's mind was numb with anger but Havland heard what Patric said and moved quickly to separate the two before damage could be done. He pushed Patric back onto the stool, sitting on his lap as he forced Thorien to focus on him instead.

"Did ye hear what the lad said, man? He killed Volkren! He avenged his father."

Patric was struggling to be free and Havland leaned back against him. "Ease up there, laddie. Give the earl a chance to hear me."

With that the haze slowly cleared from Thorien's mind and he released the grip he had on his short sword.

"Leave off him, Havland," he finally mumbled. When the man did as he was bade the earl leaned in to Patric. "Is it true that ye killed Volkren?"

Patric nodded cautiously, not entirely ready to let go of his anger.

"When?"

"On the full moon past."

"Does Brian know of it?"

"I couldn't say," Patric shrugged. "Why should it matter?"

"It matters plenty," Thorien growled. "Yer brother has been using Volkren as his excuse against fighting with Brian. With Volkren gone there would be nay reason for him to deny the king yet again he isn't with us. His actions are traitorous and when Boru finds out he'll remove him. Now tell me, are ye prepared to be Ri Tuath as yer father wanted or are ye fearful of such responsibility?"

Patric felt himself tremble as the rage built inside him. It exploded in a manner that surprised even him. "I've already told ye that my father didn't want me!" he bellowed, tears of frustration streaming down his cheeks. "He made nay announcement and left nay writ! He didn't want me I tell ye and if ye continue to embarrass me this way I don't know what I'll do!"

Thorien's eyes flew open as he realized he misjudged the situation. The lad truly didn't know what Lorca had planned for either him or his brother. He took both of Patric's hands into his own, more to protect himself from another attack than for any other reason. "Hush now, laddie and hear me out. Yer father wanted *ye* to succeed him, nay yer brother nor anyone else. If he didn't make the announcement or leave a writ 'twas because something, or someone, stopped him from doing it. Since the day ye were born he was preparing to make ye a leader. If ye think about it hard enough ye'll know I speak the truth. He believed in ye, laddie."

Patric's head was reeling. He didn't know what to believe. "But who could have the power to stop him if he truly wanted to name me heir?"

"Treachery comes in all forms, Patric," Thorien replied, "and sometimes it strikes where we least expect it. Nay doubt, yer brother had a hand it this somehow."

"Kevin? What could he do about it?"

"When a man's threatened with the loss of his power he'll make a deal with the devil himself to keep it. Yer father knew Kevin would be trouble for him that's why he wanted to leave a writ."

"Why go to such lengths?" Patric rebutted. "He could have just as easily told Brian that he wanted me and all would have been settled."

"Aye," Thorien agreed. "I offered him that advice but he was fearful that Boru couldn't stand behind it."

A look of concern dotted Patric's face and the earl moved to clear up the misunderstanding. "Not because he didn't want ye, but because of the edict he handed down about the rite of succession. Brian did it to protect the Munster throne but it holds just as true with the thrones of the lesser kings. If Lorca told Brian of his decision before it was announced, the Ri Ciocid would have been put in a position to rule on it and yer da wasn't taking any chances. He figured that once Kevin was in the abbey at Clonmacnoise it would be easily accepted that ye should succeed him as Ri Tuath and Boru and his edict wouldn't be compromised."

"The abbey at Clonmacnoise?" Patric questioned. "When was this supposed to take place?"

"Yer da sent a message to the abbot when last we saw each other. It was Lorca's hope to have Kevin on his way before the feast."

His brow wrinkled as a thought struck him. "I wonder why that didn't happen."

"It didn't happen because he changed his mind!" Patric blurted. "I did something to let him down and he changed his mind!"

"Ye're wrong!" Thorien shouted back at him as his own guilt began to grow then he lowered his voice. "If anyone let him down it was me. If only I had done what I was entrusted to do ye'd be sitting with him now, here on earth, knowing yerself how much faith he had in ye. Ye did nay a thing wrong, laddie. It was me that let him down."

Patric blinked through his returning tears as he struggled to take the earl's meaning.

"Aye," Thorien continued. "I'm the one to blame for yer da's death and for yer lost throne."

"Thorien!" Havland barked, wishing to put an end to the lament once and for all but the earl rebuked him.

"'Tis true, Havland and ye know it."

"In yer mind perhaps but not in the mind of others."

It was then that Thorien released Patric's hands, sighing deeply and hanging his head as he prepared to deliver his confession.

"He was a good man, yer da. The best I've ever known. There's nay a thing he could ask of me that I wouldn't do. I just wish…"

"'Twas his time to go and ye should accept that," Havland interrupted.

"Ye can accept it because it wasn't yer fault—'twas mine!"

Patric looked to Havland then to Thorien wondering where this exchange would take him but in short order Thorien returned his attention to the lad.

"Lorca trusted me to keep an eye out for things in Limerick but when all seemed to be well I got it into my head to take a trip north to UiFichrach Muaide to make an offer on a ship I'd been eyeing. By sea, the journey should have taken just three days and I would have been back in time for the feast, but negotiations went awry and I was forced to travel back by land. By the time I returned, yer da was gone and Cavenlow was left in ruins."

Patric considered the information and the pain in the earl's eyes as he relayed it. Following Lorca's death he had been prepared to battle anyone who had a hand in it…even Brian if that's what it came to, but in the end he knew there was no one to blame save Volkren and he had dealt with him.

"Thorien," he finally whispered, "Brian himself fought at Lorca's back that night and even he couldn't save him. If ye had known of Volkren's intentions and been there to deliver the information, there's nay certainty that Lorca would've survived. Believe me—I was there—I know. Accept his death, Thorien. I have."

Thorien looked at the lad as if he was seeing him for the first time. He had Lorca's eyes, round and crystal blue filled with life—he also had his reasoning. A feeling of calm suddenly overtook him—like he'd been absolved of a great sin. In that moment he knew that his friend wasn't lost.

"I hear what yer saying Patric and will accept it, but as ye have avenged yer father ye must allow me to avenge my friend. 'Twas yer father's wish to have ye sit on his throne and I'll move heaven and earth to see that it's done."

"But how?" Patric asked as a spark of excitement built within him.

"Of that I'm nay yet certain but ye can rest assured I'll find a way."

*   *   *   *

Ailech, Ireland: The great hall of Fladbartoc O'Neill: Two hours to midnight—2, November 983 A.D.—Kevin was now certain that he was both brilliant and lucky. Following the raid, Brian's short sword was found among the charred remains of those who washed up on shore proving that Patric was dead. And though *he* was fairly certain that it was Volkren's leg that the blade was found in, no one, save Garvin, could identify the body leaving his claim that the earl had escaped indisputable. He was finally free. Free to sit upon his rightful throne without harassment from Brian or anyone else, and free to pursue the crown of the Ri Tuath Ruire. He was positively giddy as he took another sip of sweet wine letting each precious drop slip pleasantly down his throat.

The hall of Ailech was obviously ancient, scarred by peeling paint and spotty mold growing at the junction where the thatch roof met the stone walls. It reeked of smoke and stale water but the wealth of its owner was obvious in the colorful tapestries hanging on the walls and the shimmering ornaments adorning the Ri Tuath's table.

The evening's entertainment was a bard known as Ferick. It was said that the pope himself was so impressed with his reputation that he sent a boat to carry him to Rome. Though Kevin considered the story far fetched, he did appreciate the bard's great talent. He sat back, listening to the story and the gentle plucking of the harp. When it was done he leapt to his feet offering both applause and words of adoration.

"Grand," he cried. "Simply grand."

This brought a broad smile to Malsakin's face and he joined their guest in his praise. "'Twas a good story, Ferick," he offered as he straightened the golden ring sitting upon his brow. "Mighty good indeed."

They all turned to Fladbartoc who had removed the ring from his forefinger and was busy spinning it atop the table. When he noticed their attention he brought his hand down over it and joined in, "Aye. 'Twas a good story indeed."

Malsakin released Ferick with a wave of his hand then the three kings promptly got down to business. Fladbartoc slipped the ring back onto his finger and was the first to speak, "So, Dal Cais what's brought ye to us?"

Kevin rested back in his chair, letting his eyes sweep the near empty hall again before they came to rest on Fladbartoc's face. There was a resemblance between the Ri Tuath of Ailech and the Ard Ri. Both had dark hair and both sported long beards. Yet while Malsakin's eyes were round and blue, Fladbartoc's were the color of lavender, slanted at the sides to give him a catlike appearance. Fladbartoc was also much larger.

They were both learned men and Kevin felt quite comfortable dealing with them.

He took another sip of wine before offering, "I believe our motives are the same in this, Fladbartoc. We both want to see Eire in the hands of thinking men instead of the brute warrior chiefs who are becoming far too numerous to control."

Fladbartoc raised an eyebrow at the comment then again slipped the ring from his finger to give it a spin. He never took his eyes from the spiraling gold band as he retorted, "I should think that problem is more prevalent in the southern regions than it is in the north. As ye know, the O'Neills have long been admired for their ability to reason. How else could we have remained in power for as long as we have?"

Kevin nodded his head in acceptance of Fladbartoc's point.

"Aye, ye are the great thinkers of our world that's why I thought ye might be interested in working a plan to take Boru down—but if he doesn't concern ye I'll not waste any more of yer time."

He stood to leave and Malsakin grabbed his arm. "I pray ye take nay offense, Kevin." The Ard Ri raised an eyebrow in silent warning to Fladbartoc before continuing, "It's long been the concern of the O'Neills that Eire be ruled properly that's why so many of us have taken on responsibility as leaders, but ye must admit that Brian Boru is a troublesome sort. Many have tried to take him down and all have failed."

Kevin returned to his seat as the smug smile spread across his face. "Perhaps," he offered before taking another sip from his cup, "but then again those who have tried handled the situation abominably."

"And exactly how many ways are there to skin a cat?" Fladbartoc asked as he sent his ring for another spin. "Either ye meet a man on the battlefield or ye perpetrate a raid—the only option after that is murder. While that might be the way with the Dal Cais, it's not the type of thing the O'Neills look kindly on."

It was truly amazing, Kevin thought to himself, that these were the greatest minds that Ireland had to offer yet they couldn't see the scheme unless it was handed to them on a platter. He sighed gently as he offered, "We're all in agreement that Brian's a usurper are we not?" The two men nodded and he continued, "Well then, if usurping is good enough for Brian why wouldn't it be for someone else?"

Fladbartoc and Malsakin looked at each other and Kevin smiled cunningly. "Let me make myself plain. I will help ye to get rid of Brian if in turn ye name me Ri Tuath Ruire of Munster."

"And how do ye plan on doing that?" Fladbartoc questioned, amused by the dainty man's confidence.

Recognizing Fladbartoc's obvious dislike for him, Kevin decided to ignore him. He turned toward Malsakin to ask, "Ard Ri, I notice that yer lovely queen hasn't made the journey north. Has she taken ill?"

Taken aback by the sudden change in subject, Malsakin stammered, "A-aye. Nothing to worry over, mind ye, but we thought it best that she stay behind. The trip can be grueling this time of year."

"I'm sorry to hear that," Kevin cooed, "I should think that she, above all, would be interested in my proposition."

"What proposition?" Fladbartoc huffed. It was bad enough that he was forced to hand over his hall so his cousin could hold court, he wouldn't be ignored as well.

Kevin continued to give Fladbartoc his back then lowered his voice as he addressed Malsakin, "I've a plan to take Leinster right out from under Brian's nose."

"How?" Malsakin grumbled in defense of his cousin.

Kevin read signs as well as any man. He sat up straight, turning himself so that both kings could hear. "Brian gained adoration among the Leinster Galls by giving them their freedom but if someone started to raid them, let's say a Dal Cais, they'd turn on him for sure."

Fladbartoc laughed out loud before sending his ring for another spin. "Don't tell me ye believe yerself strong enough to perpetrate these raids."

"With yer help I can," Kevin retorted.

With the palm of his hand, Fladbartoc flattened the ring against the table to give his full attention to the conversation. "Now why would I assist ye in taking Leinster? If I wanted it, I would have taken it myself."

"And if ye failed ye would have forfeited Ailech," Kevin snapped back. "My way, no one forfeits anything—win or lose."

Malsakin smiled as he suddenly saw the beauty of the plan. "Very well," the Ard Ri thrilled as he offered Kevin his hand. "I'll provide ye the men needed to perpetrate these raids so long as ye understand that when ye take the territory it will be me who names it's leader. My wife is very fond of her homeland and wouldn't look kindly on any other than her blood kin ruling it."

"Agreed," Kevin issued as he clasped the Ard Ri's hand. "And when we're through with Leinster we'll move south to Munster where ye'll name me Ri Tuath Ruire."

"Agreed," Malsakin replied.

Fladbartoc looked at the two men, smug in the success neither had yet gained. Other than Tara, Malsakin had never been in battle and he highly doubted that Kevin was strong enough to raise a sword. He chuckled as he took a sip from his cup.

"What?" Malsakin asked as he turned toward him.

"Nay a thing," the Ri Tuath replied. "I just hope the execution of the plan is as simple as the laying."

Malsakin rested back in his chair then folded his arms across his chest. "Tell me, Fladbartoc, have ye a better way to cut Boru down?"

"Nay so much better," he replied, "but perhaps more direct. If I wanted to take Boru down I'd simply meet him on the field."

Kevin offered a "hmph" before sipping his wine and Fladbartoc turned toward him glowering. "And what's that supposed to mean?"

"Nay a thing," Kevin cooed. "But if ye want to challenge him ye won't have to go far. I understand that Boru's marching his army toward Ailech as we speak."

CHAPTER 13

▼

Clonmacnoise, Ireland: The Abbey—mid afternoon—3, November 983 A.D.—Thorien decided that the broken cart axle within walking distance from the Clonmacnoise Abbey was less bad luck than it was a sign from Lorca. He didn't tell Patric and Havland where he was going in the event things didn't work out, but instead ordered them to stay behind to repair the rig so they could be quickly on their way.

He stood in the doorway of the ancient abbey, marveling at its magnificence. The ceiling was a dome painted colorfully with scenes depicting the life of Saint Patrick. On either side of the rotunda were wooden stairways decorated with elaborately carved banisters. A long hallway ran from the door to the end of the building. The floor was covered in deep red rushes.

Thorien inched in further as he noticed the beautiful pottery and polished furniture lining the walls of the hall. There was no doubt the abbey was a rich one. Suddenly the abbot appeared from the eastern hall leading into the rotunda. Thorien's heart thundered in his ears as the abbot's footsteps rang through the hall. He felt like a child who was awaiting a reprimand.

"Are ye the Viking who wishes to speak with me?" the abbot asked, half turning to the young scholar who had brought him out of his chambers.

"I am," Thorien replied, his strong voice echoing off the walls of the ancient building. He lowered his tone. "I'm known as Thorien Long Bow, although now they call me Thorien of Limerick. I was second to the man known as Lorca of Cavenlow—an ally of the great Brian Boru."

"Aye," the abbot sighed, nodding his head in recognition of the names. "I know of Lorca and of Brian but I'm sorry to say I don't know of ye."

"That's fine, father," Thorien replied with a smile. "I didn't think that ye would but I'm wondering if ye heard of what happened to Lorca?"

"He was killed by Volkren gone on two summers ago I expect."

"Aye, ye're right," Thorien cooed. "And do ye know what became of his son, Kevin, the one who was to have studied here?"

"Aye." The abbot's face was full of doubt with the line of questioning. "He became Ri Tuath."

Thorien's stomach flipped as the excitement swelled in him. It wasn't uncommon for abbots to be moved around by the church, serving where they were most needed. That he was able to find the man who could give him what he needed was an omen indeed. Now he had to gain his trust.

"Father, is there a place where we could speak in private because what I have to tell ye is not for all ears?" He looked to the scholar without turning his head.

A Viking calling in the middle of the day with thirty others just down the road fixing a cart axle made the abbot slightly suspicious. Instead of taking him into the inner sanctum where so much of the abbey's treasure was stored, he turned to the scholar to order, "Ye may leave us, Mahon. Tell the other brothers that I am out here with Thorien of Limerick and that they aren't to disturb us."

The scholar took his meaning and made off down the hall to quietly warn the others. The abbot returned his attention to Thorien. "We won't be disturbed." He motioned for him to take a seat on the ornate wooden bench in the hallway then sat beside him. "So tell me, son, what is it that ye seek?"

Thorien sensed that the abbot was nervous so he got right to the point. "As I told ye before, I was second to Lorca and I know he wrote ye requesting that ye make a place for his elder son, Kevin. He did it because he intended to give his throne to his youngest son, Patric, an excellent leader who's loyal to Boru. He was to make his announcement at Patric's coming of age—he even left a writ— but he was slaughtered before the announcement and now the writ has disappeared."

He softened his eyes as he turned to face the abbot fully. "Father, if ye still have the written message that the Ri Tuath sent ye it could assist Lorca's youngest in taking his rightful place as leader."

The abbot bowed his head then began to shake it. Ireland was full of such treachery between brothers. He hardly thought it was the place of the church to become involved in it. "I'm sorry that I can not help ye. We're a humble order and it would be best for us to stay out of the troubles."

"But father," Thorien pleaded. "I know Lorca's missive came with five ounces of gold—quite a sum for someone outside yer parish. Certainly ye could see yer way clear to help him find peace in the afterlife knowing his rightful heir is sitting on his throne."

The abbot got to his feet, openly offended by the Viking's words. "I'm sorry I can not help ye," he said again as he moved toward the door.

Thorien was angry but he was also desperate. He swallowed hard, the bile burning his throat. "Father, I don't think ye understand. The lad is a favorite of Boru. The Ri Ciocid would do anything to see him in power."

The abbot stopped short of opening the door then turned to look at Thorien. "Is this so?"

"Aye."

"Well, if Boru is so interested why doesn't he just appoint the man? He doesn't need a writ to do it. He's the Ri Ciocid."

Arguing the finer details of politics with the abbot was the last thing that Thorien wanted to do so he appealed to something the abbot would readily understand. "Boru is marching toward Ailech to face the Ard Ri. If he's successful, he may find himself wearing the high crown. Certainly he would look favorably on ye if ye were able to find the missive."

"This abbey stands at the crossroads," the abbot huffed. "We receive messages everyday. How am I to find the one ye seek? Even if it was still here it would take me hours to lay hands on it."

Thorien noticed the abbot staring at his arm ring. It was a gift from his father for his coming of age and not a day went by when he didn't wear it. He removed it then held it against the stone wall. With one swift move he pulled his sword from his back harness then hacked the bracelet in half.

The sound of the blow rang solid through the abbey and within minutes there were priests scampering down the hall and stairways to see what trouble there was. Some carried daggers while others held whatever object was nearest to them when they heard the sound but all looked menacing as their eyes alighted on the Viking.

Thorien returned his blade to its sheath before offering the abbot half of the bracelet. "Take this for yer troubles."

"Are ye alright, father?" one brother called, placing himself between the abbot and Thorien.

"Aye, Sean, I'm fine," he responded then handed him the silver. "Take this to my chamber, Sean, and while ye're there search under my mattress for the letters from Lorca of Cavenlow. I believe ye'll find them bound, three in all. Bring them to me."

He turned to the others. "The rest of ye can go back to what ye were doing. This is our friend, Thorien of Limerick. He's an ally of Brian Boru. He's here to help us."

Thorien smiled and nodded. Less than a quarter hour later he was walking down the road with his treasure tucked in his coat and a feeling that Lorca was right beside him.

*   *   *   *

Ferta Nime, Ireland: The campsite of the Munster army—Six hours to midnight—3, November 983 A.D.—The night was unusually warm making the north wind blowing down from the Sperrin Mountains a welcomed relief to the soldiers of Brian's army. There were campfires burning as far as the eye could see but only several tents were pitched to house officers—the largest being reserved for the Ri Ciocid who would join them sometime over the next two days.

The field was alive with movement as warriors refreshed themselves in the creek or exchanged war stories with comrades. In the distance a contest of strength had started sometime following supper and was still going strong. It was a boulder toss—the reigning champion being a Leinster Gall who had joined them along the way. As men continued to line up for their turn to oust this new champion, some of the losers allowed that if Thorien hadn't been detained back in Clonmacnoise he would have surely put the Leinster man in his place.

Every now and again a warrior could be seen slipping into the forest to take his pleasure with a camp follower but more often than not that type of trade happened out in the open under the cover of blankets.

Connor drew deep from his cup, the bitter ale stinging his tongue before he swallowed it. It wasn't often that he engaged in drunkenness but tonight was a turning point for him and he indulged himself beyond capacity. He squinted his eyes to focus his vision while the roar of laughter from his under captains sitting around their fire pounded in his head like a bodrahn calling him to war. He took a moment to steady himself then struggled to his feet. The noise around him suddenly stopped.

All eyes were on him. Each man wondering what news had been delivered that could put the captain into such melancholy. They held their breath waiting for him to offer it.

"Wart err ye lookin at?" Connor slurred as he rested his left hand on his hip and his right hand on the short sword protruding from his belt. Still his men stared at him—none of them being brave enough to answer.

He knew he was drunk but he decided that he must be quite the sight to have his men looking at him that way. It had taken all his courage to get this far and he wouldn't be put off from his mission because of round eyes and slack jaws. He squinted again, forcing his brain to decipher whether or not the person snuggling with Sion of Cara at the edge of the campfire was male or female. He cocked his head to one side, deciding it must be a lass due to her abundance of hair. He shouted, "Bring me thart womin!"

Sion took a moment to consider this strange turn of events before scrambling to his feet. Everyone knew that Connor was more likely to request the company of a weapons boy or water bearer than a woman, still, he offered a hand up to the camp follower then shoved her gently forward. She went willingly though she would have laid wagers that the man was too drunk to get it up. She stood very close to him, the heat of his body causing her to sweat just a bit more.

"Good," Connor crooned as he lifted a strand of her hair to sniff it. Beyond the scent of perspiration and sex was the faint scent of lavender. He sniffed it again before resting his hand on her shoulder to point her toward his tent. She turned then stepped through the flap. After surveying the environment, she moved forward to the pile of animal skins stacked neatly in the corner. One by one she spread them atop each other to make a comfortable bed.

Connor smiled as he watched her. Her thick auburn hair cascaded down her back in soft curls—the ends of which were littered with bits of grass. She had a full round face and dark eyes that shone with confidence and Connor laughed that it was nothing more than dumb luck that he'd chosen a woman of intelligence to tutor him in the ways of the fairer sex.

When the skins were laid she unpinned the corners of her lein then let it drop to the floor at her feet. Her skin was a bit grimy and her figure straight and narrow but her breasts were full.

Probably why the men like her, Connor thought to himself.

He stepped forward to touch one and immediately she threw back her head in mock ecstasy. He kissed her neck and she moaned before moving her hands along his hips to undo his belt. Instinctively he stopped her, his large hand clamping down on her wrists like a vice. She was startled. "I'll do it," he growled as he stepped away from her.

She dropped her eyes then let her hands fall to her side. Though the man no longer seemed drunk he did seem quite tense and in that moment she realized just how difficult her job would be.

By the time she lifted her eyes he was standing naked before her. His broad shoulders tapered down to a taught stomach—his legs were long and muscular. He was scarred from battle on his shoulder, hip and thigh. If it weren't for the flatulent penis nestled in the patch of golden red hair she would have thought him a perfect specimen of a man. He moved toward the pile of skins, stretching himself out across the soft hairs then motioning to her with his hand. "Come join me," he beckoned. "Show me what it is ye do that has my men rapt."

She took a deep breath as she lowered herself beside him. It would be a long night indeed.

✳   ✳   ✳   ✳

Clonmacnoise, Ireland: In the tavern run by Mangus Horn—Six hours to midnight—3, November 983 A.D.—Patric's head was reeling from excitement and the abundance of mead he'd been consuming. He hadn't had honey wine since the night of his sixteenth birthday. He'd forgotten how much he enjoyed it.

He swayed in his chair watching Havland who was in the corner singing a song in his native Orkney tongue. Patric had no idea what the words meant but the peculiar faces Havland made throughout his performance were humorous enough to make him laugh.

The crowd cheered when it was over and Patric turned to Thorien who seemed to have understood every word. "How long have ye been in Eire?"

Thorien smiled at the lad who's slurring words attested to his drunkenness. He didn't blame him. He had lived these past seasons thinking that his father had little use for him. To find out now that he was the rightful leader of his village must have been overwhelming.

"I was brought here many years ago by Olaf Curran. My father owed the old king a debt and it was me who was sent to pay it off."

"Ye were a *fudir*?" Patric asked in a loud voice, his wide eyes marking his surprise as he struggled to keep his head steady on his shoulders.

"Nay, man!" Thorien bellowed. "I was never a slave. I only came to work off the debt. After it was paid I was on my way and made a home in Limerick."

"Ye're a liar, Thorien!" a voice called from the next table. "Ye were a slave and ye ran off before yer debt was paid. Ye're nay different from the rest of yer family. Ye're all a pack of liars. Ye're born to it!"

Thorien was immediately on his feet and Patric became confused with the sudden movement. When he realized what was going on he scrambled to cover the earl's back.

Thorien's accuser stood a full inch taller than the earl, his yellow hair hanging in matted tangles about his shoulders. Though he wasn't as lean as Thorien the outline of his large muscles were clearly visible.

"It's ye who's the liar, Hagar," Thorien barked as he stood full up to his accuser, "And I suggest ye keep yer tongue still before its wagging earns ye a blade in the heart."

"And who'll put it there, Thorien?" Hagar asked as he stepped closer. "I see nay a man in this tavern who could carry out such a threat."

Thorien took a moment to look around the room, marking any who would become entangled in the conflict before chuckling, "It does my heart good to see that ye've graduated from preying on children and old men, Hagar, but if ye want to live I suggest ye pick yer battles with someone of significantly lesser skills than mine."

He gave Hagar a gentle shove. "Go now and sit down before ye get hurt. All here know ye accost me because my sister took yer land as settlement in yer divorce."

Patric turned as murmurs were heard from the tables closest to them. It was clear this feud had been going on long enough for men to pick their sides and argue the point amongst themselves, but when he looked for Havland he found the man still in the corner regaling his audience, unaware of what was taking place at the other end of the tavern.

Hagar's face reddened as his upper lip lifted into a snarl, "I never slapped yer sister in public as she claimed. I owed her nothing. My man here will attest to it." He pointed to another Viking who quickly came to stand beside him.

Patric stretched his neck to see the next Viking, bigger than Hagar. He swallowed back the lump in his throat as he wrapped his hand around his clay cup praying that Havland would finish his song.

Thorien threw back his shoulders without looking to the second Viking. "Yer man here preys on innocents as ye do, Hagar. No one will believe him now as they didn't at the time of the divorce."

He felt his waist for his dagger then pressed his nose against Hagar's. "I'll tell ye again, if ye want to live ye should back away now."

A voice from the back of the tavern called out, "Step away, Hagar or he'll cut ye for sure."

Hagar turned in the direction of the voice and for a moment Patric thought the Viking would heed the warning but instead he took his blade in hand.

With one swift movement Thorien slit Hagar from his naval to his throat.

The second Viking lunged. Without thinking, Patric toppled the table using his full weight to pin the man beneath it. He smashed the cup upside the Viking's head but that only brought a deep growl from his enemy.

The Viking struggled and Patric pressed down harder, praying that his trap would hold until he could do something further then he spied the hilt of the Viking's sword poking out from under the table. All at once he grabbed for it then rose to his feet poising the blade tip above his enemy's throat.

By this time a crowd had gathered around them. They were chanting and whooping eager for the Viking's death.

Inspired by their fervor, Patric opened his stance, placing one foot atop the Viking's forehead and the other solidly on the table to keep his enemy down. He smiled triumphantly as he looked down on his enemy but it faded when he spotted the fear in the Viking's eyes. His brain muddled.

For what seemed an eternity, Patric searched the faces of the crowd hoping someone would offer an alternative to death but they all called out for the Viking's demise—all except Thorien who watched in silence.

Patric had little choice in the situation. Releasing the Viking would find him dead in an instant, killing him would torture his soul. He looked down at the man hoping to find an answer in his enemy's eyes but instead he found it in his hair.

With one swift movement, Patric leapt from the table, grabbing a portion of the Viking's hair as he went. He yanked it back then ran the blade against the Viking's scalp until both hair and flesh were freed into his hand.

He laughed maniacally as he waved his prize above his head and shouted, "When people ask ye of yer hair tell them Patric took it because ye were sticking it in business which didn't concern ye."

Blood flowed freely from the Viking's wound, blinding him as he scrambled to his feet. The crowd grew silent, wondering whether he would fight or retreat. Their answer came when he stumbled over tables and chairs to beat a hasty exit from the tavern.

One of his comrades stepped forward, motioning to Patric who was still holding the man's sword. Thorien cocked his head in warning. "I'm sure Throdier would want the lad to keep the weapon, aye? It's only fitting since it was used to shave his head."

The man took a moment to ponder the statement then, realizing he was out-matched, nodded silently before turning his attention to Hagar's dead body sprawled at his feet.

"Lend some assistance, man," he called to his other comrade as he grabbed one end of Hagar's cloak. A moment later they carried the body from the tavern.

Patric's eyes were wide and his mouth agape as he watched the scene. It could easily have been him being carried from the tavern. He shuddered with the thought of it.

"'Tis a good weapon ye claim," Thorien thundered as he nudged him with his elbow.

Still shaken, Patric looked down at the blade. The hilt was a simple gold cross with no jewels or ornament of any kind but when he balanced the blade on his open palm it laid flat and even. He smiled. "I guess I was lucky to challenge a coward who carried a quality weapon, aye."

Havland laughed as he broke through the crowd, "When yer weapon earns yer keep ye carry the finest."

"Nay, man?" Patric blurted, lifting an eyebrow. "Ye can't mean to tell me that he was a paid warrior? Surely ye're mistaken."

He looked to Thorien who nodded in support of Havland's claim.

Patric continued to shake his head in disbelief and Thorien chuckled before slapping his back then righted a chair for him to take a seat. "The man ye embarrassed is called by the name, Throdier. He's the bodyguard of the earl Sigurd of Orkney. It's said he's the fiercest of all warriors and once cut a man's throat because he found his voice offensive."

He shook his head then took his own seat as he continued, "But I doubt he'll ever find employment again now that ye've exposed his cowardice."

"'Tis true, laddie," offered an older man who was standing close enough to overhear.

Patric looked up at him and the man clapped his back in congratulations before making his way to his own table. Soon others responded in kind causing Patric to marvel at the fact that he'd earned more respect by sparing a life than he would by taking it. Then he remembered something.

He looked at Thorien's hand and his missing pinky. "Throdier?" he questioned. "Wasn't he the one who took yer finger?"

"One in the same," Thorien responded with a nod and a gleam in his eye then he extended his hand to Patric. "He always took great pride in marking me. Now I guess he'll have to live with a mark of his own."

Patric shook the earl's hand feeling closer to him than he had since they met. The last few days were the best in his life. He could hardly wait for tomorrow to see what it would bring. He looked up when Havland cleared his throat loudly.

"Well, Patric the Shaver," the Viking cooed as he positioned a buxom chestnut haired woman to stand before him. "Maybe it's time ye took yer reward for the evening."

The adrenaline of battle was still pumping through Patric's veins but when he looked into the eyes of the woman who Havland called, Freyja, he suddenly felt drunk again. She was tall and well rounded with odd green eyes that were ringed in gold. Her lashes were long and her cheeks and lips full and pink.

"It's good to know of ye, Freyja," he offered as he extended his hand to her.

She looked to Havland then back at Patric, not knowing what to make of the situation but she had been paid good silver to keep the warrior happy and she meant to do it.

She lifted her lein then put Patric's hand between her thighs as she leaned forward to kiss him. "By the gods, woman," Thorien thundered. "Take him to the back and fix him proper."

Though he'd stolen his share of kisses, Patric had never lain with a woman. He was suddenly unsure of what to do about his swelling excitement. He tried to recall Hagar's gory death with the hope that the memory would buy him time enough to come up with a plan but it wasn't necessary since Freyja was now leading him to the back of the tavern by his very obvious erection.

Thorien smiled for the scene, taking a long draw from his pint and wiping his mouth with the back of his sleeve before mumbling, "Should the lad die in his sleep tonight, he'll die a happy man."

Freyja pulled back the tattered curtain separating the tiny space from the rest of the tavern and immediately the smell of sex filled the air. Patric turned his head but she drew him inside by the same method she got him there.

They stood together for a long while, Patric wondering how he could have so little control over his own body and Freyja wondering how a man of his age could be so inexperienced in the way of women. She conjured a thought that he might prefer male companionship to hers but it passed quickly as the evidence of his excitement continued to throb in her hand.

If they were ever to be done with it she knew she must be the one to start. She released him then pulled her lein over her head before she raked him with her eyes. Not bad for a Gael. Shorter than most of the Viking's she was accustomed to yet his carriage was straight and his shoulders broad giving him the appearance of a much taller man. He was a little worse for the wear from his travels but his hair was clean and shone with a golden glow over its ruddy hue. He smelled of apples, mead and peat smoke. There was fear in his eyes so she offered a reassuring smile. He reciprocated and in that moment she decided to be generous to him.

There was no sound as she lowered herself to the makeshift bed of straw and linen, or if there was, Patric couldn't hear it. His ears were filled with the echoing beat of his own heart and the gentle whooshing of his blood as it coursed through his veins. If it were possible, this experience was as terrifying as the first time he faced a Viking on the field in Cavenlow. He swallowed hard, willing himself not to tremble and cursing his body for betraying him so.

She was lying naked across the pallet—one leg still on the mud floor while the other was propped up offering him an unobstructed vision of all she offered. Her nipples were dark against her pale skin and she put them quickly erect as she twisted each one between her thumb and middle finger.

He remained stock still, watching her performance yet making no move to join her. Finally she stretched one leg toward him, using her toes to draw his breeches open further. Without realizing that he had done it, Patric removed both breeches and lein then took a step to stand before her.

She sat upright, raising an eyebrow in approval as she took hold of his hips to pull him close. "I never knew that the smaller warriors could carry grand weapons," she murmured before covering him totally with her mouth.

Her warmth caused every nerve in his body to twitch and suddenly it felt as if all the air had been sucked out of him. He opened his mouth to ease his breathing but instead emitted a groan so fierce he was surprised that it came from his own throat. There was no sense in him at that moment, only a base instinct to continue on his journey until its conclusion.

Control was a fleeting thought as his body betrayed him in a most fierce manner, propelling him ever forward to a destination he only half recognized as ecstasy but never as all consuming as when it came by his own hand. With a shatter of blinding light behind his eyes and a rush of warmth through his body, it was over. He thought he screamed but perhaps it was only a groan. He gulped air fiercely as his heart ended its furious attempt to escape from his chest and began to subside into a normal rhythm. He felt his legs quake a bit and reached out a hand to steady himself against her shoulder as he slowly opened his eyes. Then he looked at her.

She was smiling up at him with those odd green eyes, looking like an angel from heaven. "Happy?" she whispered.

He pulled her to him, crushing her against his abdomen with the naive certainty that this was the only woman he would ever need. He wanted to hold her forever, to protect her from harm and keep her by his side wherever he may go. "I love ye, Freyja," he sighed into her hair.

She smiled under his embrace, quickly recognizing the misguided emotions of one who had taken his first lover, but still it felt good. There were many before him and there would be many after, all too young and inexperienced to understand the difference between love and lust, but this one stirred an emotion deep inside her and she decided to play along if only to be loved for a while.

She showered his stomach with tiny kisses, massaging his legs and thighs until she felt him stir again then slid herself back on the bed, inviting him to join her.

CHAPTER 14

▼

Ulster road: At the campsite of the high queen—Four hours to midnight—28, November, 983 A.D.—Maelmora pulled back the tent flap to peer outside. His eyes raked the clearing and he smiled to himself before returning to his sister. "I think he's given it up," he said though he didn't believe it. He moved to the stool then took a seat.

She had her back turned to him but she could see his reflection in her hand mirror. "Wipe that grin off yer face," she snapped with no real feeling. "I find little humor in the situation." And she didn't. Boru was being a nuisance and her gods weren't helping her.

"Come now, sister," he cooed. "If the man meant ye harm he would have marched that army right over us instead of sending them away."

"Ah, but *he's* still trailing us, isn't he then?"

"Aye," Maelmora agreed. "But he's doing a poor job of hiding it and I can't believe that's an accident. Brian Boru was an outlaw for many years. He perpetrated some of the greatest cattle raids Eire has ever seen. Ye can't tell me that a man who can move a hundred head of cattle out of a village without detection isn't able to hide himself better than he's been. He's following ye and he wants ye to know it therefore he means ye nay harm."

"Well, he's bringing me harm by making me nervous," she mumbled.

She remembered his eyes and the way he looked at her by the stream. It was as if he touched her with his mere glance. They glimpsed each other again on the road at Ferta Nime. He was close enough to touch as he rode beside her carriage, never saying a word but only looking at her. He had spent the better part of the past season haunting her dreams and now he was haunting her waking hours as well.

"Why doesn't he go away?"

Maelmora rose from his seat, an odd expression plastered on his face as he approached her. "What kind of hold does he have on ye?"

She turned to look at him, both eyebrows rising with surprise. "He's nothing to me!"

Maelmora smiled. "Ahh, but I think he is." He tenderly touched her cheek with the back of his hand. "Kormlada, ye're blushing."

"I'm not blushing," she barked as she slapped his hand away. "'Tis hot in this tent is all."

"It's cold as the dead in here," he retorted.

"Get out!" she yelled far louder than she intended but she had begun and she wouldn't turn back. She pointed to the tent flap with the hand mirror. "Get out right now before I call my guards."

He giggled before creeping up behind her to nuzzle her neck. "Kormlada loves Brian," he sang against her ear.

"Get out ye rot!"

He danced around singing, "Kormlada loves Brian," until she rose from her seat to physically remove him from the tent.

She could hear him still singing as he walked away and she leaned against the tent pole praying that Brian Boru wouldn't be the undoing of all her well laid plans.

✳   ✳   ✳   ✴

Ulster, Ireland—Outside the round fort of Ailech: Noon—1, December 983 A.D.—The march took Connor's army through the village of Longfort past Lough Gowna and Lough Erne and over Slieve Beagh. Brian's army joined them as they entered the northern territory at Ferta Nime but the Ri Ciocid wasn't with them. He would meet them later in Ailech. They made their way up past Airgialla then east toward Beaghmore and over the Sperrin Mountains.

Ailech stood just south of the Giants Causeway on the eastern side of Lough Foyle. It was a brilliant structure of white stone nearly four hundred acres round. The forest surrounding it had recently been cleared to alert Fladbartoc of the army's arrival. It was there that they pitched camp.

Owing to the broken cart axle in Clonmacnoise, Thorien's contingent trailed behind and was the last to setup camp. It was while Patric was pitching Thorien's tent that he spotted the tent of the Ri Ciocid marked with the three lions. He turned to Havland. "Is that Brian's tent?"

Havland struggled to bring the tent rope taught then followed Patric's finger to the structure. "Aye, but Brian's not in it."

"How do ye know?"

"They say he's chasing someone," Havland shrugged. Though he professed not to care much for gossip he always seemed to have the best information.

Patric stared at the tent. "Who could he be chasing? I thought he was after Malsakin and he's here?"

"The high queen," Havland retorted, coiling the last bit of rope around the stake then tying it off.

"So, does that mean he won't be with us when we fight?"

"If we fight," Havland corrected then stood brushing the dirt from his hands.

"What do ye mean by that?" Patric retorted lifting an eyebrow in askance. "Of course we'll battle. This army has marched for more than a month for just that purpose."

Havland smiled then rested his arm on Patric's shoulder. "Do I need to explain to ye how this works?"

Patric remained silent telling him that he did.

He sighed, "Brian's after the high crown, aye. After Malsakin betrayed him at Tara he figured that the only way to get it was to have the Ard Ri call him out so he's spent these past seasons marching on O'Neills hoping for just such a thing. But the Ard Ri's nay a fool. He's been figuring that the best way to keep his crown would be to avoid a war with Brian. So far he's been able to do it too."

"So Brian marched us out here hoping that Malsakin would fight in protection of Fladbartoc," Patric added, piecing the puzzle together. "But why should he fight for him and not the others?"

The lad was quick but he was missing information that would put him on the right course. Havland helped him.

"Malsakin came to Ailech to hold court hoping that his presence would demonstrate his willingness to protect his people. Brian uncovered his plan and decided to march us up here right under his nose. It's the worst embarrassment the Ard Ri could suffer. His only hope for recovery will be for him to call us out."

Patric pondered the information for some time before asking, "If ye were Malsakin would ye call Brian out?"

"Nay," Havland answered quickly, proving that he'd already weighed the consequences of either action. "If I were Malsakin, I'd turn myself around and march right back to Tara. Sometimes it's better to keep what ye have rather than risk everything to avoid embarrassment."

"And if he does go back what will Brian do next?"

"I couldn't say," Havland offered solemnly but then he smiled. "Perhaps he's planning to kidnap the high queen."

"Kidnap?"

"Aye."

Patric's face was screwed up unnaturally and Havland chuckled, "Don't ye know that any man who possesses Kormlada also possesses the high throne?"

"Bah," Patric issued with a wave of his hand. "I don't believe in fairy tales."

"'Tis fact," Havland replied. "How do ye think Olaf Curran took the throne, or Malsakin for that matter? It was the woman who brought it to them. Not until each of them possessed her was either named Ard Ri. So, if Brian kidnaps her he can have his throne without a war."

Patric opened his mouth to refute the myth when his attention was again drawn to Brian's tent. A tall chief with flowing white hair was entering the structure. Patric grabbed Havland's shoulder. "Is that Turlog of Thomond?"

Havland squinted against the sun. "Aye. Do ye know him, Shaver?"

"Aye," Patric nodded with a grimace. Ever since Clonmacnoise he'd been dubbed with the name, Shaver. He didn't like it much but he continued on without mentioning it.

"He's Brian's uncle, youngest brother of Cennitig. After my father was killed, Turlog took his place as Brian's closest ally and confidant."

"Ye seem to know much about him," Havland offered with a shrug. "He must be a good man."

"On the contrary," Patric snapped. "Each time Turlog came to Cavenlow my father warned me to be wary of him. He believed Turlog was jealous of his nephew and would one day bring him harm."

"Och," Havland spit throwing a slap in Turlog's direction. "All the nobles are the same in that respect. They're all jealous of each other and would gladly kill their own kin to get what they wanted."

He returned his attentions to the ropes as he continued, "Let me offer some advice, Shaver. Don't get yourself involved in *their* type of politics. It'll only give ye a headache."

Patric kept his eyes on the tent, remembering the long ago night in Cavenlow when he was among the tacticians as the battle plan for Sulcoit was prepared. Turlog wasn't among them then. Lorca had told him that the uncle came late to the battle, only getting into it when he was certain Brian would win. It was unfair that a duplicitous man like Turlog could be close to the Ri Ciocid when a loyal warrior like himself was questioned as a traitor. Without realizing he was speaking he sighed, "I wonder when we'll meet, Brian."

Havland nodded his head. "Ye'll meet when it's yer destiny and nay a moment sooner."

Patric's eyes betrayed his concern and Havland continued, "I can tell ye for certain that ye'll see him if we should need to battle. Aye, when we must spill our blood for him the great Brian Boru will sit upon his horse and address us with his stirring words about uniting Eire and the treachery of the O'Neills. He'll say whatever it takes to make us fight fiercely so he can go home the victor."

Patric smiled and Havland issued him a stunning clap to the back as he barked jovially, "Now help me with this tent, Shaver! Ye're not Ri Tuath yet and I won't be doing yer work for ye till ye are."

*   *   *   *

Ailech, Ireland: The great hall—Two hours past noon—3, December 983 A.D.—Fladbartoc paced within his chamber. Unlike the villages of the south, the great hall of Ailech contained both sleeping chambers and kitchens under one roof so that the Ri Tuath wouldn't have to face inclement weather when he wanted to call a gathering. He parted the animal hides dividing his room from the hall, watching for a moment as his soldiers milled about then he turned toward his captain.

"I should have killed this upstart when I had my chance in Tara. He's nothing but trouble for any of us."

"The Ard Ri has been asking for ye all afternoon. He's desperate for yer counsel."

"Well, let him wait!" Fladbartoc barked, turning away from the curtain. "I can't give him counsel unless I know what Boru's planning. Has there been any word yet?"

"Not a one," the captain replied. "They seem content enough pitching their tents and welcoming new warriors. It's as if they're setting up house."

That brought an audible grumble from Fladbartoc who rubbed his head in wonder. "Well, he must want something. I doubt he's marched all this way for the view."

Fladbartoc's captain lowered his eyes as he shuffled his feet leaving the Ri Tuath to puzzle the situation. At length Fladbartoc looked up as a thought struck him. "If he's making house perhaps we should welcome him."

The captain looked at him. "Pardon?"

Fladbartoc stood silent while he formulated his plan then he turned to his captain to see what he thought about it.

"We are in the north and Boru's men are from the south."

The captain raised his eyebrow as his Ri Tuath stated the obvious but Fladbartoc continued undaunted, "It's winter, aye. Do ye suppose they're prepared for the coming cold?"

"Ah," the captain sighed as he finally caught on.

"Exactly," Fladbartoc replied. "He's waiting us out thinking that Malsakin will strike out of anxiety. Well, let him stay the winter in Ailech. His men will be cold and hungry awaiting a battle that will never come. They'll become disheartened and leave him, creating for him the embarrassment he thought to provide my cousin."

The captain smiled. "By the way they're feasting and celebrating ye can be sure they'll be out of provisions in a fortnight. When they find the lakes frozen over and the game all in hiding they'll be hard pressed to find anything but bark and nuts to fill their bellies. They'll be battling each other for scraps rather than battling the Ard Ri for his crown."

That statement sprung another thought in Fladbartoc's head. "Boru's so stubborn that he might remain despite his inability to feed his army. If he does we'll strike him and be rid of him once and for all."

"Brilliant," the captain sighed. "Simply brilliant." He bowed from the waist then lifted his eyes. "Shall I tell the Ard Ri that ye're ready to see him now?"

"Aye," Fladbartoc offered as he strutted around the room but as the captain turned to go he thought of something else. He smiled. "Once ye've spoken to the Ard Ri I want ye to send a few bottles of wine and several wheels of cheese down to Boru's camp. Tell him it's a gift from his host, Fladbartoc of Ailech then have someone trail the man who stows the food to locate their supply. Perhaps we can ensure their starvation a bit sooner."

The captain smiled then nodded, appreciative of the fact that his Ri Tuath was one of the most cunning men he'd ever met. "It will be as ye say."

He bowed from the waist before making his way out of the chamber to give instruction to his men.

Fladbartoc looked after him then moved to his sideboard, pouring himself a glass of wine and relishing the fact that he was still one step ahead of Boru.

*   *   *   *

Ulster, Ireland: The Camp of Brian Boru—Two hours past noon—3, December 983 A.D.—Connor and Turlog sat outside Brian's tent, the Ri Tuath of Thomond on a folding stool of hide and sticks, the captain on a rock. They were hearing a grievance brought by two warriors regarding a supposed breech in the chain of command when Thorien approached. Connor looked up.

"Do ye have time for me, captain?" the earl asked.

"Aye," Connor nodded thinking he too had a problem. He waved him to a seat.

Thorien preferred not to give his information in the presence of others, especially Turlog who he trusted least among men, but a request to speak with Connor privately would be an offense to the Ri Tuath. He turned to walk away.

"I see that ye're tending important business just now. I'll return later when ye have time for me."

Connor lifted an eyebrow. It was clear the Viking wanted to speak in private and that usually meant that his news was of some importance. He lifted himself from the rock he'd been sitting.

"Walk with me now, Thorien. The Ri Tuath has this business well in hand and I've been remiss in attending my mount. He went lame on the trail. Ye're a horseman, are ye not?"

Thorien nodded and Connor smiled. "Good. Come along then and see if ye can't assist."

They both bowed to Turlog before making their way through camp and into the sparse forest where the horses were tied up. Connor headed toward his gray gelding who lost a shoe on the journey then lifted his leg to check it.

"So, what is it ye have to say that couldn't be said in front of Turlog?"

Thorien smiled for Connor's knowing. He was a good man, ever vigilant in his protection of Brian, most likely because of the affection he held for the Ri Ciocid. All the same, he kept his preferences to himself and was a capable warrior. Any man who claimed him as an ally would be well served.

"I meant nay disrespect," Thorien apologized, "but I wasn't certain how we should handle the situation and thought it best to give ye the information in private so ye could think on it."

Connor nodded his approval then leaned against the horse's hind quarter. "So let's have it."

"Havland has brought Patric macLorca to fight by Brian's side. The lad's in camp as we speak. I think the Ri Ciocid should know of it."

"macLorca?" Connor sighed, grateful to hear the name associated with something other than treachery for a change. He thought of Kevin and a flood of emotions welled inside him. He'd been praying that the young Ri Tuath would finally shed his hatred and come to the Ri Ciocid's call—perhaps he was getting his answer.

"Does he come alone?"

Thorien nodded. "He has, and he's prepared to swear his loyalty to Brian."

"That's well and good," Connor huffed in disappointment, "but I should think that Brian was expecting the Ri Tuath."

"He is the Ri Tuath," Thorien offered with a smile. Connor screwed up his face and he continued, "It's a long story but I've proof that Patric is the rightful heir to Lorca's throne and that Kevin has committed treachery, and possibly murder, to take it from him."

The statement caused Connor's heartbeat to quicken. Rumors about Kevin's treachery had been running rampant for some time but never did anyone offer any proof of them. He was listening to Thorien's explanation of writs and letters all the while wondering how Brian would react when he learned that Patric was the true heir to the throne and that Kevin was a traitor. He needed time to put together a plan that would put him back in Brian's good favor before the truth was revealed.

"Where is he?"

"He's in my camp with the others awaiting his meeting with the Ri Ciocid."

"Ye're certain it's him?" Connor questioned. "Ye know as well as I that there are many who would wish Brian harm. The man could be an imposter seeking to get close enough to the Ri Ciocid to do him damage."

"It's him," Thorien explained with a chuckle. "All ye have to do is look on him to know he's Lorca's son. He holds the same face as his father that one does."

"Well, I'll judge that for myself if ye don't mind," Connor retorted. "And until I do, I don't want ye making any promises to the lad or bringing him anywhere near Brian. Do I make myself clear?"

"Aye, ye do," Thorien nodded. He didn't blame Connor for being suspicious—in fact he appreciated it. In these unstable times it wasn't uncommon for a captain to turn on his leader in exchange for title or lands. Connor's loyalty to Brian was a quality that Thorien found most admirable.

He began to walk away but Connor called out to stop him, "Ye're certain that the lad wasn't sent by his brother to commit treachery?"

Thorien slowly turned, letting the question settle on his mind. He thought of the lad. He was a capable warrior—he proved that when he took Throdier's hair…but a traitor? He considered Patric's personality and the way he looked when he spoke of his father—it was absurd to think that the lad could cause the Ri Ciocid harm.

When he finally opened his mouth to speak Connor interrupted him. "If ye needed to consider it for that long then I suggest ye consider it even longer. I want ye to question the lad long and hard. Leave no stone unturned. Only after ye've convinced yerself that he's loyal will ye return to me so that I can do the same. In the meanwhile, keep him clear of Brian."

Thorien nodded agreement.

*   *   *   *

Ulster, Ireland: The road to Ailech—Four hours past noon—3, December 983 A.D.—The carriage of the high queen rolled slowly up the Ulster Road that had for miles been bounded by forest on either side, but up ahead the trees were cleared. Ailech stood at the end of the road, a shimmering shape surrounded by a sea of moving bodies. Kormlada drew breath.

Thousands of warriors dotted the clearing, drinking, bathing, gambling, and training. Her gods never told her that Boru was bringing his army to Ailech.

"Bastard!" she hissed to herself once she realized his purpose. Malsakin must be beside himself. He was too weak to handle such a thing on his own. "Halt!" she called to the driver with a rap on the carriage ceiling. When the vehicle stopped she gathered up her lein and cape then disembarked with a flourish.

"Shall we turn back, my queen?" the lead guard asked, dismounting in a scramble. They hadn't yet ventured into the clearing. There was still hope that they hadn't been spotted.

"Where is he?" she questioned, her eyes searching the surrounding territory. "Where's Boru?"

"Kormlada!" Maelmora snapped. There was too much to risk for her to take a tantrum now. He leapt from his horse then took her by the elbow. "Get back in the carriage. We must turn back before they see us. It seems yer tryst has led us into a trap."

"To hell with ye!" she barked before rounding on him. "Find Boru so he can give me an explanation as to why his men are here?"

"I pray ye to get back into the carriage. Let us be on our way," Maelmora pleaded, his forehead glistening with the sweat of his fear. "'Tis nay a time for yer childish games." He again grabbed her elbow then began to drag her back to the carriage. She struggled with him, cursing and kicking him about the shins.

At that moment the Ri Ciocid rode his horse through the trees and out onto the road looking as if his only care was the protection of the high queen. "Unhand her!" he barked then with a nod of his head gave the silent message to those guards with him to ride ahead into camp.

Kormlada forced herself from Maelmora's grasp, taking a moment to leer at Brian before marching forward with her nose in the air. She'd had enough of his games and she meant him to know it. "Remove yer men from this field immediately," she demanded, sweeping her hand wide to underscore her point. "The Ard Ri is holding Christmas court in Ailech and I won't have people arriving to this rabble!"

Brian smiled causing his dark eyes to twinkle. He'd heard the woman was bold and it amused him that he could be the cause of her ire. "I'll do nay such a thing."

"Ye will and ye'll do it now!"

He leaned over his horse so that the glower he was offering wouldn't be mistaken for anything else. "Look around ye, lady and tell me what ye see."

She did as he asked, raking the field in a slow precise motion. It was dotted with tents, horses and men. Presumably the later were armed and loyal to him. Suddenly she became nervous. Malsakin didn't know she was coming and because she decided to travel modestly, there wasn't a soul who could vouch that she was there except Sigtrygg—and he was in Dublin. She could feel her skin crawl with her building fear but if she had any chance of escape she mustn't show it.

"I see a collection of worthless rabble," she replied as she swung around to face him.

"Pardon, lady," he offered with a slow nod of his head, "but that rabble ye refer to is only the most skilled compliment of warriors this territory has ever seen. I would suggest that when ye address them in the future ye do it with less hostility."

"Well, I won't be addressing them now nor in the future," she spit. "And I won't be addressing ye either."

She spun on her heel to make her way toward the carriage and Brian dismounted to head her off. Maelmora and her guards closed ranks around her.

"Step aside and throw down yer weapons!" Brian barked without drawing his sword. Any threat he needed to convey was done with his eyes. It seemed to have worked because Maelmora and the high queen's guards complied with his request, their weapons falling to the ground in a heap.

Several of Brian's men rode out to assist but he warned them to stand back before grabbing Kormlada by the wrists. He swung her around, pinning her against the large wheel with his hips.

She didn't fight him, she only leveled her green eyes at his then stated, "Unhand me."

"Aye, but first I want to get a few things straight."

She stood looking at him, her face unchanging and her eyes cold with anger. Her breathing was slightly elevated but he presumed that was due to his restraint of her. He stepped back without releasing her. "I'm taking ye hostage."

"I see," she replied, her voice even and without emotion. Only a fool would have thought otherwise but if he wanted to kidnap her she was planning to make the task as difficult as possible.

"I will keep ye until yer husband agrees to meet me on the field. If he doesn't, I'll lock ye away forever."

"He won't do it," she retorted, her surety causing *him* discomfort. "Malsakin won't buckle to yer blackmail. He'd rather lose me than give a usurper the chance to reign as Ard Ri."

His jaw twitched with the statement and he silently cursed himself for the tell. He couldn't show her that she made him angry lest it weaken his position. "So then, lady, I guess we'll have plenty of time to get acquainted with one and other." His voice carried an underlying threat, which didn't escape her.

She lifted her upper lip in mock disgust. "I'm a hostage, Ri Ciocid, not yer possession. I expect to be treated according to my station, which, I might add, is greater than yers." His disappointment at her coldness showed in his eyes. She continued, "So now, if we're perfectly clear on the conditions, I suggest ye get on with whatever it is ye're planning to do."

"Very well," he retorted, his voice as emotionless as hers. It was obvious she thought herself superior to him—that would soon change.

He took a moment to establish a plan that would demonstrate his authority without the use of violence. When he settled on one he scooped her into his arms and began to walk away. Moments later he realized his mistake.

Kormlada was a tall woman, standing only a quarter head shorter than he. Carrying her wasn't only awkward—it was backbreaking. He could feel his knees buckling with each step he took but he was in it now and there was nothing he could do other than continue on in the direction of his horse.

Maelmora and her guards took a step toward him and he offered a silent prayer of thanks that they did. He took the opportunity to relieve himself of his burden, setting her down beside him with a firm grip on her wrist. He turned toward Maelmora. "Let me be plain," he slowly drawled, taking as much time as he could to recover from his labor. "Ye're all hostages of Brian macCennitig."

Maelmora noticed the odd look in the Ri Ciocid's eyes and for a moment he thought to protest. He decided against it as he looked to Brian's guards surrounding him. In reality there was nothing he could do other than to get them all killed. Besides, Boru had a reputation for being fair. No doubt he would treat them well. Then he chuckled to himself as he looked to his sister who seemed to finally have met her match.

"Is something funny?" the Ri Ciocid asked, his eyes growing suddenly dark with anger.

"Nay," Maelmora replied. He looked to his sister for a moment before lowering his eyes then nodded acceptance of the situation.

Satisfied that he'd find no trouble from the men, Brian turned to face Kormlada. She didn't meet his gaze. Instead she looked off into the distance, never moving a muscle. He heaved a great sigh before bending down low to sling her over his shoulder, hoping that this position would make his burden more manageable. The going was a bit easier as he made his way toward his horse but when he reached it he was faced with a new problem. Kormlada was dead weight and he didn't have the strength after his long ride to lift her into the saddle.

All eyes were on him as he struggled with what to do next. If he lifted her and failed he would be shamed. If he set her down he would be admitting his weakness. He took a deep breath to buy some time but the longer he took to decide what to do the more his inability would be revealed. Finally, he did the only thing he could. He staggered forward into the woods praying that no one would follow.

As they disappeared behind the trees, Brian heard his men leading the other hostages away along the road. He offered up a silent prayer of thanks that he had successfully escaped embarrassment before setting her on her feet. She stood perfectly still.

"I want to thank ye for not putting up a fight," he offered as he circled her. "Ye're quite a load to carry."

She remained silent, looking up into the tree branches. "Come now, ye must have something to say," he cajoled. He liked the fire in her and was hoping to spark it again.

She remained silent so he moved to a log to sit and catch his breath. He looked her over. She was a lady of style. She wore a white cloak and lein trimmed in matching fur but now both were wrinkled from where he'd taken hold of them. The ends of her hair were littered with dead leaves and twigs from being dragged along the forest floor. He shook his head realizing that she must be unused to such harsh treatment and he chuckled to himself as he considered that her silence was a result of her fear of him. At length he got to his feet.

"Alright then, let's be off." He clapped his hands together then began to walk away but she didn't follow.

"Are ye coming?" he asked, eyebrows raised.

It was only then that she turned to look at him, hiding her amusement for what she was about to do. "If ye want me anywhere but on this spot then ye'll have to carry me."

"Ye can't be serious?" There was real pleading in his voice.

She continued to glare at him and he realized his mistake. He'd exposed his weakness and now she was using it against him.

Her cunning amused him but he didn't show it. He continued on in a stern voice, "If ye're thinking I'll be leaving ye behind at the risk of straining my back, ye're sorely mistaken, lady." He smiled. "Now, why don't ye make it easy on yerself and follow me because if I have to lift ye again I can assure ye I won't be so gentle this time."

His cajoling didn't faze her. She remained stone still, her only movement being the turn of her head as she reaffixed her stare on the treetops.

He growled deep in his throat then walked back to where she stood. He looked at her for a long while hoping to intimidate her but she would have no part of it. "As ye wish," he grumbled, aggravation clear in his voice. He squatted low before her, placing her hip against his shoulder so that when he stood she would be draped over him like a sack of grain.

If he thought she was heavy before, she was even more so after his respite. His legs warbled beneath him and he jiggled her a few times to distribute her weight more evenly. "Pick up yer hair," he croaked as his foot became entangled in the long golden tresses.

She did as he instructed but the movement caused him to lose his balance, sending both of them toppling to the ground. He heard the wind get knocked out of her and he scrambled forward, hovering over her to see if she was hurt. "Are ye alright?" he asked as he brushed the hair from her reddened face.

She didn't respond, only stared up toward the treetops.

"Kormlada!" he barked.

Still silence.

He stared at her for a time. It was apparent that she wasn't going to give him the satisfaction of an answer. Tired and frustrated, he crossed his legs and sat on the ground beside her while he considered the situation. "Very well," he finally sighed. "'Tis clear ye have the upper hand so now what do we do?"

"Release me," she replied, still not looking at him. If it were any other time than just then she would have gone with him willingly but both Dublin and Leinster were on the line and she wouldn't lose them to her lust.

"I'm sorry, lady but that is something I can not do."

"Leave me then," she retorted.

"Ye know I can't do that either."

"Well then, I would say that ye're in a quandary."

The anger that he felt was genuine and he ran his fingers through his hair wanting to tear it out. He thought of tying her up and going back for his horse but he'd made such a display of their leaving that it would only serve to embarrass him when his men saw him returning empty handed. He unwittingly fingered the fur of her cloak as he puzzled the situation then a thought came to him. He got to his feet.

"Will ye stand?" he asked as he reached out a hand to her.

Silence.

"Very well then," he blurted.

He stood over her then began to unbuckle his belt. That action caught her attention.

"What do ye mean to do?" she questioned, eyes burning with anger. She'd experienced his passion often enough in her dreams but under these circumstances she had no taste for it. She glowered at him, hoping he would get the message.

It was his turn to remain silent and he tortured her with unknowing as he made slow work of removing the leather belt from his waist, hoping she was worried he would rape her. That would certainly take her down a peg.

She swallowed hard, fighting back the urge to skitter away from him. She was prepared to fight him off but wouldn't move until she was certain of his intention.

His belt was off yet the woman never flinched and Brian raised an eyebrow wondering if the stories about her sexual appetite were true, but now wasn't the time to consider such things. Even if he was so inclined, the long ride and heavy lifting had worn him out. He bent down over her, glaring at her lustfully to see if he could get a rise out of her but when her expression remained unchanged he got right down to business.

He wrapped her cloak snuggly around her body to restrain her then slipped the belt around her ankles, feeding the excess strap through the buckle until it acted as a handle. He tugged a few times to be sure it wouldn't come loose before lifting it over his shoulder.

In that instant, Kormlada realized what he was planning to do. "Ye wouldn't dare!" she exclaimed, outraged that the barbarian was fully prepared to drag her through the forest. She was just about to give in to his command that she accompany him on her own two feet when she caught the smug look in his eye. He was confident that he had won his battle. Well, she wouldn't give him the satisfaction. If she was too heavy to carry she was sure she'd be too difficult to drag. Let him expend his energy if he wanted to gain his trophy.

The years of battle that Brian experienced with Grace taught him never to back down from a stubborn woman. And it seemed that Kormlada was very much like his sister. Resigned to the task at hand he gave another tug on the strap then whistled a tune as he dragged his hostage through the woods, making little attempt to avoid the bumps.

*   *   *   *

Dublin, Ireland: The great hall—Four hours past noon—3, December 983 A.D.—Kevin craned his neck as he passed through the massive doors. He'd heard that the great hall at Dublin was the only one to rival that of Tara but to see it for himself was certainly a treat.

It seemed the room was endless, crammed wall to wall with rows of tables and the men to fill them. Colorful banners hung from the rafters and tapestries covered the walls. The fireplaces were so large that a cow could be roasted on a spit without need of butchering.

When Kevin gave Malsakin the news that Brian was marching to Ailech the Ard Ri set aside his plans for Leinster and instead gave *him* the burden of traveling to Dublin to gain reinforcements. He'd left the northern round fort angry that he was being treated as a messenger but he was provided with several riders to compliment his own and enough rations to make the trip enjoyable.

He spotted Sigtrygg sitting at the head table in the glorious chair of the Dublin earl. It was clearly the chair of a great man, high backed and gilded, upholstered in blue satin. He bristled that the young lad would take the privilege while his master was away, but it seemed Sigtrygg thought he belonged there as he comfortably chatted with several warriors.

Kevin had never met Olaf but he'd heard him described often enough. The lad had the markings of his father, fine built with light hair and fierce green eyes.

He sported a sparse beard that told his age was yet tender but he held himself regally. He turned with Kevin's approach. "Sigtrygg of Dublin?" Kevin queried.

"Aye," the lad responded. "And who might ye be?"

"I'm Kevin of Cavenlow. Ye're father sent me with a message."

"My father's dead!" Sigtrygg snapped back, his left brow shooting up with his suspicion.

"Excuse me for misspeaking," Kevin retorted. "I presumed that the Ard Ri had taken over those duties."

The shiver running up Sigtrygg's spine caused him to straighten. He cursed his own tongue while praying that the man wouldn't relay his transgression. "Aye, that he did. So is it the Ard Ri who sent ye?" Sigtrygg asked suspiciously. Cavenlow had long been allied with Brian Boru but lately there were rumors that the new Ri Tuath was willing to sell his loyalty for a crown of his own.

Kevin nodded in answer to Sigtrygg's question then made his way to the chair the young prince was offering. When he was seated he was met by two serving maids, one bearing food the other drink. He nodded his appreciation then took a sip from his cup before speaking. "Boru's marching north toward Ailech to embarrass yer fa—the Ard Ri. Malsakin asks that ye gather an army so I can lead them back to him."

Sigtrygg's eyes opened wide. Obviously the rumors were true about Kevin and this bit of news about Boru being a nuisance to the Ard Ri pleased him immensely. "Don't tell me that Malsakin has finally decided to give Boru a battle?"

"Nay," Kevin offered with a shake of his head, "but he does want to show all the force he can muster. He's hoping that with reinforcements, Boru will realize he's outnumbered and back down."

"How many is Boru bringing?"

"I couldn't say," Kevin sighed, angry that his plans were being put off because of Brian's mischief.

"And did the Ard Ri say where I'm supposed to gather this army from? He's taken all his warriors with him."

Though Sigtrygg's voice was even, Kevin could see the amusement in his eyes. He set aside his anger in exchange for curiosity as he wondered what troubles the lad had with the Ard Ri. "He didn't say, Sigtrygg. He only asked that I come to ye with the request."

Sigtrygg took a sip from his cup then motioned to a large man standing behind him. The man took the few steps necessary to put himself at the lad's shoulder.

"Ivan, the Ard Ri has asked that we gather an army and send them north. How long would it take for ye to do such a thing?"

Kevin looked to Ivan. He wasn't very tall but he was forceful looking. His red hair hung in long braids to his shoulder and his face was leathered and battle scarred. Obviously a Viking.

"I couldn't say, lord," Ivan offered as he cocked his head. "I could try in Caran Balder but that would take weeks. Ferta Nime is much closer but I believe the Ard Ri has had a falling out with it's Ri Tuath."

Sigtrygg shook his head as Ivan gave him the information he already had. He only asked for Kevin's benefit. "Even though Brian was the one to kill Balder's mother, it was Malsakin who benefited from the deed. If Balder came at all it would only be with half a heart. The Ri Tuath of Ferta Nime is due at Christmas court. Malsakin invited him to smooth over the troubles but I hardly think he'll go if we tell him there may be a battle. Most likely he'd choose to wait it out in the event a new Ard Ri came out of it."

"There must be someone the Ard Ri can call on," Kevin issued, eyebrow raised in suspicion. Malsakin had sent *him* to Sigtrygg and it would be *his* neck on the line if he returned to Ailech without an army. "Ye can't deny him without an attempt."

Sigtrygg pretended to ponder the situation, but in truth he had little desire in fulfilling the Ard Ri's request. He too knew that Kevin would be held responsible for the failure.

"'Tis a pity that the Ard Ri has left Leinster to Brian. If he'd reclaimed it as my mother requested we could have a band of warriors gathered in three days time."

Kevin saw through Sigtrygg's pretense and grinned evilly as he stated, "'Tis the truth ye speak, but if Olaf had kept his hands around the territory in the first place, Brian could never have gained it."

The statement was intended to rile the lad and by the scowl on Sigtrygg's face it seemed to be working. Kevin pressed on, eager to scratch the surface of this delicate family web. "It must be galling to ye that yer mother's homeland is in the hands of a usurper. I should think that ye'd be better suited to handle it than Brian is."

Sigtrygg's anger faded with the comment. He was so desperate to be seen as a leader instead of a mere lad that he decided to boast for the Cavenlow Ri Tuath.

"Leinster would be too quiet for me. My mother prefers me to have Dublin. She knows I'm the only one capable of running it."

That statement was enough to tell Kevin that his plan would work. He chose his words carefully to ensure that Sigtrygg would answer then took hold of his cup as he leaned in to whisper, "How many warriors would ye say ye had in the hall, lad?"

Sigtrygg scowled at the use of the term but still he let his eyes sweep the room. "Half more than three hundred. Perhaps four. Why do ye ask?"

"Are they yer father's warriors or do they belong to Malsakin?"

Sigtrygg turned to look at Kevin, unsure of where the questions were leading but too intrigued not to answer. "They belonged to Olaf."

"Hmmm." Kevin considered this information as he scratched his beard then looked around the room. If nothing else he was a convincing actor. "Nay, 'twill never work," he sighed as his shoulders slumped forward.

"What won't work?" Sigtrygg asked anxiously.

"I was only thinking…" Kevin let his voice trail off as he again shook his head.

"Tell me what ye were thinking," Sigtrygg urged. "Perhaps I could offer my opinion and Ivan can offer his."

"Very well," Kevin replied with a shrug. "We'd be nay worse off with the thought out in the open than we are right now." He took a moment to sip from his cup and Ivan and Sigtrygg leaned in, eager to hear what he would say.

"I was thinking that the Ard Ri would be miffed if I rode back to Ailech to tell him that *ye* couldn't raise an army to assist him." Sigtrygg frowned and began to defend his position when Kevin continued, "Rather than suffer the Ard Ri's ire, perhaps we can use the warriors ye have here to draw Brian away from Ailech."

Ivan shook his head. "If Boru's marching to Ailech to seek a battle I doubt there's anything that can be done to draw him back."

"Even a raid?" Kevin inquired with brows raised.

Sigtrygg sat forward in his chair. "Ye mean us to raid Munster while the Ri Ciocid's away?" His eyes were wide with excitement.

"Not Munster but Leinster," Kevin replied. "Think on it. We'll raid the Galls in Leinster under Brian's own banner and send word north that it happened. Brian will have nay choice but to ride out to see what it's all about. When he does it will look like the Ard Ri frightened him away."

Ivan slowly nodded his head. "It'd certainly be easier to raid the Leinster Galls than it would be to raid in Munster. Besides, they've got it coming with the way they turned on Olaf. But I'm not certain that a raid will be enough to draw Brian's attention."

"Believe me," Kevin started, the grin on his face telling anyone who would notice of his confidence, "when Brian hears that a Dal Cais is raiding Leinster Galls he'll fly out of Ailech like a bat out of hell. The last thing he wants is to have to suffer their ire."

"But who'll do it?" Sigtrygg asked innocently. "The Dal Cais hate the O'Neills and Olaf never had any allies among them. How do we find a Dal Cais willing to work with us?"

"Ye needn't look any further than the end of yer nose," Kevin offered, swallowing his exasperation for the lad's naivety. "Ye just give me yer warriors and leave the rest to me. I promise that when the Ard Ri finds out what ye've done for him he'll give ye Dublin without question."

Sigtrygg squared his shoulders in triumph. If Kevin's plan worked he could have both his mother and Malsakin eating out of his hand.

"Let's do it!" he commanded.

CHAPTER 15

▼

Ulster, Ireland: The camp of Brian Boru—One hour past dawn—14, December 983 A.D.—The sky was dreary and heavy with clouds blotting out the sun that was rising over the mountains. Freezing rains had been plaguing the camp for the better part of a week and today promised to be no different.

Brian awoke with a nagging headache, most likely brought on by his hunger. His plan had been a good one, or so he thought. Now he was left to wonder. He'd been certain that Malsakin would be willing to fight in defense of his wife but it seemed that Kormlada's statement was true—the Ard Ri would rather lose her than to offer his throne to a usurper.

He hadn't set eyes on the woman since he dragged her back to camp—in fact he'd barely seen anyone. He'd spent the better portion of the last days holed up in his tent hearing grievances from his troops who were complaining most regularly about the cold and their hunger. They'd lost a good portion of their supplies to what they suspected was rot and due to the weather the hunting parties weren't finding much success.

He rubbed at his temples as he decided on a course of action then he rose to his feet, ran his fingers through his hair and made off to speak with his hostage.

Kormlada didn't need to hear him coming, she could feel him through her very skin. She had been thankful that he hadn't come to her sooner for in truth she didn't know what she would say to him.

On that first day, when she was dragged into camp, she had been smug and indignant over her capture so when Boru allowed her to send a message back with Fladbartoc's guards she advised Malsakin against battle no matter how long the Dal Cais held her. It seemed a good idea at the time. Boru was treating her fairly, providing a tent for both her and her brother and even allowing them to keep some of the cheese and wine Fladbartoc sent with his man, but she hadn't seen the Ri Ciocid, or anyone else besides the one assigned to care for her since that day. Now she wondered if she'd done the right thing.

Solitude wasn't something Kormlada relished—on the contrary. Since childhood she surrounded herself with people who she could talk to and who would care for her. She'd rather burn her skin with hot irons than suffer the sentence of being left alone with her thoughts—and her visions. And there were visions— thousands of them flooding her mind until she thought she would go mad. They ranged from bloody battles to the transfer of crowns, but the ones that scared her most were those of Brian.

Somewhere amongst the flashes of faces and words she was able to pick out a clear vision of Brian taking her to wife and after that, the crown of the Ard Ri. Though she couldn't tell from the visions when it would happen she did know that it wouldn't take place in Ailech. This put her in a most precarious position. If she was destined for Brian it would make sense to assist him now but if she did she would be condemned by Malsakin.

She was lying across the bed of skins pondering the situation when suddenly Brian's presence consumed her. She lifted herself on her elbows, flipping her long braid over her left shoulder as she held her breath waiting for his call. It came within moments.

"May I speak with ye, high queen?"

She let his words hang in the air while she scrambled to her feet, smoothing her lein and pinching her cheeks to bring the color. She let out a deep breath before sauntering to the tent flap. "Who calls?" she questioned to put him off the fact that she knew he was coming.

"'Tis Brian macCennitig. I've a need to speak with ye."

She took another deep breath then exhaled before lifting the flap to let him in. She was silent as he ducked his head through the opening but when she looked at him she gasped. "What's happened to ye?" she asked in a voice filled with worry. His skin was loose on his frame from weight loss and there were dark smudges on his cheek.

Embarrassed by her repulsion, he straightened his shoulders and tried to look less haggard. "Come now, lady, I didn't think I was as ghastly as that. In fact there's a lass or two out there who might find me handsome. I know my wife does."

The stab of discomfort Kormlada felt with the mention of Brian's wife brought a thought into her head. Both of them were married and in order to come together their spouses would have to be either set aside or dead. She was thinking about this when his question caught her attention.

"How much longer do ye think he'll let ye stay before making a move?"

Kormlada took a moment to consider the question then she shook her head slowly. "As I told ye before, I believe the Ard Ri would rather lose me than…"

"That's just absurd!" Brian barked with frustration. "What kind of man would let his wife be held captive right under his nose without fighting for her?"

Indeed.

Kormlada thought about Malsakin. As much as he feared losing her he also trusted her advice and she had advised him not to give in. She turned her back on the Ri Ciocid, preferring to hide her face from him so he couldn't read it. "Perhaps ye should just let us go."

"Never!" Brian barked. He had gone to her tent with the hope that he could gently persuade her to send a message to Malsakin begging him to rescue her, but there was something about the woman that got his juices flowing and he couldn't keep a civil tongue in his head.

He walked over to her, the heat within him building with each step he took. He tried to tamp it down and was certain he had a grip on himself when he touched her on the shoulder to draw her attention. "Our supplies are growing meager and I may become unable to give ye the care that's proper if he doesn't make a move soon."

She knew his lips were moving but she couldn't hear his words as the voices of others filled her head. The tent grew cloudy and suddenly all she could see was the vision that consumed her. She reached out for him, blinded with the sight.

"What is it?" he asked, his face twisting with concern as he took her hands in his.

"The lad's close," she mumbled. "He's not dead as they profess. It's a trap."

"What do ye speak of?"

"He wants to come to ye but they won't let him."

"Who won't let him?" Brian huffed, struggling to hide his fear. Her eyes were wild yet hazy as if she couldn't see him and he worried that she'd been feed some of the spoiled meat they had found among their supplies.

"Kormlada," he shouted, shaking her with force. "Who do ye speak of? Are ye ill, woman?"

All at once the vision released her and she slumped forward against his chest. Her breathing was labored and it was all she could do to lift her head so she could meet his gaze. "Go away from here now, Brian Boru. Return to yer people in the north because treachery is brewing there. Ye'll gain yer crown soon enough but it won't be in Ailech."

He searched her eyes for a time, wondering what she was talking about then at length he pushed her away from him, a grin spreading across his face. "Don't play yer games with me, woman. I'm nay yer husband."

Kormlada's back stiffened. "What games? What is it ye accuse me of?" she asked, suddenly indignant.

He laughed out loud then shoved her away until she almost stumbled over the animal furs. "Save yer visions for Malsakin. At least then the drama won't be wasted."

She opened her mouth to reply but his back was turned against her as he exited the tent. "Prepare yerself, lady. It seems yer captivity will be a long one."

✳   ✳   ✳   ✳

Torshav, Ireland in the county of Leinster: Just past noon—20, December 983 A.D.—The thriving village of Torshav was steeped in Viking history. It was settled by the earl, Ragnall, the grandson of Imar of Limerick then passed to the hands of his cousin, Gamal the Black when Malsakin drove the Vikings from Tara.

Set high atop a hill, it was bounded by Clonmacnoise to the north, Dublin to the east and the River Shannon to its far west. It was from that direction that Kevin approached with no less than three hundred soldiers riding on horseback.

They were disguised in yellow tunics with the mark of three dancing lions over their chain mail. All except, Kevin carried swords as they prepared to relieve the Viking earl of his possessions.

Gamal, who had been sitting in the yard teaching his older son, Cal, to play chess while his youngest son, Njord, looked on, rose to his feet. He lifted an inquisitive eyebrow to see the *Ri Ciocid's* men arriving without benefit of notice then turned to Cal, tightening the string of his breeches as he called, "Take yer brother into the house and tell yer mother to keep him there then bring me my blade."

The order was issued in his native Manx tongue, a hybrid of Gaelic and Norwegian spoken in both Orkney and Man.

The lad was instantly in motion, taking his brother by the hand and nearly colliding with Gamal's captain, Finn, who was coming from the other direction. Finn stopped just long enough to let the lads pass then rushed forward to offer his explanation to Gamal. He too spoke in Manx. "They say they've come for the tribute."

"Tribute?" Gamal muttered as he raised an eyebrow. Though Boru was known for seeking tribute from those he protected Gamal and the others who had stood with him against Olaf were given leave of this demand. Something was amiss.

"How much does he ask?"

"A-all your cattle!" the captain stammered.

"All?" Gamal let the words settle on his brain before cracking a smile that revealed a dimple in his left cheek and one also on his chin. "Ye're joking of course."

The expression on Finn's face confirmed the truth of the matter but before the captain could utter the words Gamal's attention was drawn to Cal who was dragging the heavy sword behind him. Gamal took it, never letting his eyes slip from the vision of the approaching horsemen as he slung the holster over his shoulders.

"Well, we'll just have to see about that," he barked. This time he spoke the words in Gaelic.

With holster securely in place, he raised his left arm in greeting as he called, "Hail Dal Cais. Welcome to Torshav."

Kevin smiled wickedly as he looked the man over. Gamal was large of both height and breadth with long, dark hair drawn back from his forehead into a tail at the back while the rest hung freely past his shoulders. The shadow of his beard told that it would also be dark and his skin glowed amber from the sun. The tiny crow's feet at the corners of his sparkling gray eyes looked more like decoration than a sign of aging. Kevin immediately resented the man for his beauty.

He pulled back hard against the horse's reins causing it to rear up over the earl. Gamal's gray eyes quickly turned to tiny slits of glowing anger as he pushed Cal back out of harms way.

Kevin issued a deep belly laugh as the Dublin warriors bared their swords. "We've come for yer cattle," he called.

Gamal looked to Finn as if to apologize for not believing him earlier then back at Kevin. "How ma.." Startled by the violence he had started to speak in Manx then quickly changed to Gaelic, "How many will ye take?"

"Why, all of them of course," Kevin responded, his smile broader than before.

"But that makes nay sense," Gamal retorted, his brain scrambling to comprehend the situation. The request ran contrary to all he knew about Boru and he meant to know why the Ri Ciocid would single him out for this harsh treatment.

"Has Boru forgotten that I stood with him against Olaf?" he called out, softening his eyes to inspire trust. "I've already sworn my allegiance to the Dal Cais. I'm certain that it must be someone else ye seek."

He let his eyes go still softer and a smile played on his face. "Why not come inside? We can sort this out over a drink and a noonday meal."

Kevin leaned forward, crossing his arms over the horse's neck as he continued to smile. "There'll be nay discussion. Boru demands his tribute and I'm here to collect. My men have already secured yer beasts and are driving them down the hill as we speak. I only came to inform ye of it."

The statement demanded action and Gamal gave it, drawing his sword then moving forward to deliver his blow. In an instant, twenty soldiers dismounted. With practiced swiftness they formed a line before Kevin's horse, goading the earl to approach as they raised their weapons in preparation.

Gamal stopped just short of them then cast an eye across the expanse of the village in search of his own guards. Noticing his actions Kevin cooed, "Och aye, I almost forgot. We've taken yer guards as insurance that ye'll not be coming after us."

This time it was Finn who was moving and before the earl could stop him he was locked in battle with one of Kevin's guards.

A distant cousin of Gamal, Finn too was large of height and breadth, but while Gamal's hair glowed blue from its blackness, Finn's carried a muddy red hue.

The blow from the soldier's fist fell squarely on Finn's bulbous nose, breaking it along old cracks. He let out a growl as he lifted his sword and immediately the sword of the soldier came up to block it, the metal ringing loudly in both their ears as it clashed.

Finn stepped back long enough to wipe the strands of sweat soaked hair from his eyes then rushed in again, fist wrapped around the sword hilt as he smashed it into the soldiers left eye. His other hand came up to deliver a blow to the soldier's gut.

The chain mail beneath the soldier's tunic reduced the impact significantly but still he doubled over. As he did, Finn unleashed an unmerciful assault upon his face sending him staggering backwards.

Realizing that it would only be a matter of time before the Dublin warrior was downed, Kevin sent a silent order for another to assist, and assist he did, lunging forward to sink his short sword deep into Finn's back causing the captain's knees to collapse beneath him. Gamal moved to assist him but Kevin held up his hand. "Leave him be," he ordered.

Gamal looked up, hatred spewing from every pore in his body as his hands trembled and his voice cracked, "What kind of a man is Boru to take everything I have as the price of tribute?"

Kevin issued Gamal a tsk-tsk look as he shook his head. "Come now, Gamal, we haven't taken everything." He nodded his chin in the direction of Cal who'd been standing silently as he watched the encounter, "We've left ye yer family which is more than yer kin did for us."

With that he cocked his head in a silent order for the soldiers to remount then he reined his horse right to make a wide circle around Finn who was squirming on the ground gasping for air.

He returned to the path leading away from the house then called back as he rode, "We'll be back soon enough to collect what's left."

Gamal rushed to Finn's side, stripping off his coat and balling it against the wound to stem the flow of blood. When he was sure his captain would survive, he looked back at the retreating soldiers and wondered what manner of man this Boru really was.

✳   ✳   ✳   ✳

Ailech, Ireland: The campsite of Brian Boru—Three hours to midnight— 24, December, 983 A.D.—"Shaver, wake up," Havland whispered while shaking Patric's shoulder, his voice hoarse from the sore throat he'd been suffering.

The lad's head was already in motion from his chattering teeth. His lips were blue with the cold and his eyelashes were slick with moisture. They fluttered with Havland's call. "Wake up! The Ri Ciocid calls!"

Patric sat up with a start, feeling as if he would snap in two. Both his back and stomach ached—the former from sleeping on the cold ground, the later from hunger. They were fleeting thoughts as he threw back the meager furs covering him. "Does he call me?"

"Aye," Havland nodded. He was gaunt and pale but a smile split his beard. "He calls us all. We're marching on Fladbartoc."

"A march at this hour?" Patric rubbed the sleep from his eyes then stood to stretch.

"Well, more like a raid," Havland admitted. "Brian's decided that he won't let us continue to suffer starvation and cold while there's food to be had in Ailech. He wants us to form up and storm the round fort. We have leave to take anything we like."

"What about Malsakin's soldiers and the guards of the other leaders at court?" Patric questioned, wondering if they could find success. "They outnumber us by hundreds and they're all well fed."

Havland nodded acceptance of that point. "Our hope is to surprise them. Besides," he said with a shrug of his shoulders, "if I have to leave this earth I'd prefer it to be in battle rather than freezing to death as we are."

Patric looked around the field of warriors preparing for the raid. They were little more than shadows against the dim light cast by the many fires but they all seemed as eager as Havland.

Their food supply had dwindled some time ago and they'd been relegated to eating what little vegetation there was to be found in order to keep up their strength. They'd gladly massacre each other for a bit of meat. If nothing else, Brian was a brilliant war strategist.

Patric shook his head as he thought of the Ri Ciocid. His early inquiries to Thorien about when he might see the man were met with a barrage of questions about Kevin and then finally the relay of information that Brian hadn't yet joined them. By the time Brian *had* joined them his time was consumed with trying to deal with the cold and tainted food rations that could leave them all starved. There was no time for meetings with old friends.

He rubbed some warmth into his hands as he followed Havland to the center of the field. Once they joined the rest of Thorien's group, they were given orders to storm the round fort and take anything they desired. However, they were forbidden to strike the Ard Ri or the Ri Tuaths—they would be left for Brian. Everyone else was fair game.

Patric looked around at the faces of the various warriors whooping in delight for their impending battle. Several had painted lines on their faces and others were stripped to their bare skin, revealing their exposed ribs from the lack of food, but all carried weapons and a gleam in their eye that told anyone who challenged them they meant business.

Suddenly the field was in motion. Patric presumed that Brian was among those men sitting upon horses at the front of the attack but he couldn't be certain since the clouds were lying low in the sky covering the moon. He trotted beside Havland until they reached the battered down gates of Ailech then he skittered behind him to enter the round fort. Once inside, sheer mayhem ensued. The O'Neill guards were overrun by the starving Dal Cais army who were fighting viciously to get at whatever food they could lay hands on. Patric's sword immediately crossed with that of an enemy. He easily disposed of him, cutting him across his cheek to leave his eye dangling from its socket. The next guard caught him by surprise and he was cut on the leg before he was able to drive his blade into the man's throat. He disposed of several more in similar fashion as he moved ever closer to the doors of the great hall.

It took just under an hour to bring the O'Neill guards into submission. Once done, their weapons were collected and they were huddled onto the field to watch as the Dal Cais raiders took their reward. Fires blazed in the field to roast the quickly butchered cattle caught by the starving warriors. Kegs of ale and honey mead were split open with battleaxes, showering the warriors with the golden liquid of life. But while the rest of the army fought to feed their hunger, Patric fought with the single minded hope that he would finally meet his king.

By the time he reached the hall, any O'Neill guard visible had surrendered his weapon. They lined the wall of the great hall but none moved to stop him as Patric pushed his way through the doors. He stopped just a few feet in, unable to get past the sea of people packing the hall right up to the front where Brian and Fladbartoc were conversing.

"Damn ye, Boru!" Fladbartoc shouted while watching Brian's warriors remove the riches. "Ye leave me barren!"

"I'm doing to ye what ye did to my people!" Brian thundered.

"That's a lie and ye know it!" Fladbartoc barked back. He was standing defiantly but his eyes betrayed his fear. He gave a quick glance over his shoulder to the guards who blocked the way to where Malsakin was hidden. Boru was embarrassing him in front of his cousin and his guests.

Brian leaned across the table causing Fladbartoc to sit with a thud. "Is it now?" he questioned smugly. "Then why do I find the communion chalice from my own abbey among yer treasure?"

Fladbartoc looked away. He'd been so certain that Boru would leave Ailech once his men were cold and starving that he talked his cousin out of canceling Christmas court. But not even poisoned provisions and frostbite could dissuade Brian from his goal. Fladbartoc was near tears as he begged the Ri Ciocid to help him save face.

"How will I feed these people now, Brian?" he whispered, leaning in close so the others wouldn't hear. "Ye've taken all my cattle."

Brian's eyes widened with Fladbartoc's plea and a smirk played on his lips. He took a moment to consider the situation then bent to his page who was standing beside him. He whispered something that sent the lad running from the hall then he began pacing and whistling happily, swinging his heavy blade between two fingers as he went.

Patric watched Brian intently. He noticed the twinkle in the *Ri Ciocid's* blue eyes. It was clear he was in good humor.

And what humor will he be in if ye reveal yerself to him now? Patric thought to himself. He remembered the way Thorien first greeted him. *Yer family has been marked as traitors.*

At length he swallowed his doubts then edged forward to make his announcement. This might be his only opportunity to reveal himself and he wouldn't fall victim to his own imagination. As if will were words, just then Brian turned, snapping his head around until his gaze seemed to be leveled straight at Patric. He ceased his whistling then moved forward slowly, eyes squinting to see further in the low light of the hall.

Patric cleared his throat, swallowing hard to be sure his voice would be heard above the din of conversing warriors then smiled as Brian opened his arms.

Could this be happening? Could this be real?

Patric's head was spinning with emotion. He moved toward Brian's embrace, tears in his eyes and a lump in his throat that threatened to take his voice. He wasn't certain what he should say but he was sure that he should say something quickly. He opened his mouth then winced when nothing more than an inaudible croak escaped his lips.

Several warriors turned to see where the noise had come from and Brian's brows rushed together in askance. Patric licked his lips then cleared his throat to try again, but before he could get the words out his joy was ripped from him when he realized Brian hadn't been looking at him at all.

A smile played on Brian's face when the page reappeared in the doorway. He was no more than fifteen summers old, tall and finely built with regal features that made Patric wonder if he was Brian's son, Murchad but then he remembered that Murchad would be much older. A thick rope was slung over each of the lad's shoulders—one attached to a bull, the other a cow. The page moved forward slowly until he was certain that the animals would follow then stepped up his pace to deliver them to his master.

Brian rubbed the lad's head before accepting the ropes then spun on his heel to face Fladbartoc. He chortled when he handed him the ropes. "Here's a gift so ye may feed yer house, Fladbartoc. Pray they act as rabbits."

Fladbartoc sat stunned while the hall erupted in laughter. Even his kin seemed to find humor in his humiliation and he glared at them in silent warning to regain their composure. Most complied but the few who still had smirks lingering on their lips caused Brian to chuckle still harder.

Though he hadn't gained his battle Brian certainly created an embarrassing situation for the Ard Ri and his cousin. The Munster army would have ample provisions for their march back home and in due time word of his deed would spread among the O'Neill leaders. Soon enough he would have his battle and his crown—he was certain of it.

He thought of Kormlada and the strange words she offered him that day in her tent. A shiver ran up his spine. He shook it off then called out to Connor, "Deliver the Ard Ri his hostages immediately."

He turned back one last time to offer a red faced Fladbartoc a gentle bow from the waist then spun on his heel to head for the door.

It was then that Patric made his move, pushing and shoving the wall of warriors to put himself in Brian's path. He recognized what Brian had accomplished and now there wasn't a doubt in his mind that his king would welcome him with open arms. His heart pounded with a sudden fury when the surge of warriors at his back threatened to displace him but he held fast, waiting for the few strides it would take for Brian to reach him.

The dozens of outstretched hands groping at Brian to offer their congratulations slowed the Ri Ciocid's exit as he stopped to touch each and every one of them. Today's victory was as much theirs as it was his and he would show them his appreciation even if it meant staying in Fladbartoc's hall far longer than he should. He reached a long arm over the head of a shorter man to shake the hands of a few men in the back when suddenly a horse came barreling through the door. Except for Brian's guards who moved to surround the Ri Ciocid to keep him from harm, all eyes turned toward the rider.

Fladbartoc bolted to his feet with the sound of the approaching horse. If a rider got through without assault from Boru's army, perhaps Sigtrygg had been successful in gaining support from Balder. Right now there could be thousands of warriors outside the door ready to battle and to send Brian packing back to Munster, or better yet, to hell. He smiled smugly with the thought of his victory but just as he was about to call for Brian's surrender, he realized his mistake.

The rider wore a yellow tunic displaying three red lions marking him as a Dal Cais rider. His expression was grim and Fladbartoc issued a silent order to one of his guards to go and see what was happening. The guard edged his way forward.

The rider dismounted with a flourish then moved quickly toward the tight circle of men where Brian stood in the center. He gained immediate access before the circle closed once again, thwarting the efforts of Fladbartoc's guard to get close enough to hear.

Patric thought the rider looked familiar. When he realized it was Kevin's man, Garvin, he thought his brother might have finally come to his senses. Overcome with joy he elbowed Fladbartoc's guard in an effort to get by him. He was met with a sudden blow to his gut. "And where do ye think ye're going?" the man growled, hatred flaming in his eyes.

Unable to keep his legs beneath him, Patric groaned before crumbling to the ground in a heap. The guard smiled wryly then drew back his foot to kick him but he stopped suddenly as a strong, brilliant cry boomed from deep within the cluster of men protecting the Ri Ciocid. "Naaaaaaaaay!"

Every head turned toward the voice, wondering what news could have caused the Ri Ciocid to call out that way but no one could see what was happening within. Forgetting his assault on Patric, Fladbartoc's guard moved forward in time to see Brian mount the messenger's horse. Suddenly the circle of men separated and the Ri Ciocid galloped the animal toward him. Fladbartoc's man jumped clear of its path but Patric remained where he had fallen, barely able to lift his head in time to see the oncoming danger. He reached out blindly, catching the strap of the horse's harness in his hand and causing it to rear up so he could roll clear of it's path. He felt his arm snap.

Not realizing what had happened, Brian struggled to keep his seat, a barrage of curses streaming from his lips. Only after he regained control of the animal did he realize what caused it to rear up. His eyes settled on Patric and it seemed an eternity passed with the glance as the young man's watery eyes begged for the Ri Ciocid to recognize him. There was no recognition. The Ri Ciocid nodded apologetically before turning his mount toward the door. "Brian, wait!" Patric shouted, reaching up with his broken arm and causing it to flop sideways.

It was then that pandemonium broke out as the Dal Cais warriors stormed the door. Brian's sudden departure would leave them vulnerable to any O'Neill warriors seeking retaliation. They drew their swords, keeping their backs pressed against each other and their eyes sweeping the room in preparation for attack. They hardly noticed Patric under their feet, or if they did, they paid him no mind.

Patric tried to protect his face with his hands but his left arm was useless. He pulled it close then tucked it under his body before the heavy foot came down on his temple, knocking him unconscious.

CHAPTER 16

▼

Ulster Ireland—Inside the tent of the hostage Kormlada: Dawn—25, December 983 A.D.—Turlog paced before the high queen and her brother, hands clasped behind his back and a scowl on his face. Brian fled without a word to anyone leaving him scrambling to decide how best to conclude negotiations with the Ard Ri. He called his new captain, Connor, to accompany him to the high queen's tent and sent Brian's son, Murchad, to gather the troops back from their feasting. Several had already made off with cattle and booty they'd taken from the round fort leaving their already outnumbered contingent that much more lean, but he knew Malsakin wouldn't formally strike until his wife was returned to him.

"Brian has ordered ye returned to the Ard Ri and so I will comply," he offered, his snarling upper lip proving that he didn't agree with the action. "However," he continued, "ye won't be turned over until our troops are well away and that will take some time."

Kormlada opened her mouth to protest but Maelmora quickly headed her off. He understood how precarious the situation was and he wasn't about to tempt fate. While Brian was known to be fair, Turlog had a reputation for going back on his word. Many was the time that he sent hostages back to their kings maimed. He, for one, treasured his well manicured digits too much to find them cut off to sate Turlog's sadistic tendencies.

"Ye'll receive nay trouble from us, lord," he offered with a nod of his head.

"Good," Turlog replied, leering at him to instill cooperation. "Ye'll travel with us as far as Ferta Nime then we'll send ye back with yer own caravan."

He spun on his heel then exited. Connor was tight behind him. It wasn't until they were out of earshot that Turlog commanded, "I want the troops out first. They'll provide escort to the high queen. Have them travel the woods wherever possible. Leave Thorien's band behind. If Malsakin decides to make a show of it I'd prefer foreign blood be spilled then that of the Dal Cais."

"Aye," Connor agreed. Turlog was a fair strategist. He saw nothing in the plan that would leave them vulnerable. He watched his new master depart. The man always looked as though he carried a great weight on his shoulders making him appear much older than his nephew who was only a year or two his junior.

Connor's face grew somber as he thought of Brian. Nearly the same age as Turlog, Brian was still virile and spry. His movements, whether in battle or in life, were always graceful and confident. He shook his head to release the image from his mind but instantly it returned when Murchad rode up on his gray stallion.

Though he was smiling, Connor's stomach tightened with the realization that Brian's son would likely replace him as captain of the Ri Ciocid's army. Murchad was a beautiful man, as much so as his father. His shoulders were broad and his legs long, similar to Brian's but in his coloring he favored his mother—dark of both hair and eyes. He raised his arm in greeting. "Hail, Connor."

Connor nodded politely then got right down to business. "What's our number?"

"I should say less than seven hundred," Murchad replied, his eyes expressionless.

Connor scratched his chin. They had started out with twice more than that. "What of the dead?" he inquired.

"The nobles have been loaded on the wagon," Murchad answered, his finger pointing south to the caravan of the dead. "All others have been burned."

"Very well," Connor stated. He rubbed the stallion's chest then patted Murchad's leg to release him. He was gone as suddenly as he had appeared.

"Connor!" Thorien called, as he ran across the field, arms waving to scatter men from his path. He was visibly troubled causing another wave of anxiety to sweep through Connor's stomach. He'd seen the earl of Limerick face down an army of men single-handedly yet he'd never been shaken—he was now.

The Viking stopped, bending low to put his hands on his knees as he struggled to catch his breath. "Patric's gone missing."

Connor stood silent for a moment before remembering the private conversation he and Thorien shared weeks earlier. With all that had been happening, Patric macLorca was the least of his worries but now he was at the center of them. "When did ye last see him?"

"He was following me into Ailech," Havland replied, suddenly appearing at Thorien's shoulder. He was as shaken as his leader. "He took down three men of his own but then we got separated and I've not seen him since."

"So he was in the hall then," Connor huffed, trying to fit the puzzle pieces together.

"I couldn't say," Havland offered, shaking his head. The lad was young—he should have stayed beside him to protect him.

"I didn't see him there," Thorien added, "but then where could he be? We searched for him among the dead. There's nay sign of him."

Connor's stomach clenched. Kevin's man, Garvin had brought news of Patric's death at the hands of Volkren. It was that which caused the Ri Ciocid to depart so suddenly. Now both Garvin and the lad claiming to be Patric macLorca were gone leaving Connor certain that someone was planning to bring harm to Brian. He took hold of Thorien, scowling so fiercely that the Viking should have melted from its intensity.

"Tell me now—was the lad macLorca?"

Without blinking an eye Thorien answered the question. "He's macLorca! I'd stake my life on it!"

Connor looked from Thorien to Havland who was nodding agreement. It was clear the men believed the lad was macLorca. If he was, then why had Kevin sent word that he was dead—and for all the saints—where was he now?

"I want ye to gather a search party to go after him. Do whatever it takes to find him and when ye do, bring him to me!"

Connor turned to leave but Thorien stopped him with a hand on his arm. He wasn't certain why the Ri Ciocid had gone or why Connor was acting so suspicious but perhaps he could help. He removed the velum from his pouch then handed it to the captain. "Just in case ye need proof of Lorca's intention."

Connor read the letter then nodded his head before slipping it into his own pouch uncertain whether it would be a gift or a curse for the Ri Ciocid. "I'll see that Brian gets it."

*   *   *   *

Ailech, Ireland: The hostage keep—Two hours past noon—25, December 983 A.D.—There was no sunlight in the room. Only the golden glow of oil lamps hanging from chains illuminated the eerie nether space. The smell of mildew hung in the air thick enough to choke the life from a man forcing Patric to keep his breathing low. The throb of his left arm matched the ache in his head—a steady beat of pain that made him wish he could crawl out of his body. He took a deep breath as he lifted his head, squinting his eyes to bring his vision clear.

The man who stood over him was an elder. His skin was grimy and his hair oily as he crouched down beside Patric offering a curious look. He held a cup in his hand.

"Will ye drink something?" he asked, his voice gruff and harsh.

Patric nodded, sending another bolt of pain shooting through his head. He winced and the elder man placed a hand at the base of his neck to help him lift it.

Patric took a sip from the cup. The water was stale and putrid tasting but he needed it badly. He gulped it quickly, trying not to taste it.

"Easy there, lad," the elder reprimanded. "We only get so much. Don't be hogging it all for yerself."

Patric's expression turned contrite as he suddenly realized that the man must be a hostage meaning that he must be one also. He tried to balance himself on his elbow but the movement sent a shooting pain up his left arm. He looked down at it. It was bloody, bruised and swollen beyond recognition. The flesh above his wrist was torn from the protruding bone. He took a deep breath as he remembered that night in Cavenlow when the servants had taken the arm of a man who had suffered similarly. They explained that it was the only way to prevent it from rotting. He blinked back his tears then ripped his gaze away from his wound to settle it on the elder. "Will ye take my arm then?"

The man looked sullen as he shook his head. "If I had a knife I'd do it for ye, laddie, but they don't allow such things down here."

Patric's stomach clenched. "Do ye mean to tell me that they'll leave me like this?"

"Aye," the elder replied, amazed that the O'Neill soldiers had even bothered to take the lad. Usually they only held nobles or those men fit enough to perform work. "They mustn't have realized the extent of yer wound."

Patric took another deep breath as he wondered whether he'd been lucky or cursed.

We make our own luck, Patric.

That's what Lorca had always told him. If there was any truth in those words, he meant to know it. He grimaced as he forced himself to sit up. "Will ye help me?" he asked of the elder.

The man nodded then helped Patric scoot back until he rested against the wall. Together they slipped his lein over his head so they could shred it into strips. The action caught the attention of several other warriors who'd been brought down to the keep and soon Patric was surrounded by five men, one of which was Yon.

"Tis nasty," the Viking confessed, looking at the broken arm. "What will ye have us do?"

Patric's eyes shifted between the Viking and the elder. He had no idea what to do. He had only hoped to cover the wound to stem the blood flow. He opened his mouth to relay that information when the elder suddenly spoke up. "There was a time when I was known as a healer. Perhaps I can offer a thought."

"I pray ye to do it, man!" Patric barked as another rip of pain shot through him.

"Ye man," the elder addressed Yon. "Ye hold his shoulder while I pull on his hand. Perhaps we can get the bone to slip back into place."

Yon moved into position behind Patric then nodded to the other men willing to help. Together they would hold him steady so he couldn't buck from the pain.

Patric braced himself for what he was certain would be torture but if there was a chance that the healer could mend him he was prepared to suffer. In truth he knew the only alternative was death—and that may still come.

"Can ye give him something to bite down on?" The question was directed to any of the men who were still sporting belts.

One man stepped forward to place the leather strip in Patric's mouth, his eyes filled with sympathy for the pain he expected his fellow warrior to suffer. Patric nodded appreciatively before preparing himself for the healer's ministrations.

The healer took Patric's hand in his then poured the half filled cup of water over the wound sending the young man reeling from the pain. He waited only a moment before he slowly drew Patric's hand toward him, guiding the bone so that it could recede beneath the skin. But the swollen tissue and muscle acted like a barrier deterring it from slipping into place. "Take a breath, lad," the healer said as he used his hand to force the bone back into place.

They were the last words Patric heard.

✳   ✳   ✳   ✳

Ulster, Ireland: Outside the Ailech wall—Two hours past noon—29, December 983 A.D.—Havland rubbed his chin as he considered the height of the granite wall. Scaling it would be impossible.

When their extensive search turned up no sign of Patric, Thorien agreed to leave Havland behind with the hope that he might uncover something. Patric wasn't the only one of his men to go missing. Yon, Mordid, Evan and Rendac had also disappeared without a trace leading him to believe they might have been taken as slaves.

"We'll not be getting in this way, lass," Havland offered to the auburn haired camp follower they called Varna.

She looked at him, her blue eyes sparkling in the afternoon sun. She knew Havland favored her over the others because of the assistance she provided him. It wasn't the first time he'd paid her to waylay a guard so he could gain entrance to a place and she was certain it wouldn't be her last. He was moving again and she followed. "Do ye think it wise that we do this while court is still in session?"

"Aye," Havland responded without a hint of irritation for the question. Varna was a clever lass and he trusted her advice. "There are more then a thousand people in there. They'll never notice two more. So long as the high queen hasn't been returned, the odds are with us that Malsakin won't strike us if we're caught."

They were making their way around to the servant's gate where the garbage was disposed of. The air was fetid. Havland looked around for a bit before settling himself against the wall. He patted the ground beside him. "Have a seat, lass. We might be in for a bit of a wait."

✳   ✳   ✳   ✳

Ailech, Ireland: The great hall—Six hours past noon—31, December 983 A.D.—Malsakin sat listening to Morgan's latest troubles. He'd never thought much of the man until now. Boru's little escapade had caused many of the leaders to lose respect for the throne. If Morgan felt similarly he certainly didn't show it.

After Kormlada sent the message that he should deny Boru's demands, Malsakin decided to hold court as if nothing had happened. The raid exposed the truth of the matter sending many of the nobles fleeing to the safety of their own villages. Those who remained pitched in to recover Ailech. Now proceedings were resuming if for no other reason then to pass the time until the high queen's return.

Morgan's issue was water and power. Dundalk neighbored a Viking village called Fjord Valor. It had been there for as long as anyone could remember but recently the central well ran dry forcing the earl to dig a new one right on the line between the two properties. Morgan argued that the earl should pay him rent since half the water in the well belonged to him but the earl refused and instead suggested that it was Morgan who owed him rent since he was the one who dug the well and outfitted it so that Morgan could get at his half of the water.

"Do ye use the water?" Malsakin asked of Morgan.

"Nay," the Ri Tuath replied. "I've my own well further north. 'Tis too far a distance to travel for our needs."

Malsakin thought for a moment then asked. "Is there nothing ye could use the water for if ye chose too?"

"I could use it for the sheep," he finally answered after mentally running through the use of his property. "The best grazing is in the south quarter. It would save us from having to drive them north during dry times."

"Well then," Malsakin answered, "I would advise ye to use yer half of the water for yer sheep. Tell the earl that ye'll be denying him rent because he dug the well without yer approval. I think he'll agree that it's the best solution to the problem under the circumstances. In the end ye get the better of it for saving the expense of the well and yer herder's time."

Morgan nodded agreement. Malsakin was always one to be able to make a silk purse from a sow's ear. He was grateful for the advice. "Very good, Ard Ri," he offered, bowing low before his king.

Malsakin smiled then urged him to a seat with a wave of his hand. Varna immediately moved to serve him, proving to the senior pouring maid that she was equal to the task she'd been hired to do. She chuckled to herself as she poured ale into Morgan's cup. Havland had thought to use *her* to gain them entrance but in the end it was *his* charm that won over the female servant who let them in.

Under the pretense that he was one of the Ard Ri's hired men who had been locked out during the melee, Havland convinced the woman not only to let them pass, but also to find work for Varna who he claimed was his sister-in-law now widowed thanks to Boru's raid. He told the woman that his brother was so in love with Varna that he couldn't bear to have her away from him so when the Ard Ri called they traveled together to Ailech. She was hiding in the woods when Boru's men massacred her husband, presumably because his mind was on his wife and not on the battle at hand.

Whether it was the story itself or the dramatic way that Havland told it that won the woman's heart, Varna couldn't be sure. What she did know was that for the first time in months she was provided with a warm bath, food and a solid roof over her head and all she had to do in return was pour ale for kings.

She turned from her duty then issued a wink at Havland who was standing against the wall dressed as an O'Neill guard. He looked different without his beard and she wasn't certain whether she liked it or not. But when he flashed his smile for the servant who had helped them and the woman began to swoon, Varna decided that nothing he did to his appearance could make him displeasing.

Malsakin turned from Morgan as Fladbartoc approached the table. "May we speak, Ard Ri?"

Malsakin nodded then offered his apologies. Earlier, he sent Fladbartoc to meet with the messenger Sigtrygg dispatched from Dublin. He was eager to know what information he brought.

They stepped from the platform and through the curtains into Fladbartoc's chamber. Apparently Havland followed because when Varna turned to look he was no longer there.

"I've word from Kevin macLorca," Fladbartoc began.

Malsakin's brow shot up in askance. When Kevin didn't return he became suspicious of the Ri Tuath. Brian's raid only served to make him more so.

"He's playing us, Fladbartoc," Malsakin grumbled. "Anything he has to say must be questioned."

Fladbartoc nodded his head. "I was of that same mind until the messenger arrived. By Sigtrygg's own mouth he was given what I'm about to tell ye."

"Very well," Malsakin offered, resting back against his chair.

"When Kevin realized they couldn't gain reinforcements he sent word to Boru that Volkren had slain his youngest brother, Patric, in a raid during the harvest months. Apparently the lad was a favorite of the Ri Ciocid's. Kevin knew he would become unnerved with the news. It was that which caused Boru's sudden departure."

Malsakin looked pensive for a moment before offering, "Too bad he didn't think of that sooner."

"Aye," Fladbartoc agreed but that wasn't the best of the information he had for the Ard Ri. "There's something else."

Malsakin lifted a brow. "Ye look like the cat that caught the mouse, cousin. Why not spit it out?"

"macLorca raided Torshav."

"He didn't?" Malsakin gasped before sitting forward in his chair.

"Aye, and now Gamal has called a meeting to discuss the matter with the Leinster Galls. They feel Boru betrayed them. Kevin's plan worked."

"How did he do it?" Malsakin asked, uncertain of whether to be suspicious or pleased by Kevin's actions. If the Cavenlow Ri Tuath could raid Leinster on his own then there was no need for him to forge an alliance with the O'Neills.

"Have nay worry, Ard Ri," Fladbartoc offered in anticipation of his cousin's thoughts. "'Twas yer men he led."

Malsakin's eyebrow shot up in askance.

"Aye, Sigtrygg lent him the Dublin guard."

"Did he now?"

"According to Sigtrygg, they were most cooperative and quite effective. One of them even thwarted a skirmish."

Malsakin pushed back his chair then rose to leave. A thought crossed his mind. "Ye say that this Patric was a favorite of Boru's and that the news of his death caused Brian to abandon his entire army."

Fladbartoc nodded and Malsakin rubbed his chin. "So if Brian and Patric are so close, how is it that Kevin doesn't share this same affection?"

Fladbartoc picked up on the Ard Ri's train of thought. "That's the thing about a traitor, cousin. Ye never know when they will turn on ye." He chuckled uncomfortably as he slipped the gold ring from his finger to send it for a spin. "I think I'll be keeping an eye on our new friend, Kevin of Cavenlow."

*   *   *   *

Northern Ireland: The Ulster Road north of Ferta Nime—Four hours to midnight—4 January 984 A.D.—Try as she might, Kormlada couldn't be angry. Boru's plan to raid Ailech and send Malsakin into hiding was nothing less than brilliant. He was well on his way to becoming Ard Ri and there was little doubt in her mind that she would be his queen. How wonderful it would be to serve beside a man of such great intelligence and strength once again.

She spent her time on the journey to Ferta Nime chatting amiably with Boru's men—pulling stories from them about the Ri Ciocid. It appeared Boru was quite lusty; humorous as well; these were traits she found most endearing. She was also happy to learn that his men were genuinely loyal to him. Brave and wise were the words they most often used to describe him, a far cry from the words Malsakin's men used to describe him. Even the Vikings seemed to think well of Boru, and she of all people knew how important that was for anyone who would lead Ireland.

She thought of Olaf but this time her sadness was fleeting. Brian carried many of the same qualities she was attracted to in her late husband. She smiled then stretched herself out across the carriage bench, relishing the thought of what their lives together would be like.

She sat back up when another thought crossed her mind. Though neither of them looked it, both she and Brian had past their middle years. If they didn't come together soon there would be no issue from the marriage. Her father had taught her that a woman's worth was in her ability to provide her husband with sons. She had wanted to give Olaf many sons but Sigtrygg was their only one. Malsakin had two sons from a prior marriage but both had died in infancy and as yet, she hadn't become pregnant by him. Her skin crawled with the realization that if she did conceive a son by Malsakin he would be cast aside when she married Brian. It was bad enough that she was forced to beg scraps for Sigtrygg and Maelmora—to have to do it for another son would be too much for her to bear. The only answer to her dilemma was to be sure that she didn't conceive a child by Malsakin.

Resigned to her plan, she luxuriated in the warmth of her carriage then let the gentle rocking of it lull her into sleep.

She dreamed of Brian. He was frantically trying to gain admission into a place where he wasn't welcomed. Her heartbeat hastened and her stomach clenched with the pain he was experiencing over the lad's death.

Patric.

Someone had told him that Patric was dead but he wasn't. He'd been so close that Boru could have touched him but now there was distance between them— darkness and aching. She tried to sense where the lad was but all she could feel was the fever ripping through his body.

There was a bolt of pain and her eyes shot open. Her heart pounded in her ears while her mind raced furiously. Patric mustn't die because if he did, Brian would never become Ard Ri.

*   *   *   *

Cenn Cora, Ireland: Four hours past noon—6, January 984 A.D.—Brian leapt from his horse before it stopped, nearly knocking over his horseman as he marched forward to burst through the doors of Cenn Cora. Unlike the darkness of Cashel, Cenn Cora's hall was filled with the dappled sunlight filtering through the trees surrounding it. Soft rushes of yellow and red covered the floor muting the heavy foot of the *Ri Ciocid* as he made his way to the center of the hall where his chair sat upon the platform.

All activity from the occupants of the dozens of tables surrounding it came to a halt leaving only the sound of the rushing River Shannon lingering in the distance. It was clear Brian's ire was piqued and no man dared to approach lest it be turned on him. None except for the good father Gable, the Ri Ciocid's confessor.

Brian flung himself into his chair, covering his face with his hands as he called out to the heavens, "How can ye do this to me yet again, Lord? Ye've taken another of Lorca's sons leaving me nothing of my old friend!"

Gable took a seat beside him then tenderly stroked his back. "Ye can't blame God for the loss of Patric. By its very design, war takes lives. Patric was lost to war not to the hand of God."

Brian's red eyes were furious when his head snapped around. "So who should be blamed? Should the blame be mine? Should I alone bear the guilt of the lad's death? Perhaps I'm not a leader at all to bring such loss onto the house of my dear friend. Perhaps I'm not fit to live!"

He pulled his short sword from its sheath then held it against his stomach. Those in the crowd who saw it gasped.

Familiar with the Ri Ciocid's theatrics, Gable eased the blade out of Brian's hand. "Ye're a good leader and ye know it. Ye fight for a cause and ye're making great strides. Ye shouldn't look to place the blame for Patric's death on any other save Volkren."

Brian's eyes went soft. "And what does Lorca think of me that I've failed to protect his family yet again? Does he believe I'm a good Ri Ciocid or an incapable rot who's been remiss in his oath?"

Gable shook his head. "Lorca knows ye've been true. I'm sure by now the lad's sitting with him in heaven telling him of yer efforts, but to be sure, I suggest ye do something for those who remain in Cavenlow."

"But what can I do?" Brian asked as he threw up his arms. "Kevin and Grace have turned their backs against me. They won't respond to my messages and refused me entrance when I went to grieve with them. The hatred they hold for me has only been heightened by the loss of Patric."

His shoulders slumped forward then he sprawled across the table sobbing, "My sweet Patric. I'd give anything to be united with ye once again. Ye were like a son to me and I loved ye truly. I can't believe I'll never see ye again."

At five foot five inches tall, Gable approached the task of bringing the giant king to his feet with certain prudence. He slipped a hand under each of Brian's arms, giving a gentle tug with the hope that the limp body would follow.

Brian acquiesced, lifting himself to half form before draping his large arm over the rotund priest's shoulder.

"Good, Good," Gable panted. "Now let's go to the chapel to pray for the lad's immortal soul."

Tears could be seen rolling down the cheeks of certain warriors in the hall as they watched the painful retreat of the Ri Ciocid.

CHAPTER 17

▼

Ailech, Ireland: The great hall—Four hours past noon—6, January 984 A.D.—Havland turned his head away as another one of Fladbartoc's guards drew near. Court had concluded and it was becoming more difficult to hide out in the open since the northern Ri Tuaths and their men had begun to take their leave. There was word that the high queen's carriage had been spotted on the road and Havland did his best to confirm that it was true. He needed the excitement of her return to cover his movements so that he could finally free his men.

Being new to the contingent, he had been assigned to the keep. It was the least coveted job in all of Ailech but for him it was testament that his luck was still with him. Though he had managed to provide clean water, bandages and healing herbs to Calder, Patric was still ailing badly. The sooner they could get the lad out of that cell, the better his chance for survival would be.

Varna was already waiting in the woods with horses they'd proffered from Fladbartoc's barn. Havland had even managed to buy back Throdier's sword from the O'Neill guard who had taken it from Patric. All he would have to do now was wait for the high queen's carriage to pull up to the gate then he would slip into the keep and set his men free.

It was early evening when the carriage appeared on the Ulster Road. Malsakin, Fladbartoc and nearly half of Ailech pressed through the gates to watch the high queen's arrival. Maelmora rode lead, waving his arm frantically to get Malsakin's attention. He dismounted. "Ard Ri," he sighed, bowing low from the waist. "Yer queen is in good health though her spirits are bleak for having missed ye."

Kormlada watched her brother's display, grateful that he was a good actor. She disembarked slowly, curving her back and hanging her head as if she'd been through a great ordeal. Malsakin rushed her.

"Kormlada, my love," he called before crushing her to him. "I thought ye were lost. I'm so glad to see ye whole."

She looked up at him, forcing a smile but never uttering a word.

"Come inside and have something to eat. Ye look so thin. Didn't the rot feed ye?"

Maelmora watched his sister's performance with a certain awe. The truth was that Brian treated them grandly but her act was so convincing that even he felt a pang of worry over her.

Malsakin had his arms wrapped around her shoulders as he escorted her through the door. "How was it that ye came to be on the road in the first place?" he asked. "I thought ye had yer mind set on remaining in Dublin."

"I missed ye, husband," she sniveled as a tear escaped her eye. "I realized how foolish I was being not to accompany ye. I couldn't stand for us to be separated for Christmas so I decided to join ye and make a surprise of it. Damn that Boru, he spoiled everything."

He placed her in a chair then knelt before her as he pushed an escaped hair back behind her ear. "But that message ye sent. Why didn't ye want me to march? Was it a vision then?"

People were gathered all around awaiting the high queen's answer. They had heard she was a seer and wanted to know if the rumors were true. "It was a vision for certain," Kormlada offered in a crisp clear voice before collapsing against her husband's shoulder, seemingly unconscious.

She didn't move when Malsakin called two guards to carry her to a room. She was weary from her trip as well as her games—in truth she was weary from everything.

From the entrance to the keep, Havland watched the crowd of people follow Kormlada and the Ard Ri through the door of the great hall before making his move. He descended the stair to the dungeon then quietly opened the doors to the cells holding his friends. Yon and Mordid were in the first one. Havland handed each of them kerchiefs, which they promptly tied around their face to cover their nose and mouth. The next cell held Evan, Rendac, Patric and the healer, Calder. They too tied the kerchiefs Havland handed them around their face before placing Patric on a litter to carry him up the stair. As they cleared the door they ran into the two other guards on duty in the keep. Like Havland, they had been spying on the Ard Ri from the gate.

"What goes on here?" the elder guard asked as he looked to Havland who wore a kerchief as well. He couldn't be more than seventeen years old.

"Dead," Havland replied, nodding his head toward the litter. "We have to bury him quickly before it spreads."

"What spreads?" the other guard asked, reaching out a finger to poke at Patric.

"I wouldn't do that if I were ye," Havland called excitedly. "It's catching."

The guard looked at him then withdrew his hand as if it had been licked by fire. "What's catching?"

"The disease that killed him," Havland replied nervously, unable to recall the name Calder had given him.

The guard screwed up his face suspiciously and just as he was about to say something, Calder stepped in to save them.

"I pray ye not to make me touch him again," he cried, hands clasped together and shaking from his obvious distress. "'Tis an awful way to die, the Black Plague is. I'll do anything if only ye'll release me from this mission."

He had been addressing Havland but when the guards stepped back he turned toward them, his eyes wild with fear. "They say it gets up into yer nose then shrivels yer innards until they become hard as rocks. And the pain—by the saints I never seen anyone suffer like the lad suffered. 'Tis bad enough I was forced to share a cell with him, must I bury him also? I'd rather have my throat slit than to suffer like that."

"Enough of that now!" Havland barked, smiling behind his kerchief. The guards looked fairly terrified but he didn't want to push his luck. "Ye'll bury him and ye'll do it quick or I'll put him back in yer cell to rot."

"Aye," the elder guard offered, suddenly taking control. "Bury him now and when ye come back ye'll find a bucket and soap to clean out yer cell."

"Thank ye, sir," Calder mumbled, casting a quick glance over his shoulder in the direction of the other men who were making off with the litter.

"May God bless ye," he cooed then reached out to kiss the hand of the youngest guard.

The man pulled back before Calder touched him, a look of terror marking his face. The last thing he needed was for the old crow to be spreading the disease to him. "Away with ye now!" he barked with a wave of his hand. "Catch them up and in the name of all that's holy, don't be touching anyone."

Calder smiled behind his kerchief then continued to bow at the waist as he walked backward. When the guards were out of sight he turned then ran the rest of the way to where his men were standing. They headed for the burial ground then turned sharply south into the woods, disappearing through the thick pines without anyone being the wiser.

$$*\qquad*\qquad*\qquad*$$

Leinster, Ireland: The Village of Laigan—Eight hours past noon—25, February 984 A.D.—The hall in Laigan was purely Viking. Dug into the side of a mountain with packed sod for a roof, it was barely visible to anyone who didn't know it was there.

Harald Bald Knee was the earl. He was a medium height man with gray hair that he wore tied at his neck. There was no mistaking that he had once been a warrior since his face, hands and arms were scarred by battle. He had one good eye—it was blue—the other was blinded in battle—it was white. His skin was leathery and tanned from the sun making his white beard and mustache stand out all the more.

He sat in a chair fashioned of animal hide and bone, his back straight and his head very erect on his shoulders. Beside him sat his wife, Sorcia. Harald never went anywhere without Sorcia because he was vein and didn't want anyone to know he was hard of hearing.

The fire that burned in the pit in the center of the hall was meant to keep it warm but on occasion there had been human sacrifices cast into it. Not so much to appease the gods as to appease Harald who believed that no one should ever question the earl or serve him cold meat.

Brian was bent low as he entered the hall. By design, Viking doorways were narrow with low lintels making it impossible for invaders to burst through them with swords drawn. By the way he was forced to wriggle into the building, Brian decided that the design served its purpose. Once inside he straightened himself then waited for Murchad and Thorien to pass before moving forward to pay homage to Harald. When last he saw the man there was a friendship between them but now Harald's eyes held disdain. He bent his knee and Murchad and Thorien bent theirs.

"Welcome, Boru," the earl called from his throne making no move to release his seat for the Ri Ciocid as he usually would if the man was truly welcomed.

"Long life to ye, Harald," Brian replied.

Gamal sat on one of the low benches lining the eastern wall of the hall. Beside him sat his eldest son, Cal. At thirteen, Cal was already showing signs that he would be as large as his father but it was Gamal's youngest son, Njord, sitting on Cal's left who most people commented about.

Njord was a beautiful child with expressive green eyes and hair as black as ebony. Though still gangly, his shoulders were broad and his limbs were long foretelling he would one day stand head and shoulders above his father. He was good-natured, loved by both women and men, but his greatest attribute was his mind. At just eight summers old, Njord was capable of conversing in three different tongues comfortably as well as being able to piece together sentences from numerous different dialects.

When Gamal left Man it was for the purpose of providing a better life for his sons. All he wanted was a piece of land where he could raise his crops and feed his family in peace. He'd done everything in his power to ally himself rightly so that his sons wouldn't face the harsh life of battle he had lived as a youth but Ireland was fast proving itself to be no different than Man.

He watched as Boru and his men took seats on the benches at the western wall. One of the men was obviously Viking but the other looked to be Boru's son. He could tell by the way the Ri Ciocid looked at him that they shared a bond of love.

How could a man who openly displays his love for his son so easily ruin another man's family?

The question whirled in Gamal's head. It would be answered soon enough. Harald began. "We've asked ye here to explain why ye broke yer word to us, king Brian. We expected that our alliance would have garnered us more fair treatment than to have one of our earls left in ruins to support yer war against the high crown."

Murchad opened his mouth to interrupt but Brian placed his hand over his son's to keep him quiet. He too was raging inside but he fully intended to let Harlad finish before answering the accusation.

"Is it the Dal Cais way to take all a man has in order to feed their need for power?"

"With respect, earl," Brian replied as he got to his feet. "The Dal Cais are an honorable clan. We keep our word when it's given."

"Perhaps to the Gaels," Harald interrupted, "but to the Galls it seems ye live under another set of principles."

"My father's word is kept whether to Gael or Gall!" Murchad bellowed as he too got to his feet.

Brian whirled then issued a silent warning for Murchad to return to his seat before offering Harald his apologies. "I pray ye forgive the outburst, Harald. This business has us all upset. My son spoke out of turn."

Harald nodded his acceptance of the apology and Brian continued. "If I may, I pray ye to allow me to address the man who's been harmed."

Harald nodded toward the earl of Torshav and Brian crossed the room until he was standing before Gamal. He smiled as his gaze swept over Njord and Cal. "Yer sons?"

"Aye."

"They're strong and handsome."

"As is yers," Gamal offered, nodding toward Murchad.

Brian turned to look at his son. Murchad was the light in his life. He smiled before returning his attention to Gamal. "He is that, and perhaps a bit outspoken as well."

That brought a chuckle from the women who sat in the gallery above. Brian looked up to offer them a smile. His eyes were sincere when he returned them to Gamal. "Ye'll receive restitution for the transgression against ye and my word that it won't happen again. But since it wasn't under my order that the tribute was taken I will ask ye to describe the man who visited this trouble on ye."

Gamal took a moment to think about the Dal Cais raider and his hands clenched in anger. He held them tight to his side when he answered, "He never dismounted but from what I could see he was average in height. He wore mail and a conical helmet. All I could see was his face. His features were pleasant enough. Blue eyes."

The description matched that of nearly half of Brian's men.

"Anything else ye can think of?"

Gamal searched his memory for anything that would help Boru find the man but nothing stood out. It was Njord who broke the silence.

"If I may, father?"

Gamal looked down at his youngest son, realizing that he must have been spying from the window. "Did ye see something, Njord?"

"His sword, father."

Gamal's eyebrows rushed together as he tried to remember the man's sword. Even Finn looked perplexed when trying to picture it. "What of his sword, son?"

"He didn't carry one."

The room erupted into conversation and Harald bent low to allow Sorcia to tell him what he hadn't heard. He began to chuckle. "Ye must be mistaken, Njord," Harald bellowed. "What man would be so brave that he would raid another without benefit of a sword? If he didn't have a blade why would yer father give anything over to him?"

Njord looked to his father for permission to address the earl and Gamal nodded. He knew his son was capable of handling the situation without embarrassing himself. He gave him a leg up so he could clear the low wooden wall separating the spectators without having to walk down the aisle then relaxed in his seat. Finn smiled proudly.

"If I may, earl?" Njord asked, bowing from the waist. "I didn't say that the raiders didn't have blades, I only said that the man who led them didn't."

Brian looked down at the lad who acted far more mature than his age. He knelt beside him so he could look into his eyes. "When ye saw him did he frighten ye?"

"Nay," Njord answered truthfully. "'Twas Finn and my father who I was frightened for. The other men had blades and they used them on their leader's order."

"Did ye think he was going to kill ye?"

"In truth, Ri Ciocid," Njord began, his voice falling low so only those closest to him could hear, "that man seemed more the type to give the order to kill then to do the deed himself."

"I see," Brian stated, then he turned to look at Gamal. The lad was quite intelligent, a sure sign of good parenting. He nodded appreciatively and Gamal nodded back then he returned to his questions. "So, how do ye suppose I should go about catching the man, Njord?"

Njord thought about the question for a while then a spark flared in his eyes. "If I were ye, Ri Ciocid, I'd look for the least brave man among yer many. A man who's afraid of weapons and battle."

Brian stood then rubbed Njord's head. "Thank ye, laddie. That's exactly what I'll do."

✳   ✳   ✳   ✳

Clonmacnoise, Ireland—In the tavern now run by Freyja ingenRagnall—Three hours to midnight—9, March 984 A.D.—It was a busy night in the tavern. Every table was filled and the air hung thick with smoke, music and laughter. Patric watched as Freyja slapped away the hand of an overzealous patron and he laughed when he remembered the first time he had witnessed such a thing.

He'd barely recovered from his fever when he spied through the open door a drunken Viking mauling Freyja. He burst into the main room naked as the day he was born and screaming as if he were possessed by demons. Not only had he managed to get the Viking to unhand her, but much to Freyja's dismay, he also managed to empty the entire tavern—a mistake that wouldn't be repeated.

He smiled with the memory then his face turned serious when a man looking like a grimier version of Havland entered the tavern.

When they arrived in Clonmacnoise more than a month ago, Patric was near death. Thankfully he had no memory of the pain and fever he endured while they traveled, but from what he had been told they nearly lost him on the way. Havland entrusted him into the care of Freyja and Calder before taking Yon and his other men south in search of Thorien. It was Calder's knowledge as a healer that brought Patric through his infection and saved his arm, but it was Freyja's care, along with his hope of being reunited with Brian, which gave him the will to live.

"Where have ye been?" he blurted when Havland drew closer. With all that he wanted to say to the man those were the first words that sprang to his head.

The Viking lifted an eyebrow then walked to the ale barrel to fill a cup, brushing back his hair from his face before taking a long draw from it. He refilled the cup then returned to the table to take the seat beside Patric. "I'm glad that ye're looking fit and well. Tis good to see ye," he remarked. Then, raising his tone to change his voice he continued, "Why thank ye, Havland. Ye look a bit worn out. I hope it's not on my account that ye've been riding around until ye thought ye would drop."

"I'll own that," Patric mumbled, embarrassed at being taken to task for his lack of manners. "How are ye, Havland?"

"I couldn't find them," the Viking blurted, suddenly in no mood for manners.

"What do ye mean ye couldn't find them? Where did ye look?"

"Everywhere!" Havland bellowed. He was as frustrated as Patric was over the situation. "I rode to Limerick only to find out that Thorien hadn't yet returned."

"And did ye go to Cashel?"

"Of course I went to Cashel!"

"And?"

"He wasn't there. Neither was Brian."

"Did ye try Cenn Cora?"

"Do I look the fool man? Of course I tried Cenn Cora but by the time I arrived they had already made off to Laigan."

"Laigan?" Patric questioned. His head was beginning to ache and he wasn't certain whether it was the ale or the way Havland was forcing him to pull the story out of him in bits and pieces that was making it so. He took a deep breath. "Why don't ye just tell me what happened."

"I'm trying," Havland sighed, "but ye keep interrupting."

Patric realized that Havland spoke the truth. He leaned his elbows on the table then willed his mouth to be still. Havland continued. "There was trouble in Leinster. While we were in Ailech yer brother rode into Torshav under Brian's banner demanding tribute from one of the Ri Ciocid's allies, but the tribute was more like a cattle raid. He took every head in the earl's possession and threatened to come back and take more if the earl managed to replenish. The incident caused quite a stir and Brian was called to Laigan to explain…"

"Wait," Patric mumbled as his hand covered Havland's. "Did ye say my brother raided Torshav?"

"Aye," Havland sighed, exasperated that he was interrupted again but then he remembered that Patric had been in no condition to receive the information when he first acquired it. "While we were in Ailech, I overheard Malsakin and Fladbartoc say that yer brother took Dublin warriors to raid Torshav. It seems he hoped to gain something other than cattle by the action."

Patric thought of Kevin. His brother was the least likely person to be leading Dublin warriors against Galls. He shook his head. "Ye must be mistaken, Havland."

"Nay," Havland replied. "I know what I heard and that's what I told ye."

"And I know my brother. He's not bold enough to do such a thing."

"But is he smart enough?" Havland asked. "I don't think it's riches he was after as much as a war between Brian and the Leinster Galls."

Patric thought about it for a time before responding, "If there's one word to describe Kevin 'twould be brilliant."

"Alright," Havland sighed, feeling his point had been made. "So the brilliant Kevin macLorca raided Torshav and the Leinster Galls called Brian to a meeting to discuss it. I was…"

"Well, did ye go to Laigan to tell Brian that ye thought it was Kevin who raided Torshav?" Patric interrupted again.

"By the gods, lad, of course I went to Laigan. I even went to Torshav."

"And?"

"And nothing. They weren't there!"

"Ye should have taken me with ye," Patric sighed before running his hands through his hair.

Havland noticed the lump on Patric's left arm where the break had healed crooked. "Och," he issued through pursed lips. "That would've been grand. I could see it now, me pulling a festering, unconscious man behind me in a carriage. It would have taken us twice as long to get everywhere and half way there I would have had to stop to bury ye."

"But at least…" Patric let his words trail off when he realized Havland was right. He would be dead now if the man hadn't brought him straight to Clonmacnoise.

He stretched his left arm across the table then unwittingly fisted it over and again. Freyja had suggested he practice the exercise as much as possible to bring strength into the arm. Now it was a habit for him. "So what do we do now?" he asked.

"Wait," Havland replied, needing no time to formulate an answer. He'd been riding for more that a month without rest. He was looking forward to spending some time away from the saddle. "Thorien knows that when I'm not in Limerick he can find me in Clonmacnoise. He'll come looking for us when Brian's ready to see ye. In the meantime ye need to rest. We both do."

"I wonder if Connor is speaking out against me to Brian," Patric mumbled, looking for an explanation as to why the Ri Ciocid wouldn't have already sent for him.

"I doubt he would have had the opportunity," Havland retorted before taking another sip.

"What do ye mean?" Patric asked, confusion dotting his face.

Havland shrugged. "It seems Connor is now serving Turlog." Then he laughed, "They say he's planning to marry the Ri Tuath's daughter when she comes of age."

"What's funny?" Patric inquired with brows lifted.

Ever the gossip, Havland leaned in to whisper, "She's not exactly his type, aye."

"What type is she?"

"She's a lass," Havland replied with a wink.

Patric took his meaning but the knowledge didn't affect him all that much. He'd seen enough of it with Kevin. He turned the conversation back to more important things. "How long do ye think it will take to have this all settled?"

"There's nay telling," Havland replied matter of factly. "I should think Thorien already told the Ri Ciocid that ye were with us in Ailech. It just depends on whether Brian believes that ye're who ye say ye are or if he believes ye're dead as Kevin told him?"

"DEAD!" The conversation was becoming increasingly more difficult for Patric to follow. He rubbed his eyes feeling like the fever had returned then mumbled under his hand. "What's gone on while I was sleeping?"

"This didn't happen while ye were sleeping," Havland replied, "Or maybe it did." He knew he was being difficult but it was the mood he was in.

Patric removed his hands from his eyes to offer Havland a glare. The Viking took his meaning and continued, "Brian was in Fladbartoc's hall when the messenger rode through the doors, horse and all. He…"

"Was that the message Garvin brought that sent Brian running from the hall?" Patric asked with wide eyes.

Havland nodded and suddenly Patric was overcome by emotion. Tears welled in his eyes to know that the Ri Ciocid held him in regard enough to abandon his army in Ailech.

"I wasn't there," Havland interjected, noticing the glazing of Patric's eyes and hoping to distract him with more talk, "but those who were say it was a sight to see.

"Aye, 'twas," Patric mumbled. He wiped his eyes with his sleeve.

"Hold on here," Havland bellowed. He leaned forward with a scowl on his face. "Are ye telling me that ye were in the hall and ye didn't reveal yerself to Brian then? Why in the world would ye pass up the opportunity, Shaver?"

Patric returned the scowl as he prepared to defend himself. "I was on my way to do it when one of Fladbartoc's guards attacked me! Brian damn near ran me over in his haste to grieve for me. It was him who broke my arm. The next thing I knew I was being trampled by a thousand feet."

Havland sighed deeply then shook his head. "By the gods, Shaver," he huffed. "I think ye must be the most unlucky man I've ever known."

*   *   *   *

Thomond, Ireland: The Ri Tuath's private chambers—Two hours to midnight—9, March 984 A.D.—Thomond was a large expanse of territory containing many small villages. The great hall sat dead center surrounded by twenty small huts used by the Ri Tuath's family. The barracks were some distance away at the outer edge of the ringed wall that surrounded the northern part of the territory. Connor passed through the gates, nodding to the guards manning the palisade before walking up the northern path to the Ri Tuath's hut.

"Come," Turlog called at the knock. He wrapped his robe around his shoulders in preparation for the draft that would come with the open door.

"Pardon the late hour, Ri Tuath," Connor mumbled as he stepped inside, "but I do want to speak with ye about something that's been troubling me."

Turlog raised a brow then waved his hand toward a stool. "Well, what is it?"

Connor looked down at the vellum in his hands, twirling it between two fingers. "Something's amiss in Cavenlow."

"Well if that isn't an understatement then I don't know what is," Turlog issued with a chuckle.

"I'm speaking about real danger here. Treachery in its highest form."

"As am I," Turlog responded, not put off by the other man's tone.

"But where is it coming from?" Connor questioned, eyes pleading for an answer. "If it was Patric in Ailech then Kevin sent a false message to draw Brian out. But if Kevin was telling the truth then the lad was an imposter."

"Either are possibilities," Turlog replied, suddenly drawn into the intrigue. He lifted himself from his chair then poured a cup of warm mead for both he and his guest. "Tell me again who it was that came to ye with the information that Patric was with us in Ailech?"

"'Twas Thorien," Connor replied. He saw Turlog's lip twitch then quickly added, "Thorien has always been loyal. He wouldn't be pulled into treachery against Brian."

"Who said anything about Thorien being treacherous?" Turlog quizzed with raised brows. "But he could've been mistaken. Think on it for a moment, would ye recognize the lad after these many years?"

Connor thought about Lorca's ten sons. Other than Kevin, he couldn't put a face to any of them. Now, with things the way they were, Kevin's was a face that he'd just as soon forget.

His stomach turned with the memory of that night before Lorca's death. He was alone sitting on the rise overlooking the river when Kevin approached him. He carried a picnic basket filled with wine, bread and cheese.

"Fancy finding ye here," he called as he got to the top of the rise. "It's so loud in there that a person can barely hear himself think. I thought I would spend some time alone but I see that ye already found the most beautiful spot in all of Cavenlow. I'll move on so I won't disturb ye."

There was something about Kevin that Connor found endearing. He never spoke of war or politics but instead spent his time studying the finer things in life such as art and music. "Ye may join me if ye like," Connor offered, turning slightly so his back rested against the tree.

Kevin's smile was genuine and the moonlight caught in his eyes. They passed the better part of the night on the rise, discussing Ireland's history and its future then suddenly Kevin leaned in to kiss him.

"Well could ye?"

Turlog's question broke through Connor's thoughts causing him to start. "Pardon?"

"Where were ye just now, man?" Turlog huffed. "I asked if ye would recognize Patric if ye saw him now?"

Connor shook his head. "Nay. I can't say that I would."

Turlog wrinkled his nose. "Remind me again of his whereabouts."

Connor's face flushed with embarrassment and he cast his eyes toward the ground. "I don't know."

They sat in silence thinking the situation over. At length Turlog threw up his hands. "If ye ask me it's a quandary for Brian to decide. But I can tell ye right now that whichever way it turns out it will be me who gets Cavenlow should the lad never be found. Once ye give Brian Lorca's letter he'll have everything he needs to condemn Kevin and remove him from the throne."

"How can ye be so sure?" Connor asked, suddenly feeling defensive of the young Ri Tuath. "Did ye ever think that Patric might have thought himself too young to rule the village?"

"Och," Turlog spit then he came to place his arm around Connor's shoulder. "How much blood has been spilled in Eire to gain land? Do ye truly believe that the lad would be fool enough to hand over his right to rule because he thinks himself too young? By the saints man, there are infants ruling entire countries. Nay. Kevin took the crown by treachery and yer letter there proves it."

He motioned his chin toward the velum Connor was holding and the captain looked down at it. The hairs on his neck rose in warning. The situation was a dangerous one but it would be left up to Brian to decide what must be done. He only hoped that whatever decision he made wouldn't get them all killed.

*   *   *   *

Tara, Ireland—In the Great Hall of Malsakin O'Neill: Two hours past noon—24, March 984 A.D.—Malsakin seemed content but Kevin was uneasy. Though his raid was successful, he'd heard about Brian's meeting with the Leinster Galls and his promise to increase his presence in the territory. Suddenly Kevin wasn't certain that his idea was as brilliant as he once thought.

"Where will ye strike next?" the Ard Ri asked, breaking into his thoughts. "If ye don't mind me saying, I'd stay clear of Torshav for a while."

He smiled at that and Kevin reciprocated. "Where do ye suggest, Ard Ri?"

"Leave it be," Kormlada called across her husband. "Brian bested ye in Ailech and now it seems that he's upended yer plans for Leinster. Don't rush into anything that might embarrass ye further."

Malsakin looked at her suspiciously. She'd been acting oddly since her return, refusing to offer advice or even to share his bed. When he inquired she only said that the ordeal had been a harsh one and that she needed time to recover. Now it seemed as if she were siding with Brian.

At length he turned his back against her. "I was thinking Caran Balder should be our next move," he said to Kevin.

"Yer own kin?" Kormlada gasped.

He looked at her wryly. "Aye. Why shouldn't we? He's refused us many times. Perhaps he should suffer for his transgressions."

"Pardon, Ard Ri," Kevin interrupted, "but Caran Balder is in Connacht not Leinster."

"'Tis the truth ye speak," Malsakin replied, "but my cousin is also the most vicious warrior of our clan. If ye strike him, he'll take his retaliation on Brian. He already hates him for killing his mother."

Kormlada laughed out loud. "Do ye really think *he* can perpetrate a raid on Caran Balder without getting himself killed?" she sniffed, nodding toward Kevin.

While he should be insulted, Kevin was as interested as she was in Malsakin's answer. He leaned in.

"He'll be successful," the Ard Ri retorted. "He'll have my men with him as well as yer brother."

"My brother?" Kormlada's head snapped around to meet the Ard Ri's gaze but his attention was on the golden haired nymph pouring his wine. "Of course ye're teasing," she cooed. "Ye know I'd never allow such a thing."

"Oh, won't ye now?" Malsakin drawled. Maelmora had been as closed mouth as his sister when it came to the details of their kidnap. If the man was hiding anything he meant to scare it out of him. "It seems to me that we're doing this so that yer brother can rule Leinster. 'Tis a grand prize ye wish for him so it only makes sense that he be made to earn it."

Kormlada was furious. "There's nay need for him to earn it. It's his birthright. If ye weren't such a cow..." She let her words hang in the air then lowered her head as she realized he was purposely goading her.

This time it was his head that snapped around. His eyes grew narrow as he asked, "If I wasn't such a what?"

She wriggled beneath his glare, knowing she couldn't hurt him with her words any longer. The spark he once held for her was slowly dying out and she hadn't been doing much to rekindle it. "Very well," she thrilled, setting aside his question. "Maelmora will go with Kevin to Caran Balder but I would like to offer my condition."

"Och, aye," he replied, chuckling loudly to draw the attention of those who were near. "The high queen wishes to place conditions on me now."

Kevin could feel the tension building between the two and it made him quite nervous. He took hold of his cup waiting to hear Kormlada's next words.

"I will accompany them to Caran Balder. When we return victorious I want ye to give Dublin to Sigtrygg. I think he's *earned* that since it was his quick thinking that helped Kevin find success in Torshav."

Both Malsakin and Kevin sat back in their chairs with their mouths hanging open. Neither one of them could believe that she would put herself in such danger. At length Malsakin broke the silence. "So ye fancy yerself a raider now, do ye?"

"Nay. I fancy myself an advisor."

Kevin didn't know what to think. If the rumors about Kormlada were true he could certainly benefit by having a seer with him on the journey. But if they weren't and she was left dead, he knew he would soon follow.

"If that's yer wish, Kormlada," Malsakin issued as he placed his palms on the table. "I don't know what Boru did to ye when ye were his hostage but if it has caused ye to fancy yerself as a camp follower now then who am I to stop ye?" With that he rose, taking the arm of the pouring maid to escort her from the hall.

Kormlada was seething, more from his words then the display, but she kept control of herself. Her prize was at hand and she meant to take it.

*   *   *   *

Cenn Cora, Ireland: The great hall—Six hours past noon—26, March 984 A.D.—Brian twirled the bitters with his finger until they were nothing but a puree of green juice and string upon his plate then he pushed it aside. The mood in the hall was somber owing to the Ri Ciocid's malaise and though there were nearly a hundred people occupying the room it was silent enough to overhear a whisper.

He looked down at the letter lying on the table through the tears welling in his eyes. There was no doubt it was Lorca's hand. "I should have known," he mumbled, stroking the velum as tenderly as he would the hand of an infant. "Lorca had been training Patric to be a leader since the day he was born, it only makes sense that he would want him as his successor when his only other choice was Kevin."

"What will ye do, father?" Murchad inquired. He'd always been jealous of the love his father lavished on Lorca's sons but he never bore them harm.

Brian raised a watery eye to look at his only son then tried to put himself in Lorca's position. Ten sons and eight of them left dead for their king. What torture the man must have suffered as he saw one after the other of his boys die in battle.

Better they die in battle than at the hands of the Vikings.

He could have taken comfort from the thought if it weren't for the fact that now even the youngest of Lorca's son—the one he meant to be his heir, was dead because *he* couldn't protect him. He wiped his face with his hands then without uncovering it asked, "Thorien, tell me again why ye believed the lad to be macLorca?"

"If ye had seen him ye would have known him," Thorien replied anxiously—although now he wasn't quite sure. "I swear he was the image of Lorca."

"So ye're telling me that for weeks the lad was running around the camp right under my nose and I never spotted him? Why didn't ye come to me with this sooner? Why didn't ye tell me in Lagain? Why did ye wait until now to reveal this information?"

Thorien and Connor exchanged glances. Oddly enough, it was Turlog who answered the question. "And if they had come to ye and it was a trap, ye might be dead now. They were right to be suspicious of him and as the situation stands, it was for good reason. Ye know as well as I that if the lad were Patric he would have moved heaven and earth to get to ye. Didn't ye always say that when it came to ye, Patric was like a fly to honey? Why would he hold himself apart awaiting a formal meeting unless he meant ye harm?"

Brian nodded agreement. It was a tangle and there were no thread ends for him to pull. He'd spent the better portion of the last months mourning the lad. He didn't dare to hope that he could be alive. And even if wishes could be truth, there was another problem. If Patric were alive it would mean that Kevin had lied to him and he refused to think of Lorca's sons as traitors. "And where is he now?"

Thorien hung his head. "I'm not sure. We didn't find him among the dead nor was he with us on the road. Havland stayed behind to see if he could locate him."

"So, even if the lad was Patric he might be dead now thanks to my actions."

"Not by yer actions, father," Murchad offered. "If he was killed in Ailech he gave his life willingly."

Overcome by frustration, Brian cleared the table with his hand sending trenchers, cups and bowls sailing in all directions. Murchad grabbed the velum then wiped it with a square of linen before handing it back to Thorien.

Brian looked to Connor with tears in his eyes. "Ye were always fond of Kevin, were ye not? What do ye think he's up to?"

"I couldn't say, Brian," Connor replied, taken aback by the question. He didn't realize that his relationship with Kevin was that obvious. He hung his head awaiting Brian's reprimand.

To his surprise, Brian fidgeted with the linen lying across the table as he pleaded, "I know I have nay right to ask this of ye but if ye'd agree to stop in on Kevin so that ye can get some information from him I'd be indebted to ye."

"What's this?" Turlog asked, his stomach clenching that his nephew could undo the scheme that had brought Connor to him. "Have ye forgotten that Connor serves me now?"

Brian's brows rushed together as he snapped his gaze around to meet his uncle's. "Is he to be yer son or yer fudir?"

His ire was fully piqued. He still didn't understand how Connor made the sudden decision to marry without even discussing it with him. Not that he would have spoken against it. Connor had as much right to happiness as the next fellow but somehow this bargain between his cousin and his uncle smelled foul.

Turlog opened his mouth to reply but Connor interrupted him. "I'd be happy to do it for ye, Ri Ciocid," he replied touching Brian's arm to draw his attention back to him. Brian jumped with the touch causing Connor to draw back but soon enough he checked his anger then let out a deep breath. He flashed Connor a genuine smile.

"I'm in yer debt, brother."

Turlog was about to state that it was his debt the Ri Ciocid was in but then thought better of it. Whatever Connor learned about Kevin would be shared with him as well. In the end it might assist him in taking the village.

Connor returned the smile then said a silent prayer that this mission would put him back in Brian's good favor.

CHAPTER 18

▼

Clonmacnoise, Ireland—In the tavern—Two hours past noon—15, April 984 A.D.—The tavern in Clonmacnoise had become a most famous place to visit thanks to the experiments of Patric the Shaver. Exercising was the only way he could regain the strength in his arm, and since Calder advised him against battle training just yet, he decided that carpentry would serve his purpose.

For his first project, he constructed wooden paddlewheels, which he suspended from the ceiling joists to spin with the rising heat. The result was the warmth of the hearth being distributed throughout the structure in cold weather and a cool breeze from the newly cut windows being distributed in the summer. That caused such a stir that people came from far and wide to see if they could copy his invention.

Next, he increased the size of the tavern by adding a wooden structure on the front then moved the kitchen inside, complete with running water.

His latest project was the construction of a service counter along the tavern's eastern wall where patrons could order food and drink. He opened a pit in the earth behind the counter to store the ale kegs, keeping the liquid cool no matter what the temperature.

While Patric kept himself busy with improvements that would attract customers, Havland kept himself busy visiting with them. He would spend hours speaking with travelers who had gossip to share. On this particular evening, he was speaking to a rather large man known by the name of Finn. They met in Torshav when Havland was there in search of Brian.

"Shaver," Havland called, waving Patric to join them. "I've someone for ye to meet."

Patric's mouth twisted with the use of *that* name but it seemed to have stuck and there was nothing he could do about it. He set his tools aside then closed the short distance between them, offering Finn his hand before taking a seat. Immediately Varna rushed forward with a pint.

"So this is the Shaver," Finn drawled as he looked Patric over. "Ye've quite a reputation for a young lad."

"Don't believe the stories ye hear," Patric replied modestly. He too had heard the exaggerations being attached to his new name. "Most of them are lies."

"So then, ye didn't take the hair of Throdier of Orkney?"

"Now that happens to be true," Patric retorted. "It's that bit about me being able to move mountains with my bare hands that's an exaggeration."

Finn laughed so hard that ale squirted from his nose then he exchanged a knowing glance with Havland. "I see what ye mean about him."

"I wouldn't tell ye anything that wasn't true," Havland replied.

"So what's this all about?" Patric inquired, feeling that he'd been left out of a secret.

"Finn and I were discussing the Dal Cais raider who paid them a visit before Christmas. I told him that ye might be willing to lend some assistance."

"Aye, that I would," Patric replied, turning to Finn to express his seriousness. "What can ye tell me about the man?"

"He was average height with a scrawny build. The only remarkable thing about him was the fact that he didn't carry a sword."

The doors of the tavern opened with a rattle and they all three looked up to see Njord rush in. His face was flushed from running and his breathing was labored. He searched for a moment before his eyes alighted on Finn then ran forward. "I won!" he cried in triumph, plopping himself on the empty stool beside Finn then reaching out to take the man's cup. He drained it then wiped his mouth with his sleeve.

The expression on Finn's face was sheer adoration. He rubbed Njord's head. "Well I knew ye would win. I bet those lads are wishing they hadn't bothered to challenge ye."

"Aye," Njord mumbled as his eyes scanned the table for something else to drink. He looked to Patric's freshly poured cup with hunger in his eyes.

"Here," Patric offered, pushing it toward him. "This one's on me."

Njord nodded politely before taking it then began to gulp it down.

"Njord, this man is Patric the Shaver," Finn offered before setting a finger on the end of the cup to tilt it away from the lad's mouth. The last thing he wanted was to bring him home drunk again.

Njord wiped his mouth then also his hand before offering it to Patric. "'Tis good to meet ye, Shaver," he said, far too manly for a lad of his age. "We've heard about ye in Torshav but I didn't think I'd ever meet ye."

"Why's that?" Patric questioned, taking a moment to gaze at the lad's face. He was a particularly handsome child with round green eyes that twinkled when he spoke.

"They say ye've been traveling the countryside battling ogres and serpents. Are ye on holiday now?"

All three men chuckled as the lad proved his age. "What's funny?" he asked.

"Nay a thing," Patric replied rubbing Njord's ebony hair. "I'm taking a bit of a respite from my battles to heal up my arm. I broke it in Ailech."

"Ailech," Njord blurted with wide eyes. "Was it a giant ye were battling there?"

"Not all of them were giants," Patric responded, unwilling to burst the lad's bubble. "But it was a battle all the same. I was taken hostage and my friend, Havland here, helped me escape."

Njord's eyes widened further when he looked to Havland.

"'Tis the truth," the Viking offered, answering Njord's unasked question. "We escaped within an inch of our lives."

Patric raised an eyebrow for the exaggeration but said nothing further.

Njord looked at Finn, his face expressing the idea that popped into his head. "We should ask them to come to Torshav with us," he rambled excitedly. "Perhaps they could help us fight back Boru's raider."

Before Finn could respond Patric interrupted. He didn't want the lad thinking that Brian was doing the raiding if it wasn't true. "I'd be happy to assist," he offered earnestly, "but I'm not quite convinced 'twas Boru who authorized the taking of yer cattle. There may be someone else behind it."

Finn scowled at him. "Well he owned it in Lagain."

"Did he?" Patric asked. He looked to Havland in surprise. "I thought ye said it was Kevin who did it."

"That's what *they* said," Havland replied.

This time is was Finn who was feeling left out of the secret.

"Who's Kevin?"

"I don't know anyone else who would be fool enough to march on someone without a sword," Patric continued, addressing himself to Havland. "He fears weapons. Doesn't want to mar his dainty skin, aye."

"That's what I said," Njord interrupted, excitement lilting his voice for being correct in his opinion. "Didn't I say that in earl Harald's court, Finn?

"Who's Kevin?" Finn asked again, ignoring the lad's question.

"It had to be him, Shaver," Havland continued. "I'm sure Brian only owned it to keep the peace."

"I think I like, Brian," Njord interrupted again, "but I'd like him more if he kept better control over his men."

Patric smiled at him then rubbed his head. "Me too."

"Who's Kevin!" Finn roared, pulling his dagger from his waist. He wanted an answer to his question and it seemed that violence would be the quickest path to gaining it.

They all looked at him but it was Patric who answered. "Kevin is my brother."

Finn looked to Patric then to Havland, feeling as though he'd been played. "And do ye think I won't strike ye because of yer reputation?" he asked, preparing to do just that.

"Hold on there, brother," Havland crooned, catching Finn by the wrist. "The Shaver had nothing to do with this. He's only inquiring so that he can assist ye in finding the raider."

Patric held up both hands to show Finn he was unarmed. "'Tis the truth."

Njord turned to Finn. "I believe him."

Finn raised an eyebrow at the lad before placing the dagger on the table. His head was aching from all the back and forth. He needed a drink.

He reached for his cup then realizing it was empty, grabbed one from Varna's tray as she passed. He took a long draw to settle his nerves. "So ye believe that Boru will seek his revenge against yer brother for his actions?"

Patric nodded his head. "If I have anything to say about it that's exactly what he'll do."

"And will ye have something to say about it?" Finn asked, wondering whether the lad was depending on his reputation or something else to gain the Ri Ciocid's cooperation.

All eyes were on Patric as the question hung in the air. He would move heaven and earth to put himself in Brian's company again. This might be exactly the thing he needed to do it. He nodded but didn't say another word.

*   *   *   *

Caran Balder, Ireland: Two hours past midnight—15, April 984 A.D.—
Located just south of Lough Conna, Caran Balder spanned more than a mile. On the east it was bounded by rolling hills and open terrain—on the west by the North Atlantic. Being the least fertile territory in Ireland, none of the five main

roads built by the early Celts reached as far as Connacht so travelers wishing to get there were forced to cross over rough mountains of limestone rising nearly one hundred feet high. It had come to be known as the edge of the world and when Kormlada finally reached it she understood why.

The wind whipped up from the sea causing her hood to slip back from her head as she scanned the mountaintop village on the next rise. The fortress of Caran Balder was built of limestone, seemingly impenetrable as it glowed in the light of the moon. She turned to look over her shoulder at Maelmora and Kevin who were sitting their horses behind her. Both faces were grim. The task wouldn't be an easy one.

"If ye look like that now, how will ye be once we get started?" she called out against the howling wind.

Maelmora urged his horse forward in an effort to hear her better. "Ye're certain we'll find victory?"

"I'm certain," she replied, catching a strand of wayward hair in her hand then tucking it back behind her ear. "But remember, we must take his ring to ensure our safe departure."

Maelmora looked down at his own hand. The gold ring on his index finger had been his since he was a child and hadn't come off his finger since he was large enough to wear it. He was certain it was no different with Balder.

"'Twill be as ye say," he called back to her.

She held her finger out toward the palisade. "He's light of guard. There are only three for the entire fort. Makes sense since he thinks himself invincible. We can do it, Maelmora."

Kevin closed in on the brother and sister, eager to get things started. They had laid their plans the night before and gone over them twice during the ride. His men were in position awaiting his call. "Shall we get on with it?" he asked, his words obscured by the howling winds.

Kormlada didn't need to hear him, she knew he was ready, as was she. "Give the word, Ri Tuath."

Kevin nodded then departed down the rise. Maelmora followed. A short while later they appeared on the next hilltop in front of the fortress wall, the three red lions visible against the glow of their yellow tunics in the moonlight.

"Open the gates! We've come for yer tribute," Kevin called from his horse.

Balder's guards looked down from the wall in surprise. They were smug in their expression as they were about to offer their protest but all at once Maelmora gave the order to batter down the gates. The wall trembled with the assault.

The raiders struck on all sides at once, gaining quick entrance into the village that boasted the reputation of never having been penetrated. Kormlada watched as the guards on the palisade scrambled but she couldn't see what was happening beyond the walls. She closed her eyes hoping to bring a vision.

While Kormlada watched the village, Connor watched Kormlada from his position of safety in the shadows of a yew tree. When he arrived in Cavenlow, he was told that the Ri Tuath had business in the north and that he wouldn't be returning anytime soon. Connor picked up his trail on the Leinster Road and tracked him all the way to Sogain. It was there that Kevin met up with Kormlada, Maelmora and six hundred men from the Ard Ri's army. Connor was astounded. Never in his life had he seen a regiment so organized and focused. They marched in neat rows over Slieve Gamph then followed the River Moy until they came to a clearing. They made camp in darkness, not daring to expose themselves to the guards looking down from Balder's fortress. They spent the next day in near silence, preparing for their battle only after the sun went down.

From what he could tell, Kormlada was their leader but Kevin and Maelmora got a word or two in when the mood struck. He shook his head in wonder. Kevin was the least likely person to perpetrate a raid on Caran Balder, but with Kormlada beside him perhaps he felt invincible.

Connor watched Kormlada sitting her horse, her head held high as if she were praying to the moon. Her blonde hair and cape were blowing riotously in the wind but she never took her eyes off her prize. Of all the women Connor had ever seen there was no doubt Kormlada was the most beautiful. Now, sitting there with the moon at her back she looked every bit the warrior.

The wind carried the sound of clashing metal up the hill. Both Connor and Kormlada leaned forward to get a better look but there was nothing to see beyond the fortress walls. Once in a while they could hear a shout and several screams but it wasn't until a full hour had passed before the first rider emerged from the gates. He raced up the hill followed by an endless stream of warriors and cattle looking like ants as they rode in straight lines. Connor looked up to see Balder, standing on the palisade watching in dismay as the wealth of his village was led away.

"He got it," Maelmora cried breathlessly when he reined his horse beside his sister. It danced around frightened by the howling wind but he kept his seat with little effort. "Kevin took Balder's ring."

Kormlada expressed her lungs but wouldn't rest easy until she saw it with her own eyes. Kevin fulfilled that desire. He rode up the mountain with the wind at his back, pushing back the hair from his face before he opened his hand for her. "Was this what ye wanted?" he asked, smiling smugly for his victory.

She nodded then took it from him, holding it up to the moonlight before sighing, "Dublin is mine."

The three sat their horses in silence, watching as the last of their regiment climbed safely up the mountain then all at once a riot of orders were given. Maelmora took charge of the cattle while Kormlada organized their men. It was left up to Kevin to lead them back over Slieve Gamph to a wooded area more than a day's ride away where camp would finally be made.

They took turns sleeping on their horses until they finally reached the clearing by the side of Lough Rae but Connor never rested. He had come this far to see Brian safe and he wouldn't miss the opportunity for something as insignificant as sleep.

Camp was made in the usual way but with the high queen present the warriors kept to their best behavior. If any drinking or gambling was taking place it was done in silence making the camp appear haunted. Connor spotted Kevin's tent closest to the water. He waited in the shadows of the trees hoping the Ri Tuath would emerge. When he didn't he decided to take matters into his own hands.

He gingerly crept past the sleeping warriors strewn across the field then made his way toward the tent. He stepped on a twig and the sound rang out across the camp, stirring two men awake. One called out and the other sat up, forcing Connor back into the trees on the southern side of the lough. Guards came around to investigate and Connor realized that his opportunity had been lost.

It was at first light that the camp stirred to life. As usual, warriors headed down to the water to relieve themselves before breaking their fast. Connor withdrew further into the trees so he wouldn't be discovered. Sometime later he watched as Maelmora of Leinster took two thirds of the men and an equal portion of cattle then headed north on the Ulster Road. Kormlada took a good portion of the rest east on the Dublin Road leaving Kevin, his twenty men and ten head of cattle traveling south toward Cavenlow.

It was only when he was certain that the camp had been abandoned that Connor crossed the clearing to retrieve his horse from the other side. He noticed the ring on the ground and bent to retrieve it, wondering how the object that was so precious the day before could be so easily discarded. He tucked it in his pocket then made a mental note not to kill Kevin before he asked him about it.

Riding slowly due to exhaustion, it took more than an hour for him to catch Kevin up on the Limerick Road. Twelve hours later, the group made camp at Port daChanoic.

If Connor had been well rested he wouldn't have waited until the warriors slept to make his move but since his reflexes were slow he decided it would be best not to chance losing when he was so close to his prize.

It was just past midnight when Kevin emerged from his tent to relieve himself. Connor moved in, sword drawn and fully prepared to strike. "For a man who despises war ye did fairly well for yerself," he growled as he came up behind Kevin. "Tell me—how did ye manage to take Balder's ring without getting yerself killed?"

Kevin jumped at the question but didn't turn. The voice was familiar to him. He was fairly certain it was a friend. "I asked him for it."

"Is that so?" Connor crooned. "Do ye always get what ye ask for?"

"Most times," Kevin replied, suddenly placing the voice. "But on occasion I've had to ask more than once. As I recall, that was the case with ye, Connor."

"Aye, 'twas. And now I'm sorry I ever allowed ye the opportunity."

It was then that Kevin turned. Though he was gripped by fear at the sight of Connor hovering so close his face never showed it. "I'm sorry ye feel that way."

"Ye lied to me, Kevin. Ye said ye didn't believe in battle yet there ye were leading a raid and under Brian's banner nay less."

"I never lifted a blade."

"Well—if ye have one with ye now I would advise ye to lift it because I mean to kill ye."

Every inch of Connor's face glowed solemn. Kevin knew that he would be a dead man if he didn't handle the situation properly. He kept his voice calm.

"I didn't realize ye held Balder in such high regard."

"'Tis not Balder that concerns me and ye know it!" Connor barked as he traded his sword between hands. "Yer raiding is bringing trouble down on Brian's head but I suppose ye knew that already, aye. That's why yer doing it."

"Every man has a right to ascend. I'm taking my opportunity where I can find it."

"Ye're Dal Cais, Kevin, nay Eaghonact. What ye're doing now is just plain treacherous."

"Ye're a fool if ye think that Brian never did such things," Kevin snapped back. "When he lived as an outlaw against Madamion's wishes, wasn't that treacherous? He did what he must to gain his crown and ye supported him in it. Even when Madamion begged ye to give it up so that the O'Neills wouldn't take innocent lives, Brian continued his raiding hoping for a full out war. He used any method he could to gain his crown. Now I do what I must to gain mine."

Connor remembered his time as an outlaw. Madamion wanted to negotiate with the O'Neills so that the Dal Cais could keep their lands but Brian wouldn't hear of it. He would rather die an honorable death fighting for freedom than to live his life under the oppression of the O'Neills and their Viking allies. He took to the hills with Connor, Lorca and less than a hundred farmers willing to die for their beliefs. They raided O'Neill villages and the Ri Tuath Ruire retaliated by slaughtering Dal Cais leaders. Madamion finally joined Brian's war to stop the massacre of his leaders.

Kevin watched as confusion dotted Connor's face. He spread his arms for the man. "Why don't ye come inside so that we can discuss this a bit?"

Connor took a step back. "Not this time, Kevin. I won't be drawn into yer seduction yet again. Now defend yerself because I mean to strike."

"With what should I defend myself?" Kevin cooed, hoping that his soothing tone would buy him some time. "Ye can see I only left my bed to relieve myself."

He could see Connor was thinking and he softened his eyes further. "Why don't ye cover yer blade and join me in my tent? I've wine and cheese to share."

That caused Connor to laugh. "The only thing we'll be sharing in the future is the celebration of yer funeral."

"Very well," Kevin stated as he took a step toward him. "If ye will strike an unarmed man—have at it."

Connor leered at him, struggling with the decision of what to do. At length he realized that he couldn't strike while Kevin was defenseless. Cutting him down in battle would be acceptable but to strike him while he wasn't armed was murder. At length he decided to bring him back to Brian. Let the Ri Ciocid decide what to do with him.

He turned his head to cover his blade but suddenly he was on his back.

Kevin landed atop him, withdrawing the blade he had hidden in his sleeve to pull it against Connor's throat. He whispered in the captain's ear as he held him in his arms, "Be still, love. Go with death. There's poetry in it—isn't that what ye once told me?"

The last thing Connor felt was the warmth of Kevin's lips pressed against his.

✳   ✳   ✳   ✳

Cenn Cora, Ireland: The great hall—Noon—30 April 984 A.D.—There was little doubt that Turlog was angry, it radiated from him like heat from a hearth but Brian tried to ignore it even though his own guts clenched with worry for what Connor might be up to. Suddenly his world was riddled with chaos. He could battle men easily enough but these mysterious entities had him deeply confused. Between the Dal Cais raider and the ghost of Patric macLorca it was all he could do to keep from screaming.

"He'll return, Turlog," the Ri Ciocid issued in the voice he used to instill confidence. "I asked him to check on Kevin and he's doing just that?"

"Ye asked him to check on Cavenlow," Turlog corrected. "Ye said nay a thing about him going north to follow the Ri Tuath."

He clasped his hands behind his back as he walked the floor in front of Brian. "I wonder—do ye think it at all odd that Kevin should have gone north at the same time Balder was visited by the raider?"

"Och," Brian issued. "Now I'm certain ye've lost yer mind. Do ye really think that Kevin could perpetrate a raid on Caran Balder and live?"

"Where is he now?"

"In Cavenlow with his mother."

Turlog stomped his foot. "If ye managed to locate Kevin, how come ye can't find yer own kin?"

Brian wiped his face with his hands. Turlog's tirade was stirring up a new set of worries for him. "I have a hundred men searching for him, uncle. What more would ye like me to do?"

"Well, I've a daughter at home who's distraught that her betrothed has gone missing. What would ye like me to do about that?"

The statement sparked Brian's own ire. He'd been waiting for the right opportunity to inquire about the match between Connor and Lara without seeming bitter and now was his chance.

"And when did this torrid love affair come to life anyway?"

Turlog was taken aback by the question. Brian pressed on before he had a chance to collect his thoughts. "Connor has no land or riches, so I wonder why ye'd accept him as a match for Lara."

Turlog quickly shook off his confusion then rallied his thoughts to shoot back, "Don't blame me because *yer* man didn't confide in ye, nephew. Perhaps if ye gave as much attention to the lives surrounding ye as ye do to gaining yer crown, ye could see that people have feelings."

It was the best answer he could come up with and by the look on Brian's face it hit him hard. He pressed on. "Something's amiss and it begins in Cavenlow."

"Will ye never tire of these accusations, Turlog?" Brian rallied. "First Lorca now Kevin—why don't ye just accept the fact that ye'll never get yer hands on Cavenlow and be done with it. Ye're becoming boring."

Turlog drew back as his nephew hit on the truth. Brian rose from his chair. "Now, if ye'll excuse me I think I'll retire. I've a splitting headache and I'd like to get some rest."

Turlog looked long at him. It wasn't like Brian to retreat from an argument he was winning but that's what he was doing now. "Something's happened," he issued, his smile riddled with knowing. "Ye only suffer these headaches when ye're concerned over something. I've a feeling it's more than Connor."

"'Tis none of yer concern," Brian snapped back.

"Ye're my nephew and my leader, whatever happens to ye affects me."

Issued by most anyone else, the statement would have portended loyalty, but Turlog's motives were always suspicious.

"If ye must know, uncle, I've been called to Tara to stand trial for the raider's action against Balder."

Turlog thought about it for a moment then huffed. "Well that's ridiculous! Ye won't get a fair hearing with Malsakin sitting in judgment. Ye just made a stand against him in Ailech. On top of that Balder's his cousin. Ye can't seriously be thinking to go?"

"I must," Brian replied. He lowered himself back into his seat then rubbed his temples.

"Why must ye?" Turlog inquired, real worry in his eyes. If Malsakin exacted revenge on his nephew it would leave him on the wrong side of things and that wasn't where he relished being.

"Whether we like them or nay, we live by laws, Turlog. A member of my clan has been striking against others and I'm left to answer for it. Would ye prefer that I deny the call and have Balder come down on my head?"

Turlog thought about it for a moment. Balder was certainly a formidable enemy. If he called Brian out with the backing of his kin, the Dal Cais could very well lose the southern territory—Thomond included. "So what do ye think Malsakin will do about it when ye go?"

"He'll force me to pay restitution. Probably make me pay back the cattle I took from Fladbartoc as well."

"By the saints," Turlog mumbled as he slumped in his chair. "'Twill ruin ye."

"Nay so much," Brian huffed, "but it will keep me poor for a bit. There'll be no more marching until I recover and that may take some time."

"So there's nay a chance that ye can make a stand at Tara?"

"After Ailech I'd say I'll be hard pressed to gather an army for sometime," Brian grumbled. "Besides, I'm eager to learn all that I can about this raider. If it costs me some wealth, so be it, but I mean to put an end to him before he sparks a war I can't possibly win."

Turlog nodded agreement. Then a thought struck him. "Ye'll not be asking me to accompany ye?"

"Nay, uncle," Brian replied sucking his teeth. Even if he wanted his uncle with him he was sure the man would find an excuse to squirm out of it. "I don't want anyone else exposed to this but me. Ye go back to Thomond and sit tight just in case Malsakin might be thinking to make a move. If he wants to strike at me it would make sense for him to raid my birthplace."

"Will ye give me guards?" Turlog asked, anxious to gain all he could from the situation.

"Aye. My guards will be scattered to all our critical sites. No one will be left unprotected."

Turlog sighed as he pondered the situation. This could very well be the beginning of the end for his nephew.

CHAPTER 19

▼

Clonmacnoise, Ireland: In the tavern of Freyja and Patric the Shaver—17, June 984 A.D.—The door burst open with a fury that could only mean one thing—Njord had arrived. Over the last weeks the lad had been a regular visitor to Clonmacnoise. Likewise Patric and Havland had been traveling to Torshav. Patric felt a certain obligation to the earl for what his brother had done to him and he was making it up by offering his services laying out plans to modernize the village. The relationship between them was solid and Patric was grateful that he'd have a strong ally if ever he were able to claim his father's throne.

He looked up from the board he'd been sanding. It took twice as long to accomplish his task using his left hand but the exercise was returning the strength to his arm. Once the lad spotted him he knew he was fair game and he braced himself for the assault, throwing open his right arm while tucking his left behind his back. He lunged forward to catch the lad so he wouldn't be knocked off his feet. It seemed to be some sort of test that Njord had to find out if his friends were worthy of him.

"He rides, Shaver! Boru rides to Tara on the new moon!" he cried as he slammed his body into Patric's. Though the news was grave he wanted to be the one who delivered it to his new friend.

"Slow down there, laddie," Patric croaked, forcing the air back into his lungs. "Tell me what's happened."

"Malsakin has called Brian to Tara to have him answer for Caran Balder. Everyone will be there!"

"Caran Balder?" Patric questioned. "That's the edge of the world. Do ye mean to tell me that the raider struck there?"

"Aye," Njord replied, his voice trembling with anxiety. "They got away with all the cattle. Thousands of them. The army was so large that they just marched right through the walls. They didn't even use the gates."

Caran Balder had the reputation of being the most impenetrable fortress ever built. Bards sung about it and kings envied it. It was hard for Patric to believe that Kevin could have successfully perpetrated a raid on such a village.

"Ye say that Brian is going to answer for this?"

"Aye. My father says that if the Ard Ri finds him guilty of the raids, Brian will be forced to hand over all his wealth." He lowered his eyes as the news became more disturbing. "My father worries that if Brian loses his wealth 'twill only be a matter of time before an O'Neill will sit on the throne of Munster."

The thought of it made Patric sick to his stomach and he worried his bottom lip as he tried to sort out the situation.

Certainly Brian knew he wouldn't get a fair trial from Malsakin. Perhaps he was going with the hope of getting information about who was doing the raiding. He looked up at Havland and Finn who were entering the tavern with far less panic then Njord had. He set the lad aside then met them halfway. "Is it true that Brian is riding to Tara?"

Havland nodded but Finn spoke. "Aye, Shaver. Balder is hopping mad about the whole of it. He's out for blood and may just get it. The Ard Ri's his kin."

"Aye," Havland agreed. "And don't forget what Brian did to Malsakin in Ailech." He shook his head and sucked his teeth. "Tis grave."

"How did Kevin do it?" Patric wondered aloud. Havland and Finn looked at him and he continued. "My brother isn't exactly a brave one, aye. He's very smart but when it comes to wielding a sword I highly doubt he even knows which end is up. I just can't believe that he did this."

Finn took the cup being offered to him by the maid behind the counter before answering, "Well, whoever it was he's definitely Dal Cais. There were witnesses who saw them on the road in Sogain. They say there were more than five hundred of them all wearing Boru's colors."

"I told ye," Njord offered, stepping on the rail so he could reach the counter. He found the cup Finn had just put down then drew deep from it. "Brian rides and everyone will be there. Ye must go, Shaver."

Patric was thoughtful for a moment then at length he spoke. "Aye, Njord, I think I should."

✳   ✳   ✳   ✳

The fortress of Cashel—Two hours to midnight—9, July 984 A.D.— Brian paced the floor of his chamber as sleep escaped him once again. He looked to his wife who was slumbering peacefully then back through the window at the night sky.

White wisps of clouds were gathering in the azure haze. It would rain soon but he didn't need to see the sky to know it—the ache in his knee where Neila had cut him was the surest predictor of the weather. He rubbed at it to loosen it up then continued his pacing. He pondered the situation of the raider with great determination.

Which of his clansmen held such hatred for him that they would do such a thing?

He ran through the list in his head, each man's face appearing before his eyes as he considered their territory and their ability. Thorien was certainly able to perpetrate such raids but he was loyal as the day was long. Besides, he was with him in Ailech when the first raid took place, as was Turlog, Rydec, Vangar and most of the others. Of the sixty who held kingdoms in Munster, only three hadn't joined them in Ailech, among them, Kevin.

He considered Kevin and Grace. It might very well be that Turlog was right about him. But of all the men in his clan, Kevin was the least capable of doing such a thing—unless he had assistance. Then he thought about Connor.

Where had he gotten to?

There was a nagging in his gut that told him something was wrong but he squelched it. Connor was given to brooding and would often go off by himself into the mountains to spend some time alone.

How long has he been gone now? More than two moons.

That was unusual even for Connor, especially when he'd been given a mission. He thought about Kevin again. He remembered seeing the two of them walking off together in Cavenlow which was exactly why he sent Connor to try to get information from him. It seemed they shared a relationship. That thought made him bristle. Then he thought about Patric. More than anything he wanted to believe that the lad was alive but more and more he was turning toward the idea that the imposter had been sent to do him harm. The only one who could do that was Kevin.

"What's wrong with ye that ye can't see things right under yer nose?" he asked of himself when he realized he had allowed his emotions to get the best of him. Kevin was his enemy; he should have moved on him long ago.

His wife stirring in their bed caught his eye and he stood stone still, watching as she shifted beneath the linen then drew it up around her shoulder. There was a chill in the air from the open shutter but he was unwilling to close it against the sweet smell of heather that was wafting up to tamp down the stale smell of smoke from the heat pot.

There was a break in the clouds where the stars showed through and he wondered where Lorca was and what advice he would give to him now. His head muddled and he rubbed it. Kevin was acting in concert with someone, but who?

"Malsakin?" he mumbled.

That thought conjured visions of Kormlada and instantly he was back in Ailech—in the forest where he had carried her and she lay beneath him after he dropped her on the ground. The memory was so vivid that he could almost smell the pine needles and leaves rotting on the forest floor. He took a step toward the window where the breeze was coming in but he was blinded by his memory and he bumped into the table that held the chamber pot. It crashed to the ground and smashed to pieces shattering the silence and waking his wife. She sat up, rubbing her eyes until they focused on him in the moonlight.

"What ails ye, Ri Ciocid? Are ye having trouble sleeping?"

"I'll be alright," he responded in hushed tones. "Lay ye down and sleep yerself."

She looked at him, his handsome features awash in the glow of moonlight. A sly smile spread across her face. She patted the empty space beside her. "Well, come to bed and perhaps we can think of something to do that will make us both sleepy."

*   *   *   *

Cavenlow, Ireland: Two hours past noon—The great hall—10, July 984 A.D.

Turlog walked into the hall feeling quite anxious. It was Eagan who told him that Kevin wasn't in the village, but that his mother, Grace, would be happy to meet with him. He offered to show him the way but Turlog declined. He'd been in Cavenlow a thousand times before—on most occasions without anyone else's knowledge.

The hall was empty causing his footsteps to echo off the walls as he made his way to the head table then out through the southern door to the courtyard.

Grace was a vision sitting in the sunlight with her long lavender coat draping around her to set off her hair. It was still mostly red although there were streaks of gray running through it. He remembered how it felt in his hands. Her eyes were as blue as the sky with only a few wrinkles at the corner. Her skin held the glow of ivory. She rose as he neared her.

"Ri Tuath," she offered before bowing her head. "'Tis good to see ye in our home. We don't get many visitors these days except beggars and warriors. I'm happy to have someone to chat with."

He considered her for a moment before moving forward. He opened his mouth to say something but then thought better of it. Instead he reached out to take her in his arms then kissed her with an urgency that only she could stir.

She reacted to him in the same manner and the kiss lingered on until they were both breathless.

"By the saints, Grace, ye look good enough to eat and I'm famished."

She smiled up at him as she took his meaning. No matter how much time they had together there were always few words between them. She nuzzled his neck and he growled deep in his throat then she turned on her heel, taking him by the hand to lead him to her chamber.

*   *   *   *

Dublin, Ireland: The gardens—Noon—14, July 984 A.D.—Kevin could hear the swords clashing from the training field adjacent to the gardens. He flinched from the noise. More than anything else he hated that sound. He returned his attention to the chessboard. With one move, Sigtrygg could have him checkmated. He moved his pawn out of the way to be certain that the lad saw it.

"Gotcha," Sigtrygg cried in triumph, moving his bishop into the black box diagonal to Kevin's king. "Checkmate."

Kevin sat back feigning surprise. "Ye certainly do know the game, Sigtrygg. Where did ye learn to play like that?"

"Olaf taught me," the lad thrilled, setting up the board so they could have another go. He had taken quite a liking to Kevin and now that he would be earl of Dublin, he thought it would benefit him to keep the Ri Tuath as his ally.

"He always said that he could tell by the way a man ran his chessboard what type of strategist he was. He urged me against using the same tactics over and again but to instead invoke the element of surprise. I've beaten every man I've ever played against except Maelmora."

"Is that so?" Kevin cooed. He too used the board to measure a man's ability. Sigtrygg's was only fair.

"What of Malsakin? Do ye ever play against him?"

"Aye," Sigtrygg responded smugly. "I beat him as well."

"Did ye ever beat Olaf? I mean really beat him?"

Sigtrygg thought for a moment then shook his head. "He used to let me win."

Kevin nodded knowingly and Sigtrygg continued, "I was a lad then."

Kevin understood, but he was loathe to encourage Sigtrygg on the subject of his father. Once started, the lad could go on for hours. Right then he would prefer to get the information he was after.

"So, tell me about Malsakin? What kind of a warrior is he?"

"Nay much," Sigtrygg replied. "He trains a bit with his men but if ye ask me they go easy on him being that he's the Ard Ri. His mind is sharp enough, though. I'd say he could lay a fair strategy if he has to."

"Or avoid one," Kevin interjected thinking about Brian.

"Aye, that too."

"I hear tell that he's a man of his word. Is it so?"

"Ye would know that as well as I. Ye know what lengths my mother had to travel to get me the throne, aye."

"Aye," Kevin nodded. "Speaking of yer mother, what can ye tell me about her? Has she always been so daring?"

"Och," Sigtrygg offered with real fear passing over his eyes. "Now there's a mind for ye. I'd say the woman could get anything she desired."

"Aye. And next she desires for Maelmora to rule Leinster. Do ye think Malsakin will give it to him?"

Sigtrygg winked his eye as a sly smile split his downy beard. "The real question is what will my mother do to get it for him. He'll have it and she'll be the one to get it for him. Ye can wager on it."

"Even if it means taking on Boru to get it?" Kevin asked with wide eyes.

"Aye, even that," Sigtrygg replied as he moved the pieces about the board.

Kevin considered the young prince for a moment. He could be quite useful to him once he became earl. He smiled smugly looking down at the freshly set board. "So, I see ye plan on giving me a chance to redeem myself," he stated as he moved his knight out in front of his pawns. This time victory would be his.

Sigtrygg smiled wide, unaware of what was coming.

*   *   *   *

Port daChanoic, Ireland: Noon—14 July 984 A.D.—The air was thick with moisture and the million gnats hovering near the river so Patric, Havland

and Finn traveled the Ulster Road to Port daChanoic instead. They stopped for lunch at a clearing that, from the looks of it, had been used as a campsite in the not so distant past. Havland took the time to investigate the tracks.

"I guess about fifteen men on horse and an equal number of cattle."

"Ye're about right on the cattle but my guess is there were ten men," Finn corrected, "and a few goats."

It always amazed Patric when men could do that. He never did pick up the art of tracking. He didn't have the patience for it. He bit into the dried meat he was holding then stepped forward to see if he could learn something from the Vikings.

"How can ye tell which tracks are which?" he asked, pointing to the marks just beneath his feet. "These look to be wiped out."

Both Havland and Finn screwed up their faces as they considered the markings Patric was pointing to.

"Those are drag marks," Finn finally replied before following the trail into the bushes. He stopped dead only a few paces in. "By the gods."

"What is it?" Patric asked. Both he and Havland rushed forward to see Finn's discovery.

It was a man, or what was left of one, buried deep beneath the bushes.

Patric dropped the meat he was gnawing as he felt his stomach flip. It was a horrible sight, the man with his throat slit covered in maggots.

Havland stepped forward, undaunted by the gory sight. He'd seen it a thousand times before on the battlefield but somehow this man looked familiar. He considered his hair and the scar running down the side of his cheek.

"It's Connor," he mumbled, hanging his head before offering the Viking death prayer. He checked the captain's hands. They were stiff and unbending. "He never saw it coming."

"Murder?" Patric asked, wondering who would do such a thing.

Finn stepped forward to inspect the body further. "I'd say it came straight at him."

"'Tis odd," Havland offered, ignoring the contradiction as he got to his feet. "He's not wearing his colors."

"Didn't ye say he had gone to serve Turlog?" Patric inquired.

"Aye, but he'd still wear his colors if he was on business."

"Maybe he was out for a ride," Finn retorted, swatting at the flies buzzing around Connor's face. "Or maybe he didn't want anyone to know who he was."

Havland nodded his head then turned to Patric. "I know 'twill be unpleasant, but I think we should bring him to Tara. Brian should know of this."

Patric nodded agreement, but he didn't relish the thought of traveling the distance with a rotting corpse slung across his horse.

*   *   *   *

Tara, Ireland: The great hall—One hour past noon—17, July 984 A.D.— There were so many people crammed into the building that Malsakin thought they would use up all the air. The trial promised to be the most exciting event in Tara since the last Fair of Taltain. He looked to Balder who was wearing his best robe. It was adorned with a ruby brooch attaching his colors, which were draped around his chest. He was a striking man with fine features and fierce blue eyes that never showed the thoughts lurking behind them. He was seated in one of the two chairs set out before the Ard Ri's throne chatting amiably with another man who Malsakin didn't recognize. The chair beside him was empty, awaiting Brian to take it.

The people in the hall continued to speak with one and other, turning now and again as the doors of the hall opened to admit someone other than Boru. Anticipation hung heavy in the air as each of them wondered whether or not the southern Ri Ciocid would subject himself to the judgment of the Ard Ri.

Half an hour later Brian appeared in the doorway. The crowd grew silent. He stood there for a moment, the sun at his back casting a glow around him. Murchad and Thorien stood just behind him, looking like giants as their tall forms filled the opening. Brian stepped forward.

He nodded his head at the spectators as he walked up the long aisle, his red cloak billowing behind him as he went. Thorien and Murchad took their place along the wall nearest the doors, prepared to thwart any danger.

"Forgive the delay, Malsakin," Brian called out before taking his seat. He was purposefully late to show the Ard Ri he didn't have the upper hand. "It couldn't be helped."

His eyes met Kormlada's and they lingered there for a moment. She was ever the beauty, dressed in a summer lein of shimmering gold with a wide neckline exposing her shoulders. She looked away quickly as if she didn't want him to know she was watching. He shrugged his shoulders, pretending that her scorn didn't affect him.

"Let's get started," Malsakin barked, his dissatisfaction for being kept waiting clearly marking his face. He knew Boru was late on purpose but chose not to mention it. In truth, he was most surprised out of everyone that the Ri Ciocid had bothered to come at all. Now that he was there it would take all his cunning to be able to punish the man without letting on that it was his own wife who raided Caran Balder.

"Balder," he bellowed, bringing the half-Viking Ri Tuath quickly to his feet. "What charges do ye bring against this man?"

Balder looked to Brian. He raked the Ri Ciocid from head to toe but his eyes never showed a hint of the hatred he felt for the man. Then he turned toward Malsakin.

"He sent a raiding party to Caran Balder two moons past. They wore his colors and demanded entrance in his name. When I refused their request they battered down my gates then threatened to slaughter innocents if I didn't offer them tribute to leave in peace."

Kormlada squirmed in her chair as Balder recounted the events of the raid. Since the moment she perpetrated it she had felt that she put Brian's ascension in jeopardy. This trial might well be the thing to doom it.

Malsakin shot his wife a curious look before returning his attention to Balder. "And did ye offer tribute to these raiders?" he asked, forcing his voice to sound as regal as it could.

"Aye," Balder responded, again raking Brian with his eyes. "The price to end the melee was two hundred head of cattle and my family ring."

Two hundred head of cattle was indeed a grand price but the taking of a man's ring was an unforgivable offense. The crowd gasped and soon they were discussing the atrocity amongst themselves forcing Malsakin to call for order in his court.

When the chatter died down he returned his attention to Balder. "Did ye ever give the Ri Ciocid cause to perpetrate such a deed upon ye?"

"Nay, Ard Ri," Balder replied. "In truth, it was he who gave me cause to offer such a deed against him."

Malsakin lifted his eyebrow and Brian turned his attention toward Balder as both of them wondered what the man spoke of. "Do tell," Malsakin finally requested.

"'Twas he who killed my mother."

That caused the crowd to gasp even louder. This time their discussions were offered in tones that were barely hushed.

Brian listened as two women sitting behind him called him an animal and a barbarian. He turned his attention toward Kormlada who was fussing with the material of her lein. He wondered if she too thought him a barbarian but quickly cast the thought from his mind. He looked back to Malsakin.

Malsakin tried to quiet the crowd by banging his fist against his chair. When their attention was his he again turned toward Balder. "Yer mother was the captain of Olaf's army, was she not?"

There was another outburst from the crowd with the mention of the ousted Ard Ri. Though mostly Gael there was a smattering of Galls among them. And whether Gael or Gall, the name Olaf Curran was enough to strike hatred in their hearts, a fact that Malsakin was well aware of.

"Yer mother died in battle," the Ard Ri continued. "I should say she knew what she was doing at the time of her death."

Balder hung his head. "Ye speak the truth, Ard Ri, but it doesn't lessen my grief over her loss at *his* hands."

Brian wasn't about to defend himself by admitting it was Connor who took Neila's life. Instead he stood to address the matter at hand. The room grew silent.

"If I may, Malsakin, I would like to address Balder directly."

Malsakin nodded his agreement.

Brian took the few steps necessary to put himself before Balder then looked directly into his eyes. "Though it wasn't me who authorized the raid on yer village, I feel it is my duty to offer ye reparations. I will deliver ye the two hundred head of cattle to replace those that were stolen and fifty more for the trouble ye suffered. What I ask in return is a description of the man who raided ye."

A fleeting look of hatred washed over Balder's face, barely noticeable by anyone other than Brian. He answered. "He was slight of build. Blue eyes. His face was unremarkable."

Just then the doors of the hall opened and Brian turned along with the others to see who was joining them. The sun was low in the sky causing rays of light to flood the hall. Tiny specks of pollen glittered in the light and the three men standing in the doorway looked to be nothing more than shadows. One of the men stepped forward just as Brian was about to return his attention toward Balder. His heart skipped a beat.

Could it be true?

He squinted against the sunlight and even rubbed his eyes. Patric took another step forward, uncertain whether he should continue on or wait for the trial to be finished. Malsakin and Kormlada sat forward in their chairs. He didn't know who the young man was but she did. "Patric," she whispered beneath her breath.

Brian didn't hear her but for some reason he turned to look at her as if she could confirm what he was unwilling to believe. Their gazes locked and she offered an almost unperceivable nod of her head. Suddenly Brian was making his way down the aisle.

Patric met him midway. His heart was hammering so hard in his chest that he had trouble breathing. He drew breath, searching for his voice and praying it wouldn't fail him this time. "I've come to serve ye, Ri Ciocid," he croaked.

Brian blinked a few times uncertain whether or not he should believe his own eyes.

Was it possible that Patric was alive or was it some sort of trick?

Patric looked up with wide eyes, praying that the look on Brian's face wasn't born out of hatred. He swallowed hard. "Are ye angry with me, Brian?"

The lad's voice was deep and husky, more manly than Brian remembered it to be but when Patric looked up at him there was no mistaking who he was. He had the look of Lorca.

He reached out a trembling hand to cup Patric's chin. "By all that's holy, lad," he whispered. "It's nay anger that I feel. Only wonder." Tears welled in his eyes. "I thought ye were dead."

Thorien smiled then let out the breath he'd been holding ever since Patric appeared in the doorway. He took a step forward but Murchad reached a hand out to stop him. He too was excited by Patric's sudden appearance in the hall but his father was in the middle of a trial. It wouldn't do his case much good if all his men went to pieces around him.

Thorien nodded acceptance of Murchad's silent warning then turned to offer Havland a wink. Only he could pull off this type of miracle. Havland nodded and smiled.

"Who is it?" Malsakin questioned as he leaned toward Kormlada.

"I couldn't say," she lied, excitement replacing the dread she'd been feeling. With Patric alive it was certain that Brian would be Ard Ri. "Perhaps it's a messenger."

Malsakin allowed Brian what he believed was the proper amount of time to receive his message but when the Ri Ciocid didn't return to his seat he barked, "Who is this man and what has he got to offer to this court?"

Malsakin's voice dragged Brian back to reality. He offered Patric a smile before returning his attention to the Ard Ri. "He has nothing for this court, Malsakin. This business is mine alone."

The statement didn't sit well with Malsakin. It was one thing to interrupt the proceeding to receive an urgent message but quite another to interrupt it without reason.

"Who is that on the horse?" the Ard Ri asked, pointing his finger in the direction of the still open doors. "Does your messenger bring a dead man into my hall?"

Brian had been so intent on Patric's return that he hadn't noticed the two men who accompanied him or the horse carrying the corpse standing behind them. He looked askance of Patric.

"'Tis Connor," Patric whispered with his mouth close against Brian's ear. "We found him murdered on the road in Port daChanoic. I thought we'd bring him to the Munster hut before the trial but when we heard it had already begun we headed straight here. 'Twas my mistake."

Brian could feel the blood drain from his face. In an instant one life was returned to him while another was taken away. As if in sleep, he walked to the horse, gently reaching out a hand to lift Connor's rotting face so he could see it. He swallowed hard then closed his eyes, saying a prayer for his immortal soul.

"Who is he?" Malsakin inquired. "I demand an explanation."

It took a moment for Brian to find his voice. When he did it trembled. "'Tis nay a thing for ye to be concerned with, Malsakin," he croaked against the lump in his throat, his back still facing the Ard Ri. "'Tis one of my men who was found dead on the road."

Thorien and Murchad looked to one another wondering who it was.

"On what road?" Malsakin demanded. He had enough of Boru's games. "Explain yerself, Ri Ciocid."

Brian wiped the tear from his eye then turned to make his way back up the aisle. Before he did he whispered into Patric's ear, "Take Connor and yer men back to the Munster hut. I'll join ye there as soon as I finish this business."

He headed toward his seat but Patric grabbed his arm. "I've information about the raider that could help ye. 'Tis why I came directly to the hall."

Brian's brow shot up as the words settled on his brain. All at once he took Patric's elbow to lead him out of doors. Havland and Finn followed them bringing along the horse carrying Connor's body.

Thorien and Murchad were quick on their heels but as Thorien began to pass through the doors he noticed the gold ring on the ground where the horse had just been standing. He bent to retrieve it, a feeling of dread washing over him as he did.

"Boru!" Malsakin called. "Return immediately."

They were nearly around the bend when Malsakin shouted, "What is it ye have there, Viking? Bring it to me now!"

Even before he spun the ring in his hand to see it's mark, Thorien knew that the ring was Balder's. "Hurry! Get yer father," he whispered to Murchad.

Murchad looked askance of Thorien and the Viking pointed to the mark on the ring.

"Ye're trying my patience," Malsakin bellowed as his hands gripped the arms of his chair.

Thorien handed the ring to Brian as he came rushing around the corner of the building. Neither Patric, Finn nor Havland had ever seen it before leaving only one explanation as to who had been holding it.

"If it was Kevin doing the raiding as ye claim," Brian asked of Patric, "then why did Connor have this ring?"

"Perhaps he was in it with him," Patric replied, lending support to the suspicion Brian had been having all along.

"More likely he was trying to stop him," Thorien offered in defense of the captain he always knew to be loyal.

It was too much for Brian to take in at one time and with Malsakin bellowing from his chair he had little choice but to answer his call. He walked up the long aisle but instead of going to Malsakin he chose to address Balder. "Is this the ring that was taken from ye?"

"Aye," Balder replied, snatching it from Brian's hand.

Kormlada drew breath at the sight of the ring suddenly fearful they would be exposed. Malsakin bellowed, "Bring me that man immediately!"

"There's nay need for that," Brian interrupted, preferring that Connor's body not be inspected by the Ard Ri before he had a chance to do it himself. "I can identify the man for ye."

"Well," Malsakin urged.

"'Tis Connor macCormac, my captain."

The room exploded into conversation and Malsakin released his breath. He winked at his wife. Somehow fate was working with him. He waited for the conversation to die down and for his heart to return to a steady rhythm before stating, "I find it hard to believe that ye didn't know what yer captain was up to, Boru."

Brian shook his head sadly. It seemed he didn't know Connor at all.

"I've testified truthfully," Brian replied. "I've offered reparations for my captain's deeds and now I ask that ye release me so that I might tend to his funeral."

"So ye believe that it should be as simple as that?" Malsakin replied smugly.

Kormlada touched his arm to draw his attention. She whispered in his ear, "Ye have won yer battle, Malsakin. Do not tempt fate."

Brian was surprised by the jealousy he felt over the exchange between husband and wife. He was pondering the emotion when Malsakin suddenly blurted, "Very well then. Connor macCormac will be named responsible for this raid and it will be left to ye to make restitution for his damage."

The words took Brian by surprise. "As ye say, Malsakin," he snapped.

He stood for a moment looking at Balder and wondering why Connor would do such a thing before he spun on his heel to exit the hall. There were so many questions that needed to be answered but he didn't know where to begin.

CHAPTER 20

▼

Tara: Ireland: The Munster hut—Two hours past noon—17, July 984 A.D.—A riot of emotions swirled through Brian's mind. He'd found Patric but in the same moment learned his lifetime friend and most loyal captain had been a traitor before his death. Beads of sweat formed on his forehead as he tried to understand all that was going on. He wiped his face with his sleeve then rested his back against the door.

"Here," Thorien stated, handing him a cup. "Have something to drink. Ye look a fright."

Brian took a sip before lifting his eyes to gaze at Patric. "And why shouldn't I? I'm in the presence of a ghost."

Patric moved forward to place his hand on Brian's arm. "I'm not a ghost, Ri Ciocid, but yer loyal servant. Flesh and blood like the rest of these men."

"Aye, that ye are," Brian replied. He rubbed his open palm against Patric's face, awed by how much the young man resembled Lorca then he screwed up his mouth in mock anger. "May I inquire as to where ye've been and why ye didn't come to me sooner?"

Matching the Ri Ciocid frown for frown, Patric replied, "The last time I tried ye nearly killed me."

Brian's eyes widened and his jaw dropped. Patric chuckled then continued, "We were in Fladbartoc's hall. Ye were in such a hurry to grieve for me that ye broke my arm and nearly caused my death." He lifted the affected appendage then rubbed the spot where it had healed crooked.

Brian looked at it. "By the saints, lad," he gasped when the memory was dredged up in his mind. It was Patric on the ground beneath his horse but at the time he thought his eyes were playing tricks on him. He had pushed the memory so far back in his mind that he didn't recall it until that moment.

As if he could read his thoughts, Patric put his hand on the Ri Ciocid's shoulder. "Ye better sit down, Brian. We've much to discuss."

Brian took a seat behind the small table in the room; everyone else grabbed seats where they could. Soon Patric was telling them all about Ailech. Finn filled in the pieces about Kevin in Torshav and Havland repeated the conversation he overheard between Malsakin and Fladbartoc, but Connor was left for Brian to mull.

"The only answer is that he must have fallen in with Kevin," he mumbled, cursing himself for having sent the man to Cavenlow. "He was acting very strange over the last months. Now it's beginning to make sense."

Murchad covered his father's hand with his. "He's been with ye for so long I can hardly believe it of him."

"Love does strange things to a man, son. The heart has a way of overpowering the mind."

"Well I won't believe it!" Thorien thundered. He had always been a good judge of character. Connor just didn't seem the type to turn against his principles. "There must be some other explanation."

Brian shook his head in desperation. The explanation was the only one that could ease his conscience and he wouldn't let it go. "We must accept what's before us and lay a plan for how to deal with it." His voice was full of authority telling them that he wouldn't accept contradiction. He turned to Patric.

"Yer brother is treacherous and he must be made to answer for his actions."

Thorien stood down. It made little sense to defend Connor at the risk of stirring Brian's ire. He'd rather hear the Ri Ciocid out on the topic of Patric.

"Tell me what it is ye wish me to do and it will be done," Patric offered in response to the statement. He'd waited a long time for this moment and his guts clenched that it was upon him now.

Brian looked at him then smiled. The love he felt for the lad as a child seemed to have doubled while he was away. He placed his hand on Patric's shoulder, fighting back the urge to grab him close. "Patric," he bellowed, his voice quite formal, "before these men I want ye to swear yer loyalty to me."

The request wasn't an unusual one for a king who had been betrayed by his closest ally. Patric did it willingly. He dropped to his knees while the other men in the room got to their feet then he dutifully recited, "I, Patric macLorca, prince of Cavenlow do hereby swear loyalty to my Ri Ciocid and master, Brian Boru macCennitig. My sword shall be at the ready if ever he shall call. I would turn it on myself before ever raising it against him."

Brian nodded then lifted him by the shoulder, again fighting back the urge to embrace him. It was a grave matter they had to discuss and he wouldn't fall victim to his emotions. "Have ye ever had occasion to be in Malsakin's presence before?" he asked. "Did he know ye when he saw ye just now?"

Suddenly Patric felt as if he were on trial. He answered in the same manner. "I have never been in Malsakin's presence, Ri Ciocid. I don't believe he knows who I am."

"How about in Ailech? Did Fladbartoc know ye were macLorca?"

A look of uncertainty passed over Patric's face and Havland jumped from the bed where he'd been sitting. "Nay," he replied in answer to Brian's question. "Both Malsakin and Fladbartoc believe Patric to be dead. I heard them say so with my own ears."

"Good," Brian mumbled, the formality going out of his voice. He was pleased and it showed in his eyes. "So then, ye must leave here immediately and not show yerself until I send for ye. Have ye a place to go, lad?"

Patric knew he could return to Clonmacnoise but he didn't understand why Brian would send him away. He was just about to offer his protest when Havland broke in. "We've been passing the months in Clonmacnoise. We can return there without anyone being the wiser."

Brian put his hand on Havland's shoulder, remembering the man's face but not his name. "How do they call ye, brother?"

"I'm Havland the Bold."

Brian smiled. The name obviously fit. "Very well then, Havland the Bold. Ye and…" he looked at Finn waiting for someone to offer his name.

"They call me Finn the Raven Eye, Ri Ciocid," the Viking offered as he too stepped forward. "We met in Laigan in the house of Harald Bald Knee."

"Aye." Brian smiled. "I remember ye, Finn. Ye and Havland must take Patric back to Clonmacnoise. I want ye to keep him safe until I call."

Both men nodded acceptance of their charge then Brian turned his gaze on Patric. "If it's the last thing I do, I'll see ye sitting on yer father's throne." He kissed both Patric's cheeks then exited the hut, feeling somehow that Lorca was right beside him.

*   *   *   *

Cavenlow, Ireland:—In the Ri Tuath's sleeping hut—Dawn—17, July 984 A.D.—Grace's body was as beautiful as it ever was. Her long legs were still firm and her waist, while a bit thicker from her ten childbirths, still had a comely curve to it. Her pale skin was covered in freckles, an attribute Turlog found quite charming.

He watched her as she slipped from the bed to cover herself with her robe. She didn't know he was awake yet so she moved about quietly. She picked up her hairbrush then turned toward the window to look out onto the forest as she began her grooming.

"Standing there in the sunlight ye look just like an angel," he called, frightening her and making her jump.

She turned and smiled, "I didn't know ye were awake."

"Aye."

She walked over to the bed then sat the edge, looking him over as she continued to brush her hair. He wasn't as thick as Lorca, but his body was taught and his features were fine. He looked more the scholar than the warrior.

"I would think that ye would have slept well into the day after the work ye did last night."

It was his turn to smile, an act he committed far too infrequently, but with her it had become a habit. He reached out his hand to stroke her arm. "I've something I must do so I need to get an early start." He noticed that she lowered her eyes and he asked, "Have ye given any more thought to what we spoke about, Grace?"

"I have."

He lifted himself on his elbow, anxious to hear her reply. "Well?"

She lifted her eyes to meet his and a shiver ran down her spine. As much as she and Lorca had shared, truth be told, it was Turlog who always suited her. He used his mind to gain his power, a trait that she greatly admired. She looked at him and she knew what she must say.

"I'd be happy to be yer wife, Turlog."

CHAPTER 21

▼

Dublin, Ireland: On the training field—Two hours past dawn—24, July 984 A.D.—The heat was so intense that it hung in the air like a great weight causing the warriors skin to glisten without effort. Some wore tunics, but many were bare to the waist as they bandied back and forth with blunted swords.

Kevin watched for a moment before turning his head. It wasn't like him to be found among such exercises but Sigtrygg had pleaded with him to watch and he was hell bent on indulging the lad in an effort to forge a deeper relationship.

Sigtrygg was swinging a two handed sword, grappling with a guard twice his size. He held his own, lunging forward every now and again to smack the guard on his rib and thigh then deflecting the blows being offered in return.

The clash of metal set Kevin's ears ringing but he managed a smile now and again when Sigtrygg glanced his way. He took the linen from his coat then patted his forehead. Instantly there was a water boy at his side, offering him a skin. He took it then drew deeply from it before nodding his head in thanks. The boy headed toward Sigtrygg.

"Did ye notice that new move?" the would-be earl called out, drawing Kevin's attention.

Kevin nodded and Sigtrygg walked toward him. "Why don't ye have a go?"

"Nay, Sigtrygg," Kevin offered with his hands lifted. "'Tis too hot."

Sigtrygg chuckled. "And yesterday 'twas too wet and the day before 'twas too windy. Honestly, Kevin, I don't know how ye can sit on a throne without the knowledge of the sword. 'Tis folly."

"Tis wise," Kevin replied, handing Sigtrygg the linen so he could wipe his face. "Some men are made for the sword and others are made to lead men with swords."

"I suppose ye fall into the latter category."

"Aye, as a matter of fact I do."

Sigtrygg took the skin the boy offered then waved his hand to dismiss him. He took a long draw before pouring the rest of the contents over his head.

"Here's my advice to ye, Kevin," he stated, sweeping his hair back out of his eyes. "If ye don't learn the sword, ye may well die by it if ever one of yer men gets it into his head to turn his on ye."

"I'll take my chances," Kevin replied.

"I wouldn't, and ye shouldn't either. Ye could learn to swing a blade just as well as anyone if only ye gave it yer attention. Ye've a good mind, Kevin. There's not one reason that ye should be shying from this."

He lowered himself to the ground then sat crossed legs watching the other men in the field before turning to look up at Kevin.

"Are ye afraid that ye're too small to hold the weapon?" he asked.

"Well, I'm not exactly afraid," Kevin replied far too quickly.

"But ye think ye're too small?"

"Those blades are heavy, Sigtrygg."

"Aye, but they could be made lighter. If ye decided that ye wanted a blade I could have my man fashion one to yer height and strength."

Kevin shrugged his shoulders as if he were thinking about it and Sigtrygg got to his feet, excited by the prospect of training his new friend. "Here," he said as he thrust the hilt of the two handed sword into Kevin's hand. "Just grip it. Ye don't even have to lift it."

At first Kevin drew back, but Sigtrygg shoved the hilt at him. He gingerly gripped the metal in both hands, feeling the power of the blade and the weight of it tugging on his arm. He slowly moved it from side to side to let the reflection of the sun bounce off it. Sigtrygg smiled. "Powerful, aye."

Kevin smiled then tried to lift the blade. He managed to get the tip mid way off the ground before he felt it slipping from his hands. "'Tis much too heavy, Sigtrygg.

"Aye," Sigtrygg agreed then held up a finger. He jogged onto the field to speak with the man he had been sparing with. The man called to a passing boy with a wave of his hand. In short order the lad ran to the center of the field to bring back a light sword adorned with a plain metal hilt. He handed it to Sigtrygg.

"Here, try this one," the prince called as he jogged forward, shoving the blade at Kevin.

Kevin took it. It was much lighter than the two handed one and the hilt fit snuggly in his palm. Again he leaned it from one side to the other but when he lifted this blade it came off the ground with little effort.

"Grand," Sigtrygg thrilled before picking up the two handed blade. "Now watch me and try to copy."

Kevin nodded agreement then watched as Sigtrygg arched his blade high over his head. Kevin copied the move then repeated it again on Sigtrygg's command. Soon they were moving in unison and Kevin chuckled that he'd been too stubborn to begin this training earlier.

All at once, Sigtrygg spun on his heel then thrust his blade forward. Without thinking, Kevin blocked it and the metal sang out across the field. The terrible vibration crawling up his right arm almost made him drop the blade. He gripped it tight then forced his weight against it to push Sigtrygg's blade back. The lad chuckled.

"Ye certainly do learn quickly, Ri Tuath."

✱   ✱   ✱   ✱

Tara, Ireland: One hour before noon—24, July 984 A.D.—Brian placed his foot in the stirrup then began to hoist himself into the saddle but the call of his name halted him. He turned to see the high queen approaching, her long blonde hair flowing freely behind her, shimmering against her plum colored lein.

"Looks like we'll be detained a bit," Murchad called to Thorien as he nodded in Kormlada's direction. "I've never known the Ri Ciocid to deny the call of a beautiful woman."

Thorien chuckled, "Even those nay so comely."

"I shan't be a moment," Brian snapped back, offering each a glower before turning toward Kormlada who was within earshot.

He took a deep breath to calm his nerves in preparation for their meeting. He felt odd whenever he was in her presence—like nothing in his world made sense.

"Ah, 'tis the fair Kormlada," he thrilled, making an effort to hide his nervousness. "How may I serve ye, high queen?"

Kormlada flashed a smile before nodding her head in acceptance of his compliment. She allowed him to kiss her ring. "May I walk with ye a bit, Ri Ciocid?"

He was fully prepared to decline but when their eyes met it was all he could do to find his voice. She was hypnotic in her beauty and before he could stop himself he was offering his arm to escort her down the path. He could almost feel Thorien and Murchad's giddy smiles against his back but he paid them little mind. "How may I be of service to ye, lady?"

Kormlada remained silent until they rounded the bend and were safely tucked behind the Munster hut then she whirled on him. "The question is—how may I be of service to ye?"

Brian swallowed hard, not knowing what to make of the gesture. "Pardon?"

"The lad who brought the dead man into the hall, it was Patric macLorca, was it not?"

Brian felt the hairs on the back of his neck rise then he mentally ran over all that had transpired in the hall. Unless she was spying at his door the only other way she could have known Patric was if they met in Ailech. He played coy. "He was a messenger delivering news of my man's death."

"Aye, that I was able to figure out for myself. But was he macLorca?" she asked again.

Her eyes were wild with excitement and Brian wasn't sure what to make of it. She seemed desperate to have the information. "Why does he concern ye, high queen?"

"Will ye answer me or nay," she demanded, stomping her foot like a child. If only he would admit that the lad was Patric she would tell him everything.

Her tone was condescending enough to spark his stubborn streak. Even if he had wanted to give her the information he wouldn't offer it now. "Nay."

She looked long at him, realizing that he was being pig headed. He was willful for certain, but soon enough he would be hers and she would make him understand that what she did was for his own good. For now she would demonstrate her cunning.

She smiled wryly. "So, it was macLorca," she thrilled, "which means that ye will be Ard Ri."

The words were offered as casually as if she were commenting on the weather. He thought about them for a moment. If it were anyone other than her delivering them he would have brushed them aside but Kormlada's words had meaning. He grabbed her by the hand to pull her against him then leveled his gaze against hers. "Kormlada! What do ye speak of?"

She noticed the spark of hope in his eyes. He was trying to hide it behind his anger but it was there. An evil grin spread across her face as she tapped him on the nose with her finger then leaned in close until her breath played on his lips. "I've seen it, Brian. So long as Patric lives ye will be Ard Ri." She leaned in to kiss him.

Her words were compelling but they weren't what he was thinking about as he stared at her lips. She was the most beautiful woman he had ever laid eyes on and more than anything he longed to taste her.

He began to lower his head when a thought suddenly struck him. She was there to gain information for Malsakin. Though he wasn't certain why Patric's identity was so important to the Ard Ri, he was certain that he wouldn't fall prey to a woman's guiles. He pushed her away.

"Ye're predictions are wrong, Kormlada."

Her face dropped most visibly and in a moment a storm was brewing behind her eyes. How dare he lie to her? The messenger was macLorca. Every sense in her body told her that he was. Why wouldn't he admit it?

"Liar!" she spit before taking a step toward him.

Either she was truly distressed or she was the greatest actress he'd ever seen. But why would she care about Patric? And why of all things would she be excited to see him sit as Ard Ri? He decided not to be pulled into her games.

"I must go," he said before turning away from her.

Her eyes glazed. Never had a man sparked the feelings in her that Brian did but it seemed that she had little effect on him. She turned to look at him as he walked along the path. His red hair was a riot of curls blowing freely in the breeze. She wanted to run to him, to throw herself at his feet and beg him to take her with him but she remembered who she was and straightened her shoulders before calling out to him, "Brian."

His head told him to continue on. He was nearly at his horse and could be away from her quickly enough but somehow her voice gripped him, forcing him to turn to face her. He stopped.

"Aye?"

There was distance between them and neither one was willing to make the move to close it. They stood there staring as if some invisible barrier kept them apart. She blinked her eyes several times to clear her tears then her hands came together as if in prayer. "He must be macLorca, Brian."

The pleading in her eyes was so intense that he felt his body shake with the desire to confess. It seemed she truly wanted him to gain his crown.

Was this the thing that had bards singing her praises? Her ability to make a man bend to her will by feeding his ego.

He fisted his hands as he took control of his own emotions then leveled a gaze at her that would have burned if it were fire. His voice was low when he spoke, urging her to believe his lie. "Patric macLorca is dead, Kormlada."

Her eyes darted over his face. She believed him. She felt her knees shake and suddenly she couldn't hold her own weight. She crumbled to the ground, sobbing for the emptiness that consumed her.

Instinctively, he moved toward her. She heard his footsteps coming closer and she looked up at him, pleading with her eyes that he should love her. He felt the draw deep in his stomach and soon he was moving more quickly. He would go to her and claim her for his own. Perhaps that would be the thing to have Malsakin give over his throne. He was resolute in his decision but then he noticed the look on her face. She was smiling as if she had won some great battle.

What was he doing?

It was obvious that she was playing him. Playing him as she did so many others. Well, he wasn't like any other man and he growled low in his throat before spinning on his heel to leave her where she sat.

"Nay, Brian, wait," she called to him, her arms extended as if she could touch him.

He didn't stop or even look back. Instead he mounted his horse then led Thorien and Murchad out of Tara.

Her body shook with frustration. How dare he leave her as if she meant nothing to him? She was Kormlada. A man would give his life to have her feel for him the way she felt for Brian.

She watched him until he was nothing more than a speck in the distance then she got to her feet, balling her fists as she called out, "I hate ye, Brian Boru!"

Though he was too far to hear them, somehow he felt her words ripping through his body. He shuddered before kicking his horse into a gallop.

*   *   *   *

Ireland: The Limerick road—Four hours past noon—24, July 984 A.D.—The air was heavy with moisture from the clouds gathering in the west. The storm looked to be a good one and Patric was thankful that they were nearing Torshav. This type of weather always made his arm ache. He stretched it sideways, trying to work out the kink. He reached back behind him to check that Njord's package was still secure. It was a bow and a quiver of arrows purchased just outside Tara. Havland had convinced them to stop for a few days in Port daChanoic to do some hunting with the new weapon. The result was eight rabbits, four pheasants and a swan, the later of which was accidentally shot by Havland when his arrow went astray.

They'd spent a few days in the village drinking in the tavern and sleeping rough at night but now Patric was eager to be back in Clonmacnoise, in his own bed with Freyja, telling her all that had transpired in Tara.

His intention was to stop in Torshav long enough to deposit Finn and his package then he would be off before dawn to head back home. He looked to the village in the distance and instantly realized that something was dreadfully wrong.

"Look there!" he called over his shoulder, drawing the Vikings from their conversation as they followed his finger to the black smoke billowing on the air.

Finn leaned forward for a moment, squinting to see the village in the distance then all at once he kicked his horse into a full gallop. Havland and Patric exchanged fleeting glances before tearing off behind him.

They gasped as they passed through the half opened gates of Torshav. Charred huts dotted the muddy pasture and no animals stood within the confines of their pens. In the distance, bodies of fallen villagers could be seen strewn across the road as if they'd been fleeing. The silence brought an unholy chill to their skin.

Finn sat his horse just inside the gates. He turned toward them as they approached. "'Tis ruined," he mumbled, tears brimming his eyes. He slipped from his horse in a slow, liquid motion then fell to his knees and wept. The scene brought a lump to Patric's throat.

"By the gods," Havland gasped as he too dismounted. There wasn't one building left undamaged.

Patric could feel his body shake as he looked around the village. It reminded him of the night Volkren raided Cavenlow. He thought of Njord and wondered whether the lad was as frightened as he had been when they came or was he brave in the face of his own mortality.

"Why would they burn a carriage laden with treasure?" he asked as his chin motioned toward the smoldering heap to the left of them.

Havland followed his gaze then moved to inspect the rubble. "Looks like a Viking grave cremation."

Finn rushed forward to poke at the contents. Three charred bodies, kitchen utensils, linens and food. "They've taken what they need in Valhalla."

"Is it Gamal?" Patric inquired.

Finn nodded sadly and Havland placed his arm around the captain's shoulder. Patric dismounted. "But who survived to provide the funeral?" he asked anxiously. He scanned the village hoping to find some sign of life.

Senses heightened by the threat of danger, Havland slowly walked around the stone and thatch structure that stood just south of the carriage. The only building that wasn't totally ravaged by fire. He opened the door, speaking in thunderous tones as he stepped inside. "I just hope whoever it is wouldn't be fool enough to attack the likes of Patric the Shaver."

No movement—he continued, "Just in case ye haven't heard, the Shaver's capable of killing twenty men without the benefit of a sword. An enemy ought think twice about an ambush unless he has an army behind him."

Still nothing.

He shrugged then vanished into the shadows of the hut.

Patric uncovered his sword then lingered in the doorway a moment to be certain Havland wasn't walking into a trap. When he was satisfied there was no danger lurking within, he made his way around to the other side of the building. He was brought up short when the slash of the Viking long blade caught him at his side.

He looked down at the rent in his lein and the tiny beads of maroon blood forming a line on the pale skin just above his hip—nothing more than a scratch.

"Damn," he mumbled, then pressed his back tight against the wall of the hut to survey his torn lein. It could be mended easily enough but he hated sewing above all else.

His ire fully piqued, he slid himself against the wall until he was at the edge of the building. He glimpsed the reflection of light off the enemy blade telling him another strike would come soon and he flattened himself against the wall in preparation. He exchanged his sword for his dirk then waited. Within moments, the sword poked around the corner again, slashing with impunity before falling to the ground with a thud.

Confused by the action, Patric quietly slid around the structure in the opposite direction to come upon his enemy from behind. When he did a grin played on his face.

It was Njord.

Patric scooped up a pebble then threw it over the lad's shoulder to distract him before moving in to grab him by the arms. "Easy there, laddie!" he cooed, jumping aside so the flailing blade wouldn't catch him again. "Ye're gonna hurt yerself with that thing!"

"Leave off me, Shaver or I'll kill ye!" the lad shouted as he struggled with Patric over ownership of the blade.

The commotion drew Havland's attention and he rushed from the house in time to see the battle. "Njord!" he cried. "Ease up before ye do damage."

He gave the blade a gentle tug, freeing it into Patric's hand. "What's gotten into ye, laddie? The Shaver's yer friend."

Njord stood staring at him for a time then all at once charged him, kicking and biting him about the shins as he growled with determination.

Havland struggled against the onslaught, pushing away each attack only to be besieged by another. The child was as relentless as a hornet finding any open area to bite.

Patric grabbed Njord by his shoulders, carefully avoiding his flailing limbs. He set him atop the water barrel, gripping his wrists and ankles in either hand as he shouted, "Stop this now and tell us what happened here!"

"Filthy bastard!" the child replied, his piercing green eyes burning with determination as he struggled to be free. "I'll tell ye nothing. Get off my land." He spit in Patric's face.

Patric's eyes narrowed as he pushed his nose against the child's face. "Don't test me, Njord. This isn't a game. Now tell us what happened here."

Njord glared at him without answering and Patric continued, "I know ye're upset but striking out at us won't bring yer family back."

Silence hung in the air as thick as the low-lying clouds, broken only when Finn came tearing around the corner of the building. "Njord! Thank the gods ye're safe."

Njord turned to the call then jumped from the water barrel to land in Finn's waiting arms. He buried his face in the Viking's neck, sobbing uncontrollably. "Why couldn't he just leave us alone? My father never did anything to cause Boru to strike at him. Why couldn't he just leave us in peace?"

"What are ye saying, Njord?" Finn asked as he shook him gently. "Who did this?"

"'Twas Boru's man, only this time he sent a different one. He had a sword and he used it."

Finn pulled Njord close to his chest, stroking the lad's head as he offered gentle hushes. He turned to Patric. "He's too distraught to speak now. Let's give him some time to pull himself together then we'll find out what happened."

"I'm nay a coward!" Njord cried, his voice muffled by Finn's chest. "I took one down myself."

"Took who down?" Patric inquired, urgency lilting his voice.

Njord pushed Finn back, wiping his face with his sleeve as his lip curled. "One of yer king's s-s-soldiers. Yer kin. I took him down with my own hand."

Havland and Patric exchanged glances and Finn grabbed the lad by the shoulders. "Can ye tell us how it happened?"

Njord nodded his head, steeling himself in preparation for the story he was about to tell. "I was in the barn with the cows when the raider rode up with his soldiers all in black masks. They came right up to the house screaming for my father to show himself. They took my mother and brother hostage until my father appeared then they demanded that he pay them silver. He explained that he had none to give but the Dal Cais insisted he had something to offer and that he'd better give it up or suffer the consequences."

He looked to Patric, eyes glowing so hot with hatred that the heat was almost tangible. "My father told them the truth but they wouldn't believe him. They cut Cal's throat and my father went berserk!"

"Are ye sure it wasn't the same man who raided ye before?" Patric asked, his guts twisting in frustration. "Ye're sure it wasn't my brother?"

Njord hung his head. "Brother or nay, 'twas yer kin all the same."

Patric nodded acceptance of the point but Havland meant to know who it was. "Can ye describe him Njord?"

"He looked to be older. His hair was white. He was much taller than the first raider. His voice was different too."

"What happened next?" Finn asked, consumed by guilt for not having been there to protect his master.

"After that, I don't remember it all. They laid fire to the house and there was blood everywhere. There was screaming and smoke and when it was all over I was alone."

"And the soldier," Patric urged. "How did ye manage to kill him?"

As if he was watching it all again, Njord's eyes held a far off look. He didn't answer the question but continued to speak. "My mother bent to kiss my father who was bleeding out from the spear in his chest. When she did they cut off her head!"

The memory was too vivid. Njord began to shake then all at once collapsed into tears.

"'Tis enough, Njord," Finn whispered, offering a silent warning to the other men not to ask further questions. "Ye needn't continue."

Havland wouldn't be put off. He placed a hand on Njord's shoulder before asking, "Tell us what ye did with Boru's man, laddie."

Njord swallowed his sobs then straightened his shoulders. "I'm not a coward!" he cried. "Ye may think I am because I hid in the barn when first they came, but I'm a warrior."

"Ye're a fine warrior to have survived," Patric replied. "Now tell us what ye did to cut down the soldier."

Njord drew a convulsive breath as he struggled to tamp down his emotions. "W-w-when they came, I was frozen with fear and couldn't move. Then I heard it—Thor, the great god of war, reminded me that I was now the earl. He told me to get the sword of my ancestors from the chest where my mother kept it and to use it to avenge the death of my family. I ran through the flames and found it in the bedroom but by the time I had it they were already gone. The filthy Dal Cais set my village aflame before stealing away like the thieves they are."

Guilt eclipsed the lad's face as he hung his head. "I cried as I dragged my family to the field and cried again as I watched the flames carry them to Valhalla. They were warriors but I was a coward."

He took a halted breath and for a moment they thought he would cry again but he held back his tears. "I fell asleep in the barn and was awakened by the sound of a horse. I saw the Dal Cais soldier in search of something. I shook with the thought that it was me he searched for but again I heard Thor speak to me. Suddenly I became brave. I picked up the sword then mounted my father's steed. I used rope to tie myself on so I wouldn't fall off then took aim before setting the horse to gallop. We flew out of the barn and before the Gael bastard knew it was coming, I pushed the sword through his throat. He gasped and squirmed and wriggled on the ground. He even reached out for me to help him but I only laughed and spit on him. He still lays where I left him."

Patric balled his fists in anger. It seemed Kevin had more allies than any of them knew. Havland broke into his thoughts. "So ye are a warrior then, laddie," he bellowed as he turned Njord to face him. "Yer father should be proud. But with my own eyes I must see this soldier ye took down."

Buoyed by the admiration, Njord smiled proudly as he escorted Havland by one hand and Finn by the other to the soldier's rotting corpse lying behind the barn. He spit on it. "I hate the Dal Cais! They're nothing but scum!"

Patric's stomach turned when he reached down to pull on the soldier's lien. "He's wearing Brian's colors but I don't recognize him from Ailech. Can ye place him Havland?"

Havland shook his head. "He could belong to any of the chiefs who didn't join us in Ailech. Not everyone came."

Patric nodded and Finn touched his arm. He was worried about the lad's safety and didn't want to remain in Torshav just in case the raider returned for his man. "We must leave here, Shaver. Can we join ye in Clonmacnoise?"

"Aye," Patric responded. "I'll send word to Brian as soon as we get back. Let's see what he thinks about all this."

"Nay," Njord bellowed. "I won't leave my land and I want nothing to do with Boru."

"Aye, ye will," Finn retorted, offering the lad a pat on the buttocks meant to instill obedience.

"Don't touch me, Finn!" Njord snapped, a veil of hatred covering his face. "Don't any of ye touch me! I'm the earl now and I won't leave my home so some Dal Cais bastard can claim it." He turned to Patric. "Ye claim to be my friend— then prove it. Stay and help me fight Boru."

Patric opened his mouth to reply but it was Havland's voice that filled the air. "Don't ye issue challenges to him. We're not fool enough to face an army with only ye to assist. Ye'll leave here and ye'll do it now!"

With that he lifted the boy who kicked and flailed against him then set him atop his horse with a thud. Finn moved forward to assist holding Njord down with one hand while he adjusted the saddle straps with the other to ensure it wouldn't slip.

"But, Finn," Njord cried in a desperate attempt to gain the captain's sympathy. "Ye can't take me away. What would my father think that we abandoned his land because we were afraid?"

Finn swallowed the guilt that began to swell in him. Acting on emotion would only get them killed. He would avenge his friend in due time but first he must protect Njord. "Yer father would want me to see ye safe and that's what I mean to do," he offered, interrupting the lad's pleading. "Now don't make this harder than it has to be."

"At least let me find my blade," Njord cried as he tried to slip from the horse. "It's the sword of my ancestors. It's all I have."

Finn forced him back into the saddle then turned in search of the blade but Patric held up his hand to stop him. He lifted Gamel's sword into the air to assure the lad that it would be brought along then tied it to his own horse so Njord wouldn't be tempted to use it on him.

He filled their water skins while Finn stood guard over Njord and Havland rummaged through the huts for extra provisions. Less than a quarter hour later, they rode into the north woods on their way to Clonmacnoise.

Traveling with Njord proved to be a maddening experience even for three skilled warriors. The lad was as wily as a fox. Every time they turned their heads he was trying to escape.

They didn't get more than a mile away before he insisted he needed to relieve himself. They made the mistake of letting him go alone and it took them nearly three hours to find him. When they did, he complained of thirst. They gave him the water skin and he drained it forcing them to stop once more so that he could relieve himself again. Even with Finn standing guard, the lad slipped them. That time it only took half an hour to find him.

Eventually they decided to tie him to his horse but by then it was too late. Darkness had fallen and they were left with no choice but to bed down for the night—unfortunately nobody got any rest.

Patric was cleaning up the remnants of their breakfast when Havland approached him. He held out Patric's cloak. "I'm afraid it's ruined, Shaver. I made the mistake of asking the lad to bank the fire and he used yer cloak to do it."

Patric shook his head as he surveyed the garment then swept back the lock of hair that came to rest on his forehead.

"Not to worry. I'll use it to sit on."

Havland raised an eyebrow in askance and Patric explained. "He covered my saddle in horse shit."

Despite himself, Havland chuckled. "He's persistent, I'll give him that. He's managed to turn a one day ride into two."

"Aye," Patric agreed. "I can hardly wait to see what he has in store for us today."

"Well, he's the only one who got any rest last night so we better be on guard."

Patric looked over to where Finn was tying Njord onto his horse. The lad was kicking and cursing as if he were defending himself against murder. "We must find a place for him, Havland for if we don't I might kill him with my own hands."

"I know ye speak the truth, Shaver," Havland laughed. "He's a handful indeed."

He thought about it for a moment then snapped his fingers as a thought crossed his mind. "Perhaps he needs the hand of a woman to rein him in."

Patric's eyes widened. "Aye. We must find him a mother. Perhaps a woman who can't have children of her own." He scratched his beard and wondered aloud, "But where can we begin our search?"

Havland frowned. He had the answer but he doubted that Patric would want to hear it. He offered it cautiously. "We're headed for it."

Patric screwed up his face for a moment before he took Havland's meaning. "Ye can't mean Freyja?"

Havland nodded then all at once ducked as Njord's shoe came sailing past his head. He went to retrieve it and Patric looked to the lad who was beating Finn about the shoulders with the hand he managed to slip from his bindings. "Christ, Havland. Ye can't be serious."

Havland smiled and Patric's shoulders slumped. It was the only thing that made sense. After all, who else would take the demon spawn?

"Ye know it's the best plan, Shaver."

At length Patric heaved a great sigh then turned his attention back to his cloak. "Aye it is," he mumbled, "but that doesn't mean I have to like it."

*   *   *   *

Thomond, Ireland: Early evening—27, July 984 A.D.—Turlog flinched as the needle pierced his skin. His carefully laid plan had fallen apart with Connor's death leaving him scrambling for a plausible cover.

"Easy there, hag!" he hissed between clenched teeth.

The old woman momentarily stopped her stitching to look up at him. "There's nay easy way to mend it. Wounds like these cause as much pain to heal as they cause when they're given."

He looked long at her, his upper lip twitching with the desire to smack the smug look from her face. He was sure she was taking pleasure in his discomfort but he'd rather have the needle pierce his skin than die from a festering wound.

"Well, get on with it then," he muttered, "but ye don't have to look so happy about it."

The woman heeded his command and he returned his attention to his son who was looking on with great interest.

"'Tis too bad that ye didn't arrive sooner in Torshav. Brian returned from Tara certain that Connor had been the raider but this new attack proves it was someone else."

"Aye," Turlog replied, wishing he'd never set foot in the village.

"So, tell me again how ye managed to happen on the whole affair?"

Turlog looked down at the needle, unwilling to let his son see his eyes. "I went to Cavenlow to inquire about Connor but neither he nor Kevin were there. I passed a few days with Grace awaiting their return but when they didn't appear I decided to ride to Torshav to speak with the earl. Connor had been acting oddly this past season and I had a suspicion that he might have been involved in the raiding. I thought Gamal could shed some light on it. When I arrived the place was in ruins with a few stray warriors making their escape. They saw me and attacked."

"And ye were unable to catch any of them?" Joseph queried.

"Catch them?" Turlog barked, "I was lucky to get away with my life. Madan went missing during the skirmish. I never did find him."

"So if Connor was already dead by the time the deed was done who could have done it?"

"Perhaps 'twas Kevin."

"Well, did ye see anyone who resembled him?" Joseph inquired before flinching in sympathy as his father endured another stick of the needle. He turned his head.

"Nay," Turlog growled, stiffening his body and biting his lip from the pain.

"But ye think it could be him?"

"Who else could it be? He left Cavenlow just before the raid occurred and we both know how he feels about Brian."

Joseph thought about that for a while but before he could respond his father was speaking again. "Poor Grace—nine sons dead and the tenth a traitor. 'Twill break her heart when she learns of it."

"Aye," Joseph mumbled. There was no one better at untangling webs then Turlog but for some reason he had a nagging feeling in his gut. "So there's nay doubt in yer mind that things are as ye say?"

Turlog ripped his attention from the needle piercing his skin to let his gaze meet Joseph's. "I've lived yer life twice over. I know a thing or two about men and how they work. Don't question me on this."

"I'm not questioning, I'm just considering," Joseph huffed. "'Tis a precarious position ye find yerself in, father. Yer daughter was betrothed to one raider and ye're planning to marry the mother of another. I wonder what people will think about ye when they learn of this."

Turlog was so angered by the statement that he leaned forward as he prepared to reprimand his son. The thread stretched against his tug but the servant didn't let go of the needle causing it to pull right through the skin. His anger at Joseph was quickly transferred to the woman. "Bitch!" he bellowed before slapping her to her knees. "If ye want to kill me why don't ye just use my sword and be quick about it?"

She rubbed her jaw as she glowered up at him, wishing that words were deeds. Turlog returned his attention to Joseph. "Never mind what people will think," he growled before taking a sip from his cup. "Gossip is the one thing I handle better than anyone else. I'll put things straight before they get out of hand."

Joseph nodded then sipped from his own cup, wondering exactly what his father was up to.

*   *   *   *

Tara, Ireland: The hut of the high queen—Just before noon—28, July 984 A.D.—Kormlada turned her head as the door squeaked against it's hinges. Earlier in the day Malsakin warned her he would be coming. Since her cycle was upon her she thought it would be safe to lay with him. She hadn't expected him so early.

She quickly covered the herbs on her table with the linen then got to her feet hoping to get it over with as quickly as possible. "So is yer business done for the day, Ard Ri?" she asked, her distaste for the matter as transparent as the sheep bladder covering the window.

He smiled as he walked toward her but he didn't answer her question, instead he reached behind her to remove the linen from the table. He looked over the assembly of her concoction then titled his head in askance. She ignored him.

"Come sit with me, husband," she thrilled as she moved toward the bed. "It's been a while since we've had time to ourselves. So many people coming and going and court was quite..."

Her voice trailed off when he moved to stand before her. She averted her eyes. "Will ye rest a while?" she asked, pulling back the bed cover with one hand as she continued to sit the bed's edge. "There's fresh linen."

His gaze penetrated her to her very core and her stomach clenched with an overwhelming feeling that he was going to strike her. She swallowed back her fear then looked up at him with adoration. "Ye look tired, Malsakin. Come and sit beside me so that I can rub yer back."

"What did ye tell him?" he asked suddenly.

His voice was flat, devoid of all emotion but because he hadn't uttered a word until then it caused her to jump. She looked up at him. "Pardon?"

He raked her from head to toe as if there were fingerprints on her skin. She squirmed under his gaze. His eyes narrowed. "Ye must know that I won't let ye go."

He had a strange look in his eyes—as if he were having a vision of his own. She swallowed hard unnerved by the thought that he could know what was in her mind. "Go where?" she cooed.

He stared at her for quite some time but never uttered a word. At length he turned to leave and suddenly she was on her feet, rushing to put herself between him and the door. "Malsakin," she barked as dread consumed her. Darkness began to envelope her. "Tell me what ye mean to do with me."

Again he looked at her. There was pain in his eyes and fear. She took a breath. "Will ye explain yerself?" she asked, desperation lilting her voice.

He stepped close to her—close enough for her to feel his breath on her lips. She leaned in to tempt him.

There was a lengthy silence as he stared at her. He made no move to take what she offered. Instead he seemed repulsed by her. He reached around her to place his hand on the door latch. She pressed herself against him but he shoved her aside, exiting without uttering another word.

✳   ✳   ✳   ✳

Clonmacnoise, Ireland: Noon—28, July 984 A.D.—The air was scented with honeysuckle and bells carried on the breeze from the north. Patric lifted his nose to it, reveling in the first peaceful moment he'd had in days. He knew it would be fleeting and he wanted to enjoy it while it lasted.

When the breeze died down he twisted in his saddle to look back at Havland. The Viking had dark smudges beneath his bloodshot eyes and his hair hung from his head in a tangled mass. Most likely the gash running down his cheek wouldn't leave a scar but Patric couldn't recall ever seeing the man look as haggard as he did at that moment.

He faced forward again to look at Finn who was riding lead. The huge rent in his sleeve was flapping in the breeze to reveal the dark red line of dried blood running from his shoulder to his elbow. Only sheer will kept the man seated on his horse and that was running out quickly.

Patric's own appearance left much to be desired. He absentmindedly wiped back a stray hair from his forehead then flinched as the pressure against his broken finger sent a jolt of pain up his arm. "Damn," he hissed while trying to shake it off.

Finn's head snapped around, his short sword poised to fend off the attack, but when Patric held up his hand in a sign that all was well he again faced forward, pushing on despite his weariness.

Patric sneered when he looked at Njord—silent now thanks to the gag in his mouth. The lad was the picture of health, sitting erect in his saddle as his green eyes darted from one side to the other taking in his surroundings.

Patric imagined the thoughts behind those penetrating eyes then issued an audible growl to warn the child against further mischief. Havland wasn't so kind.

"If ye try anything at all, laddie," he called as he reined along side Njord's horse, "I'll kill ye."

Njord's eyes widened then he lifted his chin, tugging slightly against the ropes that bound his hands as if to say that there was little he could do. Havland issued a wary laugh in response. "Even the strongest rope couldn't bind the devil."

When they reached the tavern they dismounted in turn, each warrior stretching away the soreness of his muscles before gingerly touching his wounds. Then they prepared to release Njord.

Without words it was decided that Havland would do the deed. Being both the largest and least damaged of the three it only made sense. He approached the job with certain prudence, looking over the situation before issuing his orders.

"Finn, ye take his left leg and the Shaver will take his right. Hold him down good so he can't kick at ye. Only after I get the legs untied will I release his hands, but ye better be ready because it's then that he'll be in a position to do the most damage."

Both Patric and Finn nodded their understanding then moved to take their positions but just as Havland began to execute the plan, Freyja appeared in the dooryard.

"Shaver?" she called as she lifted a quizzical eyebrow for the scene. "I didn't expect ye back so soon."

If there was fear in Patric's eyes as he prepared to deal with Njord it doubled with the sight of Freyja. He swallowed hard as he looked first to Finn and then to Havland. Each returned his glance, sympathetic for the task that loomed before him. He turned toward Freyja, opening his arms and plastering an innocent smile on his face before limping forward to greet her.

"By the gods, what happened to ye, Shaver?" she gasped.

Patric sighed momentarily when she pressed the damp cloth she'd been wiping her hands on against his heated face then he took her hand in his. "Someone raided Torshav," he replied, nodding his head toward Njord. "Only the lad survived."

"Torshav," she mumbled, confusion dotting her face. She covered his other hand with hers and he drew back in pain.

"What happened, Shaver—I thought ye went to Tara?"

"I'll explain it to ye later, aye." He was weary and he wanted to rest a bit. "Right now we need to get the lad inside."

Freyja's brows knit together as she struggled to make sense of the statement. She cast a scrutinizing gaze at Njord then noticing his restraints and the gag in his mouth it suddenly became clear to her. "Don't tell me that *he* was the cause of this."

Patric nodded and she threw up her hands.

"Naaaay," she spit. "We don't need any trouble here, Shaver."

A barrage of curses bubbled up in Njord's throat as he tried to tell Freyja just what *he* thought of *her* but the gag muffled them.

Havland took the opportunity of the lad's distraction to quickly release his bindings. He pulled him from the horse and immediately Finn moved in, grabbing Njord's ankles so he couldn't do further damage.

The action sent Freyja flying back into the tavern muttering, "Nay. I've enough to deal with around here without having a banshee as my ward."

"He's a good lad, Freyja," Patric gushed as he followed her. "He won't be giving ye any trouble."

She turned then, watching intently as Havland and Finn carried Njord into the darkened tavern like a strung up deer. They set him down on a chair, each man pressing down on a shoulder to stop him from bolting.

"Och, aye," she laughed, "I suppose that's why ye have him strung up so." She lovingly slapped his cheek. "Don't be lying to me now, Shaver. I know the lad. I've seen the fire in his eyes when he gets himself worked up. He's a handful. Just look at the lot of ye."

She walked away, waving her hand in dismissal. "I've nay a need for such trouble. I've enough to tend with the drunken rots around here."

Patric caught her by her wrist then lowered his eyes to meet hers as he began his pleading. "He could be a help to ye, Freyja and I'll pay ye for his care."

She shook her head fiercely, chuckling as she wrenched away from him. He closed in on her.

"I promise he'll be nay trouble to ye. In fact, he'll be my responsibility. Let him stay out the winter. If after that ye still don't want to keep him I'll find another home for him when next I leave."

Her shaking head continued to offer her refusal but her eyes were beginning to show her weakness. Though she would never admit it, she had fallen totally in love with the Shaver and would do anything he asked in order to keep him with her.

He stroked her cheek with his thumb as he held her chin in his hand. She sighed, "But why would ye want to keep a child who's given ye so much trouble, Shaver? Wouldn't it be better to see him off now and be done with it?"

He leaned in close to her ear sending chills up her spine as he did. "If it was my brother who sent the raiding party to Torshav then I have a responsibility to care for the lad. Would ye have me dishonored, Freyja?"

"Nay," she replied then cast her eyes toward the ground. Patric's honor was his most attractive quality. She wouldn't be the cause of him losing it. She looked up suddenly, melting with the warmth she saw in his beautiful eyes. If she kept the lad she could gain him in the bargain. "So, if he'll be yer responsibility I suppose ye're planning on staying in Clonmacnoise for a time."

Her tone revealed nothing of the love she held for him.

"If ye'll have me."

Of course she'd have him but she was wary of giving him her heart for fear he'd break it. It had happened once before and it nearly devastated her.

"What about Cavenlow?" she questioned, needing to mark the things that could make him leave.

"'Tis a long story, Freyja," he sighed. "I'll tell ye all about it when we're alone but for now will ye agree to keep the lad?"

She heaved a great sigh before looking past him to Njord who was still being restrained by the two warriors. He was thick of flesh with hair as black as coal and sparkling green eyes that seemed almost catlike in the glow of the oil lamps. She walked over to him, taking his handsome face between her thumb and forefinger then moving his head from side to side as if she were inspecting a horse. She glowered at him.

"Ye must promise Freyja that ye'll cause her nay trouble, lad," she demanded. "I won't put up with whatever mischief ye perpetrated on these three. If ye don't agree, I'll put ye out for the wolves."

She took the gag from his mouth and he wrenched himself from her grasp. "I don't need ye to care for me, woman!" he spit. "I'm a man who can care for myself! I'm a warrior."

Her soft eyes immediately narrowed. With the speed of a deer she ripped him from the chair then slapped his buttocks with her powerful hand. The crack rang solid in the empty tavern.

"Ye'll never use that tone with me again," she hissed. She spoke in Manx as she did whenever she was angry. "Warrior or nay, ye're under my care now and ye'll do as I say. Is that plain enough for ye, little rot?"

Njord's eyes flew open with the shock of the action then immediately glazed. "I'll obey ye, Freyja," he croaked in the same language she used, batting his eyes several times in order to hold back his tears.

She took a long moment to look at him but her eyes never softened. She straightened her lein then stormed off toward the kitchen, muttering loud enough for all to hear. "Now, that's how to handle the lad. Damn men can storm a village and kill everyone in it but ye can't make a child bend to your will. By the gods, I wonder how ye control this world."

Havland laughed heartily before adding his own abuse to Njord's reddening buttocks by way of a not so gentle whack. "So now, I guess ye've met yer match there, laddie."

As much as Finn was enjoying seeing the lad suffer he stepped forward to offer him comfort. He'd known Njord since the day he was born and though the lad was a handful he was showing signs of becoming a good leader.

"Come on now, laddie," he cajoled, "Be brave about it."

Njord buried his face in Finn's chest to hide his tears then shouted after Havland who was moving toward the mead barrel to get a drink, "I only obeyed for yer sake. I didn't want ye to be without a friend in the woman."

Havland chuckled so hard he spit then wiped his mouth with the back of his sleeve.

"I haven't found a friend in that woman since I first introduced her to the Shaver," he replied, nodding his head toward the back of the tavern where Patric was sitting, legs upon the table and leaning back in his chair. "It's him who'll benefit from yer obedience, nay me."

Patric issued a "hmph" before carefully crossing his arms behind his head. If anyone could control such an evil lad it would be Freyja. He closed his eyes to get some rest but in a moment Njord was at his shoulder. "I won't be staying here, Shaver and ye can't make me," he hissed. "I belong in Torshav. It's mine now and I must go back to claim it before someone else has at it."

Patric didn't look at him. "Go then," he mumbled, completing his yawn. "I'll not stop ye. But I'll tell ye right now that if ye choose to go ye best not be seeking my help when ye find yerself surrounded by an army."

There was no response from Njord. Patric opened one eye to see if the lad was still standing there. It seemed the child was thinking about the statement and Patric continued on to stress his point. He unfolded his arms, taking care not to bang his broken finger then he brought his legs down from the table and leaned forward to relay his seriousness. "We brought ye to safety and ye repaid us by causing us harm."

He slid his hand forward so Njord could see his swollen and blackened finger. "If this is the way ye repay kindness then I'll be happy to see ye off."

Njord remained silent as he looked at the hand. Patric's anger ignited. "Here," he barked, pulling his dirk from his belt then slamming it against the table. "Take this to protect yerself with."

Njord looked at the blade then to the warrior whose eyes were glowing serious. It was true—they were trying to help him and he was acting like a child instead of the earl he now was. His father would be embarrassed. His vision blurred as his eyes again glazed.

"My apologies, Shaver," he croaked. "I'm better than this and if ye give me the chance I'll prove it to ye."

At first Patric thought to rebuke him but then his heart took the place of his head. Again he remembered the night of Lorca's death and his eyes softened.

He began to pat Njord's head with his right hand then remembered the broken finger and traded it for his left. "What say ye to having something to eat?" he whispered. "We're worn out from our journey and shouldn't make any decisions until we've taken our rest. We can discuss this in the morning when our heads are fresh and Calder has a chance to set our wounds to healing."

Njord lifted his head then wiped away his tears with the back of his sleeve. He gently leaned back against Patric's arm. "That'll be fine Shaver," he sighed. "Perhaps ye can assist me in figuring out who the raider really is."

That was Patric's intention all along.

CHAPTER 22

▼

Cenn Cora, Ireland: The great hall—Early evening—3, August 984 A.D.— Murchad mulled the board anxiously. He was certain his father had laid a trap for him but he couldn't spot it. A lock of brown hair hung down his cheek and he reached back to push it behind his ear then he smiled.

"Check," he called, moving his pawn to the black square in front of Brian's king. "Very well," Brian replied, then moved his king one square to the side to threaten Murchad's knight.

"Damn," Murchad hissed. Again he considered the board with determination. In all the time they had been playing against each other, he'd only beaten his father once. His finger dangled over his rook and a fleeting smile passed Brian's lips. He withdrew then moved it to his queen.

They were both so intent on the game that neither looked up as Turlog approached. "May I speak with ye, nephew?"

Startled by Turlog's presence, Brian sat straight in his chair before waving his uncle to a seat. "Can it wait a moment? I think I have the lad on the ropes."

"Don't be so sure, Ri Ciocid," Murchad replied, moving his queen into striking position of his father's king. "Check again."

Brian returned his attention to the board and Turlog touched his arm. "I know ye heard about Torshav."

"Aye," Brian replied before taking Murchad's knight with his bishop leaving it to threaten his king. "That's checkmate, Murchad."

Murchad's eyes narrowed as he studied the board. His father had queen, knight, bishop and rook surrounding his king. There was no escape. He nodded acceptance of his defeat then set the board aside so they could hear Turlog out.

"So?" Turlog asked.

"So nothing," Brian replied. He sat back in his chair then lit his pipe. "The village was annihilated. There's no one left to demand restitution from me."

"So who do ye think it was?"

Brian looked long at his uncle then to Murchad. He'd given both his son and Thorien clear instructions never to speak about what they learned in Tara regarding either Kevin or Patric. He hoped that Connor's death would either end Kevin's raiding or draw him out. It seemed to be doing the latter.

"Why don't ye tell me who *ye* think it was?" Brian replied, turning back to look his uncle in the eye. "Joseph tells me ye saw the raider leaving the village and that ye swore it was Kevin."

"I said that I thought it was Kevin," Turlog corrected. "I never swore 'twas him."

"I see," Brian crooned. A wave of distrust prickled his skin but he didn't show it.

"I'm lucky I wasn't killed, nephew," Turlog continued. "There were better than a hundred men raiding that village."

"Aye," Brian offered before removing his pipe from his mouth. He shifted the tobacco in the bowl then lit it again by the oil lamp before drawing in the smoke. "Those are remarkable odds."

Turlog panicked as he waved the smoke Brian blew in his face away with his hand. His nephew was being far too indifferent about the whole affair. "What goes on here?" he demanded. He could feel that Brian was keeping something from him but he wasn't sure what. "Ye bring back Connor's dead body and announce that he was the raider yet ye're questioning me as if I had something to do with it."

Brian wagged the pipe under Turlog's nose setting the man to coughing when he accidentally inhaled the smoke. "I've asked ye nothing."

"Well then why do I feel that I'm being accused of something?" Turlog croaked. "I told ye what I thought. If ye can use it fine, if not then I'll be on my way."

He stood to leave but Brian stopped him with a question. "And where were ye that ye managed to come upon the raid, uncle?"

Turlog looked down his nose at Brian, struggling to keep his voice even. "I was in Cavenlow waiting for Connor but when he didn't arrive I went to Torshav to question Gamal."

"And why would ye do that without informing me about it? I settled my business with Gamal in Lagain?"

"Connor was my man! I had every right to know what he was up to."

"And ye thought he was up to raiding?" Brian questioned, his voice growing stronger as he inched his way closer to the truth. "Were ye in it with him then?"

"How dare ye?" Turlog snapped back. "After all I've done for ye, now ye accuse me of treachery?"

"What am I to think?" Brian replied. "Ye betrothed Connor to yer daughter without so much as a mention of it to me and he turns out to be the raider. Then ye just happen to be in Torshav when a second raid occurs and Cavenlow before that. Explain it to me, uncle because my head aches trying to figure it all out."

Turlog was ready for the accusation though he was surprised it would come so soon. He lowered himself back into his chair then let his eyes go cold before addressing the charges. "Let me remind ye that both Connor and I were in Ailech with ye when the first raid occurred. We were by yer side trying to win ye the high crown. 'Twas ye who came back from Tara accusing the man of treachery, not me. Ye sent Connor to Kevin and he didn't return. If ye recall I told ye that I thought Kevin was up to nay good. I went to Gamal to gain clues about Kevin hoping they would lead me to Connor, but as ye already know, I was too late."

Brian mulled the explanation. It was plausible but something still didn't sit right with him. "Ye were in Cavenlow for some time. What were ye doing there?"

"Making love to yer sister," Turlog stated plainly. "Grace and I are to be married."

That statement nearly knocked Brian from his seat. First Connor and Lara then Grace and Turlog. How could all this be going on right under his nose without him knowing about it? Lorca would roll in his grave. "Married? Ye and Grace?"

"Aye," Turlog replied. "We decided it just now. I came to get yer blessing but now I suppose 'twill be out of the question."

Brian should have expected as much. Turlog was as eager to get at Grace as he was to get at Cavenlow. Originally it was he who sought her hand but Cennitig refused his offer choosing Lorca to be Grace's husband instead. They were both widowed now. There wasn't any reason they shouldn't be married but somehow it felt queer to him.

"Ye shall have it," Brian mumbled. "But I hardly believe that my sister would care if I gave it or not."

"I care," Turlog replied, and he did. Brian's blessing would be a public statement of trust thwarting any who would mark him as a traitor due to his ties to Kevin and Connor.

Brian extended his hand and Turlog took it. "Ye and Grace always got on well. It makes sense that ye should share yer lives. I have only one question."

"Aye," Turlog responded, lifting his brow to urge him on.

"Have ye told my sister that ye think her son is the raider?"

"Of course not," Turlog huffed. "She's innocent in this. I doubt she even knows that it's happening."

"But ye will tell her in time?"

"Why would I?" Turlog replied bitterly. "'Tis obvious that ye believe Connor to be the raider. Unless ye change yer mind about it I'll gain nothing but the woman's ire for the accusation. Nay, I'll not speak about it again."

The statement was a true one. Speaking about the raider would only cast suspicion on him and that was the last thing he needed.

Brian nodded acceptance of his uncle's point. In truth, he was grateful. Until he was ready to move on Kevin it would be best to keep his intentions to himself, besides, Turlog's marriage to Grace might prove useful in gathering information about Cavenlow.

"So then, should I expect to be banned from the wedding?" Brian asked, his wry smile suggesting that there could only be one answer.

"Of course not," Turlog responded. "Grace knows her place in these matters. 'Twill be a small affair but protocol will be observed."

"Good," Brian replied then turned to look at Murchad who'd been sitting silent through the conversation. A slight shadow of confusion played on his face, unperceivable to anyone other than Brian. He stood at the same time the Ri Ciocid did.

Brian linked arms with him then descended the platform. He leaned in close to whisper, "Send word to Patric that I'll be meeting him in Torshav in two weeks."

Murchad nodded and the Ri Ciocid left the hall.

$$*\qquad*\qquad*\qquad*$$

Cavenlow, Ireland: The private chambers of the Ri Tuath—Two hours past noon—8 August 984 A.D.—Grace laid perfectly still while she waited for sleep to come to her. She had spent the whole of the morning and into the afternoon in that same position, studying the thatch underbelly of her hut. Since childhood, she rarely slept at night just in case there was an attack. Instead she would grab a few hours of sleep at dawn then sustain herself with a light nap during the day, but lately, sleep was eluding her completely.

Her thoughts were consumed by Kevin. He left Cavenlow two moons ago and during his absence another Gallish village had been raided. It was the third time such a thing occurred. She couldn't deny it any longer—he was the Dal Cais raider.

Her stomach flipped with the thought of it causing her to sit up. He was placing himself in grave danger—not only with the Galls but with Brian as well, and it was Brian that worried her most. Turlog was her only hope for protecting him and she would do anything she must, including groveling at her brother's feet, to see her last surviving son safe.

The commotion in the courtyard stirred her from her thoughts and immediately she was on her feet. Kevin sent word that he'd be home two days ago. Apparently he had finally arrived.

She grabbed up her robe then headed out the door, smoothing back her hair with her hands as she went. She caught him before he entered his hut. "Thank God ye've returned safely," she called, rushing forward to shower his face with kisses. She was a master at disguising her emotions. This performance attested to the fact. "Was the journey a hard one?"

He looked her over at arms length, never letting the smile slip from his face even when he noticed the dark smudges beneath her eyes. "Aren't ye a sight," he cooed before returning the affection she had showered upon him. At any other time he would have preferred to get himself settled before dealing with her but the news he had to share made her sudden appearance a welcomed one. "'Tis amazing that I only realize how much I've missed ye once I'm home."

She returned his smile then pushed back a lock of hair from his forehead. "Will ye tell me all about yer trip?" she asked. "How was Dublin?"

His eyes lit up with the question and suddenly he looked like a child. He reached out his arm to Garvin who was standing behind him carrying a long leather case.

"Ye'll never believe what I did while I was there, mother." He took the case from Garvin then undid the laces to expose his new blade. He held it out to her. "'Twas a gift from earl Sigtrygg the Silken Beard. He had it made especially for me and even instructed me in it's use. Can ye believe that after spending my whole life avoiding lessons I've come to learn that I'm actually quite good? I must have taken the gift from my father. Don't ye think so, Garvin?"

Garvin nodded his head then forced a smile. The blade was the only thing Kevin talked about their entire trip home and it was beginning to grate on his nerves. While he was happy that the Ri Tuath finally learned the art of weaponry, he was sore that he hadn't been the one to teach him. That pleasure had gone to the young earl, Sigtrygg who was fast becoming his rival.

Grace drew breath with the statement. She watched her son move with the blade, seemingly complete now that he understood the use of it. If there were any doubts at all in her mind that Kevin could be the raider they were erased at that moment.

"Ye handle it well, son," she muttered through her forced smile, "but I fear that I'll be worrying over ye now more than ever. Shall I presume that ye're meaning to march when next ye're called?"

Kevin momentarily paused in his exercises to look up at her then he laughed. "I can assure ye that if yer brother calls he'll be met with the same answer I've always given. But at least now I'll be ready if Volkren returns."

He handed the blade back to Garvin before moving close to her. "Ye needn't worry for me, mother," he stated with certain conviction. "Every man should know the blade for if he doesn't, he'll be left vulnerable to the machinations of others. I'm a man and I must protect ye. Now I can."

She was truly amazed that he would be so bold about the situation and decided in that moment that she must tell him of her plans to save him from himself. She nodded her head as if she accepted his point then laced her arm through his to lead him to her hut. "We must speak privately," she cooed in the voice she used whenever she wanted to gain his immediate attention. "I've something to tell ye."

He lifted an eyebrow then turned to nod at Garvin, giving him the silent message that he would join him in their bed later.

"So is it intrigue or gossip?" he asked when he turned back to her, his voice giddy with excitement.

"Neither," she replied then she opened her door and they both stepped inside. She wrung her hands while she struggled for the best way to approach the subject. In the end she decided to lay it plain. She waved him to a seat.

"On the new moon I shall remarry."

Kevin's smile faded slowly as her words settled on his brain. He looked at her with narrowed eyes, wondering what had taken place while he was away. "Married to who?"

His tone was that of superiority but according to Brehon law she didn't need his permission to remarry.

"Turlog of Thomond," she replied, looking him straight in the eye to show she was serious.

The eyes that held love for her a mere moment ago grew angry as Kevin got to his feet. "Never!" he barked. "I'll not give my consent for ye to marry Brian's uncle after all we've been through. Ye must be mad for even thinking that I would!"

"I don't need yer permission. 'Tis my right to marry anyone I wish. I choose Turlog."

She was right, of course and he could see by her eyes that she was dead serious. If he wanted to dissuade her from her cause he would have to cajole her. He took a deep breath before stepping toward her with upturned palms.

"Ye must forgive me for being so abrupt," he whispered, "but ye have to admit that this is quite a surprise for me. What's happened while I was away to make ye rush into such a decision? Aren't ye happy here, mother? Have I done something to drive ye away from yer own home?"

Her eyes narrowed with her swelling anger. He was a grand actor but he seemed to have forgotten that his audience was someone who knew him far too well.

"There was another raid on Torshav while ye were away. Rumor has it that ye were the raider. If these rumors manage to reach the Ri Ciocid's ears, I think it's best that we have an ally in his camp who can keep ye from harm."

Genuine confusion dotted his face and for a moment she wondered whether she misjudged the situation, but even if he wasn't the raider there were those who would see him hanged for it all the same. "I'll not lose ye to my brother, Kevin. I've lost too many already. Ye're all I have left."

"But I don't understand," he mumbled while taking a step back. "I've been in Dublin all this time. Sigtrygg will attest to it."

"Really, Kevin," she blurted. "Ye must think me the grandest fool of all."

His only reaction was a blank stare. She pressed him, "Do ye seriously think that Brian would take the word of Olaf's son? Malsakin's stepson? Believe me Kevin, the only way to see ye safe is for me to marry Turlog and that's exactly what I intend to do."

He sat the edge of her bed trying to digest the information. Malsakin had sent a message to Dublin telling him what transpired during court and suggesting that they put their plans on hold for a while to see what came out of it. He never mentioned this. What could he have hoped to gain by sending someone else to raid Torshav?

"When did it happen?" he asked, looking at her but not really seeing her. "When I was in Dublin I heard that Connor was the raider and that…"

"Torshav was raided after Connor's death," she replied, probing him with her eyes hoping that he would reveal the truth.

He shook the confusion from his brain. "And people believe it was me doing the raiding. I don't understand why."

"Why not?" she snapped as she finally lost patience with him. "They lay everything else at yer feet. Why not this?"

He looked at her then, realizing that she was angry with him. "Ye believe it too, don't ye?"

"Is it true?"

He shook his head then got to his feet. He rested his hand on her shoulder. "I was in Dublin, mother. On that ye have my word."

"And the other times? Where were ye then?"

He looked at her, his eyes cold and hard. She was an intelligent woman who could easily see through his lies so he chose not to offer them. Instead he asked a question of his own. "So ye believe that marrying Turlog will keep yer brother away from me?"

The fact that he didn't answer her question didn't escape her. She answered him anyway. "I do."

"Very well," he replied, squeezing her shoulder gently. He needed to be out of there quickly so that he could think about the situation. "It will be as ye wish."

He turned to exit the hut, stopping long enough at the door to call out, "Just be sure to save a dance for me."

*   *   *   *

Torshav, Ireland: The earl's hut—Two hours past noon—17, August 984 A.D.—Brian sent word that he wanted to meet with Patric privately and it was decided that Torshav would be the best place to accomplish that goal. Patric spent the better part of a week repairing the earl's hut so they would have a comfortable place to pass the time. He stepped back to admire his work just as Havland burst through the door.

"He's here, Shaver."

"Who does he bring with him?"

"Only Murchad and Thorien."

Patric nodded. He had expected as much and set six chairs around the table so they could speak comfortably. He shooed away the flies from the feast of cheese and cold fish lying on the sideboard then turned on his heel to greet his king.

The vision of Brian seated on his horse always took Patric's breath away. He looked almost holy with his long red hair blowing back in the breeze and a glint of sunlight sparking from his dark blue eyes. This day he wore a brilliant blue coat over a gold lein making him look every bit a king.

"Welcome, Brian," Patric called as he bowed from the waist.

Havland and Finn quickly did the same.

Brian dismounted then closed the distance between them, a queer expression of confusion and love marking his face. He lifted a lock of Patric's hair from where it rested on his shoulder then scrutinized the lad for a moment. "Ye look like a Viking," he bellowed before hugging him close.

"Aye," Patric replied. "Ye said ye wanted me to keep my identity a secret. I'm only following yer orders."

"And it's working," Havland added. "Ye should hear the lad when he speaks the language. Ye'd think he was from the motherland the way he's picked up the tongue."

Murchad looked Patric over, appreciating his appearance. He was thick and well muscled and his costume of a hide vest and breeches fit him well. Murchad's eyes lingered on the bronze cuffs at Patric's wrists. "I rather fancy the look," he offered as he walked around him. "I very much like the jewelry."

Patric nodded then undid the clasps of his cuffs. He held them out to Murchad. "They're yers. A gift between brothers."

Murchad smiled as he accepted them then bowed before Patric. Truth be told, he liked the man.

"Why don't we go inside to have something to drink?" Patric offered pointing toward the door. "I've managed to get at least one building back in shape. The others will take a bit of time."

Brian followed him into the hut then took a moment to marvel at its grandeur. It was large enough to house twenty men and Patric had it set up so that it resembled a small hall.

"Do ye like it here, Patric?" he tested, hoping the answer would be positive.

"Shaver," Havland interrupted causing Brian to raise his eyebrow. "We call him, Shaver for what he did to Throdier. We thought 'twould be best not to use his Christian name if we wanted to keep his identity a secret."

Brian nodded and Patric responded to his question. "Aye, Brian, I like it here fine. Set up properly the village could be quite productive and extremely defensible."

"So if I asked ye to stay here a while longer while I sort out the situation with Kevin ye wouldn't protest?"

Patric, Havland and Finn all looked at each other weighing the possibility. Finn was the first to nod his agreement. Havland soon followed but Patric had some questions. "How long do ye think it might take ye?"

"I couldn't say," Brian replied before reaching over to grab a piece of cheese from the feast laid on the sideboard. "It seems that yer mother is planning to marry my uncle. I'm hoping to gain some information from the union."

Patric's eyes flew open and his lip curled in anger. "Turlog! She's going to marry, Turlog? Lorca will haunt them every day of their married lives."

"Aye," Brian agreed, remembering the way Lorca's face would twist whenever his uncle was among them. Lorca knew Turlog coveted his wife and was always quick to remind the old man that she was his. "We were all quite surprised by it."

Patric pushed himself from his chair then began to pace the room, needing some release for his anger. The more he paced the more he thought then suddenly he whirled around to face Brian. "Her marrying Turlog is as good as an alliance between ye and Cavenlow. Does this mean that Kevin is prepared to swear to ye?"

Brian reached out to touch Patric's arm. Though he knew that patience wasn't a virtue possessed by most young men, Patric had demonstrated that he was capable of it.

"That's why I need the time," he explained sympathetically. "Yer mother's marriage to Turlog is set for the full moon. It's then that I will ask Kevin to swear to me. If he does I can't very well remove him from Cavenlow even if he is the raider. If he doesn't I'll call him out for his treachery and ye shall lead my army."

Patric thought about the relationship between Kevin and Grace. They had been in collusion on too many things for him to believe this marriage wasn't to benefit his brother.

"He'll swear," Patric mumbled, realizing that his hope of gaining his father's throne wouldn't be realized. "But even when he does, I wouldn't trust him. Ye must keep yer eye on him, Brian because if he sees an opportunity to strike at ye he'll use it."

"Aye," Brian agreed. "That's why Turlog will be useful."

"Do ye want me to remain hidden in Torshav?" Patric questioned, puzzling through his own future. In truth, he had come to like his life as it was. The adjustment wouldn't be much of a sacrifice.

"If ye agree I'd like ye to oversee Leinster for me," Brian replied. "I've always left the Galls to themselves but with the hard feelings about the raids I think it best that I have one of my own here to keep an eye out. Since there was no one left in Torshav I thought ye could take it for yer own. I'll name ye earl and…"

"Njord," Patric interrupted.

Brian lifted his eyebrow and Patric continued, "Gamal's youngest son, Njord, managed to escape with his life. I've been keeping him in Clonmacnoise with me. The village rightfully belongs to him."

Brian remembered Njord from Lagain and a smile crossed his face. "Ye mean the little lad who was smart beyond his years? He survived?"

"Aye," Patric replied. "He fancies himself as earl now that his father's dead."

Brian puzzled through the situation. "Well, he'll need a custodian. I'm certain he'd agree to let ye conduct yer business from his village until he's old enough to take it. By then, who knows what will be."

"He'll agree," Finn interjected in a clear, strong voice. Even though the plan might strip him of the opportunity to avenge Gamal's death it was important for Njord to have a friend in the Ri Ciocid when he became earl of the village. "He'll agree even if I have to redden his arse to make it so."

The men laughed at that and Brian rubbed his hands together. "So then it's settled. We're all in agreement that Patric—I mean, the Shaver, will be overseer in Leinster."

Patric nodded and the next few hours were spent laying plans for his new life as a Leinster Gall.

PART TWO

CHAPTER 23

▼

EIGHT YEARS LATER

Torshav, Ireland: Dawn—13, June 992 A.D.—The passing years were relatively uneventful. Brian spent most of his time in Cenn Cora trying to rebuild his wealth and laying plans for his ascension. He was married for the fourth time after his last wife died of illness. The only issue from his new marriage was a daughter.

Grace and Turlog were now living in Thomond. Every now and again they would travel to Cavenlow to call on Kevin who had sworn his loyalty to Brian on their wedding day. Twice a year Kevin traveled to Dublin to visit with earl Sigtrygg. He never did marry but rumors of his treachery were virtually nonexistent. Brian named Connor as the Dal Cais raider and most everyone accepted it.

Thorien continued on as earl of Limerick. The four sons Gayla had given him traveled everywhere with him, except when he was called to do battle for Brian—mostly petty skirmishes that were quickly put down.

Murchad was married to the granddaughter of Malmua of Desmumu as was arranged after the Ri Tuath's death. Desmumu now belonged to Murchad and he had two daughters and a son by his wife. They were happy.

For Malsakin O'Neill life was a bit more difficult. Suspecting that the high queen was treacherous he locked her away in the dungeons of Tara presuming that so long as he possessed her he would keep his crown. But the high queen's power was proving greater than the stone walls of the ancient village. Rumor had it that she cast a spell on the entire O'Neill clan causing many of them to fall ill or lose their wealth to the Viking raiders that were suddenly running rampant in the north.

The territory of Leinster, however, was experiencing a great renaissance. Under Patric's rule it had become nearly as impenetrable as Munster. Patric was a favorite among the Gallish leaders and was a regular visitor to the house of Harald Bald Knee where they would pass the hours playing chess and meting out justice whenever it was needed. Havland, Finn and Njord were ever at his side and when his business was done he would return home to Freyja.

The village of Torshav was thriving and Patric watched with pride as his ceiles worked the fields in anticipation of the harvest. Fudirs were scampering in and out of the pristinely painted great hall, preparing for the evening feast that would celebrate Njord's sixteenth birthday—the day he passed into manhood and took the village for his own.

As a lad, Njord was handsome but as a man he was stunning. He had grown to stand a head taller than Patric and if his gangly limbs were any indication of it, he still had further to go. His clear green eyes were sharp of vision allowing him to easily hit a small target from more than two hundred paces away and his mind was swift and sharp, able to grasp the most complicated plans with little difficulty.

Patric rose from his perch on the old tree stump as his son approached, bow slung over his shoulder and a quiver of arrows strapped to his back. He had young Falkein in tow.

"It'll be the three of us then," Patric cooed, happy to see his son take interest in the nine-year-old son of the widow, Niamh. "It's good to see ye, Falkien."

"In truth, I asked to come, Shaver," Falkien offered quite seriously. "I've a matter I wish to discuss with ye."

"Do ye then?" Patric queried, raising an eyebrow at Njord.

Njord shrugged his shoulders then walked on ahead to allow the lad the privacy he was seeking. Patric continued, "Would ye like to speak about it now or should we do a bit of hunting first?"

Falkien looked to his feet as he shuffled the loose earth with his shoes. He gave a deep sigh then a swallow, screwing up his courage to offer Patric the proposition.

"Ye know my ma's in love with ye, Shaver," he stated plainly. "She wants ye to take her to wife so that she can give ye babies."

Knowing full well that the lad was speaking for himself instead of his mother, Patric swallowed the chuckle that was brewing in his throat.

"Does she now?" he croaked.

Falkien nodded his head.

"Did she send ye to tell me this, Falkein?"

"Nay," Falkien admitted, wringing his hands nervously. "She didn't send me but I know it's true. She's been in quite good humor since we came to Torshav. I haven't seen her like that since our father died. I just know it's got something to do with ye."

"Well," Patric sighed as he bent to look the lad in the eye, "I caution ye from making bargains which yer mother may not wish to fulfill." He jutted his chin toward Niamh's hut. "I think its Havland she fancies, Falkien, not me."

Falkien's eyes widened. "But ye're the great warrior, Shaver. Everyone knows about yer skills. I'm sure it's ye she fancies."

"Listen to me, Falkien," Patric offered as he rubbed the lad's head, "Freyja is my woman and Njord's my son. Soon he'll be earl. Ye'd be wise to stick close to him. He'll help care for both ye and yer brothers until yer ma takes another husband. Though it might be sooner than ye think, I can assure ye it won't be me."

Falkien's eyes expressed his disappointment but before either of them could utter another word, Havland's voice came barreling up the hillside with the man himself following close behind.

"Come quick, Shaver!" he called as he struggled up the incline, half naked and bare foot from taking his pleasure with Falkien's mother. "It's the Ri Ciocid's messenger at the gate. He says Boru searches for ye."

Njord emerged from the woods in response to Havland's cry. When he realized there was no danger he turned to Patric, scowling as he asked, "Now what?"

It was his usual response when it came to Brian. It never did sit right with him that the Ri Ciocid accepted Kevin back into the fold without so much as a question regarding his raiding. For all these years he'd been on a mission to exact revenge for the murder of his family and there was no sign of him letting up.

Patric took a step forward and Njord took one back. "Easy there, laddie," he cooed. "Let me see what he wants before ye get yerself all riled up."

Njord placed a hand on the hilt of his sword as he began to march forward. "Tonight Torshav passes into my hands. From now on if the Ri Ciocid wants anything from us he'll have to settle things with me first. Ye take Falkien hunting and I'll see to this myself."

Patric exchanged a worried glance with Havland before reaching out a hand to halt the lad. "It's me the Ri Ciocid seeks, son, not ye. Need I remind ye that even after tonight ye'll continue to answer to me?"

He was using his fatherly tone—the one that used to gain Njord's immediate obedience. Lately it wasn't working.

"Now take yer hand from yer weapon and let me go and find out what he wants then…"

"See what *he* wants?" Njord interrupted as he rounded on his father. "What about what I want? Doesn't that matter to ye?"

The air was charged with anger as both Patric and Njord faced off. Havland forced himself between them. "Come on now, laddie," he barked, blocking Njord's path, "Let the Shaver tend to the matter and I'll take ye and the little fellow here hunting. It's his business with the Ri Ciocid not yers."

Njord screwed up his face then snapped back, "And does the Ri Ciocid care that his business is putting the Shaver's life in danger? Remember the raid on the highway last spring that nearly left my father without an eye? And the call for assistance we received two summers past that would have found us all dead if Yon hadn't realized it was a trap? If ye ask me, being Boru's ally is bringing the Shaver more harm than good."

"And ye think these things happened because of Boru?" Havland asked in the most soothing voice he could muster. Njord cast his eyes toward the ground and he continued, "Great men have enemies, Njord. The Shaver's a great man. But even if he were a ceile or fudir there would always be someone to hate him. 'Tis the way of it and there's nay a thing ye can do about it. All men can claim enemies but not all men can claim the Ri Ciocid as their friend."

There was truth in the statement but not enough to make Njord back down. He took a step closer to his father, leaning in slightly so their eyes would be level. "If Boru's such a good friend to ye then why not ask him to help me take my vengeance for my family?"

Patric huffed in frustration. It hadn't been easy to live his life in secret while Kevin roamed free without consequences for his actions but he did it out of loyalty to Brian. Njord held no such loyalty. Now with him poised to take control of the village Patric wasn't certain how long he could keep the two from conflict.

"I'll tell ye what, Njord," he finally sighed. "Let me find out what Brian wants then we'll lay a plan to deal with the situation."

Though his voice was even his eyes told Njord that any further argument would be futile. The lad nodded agreement and Patric turned on his heel to head down the hill.

He spotted Brian's messenger seated outside the mead hall, a cup in his hand while he chatted amiably with Patric's guards. They rose as he approached. With a wave of his hand Patric dismissed the guards then took the messenger by the elbow to escort him into the house.

Thanks to Patric's ingenuity, Torshav was unlike any other village in Ireland. Instead of boasting a grand hall surrounded by tiny huts that could only be accessed from the outside, Torshav's hall was surrounded by an outer ring containing individual chambers that could be accessed from within. Even the kitchen could be entered from inside the doors.

As he did for the tavern in Clonmacnoise, Patric brought running waters inside by placing a double height barrel against the exterior wall of the kitchen to catch rainwater. Fine gravel placed on a pierced metal disc kept debris out while a hollowed sapling trunk cut on a ninety degree angle poked through both barrel and wall to bring the water inside.

He led the messenger down the circular hall and into his private chamber then waved him to a seat before taking one for himself. "Quite a place ye have here, Shaver," the messenger sighed then realizing he was gushing, he turned right to business. "The Ri Ciocid has sent me to prepare his allies for battle."

Patric sat forward, surprise clearly marking his face. "When and with who?"

"After the harvest," the man replied. He took a sip from the cup Patric handed him. "It seems Malsakin has finally given in to the pleading of his kin and set the high queen free. Her price to remove the curse is the return of Leinster. Malsakin fights under the banner of Sigtrygg the Silken beard to take it back for her."

That statement caused Patric to sit back with a sigh. "Damn," he hissed through clenched teeth.

"Is there a problem?" the messenger asked, surprised that someone as loyal as the Shaver would react in such a way.

"Nay," Patric sighed, reading the expression on the messenger's face. "It's my son, Njord I was thinking of. He celebrates his coming of age tonight. I had hoped to keep him from battle for a while. 'Tis not the best birthday gift I could give him."

"I don't know," the messenger started. "I remember myself at that age. I lived for battle."

"Aye," Patric agreed. There was no doubt in his mind that Njord was ready for battle. The real question was whether or not he was willing to fight for Brian.

*   *   *   *

Tara, Ireland: Outside the great hall—18, June 992 A.D.—Kormlada breathed the fresh air deep into her lungs then threw back her head to let the sun warm her face. She took one halting step forward—then another before she realized there would be no one to stop her. She had been locked away for so long that she nearly forgot how sweet freedom could be.

Damn, Malsakin for his harsh treatment of her and damn her brother and son for not coming to her aide. She spit on the ground to condemn them but in truth it was Boru who disappointed her most.

All these years and he hadn't made one move to save her. Oh, he thought of her often enough. She made sure of that through the visions she sent him. But for all her efforts the man would do nothing to help her or himself.

"Bah," she grumbled as she headed toward the hall. As always, it would be left up to her to get the job done. It seemed to be a curse that the men in her life were too weak to do things for themselves.

She straightened her shoulders and threw back her head as the guard moved to open the door for her. She would enter the gathering of clansmen in her full grandeur, showing every one of them that she was a force to be reckoned with.

The creak of the door on its hinge drew Malsakin's attention. He swallowed hard then cast a glance at Sigtrygg and Maelmora who were sitting on either side of him. The terror he felt was reflected in their eyes. He grasped the table with both hands, determined to hide his feelings from the others gathered in the room.

Fladbartoc noticed and bent low to his ear from his position behind him. "She's only a woman, cousin. She has no power to condemn ye."

"Well, tell it to the rest of these rots, aye," he whispered back from the corner of his mouth. "It's only on their insistence that I do this thing."

"Need I remind ye that I counseled against it?" Fladbartoc retorted.

"Hush now," Maelmora blurted then wiped the beads of sweat from his forehead. "Here she comes."

The door swung full open and a beam of light shone into the hall. Kormlada was a mere shadow of darkness against it. Fladbartoc watched as all eyes in the room turned toward the woman and he chuckled to himself that grown men could believe in her curse. But as she moved toward him he felt the hair rise on his arms and he wondered for a moment whether it wasn't a warning that her freedom would do more harm than her supposed curse had done.

Kormlada moved forward in a smooth liquid motion, the material of her lein swaying with each movement of her hips. Her hair was brilliant gold and her eyes as deeply piercing as they had ever been. The years hadn't aged her a bit.

She passed among them without uttering a word, her eyes clearly focused on her husband whose hands had begun to tremble most visibly. She smiled at him, displaying a row of perfect white teeth then moved around the table to stand beside him.

"Mother," Sigtrygg cooed as he got to his feet.

He opened his arms to her and she placed herself into his embrace. "I see ye haven't gotten around to shaving that thing off," she whispered against his ear as she embraced him back. "I really wish ye would heed my advice."

He swallowed hard then released her, not sure what to make of the comment. Before he could respond she was moving past him and around the Ard Ri to place her hand on Maelmora's shoulder.

"Brother, dear," she cooed as she lowered her cheek to his lips. "Ye're looking fit as ever."

Maelmora kissed the proffered cheek then cleared his throat to find his voice. "As are ye, sister. Ever the beauty ye are."

She turned from him then, stopping only momentarily to state, "I see my exile has agreed with ye too, Fladbartoc."

He didn't bother to respond since she had already moved past him.

Finally, she placed her hand on Malsakin's shoulder. His back stiffened. "Has it been so long that ye've forgotten my touch, husband? There, there—we'll have to remedy that right away."

Malsakin reached up to grab her hand with force enough to crush her fingers. She struggled at first but soon enough relaxed into submission. "Sit with us, wife," he ordered softly. "We are all eager to hear what ye have planned for Leinster."

She looked out onto the sea of faces staring up at her. They were sheep, each of them and she planned to herd them as any good shepard would.

She took her seat beside Malsakin then rubbed her hands together before leaning forward. "Aye, I do have a plan for Leinster," she cooed. "And it took me every bit of eight years to lay it."

*　　　*　　　*　　　*

Cavenlow, Ireland: Early evening—2, July 992 A.D.—Kevin poised his finger above his rook, then thought better of it. He looked the board over more closely and when he finally realized his queen was in jeopardy he moved his knight to block Garvin's advances. He sat back, smug with the knowledge that he could have the game in several moves.

It was Garvin's turn to look the board over but he couldn't concentrate. He had so much news to share that he didn't know where to begin.

"I've had news of yer brother, Patric," he finally mumbled.

Kevin looked up from the board with a queer expression on his face. "Patric?"

"Aye," Garvin continued. "He's alive and living in Leinster under the name Shaver."

Kevin's hand immediately came to rest atop his, squeezing it with a grip fierce enough to contradict its size. There was pleading in his eyes. "Ye must be mistaken."

"'Tis true, Kevin."

"How do ye know it to be true?" Kevin whispered, desperation creeping into his voice. He had heard stories that the Shaver was kin to Brian but never in his wildest dreams did he consider him to be Patric.

Garvin slowly leveled his gaze at Kevin. The rumor was true—he'd made sure of it before offering the information. But Patric was only the beginning of their problems.

"They call him the Shaver because he took the hair of Throdier of Orkney in a tavern fight. He's been overseeing Leinster and there's talk that Brian is planning to name him Ri Tuath Ruire if they're successful in beating back Sigtrygg for control of Leinster."

Kevin's face twisted into an unnatural expression. "What do ye speak of, man?" He had been in Dublin only last season. Sigtrygg never mentioned his plans to challenge Brian. "Ye must be mistaken."

"'Tis nay mistake. Sigtrygg is calling Boru out," Garvin stated then quickly added, "Well, his mother's really."

"Kormlada," Kevin sighed, thoroughly confused by the whole of it. "I thought she had been locked away for good."

Garvin shook his head. "It seems that the O'Neill leaders truly believe that she was the reason for their suffering. They begged Malsakin to set her free and to give her what she asked so that she would remove her spell."

"And what she asked for is Leinster," Kevin interrupted.

He sat silent for a while, remembering Kormlada's passion for reclaiming her birthplace before her confinement. It must have been the one thing she thought about for all these many years. No doubt she would find success.

He laughed to himself that Malsakin was planning to reduce his risk by using Sigtrygg's crown to fight under. "Brilliant," he sighed. Then his stomach tensed when he realized that Brian would be expecting him to fight on the side of the Dal Cais.

"Where did ye get this information?"

Garvin lowered his head for his transgression. "Sigtrygg sent a messenger with it."

Kevin's eyes glowed with anger. "When?" he demanded.

"A fortnight ago."

He swept his arm across the chessboard, scattering pieces in every direction. "And ye decided to keep it from me? Why would ye do such a thing?"

"Because I wanted to be sure it was true."

"Why would Sigtrygg lie about a war?" Kevin barked, trying to understand what it was Garvin was up to. He knew that he was jealous of the Dublin earl. "What did ye hope to gain by keeping this from me?"

"Yer safety," Garvin replied.

Kevin recognized the truth. He looked around the room and noticed that his men were staring at him. He took Garvin by the arm to lead him into an alcove.

"I've managed to escape Brian for this long. Tell me why ye are so worried over things now?"

"'Tisn't Brian that I worry over," Garvin replied. "'Tis yer brother."

With all there was to think about, Kevin nearly forgot about Patric. The Shaver certainly had a reputation as a fierce warrior but if he wanted him dead he would have moved on him already.

"Brian must have had a reason for keeping Patric a secret for all these years, but ye can rest assured that I'm nay willing to wait for him to tell me why. I want ye to go to Sigtrygg and tell him we'll be in this battle with him. If I'm to see the rotten face of my brother again let it be on the battlefield, aye."

Garvin accepted the order without question. Though Sigtrygg was his rival he knew he was their only hope against Brian. "When shall I tell him to expect ye?"

"A fortnight—nay much longer. I must settle a few things here first."

Kevin wrung his hands as he paced the floor searching his mind for any points of weakness Boru might have. When he lifted his eyes he noticed Eagan sitting with several soldiers by the entrance to the hall. His brother's friend had become a fierce and cunning warrior—the champion of every match he entered.

He nodded his chin in Eagan's direction. "Before ye go I want ye to get rid of him, aye. If he ever learns that my brother's alive he'll go running straight to him. There's nay sense in giving Patric further advantage."

Garvin followed Kevin's gaze to Eagan and a shiver ran up his spine. He nodded his head without revealing his trepidation. He'd give his life to see Kevin safe. He only hoped it wouldn't come to that.

*   *   *   *

Thomond, Ireland: In the private chambers of the Ri Tuath—4, July 992 A.D. Grace watched Turlog's face as he slept. He looked so peaceful and content that she hated to disturb him but the upcoming battle for Leinster was weighing heavy on her mind and she had to speak with him.

She stroked his nose with her finger then did the same to his eyebrows, bringing a wriggle of both. Eventually his eyes fluttered open. "What ails ye, woman?"

"I need to know if Brian expects Kevin to march with him."

"Of course," Turlog yawned as he scooted back into a sitting position so he could lean against the wall. "He'll expect all of us."

"Joseph as well?" she asked, unbelieving that he too would offer up his son for Brian's folly.

"Aye."

Her eyes opened wide and her face twisted. "How do ye men do it? How can ye offer up the lives of yer sons for another man's glory?"

"'Tis not his glory alone, Grace. When Brian succeeds we all do. 'Tis the way of the clan."

"What more does he need, Turlog? For that matter, what more do ye need. Don't ye have enough? Ye have Thomond. Ye have cattle—a home—fields. What more could ye possibly need? What riches are so great that ye would offer up yer son's life to have them?"

He drew a deep breath then ran his hands over his face and through his hair to get the blood circulating. "What's this all about, Grace?"

"Ye tell me! I've lost nine sons, Turlog. Nine. I've lost a husband, two fathers, a mother and a brother all to war and I've gained nay a thing for it. What's that about, Turlog?"

He reached out to take her into his arms, pulling her close so that he could rest his chin on the top of her head. "I know ye suffer for the loss of yer sons, Grace. I suffer too for the loss of Ryan, but these are the times we live in and we must do our part to show our loyalty to the throne. Don't worry about Kevin. I'll look after him as if he were my own."

She looked up at him with the words fast on her lips. "Turlog," she started then swallowed to dislodge the lump in her throat.

When she said nothing further he looked down at her. She looked queer and for a moment he thought she might cry. "What ails ye, woman?"

"Ye must understand that I had nay choice but to keep it from ye."

"Keep what from me?" he asked with eyebrows raised. Again she was silent and he urged her, "Why not lay it plain, woman? Whether ye take yer time or lay it plain, my reaction will be the same. Tell me what it is ye have to say."

A Novel By Leticia Remauro

The one thing she knew about her husband was that he was a suspicious man, vengeful as well. She feared what he would do when he heard what she had to say, but on some level she suspected he might already know.

"It's about Kevin."

"What about him?" Turlog barked. He could feel the anxiety building within him. The one thing that infuriated him most about women was the way they made even simple things complicated. "What is it ye have to say, Grace?"

"He is yer own, Turlog."

He opened his mouth to ask her what the hell she was talking about then stopped before saying anything.

"What do ye say, woman?" he finally asked, anger clear in his voice.

She remained silent while she pondered whether or not she had done the right thing.

"Ye don't mean to say that Kevin belongs to me?"

Grace nodded and Turlog drew breath. He wasn't certain whether he was angry for being kept unawares or for the fact that the one lad the woman had given him was the least desirable of her lot.

He pushed her aside then rubbed his hands through his hair again. "After all this time, why tell me now, Grace?" he asked without looking at her.

"It made nay sense to do it while Lorca was alive."

"And after that?" he asked, peeved that he could have had Cavenlow for all this time.

"After that I was fearful that Brian would strip him from the village if he found out that he wasn't Lorca's true heir."

"If he did strip him from the village he would have given it to me, woman. What were ye thinking?"

He pushed past her then sat the edge of the bed rubbing his head. It was a mess that he was in and he didn't know what to do about it.

"Will ye watch out for him?" she called over his shoulder, desperate to protect their child together.

He heard the concern in her voice and he turned to look at her. "Ye betrayed me, Grace."

Her tears were brimming her eyes and it was all she could do to keep from sobbing. "Forgive me, Turlog."

He took a moment to think about the situation. "I don't suppose he knows about this."

"Nay," she replied with a shake of her head.

"'Tis better that way, aye."

She nodded then he continued, "I'll do what I can to keep him safe, Grace, but he's a man and must do his part on behalf of the clan. I ask nay less of Joseph."

She nodded her understanding then slipped between the covers leaving him to ponder the situation alone.

*   *   *   *

North Limerick Road, Ireland: Three hours past noon—10, July 992 A.D.—In his wildest dreams, Eagan never thought he would step foot in Dublin but that's where he was headed. He'd heard all about the city set high atop the hill that glowed at night with the light of a thousand oil lamps. At any other time the prospect of seeing such a place would have thrilled him but as he rode in silence with these new warriors Garvin had gathered the hairs on the back of his neck stood up in warning.

He cast his gaze in the direction of the soldier who rode to his left. He couldn't remember his name but the man carried the fierce look of a seasoned warrior. He recognized the same look in the face of the man who rode to his right. He looked to Garvin who was riding lead then slowly let his eyes play over the other six soldiers riding two abreast before him. They were nearing the village of Torshav when Garvin suddenly led them away from the main Limerick road and into the woods flanking Lough Derg.

"Where do ye take us man?" Eagan called out. "We had best keep to the road or else the bogs will impede our travel."

Garvin didn't turn but instead kept his eyes straight ahead while several of the other soldiers reined in their horses. In a moment Eagan was surrounded.

A shiver ran up his spine as he recognized the ambush. He drew his sword then kicked his horse, lunging forward to pierce one soldier through the heart before swinging wide to cut another in the face. He felt the bite of the blade against his leg but he had no time to tend it as another warrior grabbed his lein, threatening to dismount him. He shoved the reins under his thigh to free up his left hand then sent it sailing into the face of the warrior who'd been tugging on him. The man fell to the ground with a thud and Eagan kicked him before elbowing the next warrior who came up on his left. The man went sailing off his horse.

There were five left seated and he fought them with both short blade and long, swiping one across the throat as he punctured the lung of another by plunging the knife into his back.

He hadn't felt the blade slice his brow but the gush of blood told him it was there. He was nearly toppled when he used his sleeve to wipe his eye. He used the flat of his long blade to slap the man coming at him then plunged his short sword into his throat.

The two warriors he'd dismounted were pulling on his legs to unseat him. Eagan slammed each in the jaw sending them sailing back to the ground. He placed the reins between his teeth then pulled back to cause his horse to rear up while he sliced the air on either side of him with the blades he carried in each hand.

One warrior scrambled to his feet then sliced Eagan's calf down to the bone. When Eagan grabbed at him he was pierced in the shoulder as well. He reared his horse again to be rid of them then he galloped forward until he was riding at Garvin's side.

Garvin's eyes widened as Eagan's blade came directly at him. He opened his mouth to say something but before he could his head was separated from his shoulders.

Eagan looked back to the warriors who were scrambling to catch him up. He was weak but there was a chance he could outride them. He looked to the village set atop the next rise. If he had any luck at all he could make it there before they caught him.

✳   ✳   ✳   ✳

Torshav, Ireland: Four hours past noon—10, July 992 A.D.—Patric swatted at the gnats hovering around his face. There had been a large amount of rain in the spring leaving behind an abundance of annoying creatures. He marched up the road leading to the gate, never taking his eyes from the horse shifting its weight uncomfortably or the rider lying in a heap against the oak tree. When the wind whipped up it carried the sharp scent of blood. He raced forward to see what the matter was.

"He's badly wounded," Finn stated as Patric bent to inspect the soldier. "I would have handled it myself but I thought ye'd be interested in him since he hails from Cavenlow."

"Cavenlow?" Patric looked at the man again. He didn't recognize him.

"Aye. Says his name is Eagan and that he was ambushed on the road by his comrades."

Patric's stomach flipped.

"Jesus Christ," he mumbled, wiping back the soldier's hair to get a better look at his face. "Eagan, what have they done to ye?"

"So ye know him?" Havland asked as he stepped out from behind the horse. It was a quality animal and he thought he would claim it in the event the warrior didn't survive.

Patric nodded sadly, remembering the times he and Eagan shared together then he wondered aloud, "Whatever made him come here?"

"I don't think he knew where he was going," Finn offered. "He rode in begging for sanctuary then fell from his horse where ye see him. The ambush must have taken place close by. I've sent a few men down the road to see what they could learn."

"We'll need to tie off the bleeding," Patric barked when he noticed the slice in Eagan's calf. He ran his hands over the man's torso to find out where the rest of the blood was coming from then drew back when his finger slipped into the puncture wound at his shoulder. Eagan didn't flinch.

"Eagan," he cried, "Open yer eyes man and tell us why they did this to ye."

When Eagan didn't respond, Patric pressed his fingertips against the pulse point in Eagan's neck. The faint thumping told him that his friend was still alive.

"Help me get him to my chamber," he called to Havland. "Calder will have to tend him."

Patric grabbed Eagan's shoulders while Havland took his legs and just as they began to lift him his eyes fluttered open. They went wide at the sight of the Vikings trying to hoist him. In a moment he was bucking against their grasp, freeing himself then crouching low against the tree with his short sword in hand.

"I don't want any trouble," he barked, his eyes shifting between the three of them.

"He's a wily one, aye," Havland chuckled to Patric. "No wonder he got away."

"Aye," Patric agreed, happy to see that Eagan's wounds weren't mortal. "He always was quick on his feet."

"Who are ye?" Eagan barked, confused by the familiarity. "What do ye mean to do with me?"

Patric raised an eyebrow then realized that Eagan didn't recognize him through his disguise. "Easy there, brother," he called as he turned his palms up in a defenseless posture. "Ye'll find nay trouble here."

Eagan lowered the blade as he took a step closer. Though he didn't recognize the face, the voice was familiar.

"Patric?" he gasped, finally putting it all together. "Is that ye under all that hair?"

"Aye," Patric chuckled, "but they call me Shaver now."

"But I don't understand," Eagan started then all at once he hung his head. "So I'm dead then. Ye've come to take me?"

All three men laughed out loud causing Eagan to furrow his brow. "What's funny?"

"Ye're not dead, man," Patric snorted. "Ye're in Torshav."

"How could that be? Ye're dead. With my own eyes I saw ye burn on that ship. 'Twas me who buried yer body. H-h-how is this possible?"

Suddenly Eagan's vision blurred and the ground began to spin. He could feel his head getting light. He fell over with a thud, gasping for air.

"Ye alright?" Patric inquired, resting his hand on Eagan's neck.

The hand was flesh and blood putting to rest any thought that Patric was a ghost.

"Aye," he gasped, "just dizzy is all."

"Well breathe, man," Patric commanded as he massaged Eagan's neck. He took the water skin from Finn then offered it to him. "Take a drink, aye."

Eagan did as he was bade and when the dizziness passed he raised his head to watch as one man bandaged his leg while the other bandaged his shoulder. They made quick work of their ministrations but Patric still looked concerned.

"That should hold him until we can get him to Calder's hut."

"Who's Calder?" Eagan asked as he tried to stand but the dizziness overtook him again and he was forced to place his head between his knees until it passed.

"He's my healer," Patric replied, then he bent down to inquire, "Who did this to ye, Eagan."

"I would suspect 'twas yer brother though I never gave him any cause."

Patric was puzzling the situation when Njord walked over to offer Finn the flask of mead he had requested earlier. "Now there's a surprise," he stated, resting his shoulder back against the tree.

Patric looked up to give him a silencing glare but Njord only chuckled. "Am I wrong?"

"Hush now, Njord," Havland scolded, feeling the tension build between father and son. The lad had a natural penchant for provoking the man. "Let yer father figure this thing out."

"Father?" Eagan inquired, lifting an eyebrow at Patric. He turned his neck to look over the man standing beside him. "Ye haven't been gone long enough to have a son that age."

"It's an endearment," Patric growled, "but of late I wonder."

Njord huffed and Eagan continued, "Well, he's as tall as ye are."

"Taller," Patric stated proudly.

Eagan let his eyes sweep over Njord one last time before the dizziness forced his head back between his knees. "Broader too," he mumbled then waited for this new wave to pass before he spoke again. "Must be a good one to have around."

"That depends," Patric retorted, shoving Njord aside so he could better rub Eagan's neck. "He's the best one for fighting alright, but if it's listening ye're after ye might as well be talking to that tree he's leaning against because it'll be far more attentive."

Eagan's back lurched with his chuckle and he raised his head slowly to assess the other warriors who made up the group. He looked over his shoulder to offer, "Ye've got a good crew here—Shaver, is it?"

"Aye," Patric replied with a smile. "Better than the lot we had in Cavenlow."

"That's not saying much," Eagan blurted, then realizing he'd better explain the statement before the warriors took offense he continued, "A bunch of women could have taken down the Cavenlow army."

He let out a whelp as Patric found the nerve that seemed to be giving him trouble. He continued, "I should know, I was forced to live among them all these years."

"More's the pity, man," Havland consoled, patting Eagan's shoulder. He knew little about the man but it seemed the Shaver had a liking for him and they could certainly use another pair of hands capable with a blade. "Perhaps ye can stay and join us here."

"Aye," Njord agreed. If Eagan came from Cavenlow he might be able to assist him in finding the man who killed his family. "Stay with us and tell us what ye know about yer Ri Tuath."

"Put that aside for now, Njord," Patric huffed. "We can discuss it later. For now let's get the man inside so Calder can have a look at him, aye."

He placed his hands under Eagan's arms to help him up. "When we're certain that ye're well ye can tell us all ye know about Kevin and Cavenlow."

Eagan nodded then leaned against Finn and Njord so they could assist him down the path. When they were well away, Patric turned to Havland.

"Send a message to Brian that Eagan's with us and that I fear Kevin may know I'm alive."

Havland raised an inquisitive brow. He didn't get any of that from the conversation.

"Don't worry, I'm sure of it," Patric responded to the unasked question. "'Tis the most likely reason Kevin would have for wanting the man dead.

*   *   *   *

The Isle of Man:—10, July 992 A.D.—Brodir's black eyes radiated death and his brows rushed together as he delivered it. He wiped the spray of blood from his sallow cheek with his forearm then whirled, ready to meet his next opponent. When none stepped forward, he pushed back the long strands of blood soaked hair from his eyes then lowered his sword.

They called him the hawk because he resembled one as his sharp eyes flicked back and forth, scanning the field. He was much thinner after his captivity making his head look far too large for his neck.

The sound of battle was growing faint as the warriors of Halfden Long Leg retreated under their lowered banner. He had won.

He saw someone running toward him and began to raise his blade but he lowered it when he recognized his brother, Ospak, his bald head glinting in the sun. Ospak was the beauty of the family, full of face and chest with amber eyes that always seemed to smile. His face was as bald as his head except for a bit of hair just under his lower lip.

Brodir sighed then tucked his long black beard into his belt before moving forward. "Are we clear?" he asked, nodding to the field.

"Aye," Ospak replied, his broad smile exposing the dimples in each of his cheeks. "Congratulations, earl Brodir."

Brodir took the hand his brother offered then looked to the fortress up on the hill. "It will be good to know what the thing looks like from above ground, aye."

For more than a decade he'd been locked up in the belly of the ornate structure, barely living amongst the rats and filth. If it weren't for Ospak he would have died beside Olaf after Halfden bought them from the earl of Iona. He owed his brother everything and he meant for him to have it.

"Our lives will be good now, Ospak. There'll be riches beyond yer wildest dreams and women to keep ye warm at night. We will be powerful and everyone will seek our counsel."

Ospak's eyes lit up with the thought of it but then he turned to look at the ocean. "And what of Eire? Will ye travel there as ye said ye would?"

Brodir followed his brother's gaze. It had been a long many years since he set foot on the green island but somewhere on it was the woman that he loved. He thought of the tavern in Clonmacnoise and the fair Freyja with the odd green eyes. A sigh escaped his lips.

"All in good time, brother. All in good time."

CHAPTER 24

▼

Cenn Cora, Ireland: 21, August 992 A.D.—It had been some time since Patric spoke with Brian face to face but after he sent his message about Kevin, the Ri Ciocid decided to question Eagan himself.

The day was a glorious one. There was a gentle breeze rolling up from the Shannon carrying with it the scent of lavender and river grass. The azure sky was streaked with white wisps of clouds and the sun beat down with a comfortable heat.

Cenn Cora was alive with movement as buyers and sellers haggled in the market. Women strolled casually down the street carrying jars of water and out in the field Brian's guards went through their daily paces. Several lads sat in the grass watching the show but others mimicked the warrior's actions, squaring off against each other with sticks and branches.

It was the first time Patric had been back in Munster since he left for Ailech and he took great care with his disguise. He wore his hair loose with warrior braids at either side adorned with leather and bird feathers. His beard was braided too. He wore a gold hoop in his left ear and silver cuffs on his wrists with a matching arm ring on his left bicep. His clothing consisted of breeches and a sleeveless leather tunic inlaid with mail.

Njord, Havland and Finn were dressed similarly but Eagan was dressed as a soldier. His hair was neatly trimmed, as was his beard. Over his lein and home-spun breeches he wore a tunic emblazoned with three dancing lions marking him as a member of the Dal Cais army.

Patric looked over to a group of boys who had stopped playing long enough to ogle them. He reined his horse so they could get a better look.

"Who are ye?" one lad asked, stepping back as Patric drew closer.

"They call me the Shaver," Patric replied, adding a little growl to his voice so he would sound ferocious. "Have ye heard of me, laddie?"

"A-a-aye," the boy replied. Then he looked to the sword at Patric's back. "Is that the blade ye used to cut off the hair of Throdier of Orkney?"

It was Havland who answered the questioned as he reined in alongside Patric. "Aye, 'tis," he growled more ferociously then Patric had. "Why don't ye come closer so the Shaver can show ye how he did it?"

The boy's eyes went wide and he stood frozen for a moment before his mates grabbed him by the arm to run away. They hid behind an oak tree that was thick enough to cover them all. Patric chuckled before turning to Havland. "Ye never tire of that, do ye?"

"Let them learn to be leery of strangers. 'Twill make it easier on their parents."

Patric nodded then kicked his horse forward so he could again take the lead. Within moments they arrived at the great hall.

Each man disembarked then walked through the door but Patric stood waiting for Njord. When the lad was within reach he grabbed him by the arm. "Let me do the talking, aye. I don't want any trouble here."

"Now why would ye think that I would cause ye trouble, father?" he replied with a smile. Without another word he followed Finn into the hall.

Brian's head turned as they entered. He squinted a bit in an effort to determine who it was. Of late his eyesight was failing him. "Is it Patric?" he whispered to Murchad.

"Aye, father. Havland and Finn are with him as well but I don't know the other two men."

"Well one of them should be Eagan." He squinted a bit more then nodded his head as he recognized his colors. "The other must be Njord. My how he's grown."

"Aye," Murchad agreed, recognizing the lad's eyes. "He's the largest of the lot."

"I'm glad he's on our side," Brian offered with an elbow to Murchad's ribs. He stood then, opening his arms to the approaching warriors before he called out, "Welcome, Shaver. I see ye've brought the earl with ye. Welcome to ye, Njord the Black."

"Long life to ye, king Brian," Patric called back then nudged Njord to remind him of his manners.

"Long life to ye, Ri Ciocid," Njord mumbled.

There were a hundred conversations taking place as the warriors passed through the crowd. Patric noticed that most eyes were on Njord. He smiled. Women were whispering behind their hands using words like, "beautiful" and "handsome" to describe the lad. Men weren't so generous but every now and again Patric caught one puffing out his chest and straightening his back in an effort to match Njord's stature.

Njord too heard the whispers but he paid no mind to what they were saying. It happened wherever he went—people remarking that he was too tall or too broad. He was a giant—a freak of nature. They were repulsed by him. He stuck close by Finn's side to draw comfort from his kinsman then watched as Patric moved forward to greet the Ri Ciocid.

"Brian," Patric sighed as he stepped into the embrace. "Ye're looking well, Ri Ciocid."

"I wish I could say the same for ye," Brian chuckled, flipping one of Patric's braids off his shoulder. "Must ye be covered in so much hair?"

"Under the circumstances, I think it's best."

That brought a "hmph" from Brian. He lowered himself to his chair, waving his hand for Patric to take one also. To the other warriors he issued, "I pray ye take a seat. We were just about to have some entertainment."

The musicians began a lively tune and the other four men lowered themselves to their seats so that they wouldn't obstruct Brian's view. The Ri Ciocid looked to Eagan. "Ye're looking fit, Cavenlow," he stated before handing the man a cup. "Patric tells me that ye received quite a beating."

"Aye, that I did, Ri Ciocid."

"Why do ye suppose Kevin wanted ye dead? Ye've been with him all these years without betrayal. What could have changed?"

In truth, Eagan wasn't certain what had changed. Only Patric seemed to have an idea about that. "Kevin must know that I'm alive," Patric offered. "It's the only thing that would spark such aggression against my man."

"I see," Brian cooed. "Eagan is yer man. Well that would make sense."

"For the life of me I can't figure out where Kevin would learn the truth," Patric continued. "We've been careful in Leinster never to use my Christian name but only to call me by the Shaver. Have ye a clue, Brian?"

Brian thought for a moment. The only ones other than himself who knew about Patric were Murchad and Thorien. Turlog knew about Lorca's letter but when Brian told him that he was certain Patric was dead he accepted it readily enough. He racked his brains trying to come up with an answer. Then he remembered Kormlada.

"The high queen hinted at knowing who ye were when ye came to Tara but what reason could she have for giving it to Kevin. And how?"

Eagan sat up with the mention of Kormlada. "She's the mother of Sigtrygg the Silken Beard," he blurted. "And Sigtrygg is a comrade of Kevin's."

"Sigtrygg and Kevin?" Patric questioned.

Eagan nodded. "The Ri Tuath travels to Dublin twice each year to visit the earl. They've a solid friendship. We were on our way there when the ambush occurred."

"I was right," Patric issued, banging his hand against the table. "If Malsakin is marching under Sigtrygg's banner then it only makes sense that Kevin would be standing with him. It was Sigtrygg who told Kevin that I was alive."

Brian nodded his agreement. "So, yer brother is planning treachery in order to keep Cavenlow. Well, it's about time that he paid for his crimes."

"Aye. I can hardly wait to get my hands on him," Njord interjected.

All eyes turned toward the handsome earl whose eyes were burning with hatred. "I'll only let him live long enough to tell me who killed my family then I'm going to rip his heart out with my bare hands."

Patric knew the oath was a solemn one but Brian asked, "Ye said ye want him to tell ye who killed yer family. Don't ye believe 'twas him?"

"Nay," Njord replied, shaking his head fiercely. "Maybe 'twas him the first time, but the last time it was someone else entirely."

Brian looked to Patric who shrugged his shoulders. "I see," Brian replied.

He was mulling the situation when Turlog approached with Thorien. "Who have we here, nephew?" the Thomond Ri Tuath asked before taking the seat beside Finn.

Brian exchanged warning glances with the men before making his introductions. "Uncle, I'd like ye to meet the Shaver who's been overseeing things for me in Leinster."

Patric cautiously offered his hand and Turlog took it without recognition. Havland used the opportunity to slip from his chair and Brian quickly moved to his next introduction. "And this brave warrior is Njord the Black, earl of Torshav."

Njord barely looked up as he offered his hand but Turlog seemed fixated by the lad. "Torshav?" he questioned. His eyes held a far off look as if he were remembering something.

Brian noticed it. "Aye. He's the only surviving son of the earl, Gamal."

The hair on the back of Njord's neck rose with the mention of his father then he looked at Turlog and all the memories came flooding back. Suddenly he was back in time, watching as the raider took his mother's head. He began to shake as a wave of nausea swept over him.

"Pardon," he said as he scrambled to his feet then he turned on his heel and exited the hall.

"Now what could've come over him?" Turlog questioned anxiously.

His words hung in the air without an answer.

*   *   *   *

Dublin, Ireland: 21, August 992 A.D.—Kevin followed Sigtrygg down to the keep, covering his face with a cloth to stave off the stench. He looked to the slab carrying Garvin's dead body and all at once he began to shake.

Sigtrygg put an arm around his shoulder. He knew Kevin's relationship with Garvin went far beyond soldiery. Though his own tastes didn't run that way he understood how painful the loss must be.

"Who sent him?" Kevin inquired. He wiped at his eyes with his sleeve awaiting the earl's answer.

"Brian," Sigtrygg offered.

Kevin nodded his head. Sending Garvin's dead body to Dublin was Brian's way of telling him that his secret was exposed but if the Ri Ciocid thought to scare him off he had misjudged him. "So the day has finally come when I will declare myself an enemy of Brian Boru. God help him if I should meet him on the battlefield. There'll be nay mercy for either him or my brother."

Sigtrygg looked at the man. In an instant it seemed his face had changed. The lines at the corners of Kevin's mouth were deeper and his eyes glowed solemn with his oath. Hatred was a mask all it's own.

He placed his hand on Kevin's shoulder. "I shall help ye."

There were tears in Kevin's eyes when he turned to look at him. They shared something beyond friendship or even brotherhood—they shared a soul.

*   *   *   *

Torshav, Ireland: Two hours to midnight—21, August 992 A.D.—"Aye, that's the spot," Patric sighed as Freyja's strong hands massaged his arms and neck.

The air was heavy with moisture causing old wounds to flare up.

"Ye take on too much, Shaver," she scolded gently as she massaged more deeply. "Perhaps ye should stay put through the winter. Wait out the cold and do yer blood letting in the spring."

Patric rolled over, turning onto his back so he could see her face. He recognized her worry and reached out a hand to stroke her cheek then pushed back the gray strand of hair that escaped its braid. When they first met their age difference was almost unperceivable but now it seemed blaring.

"Come here," he whispered, drawing her near. "Lay with me a while."

She did as he bade then sighed as she snuggled against his shoulder. He kissed her head, breathing deeply to smell the flowery scent of her hair.

"What troubles ye, woman?" he asked as he rested his chin atop her head.

"I've nay troubles, Shaver." She twisted around to look up at him. "I've all I could possibly want."

"Don't be lying to me now. I can tell when ye're troubled because ye hardly bark at me at all. Ye've been quiet lately. What is it ye worry over?"

She closed her eyes as his words touched her soul. He was the only one left who was close enough to see through her thoughts. She wondered how much more time they'd share together before Brian took him from her but she dare not let him know it. Instead she sighed then snuggled closer to him.

"I worry for ye, Shaver—and the lad. 'Tis one thing to go marching off to defend a village but quite another to be marching into war with Brian."

"Why is that?" he quizzed as he continued to stroke her hair.

She shrugged her shoulders and he turned her face up to him so he could see her eyes. "'Tis not the war that troubles ye and ye know it. Now tell me what the matter is."

"Och," she issued, turning away from him to hide the truth. "I'm getting weepy in my old age. I worry over nothing these days. Leave it be, Shaver. I'll be all right."

He was about to press her on it when the argument that had been brewing all evening between Finn and Njord suddenly erupted outside his chamber door.

"I tell ye it's him, Finn," Njord barked in Manx, not wanting to expose his conversation to the Gaels that might overhear.

"I was there!" Finn retorted. "I saw him with my own eyes and it wasn't him."

"But ye weren't there the last time—remember? Ye were off in Tara with the Shaver when this one came. It was him I tell ye."

Freyja huffed then rolled off Patric's arm so he could be freed. "Ye best go out and settle it, Shaver. The lad'll stay with it until he wins the battle and poor Finn will never get any rest."

Patric expressed his lungs then nodded his agreement. Njord's combative behavior had only increased since they returned from Cenn Cora. He moved to the chair to take hold of his lein then smiled at her when it was over his head. "Remember where we were, aye. I'd hate to come back to a cold bed."

She slapped the air after him and he winked before opening the door. Suddenly he ducked as Njord's blow came directly toward him. He grabbed his arm.

"Stop this now, lad," he barked then turned a quizzical eye toward Finn who had his own hands balled into fists.

"Leave him go, Shaver. Perhaps it's time me and the lad had at it. It seems to be what he wants."

Patric looked at Njord whose face was red with anger. The vein at his temple was pumping furiously. "So has it come to this?" he questioned. "Will ye have it out with one of yer own just to prove yer point?"

With no escape for the anger bubbling inside him Njord jerked back his arm then sent his fist crashing into the mud wall. Patric wasn't sure whether the crunch he heard was bone or mud but either way the sound was enough to pull Freyja from the chamber.

"What happened?" she asked, as she looked them over. Then seeing the blood trickling down Njord's hand, she rushed him. "What did ye do, lad?"

She wrapped his fist in her robe and he bucked from the pain. "I'll be alright, woman," he responded, "'Tis nothing to worry over."

He tried to pull his hand away from her but she refused to release it. Instead she wiped the blood away then pulled on each finger individually. When he didn't react she pressed down on his knuckles. It was the middle one that caused him to jump and she issued a growl from deep in her throat. "Ye broke it. Are ye happy now?"

She released his hand then slipped through the chamber door. "Come on, I'll need to splint it."

Njord didn't follow. Instead he leveled a hateful gaze at the two men he trusted most. They watched him in silence until he spun on his heel to make his way down the hall. Freyja poked her head back through the door in time to see him go.

"Come back here, ye little rot," she called as she started after him.

Patric caught her by the shoulder. There had been enough drama already—he didn't need her getting into it. "Go back inside. I'll find out what's troubling him."

"It's more of the same, Shaver," Finn spit when his anger began to ebb. "He says 'twas Brian's uncle who killed his family. He was on his way to tell you of it but I knew yer old wounds were aching so I tried to stop him. That's what's got him all upset."

Patric's stomach flipped with dread but he dared not let Finn see his concern. He patted the captain's shoulder as he smiled at him. "I'll see to it, Finn. Go and take your rest now."

Finn nodded agreement and Patric turned on his heel to follow his son out into the night. He found him in the barn working with the horses. It seemed to comfort him to look after the beasts and these days he spent more time there than was necessary. Patric walked to the stool, removing the grooming tools before taking a seat.

"Will ye tell me about it?" he asked in a voice heavy with concern.

"Will ye listen," Njord snapped back, continuing to brush the mare's mane. "I'd rather not waste my breath if ye won't."

"I'll listen," Patric responded then steeled himself in preparation for the information.

"It was Turlog," Njord offered.

He turned to see his father's reaction. "Brian's uncle was the one that killed my family which means that Brian must have known about it."

Patric thought about the words, careful not to let his face show the thoughts going on inside his mind. "How do ye know?" he finally asked.

"How do I know?" Njord barked, throwing up his hands. "I know because I was there. I saw him, aye."

"Ye said yerself that the man who killed yer family wore a mask. How can ye be certain it was Turlog?"

Njord hung his head. It was true that the raider wore a mask but he had spent every day since they returned from Cenn Cora trying to figure out why Brian's uncle seemed so familiar to him. He was certain he was right about this.

"I don't know how to explain it," he whispered, "I just know it was him."

Patric stood, placing his hand on Njord's shoulder to comfort him. "Do ye remember the man we sent to Dublin—the one Eagan killed?"

Njord nodded and Patric continued, "His name was Garvin. He was Kevin's lover—quite loyal to him, aye. If ye remember, he was tall with light flowing hair much like Turlog's. Could it be him who did the deed, son?"

Njord sighed deeply before taking the time to consider the question. "I don't know," he finally replied, "perhaps."

The sound of his own voice infuriated him and he balled his fists then kicked over the stool. "If it was Garvin, why didn't I recognize him for it?"

"He was dead, Njord. A man looks different in death then he does in life but ye have to admit 'twould make sense that it was him."

"Aye," Njord mumbled, feeling suddenly cheated.

"Now I'm not telling ye to accept Garvin as the one who killed yer family. What I am saying is that there is more than one possibility. Try to control yerself until ye have the information ye need. Marching around like an angry giant will forewarn yer enemies and then where will ye be?"

Njord nodded slowly. As always he was acting without thinking and as always, Patric was there to put him right. "Forgive me, father," he mumbled too embarrassed to look up.

"'Tis not me ye should be apologizing to but Finn. He's been good to ye, aye. Ye shouldn't go around challenging him lest ye lose a friend in the man."

"Aye," Njord chuckled. "I bet by now ye both wish I'd been killed by the raider."

Patric pulled him close, standing on tiptoe so he could plant a kiss atop his head.

"Never," he sighed.

*　　*　　*　　*

Lagain, Ireland: Break of Dawn—21, September 992 A.D.—The field of warriors stretched out as far as the eye could see. There were thousands of them, vibrating the ground with their very movement. Patric looked to the woods to the east of the field, even they seemed alive as camp followers and family members waited anxiously for the fighting to begin. Brian's camp stood to the southwest, Sigtrygg's to the northeast—in between stood an open terrain of yellowing grass that would soon be red with the blood of dying warriors.

In the distance Patric could see the tent of the Ard Ri set high atop a rise to give the man a clear view of the battlefield. Though he wouldn't risk his crown by being in the fight, he was willing to lend his men to assist his stepson.

There had been word that Kormlada was in there with him, calling on her gods to ensure Brian's defeat. Brian wasn't surprised by the news. He remembered their parting words in Tara and decided it would be best for him to address his men to lay their fears to rest.

"Men of Munster, make nay mistake who we fight today. Though he chooses to hide behind the banner of the earl of Dublin, it's the Ard Ri's army that we face. When we take them down 'twill only be a matter of time before all Eire is ours."

There were no rousing cheers following his words. Instead there were a few mumbles as his men all expressed their concern that it was magic they were up against.

Brian continued, "Do ye tell me that the Munster army is fearful of a woman?"

Someone in the crowd called out, "She's a sorceress, nay a woman!"

Brian laughed as he held up his hand. "Those of ye who were with us in Ailech know first hand that the high queen has no magic, for if she did she would have escaped us then. She's mortal—flesh and blood. The chains that can bind ye can bind her. She has no magic against us because we have the power of the Lord on our side."

Again the warriors began to talk amongst themselves and this time Brian let them do it. They were discussing their time in Ailech; remembering how Brian dragged Kormlada in from the forest then kept her as a hostage for weeks. She was human and every one of them shed their fear of her.

"When ye fight today ye fight to protect the children of Eire. Ye fight against the slaughter of innocents."

As if the words were spoken to her, Kormlada smiled before abruptly covering the herbs on her table. She leapt to her feet with a graceful urgency then made her way to the tent flap to peer outside.

"What is it?" Malsakin questioned, his face twisting with concern.

She turned slowly, unwilling to show him that she was amused by the situation.

"Nay a thing," she mumbled as she slowly returned to her seat. "I just needed some air."

"Ye're certain we'll have victory?" he asked, his voice full of authority.

He was sitting in his field chair draped with animal fur making him appear a much larger man.

She returned to her table, moving the herbs around to draw his attention away from her face. The game she was playing was a dangerous one but it would be worth it. "We'll have victory if ye do as I say," she reported. "Ye must lead yer own army onto that field."

Malsakin sat forward in his chair. "Ye never said that I was to lead my army!" he barked. "Ye only said that they must fight!"

"Ye are yer army," she replied without turning. "A bunch of soldiers do not make an army—only the man who leads it can claim that glory."

He lunged at her, grabbing her by the hair until her head was snapped back. "Bitch! Ye've concocted this whole event to see me dead, haven't ye? Ye've brought me here so that I would fall to him, didn't ye?"

Her eyes were filled with hatred bred from years of captivity. She had brought them there to serve her own purpose. However it turned out she would win.

She swallowed the saliva welling in her throat before whispering, "Ye're here to reward me for giving yer leaders what they asked of me. Now the choice is yers, Ard Ri. Ye can lead yer army onto the battlefield and gain glory for yerself or ye can let my son do it. Either way I win."

He spied the knife on her table and for a moment thought about using it on her but his cowardice got the best of him. He wasn't certain what would happen to him if he killed her, but he was certain that if he fought this battle he would be dead by Boru's hand.

He growled low in his throat. "'Tis yer war, Kormlada, nay mine. Ye fight it!" With that he spun on his heel to exit the tent.

Patric sat by Brian's side watching the warriors as their faces lit up in anticipation. Suddenly his attention was drawn to a movement in the distance. It looked to be Malsakin mounting his horse but when the man rode away from the battlefield he decided he must have been mistaken. He lowered his gaze to overlook the rest of their assembled enemies. His eyes opened wide when he noticed Kevin sitting his horse beside Sigtrygg. He turned to Njord.

"There's yer raider," he grumbled.

Njord followed his father's finger to the smaller man sitting the stallion. He was dressed in mail overlaid with the colors of the Dublin earl, the gold hilt of his sword peeking out from above his left shoulder.

"But that can't be, father," Njord gasped. "When yer brother raided our village he didn't carry a sword."

Patric looked at Kevin, surprised that he hadn't noticed the weapon sooner. "Well it appears he means to fight. Perhaps he's learned to use that blade."

Njord's brain muddled. If Kevin learned the sword then perhaps he was the raider both times.

The sound of the battle horn broke into his thoughts and all at once he was galloping forward to meet his target. Sheer mayhem ensued as Brian's army descended on Sigtrygg's pressing them up the incline toward the Ard Ri's tent. Kevin sat upon his horse just in front of it waiting for the moment that his brother would be within striking distance. If it would be his destiny to die then he would take Patric with him.

Patric dismounted just before the rise, carrying a sword in either hand as his arms moved in swift, precise strokes, methodically cutting down his enemies. He cleaved one man at the waist then quickly turned to take the eye from another. He pressed himself against Njord's back as three more men approached. He sliced one in the face as he pushed his sword through the throat of the other then jumped over the swipe of the third man before coming down hard on his head.

Njord fought similarly, covering his father's back. Garvin was dead—Kevin would soon join him.

The battle was fierce and lasted long into the day. There was a time at mid morning when Sigtrygg's soldiers began to gain ground on Brian's army and the Munster men feared that Kormlada was working her powers. Brian took the lead to show them there was nothing to fear and by noon the roles had reversed.

Kevin fought on horseback, using the animal to cut a path through Brian's army. He was surprised by the exhilaration he felt when he took his first life—a lad who he trampled before piercing his chest with his blade. He thrilled for what it would be like to do the same to his brother and Brian.

When Patric and Njord found themselves surrounded by their own men they charged the field searching for another group of enemies to cut down. All at once the field shifted.

Brian's army was moving further up the rise, engulfing Kevin and pushing Sigtrygg's army further back. Kevin swept the field with his eyes hoping to identify Patric or Brian among the charging warriors. When he didn't find them he reined his horse to escape through the woods. Suddenly the beast reared up. He was nearly unseated and grabbed desperately for the reins. They were yanked from his hands.

"Murderer!" Njord barked as he gripped the leather firmly in his hand. "Bet ye didn't think ye would see me again, did ye?"

"Nor me," Patric barked, coming up alongside the horse to drag his brother down from it.

Kevin struggled to be free, twisting his body against Patric's grasp and kicking his legs out against Njord's aggression. He tried to free up his blade but his arms were pinned down.

"Halt!" Brian shouted breathlessly as he galloped forward. He had been fighting just south of them when he noticed the assault. He was covered in blood.

All three men looked up in wonder. "So is this the way it will end for him, Patric?" Brian asked while struggling to catch his breath.

Patric was consumed by bloodlust and it took a moment for Brian's question to settle on his mind. When it did he hung his head. Even in war there should be honor. Killing Kevin without giving him a chance to defend himself was unworthy of him. He released his grip and his brother slumped to the ground.

Kevin began to scramble to his feet but before he could release his blade Njord charged him, pushing his short sword through his chest with determination. Kevin fell back dead but Njord didn't stop. He relentlessly jabbed the blade into Kevin's chest until blood pooled up around him.

"Enough!" Patric barked, pulling his son by the shoulders to drag him from his brother's body. "He's dead, Njord!"

Repulsed by what he had witnessed, Brian jumped from his horse then looked to Njord whose face was speckled with Kevin's blood. There were tears streaming down his cheeks and his hands were shaking.

"Take him away from here, Patric," Brian mumbled.

Patric touched Njord's arm but the lad didn't move instead he shouted, "'Twas my right to avenge my parents, Brian! There was no shame in what I did. He did the same to them."

Brian nodded his agreement but it was the way Njord perpetrated the deed that put him off. "Ye should have let him clear his blade."

Njord's heart was pumping furiously causing his ears to ring from the pressure. He looked to his father then to Brian. It may not have been an honorable kill but it was deserved. He wouldn't apologize for it.

He pushed past Patric, rubbing his bloody hands through his hair as he went. Brian caught Patric's arm as he began to follow him. "Ye must teach him to be better than that if he is to live amongst us. It may be the Viking way to do such things but it won't be tolerated in this clan."

Patric nodded his understanding then turned his gaze toward Kevin whose cold eyes looked much the same in death as they did in life. "Forgive me, father," was all he said before making his way back up the rise to find his son.

"Aye, Lorca," Brian mumbled, "Forgive us all."

It was then that Turlog came barreling over the rise. Patric jumped from the horse's path, leering at the ancient Ri Tuath with the hatred bred into him since he was a child. For a moment he thought to call out to him but decided that it would be best for Brian to reveal his identity. He watched from the top of the rise as the two men came together.

"Is he dead?" Turlog called when he noticed Kevin lying at Brian's feet.

"Aye," the Ri Ciocid replied.

Turlog heaved a mighty sigh. He had been searching for Kevin most of the day, hoping to find him just as he was now. Things would have gotten too complicated if he had lived. He was only thankful that his death came at the hand of someone other than himself. "His mother will be grief stricken."

Brian looked up at him. "Ye told her that he was planning to fight against us, didn't ye? I would think that her grief would have come over that."

"Aye, it did. But at least then he was still alive."

Brian shook his head. Grace would be an enigma to him until the day he died.

He swept the field with his eyes to be certain that his army had taken it and his gaze alighted on Patric. "Perhaps her grief will be eased when she realizes that she still has one son alive."

Turlog screwed up his face then followed Brian's gaze to the Viking on the rise. "What are ye mumbling about, nephew?"

"'Tis Patric there," Brian replied, jerking his chin in the Viking's direction.

"The Viking I met in Cenn Cora?" Turlog gasped. His head snapped around and he leveled his eyes at his nephew as his anger bubbled in his veins. "Why did ye keep it from me? His mother had a right to know about it?"

"'Twas his decision," Brian lied. "At any rate, ye know of it now and so will she. Patric will rein in Cavenlow upon our return."

Turlog wrapped the reins tight around his fist to keep himself from attacking. His nephew's games had just crossed the line from insult to injury. He rode away without another word.

The wind whipped up just then and Brian noticed the banners waving atop Malsakin's tent. The Ard Ri was probably in a state over his wife's failure to help him gain his victory. "That'll teach ye not to believe in fairies," he bellowed before making his way back to his own tent.

Again Kormlada rose from the table to peer through the tent flap. It was Brian on the next rise, shaking his fist in the air as he shouted into the wind. She smiled knowingly before stepping aside to allow Sigtrygg entrance.

He barreled into the tent while pulling his helmet from his head then pushed the matted strands of hair away from his face. "What the fek happened out there?" He had a bruise on his right cheek and a scratch to his neck but other than that he seemed whole.

"Ye lost," she offered without apology.

"Ye said we would have victory! Ye said Leinster would be ours!"

She returned to her stool before offering the words she'd been practicing most of the day. "This failure belongs to Malsakin. I won't have ye make it mine. He abandoned his army. What choice did the gods have but to abandon him?"

"Abandoned?" Sigtrygg gasped. "Where is he?"

"He's gone back to Tara. Said the battle was yers and ye must live with the consequences."

Sigtrygg took a seat then again ran his fingers through his hair. Nothing made sense to him. They had gotten into this war on her say so and Malsakin agreed. Why in the world would he abandon him without explanation?

He needed to lay a plan for what to do next and the only one he trusted to help him was Kevin. He rose to leave but she called out to stop him.

"He's dead, Sigtrygg."

"Malsakin?" he gasped as the color drained from his face.

"Kevin of Cavenlow," she corrected. "It's he that ye search for, aye?"

Confusion showed on Sigtrygg's face as he tried to keep up with these ever changing events. "How do ye know this?" he asked although he already had his answer by the far away look in her eyes.

"Let's just say it was in the stars."

Every hair on his body stood on end as he turned to exit the tent. He looked over his shoulder. "I hate it when ye do that, mother."

*   *   *   *

Cavenlow, Ireland: 1, October 992 A.D.—The Munster army marched south to claim their prize. Though their battle was in Leinster, the land that they gained was a small southern tuath called Cavenlow.

They arrived to a grand celebration. Nobles from as far away as Desi and Cara traveled north to meet the new Ri Tuath, bringing with them their unmarried daughters to entice the now famous bachelor into an alliance.

Tents sprouted up wherever there was an open patch of land and food and drink were in abundance. There was a carnival atmosphere in the village with Patric as the main attraction.

"Yer cup runneth ofer," Havland belched as he plopped down in the seat next to the new Ri Tuath, sloshing mead over both of them. "There must be a hundrit womin here of all shapes and shizes for ya to shose from."

"Aye," Patric huffed back at him before returning his attention to yet another lass being escorted by her mother. "Leilach, is it?" he crooned, nodding to the dark haired woman whose eyes were set too close together. "It's my pleasure to know of ye."

"And I ye, Shaver," she giggled, sending her eyes inward toward her nose.

Patric smiled and nodded before waving her away then sighed as he slouched in his father's chair. "I don't know how long I can keep this up, Havland," he huffed. "'Tis more tiresome than battle."

"Ah," Havland cooed as he too rested back, "but ish far more rewarging, aye."

Patric looked to the endless array of women who seemed to be lingering around the great table. He noticed Njord sitting just past them and smiled.

"Do ye think the lad's enjoying himself?"

Havland frowned as the cup he was lifting missed his mouth to send more mead splashing across his lein. He brushed it away then tried again, this time using both hands to steady the cup. He took a long draw to let the sweet honey wine trickle down his throat before wiping his mouth with his sleeve. He turned his attention toward Njord then squinted to bring the blurry shapes into focus. "I shrould tink he-ish."

When Patric turned he noticed that Havland was swaying in his chair. He laughed heartily, "Viking, ye're drunk!"

"I'm nock dr-drunk," Havland retorted, "I'm jest ti-tired."

Patric gave him a gentle shove that sent him sailing from his seat. "Well lay ye down, man," he chuckled, "ye're disgracing yerself."

He heard the thump of Havland's head as it hit the platform, but if the man felt any discomfort he didn't let on. Instead, he hugged his cup close to his chest then curled into a ball. A moment later he was snoring.

"Easy there, Eagan," Finn called as both of them made their way up the platform. Eagan's foot missed the stair and he stumbled over Havland. "Go 'round this way, aye."

"Aye," Eagan agreed. He sidestepped Havland then threw himself into his recently vacated chair. "I like ye, Frinnnn," he cooed while stroking the captain's hand.

"Not ye too," Patric groaned. He wriggled free of Eagan's shoulder that had him pinned against his chair. "Will I have one man left sober by the end of the night?"

Finn pulled his hand back from Eagan who insisted on petting it then motioned with his chin toward the circle of women. "Ye should see what's going on over there."

Patric turned in the direction of his son but there were so many people surrounding him that he was no longer visible. "Go on," he urged.

Finn raised a brow. "It seems the Ri Ciocid's intent on educating our lad in the ways of women."

"Nay," Patric gasped, unbelieving that either one of the men would abide each other's company for that long. Finn nodded in testament to the truth and Patric pushed himself from his chair, standing on tiptoe to get a glimpse of the events taking place within the circle.

"But they're nobles," he gasped, watching as another woman stepped up to Njord to settle herself in his lap.

"Their eager," Finn replied then looked down at Eagan who was stroking his cheek against his hand. Finn huffed as he tried to withdraw but Eagan was insistent. After a time Finn gave up the fight then returned his attention to Patric. "Some of them managed to slip their mothers and are plying the lad with spirits in an effort to gain his favor." He raised an eyebrow then shrugged. "If they can't have the father, aye."

"And Brian's overseeing this?" Patric quizzed, wondering what great event had taken place to have the two men settle their differences.

"He's directing it," Finn chuckled, now thoughtlessly stroking Eagan's head to soothe him into sleep. "He's got them all lined up so Njord can decide which one he wants."

With that Patric slid around Eagan, pushed past Finn and hopped over Havland to see for himself. As the captain reported, Brian had Njord seated in a chair with a cup in each hand while in turn the long line of Dal Cais women bent to kiss his lips.

"Don't crowd him now," the Ri Ciocid scolded when they began to surge against each other. "He's still young enough to be able to satisfy the lot of ye. Just wait yer turn."

A buxom redhead giggled before easing herself into Njord's lap. She ran her fingers through his black hair as she prepared to convince him that she was the one he wanted. Njord took a sip from the cup in his right hand while he pressed his left against her back. He licked his lips before smiling wryly. "Ready."

She plunged her lips down onto his, holding his head steady with her fingers entwined in his hair. Brian watched enthusiastically but when he noticed Patric standing behind her he lowered his eyes. "Shit," he mumbled.

Patric raised a finger to his beard to hush the Ri Ciocid then grabbed the lass around the waist to break the embrace. He leaned close to Njord who still had his eyes closed then blew against his ear.

"Orch, I like dat," the earl stated when the shiver ran up his back. "Do it agrain," he requested.

When the lass didn't comply he opened his eyes. He was startled to see Patric so close to his face and his chair toppled backward. "Bry the gogs, fodder," he slurred when the laughter erupted around him. "Dat wras enouve to put me off wromen for life."

"I seriously doubt that," Patric replied then offered him a hand up. He nodded in Brian's direction. "Let me caution ye against letting this one talk ye into something ye're not ready for, son."

"I take offense at that, Shaver," the Ri Ciocid blurted, stumbling when he tried to stand. He steadied himself against the chair. "The lad and I were only having a bit of fun." He beckoned the redhead to use her as a leaning post. "Weren't ye having fun, lassie?" he inquired with a tweak of her nose.

She smiled then nodded and Patric pulled Njord close. "Be careful with this lot, son," he whispered. "They're looking for a husband and if ye're not swift they just might catch one, aye."

Njord's head bobbed on his shoulders and Patric worried he would become sick. He grabbed him by the arm to steady him then broke through the gathering of women with a wave of his hand. They grumbled and called out forcing Brian to intercede on Njord's behalf.

"Now, now lassies," he cooed, trying his best to console them. "The Shaver's right. 'Tis nay a way to pick a wife. Now, I suggest ye go to yer fathers to tell them that our young Njord will be returning to his own Tuath soon. So if they're planning to negotiate they best do it right away, aye."

"Och, that's grand," Patric huffed over his shoulder as he led his son to the head table, "It's not enough for ye to be marrying me off, ye have to have the lad married as well?"

"And why not?" Brian asked while he waited for Patric to place Njord in a seat then took one for himself. "If either of ye are to be accepted into the clan ye must have proper wives."

Njord straightened his back suddenly and Patric gave it a tiny rub before turning to Brian. "That's well and good for me but the lad may have different ideas, Brian."

"Hmph," Brian offered with a slap to the air. "What different ideas could he have? He's one of us now. He should have a respectable wife."

Patric looked to Njord whose head continued to bob on his shoulders. "Alright then," he huffed, "but let's do it properly."

"The lad didn't seem to have any complaints about the way things were going until ye got involved. Did ye laddie?"

"It was guuk enough fror meee," Njord replied, swaying in his chair. He leaned forward, struggling to get to his feet and when Patric tried to assist him the lad became sick all over him.

"Och, that's grand," Patric huffed, holding up his hands to limit the damage. He looked long at the Ri Ciocid before bursting out laughter along with everyone else.

Ever the caregiver, Finn stepped forward to lift Njord from his chair. He hoisted him onto his shoulder then exited the hall to find a place for him to sleep off his ale.

Brian smiled as he watched. "He's a God send, that one. Looks after the lot of ye as if he were yer own mother."

Patric stopped wiping at his lein long enough to agree with the Ri Ciocid. "I trust him with my life. There's none better."

Realizing that there was no hope for saving the garment, Patric removed his long coat then slipped the lein over his head. He crushed it into a ball then tossed it into the corner where Havland and Eagan were slumbering peacefully. "They're all good to me. Far better than I deserve."

"Och," Brian offered then took a sip from Patric's cup. "Ye're the good one, that's why they follow."

The statement reminded Patric of Freyja. She often said such things but he wondered what she would say now if she could see him sitting on display for the purpose of gaining a wife. At length, he shook his head. For him, marriage must come with an alliance and since Freyja had neither family nor lands, he was obliged to marry someone who did.

He shrugged into his coat then sipped from his cup as he leaned back in his chair. When he looked out into the crowd he noticed the redhead who had been hoping to gain Njord's favor earlier. At the time he hadn't realized how attractive she really was. "Do ye know that one?" he inquired of Brian while nudging him with his elbow.

Brian followed Patric's gaze to Lara then chuckled, "I should say so and so do ye." Patric raised a quizzical eyebrow and Brian continued, "'Tis Lara ingenTurlog. Our cousin."

"Turlog," Patric spit as if he tasted something foul. "That's unfortunate."

"Not really," Brian offered. "She has more of her mother in her. Very fierce that one. Wants to be a warrior."

"A warrior?" Patric chuckled, "Ye tease me, man."

"Nay," Brian retorted before taking another sip from his cup then he leaned in close. "Wait—I'll show ye." He pressed his palms against the table to lift himself up then called out, "Lara, come join us."

Lara's eyes lit up as the Ri Ciocid beckoned her with a cock of his head. She'd been smitten with him since she was old enough to be interested in men and only agreed to marry Connor to be close to him.

Thank goodness that never happened.

She bent her knee before him as she cooed, "And how may I be of assistance to the great Brian Boru?"

Brian flashed a smile at the petite beauty before him. Her eyes were as blue as the sky with a litter of dark lashes surrounding them and her cheeks were flushed red in contrast to her ivory skin.

"Come sit with us for a time. The Shaver here wants to hear yer opinions on war."

"Och," she issued as she waved a hand at him, "Ye tease me now."

"Nay," he blurted. "'Tis true, isn't it Shaver?"

She followed Brian's gaze to the handsome man seated beside him then bent her knee for him as well. "'Tis good to see ye again, Patric," she offered. "It's been quite some time."

Patric nodded happily as he tried to place the woman but before he could utter a word his attention was drawn by yet another woman calling his name.

"Patric," Margreg yelled out from across the room. She waved her arm in the air causing her dark hair to cascade over her shoulder. "Over here, Patric."

He looked in the direction of the call and smiled to see his cousin standing there. Suddenly it was as if he went back in time. Margreg looked just the same as always. He began to move toward her but it wasn't necessary since it only took a moment for her to clear a path so she could get to him. She stood before him, hands on hips as if she were angry that he would begin the celebration without her.

"Margreg," he sighed. "When did ye arrive?"

"Just now," she blurted in that familiar tone that brought him immediately back to his childhood. "We came as soon as we heard about yer brother."

"We?" Patric quizzed.

"Aye," she retorted with a flash of her gray eyes. "My mother's with me and…"

Patric was so excited to know that his favorite aunt was still alive that he cut her short. "Where is she?" he asked, standing on tiptoe to see over the crowd.

Gertrude was Lorca's sister and the best woman that Patric had ever known. She was as wide as she was tall with bright blue eyes and rosy cheeks and a hearty hug for him whenever he was near her.

"Gertrude," he called out as his eyes swept the crowd in search of her. He spotted her at the far end of the hall then leapt over the table to rush her.

"Patric!" she shouted gleefully when he took her up around her wide middle to spin her about. "My sweet laddie, ye've come back to us."

Tears streamed from her eyes and she showered his face with kisses. "We thought ye were lost. 'Tis a miracle that ye're alive."

They embraced each other with such enthusiasm that both of them were breathless when they finally let go. At length Gertrude took a step back so that she could get a good look at him. "What've ye done to yerself, lad?" she asked as her face soured. "Ye look the Viking."

"Aye, auntie," he crooned. "I rather like it."

"Well I don't," she admonished, wagging her finger beneath his nose. "Haven't ye even got any clothes to wear?"

He looked down at his bare chest then laughed before spinning her around again, "I've got clothes but they tell me it's easier to catch a wife if I'm not wearing any."

"Well that all depends," she laughed, clinging to his arms so she wouldn't fall. "If ye bulge the same all over yer body I should think ye'll have nay trouble at all."

He laughed again then lowered her to her feet, placing his arm around her shoulder so he could escort her to a chair. "Finn," he called to the captain who had suddenly reappeared by the table. "Can ye rid us of the rabble sleeping on my throne so my aunt doesn't think us a bunch of sots?"

"Aye, Shaver," Finn replied. He knelt down to lift Havland from the floor then pulled Eagan from his chair by his coat. They grumbled and swayed when the captain led them through the side door by the scruff of their necks.

Patric placed his aunt in the seat on his right before filling a cup for her. "Well isn't this grand?" she cooed before taking a sip. "Imagine me being tended by the Ri Tuath himself."

"It's as it should be," Brian said, nodding in her direction. He had thought the old woman was lost some time ago. He lifted his cup in her direction. "Ye've always been a good one, Gertrude. Very much like yer brother."

Those near enough to hear went silent with the mention of the Ri Tuath causing Brian to lift his cup higher. "To Lorca!" he called.

"To Lorca," they replied, lifting their cups before drinking.

Patric felt a shiver run up his spine as he sipped his ale. For a moment he thought he smelled his father's musky scent but it was fleeting.

He returned his attention to his aunt when the tiny, dark haired lass barreled onto the platform to settle herself in Gertrude's lap. "And who might this be?" Patric asked as he reached down to chuck the child under her chin.

"Nana," the child cried, clinging to Gertrude as if her life depended on it.

"There, there, Eilis," Gertrude cooed, stroking the child's hair. "Ye shouldn't be frightened of the Ri Tuath. He's a good lad. He'll be kind to ye."

The child peeked over her shoulder to catch a glimpse of Patric then hid herself again when he smiled at her. He reached out a hand to rub her dark hair. "She's a grand beauty, aye. Who does she belong to?"

"She's mine," Margreg called out, pushing her way in front of Lara so Patric could see her.

Patric smiled. "So ye finally managed to snag yerself a husband," he blurted, remembering that being married was all she ever talked about. She was a hopeless romantic. As children she would force him to listen to her recitation of love poems while she swooned. "I'll have to meet this man to offer him my condolences."

Margreg cast her eyes toward the ground shamefully and Patric looked to Gertrude for an explanation. "Tis yer brother's child, Patric," she offered without apology. "There was nay a marriage."

"Jesus Christ," he blurted while he thoughtlessly stroked the child's head. "I didn't think he had it in him."

"Neither did she," Gertrude snapped, jutting her chin at Margreg who now had her cloak drawn up around her ears.

"She goaded him into it with her sharp tongue, always chastising him for not being the man his father was until he finally snapped."

Brian lifted his head from where it rested on the table. There was anger in his eyes. "So now vengeance is served," he growled in Margreg's direction causing the woman to jump. "Ye should be shamed no longer, aye."

Margreg wiped the tears from her cheek then bowed to the Ri Ciocid before making her way around the table to take Eilis into her arms. The child fussed at her causing Patric to reach up. "Let me take her," he offered.

To everyone's surprise, Eilis went willingly, curling herself into a ball on his lap before quickly falling asleep.

"Ye seem to have a way with her, Patric," Brian cooed then cocked his chin in Margreg's direction.

Patric took the Ri Ciocid's meaning as clearly as if he had spoken the words. He responded with a quick shake of the head. If he married Margreg the child born from his brother's rape would be legitimate but he knew that he and his cousin clashed too much to share the same house in peace let alone the same bed.

Brian nodded his understanding then they both turned their attention to Lara who was reaching over the table to stroke the child's face.

"She's a dear one, alright," she cooed. The child reacted to her petting with a slumbering smile.

"My apologies, lady," Patric sighed. "I fear I interrupted ye when ye were speaking earlier."

Lara lifted her eyes to meet Patric's then drew breath. He was fiercely handsome. The child in his arms only served to make him more so. "Yer apology is accepted Ri Tuath," she replied. "Perhaps we should speak at another time when yer hands aren't quite so full."

Brian watched the exchange between them and for some odd reason he thought of Kormlada. He was just drunk enough to lose himself in the memory of a dream he once had in which they were married and celebrating his ascension to the high throne. He again rested his head against the table while mumbling to himself, "If ever dreams could come true that would be the one I want."

∗   ∗   ∗   ∗

Torshav, Ireland: Three hours past midnight—2, October 992 A.D.— Brodir rode into Torshav with the wind at his back causing his long black hair to whip around his face. The storm that had been chasing him all evening unleashed itself as he got to the gates. He held his arm over his eyes when he called up to the guards, "I search for the woman they call Freyja. Is she here?"

The young guards exchanged anxious glances as they wondered what business the Viking could have with the woman. Patric left them strict instructions that no harm should come to Freyja. No matter what transpired they were to guard her with their lives.

"Perhaps it's her brother," Steven offered to Shane as his brows knit together. Though he was beyond loyal to the Shaver he saw no need to take on trouble when it could be avoided. He looked at the Viking whose features were sharpened by the glow of the torchlight. "They have the same look, aye?"

"Aye," Shane agreed taking a moment to assess the man.

The weapon holster slung over Brodir's back told them that he was battle skilled, yet standing there in the rain he didn't look to be threatening. "Still the same, ye best ask."

Steven nodded then leaned out over the split rail of the stanchion to inquire, "Are ye family then?"

Brodir smiled wryly as long ago memories of glorious nights spent in Freyja's arms filled his head. For all the women he had ever known she was the only one to fully possess his soul. They often finished each other's sentences. And pleasing each other came instinctively to them. They were kindred spirits—as close as two human beings could possibly get.

"Ye might say so," he cried taking a step back to get a better glimpse of the man who asked the question.

When he arrived at the tavern in Clonmacnoise three days earlier, Varna told him that Freyja had taken up with the Shaver. She confessed that the Shaver was a fierce warrior and warned Brodir against seeking the woman out. But only death itself would keep him from her.

Under the cover of his cape he laid his hand atop his dagger. "Tell her Brodir of Man searches for her. She'll know me."

Shane turned to Steven then shrugged his shoulders. If this man meant trouble for them Freyja would tell them of it. In the meantime the gates would keep him out.

"Go and speak with her," he ordered. "She'll be sore if we keep kin waiting in the rain."

"Aye," Steven agreed then made his way down the ladder and across the field to the house with lightening speed.

"Freyja," he called as he pounded on her door leaving a puddle in the hall from his dripping cloak. "There's someone here to see ye."

He waited for a moment or two but when he heard no noise within he pounded again. "Freyja! Are ye awake, woman?"

The heavy door creaked against its hinge as Freyja peered through the crack. Her hair was tangled and her face creased from where the linen had bunched up beneath it. "I am now," she huffed. "What's this all about? Has the Shaver returned?"

Steven opened his mouth to answer but all at once the thought flooded her brain and she threw open the door to grab him by the arms. "Is it the Shaver, Steven? Is he hurt?"

Steven took a moment to gaze at her naked body. Despite her years Freyja was still a sight to behold, slender where she needed to be and ample everywhere else. He cast his eyes toward the ground as he felt his blood stir. "Och, woman, 'tis not the Shaver but another man that seeks ye. Says his name is Brodir of Man. Says he's kin and that ye know of him."

Her eyes went wide and her jaw slackened then suddenly her body began to tremble. "Brodir," she sighed.

Steven touched her shoulder. She shivered beneath his grasp. "Is he trouble then, woman?" he barked. "Tell me now so I can gather some men."

She thought about the question before responding. For certain Brodir was trouble—especially for her. He was skilled in all weapons and had the uncanny ability to read a man's soul. There were those who called him a sorcerer. For all she knew it could very well be true—but there was one thing she was certain of— Brodir possessed both her body and her soul. Only the news of his death allowed her to be free of him. Even then his memory haunted her.

"Are ye certain it's him?" she asked, her voice still husky from sleep.

"Freyja," he barked, shaking her a bit as he did. "Is he trouble?"

Realizing that the only way to gain more information was to allay his fears, she let her eyes go soft as she crooned, "If he's the man I think he is there'll be nothing for ye to worry over. Why don't ye tell me what he looks like so I can be sure?"

Steven held his hand above his head as he did his best to describe the Viking to her. "He's very tall, aye. Kinda like Njord." Then all at once it struck him. "Come to think of it, he's got the look of the lad. Dark of hair and very broad through the shoulders."

She nodded her head as she recognized the description. Of course Brodir had the look of Njord. They were kin. Both hailing from the line of Imar though Njord was further removed. "I'll see him," she finally answered as she stepped through the doorway but suddenly he stopped her.

"'Tis raining outside," he chuckled, "perhaps ye should put on some clothes first."

She stared at him for a moment until the words settled on her brain. She was naked. Her face flushed red before she stepped back into her chamber to get dressed.

She could feel the blood racing through her veins as anxiety gripped her. It had been twelve years since Brodir left her behind with a promise to return for her. Soon after news of his death made its way to the tavern in Clonmacnoise. At the time she prayed that death would claim her too and she did her best to have it so, but eventually she healed. Now everything was coming undone again.

With shaking hands she pulled the lein over her head then took a moment to smooth her hair and pinch her cheeks to bring the color. She stepped through the doorway but again Steven stopped her. "The ground's quite muddy," he offered, looking to her bare feet. "Ye alright, woman?"

Realizing that her thoughtlessness was arousing his suspicion, she used anger to cover it up. "Well ye woke me from a dead sleep, aye. Ye can't be expecting me to have all my wits yet."

She made her way back into the chamber, quickly slipping her feet into her shoes but taking far too much time to lace them up as her shaking hands made the task that much more difficult. When she was done she looked herself over to be sure she hadn't forgotten anything else. Deciding she was finally ready, she stepped through the door to be on her way.

Steven was Gael and as far as she knew he had no other tongue to him. "Who's on watch with ye tonight?" she asked while she strolled casually beside him.

"Shane," he answered. Then thinking that she might be angry with him for making the decision to wake her on his own he added, "He's the one what told me to get ye."

Reading his face she smiled for him. "That's fine," she replied. "Ye did right by getting me."

The only thing she knew about Shane was that he was a Gall born in Crowfjord. If he had another tongue other than the Gaelic she would know soon enough.

They stopped just short of the gate and she pulled her cloak up about her neck. Though the rain was cold against her exposed skin, it wasn't that which made her shiver. She looked to Steven. "Go and help Shane with the gate, aye."

His eyes went wide as he looked at her but before he could offer his protest she placed her hand atop his to offer, "'Tis alright. He'll do me no harm."

He nodded then climbed up the ladder, calling to Shane who had retreated back into the shelter of the overhang. Together they yanked the heavy iron chains through the rollers Patric had devised to make opening the gates that much easier.

She held her breath for what seemed an eternity before the man outside was revealed to her. She released it when she recognized Brodir. For a moment she thought she might faint. She took a deep breath to regain herself.

"*Ta shiu braew, dooiney,*" she offered in the Manx tongue he was accustomed to.

He flashed his white teeth before rushing her, pulling her head back with his hand in her hair before crushing her with his kiss. It had been a long time but still her body reacted to him, molding itself against his until the heat rose up within him.

Suddenly he broke from her. He took a step back to look her over. Though her dark hair was now streaked with gray she still had the same look as when they last laid eyes on each other. "I've come for ye, woman," he sighed against her hair in the same language she'd spoken to him. "The isle's mine."

She had no words for him as her brain scrambled to make sense of the situation. She wanted to crush him to her—to bury herself inside him so she could feel his warmth. She lifted her head to him so he could kiss her again but suddenly she glimpsed Shane descending the ladder and all at once she remembered where she was.

She began to cough when the churn of her stomach sent bile up into her throat and Brodir rubbed her back, his eyes filling with concern. "Ye can't stay here," she croaked, struggling to find her voice. "He'll be returning soon," she whispered, knowing that Brodir would know who the "he" was. "Ye must leave."

"Leave?" he chuckled then rubbed her cheek with his thumb. He had no doubt that he could handle the two guards. And no matter how fierce her new man was, he would be no match for someone who had waited so long to reclaim what was his. "I've traveled an ocean and waited a lifetime to gather ye, Freyja. Ye can't be rid of me that easily."

"But ye must," she hissed. She grabbed his arms, the fear welling up in her as Shane and Steven moved toward them. The last thing she wanted was to see them harmed.

"Ye alright, woman?" Shane called. Brother or nay the man was beginning to irritate him.

"Aye," she responded without turning. Her eyes darted around the interior of the fort searching for a place where they could be alone. "Go back to yer post, Shane. I'll be speaking with my kin in private."

They stopped at her order but didn't turn causing her to grab Brodir by the hand. "Follow me, aye," she whispered.

The fact that Brodir had his hand poised on his dagger unnerved her even more. She tugged against him with all her weight as she headed for the abandoned herder's hut at the far end of the clearing. She pushed him through the doorway then looked back to be sure that Shane and Steven weren't following before slamming the door shut and throwing the bolt.

She took a moment to let her eyes adjust to the darkness then moved quickly to the hearth where she sparked a fire with the flint stones she found resting on the table. Her chest was heaving from her efforts when she turned toward him then suddenly it was heaving from more than that.

When she looked at him she found the same man she knew so long ago. His green eyes glowed in the dim light of the fire and his sharp features were made more so by the full long beard he wore down to his waist. Though quite dark, there was no doubt he was a Viking of noble heritage. Every inch of his taught muscular body foretold the power within him. He was built like the Shaver but the Shaver was only dangerous in battle—Brodir was just plain dangerous.

He advanced and she took a step back. His strong arms quickly brought her to him and again he crushed her with his kiss.

Her mind flooded with thoughts of Patric and she struggled against him but he wouldn't release her. Soon Brodir's familiar touch heated her blood and she molded herself to him as she eagerly took all he offered her.

"Ye're mine, woman," he sighed against her cheek as his strong hand pressed her to him. "No other can possess ye as fully as I do and ye know it."

The tears welling in her eyes suddenly broke loose, streaming down her cheeks to wet his face. "They told me ye were dead and when they did I wanted to join ye but I was too cowardly to do the deed."

"Thank the gods," he whispered, kissing the tears from her face. "Ye'd be no good to me dead now would ye?"

Her tears kept coming and she pounded his back with her fists as she howled, "Why didn't ye send for me as ye promised? Ye let me live these years thinking ye were dead and having my heart ripped from me for my sadness."

He stopped what he was doing to push her back a bit then grabbed her by the wrists to end her assault. He was staring at her so intently that she could see what he was thinking. She looked away to hide her shame.

"By the looks of things here," he hissed, "I'd say ye recovered just fine, aye."

It was obvious that he knew about her life with the Shaver. She didn't question how. Brodir had always had an uncanny ability to know everything about her. Now she was faced with the most difficult decision she would ever have to make. She leaned away from him to break his grasp, knowing she'd only be free of him if he wanted it that way. He slowly let her slip from him, watching her intently as she paced the room.

"What shall I do now, Brodir?" she asked without turning to him.

She heard his answer in her head but the only sound in the room was that of his breathing. She turned to him with pleading eyes. "But how can I leave him?"

This time his answer was clear as he moved close to stroke back the hair that came to rest on her cheek. "He's left ye already," he sighed, "And ye know it."

Her eyes told him he was right but still she nodded her head. He smiled then lifted her chin with his finger as he prepared to reclaim her.

CHAPTER 25

▼

Cavenlow, Ireland—Private Chamber of Patric macLorca: One hour before noon—22, October 992 A.D.—Turlog swallowed the bile rising in his throat before lowering himself into the chair facing the new Ri Tuath. He looked to the artifacts lining the walls and his stomach flipped. He only joined in the celebration of Patric's taking of Cavenlow so that he wouldn't arouse suspicion. Now, as he sat there alone with Brian and Patric he wasn't so sure that his plan was the best one.

"So what is it ye want of me?" he grumbled as he prepared to defend himself against whatever accusation they were planning on leveling.

Brian recognized Turlog's tension. No doubt his uncle was sore over losing the village when he thought himself so close to finally gaining it. He hoped his anger would ease with the prospect of this new alliance. "'Twas a good celebration, aye?"

Turlog nodded but said nothing further. Brian continued, "It should be a relief to ye that Patric is a good warrior. Thomond borders Cavenlow. Having someone capable with a sword sitting as its Ri Tuath could be a benefit to ye if ever ye need assistance."

"What's this all about?" Turlog bristled, his patience wearing thin with the idle chatter. "It's clear ye're trying to get at something. Why not just lay it plain?"

Patric raised his eyebrow at Brian as if to say that the whole thing was a bad idea. He should have traveled to Torshav himself to tell Freyja of his intentions before rushing into a marriage bargain with someone else.

"Patric is interested in Lara," Brian offered in response to Turlog's request. "What say ye to striking a bargain to keep an alliance between clansmen?"

"A marriage bargain?" Turlog's relief was evident in his posture.

"Aye," Brian replied. "What did ye think we were after?"

Realizing his tell, Turlog screwed up his face. "Ye've been so secretive lately that I didn't know what ye were wanting, nephew."

Brian nodded as if to own the charge. "So is it agreed?"

"Hold on there," Turlog replied. "If there was a bride price offered I must have missed it. What does the Ri Tuath offer for my daughter's hand?"

Patric leveled his gaze at the man. His distaste for Turlog had been as deeply imbedded in his soul as his love for Brian was. "Take yer choice, Turlog," he replied, waving his hand through the air to indicate the many gold and silver trinkets his brother had acquired during his raiding. "For me these items are stained by the blood of innocents. A blight against our clan. If there's something among them that ye fancy, take it with good riddance."

"Well," Turlog huffed as he did his best to act insulted. "So now ye offer them to me?"

"Come now, uncle," Brian sighed, feeling the tension build between them. It seemed to be a curse that any marriage negotiation he took part in ended in bloodshed. He leaned forward as he prepared to do his best to have this one turn out differently. "He's only being generous to ye. Would ye prefer that he be less than that?"

Turlog raised an eyebrow before leaning forward to meet the Ri Ciocid. "Nay," he sighed, "but my daughter is quite valuable, as is my friendship. Mere trinkets couldn't begin to equal that which Patric will gain by taking Lara to wife. When it's done, it will put him in good standing with the clan and that's worth more than a silver cup or a few…"

"Slow down there, Turlog," Patric interrupted as he too leaned forward. "Do ye forget that I've redeemed the honor of my family by standing with Brian in Leinster. I don't need a marriage to yer daughter to do that for me." Turlog huffed and he continued, "All know what I did for Brian and this clan. I need nothing more to redeem my honor."

"Easy there now both of ye," Brian offered as he laid a hand on each of their arms. "I've not sat in on such a tense marriage bargain since I last struck my own. God knows I shouldn't want to live through that twice."

Turlog laughed out loud. He was present during Brian's negotiations for his fourth wife. When the woman learned that her intended husband had killed her father she had to be dragged kicking and screaming down the aisle then held down as the abbot recited the vows. He always wondered whether his nephew had to use that same tactic to have her concede in bed but seeing that she bore him a child he figured that she must have acquiesced.

He chuckled again then sat back in his chair leaving Patric thoroughly confused. "Alright then, we'll leave the knives out of this but I do ask for a yearly tribute."

"Yearly tribute?" Patric blurted, turning to Brian in amazement. "And what shall yer uncle do to earn this tribute? Does he plan on protecting my lands for me?"

"If it comes to that," Turlog huffed, drawing Patric's attention back to him. "My alliance brings with it my resources. I should think my army could be very helpful to ye until ye build up yer own. Didn't ye send most of yer men back to Torshav this morning?"

The point was a good one and Brian shrugged in agreement. "It makes sense, Patric," he crooned. "It might be yer best option while ye build up an army of yer own."

Patric sat back with a sigh as he realized the sense of the plan. He'd sent his men back to Torshav knowing that Njord would likely need them more than he would. The only ones who remained with him in Cavenlow were Finn and Eagan.

As much as he wanted to be done with the negotiations he couldn't help his resentment for having to pay more than he should. He countered with an offer of his own.

"Very well then," he finally sighed. "I'll offer ye a yearly tribute of silver but I want the marriage to take place by the new moon."

"Come now, Shaver," Turlog retorted, understanding that the planning of a wedding would take far longer than that. "Ye can't be meaning to recall the clan so soon after they just left. It will take us until spring to prepare properly. It can't be done before that."

Brian opened his mouth to offer his agreement but Patric quickly cut him off. "Either we do it now or we can forget about it all together. There's nay need for a celebration. We need only marry."

The Ri Ciocid wiped his hands over his face as his uncle looked to him with wide eyes. "Lara will never agree to these terms. She's not been shamed. Why shouldn't she have the opportunity to celebrate among the other women of her clan?"

Again Brian opened his mouth to offer his bit but Turlog spoke again, "I suppose next he'll be telling us that he plans to keep the whore, Margreg and her half traitor child living in the house with them."

The statement ignited Patric's ire and his hands shook with his effort to control it. It was just like Turlog to mark an innocent child so cruelly. It was those types of actions that made an alliance with the man so distasteful. "This conversation is over," he barked then pushed himself from the chair so he could leave. "Perhaps Brian's first thought was the right one. Perhaps I should marry Margreg. At least with her I can avoid being extorted in exchange for an alliance."

He laughed before adding the bit he was sure would get Turlog's juices flowing. "In the end a marriage to Margreg will bring me greater favor from the clan than a marriage to Lara ever could."

Turlog's eyes went narrow as he prepared to rebuke the statement but when he thought about it he realized it was true. If Patric righted his brother's wrong by taking Margreg to wife the clan would surely look favorably on him and support him for any position he desired. He released his breath then rose from his chair, walking across the room to meet the Shaver.

"Very well," he stated. "Ye may marry Lara immediately if ye promise to lay a celebration at Easter. She's a good woman. There's nay a reason she shouldn't get what's coming to her."

Brian held his breath as he watched Patric's face. He could see the tiny vein at the side of his head throbbing in anger but in the end he offered his hand to Turlog. "It's a bargain then."

Turlog took the hand being offered and Brian watched him. That fact that his uncle had been so nervous earlier didn't escape him. He hoped Patric's marriage to Lara would make it easier for him to keep an eye on the man.

✳   ✳   ✳   ✳

Torshav, Ireland—Great Hall: Six hours past noon—23, October 992 A.D.—Freyja sat in Njord's chair, mulling the words he just offered. At length she looked up at him. "So he'll not be returning then?"

When Njord didn't answer she reached out her hand to lift his chin with her open palm so she could see his eyes. "Worse yet, he's sent ye to do his work for him."

Njord recognized the contempt in her voice and he defended his father with his curt response. "And why not? I'm the earl. It's my place to care for ye."

She took a moment to look at his beautiful face while she struggled to hold back her tears. It was bad enough that she would have to leave him behind but she'd hoped Patric could be with her when she broke the news to him. She blinked her eyes a few times to keep the moisture from overflowing them then looked away from him to where Havland was leaning against the table. He too was a handsome man, and a great friend.

"I suppose it's yer place as well," she sighed as she recognized his embarrassment for the situation.

"Nay," he retorted, lifting his eyes to expose his discomfort for the whole affair. "I do it because I care for ye, woman. I've nay a duty to bind me."

She nodded slowly then prepared to deliver her own news. Even before Patric went to Leinster she knew their relationship was over. He knew it too. But while they had time to get used to it, it was a fresh wound for Havland and Njord.

"Come," she finally sighed as she held a hand out for each of them to take. "I've something to tell ye."

Havland's head shot up when he recognized her tone to be the one she used when she had bad news. "What is it, Freyja?" he asked, taking her hand in his.

She looked to Njord who leaned forward in his seat. She stroked his black hair then kissed his head. "I'm leaving ye. I'm going to Man."

"What?" he blurted as he lifted his eyes to meet hers. He knew she was hurting but running away wouldn't solve anything. "Ye can't make that kind of decision without first giving it consideration."

"Don't ye worry over me, laddie," she retorted with the sharp eyes of a mother. "I've given this consideration enough. I've had nearly yer whole life to think about it, aye."

Havland, who was as thoroughly confused by the situation as Njord was, barked at her, "Don't toy with us, woman, just lay it plain."

"Very well," she huffed, offering them the bitterness she would have leveled at Patric if he had been brave enough to be there. "When the Shaver finally does decide to show his face ye can tell him that I'm to marry Brodir of Man."

Their eyes went wide then they looked at each other.

"Imagine that," she chuckled. "I've found a husband of my own."

"Brodir," Njord sighed, struggling to understand what was happening. A moment ago he was peeved that his father was forcing him to offer news that he was sure would break her heart. But to learn that she'd been preparing to betray the Shaver all along was too much for him to accept. "How can this be?" he questioned as his eyes filled with contempt for her.

"Never mind how it can be," she retorted. "It just is and that's all ye need know." Then with a deep jab of anger for the circumstances that caused him to look at her that way she spewed, "Ye just tell the Shaver that I stopped being a whore some time ago and I resent him for treating me that way now. Ye tell him that I was gone when ye came and that ye never found me to give me his message, aye. Ye'll do it if ye're as duty bound as ye claim to be."

Njord made no effort to hide the distaste he held for her. She may have acted as his mother for all these years but now she was acting like the whore she professed not to be. "How can ye betray him after all he's given ye?" he growled. "He's given ye everything he had and treated ye like Mave herself and all the while ye had someone else waiting for ye."

"Och, that's rich." Her chuckle was riddled with contempt. "He sends the two of ye to tell me that he no longer has any use for me and ye condemn me for promising myself to a man who thinks I'm worthy of being his wife."

Njord didn't answer instead he looked at her as if there wasn't any skin covering her bones. She defended herself more fiercely.

"I suppose I did nothing to earn this wonderful treatment he gave to me, aye. Perhaps standing by his side caring for him, waiting for him and mending him after his wars didn't earn me the right to have him tell me he's leaving me in person."

She leaned in close enough to let her breath play on his face. "Well, my apologies fine lad if I seem ungrateful to the Ri Tuath but I think that after all our years together he could have managed something more meaningful than a message delivered by the two of ye."

"Ye are a whore!" Njord finally blurted, "And the Shaver should be glad to be rid of ye."

"Easy there, laddie," Havland broke in but he was too late. The wound that was delivered showed itself in the eyes of its victim.

Freyja hardly felt the tears as they brimmed her eyes but she did feel the heat of anger explode inside her. She emitted a growl from deep in her throat then delivered a stunning slap to Njord's face. "Never!" she spit, "Never speak such words to me again. Do ye hear me, laddie?"

He stared at her with cold eyes as the skin of his cheek warmed from her blow but he didn't utter a word. She got to her feet, looking him over with eyes so sharp there was no doubt that hatred loomed in her heart. She spit in his eye. "Give that to the Shaver for me, aye."

She turned on her heel and Havland called out before she got to the door, "Ye can't be leaving it this way, Freyja!"

She looked back long enough for him to see the pain in her eyes then disappeared into the shadows of the circular hall. "Ye must go to her, Njord," he huffed. "Ye can't send her away in anger. 'Twouldn't be right."

"Wouldn't it?" he replied.

Though he had never met Brodir, he'd heard all about him from Gamal. His reverence in Viking circles spread from Waterford to Orkney but the Gael hated him thoroughly. He was surprised by his own feelings of contempt for the man but he would be Dal Cais soon and supposed that had something to do with it.

"It's clear she's chosen her own way without so much as a drop of remorse for her betrayal of our clan," he barked. "I say good riddance to her."

His anger flared as he again thought of Patric then he waved a hand toward the open door and spit. "I'm only glad she waited until my father was away from here to show her true self. He'd be broken hearted to know that her love for him was nothing more than a ruse."

Havland sighed then shook his head. He'd been with Patric and Freyja for too long to think that the love they shared was anything less than genuine. But the lad was too young to understand the torture of his mother's heart. He searched for the words to enlighten him but in the end only offered, "Wait a while, laddie and ye'll understand all that happened. I only fear that by that time it may be too late for ye."

He exited the chamber, hoping that by some miracle she would change her mind about marrying Brodir.

*   *   *   *

Cavenlow, Ireland—The Great Hall: One hour past midnight—24, October, 992 A.D.—The weight of Patric's statement came crashing down on Margreg like a rock. She had rushed to Cavenlow hoping he would marry her to redeem the good name of her five-year-old daughter but he had other ideas.

"So I suppose ye'll be wanting us to leave after ye take Lara to wife?" she sighed, stroking the head of the child who slept in her lap. She felt the tear forming in her eye and lowered her head. "Perhaps it's for the best. It wouldn't be fair to ask Lara to bear the burden of yer brother's sins."

Patric knew she was fishing for an explanation but he didn't know how to give it. Instead he placed his hand atop hers and smiled. "I'll not send ye away, Margreg. The child deserves a proper home. She's of my blood, as are ye. Ye may remain with us as long as ye like. It'll be my great honor to care for ye."

"Will it?" She raised her eyebrow. If he were willing to care for her she didn't understand why he chose to marry someone else." I should think we'd be a hindrance to yer new wife. Perhaps ye should speak with her on it."

"Margreg," he sighed, realizing it would be best to give her what she wanted no matter how much it hurt. "Ye know things would never work out between the two of us. We've known each other for too long to pretend we could get on without ripping each other's heart out. 'Tis best for ye to wait for a man who could serve ye as ye should be, not one whose temper is as volatile as yer own."

Her eyes narrowed as she leveled her gaze at him. Though she would accept a marriage offer made in pity she could hardly accept a denial laced with it. "So that's what ye think I'm after," she huffed. "Ye think that I'm wanting ye to right yer brother's wrong by marrying me?" She turned away from him in an effort to hide the truth. "Come now, cousin, ye know me better than that. I've managed this long without the help of a man and I'll continue on until I find one that suits me. I was only worrying for yer happiness is all."

Thoroughly accustomed to her vast mood swings, he quickly offered his apology. "Forgive my foolishness. I only meant ye to know my end of it is all."

He watched her eyes, waiting for the moment that the fire in them died down before continuing, "Ye should be married to a good man, Margreg. I promise ye that as soon as I'm settled I'll begin working on a match for ye. 'Twould be good for the child to have a father's love to grow on and perhaps a brother or sister to keep her company."

That statement caused her to look up at him. Since her rape at the hands of a man who was so widely detested she was made to feel unworthy. "Do ye believe anyone could ever love me, Shaver?" she questioned with pleading eyes. "Is it possible that anyone would have me after…"

She went suddenly silent and he reached out a hand to stroke her neck. "Och, woman," he sighed, pulling her head to rest on his shoulder. "There's at least a hundred men who'd give a finger to have ye and the child as their own. Ye're foolish to even think otherwise."

He felt her shoulders lurch beneath his grasp and he soothed her with a cluck of the tongue. "Hush now, woman. It's not so bad as that. I promise all will go well."

He rocked her back and forth but her sobs only intensified until he finally moved his mouth near her ear to ask, "Will ye tell me of it then?"

She sniffled then looked up at him, the nod of her head almost imperceptible. Though many people spoke of it, none ever asked her what really happened.

She shifted Eilis' weight into her left arm as her right hand wiped the tears from her eyes. "Do ye really want to know?"

His eyes went soft telling her that he did and she settled back against his shoulder, her embarrassment forcing her gaze away from him.

"It was a hot day," she began, "Too hot to do much more than sit outside waiting for a cool breeze. That's what I was doing when one of the hired soldiers came up behind me to accost me with his crude remarks. He was naked to the waist and I could smell the ale on his breath as he moved around me, offering me my heart's desire if only I'd lay with him. I told him what I thought of his offer and he smacked me in the face. That's when I went inside to find Kevin.

"He was in his chamber with the tall man they called Garvin. I could hear by their groaning that they were committing acts against nature. I was so sickened by it that I said so loud enough for them to hear. Before I could get away, yer brother had thrown open the door and was standing in front of me wearing nothing more than a look that would have cut me in two if it had been a sword. He told me that I shouldn't speak about things that I had nay a knowledge of and when I told him that I'd rather be dead than to know of such things, he told me he could arrange for both.

"It was then that he grabbed me and dragged me into the chamber. They were both drunk, but while Garvin begged the Ri Tuath to let me go so that they could get back to their business, Kevin insisted on teaching me a lesson.

"He had Garvin hold me down while he committed his crime then he beat me to within an inch of my life. I awoke the next day in a pool of my own blood with my eyes swollen shut from the abuse. It took a month for my wounds to heal and by that time I knew I was carrying his child. I did everything I could think of to be rid of it but when my womb started to swell he again brought me to his chamber.

"He kept me there under lock and key, believing I would deliver him a son. He told me that if I did, he would marry me so that he would have a proper heir, but when Eilis was born he decided to send us away in an effort to soothe Garvin's jealousy. He called us back soon after."

She hesitated for a moment and Patric looked down in wonder that she was able to relay as much of the story as she did without tears. He had expected to see her face contorted in grief but was surprised to see her smiling.

She lifted her eyes to meet his as she offered, "Believe it or not, he cared for the child and wanted to be sure that no harm came to her. When he decided to join Sigtrygg in his war he sent us away with enough gold to live on for a year. He told me that if he was slain and ye were left alive that I should come to ye so that ye could provide for us proper. Now here I sit with the child in my arms and yer promise to see us safe."

A tiny "hmph," pushed past Patric's lips as the story contradicted everything he knew about his brother. "I'm sorry for ye," he finally offered then they both sat silent for a bit longer.

She looked at him and decided to take the opportunity to ask the question that had been nagging at her. "What will ye do with yer Viking woman?"

She felt his back stiffen. "How did ye know about Freyja?"

"Finn told me of her."

She looked up and noticed that he was frowning. "What troubles ye, cousin? Was she to be a secret?"

A pang of guilt shot through him as he thought of Freyja. He wondered how she reacted when Havland and Njord brought her the news that he was planning to marry. He was sure she had expected as much, but still he pictured her eyes glowing hot as she set her jaw in an effort to restrain the vulgarity brewing in her throat. She was beautiful when she was angry and he smiled as he remembered the many nights of passion they shared after a fight.

For a moment or two he let his mind take him back to that wonderful place in Freyja's arms but all at once his body stiffened as he realized that her passion wouldn't end with him. If she needed somebody to love it would most likely be Havland that she would turn to. Given their history it would make sense.

"I don't know what will become of Freyja," he grumbled. "I only hope I can make it up to her."

Margreg recognized his sadness and somehow felt closer to him for it. "Have nay worry, Patr—Shaver," she offered, his new name still sounding strange to her ear. "Ye'll figure it out. Ye always did have a good head in times of trouble."

He looked at her and a thought suddenly occurred to him. "Ye said it was Finn who told ye about Freyja. What else did he tell ye?"

The blush of her face with the mention of the captain's name was a welcomed surprise for Patric.

"He told me about Torshav and how ye came to meet. He told me of his people and the things he liked to do."

Recognizing that any description of Finn would hardly include the word talkative, Patric wondered what great event took place to have the captain so thoroughly bear his soul.

Before he could inquire the man himself appeared in the hall. "So that's where the lassie's gotten to," Finn cooed as his long legs brought him quickly to the table. He knelt down to stroke Eilis' cheek. "I was passing by the chamber and thought to look in on her but she wasn't where I left her and I became concerned."

"Where *ye* left her?" Patric questioned as he raised an eyebrow. Although Finn had always been conscientious in the care of his men, he had never witnessed him around a child other than Njord. "So are ye adding nurse to yer long list of duties now, Finn?"

The blush of the captain's cheeks was a sight that nearly knocked Patric from his chair. He tried desperately to hide his surprise when Finn responded; "Margreg here has quite enough to keep her busy. I thought since I wasn't particularly needed at the time that I could give her a hand by laying the lass down for the night."

"I see," Patric crooned then turned to look at Margreg whose color had heightened enough to match the wine in her cup.

"Ye're a lucky one to have the fine captain lending a hand, cousin. He's the most level headed of my lot."

"I should say I am lucky, Shaver," she replied, her eyes turning toward Finn. "The man is a God send. It's a wonder he's escaped marriage as long as he has being that he's both capable and handsome."

"Go on with ye now." Finn slapped the air modestly then lifted the child from Margreg's lap to settle her against his shoulder. "I'll take her back for ye, Margreg. Just sit there and rest yerself a bit more. Ye needn't worry."

As Finn moved off the platform to exit the chamber, Patric leaned in to Margreg. "Open yer eyes and see the things right under yer nose, woman."

She touched his arm as she took his meaning. "Do ye really think he'd want me, cousin? I thought perhaps his kindness was part of his nature"

The smile on Patric's face was answer enough but still he responded, "Indeed, the man is kind but with you there's something more. Believe me when I tell ye that I've spent enough nights and days with that one to know his heart and I've never seen him act as he did just now. Go to him and let him see that he has a chance with ye. If ye do it right, I'd say I'll be sitting with him in the morning discussing issues other than the weather, aye."

She looked long at him to be sure he wasn't teasing her. When she recognized the seriousness in his eyes she offered him a tiny kiss then scurried from the hall calling, "Finn, let me catch ye up. I'll lend ye a hand."

*   *   *   *

Clonmacnoise, Ireland: The tavern—One hour past midnight—30, October, 992 A.D.—Dark and reeking of the sweat of unwashed men, the tavern in Clonmacnoise was no different then the day that Freyja left it. She took a moment to let her eyes grow accustomed to the darkness then moved forward as she spotted Brodir sitting in the corner with another man she didn't recognize. A smile broke across his face when he spotted her and she sighed for his beauty. His hair was clean and smoothed into a long tail at his back and his long beard was braided then tucked into his belt. The torchlight bouncing off his arm rings drew her attention. She let her eyes linger there as she imagined him embracing her. No sooner did the thought cross her mind than it was happening.

He pulled her close, letting her taste the mead on his tongue until he consumed all her breath. Then he broke free, taking her chin in his hands as his green eyes bored through her soul. "Is that what ye were wanting, woman?"

She smiled at him seductively and he lowered his head for another go until the call of the stranger stopped him. "Leave off her for a moment more, Brodir," Throdier barked. "Let's finish what we started here before ye start something else altogether."

The corner of Brodir's lip lifted into a half smile as he looked into her eyes. Again he plunged his tongue into her mouth. She grabbed onto his shoulders to steady herself.

He left her breathless then winked his eye before taking his seat. "Bring us another pint, aye. I've got business to finish with Throdier before we depart."

It took every ounce of strength in her body to rip her gaze from him, but when she finally did she turned it on the other Viking. The man's naked face wasn't familiar to her but the scar on his bald head told her that he was the same man the Shaver had put down all those years ago. She wondered what business Brodir could have with him.

Deciding that an inquiry would only serve to bring Brodir's ire, she turned on her heel to bring another pitcher, stopping frequently to chat with the many patrons. Throdier leaned across the table to keep his conversation private.

"So, how do ye propose we deal with the man?"

"I'm not quite sure," Brodir responded, shaking his head. All the information he could acquire about the Shaver led him to the same conclusion—not only was he dangerous but also quite bold. The only way to be certain that Freyja wouldn't return to him was to have him dead. "I don't want any chance of him escaping with his life therefore we must be sure that the deed is done correctly."

"There's nay a need to bring up the past," Throdier huffed, knowing the point Brodir was driving at. He had made several attempts on the Shaver's life since his return to Ireland but all of them failed.

"'Twasn't meant as an insult, brother, only a statement of fact. 'Tis clear that the best way to do the deed is one on one but I doubt we can get him to shake his men." He noticed Freyja returning with the pitcher then leaned in closer to offer,

"Take some time to think on it before ye strike again. If necessary, send for me in Man and I'll come back to do the deed myself."

"It won't come to that," Throdier huffed. Brodir continued to stare until he offered his consent. "If it does, I'll send for ye."

By the time Freyja got to the table, Brodir was already on his feet. He ripped the pitcher from her hand then tossed it against the hearth causing the men who were sloshed by the liquid to grunt. He kissed her, pressing her against a chair as his body melted into hers. The man sitting in the chair got to his feet.

"Take it outside, aye," he growled.

Freyja looked at him from the corner of her eye then pushed against Brodir's chest to be free of him. If they continued on as they were he would take her right there without a care for anyone else.

"Come," she panted. "I've a place where we can be alone."

She led him to her apartment but hesitated before stepping inside. Everything in the place reminded her of Patric.

Brodir knew what she was thinking. He pushed her forward until she was sprawled on the bed then entered her with a fury only abstinence could cause. He would do whatever it took to erase the Shaver from her mind even if it meant killing her. She was his and nothing in heaven or on earth could change that fact.

✳   ✳   ✳   ✳

Cavenlow, Ireland: In the abbey—Sundown—15, November 992 A.D.— Patric shifted his weight from one foot to the other as he gazed around the ruined abbey. He watched for a moment as the droplet of rain lingered on the edge of the hole in the thatch roof then marked it in his head as something he'd have to tend as part of Cavenlow's recovery.

There were only six benches in the room that had one time held twenty, and those were sorely in need of repair. He thought of Vahn who had come to live in Torshav after Njord found him wandering in the woods. His skills as a carpenter were invaluable. He decided to send for him then looked around to see what else might need mending.

All thought went out of his head when he noticed his mother approaching.

The ever-present sorrow in Grace's eyes seemed to have gotten worse over the years and Patric wondered if Turlog was treating her well. He moved toward her with the hope that she would be happy to see him and though she looked at him adoringly he could still see her sadness. He bent to kiss her. "'Tis been a long while, mother."

"Aye, that it has, son. Ye're looking fit."

It was as if they were strangers and suddenly he was remorseful for never taking the opportunity to really get to know her. He took her hands in his, kissing each one then stroking them against his cheek. "Do ye forgive me?"

"Aye," she replied, wanting desperately to beg the same from him but she was too proud. Instead she brushed the hair from his shoulder. "Ye need a cut."

"So I've been told," he replied with a chuckle.

"A shave as well," she reprimanded before taking a seat.

It was funny, he thought to himself, that no matter how old a man got to be or what he lived through, that his mother could always manage to put him in his place. He smiled at her again before he noticed Lara approaching.

She was a vision in a lein of yellow with her red hair wound into braids and pinned up with jeweled combs. Her slender form stood quite erect as she made her way toward him being escorted by Turlog on her left and Brian on her right. She was smiling but he knew she wasn't happy. It was wrong of him to deny her a proper wedding in front of her clan because of his own weakness. But in the end he knew if he waited that long he would have returned to Freyja.

The pang of guilt that tore through his gut with the thought of Freyja was one he experienced nearly a dozen times a day. Even his sleep was riddled with nightmares as he pictured her in the arms of another.

"So then," Gable sighed down at him, breaking through his thoughts to cause him to start. "Will ye take the woman's hand, Gilla Patric?"

Patric offered Lara an impish grin before taking her hand in his. He felt her tremble beneath his grasp and he smiled as he leaned in to offer, "Don't be nervous, aye. I haven't bitten anyone yet."

Her lids fluttered as she struggled to hold back her tears. When her father first told her of the bargain she had thought it a jest. She had spent enough time with the Shaver to know that she wasn't the woman he truly wanted, but now there she was, preparing to take her vows to become his wife as a bargain between clansmen.

"Repeat after me, Lara," Gable commanded, bringing her back from her thoughts.

She looked at Patric then beyond to Margreg who was cuddling Eilis in her arms while she sat beside Finn. She envied them their ability to have a match made in love. She sighed before attending what was being requested of her.

"I take ye, Gilla Patric macLorca as my husband," she repeated dutifully. "I take ye as my master in all things on this earth and will keep honest to ye until the day of my death."

Patric swallowed hard as he prepared to give his own vows. Though she only needed to promise fidelity, he had to promise to protect her and her family in all things demanded of him. He felt the hairs on his neck rise when he looked to Turlog who was glaring at him then he remembered Njord's accusation. He doubted that anyone would ever know the truth about what happened in Torshav but at that moment he decided to keep a keen eye on the old man.

"I, Gilla Patric macLorca," he repeated after Gable, "do swear from this day forward to keep ye as my wife. To protect ye against all danger and to come without question to the aid of yer family should they request it."

He heard the sigh as it was issued from both Turlog and Brian then nodded when they both smiled at him. It was then that Gable pronounced them married and, as was the custom, he bent to kiss his new wife.

What he found when he did was surprising. Instead of receiving the gentle touch of lips he expected from the inexperienced virgin, he was met by a heat of urgency that foretold great passion. He smiled against her mouth when her arms came around his neck then nudged her hair away from her ear to whisper, "Easy there, lassie. Ye'll have me unable to leave the abbey if ye keep it up."

He broke the embrace in time to see her skin flush the same color as her hair then patted her hand as he again leaned down to whisper, "I like what ye did just now. Remember to do it again when we get to the chamber, aye."

She nodded her head as her blush deepened and he rubbed her cheek with his thumb to allay her embarrassment. It might just work out after all, he thought to himself then turned as the few witnesses lining the pews got to their feet to offer their congratulations. It was Finn's voice that halted the celebration.

"If ye don't mind Shaver, I wish to ask the abbot to stay on a bit longer."

Patric raised an eyebrow before realizing what Finn was up to. Since Kevin wasn't a holy man, he'd not kept an abbot in Cavenlow. Brian brought Father Gable from Cenn Cora to perform the ceremony and if Finn didn't act fast he'd be hard pressed to find someone to perform his rites.

"And what is it ye ask of him, Finn?" Patric crooned though he already had the answer.

"With yer permission, Ri Tuath, I wish to take the fair Margreg ingenFiland to wife."

Margreg held her breath as she awaited Patric's response. She knew Finn planned to make the request but she didn't think he'd do it at that moment. She prayed her cousin wouldn't be cross with him for intruding on his own wedding day.

Lara sighed at the prospect of the two lovers having their chance at happiness then clapped her hands together before blurting, "That's grand."

She noticed the anxious look on Margreg's face caused by the Shaver's silence then tugged on his arm to urge, "Isn't that grand, husband? We shall be married together and we can celebrate as one at Easter."

Husband.

Patric's chest swelled with the respect offered by his new wife and the couple whose fate lay within his grasp. He let a slow smile spread across his face then responded, "Aye, 'tis grand and I pray the Ri Ciocid agrees so that he can have the good father Gable stay on to perform the service."

"Well, of course I agree," Brian thrilled, nodding his head at Gable to have him perform the rites that would bring another bold warrior into his clan.

In order to marry a Dal Cais woman, Finn would have to swear an oath to the clan. It would be the same with Njord and Havland if he could manage to have them in the same position.

"I should say 'twould be good to have ye as our own, Finn," he crooned, stepping up to the altar before beckoning the man with the crook of his finger. "Give a knee then."

Finn did as he was bade. He knew that Margreg's hand would come with such a price. He turned to offer her a smile and she nodded proudly as he handed his sword to Brian who held it up by the blade.

"Speak it as I do, man. I, Finn the Raven Eye do solemnly swear my loyalty to the clan Dal Cais. Never shall I take up arms against them but come to serve when I am called."

Finn repeated the words in a strong clear voice that boomed off the stone walls of the abbey. He covered Brian's hands with his own as the sword was lowered enough so that he could kiss its hilt then offered a kiss also to Brian's ring.

"Good, man," the Ri Ciocid thrilled. He stepped aside to let Gable take over. "Come, Margreg, yer man awaits ye."

She approached and he reached out to take Eilis from her but he halted when Finn's hand came to rest atop his arm. "If ye don't mind, Ri Ciocid," Finn said as his eyes fell to the ground, "I'd rather have the child with us in that I swear to protect her as well as her mother."

Brian nodded his assent, marking the action as another reason to have Finn as one of his men then he watched intently as Gable performed the ceremony.

The cheering that ensued was worthy of warriors returning home victorious and Patric stepped up to add his bit to the celebration. "I hope ye know what ye're getting with this one, Finn," he crooned, nodding his chin toward Margreg. "She's willful if nothing else."

"Och," Margreg retorted. "Look who's talking about willful. I should say that ye're more guilty of such things then me, Patric."

"Well, that suits me just fine," Finn cooed, pulling her close to him. "I need a good woman to set me straight and she's just the one to do it."

"Ye better know that she is," Patric replied, "and she's not dainty about it either. Got a mean right cross that one."

He rubbed his jaw as he thought about a particular altercation of their youth. "So, ye remember it?" she asked pride fully. "It served ye right to get knocked down after the way ye were teasing me for my lost hair."

"Lost hair?" Lara quizzed.

"Aye. I was taking a kettle from the flame and my comb came undone. Singed nearly half my head. This one here," she nodded her chin in Patric's direction, "thought it was so funny that he didn't even help me put the flame out but instead doubled over in laughter. I beat him for it."

"Patric!" Lara gasped, a look of astonishment crossing her face. "Ye should be ashamed of yerself."

"Easy there, wife," he retorted as he held up his hands in his own defense. "That was many years ago and I took my whipping—not only from my fine cousin here, but from her mother and my mother as well."

"That he did," Gertrude interjected as she came to his defense. She patted his cheek as she cooed over him. "Ye should've seen the black eye he sported after Margreg beat him. 'Twas terrible. Do ye remember it, Grace?"

"I should say I do," Grace replied, eager to take part in the conversation. Those were the happy times when all her boys were alive. She recalled them often. "I think he cried for the better part of the afternoon, hiding behind my skirts and keeping me from the pies I had promised for the feast."

"Och," Patric issued, as his skin blushed red. "Speaking of feasts, there's one in the hall. 'Twill be cold if we stand here retelling old stories."

Grace rubbed his cheek then kissed him on it as a genuine smile spread across her face. She laced her arm through Gertrude's and the two of them walked down the aisle recanting old tales.

As Patric moved to follow them Brian caught his arm. "I'm glad of what happened with Finn because we just might need to rally again."

Patric's face contorted. "Another war?"

"Perhaps," Brian replied with a chuckle. "Rumor has it that Malsakin's so worried I might strike him after our win in Leinster that he's sending his cousin around to gather Viking support."

"Is that what ye were thinking?" Patric asked. "I mean about moving against Malsakin."

"To tell ye the truth, laddie," Brian replied with a shake of his head. "I had thought to stay put in Cenn Cora for a while and rest these weary bones. But if Malsakin is looking for a war who am I to deny him?"

"Tell me what ye need of me and I'll do it," Patric replied.

Brian chuckled, "Right now I want ye to concentrate on yer honeymoon. Make yerself a little heir to claim yer throne so Cavenlow will never be in doubt again. After that ye can assist me with Malsakin."

*   *   *   *

Tara, Ireland: In the gardens—25, February 993 A.D.—Kormlada had been spending nearly every day alone in the gardens hoping to be the first one to catch Brian when he finally made his appearance in Tara. Since Malsakin's suspicions about her only heightened after the battle of Leinster, he was happy to have her away from him and his plans so there wouldn't be a chance of her thwarting him.

She looked up at the approaching rider but her hopes plummeted when she recognized Sigtrygg. "Hail, mother," he called down from his horse. "'Tis a glorious day for a ride. Won't ye join me?"

"Where are ye off to?"

"I thought I'd ride the track for a while. I want to work out her legs since I'm planning to head back to Dublin tomorrow?"

"So is yer business with the Ard Ri done?" she asked even though she already had the answer.

He dismounted then—the expression on his face telling her that he was wary of giving her information. "'Tis done. It was nothing really. I just wanted his advice on a skirmish over a bit of land."

"Really, Sigtrygg," she huffed but before she could continue the sound of horses caught their attention.

Sigtrygg's mare pulled against her bit and they both stroked her side in an effort to calm her while the band of Dal Cais riders passed them by.

Kormlada cursed beneath her breath when she recognized Brian atop his horse, carrying a white banner to show he came in peace. She looked ahead to the great hall then watched him dismount.

"Did ye know he was coming?" she asked her son as she stroked the horse in her effort to cover her nervousness.

Sigtrygg's stomach flipped with the feeling she was toying with him. Malsakin hadn't mentioned anything to him about Boru. "I couldn't say," he replied, "but somehow I don't think it's good news."

He turned to look at her, annoyed by the smile that was playing on her lips. "Ye know something, don't ye?"

She shook her head then shrugged her shoulders. "Now how could I know anything?" she sighed. "I'm nothing more than a woman. What could I possibly know of men and their wars?"

"War," Sigtrygg huffed. "Ye think he's come to call Malsakin to war?"

Again she shrugged then laced her arm through his to direct him toward the hall. He stopped in his tracks. "Ye must tell me if ye think it'll come to another war, mother. My army's unprepared for such an event."

"Why should I tell ye anything?" she thrilled, lifting her eyebrow. "Both ye and the Ard Ri have been treating me as if I'm tainted. Why should I waste my breath advising ye only to have ye disregard my wisdom?"

She looked long at him, dismissing the pleading in his eyes as she continued, "Nay, I think ye should seek yer advice from Malsakin. It's him ye're indebted to for yer crown, not me."

That statement caused him to laugh nervously. He decided that the only way to get anything out of her was to cajole her. "We both know I owe my crown to ye. If the price ye exact for it is to give me yer counsel than I should be wise to accept it." He bent to kiss her cheek then took a step back holding both her hands in his. "Now why don't ye share yer guidance?"

Kormlada looked him over. He was a handsome man and for a moment she wondered if Olaf looked the same in his youth. "Ye're much like yer father, Sigtrygg," she sighed. "It's my hope to see ye a greater man than he was."

Sigtrygg blushed with the compliment then cleared his throat as he inquired, "So, what is it ye think?"

She was buying time trying to figure out a way to get Brian alone. At length she patted Sigtrygg's cheek and smiled. "I think we should go inside to see what the Ri Ciocid has to say for himself. Why should we stand around and guess when the event is taking place within our grasp?"

They entered the hall in time to see Brian leaning over the Ard Ri's table leveling his accusation. "I've heard it from more than one source that yer trying to hire Vikings to raid in Leinster, Malsakin," he growled. "So let me warn ye right now that if it's another battle that ye want I'm ready for ye."

Malsakin's hands trembled with anger. When they were beaten in Leinster, Fladbartoc's took it into his head to pick up Kevin's plan of raiding again. He thought it would keep Brian off balance and he wouldn't have enough time to muster forces against them leaving the territory vulnerable. Now his cousin was off trying to hire Vikings while he was left to face the Ri Ciocid alone.

He cursed under his breath that the round fort was devoid of the nobles who usually made a nuisance of themselves. He was just about to offer his cousin up as the culprit when he spotted Sigtrygg and Kormlada entering the hall.

"Ah, Sigtrygg," he cooed, "Come sit with us and hear what the Ri Ciocid has to say."

"I should say it'll be unnecessary to sit with ye if we want to hear him," Kormlada responded, her voice thick with sarcasm. "We could hear him barking at ye from outside the doors."

Malsakin screwed up his face then rose from his chair. The last thing he wanted to do was to bear witness to his wife throwing herself at the Ri Ciocid's feet. He decided to deny her the opportunity. "If ye don't mind, wife, I would rather sit with Sigtrygg and Brian alone. We've matters to discuss that will only bore ye. Why don't ye go to the solarium to take up yer sewing?"

Brian struggled with the decision of whether or not he should turn toward her. He had been relieved when he heard that Malsakin had her locked away. In truth, he prayed she would never be let out. For all this time he had been succumbing to her in his dreams. He didn't trust what he would do in her presence.

He glanced at Thorien and Murchad from the corner of his eye. Judging by the expressions on their faces she must be looking particularly beautiful. At length he decided that he must look at her—if for no other reason than to prove she had no hold on him. He straightened his back before turning towards her. Immediately he wished he hadn't.

She looked like a goddess of the Viking sagas standing there in her red lein with her long golden hair draped the entire length of her incredibly tall body. The woman was ageless. He remembered the nights of passion they shared in his dreams and his skin began to warm. The pull in his stomach told him that she did have a grip on him. He ripped his eyes from her.

"So, will ye call yer men off or must we have another war?" he barked at Malsakin without really looking at him.

"Easy there, Boru," the Ard Ri retorted, buoyed by Sigtrygg's presence. "If ye don't mind, I'd like to see my wife safely away before we discuss this further."

Malsakin rose as if he was planning to escort her from the chamber but she held up her hand to stop him. "Ye needn't bother over me, Ard Ri," she droned, willing Brian to look at her again. When he resisted she continued, "I'm familiar enough with my own home to find my way without yer assistance."

She thought to pass in front of Brian before exiting the chamber but the look on Malsakin's face told her that to do so would be begging for trouble. Instead she raked her eyes over the Ri Ciocid appreciatively before gliding from the hall.

All eyes watched her leave.

As the last of her flowing lein disappeared through the alcove, Malsakin drew Brian's attention back toward him by thrilling, "Now that she's gone ye should take a seat so we can discuss this rationally?"

Brian shook off the after effects of Kormlada before turning his attention toward the Ard Ri. He wasn't about to leave Tara with anything less than that which he already possessed. In truth, he was hoping to spark another war—this one for the high crown.

He leaned over the table until he was within an inch of Malsakin's face, hoping to goad the man into his desired outcome. "There'll be no discussion, Ard Ri. Either ye leave me in peace or call me out. The choice is yers."

Sigtrygg noticed Malsakin's hand tremble. Anyone else may have thought it was from anger but he knew the Ard Ri feared Brian most among men. He cleared his throat as he offered the solution he was sure would keep them from another bloody war.

"Perhaps ye should split the territory," he blurted. Both men looked at him and he continued, "It only makes sense. Ye fight for the same cause, do ye not?" They continued to stare. "To rid Eire of Viking aggressors."

Brian swept his eyes toward Malsakin who was looking at his stepson in astonishment then he looked back toward Sigtrygg. Some would say that being the son of Olaf Curran, Sigtrygg himself was a Viking aggressor.

"I'm not quite sure that we do fight for the same cause, Sigtrygg," Brian retorted, "but I am intrigued by what ye have to say. I pray ye continue."

"Well," Sigtrygg thrilled, eager to offer his solution, "whatever it is ye fight for, one thing's for certain—ye're both powerful men. Another war between ye may very well leave Eire without either of ye. Why not split the territories? The Ard Ri can take the north and ye can take the south. Make an alliance so that there will be peace."

Brian rubbed his chin as he offered a tiny, "hmph." By the look on Malsakin's face he wasn't thrilled with the prospect of forfeiting half his control but for him it would be a good deal. His brain scrambled for a way to seal it before Malsakin had a chance to shoot it down.

"And what will Fladbartoc think about this?" he finally offered, purposely hitting on the Ard Ri's sore spot. "I doubt he'll warm to the idea of losing control of half his country."

Malsakin ripped his attention from Sigtrygg to level his gaze at Brian. "What control does Fladbartoc have? He's not Ard Ri. He controls only the territories I see fit to give him."

Brian halted the smile that threatened to spread across his lips. "So then," he cooed, "It'll be as Sigtrygg says. Ye'll take the north and I'll take the south but I must keep Leinster in the deal."

"Aye," Malsakin agreed then without a thought he took the hand Brian extended before him.

Brian released it almost immediately, leaving Malsakin's hair standing on end. He watched as the southern Ri Ciocid began to exit the chamber then called after him, "Won't ye stay and sup with us before ye depart? I think a good meal is in order to seal this deal."

Brian stopped in his tracks, spinning on his heel to face Malsakin before offering a low bow from the waist. "If ye don't mind, Ard Ri, I've several things to tend before I return to Cenn Cora. I pray ye offer me again at another time."

Malsakin nodded slowly as he watched Brian depart then he turned to Sigtrygg. "I want someone to follow him," he whispered, regret for the deal he just made creeping into his voice. "I want to know what he's up to."

"Aye," Sigtrygg responded smugly. He knew the deal was a good one. It would just take a bit of time for Malsakin to realize it. "I'll see to it myself."

As Brian passed the alcove at the far end of the hall he noticed the flash of red material hidden in the shadows. He turned his eyes without moving his head to make out the form of Kormlada standing there. She looked at him long and hard until he could almost hear her voice calling to him.

"Meet me in the tavern at Port daChainoc."

Thorien and Murchad followed him through the doors. He wondered if they had heard it too.

CHAPTER 26

▼

Port daChainoc, Ireland: 26, February 993 A.D.—It had rained during the day leaving the air more chilled than usual for late fall so there was a fire blazing in the center hearth of the tavern. The smoke stung Brian's eyes and he rubbed at them causing his already impaired vision to blur further. He bumped into a chair then offered his apologies to the man sitting in it.

"Here, father," Murchad called, finding them seats at the western wall furthest away from the hearth. The air was colder there but at least they wouldn't have to contend with the smoke.

Thorien waved to the pouring maid to catch her attention and she smiled to see such well off men gracing the establishment. "Will it be food, drink or both?" she inquired, bending low to give them time to look her over.

"Both," Thorien replied. He slid his arm onto the table just under her bosom. "Anything else?"

He winked at her. "Nay the now." Brian's request to stop at the tavern was an unusual one and he wasn't certain what the Ri Ciocid had planned. "Check with us later, aye."

She nodded knowingly then turned to leave but Brian grabbed her by the arm. "We'll need rooms, aye."

Murchad and Thorien exchanged quizzical glances but as Murchad opened his mouth to inquire Brian issued a look to silence him.

"We only have one," she replied.

"That'll do," Brian responded then directed his attention toward the door. He knew he was acting strangely but in truth he had no answers to give to his men.

He couldn't explain what they were doing there or why he had taken the room because in reality he had no reason for it.

"I'll make the arrangements for ye," the maid said before turning on her heel.

Thorien stretched his arms out wide, deciding that Brian would offer them an explanation when he was good and ready. The maid returned to set three cups down in front of them then disappeared again.

"It suits me just fine to be sleeping in a bed for the night," Thorien sighed with another stretch. "I'm too old to be sleeping rough in the cold."

"Ye may have nay choice," Brian responded then he nodded his chin at the woman who just entered. "Is it Kormlada standing there? I can't make her out from this distance."

Thorien and Murchad turned to see the woman who was covered from head to toe by a red cloak. She was tall and slender with an abundance of blonde curls peeking out from the folds of the material. "From what I can see of her, I'd have to say, aye," Murchad replied. "What do ye think she's doing here?"

Brian exchanged a glance with Thorien. "Give us some time, aye."

Thorien nodded then patted Murchad's hand. "Drink yer ale."

Brian felt his heartbeat quicken as he made his way toward her. There was an energy surrounding her—an inexplicable force that seemed to be pulling him toward her. The hair on his neck rose in warning but he ignored it until the moment she looked up and the hood slipped from her head.

"Ye came," she sighed, her eyes sparkling in the fire glow.

He felt as if he'd been gut punched and he expressed his breath slowly before replying. "As ye requested."

The wave of terror that he experienced from his own words nearly brought him to his knees. She never said the words in Tara but yet he heard them. Now she was standing there before him though he had no earthly reason to believe that she would be.

"May we speak?" she asked, sensing his discomfort. Usually she enjoyed her mystical superiority but with him everything was different. It mattered what he thought of her and she meant him to know it.

At length he nodded then directed her to a table at the other side of the room deciding that the best way to handle the situation was to lay it plain. The fact of the matter was that he didn't believe in fairies. Once he informed her of it he planned to be on his way.

They took the seats opposite one another and sat silent for a long while, neither one willing to start. In the end it was him who spoke first.

"What is it ye want with me, woman? What ye do is unnatural."

"Is it?" she asked, uncertain whether or not to be offended by the statement. "And what exactly is it that I do?"

"Ye know damn well what it is," he replied, his voice more harsh then he had intended. She was unnerving him and he was having a hard time controlling his emotions.

He lowered his voice, trying to keep it steady. "Ye speak to me without opening yer mouth. Ye know my thoughts before I know them myself and at night…" He let his words hang in the air, unwilling to say them out loud.

She thrilled with the thought that he might actually care for her but she didn't show it. Instead she kept her voice even, urging him with her eyes. "What is it that I do to ye at night?"

He reached across the table to take her hands in his and immediately he wished he hadn't. It was as if a thousand warriors were trampling his very soul. "By all that's holy, woman! Ye know damn well what ye do!"

He tried to withdraw but she pulled him toward her. "Tell me," she sighed, her words a mere whisper but for him it was as if she were shouting in his head.

Her eyes were warm and heavy, pulling from him the things he knew were better left unsaid. "Ye come to me in the night and ye make love to me."

She collapsed against the table, her head touching his hands so that he could feel the softness of her hair. She remained that way for sometime as if she had expended an abundance of her energy then all at once she looked up at him. "I am yers, Brian. All ye have to do is take me."

An unholy chill blanketed him until he felt himself shiver against her unusually warm hands. He looked at her for a long while, knowing that she spoke the truth but unwilling to risk losing himself in her. She was dangerous and every fiber of his being told him to leave right then while he still could. He ignored it.

He rose and she came with him, a mere feather in his grasp. He placed his hand in the small of her back to escort her to the room at the back of the tavern. It was as if she were gliding on air. Thorien and Murchad watched them disappear behind the curtain.

"Jesus Christ," Thorien sighed. "I don't believe he's going to do it."

Murchad felt the hairs at the back of his neck rise. His father had never been the type to believe in magic but now it seemed that he was planning to lay with the high queen just to gain his crown.

He stood up to stop him but Thorien caught him by the arm. "Don't do it, laddie."

"Don't tell me that ye believe this business about her being charmed!" Murchad barked at him. "Malsakin only just offered to give him half the country. Do ye think it wise that he risk it to gain a bit more?"

Thorien looked him in the eye. The lad was right but he knew Brian far too well to think that anything either one of them could say would stop him. "He knows what he's doing. He came this far without yer meddling, aye."

Murchad considered the words before looking to the animal hide separating him from his father. He shook his head. "If ye ask me, he's taken leave of his senses."

He returned to his seat then pushed the roasted meat and potatoes around on the plate. There was a time or two when he was guilty of bad judgment when it came to women but at least he hadn't been risking an entire kingdom.

He opened his mouth to discuss the situation further but he was brought up short when his father came barreling back into the room.

Brian's face was as pale as parchment. He headed straight for them. "We're leaving now!" he barked before making his way out the door.

There was fear in his voice and Thorien and Murchad scrambled to their feet hoping that whatever it was that put him in such a state wasn't following too closely behind.

✳   ✳   ✳   ✳

Dublin, Ireland—Fortress of Sigtrygg the Silken Beard: Noon—15, March 993 A.D.—The Viking earl of Dublin paced before the window in his study chamber wondering just how he should approach the subject. He wrung his hands as he blurted, "I saw ye in Port daChainoc."

Surprisingly, his words didn't seem to affect Kormlada. "Did ye now?" she asked while shinning a fingernail against her lein. "And what exactly did ye see?"

"I saw ye with Boru!"

"Is that a crime?"

"Don't play me mother," he huffed. "I've not told the Ard Ri of it because I wanted to hear ye out first. But if ye continue to make light of this I'll have nay a choice but to tell him now." His voice was no more than a whisper but there was no mistaking the anger in it.

She looked long at him, feeling her heart crack for his ready betrayal of her. She gave everything she had for her son and brother but they would only take her part in things when they could gain something for themselves.

"I went to Port daChainoc to offer my counsel," she responded curtly. "I needn't remind ye that 'twas yer idea to split the country between the two. I wanted to be certain that Boru understood what that meant for him. 'Twouldn't do for him to believe that he could take more than he was given unless ye wanted Malsakin coming down on yer head for making the suggestion in the first place."

He thought about that for a moment, trying to weigh her words and the way they were delivered to decipher whether or not she was lying. "Well, did he accept yer counsel?"

She thought about that night in the tavern and her skin began to warm, but just as suddenly her stomach gripped in anger. She had laid herself bare for the man then invited him to make her his. She knew he wanted her; it was in his eyes and his touch as he stroked her body with his hands, but when she professed her love for him it was as if he had been stuck with a hot poker. His eyes went wide and he withdrew as if her skin burned him. Then he looked long at her repeating over and again, "Nay." He escaped through the curtain without looking back, leaving her lying across the bed like an unwanted whore.

She drew breath, fighting back the tears that were welling in her eyes. "I'm not certain," she offered at length. Then all at once she began to sob.

He turned from the sideboard where he had been eyeing a pastry; confusion marked his face. In all his years on earth he had seen a wealth of emotions displayed by his mother but never had he witnessed her crying. He ran to her.

"What is it, mother?"

She looked up at him through red eyes, cursing herself for her weakness. "Malsakin will put me out. 'Tis only a matter of time."

Sigtrygg swallowed hard as his world began to crumble. "What do ye say, woman? What have ye done that would make the Ard Ri set ye aside?"

She wiped her eyes with her sleeve then twisted her mouth for being forced to explain it. "Let's just say that the country isn't the only thing that's been split between them."

"Mother," he gasped, his eyes wide with astonishment. "How could ye give yerself to a usurper? What were ye thinking?"

"I didn't give myself to anyone!" she snapped back at him.

If possible, Sigtrygg's eyes opened even wider. "Ye don't mean to tell me that Boru rejected ye?"

"He didn't reject me!" she lied. "He chooses to be cautious and I agree with him. But make no mistake, we will be together."

The low throb in Sigtrygg's head that began with the start of the conversation suddenly intensified. He rubbed his temples with his fingertips as he struggled to understand what was going on. How could she still be infatuated with Boru after being locked away for so many years? Surely this time Malsakin's punishment would be far greater.

His stomach gripped with anxiety. "So what do we do know?" he finally asked, hoping that her folly came with a plan.

"Ye must side with Boru," she blurted. Gilding her words would only make things more complicated. "Help him to get what he needs to take the high crown fully."

"Side with him?" he questioned, not believing his own ears. "Are ye suggesting that I stand against the Ard Ri? Ye must be mad!"

"Ye'll have nay choice, Sigtrygg. Once Malsakin sets me aside he'll come after ye. Ye must do it if ye want to keep yer crown."

Again Sigtrygg rubbed his temples. It was as if he had died and was sent directly to hell. "I can't believe that ye put us into this position," he mumbled. "I must have done something quite evil to deserve this."

"Listen to me, Sigtrygg!" she snapped. It seemed all her nerves were fraying. "The situation is a grave one. Ye must ally rightly."

He knew how grave the situation was and try as he might he could see no way out of it. His shoulders slumped. "So what am I supposed to do to assist Boru?"

"Kill Malsakin," she blurted.

Her words were enough to knock him from his feet and he stepped back to keep his balance. "I can't believe we're having this conversation. I must have drunk too much with dinner."

She growled deep in her throat as she leveled her gaze at him. "Don't shrink from the task, Sigtrygg. 'Tis the only way."

He looked at her as if she were a stranger. Her once solid counsel had become erratic since her infatuation with Boru. Now he wasn't sure what to make of her. "Tell me the truth, mother. Are yer visions failing ye?"

His question wasn't without reason. "I've seen it," she replied. Her glare was so intense that he could almost feel her touching him with eyes.

He considered her for a moment and a shiver of fear rose up his back. She looked as though she were possessed of a demon. "Very well," he finally sighed, not wanting to fly in the face of her gods. "Should we lay a plan or have ye done that already?"

She smiled then took him by the hands. "Malsakin will be in Meath next month for his Easter celebration. I want ye and Maelmora to gather a raiding party and find him there. Let him die as he watches his people go up in flames. It's a fitting end for a man who fears the Vikings above all others."

He nodded and she gripped him still tighter. "When it's done, ye'll go to Boru and negotiate with him for the northern territory in exchange for yer support of him as Ard Ri. Tell him what ye did to Malsakin to gain his favor. In the end we'll all get what we deserve."

For a moment he wondered whether he had the capacity to do such things but he quickly put the thought from his mind, fearful that she would sense it. He stepped closer to her so that her head rested under his chin then he kissed the top of it.

"Consider it done," he stated as he looked behind her to the window that opened out on Dublin Bay. It was likely that he wouldn't have many more chances to gaze upon it.

*   *   *   *

Cavenlow, Ireland: Two hours past noon—24, March 993 A.D.—The Easter feast in Cavenlow promised to be the event of the year. Patric invited every noble, both Gall and Gael, from Clonmacnoise to Desi to join him as he blessed his new wife and home. There was even talk that Harald Bald Knee would be coming from as far away as Laigan.

The day was sunny but the air was chilled and Njord took a moment to scratch his thigh where his woolen leggings were chaffing him.

"Come on, Njord," Eilis called, tugging on his cape. "Ye have to chase me."

"Here I come, lassie," he growled then bolted in her direction.

She let out a squeal when he caught her and she threw her head back in laughter. She was a beautiful child with almond shaped eyes and chubby cheeks just begging to be pinched. Her hair was dark, like her mother's, but her skin was as fair as Kevin's.

"Gotcha!" he cried before lifting her high so he could blow raspberries against her belly.

"Ye're good with the wee ones, laddie," Finn called out from his place on the rock. "Perhaps it's time ye thought about taking a wife of yer own so that ye can get busy, aye."

Njord plopped down beside him. He was breathless from his labor but Eilis quickly climbed into his lap, urging him to tickle her. When he did she laughed hysterically.

"Aye," he replied before tickling her once more. He pulled Eilis close to him, locking his arms around her then stroking the top of her hair to calm her down a bit. "If I knew that my own would be as precious as this one, I'd jump on the first woman I laid eyes on."

"Well," Finn cooed, "I've noticed quite a few comely lassies around here for the feast. After swearing yer oath tonight ye could have yer pick."

When Eilis suddenly lifted her head, her eyes were wide with concern. "Are ye looking for someone to marry, Njord?"

Njord smiled down at her. "Perhaps."

"Ye may marry me if ye like," she replied. "I'm not so big yet but I'll grow, won't I father?"

Finn tried to hide his chuckle by scratching at the beard Margreg insisted that he grow. "Aye, lassie. Ye're gonna be a tall one alright. Maybe even taller than yer ma."

"See there," she said as she turned to Njord. "When I'm tall ye can marry me just like Finn did with ma."

Njord was left speechless and Finn moved to help him out. "Njord's a bit older than ye are, Eilis. He'll be needing a wife right away, aye."

"So then ye must give us permission to marry, father," she replied quite seriously.

He raised an eyebrow then choked back the laughter brewing in his throat. Just as he was about to reply, Njord jumped in to offer, "Do ye love me then, Eilis?"

"Aye," she responded without needing time to think. "Do ye love me?"

"As much as I love myself," he replied. "But I fear that by the time ye're ready to marry ye may think me an old man and not want me any more. I'll be old and shriveled by then and ye'll still be the great beauty ye are now. 'Twould break my heart if I wait for ye only to have ye shun me."

She thought about his words before rising to her feet to face him. She smoothed back his hair as she took his face in her tiny hands. She looked into his eyes then offered, "Ye'll always be beautiful to me, Njord."

He could see that she was quite serious and his heart sang with love for her. She was a vibrant child with a sharp mind and a quick wit, but she was also quite sensitive and he struggled for a way to escape without hurting her feelings.

He looked to Finn then back at her. "Take a good look at yer father there, lassie. It's as old as him that I'll be by the time ye're ready to marry. See those tiny lines bunching up at the corners of his eyes and the way the fat hangs over his belt?" He gave Finn's stomach a poke. "I'll look the same one day. Will ye still think me beautiful then?"

"Easy there, laddie," Finn huffed in his own defense. "I may be a bit out of shape but I'm not as bad as all that."

Njord lifted his eyebrow then turned back to wink at Eilis. "Look at him and tell me if ye think he's beautiful."

She climbed over Njord's knees to stand between her father's legs then with the same scrutiny she'd given to Njord, looked him over from head to toe. She turned his head from side to side then lifted his lip to get a glimpse of his yellowing teeth. She poked his biceps and finally his stomach before returning to her place between Njord's legs.

"He aint that bad. I could live with it."

That caused Finn to howl. "Let's see ye escape that, laddie."

Njord's brow furrowed as he considered another tact. "How old are ye, Eilis?" he finally asked.

"When the summer comes, it'll be my sixth." She held up her fingers to be certain he understood.

"As old as that, are ye now? So we'll need eight more after if ye're to be a proper bride, aye—ten if ye're to have the marriage of a noble."

She nodded her head in agreement.

"Now, I've just past my sixteenth summer. What say ye to revisiting this conversation when ye achieve seven years. If at that time ye feel the same about me I'll speak to Finn about a bargain."

"Ye don't know what ye're getting yerself into, lad," Finn warned. "When this one becomes attached to an idea she rarely lets go of it."

"That's right," she chuckled then tickled Njord under his chin before running away hoping that he would chase her.

Finn watched for a time as Njord played horse to Eilis' master. She was pulling on the ends of his long hair making him go from side to side then pulling back to make him rear up. It was a great sin that they weren't closer in age because more than anything he would be proud to have the lad for his own.

"Come on now the two of ye," he called as he noticed the carriage making its way through the gates. "There's another one arriving and there's still much to do before the feast."

Njord scooped Eilis into his arms then carried her toward the door of the kitchen where Finn was entering, sidestepping the construction material from Patric's still unfinished addition to the house. He set Eilis down then released a spray of water from the spigot with a suck on its end, splashing it over his face.

"So it'll be a mask then," he mumbled behind the linen Eilis had just handed him.

"Aye," Finn replied. "'Twas Margreg's idea to have people disguised. She says it'll be more exciting since everyone was together such a short while ago. In truth, I think she did it on yer account."

"My account," Njord blurted. He wiped the water from his ears. "What difference would it make for me?"

Finn drew him close so Eilis wouldn't overhear. "She says she wants ye marrying for love instead of alliance. She says that the best way to know a woman would be if ye didn't see her face first but spoke to her for a while."

Njord's mouth twisted with his distaste for the idea. "I think I'd rather wait for Eilis to grow up," he blurted without realizing the child was listening.

"I thought we settled that already."

They looked down at Eilis who was standing in her scolding position, hands on hips and a frown on her face. Njord chuckled. "And so we did. Not to worry, lassie, ye just stick close by me and yer mother's ideas will never have a chance to flourish."

"I wouldn't be making that bet if I were ye, laddie," Finn warned then turned on his heel to search for his wife.

"Ah," he sighed when she suddenly appeared in the doorway. "What a wonderful woman I've married. I merely think of her and here she is."

He kissed her head before letting her pass to offer Njord the object she was carrying. "There ye are," she cooed, turning the mask so he could see it.

It was a wolf's head adorned with fur and a flap of tanned hide to cover Njord's face. "I thought ye might like this as yer disguise. I made one for Finn and Patric as well."

Impressed with the handiwork, Njord took it from her. "Tis quite a costume," he replied before trying it on. He bent down to show it to Eilis. "What do ye think, lassie?"

"Take it off," she howled as she cowered between her mother's legs. "Ye look the beast."

"There, there, Eilis," Margreg cooed. "It's only Njord. He's yer friend."

"He's not my friend," Eilis cried. "He's to be my husband. Father's agreed to it, haven't ye father?"

She looked over her shoulder to Finn and Margreg's eyes followed but before he could respond Eilis continued, "If he doesn't take that mask off I may very well refuse him."

Njord removed the mask then knelt before his little friend to whisper, "I'll take it off now but I'll wear it tonight, aye. It might be just the thing to keep the other lassies away."

She giggled then threw her arms around his neck, leaving Margreg lifting her eyebrow in a silent inquiry to her husband.

*   *   *   *

The walls of Cavenlow's great hall swelled with people as those who had missed the Shaver's homecoming joined the guest list of the nobles who wouldn't dare miss his wedding celebration. Patric had roasting pits dug in the yard just outside the kitchen and ones also at the entrance of the hall. Adjacent to the pits stood tables stacked with barrels of ale, wine and mead and an array of drinking vessels for those who'd forgotten to bring their own.

Since Cavenlow had few servants, Njord brought his from Torshav. They performed their duties happily; all curious to know what kind of woman the Shaver had chosen to settle with. Mila, who ran things in Torshav, bent her knee for Patric as she offered him the silver platter layered with fresh meats, vegetables and cheese.

"Hearty appetite, Ri Tuath," she cooed then set the platter down before him.

Patric was sitting in his silver chair rubbing his fingers in the lion's head carvings as he kept time with the music. The day had been fraught with emotions. Over the months Lara had proven that she could be as difficult as her father. They had argued in the morning and now she was locked up in her room refusing to enjoy her own feast. If that wasn't bad enough, Njord's arrival brought news that Freyja had gone to Man to marry Brodir. Seeing Mila reminded him of his once happy life in Torshav.

He took a deep breath of the perfumed air from the garlands in the rafters then lowered his head so she wouldn't see the glazing of his eyes.

"Many thanks, Mila."

She looked long at him, wondering what was making him so sad then covered his hand with hers to offer encouragement. "'Tis a grand feast ye laid, Shaver. Ye should be proud of what ye accomplished. It's been a long time in coming, aye."

Her voice carried the same lilt as Freyja's and when he closed his eyes to hold back the tears he could swear it was her speaking to him.

"Will ye hand me a linen, Mila," he croaked, rubbing at his eye. "I seem to have caught a speck."

She took the linen from atop the tray then moved around the table to assist him. She lifted the flap of his mask then held his eye wide open, searching for the offending object. She saw nothing so she blew into his eye hoping to force it to the surface.

"I think ye got it."

He held her by her wrists then blinked a few times to end the torture. "Aye, it's gone now. Many more thanks."

Recognizing the ruse and the reason for it, she released the flap so that it again covered his face. He had always encouraged her to speak freely when she was in his presence. The fact that she couldn't see his eyes behind the mask made it that much easier for her to do.

"Ye did right by marrying within yer clan, Shaver. I only hope ye see to it that my the earl does the same."

Patric smiled for her knowing. "And the woman, Freyja—did she do right too?"

"We do what we must to ensure our survival, Ri Tuath. There's no shame in it."

Having said her bit, she handed him the linen then stepped from the platform to see to the other duties she had left in the kitchen.

He thought about her words as he watched her go. Freyja had done what she must—as did he. In the end they would be the only ones to suffer for it.

"Come now, man. Ye're acting the fool," he said to himself then nodded in response to his own words. He turned when his cousin took the seat beside him.

"Who are ye speaking with?" she asked, looking to the empty seats lining the head table.

"Only to myself." He turned to look at her but he could barely make her out behind the blue veil covering her face. "I was just thinking that I rather like this idea ye had, Margreg. It seems that people speak more freely when they're hiding behind masks."

"I'm glad ye're pleased, Ri Tuath," she responded before freshening his cup. "I must say it seems like everyone is having a grand time."

"And by everyone ye mean all of Eire," he chuckled with a nod to the myriad of people mulling around the hall. "I fear there may not be anyone left outside these walls."

He nodded greetings to the couple passing by, one dressed as a fox and the other as a rabbit then turned back to his cousin as he thought of something else they could do.

"What say ye to removing our masks before the oath taking so we can get a gander at who we've been speaking with all night? It'll be great fun to see the expression on peoples faces when they realize that the person they've been speaking with all evening is the same person they've been feuding with for years."

"If that's what ye wish," she replied raising her eyebrow. "But I think everyone knows who *ye* are already since ye haven't moved from yer chair all evening."

"Damn!" he blurted then got to his feet, miffed that others would now have an advantage over him. "I'll make my way around a bit, aye. Maybe they won't remember."

He leapt from the platform then strolled toward the door, hoping that the people in the courtyard hadn't noticed him earlier. When he saw a man entering the hall wearing a mask similar to his, he grabbed his arm wondering if it was Finn or Njord.

"Who are ye, man?"

"It's me, Shaver," Finn replied, lifting the flap so his master could see his face.

"Good," Patric cooed before shoving him into the hall. "Sit in my chair for a while so we can confuse them, aye."

Already confused, Finn lifted an eyebrow bringing a frown from Patric. "I don't want anyone to be certain it was me sitting up there," he offered, nodding his chin toward his chair. "If ye take the seat for a while no one can be sure which one of us is me."

"As ye wish, Shaver," Finn replied even though he still didn't grasp the plan. He smiled when he saw Margreg sitting on the platform. "Hello wife," he called as he slipped in beside her. She was startled and he chuckled, "The Shaver asked me to sit here for a while though I'm not sure why."

She patted his arm before returning her attention to the crowd. "He thinks his disguise will help him gather information. I guess he wants his guests to be confused as to which one of the wolves he really is."

"Ah," Finn sighed as it all became clear to him. He had already gathered a good bit of information from those who were uncertain of his identity. He was sure that with his great gift of gab, the Shaver would be even more successful. "I should say yer idea might have a greater benefit than just fun, dear wife." He bent to kiss her.

He heard a whistle of air rush past his ear then the clank of metal as it bounced off the chair. He threw off his mask to search for whatever it was that landed beneath the table.

"What is it?" Margreg called. She pulled on his arm to reveal the dagger in his hand. "My God, Finn," she gasped.

He stared at the blade for a while before realizing that he was nearly killed. When it dawned on him he leapt over the table and into the crowd calling, "Unmask—all of ye!"

At first there was confusion as they tried to escape the Viking with a dagger in his hand. Husbands shielded their wives from harm and servants hid behind their trays.

"Everyone—unmask now!"

Those who complied received his scrutiny, but being unfamiliar with them he had no idea who he was looking at. Nonetheless he continued to cry, "Unmask! Unmask I say!"

He cried out until nearly every mask had been shed. But in the corner, at the far end of the hall near the main doors, there was one man who didn't shed his mask. Finn charged him, growling as he held the blade under his chin. "Remove yer mask I say!"

The commotion inside drew Njord away from the lass he had been wooing. He shed his own mask before rushing to the captain's side.

"What is it, Finn? What's happened?"

Recognizing the lad's voice, Finn didn't turn to face him but instead kept his eyes on the man who refused to unmask. "Find yer father, Njord and bring him to me!"

Struggling to understand the reason for the request and the anxiety the captain was now displaying, Njord looked to Finn's hand and the blade being held in the striking position then followed his eyes to the man pinned against the wall.

"Either remove yer mask or I'll spill yer blood, man!" Finn barked as he took a step closer to his victim. The man slowly lifted his hands to his face as he prepared to heed the command.

As Njord watched intently there was a sinking feeling deep in his stomach. It was as if the scene had been played out for him before. He saw the white hair escape from beneath the black hood and all at once his stomach gripped.

"Turlog!"

"Aye," Turlog replied, quite stunned by the whole situation. "What's this all about?"

Finn released the breath he'd been holding. "Forgive me, Ri Tuath but I…."

Njord reached over his shoulder to grab Turlog around the neck. He jumped on top of him, laying him flat while squeezing his throat until Turlog's face reddened from the loss of air.

"Ye bastard," he cried when he bounced Turlog's head off the mud floors. "I'll kill ye if it's the last thing I do."

"Njord!" Finn barked, trying to release the lad's grip by leveraging all his weight against him. "It wasn't him that did it, lad," he offered, misunderstanding the situation. "Leave him go so we can find the one who did it."

Njord's fingers were pressed so deeply into Turlog's throat that they appeared to be one with the man. He shook him fiercely. "I always knew ye were the one who did it. I should have killed ye when I first laid eyes on ye."

Patric pushed his way through the crowd to see what the commotion was about. Margreg was fast on his heels. Both their eyes went wide. "Jesus Christ," he blurted then immediately raced forward to assist Finn in removing Njord from the old man.

"Release him, son," he barked. "What do ye think ye're doing?"

Turlog's tongue darted out of his mouth and his eyes bulged from their sockets. His face glowed purple against his white hair as his shrinking lungs struggled against his last breath.

It was then that Havland came, pushing his way through the crowd then standing with hands on hips as he assessed the situation. He drew back long before sending his fist crashing into Njord's jaw. He caught him before he fell backward.

With one stealth move he hoisted Njord onto his shoulders to stroll casually through the parting crowd and out into the night.

Turlog coughed and sputtered as he struggled to draw breath then he rubbed his throat. It took a few moments before he could speak but when he could he croaked, "What got into him?"

Patric looked to Finn, as eager for the explanation as Turlog was. "'Twas my fault, Shaver," he offered. He held up the dagger then leaned in to whisper, "Someone tried to kill ye."

Patric raised a quizzical eyebrow and Finn continued, "When I took yer chair someone flung this at me. I was trying to uncover who did it. When Turlog refused to unmask I thought that he might have done the deed. As soon as he removed his mask I knew my mistake but I guess the lad misunderstood what was happening. I'm sure he was only trying to protect ye, Shaver."

The weight of the words came crashing down on Patric's shoulders with force enough to buckle his knees. The attempts on his life had ceased for a time but lately they had started up again. He looked around the crowded room as he tried to spot an enemy among the many faces. While there were one or two present who didn't particularly like him, there was no one there whose hatred ran so deep as to perpetrate murder.

"So there's no way to know who did it then?" he finally sighed as he realized that the would-be assassin had most likely escaped.

"I beg yer forgiveness, Ri Tuath," Finn requested as he bent his knee.

Patric laid a hand on Finn's shoulder as a sign of his forgiveness before extending his hand to Turlog to help the old man up. "Come, Turlog," he offered. "Lay ye down in my own chamber so ye may recover from yer ordeal. I'll find my mother so that she can tend ye. I'll deal with my son later."

Turlog nodded but didn't dare speak.

With the feast ruined, the crowd surged from the hall, whispering and mumbling their theories on why Njord attacked the old man and why the captain demanded their unmasking. Throdier followed them, taking the opportunity to slip through the gate just before the order was given to seal the fort.

✳   ✳   ✳   ✳

Meath, Ireland: 24, March 993 A.D.—Sigtrygg and Maelmora crouched in the trees wondering where the crowds were. When the Ard Ri celebrated a holy day there were usually throngs of people gathered around to show their support for the high king yet the only people celebrating in Meath were villagers.

They came together in song as the abbot led them from the hall and into the church; each carrying candles to mark the rising of their savior. Maelmora eyes followed them. "I don't see him, do ye?"

Sigtrygg shook his head then realizing his uncle couldn't see him in the darkness responded, "Nay."

"Perhaps he spends Easter in Tara." The comment was issued by Sigtrygg's captain, Ivan, who was awaiting the order to strike.

Sigtrygg looked to Maelmora. "'Twould make sense," Maelmora replied. "He's obviously not here."

"So what do we do?"

"I say we strike now," Ivan replied. It was chilly in the night air and his men were becoming restless.

"But they just went into the abbey," Sigtrygg responded. "Wouldn't that be sacrilege?"

"Since when did ye become a Christian?" Maelmora snapped back.

"I'm just saying—we've had enough bad luck to last us a season, should we risk bringing down the ire of their god on such a holy day?"

"I say we storm them," Ivan persisted, "and now's the best time to do it. We'll lock them in the abbey so no one gets hurt then we'll make off with the riches and be done with it."

Sigtrygg looked to Maelmora to get his opinion, again forgetting the darkness. "What say ye, uncle?"

"I say 'twould be a shame to have come all this way to leave empty handed. Let's just move and be done with it."

At length, Sigtrygg agreed, but somewhere in the back of his head he could hear his mother scolding him.

*   *   *   *

Cavenlow, Ireland—The hut of Finn the Raven Eye: Two hours past dawn—25, March 993 A.D.—Njord awakened to Eilis' face looming over him. Her cheeks were glittering with wetness from her tears. He reached out to wipe them away then opened his mouth to ask why she was crying but the pain that shot through his jaw was excruciating. He rubbed at it then tried again, this time speaking through clenched teeth, "Why are ye crying, *m'millish*?"

Usually she smiled when he used her pet name—*my sweet.* Obviously she was too distressed to let it lift her spirits.

"I thought ye were dead," she cried before burying her head in his shoulder, wiping her running nose against his lein as she did.

"Now why would ye think me dead?" he murmured. He lifted her chin so he could look at her.

He stroked the hair back from her face and she sighed, "Because of the way Havland was carrying ye. Ye looked like a dead deer hanging over his shoulder with yer arms and legs dangling."

He rubbed his jaw again as he tried to remember what had happened last night then all at once he sat up. "Where's Havland?" he blurted, bringing another sharp pain from his jaw. "Go and fetch him for me, aye."

She stood on tiptoe to kiss the purple bruise at his jaw before scampering through the curtain that separated her own space from the rest of the hut. When she returned she had Patric, Havland and Finn in tow.

"So ye finally wake, laddie," Patric cooed as he sauntered toward him. "Ye must have had a grand bit of the spirits in ye to have a tap on the chin put ye out like that."

"I beg yer pardon," Havland issued before squaring his shoulders. "A shot like that could've put down a wild boar."

"Hmph," Patric retorted then moved closer to his son. "We'll test ye on that the next time we go hunting, aye, but for now I'd like to hear what the earl has to say for himself."

Njord heard the grinding of bone in his ear when he opened his mouth telling him that his jaw had been broken. He closed it again then waited for the pain to pass before offering through clenched teeth, "Garvin wasn't the one who killed my parents—'twas Turlog."

"Are ye certain, laddie?" Havland blurted as he rushed him.

"Aye, I'm certain." He looked to his father awaiting his reaction.

Patric stood looking at him as the thoughts ran through his brain. To level such a charge against Brian's uncle would bring more trouble then they needed right now and with Kevin, Connor and Garvin all dead, there was no way to prove it.

He knelt down beside the pallet Njord was laying on, taking the lad's hand in his as he asked, "How can ye be sure, son? 'Twas a long time ago and ye were only a lad. I thought we agreed that it was either Garvin or Kevin who did the deed."

"I know…" Njord began then stopped as the pain shot through his jaw. He held his teeth tight then tried again, "I know because I saw him with my own eyes. He was wearing the same mask last night that he wore when he came to Torshav. It's him I tell ye. We must put an end to him for it."

Finn moved forward to get a glimpse of the Shaver's face. He understood the difficulty of the situation and would stand by him no matter what his decision.

"Listen to me, son," Patric sighed as he stroked the stress from the lad's forehead. "I swore an oath to Turlog when I married his daughter. Ye can't be asking me to break it because ye *think* ye remember him to be the one who killed yer family. Ye've been in the man's company at least a dozen times before last night. Why have ye decided to raise these accusations again now? How can ye be so certain?"

"I just told ye that I recognized the mask!" Njord shouted, ignoring the pain. "Ye've always known my feelings when it came to the man. Now I have my proof!"

"Easy there, laddie," Finn broke in. He pushed Njord back into the mattress. "Yer father has a point and I think ye should listen. Ye can't be asking him to march on the man. 'Twould bring him shame within the clan and ruin any chance he has at ascending. Ye too, aye."

"Ye may have sworn an oath, Finn," Njord growled, "But I haven't. I'm not Dal Cais yet and I'll never be so long as that rot remains alive."

"That's just foolish," Patric retorted but he was cut short as Havland's hand came down on his shoulder.

"Why don't ye leave him to me, Shaver? Let me try to reason with him, aye."

Patric looked up at the man then back at his son whose eyes were glowing with anger. If he remained it would only serve to continue the argument and he could see Njord was in pain. He nodded his head as he got to his feet then followed Finn through the curtain.

"Ye too, lassie," Havland cooed, leveling his gaze at Eilis. "He needs his rest, aye. Come back later with some broth."

The look of longing in her eyes didn't escape Njord and he did his best to offer her a smile before she disappeared through the curtain.

When she was gone Havland turned to him. "So ye're certain it was Turlog then?"

Njord nodded his head then leaned back against the pillow with his arm shading his eyes against the sun.

"Alright," Havland continued, understanding that Njord's honor was at stake, "We'll have to deal with it but not now, aye. The Shaver has a point. He can't very well march on his wife's father. But there's nothing stopping ye from doing it. We'll figure it out when we get back to Torshav. For now ye must leave the old rot alone, aye."

Again Njord nodded his head as he saw sense in the plan. He had waited this long to avenge his parents death. He was sure that with Havland's help he would finally have the opportunity.

He rubbed his jaw again then winced from the pain. Havland looked down at him to offer, "I'm sorry about that, aye. If I had waited a little longer to intercede we wouldn't be needing to have this conversation."

*   *   *   *

Dublin, Ireland—Private Chamber of King Sigtrygg the Silken Beard: Four hours past noon—10, May 993 A.D.—Kormlada reclined in her chair, stretching her legs out before her as she looked around the room. As in many of the chambers in Dublin Castle, the walls of Sigtrygg's private study were covered with tapestries giving it a deep, rich glow when the torches were lit. She sighed as she stretched her arms behind her head then leaned back against them.

"I can't believe ye failed in such a simple task." Her voice was calm—almost soothing but Sigtrygg knew the storm was brewing inside her.

"One thing," she stated, her voice elevating. "One thing I send ye to accomplish and ye can't even manage it between ye."

She threw her arms up then bolted to her feet, pacing around the room until she came to her son's writing table. She lifted the glass jars atop it one by one until she found the one she considered least valuable. She tossed it in her hand then spun on her heel before sending it sailing through the air. It smashed against the wall.

"Easy there, woman," Sigtrygg scolded after ducking the missile.

With that she rounded on him, eyes glowing with anger. "Easy? Aye 'twas easy yet ye failed. I did everything except wrap Malsakin up and carry him to ye, yet ye couldn't manage to raid a Gael."

She lifted her lip in a sneer of condescension as she growled, "And ye call yer-self Olaf's son."

Maelmora pushed himself from his chair with a sigh. The last thing he wanted to do was to further peak his sister's ire but he wouldn't stand by while she placed the failure on them.

"Ah," he sighed as he closed in on her, "but we did manage to raid the village. It's just the Ard Ri we didn't get." He lifted his finger to tweak her nose as he continued, "'Twas yer information that was bad, woman, so don't be trying to lay this off on us."

Buoyed by his uncle's courage, Sigtrygg moved to encircle her. "The Ard Ri wasn't there, mother. It's as simple as that."

She looked to her brother with questioning eyes then to her son. She knew what they were getting at—she gave them the rope. "Ye can't be blaming me for the man changing his plans," she blurted as the look of betrayal played on both their faces. "Ye can't be thinking I had anything to do with it."

Sigtrygg smiled wryly as he saw an opportunity to make his mother squirm. "Well now," he sighed as he stroked his silky beard, "Maybe ye did have something to do with it after all."

Malemora quickly spotted the game and decided to play along. Though he had less to lose than Sigtrygg did, it was her fault that he still didn't have a throne to sit upon. "Aye," he cooed. "Perhaps this whole thing was a ruse to be rid of us so ye could have the territory for yer own. Ye always said that a woman would do best ruling Eire. Why shouldn't we believe that this was an elaborate plan for ye to be rid of us?"

"What?" she gasped in mock astonishment—not that it was beyond her to do such things but there was nothing to gain by it since a woman hadn't sat on Ireland's throne for centuries. "Are ye thinking that I made up the whole story about the Ard Ri being in Meath just to draw ye into folly?" She looked each over carefully as she tried to assess what was in their minds.

Sigtrygg turned his back on her causing her to bark, "Look at me, man and tell me that ye believe me to be a traitor!"

When he didn't acknowledge her she turned to her brother. "Maelmora!" she snapped.

He too was silent as he stared at her so fiercely that she felt he was looking right through her.

"So be it," she finally huffed. If they wanted to play she would show them how.

She nodded her head slowly then again took up her pacing. "If ye think I was trying to take ye down then I'll go. I've nay a need to beg at yer feet for scraps during these troubling times."

She walked to the door, poising her hand on the handle as she offered the bit of information she was sure would bring them back to her. "If ye don't want my counsel, I'll travel to Man and offer it to Brodir. I hear tell he's taken the isle for his own." She smoothed her lein as she prepared to make her exit then threw back her shoulders. "He always did have eyes for me. Perhaps 'twould be best for me to ally with those who have the courage to follow good advice when it's given even if it does come from the mouth of a woman."

The mention of Brodir was worthy of Maelmora's complete attention and he looked to Sigtrygg, raising an eyebrow in a silent message that things had gone too far.

Brodir was a great sorcerer. If Kormlada allied with him there was no telling what powers she could gain. He, for one, wasn't about to be on the losing end of such a situation.

"Kormlada, wait," he called out desperately even though he had intended to keep his voice calm. He walked toward her, reaching out to take her hands in his. He bowed from the waist. "Ye're thought of well here, woman. Yer counsel has always been good. 'Twas not yer fault that Malsakin wasn't in Meath."

She shook her head in disgust that he could be played so easily then leveled her gaze at Sigtrygg as she snapped, "And does my son believe so also?"

"Aye," Sigtrygg sighed as he too realized that her alliance with Brodir would be tragic for them. The sorcerer's abilities were the focus of sagas told from Norway to Orkney. He would rather suffer his mother's interference than her vengeance with the assistance of Brodir's gods. "We were only making things hard on ye. Ye know yer counsel is valuable to us."

She sucked her teeth as she prepared to offer her forgiveness. After all, her focus was on Brian. It would take far longer to gain him if she was forced to beg Brodir's assistance rather than use the two men she so thoroughly controlled.

"Alright then," she cooed. "Now we must lay a plan that will bring Boru to us."

"Ye're certain about this?" Maelmora asked, willing to risk her ire a bit longer to get at the truth. The counsel she offered in the war for Leinster and the raid on Meath had resulted in failures. Either her visions were faulty or she was withholding something from them.

"On this ye can be certain," she offered with conviction. "But if ye think I could be wrong we can just forget about it."

"Nay," he replied when he noticed the haze in her eyes. It was a sure sign she was having a vision. "I'll trust ye on this, but it'll be the last time, aye. If we fail this time, Malsakin will surely have our heads."

"We won't fail and we won't have to fret over Malsakin. If I know him well enough, and I do, he'll be seeking Boru's assistance in putting ye down for raiding Meath. Once that happens, everything will be on course."

Those words caused the hair on Maelmora's arms to rise. Suddenly it all became clear to him. She hadn't failed in Leinster or in Meath. It had all been part of her plan to have Malsakin release her while drawing Brian in.

He took a step toward her, lifting her chin with his finger as his eyes relayed his knowing. "Do ye ever tire of toying with the lives of men, sister?" he asked with malice.

She stroked the end of the long lock of hair that hung over his shoulder then smiled as she poked his stomach. "Never!"

CHAPTER 27

▼

Cenn Cora, Ireland: Noon—2, June 993 A.D.—To Brian Boru macCennitig, the rush of the River Shannon as it flowed south past Cenn Cora was one of the most heavenly sights on God's earth. He stood on the riverbank with hands on hips breathing deeply to let the scent fill his lungs. "Did ye hear me?" Malsakin asked, bursting through his thoughts. "I'd rather not have to repeat myself if it could be avoided."

Brian turned his head to glimpse the Ard Ri over his shoulder, causing his hair to fall forward against his face. He took a moment to untangle it from his earring before sauntering back to the table and the grand feast that had been laid.

The Ard Ri had come for assistance and Brian wouldn't think of having their conversation interrupted by the goings on in the hall so he laid a table in the field near the smithy's shack to be certain they wouldn't be disturbed.

He reached across Malsakin to gather a handful of tayberries from the bowl then settled himself into his chair, stretching his long legs out before him as he popped them into his mouth one by one. "Tell me again what it is ye want of me Malsakin," he sighed. "I need it to be perfectly clear."

Malsakin raised his chin so his eyes would be level with Brian's then cleared his throat to draw the Ri Ciocid's attention from the pouring maid who was serving him.

"Since I've set Kormlada aside Maelmora and Sigtrygg have taken it into their head that I too should be set aside—permanently. They raided Meath and I hear tell they're planning to raise an army to storm Tara. I want ye to lend yer assistance so that we can end their plotting. It only makes sense that we stand together in this seeing that it'll be Leinster she's after next."

"Aye," Brian agreed as he watched the pouring maid make her way around the table to freshen Malsakin's cup. "And what benefit will I derive from this?"

"Ye're not asking me for a tribute, are ye Boru?" He noticed the slight nod of Brian's head. "I thought we agreed to split the territories and be done with it? Ye've nay a right to ask me for tribute if we're planning to stand side by side."

Brian looked at him then chuckled. "Ye may be fearful of yer wife and her family but I'm not, Malsakin. Meath isn't under my jurisdiction and neither is Tara, therefore, what ye ask of me demands a tribute."

"That's absurd." He threw up his hands, inadvertently hitting into the girl's arm to send mead from the pitcher splattering across the table. Other than the hiss of breath he issued for her clumsiness, he showed no acknowledgement of the situation.

"What's fair is fair, Boru, and it's fair that ye help me in this since we share the territories. If we don't act as one 'twill weaken us."

Brian popped the last of the tayberries into his mouth then chewed them slowly to let their tart juices run down his throat while he considered Malsakin's request. Since that night in Port daChainoc, Kormlada had been ever present in his thoughts. He remembered how she looked sprawled naked across the bed. She was a heavenly vision and he had worried that if he touched her she might disappear. When he moved to do it he felt a deep pulling in his soul—almost like a voice calling out to him—drawing him near. That's when he broke from her. Flesh and blood he could deal with but fairies were a different thing altogether.

He looked at the Ard Ri sitting across from him. Suddenly he remembered the words that Kormlada had offered him in Tara. At length he got to his feet. "Ye're right, Malsakin. It's from Sigtrygg and Maelmora that I shall demand my tribute once I help ye put them down."

Malsakin raised a dark eyebrow. "That's rich. And what do ye expect to get from them?"

"Not to worry, Malsakin, I know exactly what I want. If they won't pay it I'll simply have to take it from them."

Malsakin had no idea what Brian was speaking of but if the upstart was willing to lend his army with no cost to him he had no desire to question him further. He nodded his head in agreement then stretched out his hand to seal the deal. Brian clasped it then pulled him close. "When I do take my tribute, Malsakin, I expect ye to support my claim."

Whether it was the words themselves or the manner in which they were issued that caused the hair on Malsakin's neck to rise he wasn't sure, but rise it did. He shuddered against it before trying to withdraw his hand. Brian pulled him still closer, the muscles in his forearm bulging from his effort. Malsakin's jaw locked with the challenge but there was no escape from Brian's great strength. He lifted his head then let his own eyes narrow as he exposed his distaste for the situation.

Brian returned the glare. It was as if he wanted to draw everything the Ard Ri possessed right through his skin until it rested deep inside of him. His muscles twitched as his grip tightened. "Damn ye, Boru!" Malsakin finally snapped. "Is it yer intention to leave me without a sword arm before the battle?"

Brian continued to grip Malsakin's hand until the ring the Ard Ri was wearing bit into his skin. He loosened his grip then turned his hand over to get a better glimpse of it. It was a simple band of gold inlaid with a brilliant disc shaped ruby—one Brian was certain he had seen before. "Where did ye get it?" he inquired flatly.

Malsakin broke the embrace then hid his hand in the folds of his coat. "Let's just say it was a gift from a friend."

Brian pursed his lips as he nodded his understanding. He'd given that ruby to Kevin long ago. Malsakin's owning it was proof that the two had shared a relationship giving him one more puzzle piece to add to his collection. He turned on his heel before offering, "Call me when yer ready, Malsakin. This battle becomes more intriguing by the moment."

He stopped to scoop up another handful of tayberries as he passed the table then tossed one into the air, catching it deftly in his mouth before marching up the field toward the main hall.

$$*\qquad*\qquad*\qquad*$$

Thomond, Ireland: 13, July 993 A.D.—Patric and his men rode into the village as if hounds were chasing them. Though he wasn't surprised that Turlog could be attacked on the road, he did worry about who perpetrated it. He dismounted then marched directly to the Ri Tuath's chamber with Finn following closely on his heels. "Mother," he called as he pounded on the door. "Are ye in there, woman?"

It was a servant who gave them entrance to the tiny room crammed with ornate trinkets of foreign origin. Patric glanced at them before turning his attention to the old man lying in the plain box bed. There was a badly sewn gash running from Turlog's forehead to his cheek, splitting his socket and leaving him blind in that eye. His hands were covered in defense wounds and he was missing his left pinky. The blood from where the blade pierced him just below his heart soaked the linen wrapped around his chest. He was unconscious.

"Jesus Christ," he whispered to Finn before moving toward his mother.

"Will he live?" Finn asked Grace anxiously. Like Patric he suspected who the perpetrator might be and wanted to know what they were up against.

"It looks worse than it is," Grace replied, her voice flat and even. She never did run toward the emotional. "His healer thinks he's strong enough to pull through if the wounds don't fester."

Patric ripped his attention from Turlog then took his mother's hand in his. He looked down at the bandage covering it and felt his anger ignite. "What's this?"

"I'll be alright," she sighed but her eyes displayed her fear.

Finn noticed Patric's jaw tighten and he stepped forward to draw Grace's attention. "Can ye tell us about it?"

She shuddered beneath his touch then nodded. Her eyes glazed and she settled them on Turlog. "We were headed to Cavenlow, aye. Our guards were light— only four of them, but *he...*" she nodded toward Turlog, "didn't think we needed more than that. There's been little trouble in the area of late. At any rate, we were on the Limerick Road when two men rode out from the forest. Their faces were covered in black masks. They rode along side us for quite a distance before they jumped the guard. They fought viciously until all four were downed then they moved to the carriage to drag Turlog out. I chased after them, trying to draw their attention so Turlog would have time to go for his weapon but one cut me and pushed me to the ground."

A shudder ran up Patric's spine as anger gripped him. She could have been dead for their antics. He wondered how frightened she must have been.

She looked at him then cocked her chin toward Turlog. "It only took them a moment to cause the damage ye see there. If the messenger hadn't happened on us when he did, I'm certain they would have killed us both. They fled through the woods and that was the last we saw of them."

He clasped his hands together in an effort to keep them from shaking. "Ye're a wise woman, mother. Tell me what they were after."

"They were assassins," she replied without needing time to think about it. "They took nothing from us."

He was so angry that he wanted to tear the room apart. How could his son be so foolish as to perpetrate such a deed—and with his mother present no less? He whirled around to pound his hand against the wall but before he could his attention was drawn to one of the cups lining the shelf. He moved toward it then lifted it, turning it in the dim light so he could see the mark on it. His stomach dropped. It was a stallion—the mark of Gamal the Black.

The twisted plot that was his life had just become a bit more complicated. He placed the cup back on the shelf then turned to his mother. "Will ye be alright if I leave ye?"

She had hoped he would stay out the week with her but it was clear he had other plans. She nodded her head even though her eyes revealed her fear. "Aye."

"I can leave Finn behind for ye?" he offered, seeing the disappointment in her eyes and hoping that would be a suitable solution. If he were to deal with his son, it would best be done immediately.

She recognized the struggle within him. "What is it that ye plan to do, Patric?"

"I mean to find the men who did this. I'll leave Finn behind so that ye won't worry."

"Nay," she replied. Riding alone in search of assassins was a dangerous proposition. She preferred that he rode with Finn so she would be sure of his safety. "Turlog's guards are capable enough. Take yer man with ye and let me know what ye find out."

She swallowed hard before she offered her next statement. "Tell my brother of this, aye. Let him send his men to protect us and help ye. 'Tis his duty."

Patric hadn't even considered Brian in his plans. Sooner or later the Ri Ciocid would find out about the attack on his uncle and an official investigation would ensue. It would be best for *him* to deliver the information so he would have time to protect Njord.

"Aye," he mumbled then bent to kiss her.

Before they departed they stopped at the barracks to offer the message that would be delivered to Brian.

Turlog of Thomond was attacked by marauders on the Limerick Road. Send guards to Thomond to protect yer sister and a healer for yer uncle. My men will investigate. I'll send word of any news. Patric of Cavenlow.

An attempt on the life of a wealthy Ri Tuath wasn't unusual, in fact it was quite common. Most likely the culprit would never be discovered. With any luck, Patric could buy enough time to cover Njord's tracks.

They were riding north on the Limerick Road when Finn finally broke the silence.

"What will ye do with him, Shaver?" He half wished that Njord were still a lad who could be thrown over his knee and beaten.

Patric didn't need to inquire as to who the *him* was. The captain cared as much for Njord as he did—perhaps even more in that they were blood kin and Finn had known Njord all his life. "I've a thought or two but first I want to hear him out."

"Surely ye don't think there's a chance 'twasn't him?" There was hope in Finn's voice.

"'Twas him, but I still want to hear what he has to say about it."

Patric thought about the cup carrying Gamal's mark. What was Turlog doing with it? Did Brian know about it? The questions whirled in his head for the entire length of the trip, which was taken in near silence. They stopped to make camp late in the day then took to the road again at first light. By the time they rode through the gates of Torshav it was coming on noon and Patric was besieged by a whole different set of emotions.

It was the first time he'd been in the village since he left Freyja a year earlier. He hadn't expected it to affect him so adversely. A queer feeling came over him when he looked around the place. It was just as he left it except for a fresh coat of paint on the great hall and the barracks but somehow everything seemed alien to him. He shook his head hard, hoping to rid himself of the uneasy feeling plaguing him.

They rode up to the massive entrance of the hall where young Falkien was entering with a mead barrel on his shoulder. "Shaver," he called, waving his free hand to draw Patric's attention. "'Tis good to see ye."

Patric forced a smile before he dismounted. He mussed the lad's hair playfully. "Ye've grown a bit, laddie."

"Aye. Njord says that when I'm done growing I'll stand nearly as tall as ye."

"Well that's grand."

Patric turned his attention from Falkien to sweep his eyes across the field where the guards were running through their exercises. It would be usual for Njord and Havland to be among them. "Is the earl out there?" he asked without looking at lad.

"Nay, Shaver. They're inside with Yon."

Patric turned on his heel to head through the doors. "Are ye coming in?"

Finn smiled then let the lad go ahead of him. As Falkien predicted, Njord, Havland and Yon were sitting at the head table surveying the map that rested before them. Njord stood.

"Father." His voice was even but his eyes betrayed his surprise.

Havland's head turned toward the door and in a moment he was sailing over the table to intercept what he was certain would be a confrontation between the two. There was no doubt in his mind that Patric was spitting mad, he could see it in his face and the stiff way that his body moved as he made his way up the aisle.

"Ease up there, Shaver. 'Twas my idea, not his."

Havland tried to hold Patric back by placing both hands against his chest. Patric pushed against him. "I'll deal with ye later, Havland. For now I'd like to have a word with my son."

Njord stood stone still as Patric moved toward him. He had nothing to apologize for. He wouldn't be made wrong in this. "Leave off him, Havland," he called out. "My father has every right to say his bit. When he's done perhaps he'll allow me mine."

Finn looked at Havland, nodding his agreement. Havland was ever the conciliator, trying to keep peace between father and son where there obviously was none. Njord and Patric were bound to have it out. It might as well be now.

Havland removed his hands from Patric's chest then stepped aside to let the Ri Tuath pass. "My own mother was in that carriage!" Patric barked at Njord, spittle spewing from his lips. "How could ye do such a thing?"

"I didn't realize that she was," Njord replied, his face awash with guilt. "Havland tried to keep her from it. We meant her nay harm."

While it may have been true, the explanation wasn't good enough and Patric continued to move forward until he was leaning against the table, his hands gripping the edge as he stared up at his son who was towering over him from his place on the platform. "My own mother, Njord! Do ye realize what that means? That means I've as much a right to accost ye as ye have to accost Turlog."

Falkien moved to deposit the mead barrel on the table. His eyes were wide with fear that the men would strike at each other. Yon shoved the lad aside just in case they did.

"So ye believe me now?" Njord responded, honing in on the fact that his father agreed he had a right to revenge.

"Aye." Patric lowered his voice but his eyes still burned with fury. He must make Njord understand his position in this. It wouldn't be easy. "I believe Turlog was the one who killed yer family but there's nothing ye can do about it now unless ye want to stand against me!"

The words caused Njord to sit with a thud. He looked away, trying to make sense out of the statement. "Ye would defend him against me?"

"I wouldn't have a choice!"

Havland understood Patric's position but by the gleam in Njord's eye it was obvious the lad didn't. The young earl looked as if he was about to erupt.

Havland ran forward, leaning against the table beside Patric to draw Njord's attention. "He's right, laddie. Ye've nay a cause to be angry about it. We failed and now we'll have to suffer the consequences. Ye can't expect the Shaver to be standing with us in this. 'Twouldn't be fair after all he's done for ye."

Njord heard the words but didn't let them really sink into his brain. Instead he rose to ask, "Tell me now, father, if it comes to a war between me and Turlog will ye fight on his side or mine?"

Patric looked to his son who was doing a fine job of controlling his anger. Perhaps he was beginning to understand things. "I've just given ye my answer, lad."

"Nay," Njord said, shaking his head as if he didn't believe him. "I want ye to say the words to me. Say them so I can hear them coming from yer mouth."

At first Patric wondered what purpose Njord could have for the request but when the guilt rose in him before delivering the statement he understood. "If it comes to a war between ye and Turlog I will fight on his side."

The words sounded very much like a betrayal and Patric looked to the mead barrel feeling the need to rinse the bad taste from his mouth. Njord began to tremble.

Finn noticed and moved closer. "'Tis the way of it, Njord. There are no other options here."

"Ye too?" Njord's voice was desperate. His eyes glazed.

Finn wanted to run to him—to offer him comfort in the same way he did when Njord was a lad but he held himself back. He was duty bound to the Dal Cais and it would be best for Njord to know it straight away. "Aye," he replied, unable to keep the hurt he felt from displaying itself in his eyes. "'Tis the way of the clan."

The words hung in the air and then there was silence. At length the men all looked at each other, wondering what cruel trick fate was playing on them. It was Yon who finally spoke up. "Is there no escape from this?" he asked, unwilling to accept the breaking of their bond without a fight. "Is there nay a thing else that we can do besides stand against each other for a man who isn't worth it?"

Patric looked at him for a long while then nodded. There was something else that could be done but he wasn't certain that his son would accept it—or that he himself could bare it.

He began slowly, "Njord and Havland can leave here until I can figure out what to do about this."

"Nay," Falkien bellowed. Yon quickly covered his mouth.

Njord's eyes looked like tiny slits in his head as he leveled his gaze at Patric. "And where shall we go, *father?*"

The answer to the question was nearly as distasteful for Patric as his oath to Turlog was. He gave it anyway. "Ye shall go to Man."

Havland's eyes lit up with the brilliance of the plan. He was so eager for a solution that he didn't give a thought to the pain it would cause. "Aye, we'll go to Freyja in Man. Certainly she would accept us."

The thought of Brodir having the benefit of his son made Patric sick to his stomach. It must have shown on his face because Finn moved in to rub his shoulders.

"There's nay other choice, Shaver."

Patric drew a deep breath but it did little to calm him. He looked at Njord. "If ye agree to stay out a year in Man, Finn will keep Torshav for ye and I'll do my best to shield ye from suspicion. I'll call ye back when things blow over."

Again there was silence but this time all eyes were on Njord.

The earl busied himself fingering the curled corner of the map while struggling with his decision. His head was down, making it impossible to read his expression or the thoughts that were going on in his head. At length he stood. "Very well."

Njord's easy agreement caused the hair on Patric's neck to rise up in warning but he didn't dwell on it. Instead he threw back his shoulders then stretched his hand toward Njord. "Man it shall be."

Njord looked at the proffered hand as if it repulsed him. He turned on his heel then left the hall.

CHAPTER 28

▼

The Harbor—Isle of Man: Five hours past dawn—14, August 993 A.D.—
The thick fog rolling in from the ocean gave the Isle a mysterious feel. Njord's stomach gripped while he imagined what awaited him there. He swept his eyes over the mountaintops covered in shadows of dark green and brown, then to the cliffs jutting out into the water. He watched the surf crashing against the rocks with a fury and his heartbeat quickened with anticipation.

Havland must have been similarly affected because he let out a deep sigh before offering, "Look at her, laddie. Have ye ever seen anything so magnificent?"

Njord shook his head then looked to Falkien whose mouth hung open in awe. The lad had spent most of the trip in a flurry of conversation, questioning deckhands on the operations of the ship, pointing out sea creatures for them to look at, even watching with interest as Njord became sick over the side. But in all their days at sea this was the first time he'd been truly silent. "'Tis quite a sight," the earl agreed. "Much different then Eire, aye Falkien?"

The lad nodded but didn't utter a word. Havland poked him in the ribs. "So do ye think the men here are as fierce as the terrain?"

That question pulled Falkien from his daze. He puffed out his chest then screwed up his face. "They may be fierce but I'm sure they'll be nay match for ye."

Havland and Njord both chuckled at the statement. Ever since Havland revealed himself as the one sleeping in Falkien's mother's bed the lad had become smitten with him. He rubbed Falkien's head before replying, "I'd say that we three could take on any army the earl would throw at us."

"Let's hope it doesn't come to that," Njord huffed as he again worried how Freyja would react to his presence.

"Och, laddie," Havland replied then returned his attention to Falkien. "They say that the men here are very short tempered. They kill each other just for looking the wrong way. That's why the lassies outnumber them."

Deciding that the conversation needed some facts, Njord broke in with his own bit. "Gamal was born in Man. He used to speak of it often. He said the men here are fierce because they battle for both territory and honor. They prove themselves in the Althing, fighting battles to the death while the nobles place their wagers."

"Well now," Havland crooned remembering the fame he'd won in Limerick as the hero of similar competitions. "Sounds like my kind of place, aye. Perhaps we can pick up a little loot for ourselves while we're here."

"Aye," Njord sighed. "I only hope that Brodir welcomes us warmly so that we have that opportunity."

"And why wouldn't he?" Havland remarked as if anything to the contrary would be absurd. "Ye're kin, aren't ye? Ye've done nothing against the man except insult his wife. Seeing that the woman is yer own mother, I should think 'twill go a long way toward easing ill feelings."

The swelling boards of the ship creaked loudly as the vessel made its way into shallow water. A flurry of activity ensued as sailors slid down ropes to secure the ship to the dock while others lowered the sails and prepared the gangway.

"Come on, laddie," Havland cried, taking Falkien by the arm then directing him toward the gangway. "Don't ye want to make the first ferry?"

Falkein's eyes lit up with excitement. Njord handed him a bag then slung one over his own shoulder before pressing his way through the crowd to the gangplank and the awaiting ferry below. The old man guiding the vessel plunged his pole into the water, releasing an odor of salt and rotting fish. Njord turned his head aside to avoid it and his gaze rested on the fortress of Man glowing white against the clear blue sky. It was a brilliant palace with balconies running the length of the first and second floors and stanchions above for the guards to keep their watch. Embedded atop the stonewall surrounding the palace were spokes of iron jutting up toward the sky, making it impenetrable against any who thought to scale it.

"Brodir certainly protects himself," Falkien observed. "Must have a lot of enemies."

The other men on the raft turned to look at the lad and the old man's eyes lit up with excitement. "Are ye a Gael?"

"Nay," Njord retorted then continued on in Manx, leery of falling prey to the others who were listening. "My people were from Man. I'm of the line of Imar."

"Ah," the man sighed then nodded his head toward Havland.

"*Ta eh ayd braar?*"

Havland's face revealed his struggle as he tried to make out the strange dialect. He recognized the word *braar* as meaning brother then, following the man's gaze, put it together that he was asking if he was Njord's brother.

"Aye," he replied, quite pleased with himself for figuring it out. He didn't have Njord's ear for tongues.

"*Ta hooill ec shiu,*" the man issued flatly then turned his attention back to his pole to be sure they wouldn't run into the rocks jutting out from the shallow waters.

Havland looked to Njord to translate but the earl only laughed then called to the man, "*Er nagh s'cooin lesh yn chengey.*"

The man raised an eyebrow. "Well, I'd say he'd better get the language if he's planning on staying."

Havland's face flushed as his shortcoming was revealed to the other passengers. He recovered as best he could. "How is that ye have the Gaelic?" he asked, hopeful that others on the island would have it as well. If they didn't, his inability to communicate could very well pose an impediment to gaining any profits.

"Cause I'm a Gael," the man stated flatly. "The Vikings took me from my home in Connacht just after I passed my thirteenth winter. Been here ever since."

"Oh," Havland blurted. By the looks of him, it was obvious the man had passed thrice that time on the island. He hoped it wouldn't take him *that* long to pick up the dialect.

"Have ye any words at all?" the man asked, reading the worry on Havland's face.

"He'll do fine," Njord interjected. Though Havland's language skills might be limited he had an innate ability to make himself understood. "I'm Njord the Black, earl of Torshav and this is my captain, Havland the Bold," he offered by way of introduction. "This young lad is Falkien."

The man placed the pole under his arm to accept the hands offered. "Flori is what they call me here." Then he set the pole back into the water to guide the raft safely onto the beach. When it was docked the three travelers hoisted their bags over their shoulders then stepped onto the shingle beach waiting to see which way the others were heading. "I'll see ye all later," Flori called out by way of parting then shoved off again to gather the remaining passengers from the ship.

"That was a warm welcome," Havland sighed while he struggled up the slippery path that would lead them to the fortress.

"Aye," Njord agreed. "I only hope we get the same from Freyja and Brodir."

They entered the stronghold as part of the group then broke off to make their way to the main house. A rotund young guard with mousy brown hair listened intently as Njord explained who he was and why he had come. The lad nodded his head sympathetically. "I'll see what I can do for ye, earl," he stated before leaving his post to inform Freyja of her visitors. Instantly, another guard took his place.

"I don't know, Havland," Njord worried as he paced in front of this new guard. "I've played this over in my head a thousand times and I can't for the life of me imagine why the woman would welcome us."

"She's yer mother," Havland replied. "She'll welcome ye."

Falkien nodded his head in support of Havland's statement but Njord only shook his as he continued pacing. A short while later the gate swung open to reveal Freyja standing there.

She was dressed in a lein of deep purple with tiny gold beads adorning the hem and neckline. Her hair was covered by a gold kerchief but the heavy brown plait entwined with gold rope peeked out from under it as it hung over her shoulder. Her color was high and her eyes were wide and clear. She looked every bit the beauty men spoke about.

"By the gods, Njord," she sighed. "Is it really ye standing there?"

Unable to decipher whether the look on her face was joy or anger, Njord hung his head. "It's me, mother. Havland and Falkien as well. Will ye accept us?"

She scrutinized him with her gaze, taking in the way his stained clothes hung loosely on his body. His skin had a gray tinge to it and there were dark smudges under his eyes. "With the way ye feel about ships, ye're the last person I expected to see in Man," she said as she reached out a hand to him. "Come. Come inside all of ye so that I may care for ye proper."

The three men followed her through the gate in silence, bewildered by the calm way she received them. At length it was Njord who spoke, "Life here seems to agree with ye, mother."

"Aye it does." She pushed back a lock of hair that had escaped her kerchief then pointed them toward the main house, looking each one of them over as they passed her. "But I must admit that ye look a fright. Have ye been eating at all?"

"Well, we've established that he's not much of sailor," Havland replied before poking his head through the heavy oak doors leading to the cavernous feasting hall. He stretched his neck to see the carved rafters rising nearly thirty feet above the floor then glimpsed the many tapestries hanging against the wall. He nodded at two warriors who were engaged in a game of chess at the table closest to the doors then stepped back out into the entranceway. "Quite a place ye have here, queen."

"Och," Freyja replied, dismissing the opulence with a wave of her hand. She turned her attention back to Njord. "Ye're still a bit green. What say ye to some broth and a bath before I present ye to Brodir? We'll lay a feast for ye tonight, aye."

He opened his mouth to say that there was no need to fuss but she was already in motion. "Come," she issued as she turned on her heel to make her way up the stone staircase lining the north wall. "I'll show ye where ye shall sleep."

They silently followed her up the stairs and onto the balcony where she stopped to unhook the large hoop of keys from her belt. Possessing them marked her as Brodir's wife making her duty bound to see to the comfort of all within the fortress. "Here ye are," she stated proudly as she threw open the heavy oak door to reveal an opulent chamber replete with a box bed and a chest of drawers. "Ye may stay here, son. It's my favorite room in that the sunlight keeps it bright most of the day."

She exited that chamber to walk the short distance to the door following the next. Again she easily found the key then turned the lock to reveal a smaller room with furniture of equal quality. "Ye'll stay here, Havland," she ordered then worried her bottom lip as she thought of something. "I should warn ye that the daughter of Eric of Denmark is a guest in the room just there." She nodded toward the door between the two chambers. "Her name is Ermagh. Her father has sent her to Brodir to escape a marriage contract with a very persistent Thorstein of Norway. She's to be kept safe and unspoiled."

Havland raised an eyebrow. "And what does this have to do with me?"

Freyja gently tapped his cheek with her open hand. "Do ye forget that I know ye all too well, Havland? Ye'll just be leaving off the lass, aye. There's plenty here who'd be happy to keep ye company."

"Well, what are ye waiting for then, woman?" he blurted as his eyes went wide. "Bring them on."

"Och," she spit. "Ye're nay better than a beast, always thinking with the little head. I think Falkien should stay with ye to keep ye honest, aye." She turned Havland by the shoulders then gave him a tiny shove through the door. She cocked her head so Falkien would follow. "Go and clean yerself up because no one will be wanting ye reeking as ye are."

Njord gave a sniff to his own clothes, which had been soiled by vomit and sweat. "'Tis not a bad idea I think, Havland. Neither one of us is quite the bed of roses."

"That's never hindered me before," Havland retorted.

Freyja scowled at Havland giving Njord the opportunity to look her over. Though her hair was streaked gray her skin carried the blush of youth. Her posture was tall and erect instead of stooped as it had been in Torshav for the work she was forced to do there. There was a fine silver brooch attaching her ankle length lein marking her as a noble. She was every bit a queen and Njord cursed his own tongue for thinking he could prevent her from living such a life.

"Will ye sit with me a while, mother," he called to her as he stepped through the doorway of his own chamber. "Tell me of yer life here while I clean myself up."

Instantly she was at Njord's side, following him through the doorway to take a seat within the chamber. In all the time they'd known each other he had never purposely requested her presence. Those things were reserved for Patric. Her stomach clenched with the thought of *him* but still she asked, "How is the Shaver?"

Njord stripped the filthy lein from his body then poured water from the pitcher into the bowl before answering, "I suppose he's doing well. He has the respect of his clan, which seems to be important to him."

The sarcasm in his voice didn't escape her. "What brings ye here, son?"

Even though she couldn't see his face, he dropped his eyes to the ground. "I fear that the Shaver and I parted badly. It seems to have become a habit for me to leave my parents in grief."

"Och," she issued as she slapped the air. "If ye're speaking of us, all's forgiven. Ye were wounded and confused. I should've expected as much."

"Were ye also wounded?" he inquired without turning to look at her. He desperately hoped their misery could bind them. "By the Shaver I mean."

"In a way," she admitted then dropped her eyes. "I figured it would end up as it did, but I never expected he would send someone else to tell me of it. I always knew him to be honorable. Perhaps I misjudged him."

"Perhaps," he agreed then turned to walk the few steps necessary to stand before her. He fell to his knees with the linen still clutched in his hand. "Do ye think it's possible for a man to lose his honor when he gains power?"

She raised a quizzical eyebrow. "What is it ye speak of, son?"

He drew breath. "I'm not quite sure that the Shaver has his priorities straight. I was wondering what ye thought about…"

He stopped when she took the linen from his hand to wipe a smudge of dirt from his forehead. Though she wasn't looking at him, he could see the struggle within her. She sat silent for a time, the lines at the corners of her mouth growing deeper as her lips tightened. At length she spoke, "When it comes to the Shaver, any advice that I give ye will be tainted by my own hurt. If ye're seeking advice about the behavior of men, I suggest that ye speak with Brodir."

Even though he was struggling with his own feelings of betrayal by Patric, Njord couldn't sit by while his mother extolled Brodir's intelligence. "And what would Brodir know of my father?" he snapped.

The anger in his voice didn't escape her and for a moment she worried that he had come there to cause trouble. "Brodir knows a thing or two about what makes men go. Ye'd be wise to take his counsel. While ye are in his home I'll expect ye to treat him proper. He'll not be as forgiving with ye as Patric was."

"I'm here as his guest, mother, nay his ward," he offered with a sly smile.

"Aye," she agreed. "Ye best remember it too." She gazed at him for a moment, marveling at the resemblance between he and Brodir. "Ye know he's yer kin, aye?"

He nodded his head. "I know that much to be true, it's the rest I'm nay so sure of."

"And I suppose ye want me to fill ye in on it."

"I think 'twould be best. I'm hoping to stay for a while. Knowing a thing or two about the man might make the experience more pleasant."

She took her time considering how she should begin her description of Brodir. He was a complicated man. Misunderstood by most. At length she decided to lay it plain. "He's an assassin," she sighed then searched Njord's face to see his reaction. When he didn't show any, she continued, "After Olaf Curran took the high throne he sent for Brodir to help him keep it. There were two men who Olaf feared could take him down; one was Fladbartoc O'Neill and the other was Brian Boru. He called them to a meeting in Tara where he secretly planned to have them killed. Fladbartoc agreed to the meeting but Brian smelled the trap and declined."

He shook his head then patted her hand. "I know that Brodir was sent to kill Brian. What I don't know is how ye came to be with him."

"Oh," she replied then her cheeks blushed red. "I don't know that I feel comfortable telling ye about it."

He looked at her. "Do ye love him, Freyja?"

She thought about that for a moment. What she felt about Brodir was far more than love. "Let's just say that I belong to him, Njord."

"Well, if ye belonged to Brodir, how is it that ye came to be with the Shaver?"

"I thought Brodir was dead, Njord," she said as she hung her head. "When he showed up in Torshav I could hardly believe my eyes. I didn't know what to do."

"He came to Torshav?"

"Aye. We had only just received news that ye beat back Sigtrygg when he appeared in the night. It was as if he knew that the Shaver would cast me aside and he waited for that moment to come back to claim me."

"So he saved ye from yer grief," he said, finally understanding how she could go to him so easily.

She nodded her head and he took her hands in his deciding to be generous despite his own anger. "Do ye know why the Shaver didn't come to ye himself?" he asked.

"Probably because he was ashamed," she replied, trying to hide the hurt she still felt over it.

"Nay. He didn't come himself because he feared that if he did he would never return to fulfill his obligation." He lifted her chin with his hand. "He loves ye that much, woman."

She felt the tear as it rolled down her cheek and she quickly wiped at it. Deep in her heart she longed to hear those words but now that they were upon her a shiver ran down her spine.

"Never," she whispered as she took Njord's hands in hers. She looked around the room to be certain they were alone. "Never let Brodir hear ye say such things."

Though the room was quite warm Njord felt himself shiver.

*   *   *   *

Dublin, Ireland—Outside the Fortress of Sigtrygg the Silken Beard: Two hours to midnight—23, December 993 A.D.—The Dublin road was lined with trees keeping the Dal Cais army quite paranoid as they marched east. Patric rode on Brian's right to protect the Ri Ciocid's weaker arm, making them a dreaded duo against anyone who should choose to ambush them. He could see the glow of Sigtrygg's hall looming high above them and he wondered how long it would take to get the Dublin king to concede. There wasn't one thing about this battle that made sense to him. It wasn't so long ago when Sigtrygg offered up the idea that Malsakin should share the high kingship with Brian and now here they stood, ready to cut the man down because of some type of family discourse.

If anyone had bothered to ask him, he would have advised Brian to stand with Sigtrygg instead of Malsakin.

He spotted the Ard Ri's tent in the center of camp, colors flying and guards surrounding it, making the whole affair look quite official. He spit the bile from his throat then turned toward Brian. "I thought ye said that ye would be standing together? From the looks of it the Ard Ri has things set up so that he's in control, aye."

Brian followed Patric's gaze to the grand white tent then smiled as he turned to him. "We shall see about that."

Patric lifted a quizzical eyebrow. "So how do ye keep him from betraying ye again? I wouldn't trust that one as far as I could throw him."

Brian smiled wryly. "Fool me once shame on ye—fool me twice…" He let the words hang in the air certain that Patric knew the rest. "Ye'll soon see what I plan."

Though he was slightly miffed that the Ri Ciocid would lay a plan without him, Patric knew better than to press Brian on it. He'd get information quicker if he pretended not to care than he would by asking again. "As ye wish," he stated before urging his horse in front of Brian's to lead them into the camp. "Just let me know if it was successful or not, aye."

Brian smiled even though Patric's back was already against him. He'd worked the plan out when he called Sigtrygg to battle but he didn't want to share it with anyone lest it come undone. In the end Patric would forgive him. After all, what choice did he have?

Patric sent Eagan to find Finn's tent among the many that dotted the field then again reined his horse next to Brian's. "So will ye speak with the Ard Ri now or would ye prefer to have him visit ye in yer own tent once it's made?"

"I'll see him in his tent," Brian responded, offering a friendly smile to ease ill feelings. "Why don't ye go and arrange it, aye?"

"So long as ye think I'm up to it," Patric stated curtly then beckoned two Dal Cais soldiers to act as escort.

They rode to Malsakin's tent. Patric remained mounted as he waited for the soldiers to announce him to the O'Neill guards. He cast a scrutinizing gaze across the field in search of danger and when he found none he returned his attention to the tent flap.

"The Ard Ri will see ye, Shaver," the guard stated.

Patric dismounted. He held his posture quite erect as he entered the Ard Ri's tent. He took a moment to survey the opulence then sucked his teeth before bending his knee to Malsakin. "Brian has arrived." Patric peppered the statement with a bit of superiority to cause the Ard Ri discomfort.

Malsakin lifted an eyebrow but didn't bite. "Good," he crooned. He arrived early so Boru would be forced into place behind him. It seemed his plan was working. "Bring him to me then. I wish to have a word with him before the negotiations."

If Patric's tone was superior, Malsakin's was sheer arrogance. Patric's stomach gripped and his fists clenched. "As ye wish," he responded then spun on his heel to exit the tent, forgetting to bend his knee.

He was near seething as he mounted his horse. There was nothing to gain by giving Malsakin the upper hand and he had every intention of letting Brian know it—that is once he found him. With so many tents and people dotting the field it took quite a while before he spotted Brian standing near the northeast corner of the Dublin wall, speaking with some of Sigtrygg's guards. Thorien and Murchad were with him, standing ready in the event of trouble. Another wave of anxiety struck him when he realized he was being left out to the negotiations as well.

He rode up to them then dismounted with a flourish, releasing his short sword under the cover of his woolen cape. He marched forward with a look of foreboding on his face then squinted against the darkness to see what expression Brian held. When he noticed that the Ri Ciocid was laughing he offered snidely, "What is it? Have we won already?"

They all turned and he noticed that Thorien and Murchad were smiling as well. Brian pulled him close. "The answer is, aye. Sigtrygg's men have just offered me his surrender."

Though Patric was surprised he didn't let it show on his face. "And his conditions?"

It was Sigtrygg's soldier who offered, "The earl will surrender to Brian alone."

"That's absurd," Patric barked, mistaking his meaning. He stepped close enough for the soldier to see he was ready to fight. "Brian goes nowhere without me."

"Ye may tend yer king," the soldier retorted. "It's Malsakin that's forbidden from entering the hall."

"Oh," Patric stated with wide eyes. Suddenly it all became clear to him. The surrender had been prearranged though he wasn't sure how. He chuckled before turning to Brian then winked his eye to mark his gleaning. "Very good, Brian, but who shall tell the Ard Ri of it?"

Brian issued a "hmph" when he realized he hadn't thought that far. At length he looked to Finn who was now standing beside Patric. "I think we shall send our newest Dal Cais to break the news, aye Finn? It would be best to send a Viking since Malsakin fears ye above anyone else. When it's done ye may join us in Sigtrygg's hall."

Finn bent his knee then slipped his blade into its sheath before heading off towards Malsakin's tent. "Take the soldiers, aye," Patric called out, demonstrating he was still in control. Finn nodded and Patric remounted.

Soon he reined his horse along side Brian, Thorien and Murchad to follow the Dublin guard through the gate. They crossed the Liffey River Bridge then rode up High Street attracting the attention of the sailors and whores plying their business at the docks. "So, Brian," Patric mused, not quite ready to release his anger over being left out of the plan, "Ye're new city may be rich but 'tis also unruly. Ye'll need every waking hour to oversee things properly."

"'It won't be me overseeing it," Brian snapped back. He knew Patric was angry but he wouldn't allow him to belittle his accomplishment. "I'll leave Sigtrygg to run it if he gives me what I want."

"What ye want?" Patric questioned. "I thought the city was what ye were after."

Brian drew back on the reins then leveled his gaze at Patric. He knew the information he was about to give would be difficult to hear. He only hoped Patric would trust him on it. "It wasn't Dublin that I was after, 'twas Sigtrygg's mother. The city was a bonus."

"Kormlada?" Patric asked, his confusion slowly turning to dread as his brain slowly grasped the information. It was widely known that Kormlada was the most troublesome woman God had ever put on earth, capable of guiling a man with her beauty while totally dominating his soul. By the time he had pulled himself together enough to offer his warning, Brian and his men were already far ahead of him, dismounting in front of the massive oak doors of the hall where Sigtrygg stood awaiting them.

"King Brian Boru, welcome to Dublin," the earl cooed, bowing deeply as he did.

Brian spared Patric a glance before stepping into Sigtrygg's embrace. He knew what Kormlada was capable of but his mind was made up and he didn't need his friend trying to talk him out of it. "Will ye join us then, Shaver or will we celebrate without ye?"

He didn't await Patric's response but instead followed Sigtrygg into the crowded hall. He took a cup from the serving maid then smiled as the crowd cheered him. "Ye show me great respect Sigtrygg," he thrilled before lowering himself into the gilded chair. "I only pray ye continue yer homage in the future."

Patric, Thorien and Murchad made their way up to the platform while Sigtrygg fumbled to take the seat beside Brian. His mother had arranged the event down to the last cheering villager and it wouldn't do well if he didn't take the seat she had assigned him. "It'll be my pleasure to pay my respects to such a great man as yerself, Ri Ciocid—or is it Ard Ri now since yer agreement with Malsakin? At any rate, I'm certain our alliance will prove a beneficial one."

Brian waited for his men to take their seats at Sigtrygg's left before replying, "If ye pay me what I ask, earl, I'd say we'll get along splendidly."

"Pay ye?" Sigtrygg blurted. It had been agreed that if he surrendered to Brian alone he would be allowed to keep Dublin. There was no mention of anything more. He looked to Brian whose head had snapped around in anger then realizing that Ri Ciocid's men were close enough to do damage, he changed his tone to something more civilized. "I only mean to say that ye didn't ask for anything more than the city. And indeed I have little else to give. So I'm wondering what it is that ye seek?"

The air was thick with tension. Patric and Thorien poised their hands on their short swords awaiting the movement from Brian that would call them to battle. Fortunately it never came.

Suddenly there was a stir at the back of the room and the crowd parted to reveal Kormlada. She was dressed in the same white lien she wore in Ailech. Her golden hair shone brilliantly against it. Her color was high and her eyes sparkling as she floated through the crowd, stopping now and again to chat amiably with her guests.

Brian turned to watch her. He felt his stomach tighten and suddenly it seemed as if he had no air in his lungs. She looked up at him and their eyes locked. Every thought in his head centered on her. She headed right for him. "Tis good to see ye again, high queen," he said then stood, reaching out a hand to her. "And under such favorable circumstances."

Her hand trembled as she placed it into his but otherwise she showed no sign of how he affected her. "Aye. I only hope that this time ye will stay."

There was meaning beyond their words but those looking on were thoroughly confused. To Sigtrygg's amazement, the flush of his mother's cheeks was genuine. He had never seen her swoon in a man's company before—that action was reserved for the men—but that's what she was doing now, giggling like a lass and holding her breath so her chest would swell. He cleared his throat to gain their attention.

"Mother, king Brian was just advising me that he expected further payment than what had already been agreed upon. Do ye have a thought on that?"

The hair on Kormlada's neck began to rise. Certainly Brian wouldn't go back on his word. She looked for a tell in his eyes but all she could see were the charming deep blue orbs that called so many to his bed. "Of course ye're mistaken, Sigtrygg," she offered without turning. "King Brian is a man of his word. He wouldn't act in a duplicitous manner. Nay. Such actions are unworthy of him. More likely that would come from the man who sits outside waiting for him."

The words were meant to draw Brian out but he wouldn't give her the satisfaction. Instead he leaned close to her ear to whisper, "Ye look especially fit this evening, my queen. I pray ye didn't go to such trouble on my account."

It was a backhanded compliment at best—something she wasn't accustomed to. She tried to draw back from him but he refused to release her hand. "Getting back to the matter of the additional payment ye were requesting, Brian," she thrilled, unwilling to be goaded by him. "The terms of our agreement were one hundred head of cattle each year that ye allow Sigtrygg to remain as earl. Have ye suddenly a different notion?"

He nodded his head slightly but offered neither words nor change of expression to tell her what he might be seeking.

"Will ye speak on this, king Brian?"

The sharp edge in her voice told Brian that he'd achieved his goal. If he were to take Kormlada to wife she must understand her place in their relationship. He wouldn't fall victim to her whims as Olaf and Malsakin had. Nay, their relationship would be of a different nature and he meant her to know it. "I shall give ye my terms in the morning, Sigtrygg—only after I've had a chance to know what it is ye have to offer."

Though the statement was addressed to the earl, Brian never took his eyes from Kormlada. She bristled that he would be so forward with his expectations even though she was prepared to offer the same only moments earlier. "How intriguing," she blurted then all at once she withdrew her hand. If he thought he would bed her like some common whore then he had another think coming. "Than I shall retire and leave ye to yer business. We'll reconvene in the morning after ye've decided on yer terms."

She turned on her heel half expecting Brian to grab her back but when he didn't she continued down the platform and through the crowd. She thought she felt his eyes on her but she dared not turn to be certain. She would make him grovel and in the end be better for it.

Brian didn't turn to watch her retreat but instead looked at Sigtrygg. "I hear that ye're planning to trade in coin as they are in Rome. Is it true?"

Everyone at the table was captivated by the exchange, so much so that they jumped when Brian changed the subject. Patric was happy to see Brian let her go. Mere rumors of Kormlada made him fearful—to see her in person only made him more so. Sigtrygg, on the other hand, wasn't certain how he felt about the situation. His mother had told him that the only way Brian would be Ard Ri was if he took her to wife. By the looks of things that didn't seem to be part of the Ri Ciocid's plan. Suddenly he was overcome with worry that he had chosen wrongly. Still he smiled before offering, "Aye, Brian. 'Tis my hope to have coin become the means of trade in Dublin. Much easier than cattle to transport, aye."

"I'm quite curious about it," Brian replied, showing no outward sign of caring about anything else. "Perhaps ye can tell us how ye plan to have it happen."

"I'll do better than that," Sigtrygg offered. "Why don't ye come with me and I'll show ye how we make them?"

Brian cocked his head toward Patric inviting him along then spun on his heel to follow Sigtrygg to the underbelly of the castle where his coins were being made. They descended a narrow winding staircase with chambers opening to the left of every twelfth step. It wasn't until they were at the very bottom that Sigtrygg opened the door to enter.

The room glowed orange from the flames in the hearth where the silver was melted. The air was intensely hot and Brian could barely see his way for the amount of smoke in the room. Knowing that the Ri Ciocid had problems with his vision under favorable conditions, Patric took the lead, placing Brian's hand on his shoulder to act as his guide. Suddenly Sigtrygg stopped short. "Open the vent," he called to one of the six men who were working in the room.

The man moved to retract the leather coverings from the windows and almost immediately the smoke cleared. "Pardon, earl," he offered in a deep baritone. "We didn't expect ye this evening. The cool air was working against the metal."

Sigtrygg nodded his understanding then motioned for Brian and Patric to come closer. To the right of the hearth stood a press fashioned of both wood and iron. Sigtrygg explained that when the silver was sufficiently heated it would be poured into a mold then plunged into a trough to cool down. He released a coin from one such mold then tossed it to Brian as he thrilled, "It's for ye to keep. Perhaps ye'll come to understand the value of such a thing if ye can manage to disengage yerself from trading in beasts."

Brian turned the coin over in his hands as the light of the torches caused it to glimmer. "'Tis a good likeness," he offered, holding it next to Sigtrygg's head.

Sigtrygg nodded and Brian continued to consider the coin. It would certainly be easier to trade in such a way but he had serious doubts that his country was ready for such a thing.

They returned to the hall sometime later to find that Finn, Eagan and Margreg had joined Thorien and Murchad at the table. By the looks on their faces they were enjoying themselves quite well. "Margreg," Patric called, surprised to see his cousin in Dublin. "Fancy ye acting as a camp follower."

"I go where my husband does," she offered flatly, laying to rest any thoughts of a challenge.

"Easy there," Patric cooed, "I'm not displeased with it I'm only surprised is all. Ye never were one for battle. I would've thought the threat of bloodshed would have kept ye away."

"Well, so long as there's a chance that my husband might need me ye'll find me by his side nay matter the danger. Besides, ye could have use of me as a healer should it ever come to that."

"I guess that's settled then," Brian offered before he took his seat. He had hoped Kormlada would have rejoined them in his absence but it was clear from the lack of excitement in the room that she hadn't returned. "So where do ye suppose yer mother has gotten to, Sigtrygg?" he asked quite casually.

Though he was happy to have it asked, the question took the earl by surprise. "I believe she said she would be retiring for the evening, Brian. Did ye not hear her?"

"Och, aye," he replied, playing as if he didn't remember. "'Tis odd, don't ye think, that she would miss such a lovely feast. I've heard she was a great one for celebration."

Sigtrygg took sometime to weigh his response. Though Brian was trying to veil it, it was clear he desired the woman's presence. It would be best for everyone if it could be gained. "Aye, that it is," the earl mumbled, playing as if there had been a mix-up. "Perhaps she didn't realize that ye would be returning." He snapped his fingers as if a thought suddenly occurred to him. "I'll tell ye what we should do," he cooed. "Why not follow me to the upper level where I've opened a chamber for ye? Ye can freshen up a bit, aye, and while we're there I'll tell my mother that ye plan to stay on. I'm certain she'll agree to rejoin us if she knows that our esteemed guest will be remaining."

It was a very poor attempt at a ruse and they both knew it, but still Brian rose as he nodded his agreement. Patric rose also causing the Ri Ciocid to issue, "I think I can attend this on my own, aye." He winked his eye and suddenly the dread Patric had felt earlier returned. He wanted to issue a warning but no matter how he played the words over in his mind they all seemed insulting. In the end he nodded then returned to his seat.

"No good can come of this," Murchad mumbled as he speared a hunk of lamb with his knife.

Patric nodded then sat with a thud, watching uncomfortably as his king moved toward a destiny he was certain would be trouble for him.

Again Brian followed Sigtrygg to the narrow winding stairway but this time they ascended. They stepped into a vast square hall with giant hearths both north and south and doorways at all the four corners. It was decorated grandly with rushes strewn across the cobbled floor and heavy carved furniture standing against the walls.

"Here," Sigtrygg called, crossing to the door at the northwest corner. "This is where ye shall be staying."

Brian placed his hand atop Sigtrygg's as he reached for the latch. "The other doors?" he inquired. "Where do they lead?"

"My chambers are just there." The earl pointed to the southwest corner. "If ye'd prefer ye may take them as yer own."

Brian shook his head. "Nay, this will be fine for me. And over there?" He nodded to the northeast corner.

"Those would be my mother's rooms," Sigtrygg replied.

"And there?" Brian nodded to the southeast corner.

"Empty," Sigtrygg replied, knowing Brian had no need for the information. He already gained what he wanted with the second question.

"Thank ye, Sigtrygg. Ye may go now," Brian offered then released the latch to the door of his chamber. "I will join ye later."

"But I thought I would speak with my…"

"There's nay a need for that," Brian interrupted. "I'll handle things from here."

Sigtrygg hesitated for a moment before heading for the stair. Though he was fairly certain that Brian meant his mother no harm, he wasn't quite sure how she would react over it. After taking a moment to size up the situation he decided that he would rather suffer his mother's ire than Brian's. He headed down the stair, whistling as he went.

When he was certain Sigtrygg was gone, Brian moved to the door at the northeast corner of the hall then pressed his ear against the thick wood. He could hear the rattle of glass jars and decided that the woman was still awake. "Kormlada," he called through the door. "'Tis Brian macCennitig. Will ye open, woman?"

He waited for what he expected was the proper amount of time for a woman to respond to his call but when she didn't open the door he tried again. "Kormlada. Open up. I would have a word with ye."

Still nothing.

He pressed his ear against the door but this time there was silence.

"Kormlada!" he thundered, pounding on the door with his fists. "Open this damn door before I kick it in."

He prayed that she would obey. Having attained more than fifty years on earth he wasn't certain that he had the strength to kick the door in no matter how valuable the prize was on the other side.

Still nothing.

He tried the handle, chastising himself for not thinking about that sooner but it was locked. With no alternative he made good on his promise. He walked the long length of the hall so that he could get a running start then rammed his shoulder into the door. It barely squeaked on its hinges.

The crash caught the attention of a maid who was descending the stair. She stepped into the hall, eyes wide for what she saw. It was Brian Boru himself making a flying leap into the door leading to the high queen's chamber. His shoulder hit the door with a forceful thud for the second time. The hinge bent slightly but the door still didn't open. "My, lord," the servant gasped as she rushed forward.

He was slumped against the portal but when he noticed her coming for him he held out his hand then barked, "Stand back."

Again he marched across the hall to get a running start. The servant was calling to him but he ignored her as he slammed his body into the door a third time. This time it gave way and he went rushing through. He caught himself on the balls of his feet just before he toppled then straightened his short lein as he turned toward the bed. It was empty.

He looked up at the servant who was peering at him from around the mangled door. "Pardon, lord," she said in a timid voice. "If it's the high queen ye seek she's above in the solarium."

Brian's face twisted in confusion. He could swear he heard her moving about the room only moments earlier. A sick feeling came over him with the thought that she was possessed of the ability to transport herself through thin air but then he noticed the cat sprawled across the window ledge and he began to laugh.

"Are ye unwell, lord?" the maid asked. "Are ye in need of a healer, perhaps?"

"Nay," Brian replied, brushing the dust from his breeches before slipping past the broken door. "What I need is for ye to point me toward the solarium."

She nodded then crossed the hall to the staircase at the southeast corner. She pointed upward. "'Tis the only door."

He nodded his understanding then began to ascend but suddenly he stopped. "Is it locked?"

"Nay, lord."

"Good," he sighed then called back to her, "Have someone tend to the queen's chamber immediately." He preferred Kormlada not know the folly he had perpetrated to get to her.

He took the stairs slowly, rubbing at his aching shoulder while praying he would be up to fulfilling his intentions. He had been riding all day and after that last bit of enthusiasm he was suddenly quite fatigued. He stood before the door for a long while considering retreat but then he heard her call, "Ye may enter, Brian."

Damn the woman and her sixth sense. It was infuriating and he meant to tell her so.

He barged through the door with the words hot on his lips but when he looked at her he went mute. She was stretched out on her daybed, her long golden hair the only cover for her ivory skin. The moon was high in a sky dotted with stars casting blue light across the room in a beam that touched only her. She offered him a predatory look and suddenly he felt invigorated, as if God had given him back his youth. Even the ache in his shoulder had ceased.

She stretched her arms toward him. He shook his head then chuckled before moving forward slowly. "Damn ye, woman. Whatever will I do with ye?"

"Come to me and I shall show ye," she purred.

✳   ✳   ✳   ✳

Malsakin's face contorted with rage as he struggled to restrain the fist that was forming in his right hand. How dare his stepson surrender to Boru while shunning his presence? He was every bit his mother that one and he cursed the day he took him under his wing. "Leave me!" he growled at the serving maid who had brought him a tray.

She bowed from the waist before preparing to do what she was bade but her eyes went wide when Fladbartoc barreled into the tent. A fleeting thought of offering a warning to the man passed her mind but she let it go when she spotted the determination in his eyes.

"What happened?" Fladbartoc demanded as the tent flap fell closed behind him. "I'm told Sigtrygg has surrendered yet ye remain. Where's Boru?"

Malsakin hid his embarrassment by turning his face into the shadows. It was bad enough to be shamed by losing such a valuable city, but to have it be done before his kin was nearly too much for him to take. "The brat didn't surrender to me," he finally admitted. "It's Boru who'll have Dublin."

"Fool!" Fladbartoc spit as he stormed him. "I told ye not to pull Boru into this but ye wouldn't listen to me. If ye had waited as I advised, we could have done the deed ourselves. There are nearly three thousand men in this territory who would've come if they knew it meant taking down the Munster king, but ye had to do it on yer own. Now look where it's gotten ye."

The blood in Malsakin's veins had come to a full boil, blazing through him with a heat so intense he was certain it would singe his hair. He rounded on his cousin as the deep growl escaped his throat then he took the northern Ri Tuath Ruire by the scruff of his neck as he barked, "Lest ye forget, it's me who's Ard Ri, not ye, Fladbartoc. So unless ye'd like to have this neck stretched by a yard or two, I suggest ye refrain from speaking to me as ye just did. I know full well what I'm doing and I need nay further counsel from ye."

He looked deep into Fladbartoc's eyes but instead of fear he saw anger equal to his own burning within them. "Do I make myself clear?" he questioned.

Fladbartoc continued to stare at the Ard Ri as he let the growing contempt he held for his cousin bubble to the surface to be revealed in his eyes. Through the years it had been him the Vikings feared, not Malsakin. Even Olaf feared him, that's why he captured him. It was a cruel twist of fate that had his cousin sitting on the high throne. It could easily be undone with a flick of his blade.

"Be careful of throwing yer weight around too casually, Malsakin," he spit. "Because it's only my good nature that allows ye to continue on as ye do. If ye push me too far I can guarantee that Boru will be the least of yer troubles. Now leave off me and tell me what it is that ye plan. I've as much a right to be a part of it as ye do."

Malsakin swallowed the truth quite bitterly then released his cousin with a shove. He had his hands full enough dealing with Boru, he didn't need to buy trouble within his own clan. "We must go to Vikings as ye planned before," he finally sighed. "They hate Boru as much as we do. They're our only hope."

Fladbartoc moved to a stool then sat with a thud. "So ye think it's as easy as that, do ye? Just go to them and they'll come?" His face was twisted in anger so fierce that the hairs on Malsakin's neck began to rise. "'Tis nay a game, cousin. Ye can't just move yer men around a board at will without a thought for the consequences. When last I went to them they demanded a price, which I had to pay even after ye decided to call them off. What will they think of us now that we're seeking their assistance yet again?"

Malsakin didn't answer causing Fladbartoc to bolt to his feet. "They'll think us weak! They may well strike us instead of Boru!"

"Not Throdier," Malsakin replied. The Viking could care less about Boru but he very much wanted to see the Shaver dead. "He'll come if ye call him."

"Oh really?" Fladbartoc retorted. "Very well, let's just say that we get Throdier into this. How do ye suppose that we manage to know what Boru's up to? Kevin's dead now thanks to yer wife. Ye've no other spies in Boru's camp do ye?"

Malsakin sat silent for a moment pondering the situation. It had been Kevin's opinion that given the right incentive, Turlog of Thomond might turn on his nephew. It was worth looking into. "Give me a bit of time and I just may be able to get ye that spy," he cooed. "When I do, I mean to take Boru down once and for all."

PART THREE

CHAPTER 29

▼

SEVEN YEARS LATER

Cashel, Ireland: Two hours to midnight—30, April 1000 A.D.—The story of how Brian took Dublin became legend throughout Ireland leaving Malsakin O'Neill struggling to maintain his last shred of dignity.

With Turlog making himself scarce, Patric sent word to Njord that it was safe for him to come home but the earl replied that he was chasing a prize and wouldn't return until he had secured it. In his absence, Finn ruled in Torshav.

In Cashel, miracles were taking place.

Every muscle in Kormlada's body ached with tension. She absentmindedly rubbed her arm guessing that the throbbing came from gripping the bedpost when she was trying to push the child from her body. She carefully hoisted herself onto her elbows so she could lounge against the pillows at her back then ran her fingers through her long golden hair to clear away the sweat knots. When she was younger childbirth hardly affected her, but now it was as if she'd been run over by a wayward wagon. She had wanted to rest before allowing Brian to see her but that was hopeless. He'd been coming around every hour since the child was born loudly demanding an audience with her. She finally decided to let him in but she would be damned before she let him see her as she was.

She leaned across the bed to get the hand mirror from the side table then pinched her cheeks to bring up the color. It quickly faded and she grimaced as she realized that her appearance wasn't likely to get much better without real rest.

She bit her lips hard enough to swell them then ran her fingers through her hair one last time before returning the mirror to the bed stand.

She chuckled as she imagined what people would say if they knew the pain she was really in. It was widely rumored that her pregnancy at such an advanced age was proof that she was a fairy queen of the Tuath daDannan Clan and nearly every woman in Cashel passed through her chamber while she labored, hoping that she would cry out to prove she were a mere mortal. But Kormlada didn't cry out or even whimper. Not even when she pushed the healthy nine-pound baby boy from her body did she show any sign of distress proving absolutely that she was the immortal fairy queen returned to protect the people of Ireland.

She looked down at her still swollen womb with distaste. "Some fairy queen," she offered as she covered it with the bed linen then pulled it up higher to cover her breasts as well. Recognizing that there was little more she could do help her appearance she finally called out, "Ye may enter, husband."

The door flew open with force, banging against the mud wall as it swung on its hinges but Brian didn't rush forward. Instead he stood in the doorway staring at her as if he'd never seen her before.

She smiled as she looked at him. No matter his rank he was every bit the warrior. His red flowing hair was a perfect frame for the deep chiseled features of his face and his strong jaw line jutted out proudly beneath his close cropped beard. He was dressed in the golden lein and fur trimmed sleeveless black coat she liked so well, exposing his long muscular arms as he settled his hands on his hips. "Ye've given me a great gift, woman," he issued in a tone so flat that it was obvious he was trying to hide his feelings. "He's a bonnie lad, every bit as handsome as his mother."

"Really?" she cooed. Her smile deepened. "I rather thought he had the look of his father."

It was then that Brian went to her, slowly taking the few paces necessary to close the distance between them. He eased himself down to take a seat at the edge of the box bed, careful not to jar the mattress so she wouldn't experience discomfort. He sat silent for a long time while he looked at her then all at once he grabbed her to him, opening his mouth to crush her with his kiss. Through that kiss he offered the words his lips would never speak.

She was breathless when he broke from her. She patted her chest as she struggled to regain her composure. "Shall I take that to mean that ye're wanting another?"

For a moment he stared at her as if he didn't take her meaning then he chuckled while massaging her hip. "I've nay doubt that ye could deliver on such a promise but I'm happy enough with the lad ye gave me, aye. If in time the good Lord should think it proper to give us another, that'll be just fine."

In truth it would be a miracle.

The glimmer in his eye when he spoke invigorated her and she felt herself swoon. Of all the men she had ever known, Brian was the only one capable of stirring her lust so thoroughly. She was surprised that she could experience those feelings so soon after giving birth and it showed in the crimson glow of her skin.

"Kormlada," he huffed with a lilt of both hope and astonishment in his voice. She had been a bevy of surprises to him when it came to the act of lovemaking. "Ye can't be wanting to commit the deed now, can ye?"

The statement caused her to blush more deeply and she lowered her eyes from his gaze. She had always used sex to control her husbands but he made her want to do the deed for the sheer pleasure of it.

He felt himself stir as the beautiful woman who sat before him openly displayed her desire of him. He'd been married five times to her three, yet none of his wives made him feel the way that she did. He lowered his head toward her for another kiss and he felt her brace herself for the pain of it. She was perfectly willing to suffer so that he could find happiness.

"Nay," he whispered into her ear. "'Twouldn't be right. Rest yerself now. There'll be plenty of time for that later."

When he rose to leave the extent of his excitement was revealed to her. She quickly pulled him back. After seven years of responding to his call it didn't make sense for her to relinquish him into the hands of a servant now. It would weaken her hold on him.

She bit her lip against her pain then sighed seductively, "Ye won't escape me that easily, husband." She patted the space beside her until he took the seat then lifted his lein to take him with her mouth.

Every muscle in his body trembled as he gave himself to her. When he was done she rolled onto her side, gazing at him with heavy lids. "Ye're mine, Boru," she stated. "I'll not share ye with another."

He fell back on the bed with his arm shielding his eyes. "Aye, that I am, woman," he sighed breathlessly. "I pity anyone who'd try to have it otherwise."

She clenched her teeth into a false smile against the pain while scooting herself back against the pillows then quickly pulled the linens up around her waist to hide her postnatal bleeding. "Come to me," she cooed. "There's something I've been meaning to speak with ye about."

Still recovering from his release, Brian slowly moved to the head of the bed. He draped his heavy arm around her shoulder so she could lean her head against his chest. Again she grimaced but she struggled to hide it as she purred, "As ye know, my son, Sigtrygg is without a wife and yer daughter Sadhbah is now old enough to wed. I was thinking it might make sense to have them marry."

She felt his muscles tense with what she supposed was surprise but she continued on, pretending not to notice. "It could only further yer strength to have the other kings know that ye have Dublin in yer pocket."

He kept his head back against the bed board and his eyes closed as he stroked the lock of her golden hair resting in his hand. "Ah, but I already have Dublin. Do ye forget that's how ye captured me?"

"Nay," she cooed as she snuggled closer against him. "But if an alliance made through marriage once is good, one made through marriage twice is even better."

He opened one eye as he thought about the statement then closed it again before blurting, "That makes nay sense, woman. A bargain only needs to be struck once to be a bargain. If ye have to keep negotiating it isn't a bargain at all, aye."

"Very well," she sighed, preparing to take another tact. Among the many things she learned about Brian Boru during their marriage was that he used his words precisely. By twisting them she could usually gain what she was after. "If ye'd prefer they didn't marry then we'll dismiss the whole thought."

That caused both his eyes to open. He tugged back her head with his hand in her hair then lowered his head so he could see her face. "That's not what I said, woman," he stated firmly. "I only said that ye needn't strike a bargain twice. I said nothing about whether I preferred them to be married or nay."

"So then ye do believe they should be married?" she asked, her eyes growing wide with excitement.

His brow furrowed as he retraced the conversation so he could understand how he wound up in such an awkward position. If he contradicted himself it would demonstrate his weakness so the only answer he could give was, "Aye."

The more he thought about it the more it made sense to him. The corners of his mouth turned up slightly. "Come to think of it, 'twould be a good match at that."

"So it's settled then," she thrilled before sealing the bargain with a tender kiss. "I'll send word to Sigtrygg by messenger and ye can tell Sadhbah of it in the morning."

She stroked his cheek before sliding herself down beneath the covers then tugged on his lein to have him do the same. "Let us sleep now, Ri Ciocid for tomorrow will be a busy day."

Brian closed his eyes to take his rest. Somewhere in the back of his mind he had a feeling he'd been played though he wasn't quite sure how.

*   *   *   *

Isle of Man: In the mead hall—Three hours to midnight—10, July 1001 A.D. The mead hall of Man was a potpourri of music, food and drink as the many guests celebrated the marriage of the young nobles. It was said that the gods preordained their coming together. Fate brought each of them across separate oceans so that they could find each other in the house of earl Brodir. It was a touching story that had already sparked a saga or two but for Njord, who was being forced to listen to it for the hundredth time, it was nothing more then boring.

"Here, take a drink, man," Havland urged, pressing the cup into Njord's stiff hand. "Ye look as if there's a mast stuffed up yer arse. Relax and enjoy the celebration, aye."

Njord looked to the rotund woman who was marching up to him with a rooster beneath her arm. He took a sip from his cup then spoke to Havland from the corner of his mouth, "I'd just as soon poke my eye out then suffer another ritual." The woman stretched the rooster's neck and Njord nodded before plucking the knife from the table where he had stuck it after the last request.

"*Gura mie mooar ayd*, Njord," she said when he cut the bird's throat. Then she pulled a bowl from her apron to catch the precious blood.

"*She dty vea*," he replied.

When the bird had bled out she handed it to him then gingerly cupped the bowl with her hands before turning to leave. "Tell me again what that's supposed to mean?" Havland requested, picking up the dead bird by its feet to add it to the pile of others at the side of the platform.

"She said thank you and I said she was welcome," Njord huffed. "I should think ye had at least that much of the tongue by now, man."

"Not the words," Havland retorted, "the deed."

"Och, that," Njord crooned. He rolled his eyes. "It's a fertility rite, aye. They mix the rooster's blood with the hen feed so the chickens will lay more eggs."

Havland raised an eyebrow then scratched his head. "I still don't understand why ye have to kill the bird."

"I thought ye said ye were a Viking?" Njord grumbled. Havland remained silent but his eyes were insistent telling Njord he would continue to stare at him until he got an answer. "Because I'm the new groom, aye. I'm supposed to have some great power now that I've taken a wife."

"How long does this power last?"

"Och, man!" Njord spit. "How should I know? Why don't ye go and ask some of those women ye've been spending so much time with? Perhaps they can enlighten ye."

"Nay," Havland shrugged. "It's not so important. Besides, I'd rather work on the language than the rituals. I don't know why I keep mixing up the words."

Njord chuckled as he took a sip from his cup. "Me either. What was it ye called me during yer speech?"

"Milk," Havland responded with a chuckle of his own.

"Aye," Njord remembered then shook his head. "Man is *dooinney* not *bainney*."

"Aye, aye," Havland grumbled, dismissing him with a wave of the hand. "I have it straight now." They looked up from their cups to see Brodir heading straight for them. Havland smiled wryly. "I think this is it, laddie."

Brodir's face was stern and his body stiff. Just then Njord realized that in all the years he had been in Man, the only time he ever saw Brodir smile was after he killed a man at the Althing. "Are ye ready?" the earl inquired with a nod.

Njord looked past him to Eric of Denmark who was fast approaching. He was a bit uncomfortable that the girl's father would be accompanying him to his marriage bed but Ermagh had begged him to keep with the rituals and so he responded, "Aye, I'm ready."

It took him some time to unload the various fertility trinkets from his lap before he could get to his feet. Havland fingered the animal paws, feathers and strung beads that Njord placed on the table then leaned over to whisper in his ear, "Well at least ye didn't have to hold the hammer."

"Hush," Njord replied before turning his weak smile toward Eric. "Do ye want the man to think us a bunch of peasants?"

"*Gown my lethal*," Havland offered by way of an apology then he pushed his way ahead of the new groom so he could join the men leading Njord to his bridal chamber.

Ermagh had been taken away some time ago and since there was only a short distance between the mead hall and the bridal chamber, Njord worried about the various rituals her women might be performing on her. The one thing about Ermagh, she was definitely superstitious.

Njord remembered the first time that they met. The lass was in a dither because a black crow had flown into her room. It took Njord a quarter of an hour to get it out, but it wasn't enough for Ermagh that the bird was gone. She also needed to have every corner of the room swept with salt so that no evil would remain. From that moment on Njord had been attracted to the golden haired beauty whose round blue eyes expressed her emotions. There were hardly any words between them since Danish wasn't one of the languages that Njord was fluent in. Instead they communicated through hand gestures and eye rolls until Njord managed to teach her to speak Manx. He even picked up a few words of Danish in the bargain.

The trouble began when Njord, thinking that Ermagh was free to marry, decided to offer for her hand. Ermagh's father, Eric, was a greedy man who immediately snatched up Njord's offer. The only problem was that years earlier he had done the same with Thirsten of Norway and now the Viking wanted either a wife of his money back. Not being one to part with money, Eric suggested a competition between the two for his daughter's hand. Njord won the competition easily but when he requested that the marriage be performed immediately Ermagh's mother refused. She wanted a proper wedding for her daughter, which meant they would have to wait a full cycle of seasons between the betrothal and the ceremony. Given Eric's record of selling his daughter off to the highest bidder, Njord decided that the only way to keep the man honest was to have Ermagh returned to Brodir's house until they could be married. It seemed like an eternity passed while he awaited the delivery of his new bride. Now, as he walked to the chamber where he would consummate his marriage, he only hoped it was all worth it.

He looked to the witnesses walking along side him then fisted his sweating hands, wondering if he would be able to perform under such scrutiny. The door opened and he let out a sigh when he noticed the box bed draped with a curtain. Somewhere behind those yards of material was the wife he waited so long for.

He quickly stripped off his clothes then handed them to Havland who jiggled his eyebrows and deadpanned in Gaelic, "I'll be right out here should ye find yerself in need of assistance."

Brodir's head snapped around and suddenly he flashed Njord a smile. "Don't ye worry, laddie. The gods will be with ye tonight."

Njord smiled back at him then walked to the bed wondering what great miracle had occurred to cause that.

*   *   *   *

Desmumu, Ireland: Dawn—21, August 1001 A.D.—The territory of Desmumu was located south of Sulcoit bordered on the west by Lough Leanne and on the east by the Derrynasaggart Mountains. It was there that they would fight, in the clearing just north of the Kenmare River.

Since Brian captured Dublin there had been a rash of Viking aggressions in Munster. Not raids, but battles called by earls who had previously given the Ri Ciocid peace. The one they prepared for now was against the Viking earl, Rolo of Wexford who claimed that Brian's demand for tribute was exorbitant.

The field was dry owing to the peculiar lack of rain so when the wind whipped up it carried a fine layer of dust. Margrag covered her nose with her cloak then shielded her eyes with her hand as she scanned the field in search of her husband. He had been sent into Rolo's camp some time ago in search of information yet he still hadn't returned. She gave a last look to the rise in the distance but when there was no sign of him she turned her back against the wind to spit the dust from her mouth. She allowed herself a moment of worry before taking the ladle from the simmering kettle to wash the dust from her hands.

The first time she worried over him it had nearly gotten him killed. Finn was locked in scrimmage with a young soldier who drew a blunted sword. When Margreg saw it she called out to him in warning and Finn turned at precisely the wrong moment. Thank goodness the blade only caused a bruise. Finn blamed himself stating that a soldier should never turn to anyone's call but she knew it was her fault. She vowed never to engage in useless worry again.

From the corner of her eye she saw Patric running past the provision tent with Brian quick on his heels. She looked up to see Finn, Eagan, Thorien and Murchad riding swiftly over the rise. They came to a stop just before the tent. "What is it?" Patric queried. The expressions on their faces told him the news wasn't good. "How many did they bring?"

"It's not the number that concerns us, Shaver," Finn replied before leaping from the stallion, "but who they belong to."

"Out with it man," Brian barked, taking him by the arms. "Who is it?"

It was Eagan who stepped forward to answer, "'Tis Malsakin. The Ard Ri brought his army to lead the battle himself."

Brian staggered backward remembering Kormlada's words. The battle for the crown wouldn't be a battle at all. He rubbed the trinket in his pocket, hoping for some guidance. "So he means to put an end to me through Viking alliances. I'd say 'twas a strange proposition for a king who found his fame by ridding Tara of the barbarians."

"My God, Brian," Patric gasped as the notion settled on his brain. "Malsakin means ye to battle for his crown."

Brian offered a "hmph" then stroked his beard as he walked away several paces toward the rise. The only reason Malsakin would choose to battle now was if he knew he had the upper hand. He turned on his heel then walked back to where the assembly was gathered. "How many did ye see, Finn?" he grumbled.

"Near a thousand I'd say," the captain responded.

"Aye," Eagan agreed.

"Horsemen?" Brian asked as he furrowed his brow.

"Most," Eagan replied, "but I don't know that they'll use them with the field being so dry. Too much dust."

"Hmph," Brian offered again. Rolo wasn't given to using horsemen in battle, which is why Brian left his behind in deference to his archers. He looked to the trees flanking the clearing as a thought occurred to him. "Did ye ride through the woods or through the field?"

"Through the field," Eagan replied.

"What is it ye smell, Brian?" Patric blurted, his voice thick with anxiety.

"An ambush!" Brian spit then looked to the sky to mark the position of the sun. He was certain that Malsakin had additional warriors in the woods. If he could eliminate them before the battle he would have the advantage, but with the sun still high in the sky his soldiers would be exposed by the light shinning off their blades. He growled low in his throat as he again walked a few paces toward the rise, standing and looking as if he could see the great army that stood just beyond. When he settled on a course of action he turned on his heel to march back to them.

"We'll not march tomorrow," he blurted, nodding his head to underscore his decision. "It's too risky."

"Are ye certain, Brian?" Patric asked already knowing the answer.

"Aye, I'm certain. When I take Malsakin's crown it'll be on my terms not his. But from this moment until that, everything I do will be for that purpose alone." He turned to Murchad. "Is that good for ye, son?" It was Desmumu that Rolo was after so it was only right to get his son's consent.

"Aye, father," Murchad agreed. "I'll be able to protect the tuath until then. Ye'll not have to worry over it."

"Good, son," the Ri Ciocid sighed then again looked toward the rise before spitting on the ground. "We'll ride to them in the morning. Shaver, ye'll have the men standing ready in the event that there's trouble but I want camp broken before that, aye."

"Aye," Patric agreed easily although Brian's request was anything but. Breaking camp ahead of delivering the message would demonstrate its sincerity to their enemy but it would also mean working through the night with little sleep.

Margreg read her cousin's face then stepped up to offer, "Ye needn't worry, Shaver, I'll see that it's done."

"I'm obliged to ye, Margreg," he replied then he too turned toward the rise, cursing the Ard Ri for his actions.

News of the cancelled battle spread gloom throughout the camp. The night before a battle was usually marked by feasting, games and raucous music that would produce the adrenaline needed for the next day. The Dal Cais camp was eerily silent as warriors quietly took their meals with their respective regiments, watching the trees for any signs of aggression. They could hear the music emanating from Rolo's camp in the distance. Patric chafed with the desire to put an end to it. He was as much a warrior as any other man sitting on that field and he cursed the fact that there'd be no release for his hostility.

As others took notice they began milling about, looking to the rise with longing. One soldier called out toward the enemy camp, "Go home already, the battle's been called off." Moments later he was knocked to the ground by Adin, a thinking soldier who began pummeling his face. Soon the two soldiers were swinging viciously at one another. The other warriors encircled them cheering wildly as they urged their respective man on. Young Aidin emerged the victor but it didn't take long before a fresh warrior challenged him.

The competitions went on well into the night with the fallen soldiers being tended by camp followers eager to ply their trade. Patric was the latest loser. He brushed aside the attentions of the young blonde with a shake of his head then moved forward to join Margreg and Finn who were watching the competition from their place in front of their own fire. He wiped the blood from his brow with his sleeve as he neared them but when he noticed their romantic posture he turned to leave them in peace.

Finn scrambled to his feet then rushed forward to meet him. "Shaver," he called as he reached out an arm to him. "I've something I need to be speaking with ye about."

Patric dabbed at his wound with his sleeve while he waited for Finn to catch him up. The captain walked him to the edge of the camp so their conversation wouldn't be overheard. "I didn't want to tell ye this while the others were around but there's a thing ye should know."

"What is it, Finn?" Patric asked, lifting his brow.

Finn released a great sigh before offering, "Though I can't swear to it on my life, I'm almost certain that I saw the Ri Ciocid's uncle in Malsakin's camp."

"Turlog?" Patric asked, his eyes going wide. There was a time long ago when he would have accepted the information without question. It was abundantly clear that Turlog resented Brian for what he was able to achieve but now the man was blind in one eye and of late his health was failing. Patric could hardly believe that Turlog would risk the comforts of Thomond at this late stage of his life.

"Are ye certain, man?"

"Fairly," Finn replied. "He was sitting with Fladbartoc. His head was down when they were talking but when he looked up at me I could swear 'twas him."

"Ye must be certain, Finn? The accusation is a grave one. Perhaps one of the others saw him as well."

"I don't think so, Shaver. We split up so we could get a better look at things. I was alone when I saw him."

"By all that's holy," Patric mumbled. He began to pace. If it was Turlog they must tell Brian of it, but with only one set of eyes glimpsing him in the distance the story may not be accepted. "Did ye see his colors, man?" Patric asked. Perhaps Brian's uncle was planning to proclaim his treachery.

"Nay," Finn replied. "He was dressed in homespun. I suspect he doesn't want his nephew to know he's here."

"But the Ard Ri's colors were flying, were they not?" Patric inquired realizing he'd not asked the important question earlier.

"For sure," Finn snapped back. "I'd not have brought the information so publicly if they weren't."

"Good," Patric sighed. He never had cause to doubt Finn's word before but he was just as happy to have proof that the information was true.

"So what shall we do?" Finn asked.

Patric nodded his head slowly as his brain worked through the problem then he looked up. "If Turlog is planning to be in this we'll know about it on the morrow. He'll be lined up with the rest of them, aye." Finn nodded and he continued, "But if he's a spy, there's little we can do to prove it unless he reveals himself."

"Aye," Finn agreed.

"Alright then," Patric offered as he clapped the captain's back then moved him back toward the camp. "Let's keep this information between us. But on the morrow I expect those raven eyes of yers to be on the look out for the man. I would rather have Brian see him with his own eyes than to cast accusations that can't be proven."

"Ye can count on it," Finn replied.

He looked back towards the camp where his wife was awash in the glow of the campfire and a sigh past his lips. Patric slapped him on the back. "Ye should go to her. There may not be a battle tomorrow but with Brian ye never know."

Finn smiled his agreement then rushed forward to scoop Margreg into his arms. Moments later they disappeared into the privacy of their tent.

Camp stirred to life several hours later with each man doing his part to dismantle tents, pack up wagons and bank the many campfires. When it was done Patric, Eagan, Finn, Brian, Thorien and Murchad donned their full regalia then mounted their horses to make their way over the rise with a flag of peace marking their journey.

Throdier's horse danced around the field, trying to escape the debris being stirred up by the rising wind. The Viking squinted against the light of the oddly glowing sky to spot the five riders making their way over the rise. "Ye don't think they mean to surrender, do ye now?" he asked of the Ard Ri who was also looking toward the riders.

Malsakin shielded his eyes with his hand. "Nay," he spit, recognizing the flag to be one of peace instead of surrender. "They come to negotiate."

"Negotiate?" Rolo asked as he raised an eyebrow with interest. "Ye mean he may give over his lands?"

Malsakin thought about the question then took a moment to consider Boru. If he knew anything about the man, he knew he wasn't one to concede easily. There must be another reason for him entering the camp without his army. "Let's wait and hear him out." He beckoned Fladbartoc with the cock of his head. "Where has Turlog gotten to? We may need him, aye."

"I've not seen him since we formed up." A bit of bracken blew into Fladbartoc's mouth and he pulled it from his tongue before continuing, "I'll send a man for him."

Brian looked to the sky as the heavy storm cloud sailed across it. He could smell the static in the air marking the storm as one that would be riddled with lightening. He rubbed Kormlada's trinket between his fingers before looking to the line of warriors poised before them in the distance then turned to Patric to inquire, "Are they all mounted?"

Patric knew Brian had difficulty seeing things in the distance so he described the scene for his king. "They're all mounted. Malsakin sits in the center. Rolo is on the right and Fladbartoc on the left."

"That's Malsakin's left," Murchad interjected to be sure his father understood the lay out.

Brian smiled at him then inquired, "Who else is with them?"

Patric scanned the field with the hope of spotting Turlog but there was no sign of him. Instead his eyes alighted on the Viking who made him famous. "Throdier of Orkney," Patric stated plainly.

"Hmph," Brian offered, wondering what great event had taken place to draw the man back to Ireland. He scanned the field again but still the shapes blurred. "How many Vikings?"

"Not nearly enough," Murchad replied. "We have more with us than they do."

"Aye," Brian replied as he smiled at his son, "But it won't matter in that we'll not be using ours."

A wave of anxiety washed over Murchad with the statement. He'd never doubted his father's battle instincts but he couldn't help feeling vulnerable for the antics they were now perpetrating. "Just in case," he muttered to himself.

"Alright then," Brian called. He again looked to the sky glowing ominously around the black storm cloud. If his timing was right it could be very useful to him. In that moment the wind whipped up to push against their backs and he called out as he kicked his horse, "Everyone—follow me!"

Brian's troops sailed over the ridge just as the roll of thunder boomed through the sky, presenting a fierce scene to Malsakin's army. They reined in just yards short of the front line. "Malsakin the Great," Brian called out as the wind whipped his hair around in a swirling riot. The flash of lightening that streaked the sky reflected in his eyes and the golden ring he wore around his head. "Do ye plan to lead this army?"

The bits of dust being carried on the wind stung Malsakin's eyes but he refused to close them as he returned Brian's glare. "Indeed I do, Boru."

"And what is it ye think ye'll gain by it?" Brian called as another roll of thunder sounded around them.

"I'll gain the knowledge that I've put ye down once and for all," Malsakin responded. He spit a bit of dust from his tongue then he turned his head slightly to continue, "Ye betrayed our deal when ye took Dublin. Ye're a usurper, Boru and I mean to put an end to ye."

Brian raised an eye toward the sky to track the storm cloud then returned his gaze to Malsakin, calling out loud enough to be heard over the wind, "Ye should know about betrayal, Malsakin. Ye've offered it up often enough."

Malsakin's hair whipped around his face and he pushed it back with his hand as he looked to the rise. No warriors stood atop it. Whatever Boru had planned could be easily put down by his own army hiding in the trees. He offered a wry smile as he too spoke loudly, "If ye question my right to Tara I should say 'twill be settled soon enough." He waited for the next roll of thunder to die down before he continued, "Now make yer offer or gather yer army. I grow weary with this talk."

Brian continued to stare at the Ard Ri as the shadows moving across his face told him that the storm cloud was hovering overhead. He gripped Kormlada's trinket before leaning forward in his saddle to offer, "The mistake that was made on that day will indeed be rectified, but not by this battle, Malsakin."

Malsakin's brows knit together and his cape whipped around his neck as a fierce wind came howling over the rise. He grabbed the ends to tuck them beneath his thighs and Brian continued, "Ye've broken a covenant by being here today. God is expressing his dissatisfaction for it. He's called upon me to right this wrong and I do it willingly."

Patric shifted his gaze toward the Ri Ciocid without turning his head as he wondered what he was up to, but suddenly the wind whipped up again blowing the dust from the field directly into the faces of Malsakin's men. They sputtered and coughed as they turned their backs against it. A deafening clap of thunder broke out followed by a fierce crack of lightening that vibrated the ground. Minor chaos ensued when skittish horses bolted northward away from the storm. Then all at once the eastern woods became a ball of fire sending Malsakin's hidden army out into the open field, choking from the smoke.

Malsakin struggled with his own horse as warriors scattered in all directions then realizing he was losing control he bellowed, "Do ye surrender, Boru?"

Brian smiled slyly as the wind at his back whipped his hair around his face. There was another roll of thunder followed immediately by a flash of lightening which hit a nearby tree. "Far be it from me to abandon a war sanctioned by our Lord," he bellowed as the wind howled around them.

He watched as the forest fire became more intense, sending black ribbons of smoke directly into the faces of whatever army Malsakin had left behind him. They choked and coughed. Some fell back completely as the orange flames lapped out from the trees. It was a riot of nature as heat mixed with air to cause tiny whirlpools of dust to dart across the field. Thunder continued to roll and lightening continued to flash revealing the fear on the faces of Malsakin's warriors.

Brian nodded and smiled at Patric then turned to reassure his other men before spreading his arms on the wind to call out, "Let all men bear witness to God's will for today I, Brian Boru macCennitig of the clan Dal Cais and Ri Ciocid of the southern territory, do level charges against Malsakin the Great of the clan O'Neill and Ard Ri of the northern territory for collusion with Viking outlaws. As it is my right to assuage such trespass, I call him to war on the day of my choosing to claim the high kingship of all Eire from north to south and from east to west so that no lands will lay beyond the victor's control."

Malsakin struggled to stay seated as his horse danced around the field. "That's absurd," he called out. A gust of wind nearly blew him over and he covered his eyes with his arm. "Ye have no claim, Boru. I've allied with no outlaw."

Brian looked to Rolo who was edging his horse back in preparation for his escape. He called out to Patric, "Take him, man!"

Patric followed the Ri Ciocid's gaze then sailed forward to do as he was bade. Brian continued, "From this day forward, each house in the southern territory will make hostages of any Viking who refuses to swear to the Dal Cais. For according to God's will they shall be named outlaws."

Another crack of lightening flashed across the sky as if bearing witness to the truth. The tree that it struck snapped then teetered before crashing to the ground several feet from Malsakin horse causing it to rear up. Patric's horse skittered sideways but he quickly reined it in as he pressed his blade against Rolo's throat. "Down, man," he barked loud enough to be heard over the wind.

Rolo protected his face from the debris being blown into it but Throdier, who sat his horse beside him, only fingered his dagger as he calculated the time necessary to have it pulled from its sheath then flung into Patric's chest. He took hold of the weapon but as soon as he raised his arm he felt a searing heat bite into his shoulder. He looked to the dagger handle protruding from the joint then to its owner who loomed over him. "Bad move," Finn bellowed before ridding forward to rip the dagger from Throdier's shoulder.

Throdier's howl was lost to the wind as he grabbed the wound to halt the flow of blood. He was thrown from his horse when Finn's meaty fist crashed against his jaw.

Patric nodded his appreciation to the captain then worked to bind Rolo's hands behind his back. He led the earl from the field.

Eagan, Finn, Thorien and Murchad looked to Brian for further instruction and the Ri Ciocid nodded his head toward Patric. He reined his horse to follow as his warriors retreated into the oncoming storm but before he did he called out,

"I'll send word when we're to meet, Malsakin. For now I would suggest ye depart these lands before our Lord truly demonstrates his anger."

With that he galloped over the rise, shielding his face with his cloak against the pelting rain. He thought of Kormlada. All these years together hadn't yet brought him his crown but now there was hope.

✳   ✳   ✳   ✳

Dal Naraide, Ireland—Two hours past midnight—28, September 1001 A.D.—Located on the eastern shores of Lough Neagh, Dal Naraide belonged to Ladolin O'Neill, second cousin to the Ard Ri. Accompanied by four hundred warriors all bearing his mark, Brian Boru macCennitig ferried across the lough then marched six hundred head of cattle out of the village to his awaiting boats where they were transported to the other side. Before he departed he ordered the village completely destroyed.

✳   ✳   ✳   ✳

Dal Fiatach, Ireland: Two hours past noon—31, October 1001 A.D.—Billows of black smoke darkened the sky as every hut in the village was set aflame by soldiers bearing the mark of the Dal Cais. The loss to Milrud the Braw, ally of Malsakin O'Neill, was total as three hundred and fifty head of cattle followed a raging black bull being ridden by Brian Boru through the village gates. Those villagers who escaped death by blade or by fire, were deposited in Lough Strangford where they were drowned.

✳   ✳   ✳   ✳

Dundalk, Ireland: Midnight—14, November 1001 A.D.—Morgan O'Neill was ripped from his bed by a pair of hands so strong that he would swear they were inhuman. Both he and his wife were dragged from their hut then made to face each other before their throats were slit. Their bodies were deposited in the new well located at the southern edge of the village. Five hundred and thirty nine head of cattle were marched down the road while the village burned.

*   *   *   *

Comaille Muirtemne, Ireland:—Noon—24, November 1001 A.D.—Six hundred warriors on horseback barreled through the gates of the village causing the stanchions to creak then fall atop the wall of soldiers who were ordered by their Ri Tuath, Mirminadh O'Neill, to stand ready for the attack. The battle that ensued lasted well into the night and when it was over, three hundred warriors, both Dal Cais and O'Neill, lay dead upon the field. The village was burned and Brian Boru macCennitig claimed seven hundred and eighty nine head of cattle as his prize.

*   *   *   *

Airgialla, Ireland: One hour past midnight—21 December 1001 A.D.—Ardmore O'Neill fell to his knees as he begged the Dal Cais Ri Ciocid to leave him his wealth. Brian responded by taking his head as well as all his cattle.

*   *   *   *

Meath, Ireland: One hour to midnight—26, February 1002 A.D.—Showing no sign of aggression nor demand for tribute, one thousand Dal Cais warriors led by Brian Boru macCennitg camped outside the walls of Meath for three days until every one of it's inhabitants swore their allegiance under terrified duress. Not a weapon was raised nor a drop of blood spilled, but when the Ard Ri arrived a day too late there wasn't a soul in the village who would acknowledge him as their leader.

CHAPTER 30

▼

Torshav, Ireland: Four hours past noon—20, April 1002—Ermagh kept her eyes trained on the orange flowering bushes dotting the passing terrain of her new country hoping that their beauty would take her mind off her swelling sickness. Gorse is what Njord called them. Being so plentiful she thought they were a sacred plant but Njord told her that they were a plague on the farmers, often drying out enough to catch fire which spread on the ever present winds.

She shook her head in amazement that something so beautiful could be so troublesome but the thought was jarred from her when she lurched forward with the abrupt stop of the carriage. Njord jumped from his horse then stepped on to the running board to peer inside. "Ye all right?" he asked, sticking his hand through the window to pat her swollen womb. "'Twas a rock."

She smiled up at him then wiped her sweating brow with her sleeve. "Aye, I'm all right," she replied in Manx, too weary to recall the Gaelic words he'd taught her. "How much longer will it be?"

He smiled in that way she liked so well, making him look like a mischievous lad. "We're here."

A wave of anxiety passed over her with the thought of being presented to Njord's people. She had wanted to remain in Man until she was delivered, preferring not to have them see her all bloated and swollen with child, but Njord argued that he'd been away too long and needed to get back before the changing politics of his country left him without a village to tend. He pulled her to her feet then stroked her womb again, marking the cause of her discomfort. "We're home now, aye. Ye shan't suffer any longer."

He jumped down then reached up to take her in his arms. "All will be well once Hecca has at ye." She nodded her head then rested it against his shoulder as he carried her to the great hall.

Havland, who was walking ahead of them, looked around the village that was devoid of warriors. On their trip from Dublin Shane had explained that Finn and Patric took Njord's army to Tara to stand with Brian as he claimed the high crown. "So he's finally going to do it," he sighed to himself, wishing they'd returned sooner so they could have accompanied them.

"Aye," Shane replied, not realizing that the statement didn't need an answer. "It didn't come easy either. Brian raided nearly every O'Neill leader to be sure they couldn't be in it when he called the Ard Ri out."

Havland raised a knowing eyebrow. "So he's back to that again?"

Shane shook his head sadly. "This time 'twas far worse than the last. Quite a bit of bloodshed."

Knowing that Shane was anything but squeamish, Havland presumed that the raiding had been truly gruesome. He shook his head in sympathy for the lost souls then moved forward to open the door for Njord who was struggling under his burden. "Good to be home, aye," he asked of the earl then curled his lip at the bundle he was carrying.

Njord nodded to him then began to make his way through the door but Ermagh stopped him. "Put me down, husband. I'm not lame." It was bad enough that she was swollen with child she didn't want to appear weak as well.

"Ye'll be carried and ye'll be glad of it," he responded. He was eager to catch up on news and was in no mood for her childish games. "Between the ship and the carriage, yer legs may not be sturdy. 'Tis far better that ye appear to them in my arms then falling down on yer face as if ye'd been nipping too much mead."

Havland smiled triumphantly as the young earl finally put his wife in her place but Ermagh scowled then rested her head against her husband's shoulder. If he must carry her then at least their posture should look romantic.

They had barely crossed the threshold when the sound of Eilis' running feet reached their ears. She appeared in the archway leading from the circular hall, smiling broadly when her eyes alighted on Njord. As she slowed to a more lady like approach her face expressed her curiosity over the woman he was carrying. "What's happened, Njord?" she gasped, her concern for the scene squashing her enthusiasm. "Is she wounded then?"

Njord looked down at the comely dark haired lass and for a moment he couldn't place her but when he looked into her gray blue eyes his recollection took hold. "Eilis," he sighed, the smile on his face expressing all the love he held for her. "I can hardly believe it's ye. Have I been away so long that ye've blossomed into a woman with yer pretty apron covered in roses? All ye need now is the kerchief, aye."

She smiled then nodded, certain that the kerchief would come from him. If he hadn't been carrying that woman in his arms she would have greeted him in the manner that a betrothed should. As it was she was left to twirl around to let him get a better look at her. She had filled out quite nicely while he was away. In fact, she was a year past marrying age. But since he expressed his desire to have a wedding of nobles she supposed they could wait one more.

"Do ye like them?" she asked, her smile twinkling in her eyes. "I did them especially for ye." He nodded then her face turned serious. She chucked her chin toward Ermagh. "Who is she, Njord?"

He opened his mouth to answer then closed it again as he thought about the words they'd just exchanged. It appeared she still carried her childish crush for him. Telling her of his marriage to Ermagh without the proper explanation would cause ill feelings. He would have to wait until he had more time to spend before he made the introduction.

Noticing his hesitation, Ermagh looked up at him scowling. She awaited his answer but when none came she introduced herself. "I'm his wife!" she said to Eilis, holding up her nose in the haughty way she did whenever she felt threatened.

Njord scowled at her before turning to see Eilis' reaction. The lass lifted her eyebrow as if she didn't understand a word Ermagh had said.

Njord smiled then looked down at his wife. "She doesn't have the tongue," he explained in the same Manx Ermagh had just used. "And if ye don't mind, I'd prefer to deliver the news to her myself. It seems that she's still a bit fond of me. I'd rather not hurt her feelings by telling her I married another."

That brought a deeper scowl from Ermagh but even if she thought to disobey him she couldn't recall the Gaelic words to communicate with the child. "If I'm to be a secret, husband, ye should have brought me in from the back way!"

"Hush now, woman," Njord snapped back. "I'll tell her in my own time and ye'll abide."

Ermagh looked down at the child with distaste. She wasn't accustomed to being kept a secret from anyone, least of all a little scamp who fancied herself good enough to possess her husband. She tried once more to recall the Gaelic words he'd taught her but she was so angry with him that she could barely manage to croak out the Manx. "Very well, husband," she growled. "Bring me to my bed now so that ye can come back and tell her who I am!"

His back stiffened as her ungenerous nature was revealed to him once again. He decided that chastising her for it would only cause a scene and he was too tired from the long trip to suffer an argument. "Aye," he huffed then turned his gaze on Eilis whose confusion was displayed on her face.

"Go and get yer mother for me, child," he offered, his smile so large that she could see the dimples in his cheeks. "Tell her I've people I wish her too meet, aye. We'll speak together after that."

"But she's not here, Njord," Eilis responded, standing on tiptoe to get a better look at the woman in his arms. "She's off to battle with my father."

"Off to battle?" Njord questioned as he shifted Ermagh's weight against his knee. "Yer mother?"

"Aye. She says her place is beside her husband. She's been marching with him on every trip he takes. I'll do the same for ye." Though her words were for Njord, her complete attention was on Ermagh.

Njord swallowed hard with the realization that his explanation would be more painful than he thought. He shifted Ermagh's weight in his arms wishing he could dump her right there so he could have a private word with the lass.

"Is Gertrude with ye then?"

"Aye," Eilis responded, now leering at the woman snuggled close against the man she loved. It was clear she was with child. Her stomach gripped as it all became clear to her. She felt her knees go weak and her head start to swim but she was drawn from her thoughts when Njord spoke again.

"Go and fetch her then, aye."

Her face was desperate. She nodded but didn't move bringing Njord to the realization that she had put it all together. Frustrated that he couldn't offer her comfort with Ermagh in his arms, he turned to Hecca who was standing behind him then barked, "Ye follow me." He spun on his heel and the rotund woman offered Eilis a fleeting smile before following her master through the archway and into the circular hall. Eilis erupted into tears.

"There, there, Eilis," Havland cooed taking her into his arms then kissing her neck. He knew how she felt about Njord but no one expected that the childhood crush would have lasted through these years. "He's the earl, lassie. He needed a wife to provide him an heir but I promise ye that he still loves ye."

She pulled back far enough to look at him without going cross-eyed, feeling as much betrayed by him as she did by Njord. "But we agreed to be married," she mumbled, wiping her tears with the sleeve of her lein. "She can't love him as I do. Why couldn't he wait?"

"I know ye love him," Havland sighed then lifted her chin with his open palm, "but ye'll find someone else to love in time. Ye can trust me on that. I know about such things."

She had no choice but to accept his words. Njord didn't want her and there was nothing anyone could do about that now. She politely gave him her knee then slowly exited the hall in search of her grandmother, the great weight of her heartbreak slumping her shoulders as she went.

Njord led Hecca down the circular hall then stepped up his pace as the door to his chamber came into view. Although she was plump with stubby legs she matched his pace easily, releasing the latch that would gain them entrance before looking up at him with her smiling, bright blue eyes.

Once she had been married to Flori of Man. After his death, Njord convinced her to come back to Torshav with him so that his wife would have someone familiar to keep her company. She was a good woman with a natural instinct for protecting all she thought worthy of caring for. She let him pass through the door first then rushed to the bed to turn down the covers so he could deposit his wife there.

"Go away now," she ordered as she shooed him with her hand. "Let me get her cleaned up so that she can rest easy."

He smiled at her as he backed away. "Don't be so bossy, aye. Perhaps she's not ready for me to leave yet."

Still stinging from their encounter with Eilis, Ermagh waved her hand in dismissal. "Ye may go, lord," she offered curtly. "I know there's important business ye need to tend and it best be done now."

"So it's like that is it?" he retorted, chucking her beneath the chin playfully. She turned from him with a scowl.

Since she had gotten with child she'd become fiercely jealous, casting accusations whenever he got near another woman. At first he thought it charming but now it was beginning to wear on him. For her to be jealous of a child was taking things too far and he let his anger for her foolishness show. "I'll tend my business, wife and be happy to do it in that Eilis is the sweetest lass I've ever known. There's not a hateful bone in her body which is more than I can say for ye."

He turned on his heel to exit the chamber but ran squarely into Gertrude as he did. "Njord, laddie," she huffed when she bounced off him. "Ye've come back to us."

At first he was startled but soon enough he smiled his recognition. He bent his head to her so she could shower it with tiny kisses then he took her for a spin as he thrilled, "So I have, fair lady and it's good to be welcomed by ye."

As he set her down he thought to introduce her to his wife but when he looked to Ermagh she snapped her head around then tucked herself into her pillow. He rolled his eyes then returned his attention to Gertrude, holding her at arms length. "Don't ye look particularly well? I should say my absence has done a great deal of good for this household."

"So ye've seen Eilis then?" she asked, pride showing on her face. "Isn't she grand?"

"Aye," he replied then shot a hateful look toward Ermagh. "She'll be a great beauty once she's fully grown. Finn will have his hands full keeping the lads from her."

Gertrude looked past him to Hecca who had moved to join them then back up at him for an explanation. He offered it cautiously, knowing both of them were predisposed to marking their dominion. "Hecca," he called as he opened an arm to her while the other came to rest on Gertrude's shoulder, "I'd like to present Gertrude, the keeper of Torshav."

Each woman looked the other over as if their abilities could be assessed through their appearance alone. Finally Hecca bent her knee. "It's good to know of ye, Gertrude," she offered in the impeccable Gaelic taught to her by her late husband. "It'll be my great pleasure to assist ye."

Njord smiled as Gertrude returned the gesture, hoping it was a sign that all would be well and that he wouldn't be forced into making a statement about the pecking order.

"Ye're a strong one, aye," Gertrude sighed when she took Hecca's hand. "Remind me a bit of my sister when we were younger." She turned to Njord as if reading his mind then stated, "I think we'll get on just fine, earl. Now, why don't ye introduce me to this lovely thing that's lying in yer bed. Is it yer wife, then?"

"Aye," Njord huffed, preparing for the next introduction, which he was certain wouldn't go as well. He led her by the hand to the side of the bed then barked, "Ermagh! Face me so I can introduce ye to Eilis' grandmother, Gertrude."

Ermagh wrinkled her nose in distaste then pretended he had woken her. She yawned and stretched a bit before rolling over to face him. "Njord?" she cooed too sweetly to be sincere. "I must have fallen asleep."

He issued a, "hmph," before rolling his eyes at her then turned to smile at Gertrude offering, "May I present my wife, Ermagh who seems to have lost her manners since she's become swollen with my child."

Choosing to acknowledge the good news instead of the tension between the man and wife, Gertrude held her hands to her cheeks then gasped, "Ye'll be a father then, Njord. 'Tis a happy surprise indeed. The Shaver will be greatly pleased."

The mention of his father caused a shiver to run down Njord's spine. It was Brodir's opinion that his first loyalty was to his slain family even if it meant the destruction of his relationship with the Shaver. Though he knew it was good advice, he couldn't help being uncomfortable seeing the situation through. He took a moment to gather his struggling emotions before inquiring, "Speaking of the Shaver, do ye know what will become of him when Brian becomes Ard Ri?"

There was a twinkle in Gertrude's eyes when she straightened her shoulders and offered proudly, "There's been talk that he'll be named Ri Ciocid." Njord's eyebrows shot up in surprise and her eyes sharpened. "I should think he's deserving of it after his service to the man."

Ignoring her defensive posture, Njord spit on the ground to mark his distaste before inquiring over the man he was truly interested in, "And Turlog?" he grumbled.

"Och," Gertrude issued, screwing up her face to mark her own dislike of the man. "I doubt he'll be getting anything with the way he's been acting lately. Hasn't come to a battle since he lost his eye. There's been talk that he may even be treacherous."

Njord's eyes widened and he looked askance of her. She smiled. "Ye didn't hear it from me, aye." He nodded and she looked over her shoulder to see if anyone else entered the room. "Finn thinks he saw him among Malsakin's troops at Desmumu."

"Take a breath woman," Njord blurted eagerly, grabbing her arm to gain her full attention. "Have ye forgotten I've been away? Start at the beginning and tell me all that's happened here."

Gertrude's eyes twinkled mischievously as she prepared to relay the story Njord was so eager to hear but just then Ermagh cleared her throat to remind them of her presence. "Shall I return to my nap?" she huffed as she plumped her pillow with her fist.

Gertrude gave Ermagh her full attention but Njord only half turned. "Aye, return to yer nap so I can find out what's been going on around here."

She growled low in her throat before throwing herself down then pulled the covers up over her shoulder. Hecca saw it and quickly moved in to ease ill feelings. "Why don't ye go on now, Njord," she issued as she shoed them away from the bed. "Ye've important matters to discuss. I'll take care of the lass, aye."

Gertrude smiled, marking Hecca as a loyal servant then looked up at Njord who had taken her hand to lead her away. "She's a good one, that," she whispered, chucking her chin toward Hecca. "I'm glad ye brought her."

Njord squeezed her hand then led her through the doors and into the kitchens, bombarding her with questions while she busied herself preparing him something to eat. She told him how Brian took Dublin to marry Kormlada. And of Turlog's supposed betrayal of Brian in Desmumu. And the unmerciful siege Brian waged against Malsakin's kin in an effort to get him to forfeit his crown.

He sat back with his hands folded behind his head then sighed, "So it seems I've come back just in time, aye."

"Aye," Gertrude offered with a smile then began picking at the half eaten biscuit from his plate. "The best of it is that Kormlada managed to give Brian a son at her advanced age proving that she's a fairy."

Njord chuckled, "Some fairy. He's still not Ard Ri."

Gertrude extended two fingers then spit on them to keep the spirits away. "Don't say such things, Njord. Ye mark my words, when the day is done Brian will have Malsakin's crown."

He chuckled as he realized that Gertrude and Ermagh would likely get on well then sat watching her for a moment before he asked his next question. "What of Eilis?"

"Hasn't she grown then?" Gertrude thrilled. "Such a bonnie lass—helpful and kind."

"Ye don't think she could still be fond of me do ye?" he asked, his eyes sparkling with the glimmer of hope that Eilis wouldn't take his news badly.

"I'm afraid it's worse now, laddie." She patted his hand. "She's of that age, aye, when all things romantic come into her head. She's been pining for ye ever since ye left."

"Hmph," Njord issued, worrying the situation would be more difficult then he'd expected. He'd rather fight a battle than to do anything that would hurt the lass. In the end he screwed up his courage then got to his feet. "So where do ye think she's off to?"

"Ye'll most likely find her in the stables." She nodded toward the door. "She knows ye're fond of the horses and had Finn teach her how to ride so she could impress ye."

"So I suppose I should go to her," he mumbled, moving slowly toward the door.

His discomfort was obvious and Gertrude sighed to know a giant warrior could be so tender. "Just lay it plain for her," she offered with a sympathetic wink of her eye. "There'll be a sting of pain but she'll get over it soon enough."

"Aye," he mumbled then forced a smile.

As Gertrude predicted he found Eilis sitting on a stool outside the stall of one of the mares that was about to fowl. "So then," he sighed as he made his way toward her. "I hear ye're riding now."

"I'm not very good yet," she mumbled, lowering her head in an effort to hide her grief. If it was possible, he was more handsome than she remembered him to be making the whole situation that much more difficult. "I'll need some time before I can ride as well as ye."

"Aye," he replied. "Perhaps I can help ye with that."

She nodded her head causing her hair to fall in front of her face. He pushed it behind her ear as he had a hundred times before. Though she was a woman, somehow he found it difficult to think of her as anything other than the child he once knew. He took her by the hand to bring her to her feet then sat down on the stool himself before drawing her into his lap. "I've a thing I wish to speak with ye about, aye."

She could barely breath for being so close to him. Her chest heaved as both desire and sadness whirled around inside her. She kept her head down for fear she'd cry if she looked up. "Is that so?" Her voice trembled.

He lifted her chin with his open hand then looked long at her, assessing every inch of her face and her gray-blue eyes that were glazed with her tears. He cursed himself for not having the good sense to wait for her. If he had he could've been married to a jewel instead of the bitter beauty he was now strapped with.

Realizing Gertrude's advice was sound, he finally blurted, "The woman ye were inquiring over is named Ermagh. She's the daughter of Eric of Denmark."

"Oh," Eilis replied then lifted her head wondering if he was forced into the marriage.

It was his turn to look away as he mumbled, "She's my wife, Eilis and the child that she carries is mine."

Though she had the information from Havland, hearing the words from Njord ripped through her like a knife causing her to draw breath. She chewed on her bottom lip in an effort to hold back her tears then pushed herself from his lap. "Did ye make the bargain for the sake of peace?" she inquired while she looked to her shoes.

A fleeting thought of lying to her crossed Njord's mind, but Havland knew how hard he had pursued Ermagh. He wouldn't risk Eilis finding out that he'd been dishonest as well as stupid. "Nay," he mumbled, trying to catch her eye from beneath her hair. "I wanted her."

"May God be with ye then," she stated, trying to keep her voice from shaking. She offered her hand without looking at him. "She looks to be a fine woman, Njord."

"Listen to me, Eilis," he began. He took her hand but in a moment she ripped it from him then ran from the barn tearing the apron from her body as she went.

*   *   *   *

Tara, Ireland: Noon—20, April 1002 A.D.—Patric turned his head toward the oncoming wagon then screwed up his face in distaste as he realized it was Turlog joining them. The man hadn't ridden by Brian's side in years. Like some of the others doting the field, he only decided to come when victory was eminent.

"So the old turd finally joins us," Margreg huffed as she ladled the stew into the bowl he was holding. "I'd say it was about time but there's no doubt that his presence could only mean trouble."

"Hush, woman," Finn snapped when his stomach gripped with the sight of Turlog. Since that day at Desmumu he was haunted by the question of whether or not he had really seen him. A pain shot through his head with the familiar confusion and he thrust his bowl out for Magreg to fill. "Will ye feed me or nay?"

"What's got ye all boiling then?" she asked before emptying the contents of her ladle into Patric's bowl. She dipped it again to fill her husband's. It was unlike him to act as he was but she decided it was his anxiety speaking. Many of the men were acting similarly as they awaited word about whether or not they would fight.

He smiled when he looked at her, ashamed for his behavior. He stroked her arm. "I'm hungry is all. I didn't mean to snap at ye, aye."

She nodded acceptance of his apology but before she could say anything further, Patric jumped in to offer, "I understand what ye're feeling, man. It's not easy seeing him here after Desmumu, but now that ye do, can ye be certain that it *was* him?"

Finn looked up to see Turlog headed straight for them. His hair was cropped short and he sported a patch over his bad eye. Nothing about him now looked as it did that day in Desmumu. "Nay," he huffed before spooning the stew into his mouth. "But still, I would rather that he wasn't here now, aye."

"I think it was him in Desmumu," Margreg huffed taking a moment to look over her shoulder before ladling stew into her own bowl. She sat on the rock next to her husband. "I think Brian believes it as well."

"What makes ye say that?" Patric inquired lowering his spoon then eyeing her over his bowl. She was a good one for gathering gossip and by the look on her face she had some interesting news to share.

"Why else would Brian overlook him to name ye Ri Ciocid?" she asked before blowing on a steaming spoonful of stew.

Patric lifted his eyebrow then turned his gaze to his bowl, trying to cover his excitement for the statement. He had heard such rumors but he refused to get his hopes up for something that might not happen. "I'll believe that when it happens, aye."

She knew what he was thinking and smirked at him before offering, "He will name ye. I heard him telling his son as much. Murchad will be named northern Ri Ciocid and ye will be named Ri Ciocid of the South."

Patric looked at her over the top of his bowl before taking another spoonful then chewed for a moment as he considered her words. "Ye heard them?"

"Aye," she chuckled. "Didn't ye expect as much?"

He had hoped for such a thing but to know it was true was something else entirely. He felt the goose pimples spread across his skin but did his best to hide his smile. "Well, if it happens I'll be honored. Just let's not celebrate the thing before it does." He lifted his eyes toward Turlog then nodded. "We should end this conversation now, aye. There's nay a reason for *him* to know of it."

Finn nodded his agreement then all of them turned toward Turlog's call. "There ye are, Patric," he thrilled, bending his nose toward the kettle then smiling when the aroma reached his nose. "Yer mother sends her greetings. Wanted me to see ye with my own eyes to tell her whether or nay ye were fit. I should say ye're a lucky one to have a woman in yer camp. She feeds ye well."

"Greetings Turlog," Patric offered bitterly. He cocked his head toward Margreg to have her bring another bowl. "Won't ye join us? We've plenty to share."

"Well, I wouldn't mind a taste," Turlog agreed then settled himself on the rock that Margreg had just abandoned. He took the bowl offered before raking the Viking he had seen in Desmumu with his one good eye. "It's good to see ye well, Finn," he thrilled in a tone too joyous to be sincere, "I heard ye found some trouble in Dundalk."

"Bah," Finn replied as if the matter wasn't worthy of mention, but in truth he wondered how the Ri Tuath knew of it.

After Brian's raid on Dundalk Finn had volunteered to stay behind with a contingent of soldiers to secure the round fort. It was the dead of night and he was relieving himself against a tree when a man jumped out from the shadows to attack him. They struggled and he suffered a slash to the face but in the end managed to wound his attacker and send him retreating into the shadows from which he came.

They never did find out who perpetrated the deed or how he managed to get past the heavily guarded gates. Ever since that day, Finn lived with the feeling that he was a marked man.

He took another spoonful of his stew, chewing it slowly while he wondered whether Turlog had something to do with the ambush. "Nothing to worry over," he offered between gulps. "'Twas only a scratch. The wife had me back on my feet in no time."

Turlog recognized Finn's anxiety and smiled before looking to Margreg. "So ye're a camp follower now, lass. I should say 'tis a step up from a whore."

There was utter silence as Patric, Finn and Margreg presumed they had heard incorrectly. "Pardon?" Margreg asked, her wide eyes blinking in disbelief.

"What's the matter?" Turlog snapped back. "Are ye deaf as well?"

Finn threw his bowl to the ground before getting to his feet. In one swift move, he had Turlog by the collar and was dragging him upward so their eyes were level with his. "I'll kill ye with my bare hands," he growled, wrenching his elbow away from Patric who was trying to calm him. "That's my wife ye're speaking about, old man. Now, give her yer apology or I'll kill ye where ye stand."

Turlog's one good eye held a maniacal look as he leveled it against Finn. "Unhand me now."

Patric and Margreg looked on wondering what Finn would do. He was within his rights to beat the man but if he did so he would certainly lose favor within the clan. Turlog was an elder who was no longer fit to battle. No matter what his crime, it would be wrong for someone of Finn's ability to take him on.

Apparently, Finn considered the consequences because he lowered Turlog to the ground then growled low in is throat. "Ye owe the woman an apology. Why don't ye give it and be gone?"

At length they all stood around the fire. When it was clear Turlog wouldn't issue an apology, Margreg laced her arm through her husband's then turned to offer. "Let us be away from here, Finn. I've suddenly no appetite."

She could feel him tremble beneath her touch and she rocked herself up on her toes to whisper in his ear. "He's a sick old man. He doesn't know what he's saying. Let's leave him for Patric to deal with, aye."

He knew she was right but he felt he was letting her down by not defending her properly. Reading his thoughts she continued, "Ye'll do more for me by remaining in the clan's favor. When Patric relays the tale, they'll be grateful to ye for not starting a row when we're so close to gaining the high crown, aye."

He pulled back from her so he could see her face then smiled before kissing her. When it came to such things, he trusted her guidance. "Aye, wife," he sighed as he drew back from her then turned her with his hand in the small of her back.

Patric watched them go, grateful that his cousin wasn't one of those women who demanded her husband fight for her at all costs. At length he turned toward Turlog. "What's gotten into ye, man?" he growled. "He was within his rights to kill ye. Have ye lost yer mind?"

"I've lost nothing," Turlog snapped, retaking his seat on the rock to finish his stew. "I only spoke the truth. Nay different than what's being said behind her back all throughout camp."

Patric knew he was lying. Margreg's presence in camp was a great comfort to Brian's men but he decided not to challenge him. "Why are ye here, Turlog?"

"I have every right to be here," he replied, his voice indignant. "My nephew will be Ard Ri and I've come to collect what's rightfully mine."

"And what would that be?"

"Never ye mind that, Patric," he snapped back. "Just ye remember that I've stood beside my nephew far longer than ye have, aye."

Patric wondered what Turlog was getting at but just as he was about to open his mouth to inquire, Eagan rode up towing Patric's horse behind him. "Come quick, Shaver," he blurted throwing down the reins to him. "Brian needs ye now!"

Patric threw down his bowl and the contents splashed up over Turlog's lein. In a moment he was mounted then he followed Eagan who was riding in the direction of Tara. Brian sat atop his horse waiting outside the gate. Murchad and Thorien flanked him. "Come on," he called with a wave of his hand to urge them. "Ye'll miss it for your dawdling. Malsakin wishes me to join him in his chambers. Let's ride!"

They followed the two O'Neill guards through the gates then dismounted before the doors of the great hall. When they entered, they spotted Malsakin sitting behind his table, his eyes blackened from lack of sleep and his hair quite disheveled. He looked as though he hadn't bathe in a week and was obviously drunk as he tried to stand to greet his guests but became shaky then sat with a thud.

"Come in, Brian Boru," he slurred as he bobbed in his seat. "Come in and take some mead." He chuckled. "And why not—ye've taken everything else I have."

Brian nodded to his men, relaying his desire for them to stand back. He took the seat across from the Ard Ri then brushed away the servant who brought him a cup. He leaned in eagerly. "So, will ye forfeit yer crown, Malsakin?"

"Och, right to business," the Ard Ri grumbled. "Not even the manners to take my hospitality."

"Will ye forfeit the crown or nay, Malsakin?" Brian pressed.

The hatred Malsakin felt for the man who sat before him bubbled up to scorch his tongue. "Never!" he belched with his upper lip curling in anger. He again failed to get to his feet but leaned forward instead to relay his seriousness. "I'll never deliver my crown to ye."

Brian rose from his seat with a nod. "Then on the morrow I'll just have to take it."

He cocked his head toward his guards, telling them to follow then slowly walked the length of the hall with his head held high. He was nearly at the door when Malsakin called out, "Nay, wait! Come back here!"

Brian slowed his pace but didn't stop forcing Malsakin to call again, "I beg ye, Boru, return and speak with me. Surely there's some way we can settle this without swords."

Brian winked at Thorien and Patric who had come up along side him then spun on his heel to march back to the front of the hall. "Take yer crown from yer head and hand it to me now and it will be settled without swords," he demanded of the Ard Ri as he leaned over the table. "Anything less will mean a battle."

"Why do you do this to me, Brian?" Malsakin wept. "What have I done to ye to draw such hatred?"

Brian's eyes disappeared in his head as his long building rage was finally unleashed. "What have ye done?" he bellowed, spittle flying from his mouth to land on Malsakin's lein. "Ye must be deluded to even ask such a thing! Ye betrayed me man...not once, not twice, but more times than I can count. What's worse is that ye betrayed yer own people!" He mumbled to himself as he marched to the side table laden with silver bowls then held one up before continuing, "Ye pretend to want to rid Eire of the Viking's yet ye allow them to plunder our lands so that ye and yer kin can have a little more wealth!"

With a swipe of his hand he cleared the sideboard sending bowls, pitchers and chalices clanging to the floor. He marched back to Malsakin causing him to shrink further into his chair. "Ye've sold our people into bondage to feed yer greed. It's not wine ye feast on but the blood of children and old men. Ye're a poor excuse for an Ard Ri and an even poorer excuse for a man!"

Patric stepped into Brian's line of vision, lifting his eyebrow to relay the message that his ranting was making him seem more a mad man than a leader. Brian caught his clue then nodded his thanks as he balled his fists to bring his emotions under control. He let out a deep sigh before spinning on his heel to march over to Malsakin. With one swift movement he uncovered his sword then held the tip beneath the Ard Ri's chin. "Will ye hand over yer crown or will I have to take it by force?"

The sounds of metal being pulled from its sheath rang out across the hall as Malsakin's guards bared their blades. Thorien, Murchad, Eagan and Patric bared theirs. Brian and Malsakin were locked in a visual embrace but Thorien stepped forward to place himself between his king and the Ard Ri's guards. "Don't be foolish, men," he said as he poised his sword in one hand while the other was held open in a sign of trust. "Let's all take a breath and put down our weapons."

Malsakin leered at Brian through his tears. He had always been a formidable opponent but any hope of toppling him was put down with his unmerciful sieges against his kin. The usurper had taken his wife and his reputation. Now he would take his crown.

He spit across the table before lifting his hands to his head to rip the golden ring from it. He flung it with all his might. "Here's yer crown, Boru. I pray ye wear it in good health."

The O'Neills covered their blades and Murchad took a few steps forward, never taking his eyes off them as he bent to pick up the gold circle rolling across the ground. He looked to Eagan who nodded that he had his back covered then spun on his heel to bring the mantle to the new Ard Ri.

Brian took it from him, twirling the ring between his fingers as he again leaned over the table. "I've many enemies, Malsakin," he cooed, "but I hope ye won't be counted among them. For those who hate me have no love for Eire. In the end, ye'll see that what I do is for the best."

"Maybe for ye, Brian Boru," Malsakin laughed without humor, "but I fail to see how this can benefit me."

✳   ✳   ✳   ✳

Turlog sat on a rock in front of his tent while all around him Dal Cais warriors celebrated their victory. Malsakin had been dispatched some time ago, back to Meath, which Brian returned to him as a reward for the forfeit of his crown.

Patric walked along the row of tents in search of Finn and Margreg. He stopped now and again to receive the well wishes being offered him. He turned to Turlog's call.

"Patric, lad. A word if ye don't mind."

Patric excused himself from the conversation he was having then closed the distance between him and his father in law. He looked down at Turlog who was obviously in his cups. "Aye."

"Have a drink, laddie," the one eyed man gurgled, holding the clay cup out for him to take.

"Nay the now, Turlog, though I thank ye all the same. What is it that ye need of me?"

"Word's around that Brian will name ye southern Ri Ciocid."

"Aye." Patric nodded but cast his gaze away from the man. He knew Turlog coveted the position for himself. "I'm quite pleased."

"As ye should be," Turlog huffed then raised his eyebrow as he called him closer with the crook of his finger. "Just be careful, aye. Ye'll have many enemies now. Ye shouldn't be walking around here without benefit of a guard."

"I've had enemies before, Turlog, and I expect I'll have them again. I can take care of myself."

"Well, mind that ye do," Turlog continued, failing to push himself to his feet. He gave up then sat back down with a "humph." "Ye're mother would have my head if anything should happen to ye. I don't want her tongue wagging at me." He looked up then squinted his good eye to bring Patric into focus. "Where's that Viking ye call Finn? He should be minding ye, aye. Or Eagan. Go and fetch one of them to keep ye safe."

Patric stared at him for a moment, wondering what message he was trying to deliver. He knelt before him, pulling him by the collar to shake him. "What do ye mean by that, Turlog? What is it that ye're trying to tell me? Just lay it plain."

"Och," Turlog belched as he tried to release the grip Patric had on his clothing. "Leave off me now, laddie. I was only trying to warn ye to be careful."

Turlog's eye rolled in his head and Patric considered him for a time. At length, he realized that the old man was just bitter and he gently released him. Turlog's head lolled then his eye closed as he fell asleep.

He was snoring when Patric left him on the rock and the new Ri Ciocid looked up in time to see Margreg dumping the water from the boiling pot in front of her tent.

"Margreg," he called when she turned to go inside. "Brian is about to announce his appointments. I wanted ye and Finn with me when he did. Where is that scoundrel husband of yers?"

Margreg cast her eyes toward the ground. Finn had been doing everything in his power to avoid Turlog but the old man wasn't making it easy, sitting on his rock drinking while he called out to anyone who passed him by.

"He's gone hunting. He's making a rabbit fur cloak for Eilis and he needed another pelt. He thought he saw one of the right color at the edge of the woods. He'll be back in a bit."

Patric chuckled but confusion dotted his face. "Ye mean to tell me that while Brian's about to name me southern Ri Ciocid, our man is off hunting rabbits?"

Margreg's eyes lit up. "Shaver," she thrilled, taking him by the shoulders as the smile played on her face. "I was right then."

"Aye," Patric replied, "but why would Finn choose to go hunting now of all times?"

She cast her gaze at the sleeping Turlog then curled her upper lip. Patric took her meaning. "Aye. That explains it."

"He hasn't moved from that rock since ye left to meet Brian. Finn didn't trust himself around the old man. Figured that the best way to keep from killing him was to avoid him altogether."

"Smart man, that husband of yers but we must find him so that Brian can make his announcement. I won't be taking a crown without my best warriors present, aye."

"Aye," she agreed, linking her arm through his to lead him to the place where she saw Finn enter the woods.

The trees were set close together forcing them to walk single file between them. Patric kept hold of his cousin's hand as his eyes adjusted to the darkness. "Finn!" he called out in his strongest voice, hoping that the man would answer so they needn't travel any further. "Where are ye man?"

There was no answer and Patric turned to his cousin then shrugged before moving deeper into the woods. He used his short blade to cut the underbrush that was threatening to trip them up. As he labored through it, he realized that Finn hadn't passed that way, or if he did, he didn't find it as hard going as they did. Patric cursed himself for never having picked up the art of tracking as he called out again, "Finn, ye rogue. Where are ye man?"

They looked around but all they could see was the dappled sunlight as it filtered through the trees. Large ferns stood in tufts along the forest floor with bells and bonnets glowing every now and again from where the sunlight touched them.

"Finn," he called. "Show yerself man!"

The forest was eerily silent and suddenly there was a gust of wind carrying with it a strong stench of blood. Patric held up his nose, pulling his cousin behind him as he headed in the direction of the scent.

"Finn," he called again. "Finn!"

His words were left hanging in the air and suddenly his heart began pounding in his chest. Apparently Margreg was nervous too because she squeezed Patric's hand then began to tremble.

He pulled her northward and the scent became stronger. He could feel the bead of sweat break out across his forehead as he struggled to cut the underbrush.

"Finn! Answer me damn ye!"

He heard the rustle of leaves from somewhere beyond the blood spattered tree trunk lying across their path. His heart beat ever faster. "Finn!" he called. "Finn!"

"Aye," Finn replied, popping up from behind the bush. He had a knife in his hand and was covered with blood from the deer he was butchering. He noticed the expressions on their faces then turned anxiously to face them fully. "Is there trouble Shaver? Margreg, are ye alright?"

Patric and Margreg exchanged knowing glances then released the breath they'd been holding before chuckling. "What's funny?" Finn asked. He flung his knife into the tree trunk before climbing over it.

Patric smiled. "There's nay a thing wrong. I just…."

The hum of the object sailing through the air then the thud as it landed caused Patric to fall silent. Finn stood stone still for a moment before slowly sinking to his knees. His eyes were wide from the shock of the blow and he opened his mouth as if to say something. Margreg reached him in time for him to come crashing down atop her. "Finn!" she cried, pulling the dagger from his back to cause a geyser of blood to pump furiously from the wound. She held her hand over it, trying to stem the flow as she called to him again, "Finn. Come on now. Speak to me."

Patric's heart sank with the scene that unfolded before him. Time seemed to slow to a crawl as he lifted Finn's body from Margreg so she could minister to him but in the end the captain closed his eyes without uttering a word as death claimed him.

"Please, Finn," Margreg sobbed, burying her head in his neck. "Don't leave me now."

Patric slowly moved forward to lift her from Finn's body but suddenly he heard the rustle deep in the woods. He turned toward the sound that seemed to be coming closer then drew his sword before running forward.

The tears streamed down his face as he searched the woods aimlessly, viciously slashing the undergrowth only to come up empty then he fell to his knees and sobbed.

Throdier held his breath for fear that he would be found out then silently cursed himself for not having another weapon handy. He took a moment to assess whether or not he could use his advantage to take the Shaver down without a blade then decided that it would be safer to wait. After all, it would be easier to kill him now that he had one less guard watching his back.

CHAPTER 31

▼

Tara, Ireland: Seven hours to midnight, 1, September 1002 A.D.—The raven circled overhead as thousands of people gathered within the walls of the ancient fort of Tara to celebrate the coronation of the high king. There was breeze enough to lift the hair and swirl the cloaks of those gathered as their attention was given to the high priest who stood before the ancient stone of Fal.

Legend had it that the stone was connected to the underworld where the fairies of the Tuatha daDannan clan now resided. It would scream out when Ireland's true king stepped upon it, marking a renewed alliance between the people and the fairies.

Brian stood beside Gable, his hair blowing in the wind while his purple cloak whipped behind him. Kormlada stood beside him, dressed in gold from head to toe. She held Donchad in one arm while she entwined her other hand with Brian's. She issued a tiny wink to her husband before he stepped upon the stone.

The cry that rang out was crisp and clear, echoing through the air like a battle horn. Brian threw his arms up then raised his eyes toward the heavens. Kormlada called out, "People of Eire, behold yer one true king, Brian Boru macCennitig."

The event caused such a stir that Brian's guards were forced to hold back the throngs of people eager to lay hands on the new king. It took the better part of an hour to regain control. When they did, all attention was drawn to the raised platform just east of the stone.

Murchad and Patric stood upon the platform awaiting the crowns that would name them Ri Ciocids north and south. Behind them stood no less than one hundred men, mostly Gall, who had sworn their allegiance to Brian. Havland was among them.

Lara stood in the audience with Saroise in her arms. The child squirmed away from Eilis who was standing too close. "Step back a bit, aye," Lara barked at Eilis. She took both Saroise's hands in hers. "I don't know why ye two must choose this moment for yer foolishness but I for one would rather listen to the priest then act as yer go between."

Eilis wrinkled her nose in distaste before heeding Lara's command. Since she, Margreg and Gertrude had gone to live in Cavenlow Saroise had become a thorn to her, always whining and crying to have whatever object she happened to be holding at the moment. She slipped the apple from her pocket then held it up so Saroise could see it. She took a huge bite then rubbed her belly mockingly as the sweet juice ran down her chin. Saroise's eyes went wide. "Mama," she whined. "I want an apple."

Lara turned her attention from the platform where Murchad had just begun taking his oath then screwed up her face at Eilis. "Put that away, aye. Ye know she'll be wanting it. Why do ye have to tease her so?"

Eilis lowered her head then moved to Margreg's other side seeking protection from her mother. Margreg scowled at Lara before returning her attention to Murchad. He was as handsome as his father, all decked out in blue and gold while his dark hair glimmered in the sunlight. She took a deep breath as her pride swelled for having been part of the army that gained him his crown then she looked up to Finn. "We did it, husband. The high crown is ours. Ye should be proud."

Eilis frowned at her mother. Margreg's habit of communicating with her dead husband as if he were still alive was unnerving in the beginning, but now it was just plain embarrassing. She turned her attention toward the white wisp of cloud her mother was addressing and wondered for a moment whether or not Finn could see them. Deciding that he couldn't, she took another bite of her apple before returning her attention to the platform.

"I want the apple," Saroise cried again as she squirmed out of Lara's grasp to tug on Eilis' lein. "I'm hungry."

"Here," Eilis blurted, shoving the apple into the child's hand. "Ye can have it if ye shut yer mouth."

"Mama," Saroise whined again. "She ate my apple."

"Och," Lara issued before marching over to take the child by the hand. She rounded on Eilis. "Ye know better than to show her something if ye haven't got one for her too. Now she'll be nagging me until I get her an apple of her own." She ripped the half eaten apple from Saroise's hand to shove it into Eilis' then marched off in search of a vendor to satisfy her daughter's whim.

Margreg looked down at her daughter with the scolding fast on her lips but when she glimpsed the expression on Eilis' face she burst out laughing. "She's an evil little rot, aye."

"Which one, the mother or the child?" Eilis countered. They both laughed.

"Hush now," Gertrude whispered from her place beside Margreg. She thrust her chin toward the elder Dal Cais woman who was scowling at them. "We don't want them to hear us speaking ill of kin."

"As if they don't do the same with us," Eilis snapped back, returning the old woman's scowl then sticking out her tongue for emphasis. The woman huffed loudly before turning away. Eilis smiled. "Their tongues are constantly wagging with their hateful words about us."

"Well, all the same," Gertrude replied through the false smile she was offering the offended woman. She shrugged her shoulders hopelessly then scowled at Eilis for effect. "Ye don't need to be bringing trouble on us. 'Tis a grand day and it shouldn't be spoilt by bitter words. We owe that much to the Shaver."

Eilis huffed with the truth then turned around and stood on tiptoe as she scanned the crowd for Njord. She'd not seen him since their departure from Torshav but heard he might be present in honor of Havland's oath taking. Patric had tried to coax him into doing the same but he refused saying he'd never swear loyalty to a clan that allowed a murderer to be counted among them.

She thought of Turlog then spit on the ground as her hatred swelled. She never liked the old man much, but to know that he was the reason that Njord would never become Dal Cais was enough to make her wish him dead.

"Pay attention now," her grandmother called with an elbow to her rib. "The Shaver's up next."

Margreg looked around to see if Lara had returned then huffed when there was no sign of her. It didn't surprise her that the woman would miss her husband's coronation in deference to her child's whims. She was wrecking the lass with her indulgence. The monster Saroise was becoming was the proof of it.

She returned her attention to her cousin who stood regally as he prepared to take his oath. He was glorious in his ruddy lein and golden fur trimmed coat—beams of sunlight glimmering in his clear blue eyes. He held his head high and his posture quite erect while he listened proudly to the recitation of his bloodline. Then he rested his hand on the hilt of his sword before bending his knee to receive his crown.

"Ye should be proud, Finn," she called out to the heavens. "Yer brother has brought us great honor this day."

Gertrude turned to look at her daughter. She could see the tears brimming her eyes and stepped up to embrace her. She held her close to her bosom then sighed, "It's ye who should be proud, Margreg. Ye did well by them all."

That statement drew a flood of tears and Margreg laid her head upon her mother's shoulders to finally release her grief. She'd not cried since the moment of Finn's death, worrying that she didn't have the right to grieve for him since she couldn't save him. "I miss him so," she sniffed with a wipe of her nose against her sleeve. "Will the aching ever cease, mother?"

Gertrude remembered the death of her own husband many years ago. Unlike Margreg and Finn, their marriage was negotiated for the sake of peace but still the same she cried when she lost him. "It'll pass," she cooed hoping it would be as true for a marriage made in love. "But ye must stop whipping yerself for it, aye. There was nay a thing ye could do for him."

Margreg's back stiffened with the reminder of her failure and Gertrude pulled her closer. "It was God's will, woman. Though I know ye to be stubborn, even ye can't argue with Him."

"I could've tried," Margreg sobbed then hung her head.

At that moment Gertrude stepped back from her, taking her by the shoulders so she could look into her eyes. "Ye did try. Ye may not remember it, but the Shaver told me how hard ye worked to save him. Ye did what ye could and now ye must leave it alone."

Only bits and pieces of the moments before Finn's death survived in Margreg's memory. She'd been spending so much time trying to piece them together that she was neglecting to live her life. At length she nodded when she realized that Finn would have wanted her to go on. She let her mother stroke her face bringing a fresh stream of tears.

"Come on now," Gertrude issued as she took Margreg by the hand. "Let's pay our respects to the man yer husband revered most. It'll do Patric good to see ye. He grieves nearly as deeply as ye do." She took Eilis with her other hand and they all made their way to the platform, pushing through the crowd surging against them.

Havland stepped to the edge of the platform. He had taken his oath as a Dal Cais earlier in the morning along with a thousand other Vikings who had come to join the new Ard Ri and now he awaited his wedding. He smiled at Niamh who was bedecked in a rose lein and matching shawl then bent his knee so she could hear him over the din of the crowd. "Where are the lads?" he called down to her. "I've not seen them since the oath taking."

"They've gone to get us a wedding present," she replied, standing on tiptoe to see over the man who had just pushed in front of her. "They'll be back in time for the wedding."

"I should hope so," Havland responded then he turned to accept the good wishes being offered by another man who came to lean against the platform. When he released the man's hand, he noticed a familiar form moving through the crowd and his eyes went suddenly wide. "Shaver," he called then elbowed the new Ri Ciciod to gain his attention. "As I live and breathe. I believe yer son has come to join us."

Patric followed Havland's finger to the vendor booths then drew breath as he recognized Njord in the distance. He held young, Tyr, against one hip while Saroise held his hand. Lara walked beside them, engrossed in conversation with Ermagh. "I thought ye said he wouldn't come." Patric stated as the sadness he'd been feeling all day was suddenly lifted.

Njord's trip to Man did little to mend their relationship. Though he was pleasant enough when he was in his father's company, there was a strange coldness between them. Patric had hoped to convince Njord that the best way to exact revenge against Turlog would be to join the clan and ascend on his own, but the lad sent word through Havland that he would neither swear the oath nor be in attendance when his father took his crown. "I wonder what changed his mind," he sighed as he followed Njord's progress through the crowd.

Havland wondered too. He had spent quite a bit of time trying to make Njord understand how important it was for him to swear to the clan but as always, the earl was too stubborn to listen. The only thing that seemed to interest the lad was the fact that Havland was planning to marry. He issued a tiny "humph," when it occurred to him that Njord was there out of loyalty to him rather than Patric. He tried to cover it up. "Ye're his father, Shaver. He must have realized what an ass he was being and decided to offer ye his blessing."

As much as Patric wanted to believe the words he knew Njord was the least likely person to have an epiphany. He grabbed Havland's arm as a thought suddenly occurred to him. "Ye don't think he's here in search of Turlog, do ye?"

Those words were enough to make Havland shiver. He stood on tiptoe, peering over the many tents and wagons in search of the Thomond Ri Tuath. If the man were there, no doubt Njord would find him and put an end to him. "I don't see him just now," he reported, his voice thick with his own anxiety, "but ye never know when he might turn up. 'Twould be best if we kept the lad with us, aye."

"Aye," Patric agreed then skittered sideways to get a better view of his son.

"What are ye searching for?" Eilis inquired while tugging on Patric's lein.

He opened his mouth to answer but Havland reached down to pull her up onto the platform. He pointed in Njord's direction. "It's yer sweetheart, aye. I guess he missed ye."

Eilis' heart leapt as she watched Njord move through the crowd. He was carrying Tyr who busied himself playing with the beads dangling from the end of his father's warrior braid. She sighed when she realized that the child was as beautiful as Njord.

"I see he still has the power to take yer breath away, lassie," Havland whispered against her ear. "Or is it the fact that I'm standing so near that's causing ye to struggle for air."

"Leave off her," Niamh scolded before swatting at his shin. "She doesn't need an old goat like ye teasing her so."

Eilis ripped her gaze away from Njord long enough to flash Niamh a smile of gratitude. "Go to him," Havland urged. "Ye know ye want to. Don't let his sow of a wife give ye cause for concern. She's as nasty as the day is long. She gave him the son he was after. He has no further use for her now."

"If ye keep it up, Havland," Niamh chastised while shielding her eyes from the sun, "ye'll be spending yer wedding night sleeping alone."

That was enough to have Havland jump from the platform. He slapped her full rump before issuing her a bruising kiss. "If ye don't wish to spend my wedding night with me that's one thing," he crooned, "but I can assure ye I won't be spending it alone."

"Ye're a beast," she chuckled as he kissed her again then he led her away with his arm around her shoulder. "Ye should go to him, Eilis," he called back in all seriousness. "He'll be glad to see ye. He hasn't stopped talking about ye since ye left Torshav."

Eilis' heart pounded so loudly that she was sure everyone else could hear it. She turned to look at her mother and Gertrude who were locked in conversation with Kormlada then she looked to Patric. He seemed to be in a world of his own, staring at his son with no care for the goings on around him. She sidled toward him until she was close enough to clasp his hand. She looked to him and he smiled.

"I've missed him too, lassie," he offered then lifted her hand to kiss her knuckles. "Perhaps we should go and tell him so, aye." She nodded shyly before moving forward so Patric could help her down from the platform. Then hand in hand they made off to greet the man they both loved.

It didn't take long for them to reach Njord who was now conversing with Havland. Patric stood behind him, waiting to draw his attention. It was Tyr who noticed the southern Ri Ciocid. He lifted the silver ring from Patric's head and began to gnaw on it.

"Och, lad," Njord scolded. He pulled the ring from his son's hand then handed it to Patric. "My forgiveness, father. It seems that he believes everything belongs in his mouth."

Patric chuckled then pinched the lad's cheek. "Ye're a braw one alright, take after yer da."

"Don't say it too loudly," Njord whispered. "His mother has a thought that he might just be an angel. I don't want to disillusion her, aye."

The memory of Njord as a child flashed through Patric's mind and for a moment he yearned for those days again. He opened his mouth to state as much to Havland when he suddenly realized why his son had come. "So ye've come to see the great bachelor married, huh. 'Twas good of ye to travel so far for him."

"And look how far he traveled to see me married," Njord replied. He absently swung Saroise's hand. "I should say it's the least I could do after all he's done for me."

The stab of jealousy was like a blow to Patric's gut. He covered it by adjusting the silver ring on his head then struggled to think of something else to say. When nothing else came he turned his attention to his daughter. She was clinging to Njord like a leech. Patric tweaked her cheek then smiled. "So what do ye think about Njord's wee laddie? He's bonnie is he not?"

"He smells bad," Saroise whined while pinching her nose between her fingers.

"Aye," Njord agreed with a chuckle. "I'm afraid he's messed his nappy. We'll have to give him another one, aye."

Saroise continued to pinch her nose then wrenched herself from Njord's grasp to skip away into the crowd. "Ye come back here, lassie," Lara called before chasing after her but the child was too quick. "Eilis!" she cried, "don't let her get away."

"Eilis," Njord blurted when the comely woman darted out from behind Patric to chase after the child. He smiled. "Speaking of bonnie, aye," he offered with a nod of his chin in her direction. "I don't envy ye the task of making plans for her. Ye'll be needing a big stick to beat back the lads."

Eilis grabbed Saroise by the wrist then dragged her back to her mother. The little wretch stomped on her toes and it was all Eilis could do to stifle the curse brewing in her throat. She looked up in time to see Njord staring at her. Her cheeks flushed as she bent a knee for him. "I'm happy ye came, earl," she stated before casting her eyes toward the ground.

"So, it's like that is it?" he replied with a bow from the waist. "I didn't think we would be so formal but if it's what ye prefer then I'm glad to see ye too, princess."

Ermagh issued a "humph," before ripping Tyr from her husband's hands. She'd seen enough of their affection while Eilis was in Torshav. She had no desire to witness it again. "We should tend to yer son, lord," she growled, pushing past both Patric and Eilis with Tyr dangling from her arm. "He's no bed of roses as he is just now."

"Ye go on," Njord replied without looking at her. He took Eilis by the hand. "I'm sure Lara will let ye use the Shaver's hut to tend the child."

Ermagh tapped her foot as she leered at him but he paid her no mind. He was eager to know how Eilis was holding up. Following Finn's death, he'd spent every moment he could with her, hoping to ease her grief—and perhaps some of his own. In the end he knew it wasn't enough. "Are ye well then, Eilis?" he inquired looking deep into her eyes.

"Aye, Njord," she replied. Her cheeks flushed for the way he was looking at her. "The Shaver's been good to us."

Njord looked to his father whose eyes also expressed his heartbreak over Finn's death. "Finn was a good man. We all miss him."

"Aye," Njord agreed. "I can't tell ye how many times I've started off in the direction of his chamber to seek out his counsel before remembering that he's gone. It still seems unreal to me."

Eilis tried to pull her hand free of Njord's grasp so she could wipe the tear rolling down her cheek but instead he wiped it for her. "It's alright to cry for him, lassie. I do it all the time."

Ermagh continued to stare at them while the heat swelled within her. It was clear her husband would always share a bond with the lass but she needn't witness it. Lara noticed her chaffing and stepped forward to take her arm. "Come, Ermgah," she commanded before tugging her forward. "Let them have their time together while we settle Tyr and Saroise down for a nap."

"Fine," Ermagh huffed. She began to storm away but before she got too far she called over her shoulder, "Ye shouldn't be long, Njord. There's something I'd like to say to ye."

Njord waved her off without looking at her then lowered his head to offer Eilis the words he hoped would comfort her. "When I take my revenge on Turlog, it'll be for the both of us, aye."

She looked up at him intently and Patric's heart skipped a beat. If his son believed that his vengeance against Turlog would also serve the lass, there was nothing that would stop him from getting it. He watched them as they chatted and suddenly it was as if Njord was a stranger. His visit to Man had changed him greatly—not only in the way he looked but also in the way he thought and acted.

"Will ye speak with me a while, son?" Patric asked as he touched Njord's shoulder. "I've a thing or two I'd like to say to ye."

Njord ripped his attention from Eilis who he managed to get smiling with a funny story about Tyr then looked at his father with solemn eyes. He knew what it was that Patric had to say but he didn't feel much like hearing it at the moment. "Aye," he finally offered with a nod of his head. "I'll speak with ye on any subject except Turlog."

"But we must speak about it," Patric retorted, urgency lilting his voice. "Ye can't just murder the man. Why can't ye get it through that stone head of yers that the best way to avenge yer parents would be to rise within the clan?"

Njord's eyes flamed with the statement. He pushed Eilis behind him then placed his toes against his father's so he would tower over him. "No matter if I meet the man on the battlefield or cut his throat in his bed, there'll be no murder only revenge."

"So yer mind's made up?" Patric asked, stretching his neck to look into his son's face. "Ye'll not even give me the benefit of hearing me out?"

The tension growing between them was so thick that Eilis could feel it from her place behind Njord's back. If Njord murdered Turlog he would be an outcast amongst the Dal Cais and both Patric and Havland would be forced to turn against him. She might never see him again. She laid a hand on his arm then let it slip down to his silver bracelet so she wouldn't become unnerved by the touch of his skin. "Please, Njord," she sighed, drawing his attention to her, "give the Shaver a chance to work this out. I couldn't bear to see ye outlawed."

His rebuke was quick on his lips but when he looked into her eyes he realized something that he hadn't thought of before. She had spent her whole life being scorned by her clansmen because her father was a traitor. Though he was fully prepared to bring such scorn upon himself, he wasn't prepared to have his son suffer it. Being named an outlaw and a murderer would bring shame upon Tyr, the same type of shame Eilis was forced to live with. He hung his head with the realization that he had nearly destroyed his son's life then lifted her chin with his open palm. He took a moment to look deep in her eyes, silently conveying his gratitude.

"It'll be as ye ask, *m'millish*," he whispered before lowering his lips to hers.

Her knees grew weak and a tingle ran across her belly as both her arms came up around his neck. He drew her close with his hand in the small of her back and she molded herself against him. It was a kiss like none he offered before and for a moment she wished she could die right there in his arms. Njord felt the moan escape her throat and it took all his determination to push himself from her before he lost control.

He brushed the stray hair from her forehead then turned with his arm around her waist so they were both facing Patric. "Lead the way, Shaver," he stated, struggling to tamp down the desire the lass had stirred in him.

Patric looked from Njord to Eilis wondering how that simple kiss could have changed his son's mind but he wasn't one to look a gift horse in the mouth. Instead of questioning him on it he simply stated, "Let's have a cup and find a place to sit while we speak. Whatever it is that the lass did, I think she deserves something for her efforts."

"Many thanks, lord," Eilis replied, her voice a bit shaky. She wasn't certain what had just happened but she would give anything to have Njord continue walking along side her with his heavy arm resting on her waist.

They purchased a skin of mead from a vender then strolled up the rise to sit in the shade of an oak tree. Eilis was entertaining them with her account of the day her mother was chased around the stable by a bad tempered stallion when Brian caught their attention with his call. "Alas the good son returns," he shouted before making his way up the slope with Donchad in one arm and Kormlada clinging to the other. "I'd say it was about time ye got here though I'm sore ye didn't come for the oath taking. Am I to believe ye'll be shunning us then?"

The bulging vein at the side of Njord's neck revealed his struggle to restrain himself. He stood then bent his knee for Brian. "If ye don't mind, Ard Ri, I'll leave that explanation to my father. I would, however, like to offer ye my congratulations. It's grand that ye've taken the crown. With Murchad and the Shaver at yer side, I've no doubt that Eire will be kept safe."

The smile Kormlada wore while assessing the handsome earl was just enough to reveal the tips of her white teeth. She moved her eyes over him, taking in his dynamic proportions and the strong slant of his chin. It was clear by his well muscled arms and his flat belly that he kept in good health and she wondered if it was battle training or lovemaking that made it so.

Brian followed his wife's gaze. "I don't believe the two of ye have ever met, aye."

"Nay," Kormlada responded, her voice deep and husky. "Who might this young warrior be, husband?"

"'Tis the Shaver's son, Njord the Black, earl of Torshav. He's just returned from Man."

Brian noticed the slight flush of Kormlada's cheek and he patted her hand with force enough to warn her against what she might be thinking. "He's a handsome one, don't ye think? As I recall, he has the ability to have women line up to offer him their innocence. But I should caution ye that his new wife is quite protective of him."

"Och," Kormlada issued before offering Njord her hand. Her skin tingled when he took it and she turned her head toward Brian to offer, "There's nay need to caution me, husband. I've all I can handle with ye." She stroked Donchad's head. "Not every man can issue a child to a woman of my years. I'd say I'm fortunate to be the wife of one who can."

Patric stood silent as he watched Kormlada weave her web. It was apparent from the expression on Brian's face that her words had done their job in soothing his ego. It was also apparent that they did little to dissuade his son who seemed to be leering at her like a cat stalking a mouse. "So, where are ye off to then?" he called to break up the situation. "I would've thought ye'd be tied to yer throne all day with so many leaders gathered. Are we to believe the affairs of Eire could be settled simply by yer taking the crown?"

"Och," Brian issued before releasing his son into Eilis' care where it seemed he wanted to be. He straightened his lein as he turned to face the Shaver. "If only it were that simple," he grumbled. "They've a list as long as both me and Njord put together but I'm putting off hearing it until the morrow. I'd prefer to enjoy this day unmarred since we've waited so long to achieve it. Their business will keep."

Patric nodded his agreement then took the opportunity to prove his loyalty to his son. "I notice Thomond isn't represented by it's Ri Tuath," he stated before taking a sip from his cup. The statement drew the complete attention of both Brian and Njord. "What will ye do with yer uncle?"

Brian drew breath as the question he'd been hearing all day again touched his ears. Murmurs about Turlog's treachery had been traveling around the country like a plague. "I don't know," he finally sighed then placed an arm around each of their shoulders. He hung his head as he spoke, "There's no denying that something is terribly wrong with Turlog but I can't quite put my finger on how best to address it. My wife believes I should call him to Tara once the clan leaves. I may just do it. What say ye, Shaver?"

Patric smoothed his cropped beard before looking up at the Ard Ri. It was the best opportunity he would have to warn Brian against his uncle. He chose his words carefully. "I'd say that if ye're going to meet with him ye best have a guard at the ready," he sighed. "My mother tells me that he hasn't been in his right mind lately. I wouldn't want to see him unleash on ye."

"Hmph," Brian offered as he considered his words. Next he turned to Njord. "And ye," he asked as he lifted his head just enough to look into the earl's eyes, "what advice can ye offer?"

"Kill him!" Njord blurted without needing the time to think it over. "'Twould be best for ye to start off with a clean slate rather than have rumors of yer uncle's treachery flying around the country. I say kill him and show those of us who care that ye'll not tolerate such behavior—especially from yer own kin."

His eyes searched Brian's looking for any sign of the Ard Ri's thoughts but when he saw nothing other than cold blue orbs staring back at him he continued, "If ye do this thing I can guarantee that every Gall in the region will swear to yer clan."

"*My* clan?" Brian stated without changing the expression on his face. Though he didn't show it he was quite sore that the lad refused to take his oath. "Are ye not one of us then?"

Unable to keep his disappointment for Brian's inaction from his eyes, Njord shifted his gaze. "I can't," he blurted. He paused for a moment, taking control of his emotions before looking back at him. "So long as Turlog still carries the Dal Cais colors, I'm unable to wear them."

"Ye'd let one man keep ye from yer destiny?" Brian questioned angrily. He didn't even try to keep the disappointment from his voice. "Yer father is the Ri Ciocid now, Njord. Ye have a responsibility to him as well."

"My responsibilities are torn between two families and sometimes I think I'll go mad trying to figure out which one I should be serving."

Patric stepped forward, hoping to ease the tension between the two men but Njord continued to speak. "I'll give ye this Ard Ri." There was a desperate lilt in his voice. "If ye cast Turlog out and let me take my revenge on him for killing my parents, I will swear to ye and be forever by yer side."

Njord's belief that Turlog killed his parents wasn't news to Brian. In fact he had begun to believe it himself. But he needed to show the lad that the best way to handle such things was within the clan structure. "I'd be more willing to give ye that opportunity if ye had sworn already," he countered flatly. "Many here have benefited from my uncle's actions. Do ye seriously think they'll accept ye over a man of his station?"

"Are ye telling me that I must take yer oath before ye'll take my word?" Njord barked as desperation turned to anger.

"I'm telling ye," Brian whispered so that Njord would have to strain to hear, "that much has transpired since ye've been away, lad. In Desmumu I laid down an edict that any Gall who didn't swear to the Dal Cais when asked would be considered an outlaw and taken as hostage. If yer interest in me starting off with a clean slate is true then I suggest ye swear now so I won't be forced into doing something I'd prefer not to do."

Patric drew breath then looked to Njord who stood silent for a time. His hands trembled with anger. Swearing to the Dal Cais while Turlog was still alive would dishonor his family. If he didn't swear he'd be taken as hostage, disgracing himself as well as his son. "How long will ye give me?" he asked when he finally regained control of himself.

"One season," Brian replied. "If ye've not sworn by then ye'll leave me no choice."

Njord nodded bitterly and Patric quickly placed a hand on his forearm to draw his attention. "It's for the best, son. When ye swear, we'll be able to convince the council that yer story is true. In the end ye'll have yer revenge."

Njord's lip twitched in anger and Kormlada watched him with interest. He reeked of both power and ability and she could sense the danger in him. If he did swear to the clan she was certain that it would only be a matter of time before he gained a foothold in the pecking order of the hierarchy. "Njord," she called, pulling the young man's attention to her. "My husband said ye were in Man. Who do ye have there?"

"My mother, Freyja and her husband, the earl Brodir," he replied without really looking at her.

She offered a "humph," then turned her attention from Njord to Brian. Though she was eager to know the man's mind she decided that now wasn't the best time to do it. "Husband, why don't we continue our walk now? Ye said yerself that ye'd be leaving business until the morrow. Give the young earl some time to digest yer words while we spend our time together."

Brian turned toward his wife, wondering what information she had taken from the answer other than what was obvious. He momentarily returned his attention to Njord. "I think she's right, aye," he offered with a wink of his eye. "We'll speak of this on the morrow."

Njord agreed then watched as Brian descended the slope to be enveloped by the crowd below. Eilis, who had been more intent on keeping Donchad entertained then following the conversation, moved to Njord's side, looking up in wonder for the somber expression that suddenly appeared on his face. "Ye all right?" she asked as she touched his arm.

"He'll be fine," Patric issued. Things hadn't gone exactly as he planned but he was certain that once Njord had time to think the situation over he'd come to realize that his only option was in joining them. "He only needs time to consider his future."

He took her hand to twirl her about as the distant music was carried to them on the wind. "What say ye to having a dance, aye? I'm suddenly of a mind to move these old feet." He led her down the rise and she looked over her shoulder to Njord who was leaning against the tree. He looked so sad that her heart ached to be near him but she was left with little choice as Patric pushed her through the crowd to the circle of dancers now gathered before the platform where the musicians had taken up residence.

Njord looked over the crowd as his fingers kept time with the music then, deciding that it was too noisy for him to think there, he made his way down the rise to purchase another skin from the mead vender before climbing the stairs to sit atop the glistening wall of Tara.

He remained there most of the day, watching the festivities below become more raucous. The sun sank slowly in the sky, casting colored bands of red, purple, orange and gold across the deepening blue background. He lifted his head to see it and suddenly realized that he was very drunk. He rested his head against the cold stone on one side of the wall as he pressed his feet up against the other before falling blissfully asleep.

He dreamt he was kissing Eilis. He could smell her perfume and feel the light wisps of her hair as it fell around his face. He embraced her gently, laying his hands across her back to pull her close to his chest as the sweet taste of wine was given to him from her tongue. He felt himself stir.

She undid the laces of his leather breeches with practiced dexterity and for a moment he wondered where she learned such things but the thought was quickly lost when she took him in her mouth. The warmth of her was sheer heaven and a smile broke across his face to know that the one he loved most had grown into a woman who could please him so thoroughly.

His head was lolling on his shoulders from the mead and his pleasure and he pressed it forward so that he could see her while she made love to him, but when he forced his eyes open he saw a wealth of blonde hair cascading across his lap.

Though his mind told him to push her away, his body became a slave to her movements and all at once he shuddered as she brought him to climax. His heart was pounding and his hands trembling when she lifted her head to reveal herself.

He furiously sucked air into his lungs before his mouth moved to release the name that came out more of a groan than a word.

"Kormlada."

She looked long at him, boring into his soul with her piercing green eyes as if she was taking the energy directly from him. Then she brushed her sleeve across her swollen red lips before rising to her feet. She took a moment to straighten her lein then gathered her hair into her hand to inspect it for debris before tossing it back over her shoulder. It dangled down her back, nearly brushing her heels as the moonlight caused it to glisten. She turned to smile at him. Then, without uttering a word, she walked away leaving him to wonder if it *was* a dream.

CHAPTER 32

▼

Dublin, Ireland: The great hall—High noon—18, October 1002 A.D.—
Sigtrygg stood behind Maelmora while Gable read the names of his ancestors
marking him worthy to receive his crown. It was Kormlada who convinced Brian
that naming her brother Ri Tuath Ruire of Leinster and an ally of the Dal Cais
would irritate Malsakin while increasing his own power. Brian agreed readily and
now Maelmora beamed as he bent his head to receive the brass ring. It had been a
long time since a member of his line held it and he was proud to be able to
reclaim it in memory of his father.

Maelmora looked to his sister who was standing beside him, as prideful as he
was. He moved his lips to silently form the words, "Thank you."

She leaned in to kiss his cheek. "Didn't I tell ye that it would be yers if only ye
would listen to me?" she whispered in his ear.

"Aye, ye did," he replied once Gable had completed his task. "Ye're an amazing woman, sister. I wonder what more ye may have up your sleeve."

She looked toward the crowd in search of the man she was certain would play
a role in gaining her further power then nodded confidently when she spotted
Njord. "I think ye must wait and see," she cooed.

She broke from him to search for Brian. The Ard Ri was off to the side of the
platform speaking with Murchad regarding the latest siege to hit Osraige. When
he noticed her coming he opened his arm to invite her into the conversation.
"Murchad was just telling me that Cellach macDiarmait has been slain. It seems
Throdier of Orkney has found an unnamed ally to begin a campaign of his own.
Murchad thinks it might be Turlog but I'm wondering if it couldn't be Malsakin.
What say ye?"

She leaned into her husband's embrace while she looked Murchad over. The man had never accepted her marriage to his father or his younger brother making their relationship adversarial at best. Though her senses told her that Turlog was most likely the one assisting Throdier, she dared not agree with Murchad lest it gain him Brian's favor. "It could very well be Malsakin," she stated, narrowing her eyes at Murchad. "It only makes sense since he was the one who brought Throdier to Desmumu."

Murchad's lip curled. Kormlada's opinion carried great weight with the Ard Ri but he wouldn't be intimidated. "Nay," he stated with conviction. "Rolo called Throdier to Desmumu, not Malsakin. I'm telling ye, father, our uncle is moving against us and we best do something about it."

Brian traded his glance between Murchad and Kormlada as he tried to assess which one was most invested. They both seemed to be guessing. While striking Malsakin would be an easy decision, striking his uncle would require precise political maneuvering to keep peace within his clan. He looked away from them and into the crowd hoping to find a solution in the endless sea of faces surrounding them. When he noticed Njord speaking with Patric, a plan began to form in his mind. "Let's wait a while to see whether Throdier will strike again. If he does, we'll move on him. In the mean while I want ye to gather as much information on Turlog as ye can, Murchad. Set up spies in Thomond if ye think it will help us gain the information necessary to march on him. While ye're at that I'll do a little spying of my own."

"Hmph," Kormlada issued as if to say it was a waste of time but in the end she smiled at her husband as he placed his arm around her hip to lead her off in the direction of Njord and Patric.

They had traveled to Dublin alone, deciding that this event wasn't one that warranted the uprooting of their families so soon after returning from the Fair of Tailtan. Instead both men left their families in Torshav under Havland's watchful eye. Though he hadn't made a final decision yet, these days Njord had become more open to the idea of swearing to the Dal Cais. Patric's many toasts to urge him on found them both in their cups by the time the Ard Ri approached.

Brian smiled when he joined them, envying them their freedom to enjoy the feast without being strapped by the need to attend their women. "I believe Dublin boasts the best mead of any city in the land," he cooed before taking the cup from Patric's hand to drain it. "Ye better be careful not to get too drunk or ye'll be pulled into the competitions before ye know it."

Patric nodded slowly, fearful that any quick movements might cause him to vomit. "'Twouldn't be the first time for either of us," he replied with an elbow to Njord's ribs. "My son here could best any man in the city."

"Perhaps," Njord replied, trying to hide his drunkenness. "But I think the long ride has left me too weary to get into them today."

"Really?" Kormlada sighed. "As strong as ye are I wouldn't think ye ever needed to take yer rest."

Njord was sobered by her presence and the memory of the dream he had in Tara. He cleared his throat before replying, "I've been known to nod off when I've taken too much mead. Though it's a bad habit, sometimes I have the most pleasant dreams."

The corner of her lip lifted ever so slightly as she took his meaning but instead of continuing with the banter she turned to Brian to ask, "Will ye dance with me, husband? We've not danced together in such a long time. I'm feeling a bit neglected."

Brian pulled her close then touched her nose with the tip of his finger. "If it pleases ye to dance then dance I will." He bowed to Patric and Njord. "Excuse me while I satisfy my wife's desire. When I return there's a thing I'd like to discuss with ye."

He led Kormlada onto the dance floor where they were quickly swallowed into the crowd. Njord followed them with his gaze, silently cursing himself for the jealousy he was feeling. Of late Kormlada had been consuming his thoughts. In fact, he only came to Dublin with the hope of seeing her again. But with his life a tangle of oaths and petty battles, the last thing he needed was to be getting into mischief with the high queen. He looked away, wondering whether or not he could help himself.

He caught the eye of Sigtrygg's wife, Sabdah who was watching the festivities from her place just outside the ring of dancers. She nodded her salutation to him and suddenly a thought occurred to him. "Will ye excuse me, father?" he asked, already halfway across the room before Patric could answer.

He took Sabdah's hand in his before bowing to her husband. "Well, Sigtrygg," he offered, interrupting the earl's conversation with Maelmora. "It seems ye're more interested in business than dancing with this lovely wife of yers. I was wondering if ye wouldn't mind my asking her to accompany me?"

"Not at all," Sigtrygg replied jovially before leaning down to kiss Sabdah's cheek. "Just be careful of him, aye," he whispered loud enough for all to hear. "There's a rumor floating that he's been a student of Brodir's sorcery. I wouldn't want him to change ye into a snake."

Sabdah smiled appreciatively at Njord before returning her husband's affection. "Snake or nay, I think I would enjoy dancing all the same."

She followed Njord onto the dance floor where they broke into the line in time for the jig to be called. Their fresh bodies moved energetically amongst the others who'd been worn out from their previous dances and soon they were left to dance with Brian and Kormlada alone.

The next song called for the trading of partners and when Kormlada fell into Njord's grasp she whispered, "Will ye meet me on the top of the wall? I've a thing I'd like to speak with ye about."

Surprised by the request, Njord only smiled at the high queen before returning her into her husband's arms. There was a strange look in Brian's eyes when he did and Njord offered him a weak smile, hoping that his guilt didn't show on his face.

Other couples joined the dance for the next tune. Brian and Kormlada retired but Njord and Sabdah continued on until finally she patted her chest and huffed, "I pray ye to take another partner, lord. 'Tis clear that ye have tremendous energy. I shouldn't want to hold ye back from yer enjoyment."

Njord smiled and the dimple in his left check flashed. "I draw my energy from ye, fair lady," he panted. He too was exhausted but dancing was keeping his mind off Kormlada. "I shall return ye to yer husband only if ye promise to seek me out when ye're in the mood to dance again."

She smiled for the compliment and Sigtrygg rose to help his wife to her seat. Her skin glistened with moisture and her cheeks were flushed giving her an attractive glow. "I see ye managed to escape his spell," he sighed as he nodded his chin toward Njord. "I'm happy because I've grown quite fond of ye with all yer appendages, aye."

She gave him a tiny shove then pulled her lein away from her sweating chest to cool herself off. "I think he *was* working a spell," she panted before resting her head against her husband's shoulder. "My legs and arms are so weak I fear I may not be able to dance until the new moon."

"Good," Sigtrygg blurted. He liked dancing least of all things and was happy that the earl's efforts would relieve him of those duties for the evening. "I owe ye a debt of gratitude, Njord."

"It's I who owe ye, Sigtrygg," Njord replied then bent to kiss Sabdah's hand. "Yer wife is utterly charming. I'd be happy to act as her partner whenever she may call."

"So long as we're speaking of dancing then ye may have yer wish," Sigtrygg replied with a wink of his eye. He waved the maid over to bring his wife a cup. Njord took one also then excused himself to search for Patric.

He wandered leisurely through the crowd, taking his time to consider the many faces enjoying the festivities. When he came to the steps leading to the Dublin wall he noticed Patric speaking with Brian in an alcove just beyond. Though he knew he should join them, he was curious to know what Kormlada wanted from him. He took the steps two by two until he came to the top of the wall.

Unlike Tara, Dublin's wall was wide, fitted with alcoves and benches where guards could take their rest. He slowly walked the expanse hoping to find Kormlada hidden in one of the nooks but when he realized she wasn't there he took a seat and silently chastised himself for his weakness.

As he sat in the alcove sipping from his cup he couldn't help but wonder what it was that brought him there. Certainly Kormlada was a great beauty, but so was Ermagh—and he for one had never been the type of man who would let desire drive him to the exclusion of rational thought. No, it was more likely the power Kormlada could provide that made him act the way he was. Power to control his destiny as well as the destiny of his enemies. He had witnessed such power with Brodir. But while Brodir had the ability to call down his gods it cost him greatly to keep them happy. Njord knew he could never live such a life so he resigned himself to leave that place before he did anything that would bring Kormlada's ire down on him.

Grateful for his decision and eager to make his escape, he stood to leave. When he did his attention was drawn to the faint footfall growing nearer. His stomach gripped and he set down his cup on the bench before edging himself from the alcove.

Kormlada was heading right toward him. She was looking over her shoulder to be sure she wasn't being followed so she didn't see him at first but suddenly she stopped then turned toward him.

All rational thought left him in the moment that their eyes met.

She gasped when Njord dragged her into the alcove. He entangled his fingers in her long blonde hair then forced her head up so she could see him. There was a hunger in him, an animal need that drove him past all reason. She saw it and reacted.

He ravished her mouth and she pressed her body close to his. Her strong arms massaged his back until finally she ripped his coat from his shoulders then threw herself atop him. In that moment he knew there was no hope for escape.

*   *   *   *

Torshav, Ireland: Two hours past noon—24, October 1002 A.D.—Saroise threw herself on the ground then sobbed uncontrollably. She wanted to ride the horse but that terrible Eilis wouldn't let her. She begged Havland to give her a turn but the warrior refused.

"Come now, Saroise," Lara huffed as she struggled to lift the child to her feet. "That horse is too big for ye. When we get home ye can ride yer wee one, aye."

"I want to ride the big horse," Saroise cried, wriggling from her mother's grasp to again throw herself on the ground. "It's not fair that Eilis gets to ride when I can't."

"Hmph," Margreg offered before marching forward to try reasoning with the child. She'd had all she could stand of Saroise's tantrums and she meant to show Lara that a firm hand could control the child. "That horse belongs to Eilis," she issued in a voice tempered with authority. "It was a gift from her father before he died."

Saroise stopped crying long enough to screw up her face. Margreg was mean and never let her do what she wanted. She pushed herself to her knees then wiped her hands against her lein before getting to her feet. With hands on hips and a fierce growl low in her throat, she marched the few paces necessary to stand directly before Margreg. "I want the horse," she blurted then drew back her foot to kick the woman square in the shin.

"Why, ye little rot!" Margreg blurted, hopping on one foot while trying to rub the pain from her leg. "Ye're a monster is what ye are!"

"Margreg!" Lara barked. She shielded Saroise whose face was buried between her legs. "How can ye say such things about a child?"

Margreg could feel the blood boiling in her veins. She had heard Lara say much worse about Eilis when she didn't know she was listening. She had never called her on it for the sake of peace but now she let go with an explosion. "The way ye spoil that child it's a surprise that she isn't worse than she is already. Everyone says ye're too lazy to take the time to teach her the proper way to act."

Lara's eyes glowed with her anger as she prepared to do battle with the ungrateful woman. If it weren't for *her* generosity, all three of them would be fending for themselves instead of living grandly in Cavenlow. "Ye're the least likely one to give advice about how a person should act," she spit then pushed Saroise back behind her. "I'd sooner take child rearing instruction from a dog than a whore such as yerself."

Eilis sat upon her horse holding her breath as she watched the vein at the side of her mother's neck throb with anger. Havland chuckled. "I'd say *that* was a big mistake."

The words had barely left his mouth before Margreg sailed forward to land squarely on top of Lara. She pummeled her about the face and neck but eventually the other woman got in a few blows of her own. They were a tangled mass of hair and cloth rolling to and fro, cursing as they did their best to beat each other to death. Saroise stood nearby sucking her thumb.

Havland chuckled again then leaned back against Eilis' horse, arms crossed so he could enjoy the competition. But just as it was beginning to get good, Niamh appeared.

He spit on the ground before moving forward to break them up. She would kill him if she knew he was doing nothing other than watching.

"Come on now, the two of ye," he called as he took an arm in each of his hands to try pulling them apart. "Is this any kind of example to be setting for yer lovely lassies?"

"What in the name of the Lord are ye doing?" Niamh called out to the women before rushing forward to scoop Saroise into her arms. "Have ye gone mad then?"

Lara stood up slowly, spitting the dirt from her mouth as she held the ends of her torn lein together to protect her modesty. Margreg, on the other hand, nimbly shot to her feet before pushing back the mass of thick hair that came to rest over her face. They looked at each other, their chests heaving with exhaustion but neither one spoke as Havland held them apart at arms length.

He smiled at his wife then nodded his head at the two women. "So, tell me again how we *men* have a penchant for war."

Niamh scowled when he reminded her of their conversation over whether or not he should have ridden with Njord and the Shaver to Dublin. He had insisted on staying behind to mind the fort but she tried to convince him that there wouldn't be any need since no trouble would break out among women. Now she was made to eat her words.

"Never mind," she huffed then stepped in closer to better assess the damages they had inflicted upon one another.

Margreg had a huge gash running down the side of her eye which she was certain had been caused by one of Lara's fingernails. Lara's eye was beginning to swell shut.

"I can't believe the two of ye," she chastised after deciding that they would both survive their wounds. "What in heavens name started all this?"

Each woman hung her head in shame leaving Havland to answer the question. "I believe they were speaking about the gentle art of child rearing," he blurted, winking his eye at Margreg. He held the same opinion as she did about Lara and was certain she would've gotten the best of her if he hadn't been forced to stop the fight when he did.

"Is that so?" Niamh sighed before handing Saroise to her mother with a cluck of her tongue. "Well, I should say that ye've set a grand example for yers rolling around on the ground like a pair of cats. I might expect as much if ye were rearing lads but to do it in front of the lassies."

She offered another cluck at Margreg before turning on her heel to head for the kitchens. "Come on now," she called over her shoulder. "Why don't ye let me draw some water so we can clean ye up?" She disappeared through the door.

They heard the rise and fall of her voice as she relayed the story to Ermagh, Gertrude and Hecca who had been working in the kitchens. In a moment, all four of them appeared in the doorway, clucking their tongues and shaking their heads as they moved forward to claim their own.

Ermagh and Niamh flew to Lara's side while Gertrude and Hecca tended Margreg. Then they made their way back into the house leaving Tyr sitting alone on the path playing with some object he found lying on the ground.

Eilis noticed him and dismounted. She raced forward just in time to keep him from putting it in his mouth. "Let me see that?" she called as she took the flat stone from him. "Ye shouldn't be putting things in yer mouth. Ye could choke."

She took the stone from him then flung it into the grass. Tyr chuckled then picked up another stone. He was about to place it in his mouth when Eilis scolded, "Bad laddie." She gently smacked his hand.

All at once she was on her back as the crack of Ermagh's open palm fell across her face. "Don't ye ever lay hands on him again," she bellowed before scooping Tyr into her arms.

"Ermagh!" Havland shouted. He rushed forward to lift Eilis to her feet. "She was only minding the lad for ye. He was putting the stone in his mouth and she was afraid he would swallow it. Ye should be thanking her instead of abusing her as ye just did."

Ermagh looked at the young woman who would have her husband. She was growing lovelier with each passing day. It would only be a matter of time before she was fully blossomed. Then she was certain that Njord would never be away from her.

"Leave off my child," she issued, her eyes filled with hatred. She turned on her heel to head for the kitchens but before she did she called over her shoulder, "And while ye're at it, ye can leave off my husband as well."

*   *   *   *

Torshav, Ireland: Four hours past noon—26, October 1002 A.D.—The band of warriors sang an uplifting tune as the gates of Torshav came into view. There were twenty of them in all and each had taken full advantage of all the best Dublin had to offer. The supply wagon was well loaded with the orders placed by their wives, lovers and children. It rocked to and fro as it rolled up the slope of road leading to Njord's keep.

"Halt," Vahn called to the driver as he noticed that the rear wheel had nearly jumped its axle. He dismounted then bent to check it.

"What is it?" Patric called, looking over his shoulder with a sigh that their travels should be halted when they were so near.

"Just in time," Vahn replied then he kicked the wheel back into place. "'Tis a good thing we're home. This wheel wouldn't have lasted much longer. Broke a pin." He held up the splinter of cracked wood for Patric to see.

"Well, leave it behind and we'll come back for it," Njord snapped, jerking his chin toward the gate. His overwhelming regret for his infidelity with Brian's wife was beginning to fray his nerves.

"No need," Vahn answered. He wiped the dust from his hands before mounting his horse. "It'll hold together until we get inside."

Relieved that at least one thing was simple, Njord nodded then led the way through the gates and up the road to the great hall.

Almost immediately upon their appearance, the round fort began to buzz with welcoming cries from children and family members. Saroise led the way, scurrying around the wagon then leaping into the Shaver's waiting arms as he bent a knee for her.

"Daddy's home," she cried before shoving her hands in his pockets in search of treasure. "What did ye bring for me?"

Margreg raised an eyebrow at Havland who had been walking beside her. They both chuckled and Lara glared at them when she took their meaning. She rushed forward to scold the lass. "That's no way to greet yer father, Saroise," she huffed then patted the child's rear with intention. "He's been riding for days and must be quite weary. Ye should ask him how he enjoyed his trip rather than looking for a gift for yourself."

Surprised by her statement, Patric lifted his head to inquire where this sudden penchant toward discipline came from but when he did, his eyes went wide.

"Jesus Christ, Lara," he issued. He took her by the chin to better assess the black eye she sported. "What did ye do to yerself?"

"'Twas Margreg," Ermagh blurted, pushing her way past the gathering crowd to stand beside her friend. She was eager to relay the story so that her husband could finally see that *those* women were as much trouble as she professed.

She stopped to retrieve the ball of twine Tyr had thrown into the road and Patric huffed, "Margreg?" He looked askance of his cousin who came up behind Lara sporting her own assortment of bruises. "What the hell happened here?"

Njord looked to Ermagh who opened her mouth to say something but when he realized she only wanted to stir the pot, he covered it with his own.

She was breathless by the time he released her. He patted her rump before warning, "If ye didn't have the courage to be in it at the time then I suggest ye keep out of it now, aye. It wouldn't do ye justice to be sporting all those pretty bruises now would it?"

She huffed at him then pushed against him trying to escape. But he held her tight around the waist, yanking her hard to ensure her silence while Margreg and Lara prepared to relay the story.

Margreg stepped past the crowd gathering around the wagon to give her cousin the explanation he sought. "We fought over the children, Shaver. 'Twas nonsense really. We're both sorry for it."

"Nonsense was it?" Lara huffed as she bent to scoop up the ball Tyr had thrown down again. She held it out so Saroise could return it but the child kept it for herself, rolling it along the road with the stick she picked up from the grass. "I should think that the Shaver might have a problem or two with ye calling his daughter a monster," she continued, folding her arms beneath her breasts and tapping her foot as she awaited her husband's reaction.

There were murmurs from the crowd as they began to take sides in the altercation. Margreg rolled her eyes with the realization that she would be their entertainment for the evening. "I didn't mean it, Shaver," she retorted, eager to be done with it so the crowd wouldn't have anything else to gossip about. "The lass kicked me in the shin. The words came out before I had time to think."

"That seems to be a continuing problem with ye, Margreg," Lara scowled. She stepped closer, certain she had the support of all gathered. "I should think ye'd have better control over that loose tongue of yers after the shame it's wagging brought ye with Kevin."

Margreg's concern over making a spectacle out of herself evaporated with those words. She rounded on the woman, balling her fists and narrowing her eyes as she bellowed, "If ye're speaking about my daughter I should warn ye that I'm not beyond beating ye senseless for it."

Njord's total attention was on the argument. Ermagh shoved Tyr into his arms before marching forward to assist her friend against their common enemy. "Ye may as well face the fact that yer daughter is an issue, Margreg," she blurted. "Every chance she gets she's sticking her nose into business that doesn't concern her."

Gertrude, who came to stand behind her daughter, gasped that the woman could be so bold. But before she could offer her own comments she noticed Margreg draw back her arm to strike. She lunged forward, grabbing her by the wrist before the blow could be delivered.

"That's enough of this," she barked, struggling to pin Margreg's arm behind her back. "Let's go inside and let their husbands handle them."

At first Ermagh was startled by her near brush with violence but soon enough surprise turned to anger. Her eyes narrowed and she spit in Margreg's face. "Whore!" she blurted, "I should have put ye out days ago."

"Whore, am I?" Margreg replied, struggling to be free of her mother who had all her weight leveraged against her. When she couldn't free her arms she kicked out her leg, narrowly missing Ermagh because her foot got caught in her lein. "I'll show ye how much a whore I am, ye hoity bitch." She huffed then stumbled forward. "Come over here and I'll make ye eat those words."

Margreg's face was completely red and spittle trickled from the corners of her mouth as the vein in the side of her neck bulged from her restraint. Patric knew that look well enough to be frightened by it. She could easily commit murder when she was in such a state. He edged forward slowly as he held up his hand then gingerly stepped between them.

"Easy there, lass" he offered before placing his hand gently upon her shoulder. She wriggled away from him and he assessed the situation more thoroughly before trying again.

Gertrude had Margreg's arms secured tightly behind her back and he was fairly certain that her lein would restrain her from kicking her legs high enough to cause damage. He grabbed her again, this time more tightly, screwing up his face as he continued, "Don't ye think there's been enough violence done already?"

"Violence," she huffed, pushing against the open palm pressing against her chest, "These women don't know just how violent I can be, Shaver!"

With that she broke free of Gertrude then reached over Patric's shoulder to grab Ermagh around the neck. He stood full up to block her, catching the blow on his shoulder and wincing as it was delivered.

Obviously Margreg was dead serious about beating Ermagh and Njord took a moment to consider whether or not to let her do it. It wasn't until he realized that his son was watching that he moved in to save her.

"I thought I told ye to keep out of this!" he bellowed as he yanked Ermagh back out of harms way. "Ye've no business in this. Ye best keep back before *I* slap ye senseless."

Someone chuckled and Ermagh snapped her head around to leer at her husband. It was embarrassing enough to be accosted by the whore—she didn't need him siding against her as well. She narrowed her eyes at him. "I'll not keep...."

"Hush!" he barked loud enough to draw another chuckle then he turned his back against her to underscore his point.

Gertrude was red in the face as she again took hold of Margreg's wrists. She used all her weight to pull her daughter out of the road then shoved her toward the house. "That's enough now, lassie," she huffed when she gained the advantage but Margreg broke free of her again, stomping her feet to cause the dust in the road to rise up as she marched back to stand directly before the Shaver.

"Is this my repayment for tending ye during yer wars?" she blurted. She shoved her hands onto her hips then tapped her foot awaiting his response. "Am I to be treated like a common whore by yer wife and daughter in front of all these people?"

Knowing full well that this wouldn't be done until Lara apologized, Patric drew breath then let his eyes go soft. "Come now, Margreg," he cooed, praying that his soothing tone would ease her anger, "Lara didn't mean what she said." He turned to his wife then lifted his eyebrow in a silent message to follow along but it seemed the message escaped her.

"The hell I didn't!" Lara blurted, pushing past Hecca who had slipped in between them to use her girth as a barrier. "I've had all I can stand, Shaver," she spewed as she leveled her gaze against her husband's. "I want her out of my house! Ye owe her nothing and I'll not have ye treating her as if ye do. Leave her here with yer son! Let him care for her!"

That statement caused Ermgah's eyes to go wide. Before Njord could stop her she skittered around him, nearly tripping over Saroise who was swatting her ball from one side of the wagon to the other. She broke into the circle to have her say. "Ye can't be meaning to shove her off on us, Lara," Ermagh spewed as she poked her finger into her friend's chest. "We housed the whore and her little devil spawn long enough!"

"Devil spawn?" Margreg blurted, then she sailed forward to entangle her fingers in Ermagh's hair.

Ermagh squealed with pain as her desperate attempts to free herself only served to have Margreg's grip cinched tighter. When she finally broke free, a good portion of her golden tresses were missing.

"If ye ever speak that way about my daughter again it'll be yer neck that's twisted instead of yer hair," Margreg spit as she tossed the golden strands on the wind.

From his place beside the wagon, Njord could see the bald spot left in Ermagh's head and he chuckled to himself as he wondered how she would cover it up. Then he caught sight of Eilis who was standing beside her grandmother and the situation lost its humor.

Eilis' eyes brimmed with tears when she realized the hateful words being spewed were about her. She was old enough to understand what they were saying and the reason for it. It tore him up inside to know she would be made to suffer this abuse for the rest of her life.

He walked over to her then placed his arm around her shoulder so he could kiss the top of her head. Her arms came around his waist and she sobbed into his chest. All at once his anger ignited.

He pushed her back away from him then thrust Tyr into her arms. "Take him to the barn so that I can put an end to this, aye."

She nodded as she held the child close then turned on her heel to do as she was bade. "Stay there until I come for ye," he called back to her. She turned long enough to nod and smile then shifted Tyr's weight in her arms before making off to the barn.

When they were safely away, Njord marched forward to take control of the situation. He grabbed his wife by the hair then marched her toward the wagon. He gave her a shove and her eyes widened as she bounced off the running board. "I thought I told ye to stay out of this!" he bellowed then wagged his finger under her nose. "If ye move a muscle, I swear I'll thrash ye myself!"

He stormed off back in the direction of the altercation that had only paused long enough to be sure that Ermagh wouldn't be returning. "What needs to be settled here?" he inquired as he stepped between Niamh and Gertrude who seemed to be sharing a few words of their own. The women parted to allow him entrance and he glared at them as he continued, "Are ye still fighting over which of yer children is the most rotten or did ye move on to something more interesting?"

That statement drew a hearty belly laugh from Patric but when his son turned his glare on him he took a few steps back, happy to let someone else have their turn at playing Solomon. He leaned against the wagon on the opposite side of Ermagh then turned to Havland who came to stand beside him. "It's good to see ye in good health, Shaver," the Viking offered as he extended a hand to him. "Did ye have a grand time in Dublin?"

"Aye," Patric replied, shaking Havland's hand before returning his attention to the festivities. "But I dare say the competitions there were far less intriguing than the ones right here."

Havland turned back to the scene just in time to see Njord duck Margreg's blow as she tried to reach around him to sucker punch Lara. "I'll wager my best laying hen that the lass can take yer wife down."

"Och," Patric issued from the side of his mouth as Hecca stepped forward to scold Margreg for her bad manners. "There's no sport in that," he huffed then winced as Gertrude accidentally poked Niamh, who was trying to assist her, directly in the eye.

"Here's something," he cooed. His eyes turned mischievous. "I'll bet ye that Margreg can take down the lot of them—Njord included."

Havland leaned forward just long enough to see that the damage his wife incurred wasn't permanent. When she began screaming at Gertrude he resettled himself back into the negotiations. "Hmph," he offered, stroking his beard while trying to assess which of the many flailing arms belonged to Margreg. He watched as Njord stealthily ducked the blows flying around him. He was just about to take Patric's bet when Margreg landed a blow square on Njord's chin.

"Och," he finally issued, suddenly deciding Margreg *could* take them all down. He slapped the air before crossing his arms over his chest. "Perhaps we'd do best to leave the wagering for another time. I don't think it's proper for a man to be betting against his own wife."

Patric lifted an eyebrow as he considered the statement. It was unlike Havland to refuse a wager he thought he could win. He smiled smugly for his victory before settling back to watch the rest of the sport in silence.

With Njord's attention being otherwise engaged, Ermagh slid along the wagon to peer around the corner but jumped back when she saw Patric and Havland standing there. She cursed silently as Njord's broad shoulders blocked her view then stood on tiptoe to try to get a better look. She felt the ball of twine bounce off her heel then kicked it back behind her as she strained her head so she could at least hear what was going on.

"Where's my ball?" Saorise questioned as she tugged on her lein.

"Hush, child," Ermagh issued, waving her away. "I can't hear what they're saying."

"I want my ball!" Saroise whined then she bent down, noticing it was stopped just in the center of the road beneath the wagon. "Get it for me, Ermagh!" she demanded.

"I don't know where yer ball is, child," Ermagh replied, struggling to disengage the tiny fingers from her lein. "Go away now and leave off me."

"It's right there," Saroise cried, tugging harder to draw the woman's attention. "Get if for me, Ermagh. I can't reach it."

Realizing she'd have no peace until the child got what she wanted, Ermagh huffed then bent to get the ball from beneath the wagon. It rested just far enough away so it couldn't be grabbed from any side. "It's stuck," she sighed then straightened herself, clapping the dirt from her hands before returning her attention to the argument that was still raging.

"But I want it!" Saroise demanded again then she threw herself on the ground and began to cry.

"Och," Ermagh issued, wondering if Margreg wasn't right about the child after all. She screwed up her face before lifting her lein up to her thighs so she could try to reach the ball. She was on all fours, half under the wagon's floorboard but still she couldn't reach the ball. "Give me yer stick," she ordered as she reached her hand back behind her. "I can't reach it as I am."

"I lost it," Saroise replied then all at once remembered where she put it. She tore off to find it.

Worried that the argument wouldn't last much longer, Ermagh decided to crawl beneath the wagon rather than await the child's return. She laid flat on her stomach then shimmied forward with outstretched hands but was left short of the ball as her apron caught on a tree root protruding from the ground. She leveraged her foot against the wagon wheel then kicked forward to dislodge herself. All at once the wheel tilted and the wagon swayed precariously.

She heard the creak of the axle as the weight of the cargo shifted above her head. She tried to lift herself on hands and knees to move clear of it before it collapsed. Her heart pounded in her chest as the sound of cracking wood nearly deafened her then all at once the axle snapped.

With a thunderous crash the floorboards caved sending cargo rolling into the road. The mounting braces for the horses shot up into the air lifting the animals' front legs when they did. They pawed the air, snorting and foaming as their eyes rolled wildly in their sockets from their struggle to be free.

"Release the horses!" Patric yelled to Vahn whose head shot up with the noise. Then he moved forward to try to bring the braces level.

Realizing what was happening, Njord raced forward to assist Patric and Vahn but the horses were wild, rearing up against their harness making it impossible to set them free. He used his long sword to cut through the straps binding the beasts then called out to Vahn who was still struggling to unbuckle them, "By the Gods, man! Use your blade! It'd cost me more to replace the beasts then it would the harness."

All at once there was a flurry of blades as each man standing near enough sawed through a strap so the horses could be released. They whinnied and reared before galloping down the road toward the open gate. Then there was a flurry of running feet as men took off after them.

"Damn!" Patric spewed, looking over the ruined cargo. He caught sight of Lara who looked as if she'd seen a ghost. "Don't mind it," he said in an effort to put her mind at ease. She had a sickly look about her that made him nervous. "All's not lost."

"Where's the child, Shaver?" she asked, her voice trembling. "She was playing by the wagon when last I saw her but she's not here."

Patric's stomach gripped in panic and soon his expression mirrored his wife's. "Saroise!" he bellowed as he scanned the field in search of her, his heart thundering in his chest when she didn't come to his call.

Njord saw their concern and his own stomach gripped when he momentarily forgot that he had sent Tyr to the barn with Eilis. When he regained his control he moved toward the front of the wagon so they could jack it up to see if the child was caught underneath. He rounded the corner and found her sitting in the grass sucking her thumb.

"Saroise," he cried out while rushing her. "Thank the god's ye're safe." He scooped her into his arms then showered her head with tiny kisses. "She's alright," he called out to Margreg who had just made it around to the front of the wagon. "Tell the Shaver of it, aye."

Margreg smiled and nodded as she patted her chest with relief then turned on her heel to spread the good word. She stumbled over the ball of twine lying just beyond the wagons front wheels. As she kicked it away she noticed the streak of blood splattered upon it. "Njord come quick!" she blurted.

"What is it?" Njord questioned as he handed Saroise off to Patric who had just rounded the corner. He followed Margreg's gaze to the dark form lying beneath the wagon.

"Ermagh," he sighed then sank to his knees burying his face in his hands. The gods were already exacting their price.

CHAPTER 33

▼

Isle of Man: The Stables—Two hours past dawn—3 April 1003 A.D.— Ermagh's death was met with a ceremony nearly as grand as the one that celebrated her marriage. It was only right that she be buried in Man since it was there that people loved her most.

Njord spent his six months of mourning in the company of bards and scribes as each day brought a new poem or ballad singing the praises of the Danish beauty and the sorrowful earl she left behind. But the attention that was lavished upon Ermagh in death was only half that which was lavished upon her son. Being the only issue to come out of the great love between the earl and the princess, Tyr became the focus of many sagas.

The lad squealed as he scampered between his father's legs in an effort to escape the monster chasing him. Njord looked down and chuckled. He had to admit that Tyr was the smartest little lad he had ever known. He started walking at ten months and was already speaking words. He peered around the stall, sticking out his tongue at seven-year-old Jared who'd become his playmate and champion. Freyja and Brodir had taken Jared in after his parents were killed in a wagon accident making him an excellent companion for Tyr.

"Go easy there, laddie," Njord called out when his son scampered into Thor's stall. Though the stallion was of an excellent temperament, he was the largest of the lot and his long legs could easily crush the toddler. "Why don't ye go and find Hecca so she can give ye some sweets, aye?"

Tyr's round blue eyes widened with the mention of a treat and he quickly made his way toward the doors singing, "Hecca, sweet," as he went.

"Ye too," Njord told Jared in the Gaelic. It was his intention to teach the lad the tongue so he'd be better prepared to travel. "And take him by the hand, aye."

The boy nodded then spun on his heel to catch up with the child before he got away but as he passed through the door he slammed into Brodir.

"*C'raad ta aile?*" Brodir asked when he recovered the wind that was knocked out of him.

"*Na aile,*" Jared responded, rushing his explanation so Tyr wouldn't get too far ahead. "*Ta shin geddyn millish voish,* Hecca."

"*Mie,*" Brodir responded but as the lad began to race off he grabbed his arm to scold, "*Na roie, aye!*"

Jared nodded then spun on his heel again. As he was about to tear off, he remembered the warning then walked as fast as he could without breaking into a run.

Brodir shook his head then turned toward Njord. "*Eh ta mie guilley,*" he sighed.

"Aye," Njord agreed, pulling Brodir into the Gaelic. "He's good with Tyr though they both run around like they have hounds at their feet."

"I'm sure we were nay different at their age," Brodir offered then moved forward to rub Njord's shoulder. "I've a thing I'd like to speak with ye about."

Recognizing the seriousness in Brodir's face, Njord put down his grooming tools then pulled out a stool for the chief while he leaned against the wall. "Aye?"

Brodir lowered himself onto the stool taking more time than was necessary to offer his next words. Njord surmised that he was playing the Gaelic phrasing in his mind. He was a man of many languages but he always used his words sparingly, preferring not to say more than was necessary to get his point across.

"I've something to show ye," he said then took his hand from his pocket to reveal what seemed to be golden teardrops.

"What is it?" Njord asked. He stepped forward to take the objects being offered to him.

"Almonds," Brodir replied. "They grow in Italy."

Njord lifted an eyebrow in askance and Brodir popped one of the almonds into his mouth, using his teeth to crack the shell then peeling it back to reveal the brown seed. He held it up to Njord before returning it to his mouth. "Try one."

Mimicking Brodir's actions, Njord cracked the shell then tasted the sweet meat of the nut. "It's good," he offered, cracking another one just to be certain. "And what shall we do with them?"

"They're a gift from the Venetian doge, Pietro Orscolo," Brodir replied. "He's assisting the emperor, Basil to keep the Sarcens from the Dalmatian Coast."

Njord lifted an eyebrow as his mouth fell open. Basil was a crusader. Brodir was the least likely person to be taking part in holy wars. "Do ye plan to take the oath?" he questioned.

Brodir shrugged his shoulders. Pietro had promised him a high position in the church should they find success. He was considering it. "I'll make that decision when the time comes. For now it wouldn't hurt to have the emperor as our ally."

"I see," Njord stated plainly then his eye caught Brodir's and he knew what was expected of him. "When do we leave?"

The corner of Brodir's lip lifted ever so slightly as he rose from the stool. It was that which he was after. Now that he had it there was no need for further discussion. He patted Njord's shoulder before making his way to the door. "By the full moon," he called back then exited the stable.

A shiver of excitement ran down Njord's back as he wondered what he would find once they got to Italy. Basil was the cesar of the eastern empire who had been waging holy wars since anyone could remember. His primary focus was Bulgaria but he had been engaging alliances with others for lesser territories.

The Sarcens had a stronghold in Sicily and of late had been menacing the Dalmatian coast. Pietro needed access through Ellispontus in order to continue his trading. So it only made sense for him to seek alliances with notorious seamen such as Brodir to keep the waterway open.

There was talk that Basil possessed a magical liquid that, once ignited, couldn't be doused by water. They called it Greek Fire and it was said that the use of it brought Basil his victories. Njord hoped that the cesar was planning to share the weapon with Pietro.

He picked up his brush to continue grooming the horse as he wondered whether or not this offer to expand his power had anything to do with Kormlada. Though he'd only lain with her once he understood that no more than that had been necessary for Brian, Malsakin and even Olaf to be able to claim their prize. But Italy was far from Ireland and no matter how hard he tried he just couldn't manage to connect the two in his mind.

The horse whinnied and nudged him as the brush caught in his mane. Njord clucked his tongue apologetically before stroking his nose. "It'll be alright, laddie," he offered but in the end he wasn't so sure.

*   *   *   *

Thomond, Ireland—One hour past dawn—3, May 1003 A. D.—Turlog woke with a start but the creatures of his nightmare continued to gnaw at him.

He clawed at his legs, watching the black specks as they crawled down his calf to the under side of his feet. It was there they did the worst damage, constantly biting at him until he thought he'd go insane.

He leapt from his bed, raking his feet through the packed dirt floor in an effort to thwart the itching then he threw open the shutters. The light usually made them disappear. He heaved a sigh when it seemed to work then made his way to the pot to relieve himself.

Even as he stood there waiting he winced for the burning that was sure to come with urination. It had been going on for sometime and no herbs or cleansing potions worked against it. He cried out as the liquid passed from his bladder. When he was finished he collapsed on the bed.

"Turlog?" Grace called, poking her head through the window when she noticed the man's distress. "Are ye alright?"

Turlog waved his hand in the air but didn't open his eyes. "I'll be alright. It's worst in the mornings."

The room was cast in shadows but still she could see his naked form sprawled across the bed. At his insistence, they had taken separate chambers and hadn't come together in a marital way in several years. He'd lost a considerable amount of weight and his hair had begun to fall out, but most disturbing of all was the unnatural paranoia he had been displaying lately.

He had hidden it for some time but now it was blaring in that Turlog had nearly every servant in Thomond hung or beheaded for some perceived betrayal.

"Will ye come to breakfast or shall I bring ye a trencher?" she called when he seemed to stir.

"Go away from here," he snapped then he got to his feet, grumbling and growling as he made his way to the window. "Why do ye spy on me? What is it ye're after?"

She backed away just before the shutter closed then stood outside for a time listening to his continued ranting. There was no doubt about it, the chief of Thomond was terribly ill. Soon everyone would know of it.

*   *   *   *

Tara, Ireland: Four hours past dawn—30, May 1003 A.D.—The midday sun streamed through the long rectangular windows lining the walls of the great hall causing the golden thatch to glow against the whitewashed walls. Shadows moved along the colorful tapestries bringing their characters to life in a dance of light. Brian closed his eyes then held up his nose, taking a long whiff of the breeze being carried through the hall. He was uncomfortable spending time so far north but as Ard Ri he was forced to hear out the complaints and disputes brought to him from the many Ri Tuaths across the land.

There was a low din in the hall as men and women sat side by side along the many rows of benches forming neat columns on either side of the room. Larger than his other keeps, the hall of Tara resembled that of Cashel.

He took a deep breath before opening his eyes to level them against the messenger who stood before him. The news he brought was unpleasant but there didn't seem much that he could do about it. Since Malsakin's surrender there had been discourse among the many clans, mainly the O'Neills who denied Brian respect as they continued to mark him as a usurper. They were traveling the countryside engaging the leaders of smaller kingdoms in their attempt to remove him, offering tales of his incompetence and fueling worries that his relationship with the king of Dublin and the Leinster Galls was proof that the Vikings would soon return.

He chuckled without humor that a clan known for their alliance with the barbarians could be successful in spreading such false propaganda. But in the end he knew that it was exactly those types of actions that had won him the throne he now occupied.

He looked to his wife who was sitting beside him holding their son on her lap while she endeavored to shovel food into his tightly clamped lips. Their relationship had been strained as of late owing to her unreasonable jealousy of Murchad and her seeming infatuation with Njord. It showed in the way he leered at her. "Don't force it on him, aye," he snapped before slapping her hand down. He reached out to take the lad from her. "Did it ever dawn on ye that he might not be hungry?"

The anger that seemed to have taken up a permanent home just under Kormlada's skin erupted with the reprimand. "Don't ye take that tone with me, lord," she huffed before narrowing her eyes at him. He never bothered to hide his preference for Murchad over Donchad. Playing as if he cared was hypocritical at best. "Save it for yer men who grow lazy with the plentitude of yer newfound position," she barked, jutting her chin in the direction of the crowd. "It's them that's sapping the respect ye ought to be getting because they refuse to move on yer enemies."

His upper lip raised into a snarl as he prepared to lash out at her but in the end he bit his tongue. She was right and he knew it. The plague of skirmishes was now moving north, traveling like an illness causing people to think him weak. They weren't full out Viking raids but they were similar in that a band of marauders would besiege a village then relieve its owner of a few trinkets or heads of cattle before retreating. There was little death, and even less destruction, but still the same the actions were causing people to fly to the O'Neills in search of protection.

He rubbed the soreness from his head as he again ran down the names of the villages that had been raided. Try as he might he couldn't find any particular pattern. If he didn't know where they would strike next he'd be hard pressed to offer protection against the raids.

"I just don't understand it," he huffed as he pulled Donchad's head against his chest then leaned back in his chair. "The last time they raided a Viking village in the north and this time it's a Gael village in the south, but there's no way they could've traveled so far that quickly."

"Well," Kormlada huffed as she shined her fingernail against her lein, "Did it ever occur to ye that there might be more than one of them?"

"Of course it occurred to me," he barked before screwing up his face, "The problem is, there's only one of me."

She shook her head in disappointment, wondering if she should even offer the advice to help him protect his throne. No doubt he would lavish whatever he gained on Murchad, leaving Donchad to beg for scraps from his elder brother should anything ever happen to Brian.

She twisted herself in her chair then leaned in close to look into his eyes. At length she offered, "Perhaps ye should act as the aggressor then." He raised an inquisitive brow and she continued, "Why don't ye get these lazy rots off their arses and take them on a journey, aye?"

"And who exactly should we be marching on?" he snapped back in frustration. Though her counsel was usually good it had become inconsistent of late. He wondered if her age wasn't catching up to her.

"I didn't say ye need to march on anyone," she blurted, having adopted his habit of taking words quite literally, "All I said is that ye should go on a journey."

Again she jutted her chin toward the assembled crowd causing her silver earrings to dangle against her cheeks. "Most of them have spent the full cycle of seasons right here begging ye for assistance in things they should be capable of handling themselves and ye've indulged them. Now ye must gather them up along with their armies and march them around so that yer people can see how great ye really are."

There was a mischievous twinkle in her eyes making her look much younger than she was. In that moment he wanted to kiss her. He fought back the urge, choosing instead to stroke Donchad's hair as he weighed her words.

The one thing that couldn't be sapped from him was his ability at war. March-ing an army through the country would certainly remind his enemies that he was capable at bloody campaigns. A slow smile split his beard.

At length he gave in to his desire. He drew her close by the nape of her neck then pressed his lips firmly against hers until she groaned deep in her throat. "Ye're as brilliant as ye are beautiful," he sighed when he finally broke from her. "I'll take Sigtrygg and Maelmora along with me to show everyone that my alli-ances are a benefit not a threat."

It had been a long time since they laid together and the kiss only served as a reminder of their abstinence. Kormlada thought of Njord and the passion they shared then ran her fingernails against the skin of her husband's forearm, raising goose pimples in their wake. "Ye may want to go further than that," she cooed.

He shifted Donchad in his lap so he could get a better look at her. "Go on," he urged. "What is it that ye have to offer?"

"Why not call Njord back from Man so that he can stand with ye?" she stated plainly. "It's the Vikings that the people fear most of all. Having the son of a great Viking chief standing with ye may well end their concerns."

The mention of Njord ripped through Brian like a blade. She'd made little effort to hide her infatuation with the earl and he wondered what she hoped to gain by taunting him with it now.

He trailed his fingernails over her arm hard enough to leave red marks. "Doing that could buy more trouble than either one of us are willing to pay," he replied before looking around the room for the one thing he knew would hurt her as deeply as she had just hurt him. When his eyes alighted on the Byzantine beauty, he handed Donchad to his wife then rose from his chair. "Perhaps I should forget the whole thing and go to Basil instead. He's been after me to assist him with the Sarcens. I'd rather have a cesar indebted to me than have to pay Njord to come back from Man."

With that he stepped from the platform to exit the hall, cocking his head toward the woman Basil had sent to induce his help. She nodded politely, her dark eyes expressing her understanding for what he was asking of her. She stepped into his outstretched arm to let him lead her from the hall.

Kormlada watched after them, her own jealousy sparking to ignite an inferno in her gut. The Ard Ri should be made to pay for his action. She turned her attention to Donchad while she considered what that payment would be.

*   *   *   *

Sil Anmchada, Ireland: In the great hall of Doncha—2, June 1003 A.D.—Nestled in the Galty Mountains just south of Cashel, Sil Anmchada was a small Eaghonact village that had been captured by Cennitg decades earlier. It's current Ri Tuath, Doncha, returned to the ways of his ancestors as a result of Brian's bloody campaigns.

Turlog sat eyeing the man whose hair had gone thin enough on top so that the lamplight reflected in his head. His face was unremarkable, not handsome, not ugly, but he did have the straightest white teeth Turlog had ever seen.

"Brian goes to Rome to meet with the cesar," he blurted before plunging his mouth against the wide brim of his cup to take a sip. "He'll be gone most the year."

Doncha lifted a brow. "So, will it be Murchad overseeing things here or the Shaver?"

"The Shaver's gone with him," Turlog grumbled. "His Vikings as well."

"That's interesting," Doncha sniffed then took up his pipe to light it. "With all that's been going on ye would think Boru would be fearful about leaving Eire for such a long period of time. He must have great faith in that son of his."

Turlog thought of Murchad and his stomach clenched. How dare Brian give such responsibility to a lad while someone with his experience was overlooked?

"Faith can be shaken with bloodshed," he stated flatly, hoping that Doncha would take his meaning.

"Fladbartoc is doing fine," Doncha replied, drawing on his pipe to bring the heat. He released the smoke directly into Turlog's face. "He does what he must to gain his throne."

Turlog banged his hand on the table. "Well then, he had better do more than steal a few cows, aye. I don't know what's gotten into the man, raiding for trinkets as he's been. Have ye spoken to him on it?"

Doncha lifted an eyebrow. Though it was Turlog's opinion that obedience came with bloodshed, he believed that fear could be struck without violence. "I've spoken to him about stepping up his raiding but I don't believe ye're correct when it comes to the massacres. Sometimes the unknowing is better. Fear is a powerful thing."

"Damn ye Eaghonacts!" Turlog roared, drawing the attention of those gathered in the hall. "When will ye learn that the only thing people understand is blood? How do ye think Brian won the throne in the first place?"

"I'll thank ye to take yer seat, Turlog," Doncha stated, his voice calm and even. Turlog looked at him for a time before he obeyed. Doncha continued, "I said I would lend my men to do this thing but I won't have them taking part in murder. Killing in self-defense is one thing, but to do it as a display of power is something I won't abide."

Turlog's one eye went wide while he considered Doncha then all at once it narrowed. "Why do ye hate me?"

"Pardon," Doncha replied, sitting back in his chair as Turlog began to crowd him.

"Ye never really wanted to help me in this did ye? It's because I'm Dal Cais isn't it?"

His eye held a queer look that set Doncha's skin to tingling. He felt his hand tremble then swallowed. "I like ye fine, Turlog. Why do ye act this way?"

Turlog smiled then he covered Doncha's hand with his own. "I'm glad ye like me, Doncha. 'Twould be a pity if I had to kill ye."

*   *   *   *

Rome, Italy—The Basilica—Three hours to midnight—12, October 1003 A.D.—Brian sat regally beside the great emperor Basil as they both enjoyed the aria being sung for their benefit. His Italian was spotty at best but the singer performed with such passion that the story was formed through the lilt of her voice. Brian turned to the cesar and smiled.

Basil's father was an escaped Bulgar slave who was forced to serve the empire as a stable boy. His reverence for horses was so appreciated by the childless cesar that he was named successor to his throne. He served for many glorious years. When he died the throne was given to Basil and his brother to share. Since neither one was of the age to rule on their own the task was left up to their treacherous uncle. The uncle murdered Basil's brother and in turn Basil murdered him. Now the throne was his to rule alone.

Basil lived simply, choosing to forego the colorful dress of the hierarchy so as not to call attention to himself. The feast he had laid was delicious yet understated, with simple fruits, cheeses and wines to set off the taste of the lightly seasoned hens. There was no pig roasting on spits and no sweet meats or pies as there would have been in even the poorest halls of Ireland, but still the same it was delicious and Brian decided that if a man such as Basil could enjoy the simple pleasures then he was a man who understood what was truly important.

He turned to Patric whose fingers were fluttering as if he were conducting the singer's notes. "Ye were right to press me to come," the Ard Ri offered as he leaned over Patric's chair. "'Twould not do well to have Basil miffed with us. I smell great power from this man."

"He has control of half the world," Patric replied. "Ye could do worse than to have such a man as yer ally."

Brian offered an agreeable, "humph," then sliced cheese from the block to dip it into his wine. The taste of it brought a sigh from his lips and he leaned back in his chair to enjoy it.

He looked toward Margreg who was seated at Patric's left, her dark hair falling in waves down her back. Though she was smiling, her eyes held a look of sorrow. He guessed she was missing Finn. "Do ye think it was the best thing to bring her with us," he whispered in Patric's ear as he nodded his chin at her. "The march is hard for a woman without a husband to tend."

Patric shifted his gaze to his cousin who seemed to be enjoying the feast. He hadn't considered bringing her until she approached him on it. But once she did it made perfect sense. "It was her idea," he finally responded, turning to look into Brian's eyes. "It's for Finn that she wants to be here. She believes her presence will keep him with us. In truth, I think she may be right."

"But she can't go on like this," Brian retorted. "She should be remarried with a home of her own instead of traveling around with a band of warriors. She deserves better than that."

"But if she…." Patric words hung in the air when Margreg turned to glower at them.

"Do ye think I can not hear ye?" she questioned, leveling her gaze at the Ard Ri. "I'm sitting right beside ye yet ye speak as if I'm a piece of furniture."

The side of Brian's lip twitched then his grin split his beard. His eyes began to twinkle. "Forgive me, lady," he offered with a bow of his head. "I was discussing yer future with Patric."

"Aye," she replied, leering as if she were trying to see inside his mind. "I heard ye but I wonder why such things concern ye. I'm fine as I am. Is there a reason that ye wish to have me married off again?"

Patric noticed the glint in her eye and he leaned back in his chair so he wouldn't be in their line of vision.

Realizing that any answer he offered would be the wrong one, Brian squirmed before clearing his throat. "One of the senators inquired over ye earlier and it put me to mind of yer situation."

"I see," she offered. She nodded her head slowly then narrowed her eyes. "And what exactly is my situation, Ard Ri?"

Brian offered a boyish smile. "That's what I was discussing with Patric," he replied, hoping she wouldn't take offense.

"Well, in the future," she snapped, "I'd prefer any discussions about my—situation—be taken up directly with me. The Shaver has enough to think about besides worrying over whether I'm married or nay."

"Margreg," Brian began, eager to ease any hurt he had caused, "I only want ye to be happy."

With that her eyes turned soft. He could see the pain in them as she responded, "If that is what ye're after then I'm afraid ye may be disappointed. My happiness died on the day I lost my husband."

She turned away and he knew that she was crying. He stretched his arm so he could stroke her hand but Patric caught it, shaking his head in a silent message that she should be left alone. Brian withdrew then sat back in his chair to consider the situation. Basil's voice broke into his thoughts.

He turned toward the cesar who was speaking with a man of slight built but who wore the clothing of a warrior. By the medallion hanging from his neck it was clear he was a captain and from the look on his face it seemed the news he was delivering was grave.

Brian leaned into the conversation, hoping that he could understand what was being said by the expression on Basil's face but there was no hope for it. Basil was a man who kept his emotions under tight control. "Forgive me, lord," the cesar offered in Latin when he finally turned to speak with him. "It wasn't my intention to have my back against you but I fear the news my captain brings is not good."

Brian lifted an eyebrow to urge Basil on but the cesar returned his attention to his captain who continued with the message he had begun to deliver. Brian watched the man's hands move in a frenzied manner. His dark eyes expressed his concern. Brian turned from him when Patric touched his arm. "What is it? Do they march?"

Brian shook his head. "I'm not sure," he whispered from the corner of his mouth, "but by the looks of the man I'd say the cesar has a problem."

Again Basil turned toward Brian, this time a grave expression marked his face. "The Sarcens march on Bari. They killed the capitano and hold two thousand civilians hostage. They have sent word that they plan to kill one hostage for every day it takes me to bring my army to stand up to their challenge."

"Hmph," Brian offered before sitting back in his chair. The action was barbaric at best, blackmail at worst, but either way Basil would have no choice but to acquiesce.

"Do ye have troops in the vicinity?" he asked, looking deep into Basil's eyes to see his reaction as well as hear his words.

Basil nodded his head. "Pietro Orscolo is the doge. He has amassed a flotilla of foreign ships to assist him in protecting the Dalmatian coast. I expect they'll fight on land for him as well."

Brian nodded. "So then, what would ye like me to do?"

"Meet Pietro in Bari. I expect he'll need assistance handling these foreigners. I know of yer reputation with the Vikings. I'm sure you can make it clear to them what needs to be done. If we win this, Brian, you will have the undying gratitude of both myself and the Pope."

Brian nodded then translated the words the cesar had just given him to his men. Patric sat back with a sigh. "Ask him where these foreigners have come from."

Brian turned to inquire of the cesar and he responded, "Some are from Orkney, the rest from Man."

Patric didn't need Brian to translate that last bit. He understood the familiar names well enough. He took a sip from his cup then again sat back in his chair, wondering whether or not his son could have gotten dragged into this.

*   *   *   *

Venice, Italy—Onboard the ship of Brodir of Man—13, October 1003 A.D.—Pietro was a Venetian of extraordinary proportion with dark hair and eyes and a complexion so fair it seemed almost translucent. He held his back very stiff seeming formal in all things, but when he smiled it was as if all the humor in the world were captured in his eyes. He was quite demonstrative, moving his hands about chaotically as he spoke, always ready with a hearty slap to the back or a hug for a job well done. His troops were no different, celebrating and joking even under dire circumstances.

He had come aboard to inform Brodir that the Sarcens had taken Bari and that Basil was sending the mighty Brian Boru to take charge of the Vikings. Njord sat very still, watching Brodir intently to see how he would react to the news.

"Boru, huh," the earl stated, spitting the seeds from the pomegranate into his hand. "That's rich."

"Boru is a great leader, is he not?" Pietro asked with brows raised. "He has many Vikings under him in Eire. Should he not be in charge of them here as well?"

"Listen to me, Pietro," Brodir offered as he sat forward in his chair. "Boru is Gael and the ways of Eire are different than the ways of Man. You may place him over your other allies but the earl and I will take our direction from you. It would be too complicated, politically speaking, to have us answering to Boru. Do you understand?"

Pietro knew that Njord's stronghold was in Eire. The last thing he wanted was to be the cause of a problem for the man. He nodded his head. "It will be as you say, Brodir."

"And our tribute?" Njord asked in his impeccable Latin. "What will you give us when we win the day for you?"

"You will have lands in the south. Basil understands your actions to be loyal and he will want you to have a stronghold here."

"Only if we swear to the Catholic church," Njord added.

"Aye," Pietro replied, raising an eyebrow as if that had been understood all along. "Basil fights under the authority of the Pope. All those who hold title in his territory will be baptized."

Njord nodded his understanding and Pietro got to his feet with a smile. "Good," he cooed, slapping Njord's back then bending to kiss him on both cheeks. He did the same for Brodir. "We will sail on the day after tomorrow. We will meet Boru and his troops in Bari then we will lay waste to these Sarcens once and for all."

"Very good," Brodir replied, returning the doge's kisses.

They both watched Pietro depart. When Njord retook his seat he filled their glasses with the rich red wine the man had left behind. "So, ye'll be baptized then?" he asked of Brodir.

"Aye. Won't ye?"

"I don't know," Njord replied. "Patric tried to talk me into it years ago but something about it didn't sit well with me. I've always preferred to believe that Garrel's gods have been watching over me."

Brodir nodded knowingly. He had a strong relationship with his own gods, so much so that he had come to be known as a sorcerer in many circles. "I'd say 'twas a small price to pay to hold title to land on one of the busiest causeways in the world. I'll be baptized. Perhaps even make a home here if it proves to be worth my while."

"Ye'll leave Man?" Njord asked. He had never considered that as a possibility.

"Perhaps," Brodir nodded. "If I do, then ye shall keep it for me."

Njord thought about those words. Being named as Brodir's heir would certainly expand his power. Suddenly he was overwhelmed by the scent of Kormlada.

*   *   *   *

Bari, Italy—On the Margharetta Peninsula—20, October 1003 A.D.—
The Sarcen ships lined the southern side of the peninsula in the gulf of the Adriatic Sea. Pietro brought his allied ships down the Mediterranean where they lined the northern side. The terrain was like none other that Njord had ever seen before. Colorful flowers of delicate beauty climbed up the hills and rises glinting in the rays of the intense sun. Tall trees with a canopy of slender spear like leaves jutted up from the ground to provide shade. There were berry bushes everywhere. Italy was the land of water and sun with people as robust as the food that they offered.

They laid anchor just off the coast then made the two-day journey over land to meet their enemy. To Brodir's dismay, Njord found Patric almost immediately upon disembarking. The Viking earl marveled that in all these years Throdier hadn't managed to kill the man, but his bloodlust for the deed was lost long ago. He had Freyja and he had Njord. Patric no longer posed a threat for him.

They marched their regiments side by side. When they made camp on the first evening Brodir invited the Ard Ri and his men to join them. Brian leaned back in his chair sipping the robust red wine Pietro had graced them with. "I could grow accustomed to this lifestyle," he sighed, popping a cube of aged provolone cheese into his mouth to mingle with his wine.

"It's a far cry from mead," Njord agreed, choosing a slice of salted ham to savor. He looked to his father who seemed to be lost as he picked through the platters searching for food he recognized. "Will ye eat something, father?"

The stiffening of Brodir's back when Njord spoke the endearment was imperceptible. He reminded himself that the man was no longer a threat to him. "Try the fish," he offered in Gaelic before passing the trencher of brined octopus down to the Ri Ciocid. They had been conversing in Latin so that Pietro and his men wouldn't take offense but Brodir learned earlier that Patric and Margreg didn't have the tongue.

Patric's upper lip curled. "I mean nay offense, Brodir, but I'd prefer my food to be a bit less wiggly."

Brodir laughed at that. "Very well. Perhaps some bread then. It's wonderful when ye dip it in the oil."

Brodir demonstrated for Patric and the Ri Ciocid followed. He smiled and Pietro helped him to choose a mixture of olives, cheese and bread to heap onto his plate. "Like a true Venetian, eh," the doge crooned, slapping Patric on the back then looking for someone to translate his words for him.

Njord did the duty and Patric smiled at the doge. "Aye."

Brodir turned his attention toward Brian, assessing the Ard Ri through a measured stare. "I'd be lying if I said I wasn't surprised to find ye here, Boru," he offered in Gaelic. "I wouldn't have pegged ye as much of a traveler."

"I'm here for the same reasons that ye are, Brodir," the Ard Ri responded in the same language. Pietro looked for someone to translate.

Njord leaned in to explain that they were only exchanging pleasantries. Pietro nodded then returned his attention to Patric who was eating as if he hadn't been fed in a month.

Happy to see the Gael finally enjoying the fare, the doge placed a bit of salted cod on the Ri Ciocid's plate then motioned for him to take a bite. "Mangia," he said, making a shoveling motion with his hand to his mouth.

Patric took a suspicious bite of the fish then smiled. He rubbed his belly. "Mangia is good. Mmmm."

The doge laughed and seeing that the two were contented with trying to communicate amongst themselves, Brodir again addressed Brian. "My appearance here is for business purposes. I've ten ships that I plan to sail from the Dalmatian coast to Norway for the purpose of trade. Are ye telling me yer intentions are the same?"

"I misunderstood," Brian replied. "I presumed ye were here to setup alliances as I am."

"Aye, that too," Brodir agreed. "But my primary concern is business."

Brodir held out his cup for the serving boy to pour more wine then he popped a green olive into his mouth, working off the flesh before spitting the pit onto the ground. "If ye're seeking alliances I presume that yer reign isn't going too well."

The hair on the back of Patric's neck rose and he stopped eating long enough to look up at Brodir. But Pietro, who had decided to make the Ri Ciocid his pet, drew his attention with a pastry filled with greens. Patric took a bite of it then smiled as the sweet taste of garlic mixed with the buttery flavor of the pastry in his mouth. The expression on his face was sheer ecstasy and Pietro became so excited that he clapped him on the back hard enough to make him choke.

Brian and Brodir watched as the doge endeavored to feed Patric wine in order to clear his windpipe. When they were certain he was recovered, the Ard Ri replied to Brodir's comment. "Eire's location makes her a prime target for raiding. I'd prefer to make allies instead of enemies so that my people will no longer suffer. I'm sure ye can understand that since Man is in a similar position."

"Aye," Brodir agreed. "We've suffered our share of invaders throughout the years." He took another sip of wine then turned the subject. "Is it true that ye've taken Kormlada to wife and that she's born ye a son?"

Brian lifted a quizzical brow before recalling that Brodir had once been Olaf's man. "Aye, 'tis true enough. Bonnie lad. He's called by the name of Donchad."

"Good Gaelic name," Brodir replied lifting his cup. "Long life to him."

Brian accepted the blessing before taking a sip. "And ye, Brodir?" he asked. "Do ye have any sons?"

"Nay," the earl replied. "Freyja is barren. Njord will be my heir."

When Patric choked this time it was in earnest. Pietro pounded him hard on the back to dislodge the food but Patric scrambled to his feet before running from the tent. Njord followed. "Father! Are ye alright?"

"Aye," Patric gasped after coughing up the olive pit. He rested his hands on his knees in his effort to recover then all at once looked up to bark, "Damn ye! Why didn't ye tell me that ye were going to allow him to name ye heir?"

Njord hung his head. "It hadn't been decided yet."

"But ye suspected it was coming?"

"Aye. I thought that we'd have a chance to speak about it after dinner."

Brian poked his head out from the tent. He glimpsed the expression on Patric's face then went to stand by him. "Are ye alright, man?"

Patric nodded then cleared his throat a bit. Brian turned his attention to Njord. "I don't want to offend our host by staying away too long but I would like to say something to ye, Njord."

"Aye, Ard Ri."

"I understood yer returning to Man following yer wife's death but now things look to be a bit more permanent for ye. Be certain that this is the right thing ye're doing, aye. There's much at stake here and I suggest that ye seek yer father's guidance on the matter." He turned to Patric. "Speak with him, Shaver."

Patric nodded. It was more than advice. "Make my excuses to our host, aye. I'm going back to my tent."

Brian nodded then patted him on the shoulder. He stopped long enough to look Njord over, disappointment clear on his face. He clapped him on the back then shook his head before returning to the tent.

Njord followed his father back to his tent then took a seat while Patric paced in front of him. "'Tis bad enough that he has my woman, must he have my son as well?" he asked, wondering what he ever did to deserve this fate.

"Ye're the closest thing I have to a father on this earth, Shaver. Nothing will change that."

"So, is yer mind made up then?"

"Nay," Njord sighed, "but I was thinking 'twouldn't be so bad." Patric raised an eyebrow and he continued, "How can I swear to the clan while they continue to hold Turlog in high esteem?"

Patric opened his mouth to protest but Njord held up a hand. "Hear me out, father. Put yerself in my position. Can ye honestly tell me that if the rot brought harm to yer family ye wouldn't move heaven and earth to seek yer revenge?"

Patric looked at him for a time before hanging his head. "I would do it."

"I know ye would," Njord replied, his eyes going soft as he prepared to make his case. "We both know my temper so ye must agree that I've been good about this whole thing. I understand about the clan and Brian's edict so I've done my best not to bring shame on either of ye but if I return to Eire I'll have nay choice other than to march on Turlog. Every day that I live without taking my vengeance is another day that I lose a bit more of my honor. Up until now I've been able to make my excuses to myself, but if I return to Eire, I'll be duty bound to take action. Now which would ye prefer?"

Patric's hands shook with the desire to put an end to Turlog so it would be over with once and for all. "He's dying, ye know."

Njord lifted an eyebrow and Patric continued, "Turlog. He's quite ill. My mother wonders whether he'll last another season."

"If ye ask me, he's lasted too long already."

Patric nodded. "If ye accept Brodir's offer is there a chance that ye would return to Eire after the turd is gone?"

Njord lowered his eyes as he struggled with the decision over whether or not to confess to his father all the things affecting his decision.

"Njord?"

"There's a thing I need to speak with ye about," Njord mumbled, still unsure of whether or not to say it.

"Go on," Patric urged. He wasn't sure why but a feeling of dread gripped him.

"The high queen has decided to make me her pet."

"Jesus Christ," Patric huffed, wiping his hands over his face before sinking down onto a stool. "I pray ye to tell me that ye didn't give in to that."

Njord hung his head and Patric had his answer even before the words were spoken. "I didn't have much of choice in the matter. She came to me when I was drunk. I gave in before I realized what she was doing to me."

"God damn her," Patric spit. He always knew the woman would be trouble for them but he never expected this. "Ye don't plan to be continuing on with her?" he asked, the expression on his face teetering between terror and anger.

"It seems that power lays solely within her hands," Njord replied, shrugging his shoulders in surrender. "I fear that she's as powerful as people say."

Patric was the least likely one to believe in fairies but he would also have never believed that his life could have come to this. "It mustn't continue," he barked, rising from his chair to stand before his son. "It's the one thing Brian won't tolerate."

"I'm sure of it," Njord replied, shame showing on his face. "But there may not be a choice."

Patric looked long at him, suddenly unsure of what he was up against. At length he placed his hand on Njord's shoulder then heaved a great sigh. "Ye must take Brodir up on his offer, son. If ye're in Man, perhaps she won't be able to work her magic. I'd rather have ye whole and living far away than have yer head separated from yer shoulders for the wretched woman's whims."

Njord nodded his agreement but in the end he wasn't certain that distance alone could keep Kormlada from gaining her whims.

✳   ✳   ✳   ✳

Dublin, Ireland: The solarium—20, October 1003 A.D.—Kormlada luxuriated in the softness of her new horsehair filled chair. It was covered in a rose silk she purchased from one of the merchant ships in the harbor. Maelmora looked down at her before turning his gaze to the expanse of window. "I don't know what ye hope to gain by this except yer husband's ire," he huffed, hanging his head and sighing over the fact that his sister could never be contented to leave well enough alone. "As I recall, ye moved heaven and earth to get this man to marry ye and now ye're going to drive him away."

"I'm not going to drive him away, I'm merely going to teach him a lesson. His son isn't capable of running the territory and I don't want ye to suffer for it. It only makes sense that ye gather the Galls to share yer hospitality. They're under yer control more so than Murchad's. A simple feast to encourage good relations makes perfect sense."

"That I agree with ye on. It's the fact that ye want me to keep Murchad unawares that has my hair standing on end. I can garner the same respect if he were with us—more perhaps. If I make him the guest of honor they'll understand that I have his support in all things that I do."

"Wrong," she huffed. She shined her fingernail then picked a bit of crud out from beneath it. "Ye know as well as I that Harald checks everything he does with the Shaver. He hasn't accepted ye as Ri Tuath Ruire and unless ye show him that ye're capable of acting on yer own, he'll never accept ye." She threw her legs down then lifted herself from the chair to join him. "This is the best way and ye'd be wise to heed me on it. Show them yer power and generosity so that they will come whenever ye call."

He looked at her for a moment then brushed the hair from in front of her eyes. "What is it with ye, sister that ye can't be happy with what ye already have? 'Tis a most disturbing trait."

Her eyes went narrow. "And what is it with ye that ye never know good advice when it's given?" she snapped back, grabbing him by the wrist then brushing his hand aside. "What will it take to have ye do as I say without question? Why must ye always fight me on things when it's yer future I worry over? I wonder if ye realize how useless yer life would be without me to help ye along."

His back stiffened and anger flooded his eyes. It was true that without his sister he would most likely never have reclaimed his throne, but the price for her assistance was the deterioration of his ego and an almost total abandoning of his free will.

He turned from her, his hands balling into fists as he stepped into a shadowed alcove. "Very well, sister," he drawled. "I'll do this thing as ye say but I have a condition that I want to place on it."

Her sculpted brow shot up with curiosity. "And what would that be, sweet brother?"

"That ye act as my hostess for the evening."

She swallowed at that. Acting as his hostess would remove her ability to deny knowledge of the event should Brian take exception with it. She thought about it for a moment. "Won't yer new wife take offense at that?"

Whether she did or not, it made no difference to him. He'd rather suffer her chattering mouth than be hung out to dry by his sister. "She hasn't the ability to entertain such men. Besides, she fears the Galls most terribly. It wouldn't do to have them offended, aye."

Realizing she was beaten, Kormlada drew a breath then stepped forward to rub a well-manicured thumb over his chin. "Very well, brother. I'll act as yer hostess and when I do, ye'll watch me carefully. It's about time that ye learned how to handle a Viking."

His stomach dipped. There was something other than her agreement in those words.

✻   ✻   ✻   ✻

Bari, Italy—On the beach of the Margharetta Peninsula—22, October 1003 A.D.—Njord's toes curled around the sand resting in his shoe as he looked to the line of Sarcens forming up before him. They were covered in cloth from head to toe and they carried broad curved blades, so long and so large that it seemed they could cleave a man with little effort.

Basil's army was dressed in light cotton, more comfortable than the leather and mail worn by his Viking reinforcements. Njord could feel the drops of sweat trailing along his chest to rest in his belly button. He tugged at his clothing, trying to get some air behind it.

On Brian's order, the army moved forward, falling upon the Sarcens most viciously. Eagan covered Patric's back while Njord covered Brodir's but all four fought in a tight circle, keeping an eye out for trouble then beating it back when it came.

The field was alive with glints of light as the intense Mediterranean sun bounced off their blades. Njord found a way to use the sun to his advantage, letting the rays reflect off the metal to temporarily blind his enemies while he struck at them with his short sword. By midday the white sand of the beach was tinged red and the granules were compacted with the blood that was spilled upon it. Njord broke from the circle, urging himself forward by digging his foot deep in the sand to gain momentum.

He was inside enemy lines, slicing fiercely as he hoped to make quick work of the task. He needed something to drink but the water boys had long since withdrawn into the cool shade of the palm trees lining the beach. He cut one man in the chest, splitting his leather breastplate in two until the deep maroon blood oozed out from beneath it. Another lost his head to his blade; still another lost his arm.

There was an enemy before him, an older man with flowing white hair reminding him of Turlog. He was turned against him and Njord traded his long blade for his short sword before pulling on the man's flowing hair to expose his throat. Before he could slice, he felt a burning sensation rip through his chest. He looked down to see the short blade in the man's hand then watched as he twisted it further into his breastplate. He felt the tear of muscle with the blade's movement then all at once his legs gave way and he found himself on his knees.

It was Njord's deep groan that caught Patric's attention. He ran forward, driving his blade through the man's back to cause him to fall forward against his son. He removed him by the scruff of the neck. "Njord!" he cried, alarmed by the amount of blood spilling from the wound.

Njord's mind muddled when he looked into his father's face. Patric was speaking to him but he couldn't make out his words. It was as if he were under water. All sounds around him were garbled. He could feel the warmth of the sun on his face but suddenly he was cold; he held up his head, hoping to be warmed by the heat.

In all his life he never remembered the sky being so blue or the clouds so white. He reached up his hand to see if he could touch them but they were far beyond his grasp. Suddenly his arm was too heavy to hold and it dropped to his side. The weight of it caused him to fall backward and soon he was lying on the warm sand staring at the sky that seemed to be closing in around him.

He thought he heard Patric's voice calling to him but he couldn't be sure. He blinked a few times to clear his vision but there was a blinding bright light that made it impossible for him to see anything.

Though he was breathing deeply he couldn't get enough air into his lungs. He needed to rest. Perhaps if he slept he would be able to recover his strength. He closed his eyes and smiled as a vision of Gamal appeared before him. He took him by the hand then turned to lead him into the light that had suddenly engulfed him.

CHAPTER 34

▼

Armagh, Ireland: Two hours to midnight—1, November 1003 A.D.—The sound of Murchad's feet hitting the stone steps as he descended from his chamber caused a low rumble. Over the years the Vikings had besieged the church of Armagh more times than anyone could remember but for it to happen now, when he had control of the territory, was disturbing indeed.

"What's the damage?" he demanded of his guard as the sword was thrust into his hand.

"Almost total, Ri Ciocid. They've burnt everything."

Murchad strapped the holster around his back then pulled on his gloves. The last thing he wanted to report to his father was another raid. "Was it Vikings?"

"No one can be sure, but there is something disturbing, lord."

They had made their way to the courtyard and Murchad was just about to hoist himself into his saddle when he suddenly stopped. "What could be more disturbing than losing the church?"

"We've lost the clergy as well?"

"What?" Murchad rubbed his hands over his face. "How many?"

The guard hung his head then crossed himself. "All of them, lord."

Murchad leaned against his horse. "Jesus Christ. They massacred holy men."

"Aye. Quite gruesome. I'm told their heads have been set on poles lining the road."

Murchad crossed himself before mounting his horse. "I want ye to send word to Harald Bald Knee that I want a meeting with him. We'll get to the bottom of this once and for all."

"Pardon, lord," the guard called just as Murchad was about to ride away. "Harald Bald Knee and the rest of the Galls are in attendance at Maelmora's feast. Should I also ask the Ri Tuath Ruire's attendance?"

Murchad lifted his brow. "What feast? How do ye know this?"

"The messenger ye sent to Torshav returned with the information. It seems he had to travel to Leinster to find Havland so he could deliver yer message."

"Is that so?" Murchad asked, wondering what mischief Maelmora was up to. "Very well. Send a message to the Ri Tuath Ruire that he's to attend as well."

With that he kicked his horse into a gallop then headed toward the church.

*   *   *   *

The Isle of Man—21, December 1003 A.D.—Patric was awestruck as he looked around the hall belonging to Brodir. It was stunning, decorated with fine silken draperies over long windows that looked out onto the expanse of the harbor. It was a hall of conquest with thick torches resting in ornate metal cages, showering a golden glow upon the heavy furniture contained within. The servants, mostly women, were scantily clad revealing the earl's lusty appetite. The bowls they offered were no less glorious than their own golden hair, brimming with fruits, cheese and meats of various types demonstrating the wealth of the household they tended.

"Some place he's got here," Thorien whispered, though his strong voice seemed to boom from the rafters.

Patric jumped at the sound of it. "Aye," he agreed. "I could see why Njord was attracted to the place."

Thorien hung his head with the mention of the young earl. He knew how hard it was for Patric to lose him but he had been gone for quite sometime before his return to Eire and he hoped that the separation would make this one more tolerable.

"So, where did they put him?" Thorien asked. Being the ships captain he didn't disembark with Patric and Eagan but stayed behind to be sure the vessel was safely docked.

Patric sighed then said a silent prayer for his son. The injury Njord suffered in Bari was grave but once it was determined that he would survive, Brodir decided to stay behind to claim his prize leaving it up to Patric to deliver him to Man. "He's above," Patric replied, his voice sorrowful with the recollection of his men carrying Njord up the stairs on a litter. "He was still too weak to walk on his own. I suspect his mother's tending him by now."

Thorien stood silent for a moment before making his next inquiry, knowing how anxious Patric had been about it. "Did ye see her, Shaver?"

Patric shook his head by way of a response then made his way to the head table. He wasn't at all certain how he would react when he saw Freyja again. He decided it would be best if he took something to drink first to steel his nerves. He picked up a cup and immediately there was a servant girl standing beside him holding a pitcher. "What is yer preference, lord?" she asked in Manx.

Patric took a moment to consider the dialect before answering, "Mead."

She smiled for him and her crystal blue eyes sparkled in the torchlight then she reached for the pitcher containing the honey wine to fill his cup. He sipped it and immediately recognized it as Njord's special blend. He added nutmeg to it to bring out the flavor of the honey. "Would ye care for something to eat, lord?" the servant asked.

Patric shook his head then moved nearer to the fireplace to warm his hands.

"I'll have a bite," Thorien called out while stepping closer to the woman. She had the most beautiful golden hair and a fine narrow waist, suiting his taste most perfectly. "Is that duck ye have there?" he asked, surveying the platters with his arm resting comfortably on her hip.

Patric chuckled with the thought that Gayla would likely pummel him if she ever knew he'd been acting in such a way then he returned his attention to the fire, watching as the flames changed from orange to yellow to blue. He thought about Lara. Most probably she would be sore when she found out that he wouldn't be returning in time for Christmas but Njord needed him and he couldn't very well deny his own son.

"'Tis good to see ye again, Shaver," the familiar voice called from behind his back.

His shoulders tensed and he nearly lost his grip on his cup. He turned slowly to see Freyja standing behind him, her hair loose and hanging to her waist in a wealth of soft dark curls. Her odd green eyes smiled at him familiarly.

There was a lump in his throat keeping him from speaking but he dared not clear it for fear that she would recognize his nervousness. Instead he swallowed hard. "'Tis good to see ye, Freyja. How is the lad?"

"'Tis a grave wound but he's resting now. Would ye like to see him?"

"Nay," Patric shook his head then looked down at his cup to escape her gaze. "Let him rest, aye."

Freyja raked him from head to toe, making no effort to hide the fact that she was surprised by his appearance. Though his body was fit, his hair had dulled and there were tiny lines at the corners of his eyes and at his jowls. He looked older.

"Will ye take something to eat, Shaver?" she asked, sweeping her arm toward the table laden with food. "If I knew ye were coming I would have laid out the salmon that ye like so well but there's mutton and potatoes. Will that do?"

He watched her every movement, so graceful and refined. It seemed that she was born to the life she was now leading. If it was possible, she appeared to look younger than the last time he saw her. "I've no appetite just now," he said in response to her question.

"I see she said," then stood silent for a time.

She was having trouble figuring out what to do with her hands so she began playing with a stray thread from her purple lein. She twirled it over and again against her finger until finally it snapped. Then she rolled it into a ball in her hand. He watched her and it suddenly put him to mind of the first time they met. He chuckled.

"What's funny?" she asked, looking at him as if he had two heads.

"Nay at thing."

Again they stood silent and when they spoke next it was at the same time.

"I heard ye had a child."

"Man is certainly beautiful."

They fell silent again, each waiting for the other to speak but when neither one did they both started again.

"I like it here."

"Her name is Saroise."

She chuckled again then reached out to place her hand on his wrist. He thought he would melt where he stood. "Ye go first, Shaver," she cooed, her eyes as soft and loving as they had ever been.

"I'm sorry, Freyja," he said without thinking. He had wanted to speak the words for so long that they were on the tip of his tongue.

Time seemed to drag as she considered his statement. A wealth of emotions swirled around her. She wanted to yell at him; to kiss him; to beat him about the shoulders but in the end she only smiled. "I know ye are," she replied then turned on her heel to pour herself a drink.

When she returned her face shone with the tenderness of her heart. "I'd be lying if I didn't say that I was angry for what ye did but that's over now."

"Why is it over?" he asked, wanting to know what great event took place to make her forgive him.

She thought about that for a moment before answering, "Njord told me the reason ye did it. He confided that if ye faced me yerself ye probably wouldn't have gone through with yer marriage or taken yer crown."

"He spoke the truth."

"Aye? And if ye had returned I would have done everything in my power to keep ye with me."

"Even though ye knew Brodir was alive?"

"Aye, even then."

He heaved a great sigh, wondering what their lives together would have been like if they'd chosen that path. She read his mind. "We chose right, Shaver. We were good together but there were others that we needed to consider." She hung her head then mumbled again, "We chose right."

He lifted her chin with his open palm. "So, if we chose so rightly, why then do I feel the need to scoop ye into my arms and make love to ye?"

She did her best to avert her eyes from his gaze but it was no use. She felt him boring a hole in her with his stare and she looked at him. "It always was that way with us."

"And now?"

At length she shrugged. "Old habits die hard," she whispered.

He took a step closer to her and she took one back. If she let him touch her in that way she was worried that she'd never let him go again. "Don't, Shaver," she whispered, but it was too late, his mouth was already descending to meet hers.

✳   ✳   ✳   ✳

Cashel, Ireland: The great hall—30 November 1004 A.D.—Patric remained in Man until the turn of the year. Njord's strength had begun to return and Freyja prepared to join Brodir in Italy. Though it was hard to let her go, they had both grown accustomed to their separate lives. This time they parted well.

Cashel was bursting with people gathered for the marriage celebration of Eilis to Balder. The marriage negotiations had been started by Brian upon his return from Bari and were concluded once Patric returned from Man. Eilis understood the importance of the alliance between the clans but her heart was breaking to know that she would be taken so far away from her family. Margreg and Gertrude did their best to console her.

"They say that Caran Balder is the most beautiful kingdom in all of Eire. Ye'll have the ocean as yer doorstep and the mountains to watch over ye."

"Don't fret over it, mother," Eilis replied. "'Twill be fine."

"Aye," Gertrude interjected, brushing back the stray curl that came to rest on Eilis' forehead. "Balder is a comely man. Generous too. He'll make ye feel right to home there."

"His mother was a Viking!" Margreg spit before she could stop herself.

Gertrude screwed up her face behind Eilis' back to warn her daughter against being negative. "But his father was a Gael. A great warrior I'm told. My own husband had occasion to meet him. I'll never forget what an impression the man made on him. Said any son of his would be a grand success. He was right about it too because Balder is certainly that."

Eilis patted her grandmother's hand when it came to rest on her shoulder. "At least when I'm there I'll be treated with dignity instead of the disdain I face from my own people. I'm actually looking forward to a time when I can walk out amongst a crowd without hearing whispers behind my back."

"Och, child," Gertrude replied. "Ye'll be queen. There'll be as much tongue wagging over that as there is over yer heritage."

"Aye, but at least I won't know what they're whispering about."

Margreg stroked her daughter's face and her eyes went suddenly soft. "If ye want me to come with ye, ye know that I will."

"Nay, mother," Eilis responded. "Ye're far too important to the Shaver to be holed up at the edge of the world. Both he and Brian have come to depend on ye when they march." She was thinking of the wound Njord suffered in Italy. Patric told her that it was Margreg's great skills that saved him. She made the sign of the cross to thank God for sparing her beloved then sighed for the fact that she would most likely never see him again. "Ye just keep on as ye've been and let me make my own contribution to the clan."

Margreg stroked her face again wondering when the child grew into the woman who sat before her now. She was every bit the beauty with gray blue eyes that expressed her emotions and a wealth of chestnut hair that framed her beautiful face. She was the most courageous woman Margreg had ever known and for a moment she wished she had spent more time with her. "If ever ye need me, just send for me and I'll be there, aye."

The doors of the hall opened again to admit yet another guest. All three women lifted their heads to see who it might be. Eilis blinked a few times to be sure her eyes were not deceiving her then she held her breath. It was Njord standing in the doorway. Vahn on his one side and Yon on his other. "By the saints," she sighed. "It can't be him. He's in Man, recovering from his wound."

There was no doubt that it was Njord. Both Margreg and Gertrude placed their hands on Eilis' shoulders as much to keep her seated as to soothe her. It was Gertrude who spoke. "Now what could he be doing here?"

It was at that moment that Saroise made her way over to them. She was a vision in her blue lein with her stunning red hair swept back from her face to hang down her back in a wealth of curls. "Isn't that yer great love who's joined us, Eilis? Perhaps he's come to stop the wedding."

"Why don't ye just shut yer mouth and go back to yer mother?" Eilis snapped. She'd suffered enough of Saroise's mischief to last a lifetime. She was certainly in no mood for it now.

"Well," Saroise huffed before spinning on her heel to do exactly what Eilis suggested. "I'll be glad to see ye off to the edge of the world. It's exactly where a shrew like ye belongs."

"Pay her nay mind," Gertrude offered with a pat to Eilis' shoulder. "She's just another reason for ye to be glad to be away from here."

"One of the biggest," Margreg agreed, but neither one of their comments was responded to by Eilis. She was too busy watching Njord's movements and worrying whether or not a broken heart might kill her.

Njord marched directly to the head table where Brian, Patric, Thorien, Havland and Eagan were all locked in conversation. Patric looked up in time to see his son offer his knee. He was startled enough to sit back in his chair but it was Havland who actually spoke.

"By the gods, laddie," he thundered before leaping over the table to grab Njord by the shoulders. "Aren't ye a sight for sore eyes? When the Shaver told us what happened to ye in Italy we thought sure ye'd need a full season more to recover. What the hell are ye doing here?"

It was a question Patric was eager to have an answer for. He leapt from his seat waving for Njord to join them. "Will ye sit?"

There was a strange look in Njord's eye that made Patric quite uncomfortable. He didn't answer the question. Instead he bent his knee for the Ard Ri. "Long life to ye, Brian."

"And to ye, earl," the Ard Ri replied then swept the room in search of his wife.

Njord didn't notice. He was intent on Patric. He leaned over the table to whisper, "Can we speak privately, father? I've a grave matter I wish to speak with ye about."

Patric lifted an eyebrow in askance. "Is there trouble?"

"Not yet, but there could be."

All eyes were on them as Patric made his way around the table to take Njord by the arm. Havland started to join them; Vahn and Yon as well but Njord halted them with a shake of his head. He could feel Brian's gaze on his back right up until the time the doors closed behind them.

Patric followed Njord up the path to the graveyard, his stomach growing tighter with each step they took. Something was terribly wrong to bring the lad across the ocean so soon after suffering his wound. He wanted to stop and demand that the lad speak but he bit his tongue waiting until Njord was ready.

They finally stopped and Patric sat upon the rock Njord pointed to while his son paced before him. It was obvious he didn't know how to begin. Patric urged him, "Well?"

Njord had been struggling with what words he should use since he first decided to make the trip but now that the moment was upon him he didn't know what to say. He finally decided to lay it plain. "Freyja is dead, father."

With all the possibilities for why Njord would travel to speak with him, this was the last bit of news Patric expected to hear. He got to his feet, not knowing what else to do or how exactly to feel about it. "How?"

Njord understood the strange expression on Patric's face. Freyja was a woman who no longer belonged to him. News of her death wasn't something that warranted an urgent trip. He wasn't even certain that his next bit of information did. "She died in childbirth."

"W-w-what?" Patric stammered, thinking he had misheard the statement.

"Aye," Njord replied then cast his eyes toward the ground. "Brodir returned with the babe last month. He said it was the greatest gift the woman could ever give him."

Patric stumbled back to his seat on the rock. He was mystified. "'Twas good of ye to tell me of it, son," he said, still not fully grasping the situation but wanting his son to know how much he appreciated the sacrifice he was making to bring him the news. "It wouldn't have felt right to hear it from a messenger."

There was a long silence between them and Njord hoped that his father was putting the situation together. When Patric spoke nothing further, Njord stepped forward. "There's more."

More? What more could there be? Patric thought to himself. Freyja who had been barren for all her life finally received her greatest wish—a child. But as with all things when it came to her, she would never have the opportunity to enjoy it. She was dead—gone for good this time. Not merely across the sea into another man's bed or to Italy where there was a chance she might have happiness, but dead—gone to the Lord who she had obviously offended because he cursed her so. She would never lay eyes on the child she longed for; or Tyr; or Njord; or Brodir; or even him. She was dead!

Slowly the tears rolled down Patric's cheeks as the sorrow in his heart overflowed. She was a good woman. Deserving of far more than the fate she had suffered. Still he couldn't understand why Njord had made the journey to tell him of it.

Suddenly he remembered their conversation in Italy. It must be something to do with that, which brought Njord all this way. Dread took the place of grief and this time he leapt from the rock as he asked, "What else?"

Njord leveled his gaze at his father, recognizing the myriad of emotions playing behind his eyes. Again he struggled with how to deliver the news. He blew the anxiety from his lungs and his still healing wound pulled at the edges. "Brodir knows that the child isn't his."

They were back to Freyja again and Patric shook his head still not understanding where his son was going with this. Again he sat the rock. When he looked up at Njord he knew he was scowling.

"The lad is yers, Shaver."

"Mine?" Patric questioned then he shook his head. Freyja was an older woman by anyone's standards. Even if she weren't, in all their time together she had never conceived. He had presumed that her conceiving at this late stage in her life was a result of Brodir's sorcery. It was the only thing that made sense. And even that explanation was weak. "Why would ye say such a thing, son?"

"I know ye were together on Man, father. Though Brodir professes that the child was ahead of its time, all ye have to do is look on him to know it isn't true. He has yer coloring, Shaver. Red hair and blue eyes. He took nothing from Brodir or his mother."

"Stop!" Patric screamed as he got to his feet. He pulled at his own hair until he felt a few strands break free into his hands. This was ridiculous. The whole thing had to be a dream. Njord couldn't be standing there before him. He was back in Man recovering from his wound—a wound so grave that it nearly killed him. Even if he were recovered he would never be in Ireland. Kormlada was after him. He'd never risk her ire by coming back. And Freyja! He left her perfectly healthy—glowing in fact—as he placed her on the boat to travel from Man to Italy. She was there now, basking in the hot Mediterranean sun with her husband, Brodir. It was true that they came together one last time before she departed. They were weak and gave into their emotions. Most likely brought on by their concern over Njord. But there could be no child. It was impossible! Impossible!

Suddenly the ground shifted beneath Patric's feet and the air grew thick. His chest heaved and he opened his mouth wide, struggling to fill his lungs. Everything was blurry. The figure of the man standing before him drew closer—calling out to him, "Father! Are ye all right, father?"

Patric slumped back then slipped from the rock. Everything was spinning. The figure reached into his coat pocket to extract a vile and a linen square. He struggled with the cork then poured the liquid onto the linen. It came to rest under Patric's nose and a sharp, peppery odor wafted into his nostrils to burn his eyes and throat. He coughed and wretched then finally his vision returned.

"Father," Njord called as he lifted Patric by the armpit to have him sit on the rock. "Can ye hear me?"

Patric looked up at his son then reached out a hand to touch him. It was real. He was there, which meant that the conversation they had just had wasn't a figment of his imagination. "But how could this be?" he finally asked.

Njord shook his head. "I have no explanation for it father," he said as he recorked the bottle then placed it into the pocket of his coat. Hecca made the concoction to help him through his journey given his still weakened condition. It had been helpful to him on board ship. He was grateful it worked for Patric as well. "I came to stand by ye. What to do about the situation is a decision for ye."

Patric lifted his eyes. "So ye're telling me that Freyja died giving birth to my child and now Brodir has taken him as his own." Though the news was important it wasn't unusual given the times they lived in. Such things happened often. The unusual thing was for anyone other than the child's mother to know of it.

"Aye," Njord replied anxiously. It was clear that his father didn't understand the danger he was in. Danger grave enough to pull him back to Ireland. "Ye took Brodir's wife from him, father. Worse yet, ye gave her the child he couldn't. He'll not rest until he knows that ye won't be claiming the child for yer own. He wants ye dead, Shaver."

The dread that filled Patric's heart was genuine. His emotions raged and his mind muddled. His list of enemies was long enough. He didn't need to add Broir to it even though at some level he had always been there. "Is there any chance ye could be mistaken?" he asked, groping for anything that would ease his mind.

"Not likely, father. If ye think about it ye'll know it was the truth. She took a wet nurse with her on the journey and insisted on leaving right away. She knew before she left. I don't know why she didn't tell ye of it."

Of course she wouldn't tell him. How could she? She couldn't leave Brodir. Even if she did he would have hunted her down. He did once before. And Patric had his own life. There was no choice for the woman other than the one she made.

"Ye came all this way to inform me about this. I can't believe ye haven't any advice to give."

Njord hung his head. "What's to say? The lad belongs to Brodir. I only came because I know the earl well enough to understand his need for revenge. He'll care for the child but he'll never let ye live. He couldn't bear the thought of having to share him with ye should he ever find out his true paternity. In case ye hadn't noticed, he's a jealous man."

As much as the situation with Brodir troubled him it was Njord's future that truly concerned him. He looked deep into his son's eyes. "So if ye came to stand by me it must mean that ye've returned for good."

"Aye," Njord replied. "Brodir plans to raise the lad in Man so there's nay a need for me to stay there. I've brought Tyr and Hecca back with me. They're in Torshav."

"And what about Kormlada?" Patric asked. There was no mistaking the fear in his voice.

"I'm nay certain that distance alone could stop the woman from getting what she wants but there may be something I can do to beat her at her own game."

Patric was intrigued as well as nervous. "Go on."

"Would ye agree with me that things would go harder on her if I took a wife?"

"Perhaps." Patric spoke the word slowly, taking a moment to think about Ermagh. When he decided that it was just too incredible to believe that Kormlada had anything to do with her death he continued, "Alright, aye."

Njord shared Patric's trepidations but this was the best plan he could think of so he stuck to it. "I've decided that the best way to keep Kormlada at bay would be to take a wife. I couldn't think of a better alliance to forge than with the Dal Cais."

Patric's forehead wrinkled with this new revelation. "The Dal Cais? But what about Turlog?"

"Perhaps ye were right about Turlog. I'll take my revenge once I'm a member of the clan."

Patric's smile couldn't have been broader. He lifted himself from the rock to hug his son about the shoulders. "May I ask what caused this epiphany?"

"Aye," Njord responded with a nod of his head. His eyes went soft. "Having come close to death I've finally realized how important life is. Yet all this time I've been squandering mine seeking vengeance for those who are already dead. Our time on earth is too short. I want to spend mine living in peace surrounded by the people I love. With Freyja gone, there's no one left for me in Man. Everyone I care about is in Eire."

"Good for ye, son," Patric crooned.

When Njord was first injured he thought it would be the death of him. Now he realized that it might well have saved his life. He noticed Njord wringing his hands and wondered what other news he had. "Is there more?"

"Since we're alone now, perhaps this would be the best time to tell ye that I want to offer for Eilis' hand. She's of an age and we're fond of one and other. I believe it will be a good match. I hope that ye and Brian will agree."

Any joy Patric had been experiencing was ripped from him at that moment. Njord found him in Cashel so he presumed his son knew they were there to celebrate Eilis' marriage. The sorrow in his eyes was genuine. "I'm sorry but that can not be. Eilis is to be married tomorrow."

Njord took a step back, disbelieving of the words he'd just heard. "Married? To who?"

"Balder," Patric replied letting his eyes fall to the ground. It seemed that he was incapable of giving his son even one thing that would bring him happiness. "It was arranged while I was in Man."

"Certainly it could be undone," Njord blurted. He had wealth; he could buy out the contract easily enough.

"'Tis not as simple as that and ye know it. If it was anyone other than Balder I would advise trying it, but this is an important alliance, aye. The man is powerful. The clan needs him as an ally to put down the raiding that's been taking place."

Njord spit on the ground as he cursed his luck. He should have offered for Eilis before he left for Man but at the time he was supposed to be grieving. His shoulders slumped and he drew a deep sigh. "What is it with me and Eire, father? Is my price for living here perpetual unhappiness?"

Patric rubbed his shoulder. "Perhaps there is someone else for ye here, son. With yer return ye'll need allies. Many of the leaders are in attendance for the celebration. Why don't we return inside to speak with Brian about it? I'm certain we can find the proper match for ye."

Again Njord's shoulders stiffened. "But won't *she* be with him?"

They both knew who *she* was. Patric took a breath than nodded. "Just steer clear of Kormlada. Stick by me. Don't give her the opportunity to get ye alone."

Njord nodded but neither of them was certain it could be achieved. If they would escape her they would need to strike a marriage bargain as quickly as possible.

When they returned to the feast Brian and the others were half in their cups. They had spent most of the afternoon huddled together regaling those who weren't with them with stories about Italy. Brian welcomed them happily. "Ah, Njord. Ye're just in time to tell these lads about how ye came to be wounded."

Happy to lose himself within the circle of men, Njord took the seat beside Brian then began his story. He had finished with Italy and moved on to the subject of marriage when Kormlada suddenly appeared. A near hush fell over the group.

"If it isn't Njord the Black," she thrilled, her smile exposing the lust in her heart. She raked him with her eyes, ignoring Brian's gaze upon her. "Have ye come all this way to celebrate a wedding or is it something else that brings ye to Eire?"

His back stiffened as he did everything in his power to avoid her gaze. "I'm happy to say that I've returned, high queen. I will make my home in Eire and take a wife."

"Really?" she cooed. She smiled to cover the bite of anger. "Well that *is* good news indeed, isn't it husband?"

Brian leered at her before breaking into a false smile of his own. "Aye, it is. We were only just discussing it when ye came upon us." He stood then opened his arm to her. "Sit with us, wife. I wish to seek yer counsel on a match for the young earl. Ye keep up with the gossip. Which of the leaders has a comely lass for our Njord to marry."

She growled low in her throat with the thought of Njord marrying another. She knew Brian requested her counsel on purpose. She looked around the room before slipping into a seat. "Hmmm," she offered while tapping her chin with her index finger. "Which one would our Njord prefer?"

Patric noticed the look on the Ard Ri's face. It was clear that Brian was aware of Kormlada's desire and only put her into the position of picking a wife for Njord to cause her pain. Patric wanted to smile but he kept his face expressionless as he leaned in to hear what she would say.

"Be generous with him now," Havland interjected innocently. "He's a good man. 'Twouldn't be right to strap him with a sow."

She smiled at that but her heart wasn't in it then her eyes alighted on Saroise and it suddenly became genuine. Saroise was a great beauty but as yet, too young to marry. If she chose her for Njord, Brian would be hard pressed to find a reason to deny it and Njord would be forced to wait giving her the time she needed to figure out what to do with him.

"What we need here is an alliance to show strength, aye," she cooed as she turned her gaze on her husband. "Njord's a great Viking. We wouldn't want him forced into an alliance with one of our enemies."

Brian smiled for the fact that she was giving her full consideration to the task. Perhaps her infatuation had faded.

"And as Havland rightly pointed out," she continued, "we can't have him betrothed to a—what was it ye said?—och, aye—I believe the word ye used was sow."

Both Patric and Njord held their breath as they wondered where the high queen was going with this. They leaned in, as did Thorien, Eagan, Yon and Vahn. She clapped her hands together and her smiled broadened. "I've got it," she offered, her pride for her decision displaying on her face. "Njord should take Saroise to wife."

There was complete silence as all gathered considered the statement. Brian's mouth lifted into a smile. Marrying Njord to Saroise was nothing less than sheer brilliance. It would bind him to the Dal Cais once and for all by way of contract if not by an oath. At length, Patric smiled too. To keep his son attached to his family would please him greatly. He turned to look at Njord. "Son?" he asked, wondering what thoughts lurked behind Njord's green eyes.

Njord turned to look at Saroise who was giggling with the group of lassies huddled in the corner. Though still young, the promise of her beauty was evident. If he couldn't have Eilis perhaps the next best thing would be to marry Patric's daughter. It was a much better prospect to bind himself to his father than a stranger who he had no ties to.

"How old is she now, father?" he asked, a slight smile evident on his lips.

Patric's stomach tightened when he realized his answer would leave a hole in their plan but he couldn't see a way to back out of it. "She's coming upon her twelfth summer," he replied with sadness in his voice.

"Well that's a bit too young," Kormlada interjected slyly, "but I'm certain Njord wouldn't mind waiting for a jewel such as Saroise." She leaned in to Njord. "I married in my twelfth summer, and if ye don't mind my saying, I think 'twould be a mistake for someone of yer experience to take someone that young."

Her hot breath on Njord's face unnerved him. Brian interrupted saving him from having to respond, "I think it's a grand plan."

Patric and Njord exchanged glances but what was done was done. "Is it good for ye, Njord?" Patric asked even though he couldn't see any choice in the matter.

Njord continued to stare at Saroise. Even though she was young the match might be a good one. After all, Kormlada would be hard pressed to act out against Patric's daughter. And where Turlog was concerned, the contract would mean that Patric would be bound equally to both of them.

Havland watched his friend mulling the situation and desperately tried to catch his attention to warn him off it. The only imp nastier than Saroise was

Ermagh and Njord had already had his fill with that. It couldn't have been a worse choice for the lad.

At length, Njord sighed then answered, "I think 'twill be a good match."

Havland hung his head but Brian threw up his hands in celebration. "Splendid. We'll work out the details later. For now let's have a toast." He called to the passing maid to bring Njord a cup then filled it with the wine Basil had gifted him. When they were all poured out he raised his cup. "Long life to the earl and to his new bride, Saroise."

Njord lifted his cup then looked to Kormlada who resembled the cat that caught the mouse. It was obvious she thought herself the winner of the game causing Njord to worry that he had missed something. He averted her gaze so that he could think more clearly and his eyes alighted on Eilis.

She was more beautiful then he remembered her to be with her hair loose around her shoulders and her skin darkened by the sun. He thought she looked a bit frightened and in that moment he was overcome with the need to soothe her. "If ye'll excuse me for a moment," he asked of the Ard Ri. "There's something I'd like to attend."

Brian nodded and Njord turned to leave. Havland watched him go. It was a pity that the lad seemed doomed to bad marriages but he assumed there must be a reason for it. He noticed that Njord was heading in Eilis' direction and he sighed to himself, "Now that's the lass for ye, laddie."

"Good day, ladies," Njord called when he was within earshot of the three women. "I came to pay my respects to my savior."

"Njord," Gertrude cooed as she lifted a hand to him. "It's so good to see ye looking fit. We've been praying for ye, laddie. Bloodthirsty lot, those Sarcens."

"Aye," Njord agreed, "but believe it or not, they did me a favor."

"Oh?" Margreg asked. "I'd be interested in knowing what that favor was. It took me the better part of a week to patch ye together."

"Ye did a grand job, Margreg. I owe ye a great debt." He took her hand to kiss her knuckles. "I don't know what would have become of me if ye weren't with us."

"Ye would be Italian worm food," was her reply.

He chuckled at that but Eilis gasped, "Mother, really."

"'Tis the truth she speaks," he replied to Eilis. "Had she not been there to tend me, I'd be dead for certain. Ye're mother has a great gift of healing. Brian should be proud to have her willing to tend his men."

Suddenly any resentment Eilis had for her mother spending so much time away was diminished. She smiled at him and his eyes lit up. "Well then," she cooed. "I should say that I too am in her debt, earl, for I don't know what life would be like if ye no longer trod the earth. 'Twas difficult enough to find out that ye planned to live so far away." She lowered her eyes as her sadness gripped her. "So, what great event has brought ye back for a visit?"

"Ah," he offered, trading her mother's hand for hers. He couldn't get over what a great beauty she had become. "That is the favor the Sarcens did for me. When I realized how close I came to death I decided that 'twould be best for me to return to Eire to live amongst the people I care for."

Eilis' back stiffened with his words but Gertrude jumped to her feet. "Och, Njordie," she thrilled, taking his face in her hands to shower it with kisses. "So, ye're home then. 'Tis grand news indeed."

"Aye," Margreg agreed with a smile. She knew how important it was to her cousin to have his son with him. "I'm happy that ye're back."

He turned to look at Eilis. "And ye, lassie? What is that ye think about my return?" He knew he had no right to hope that she still cared about him but he wanted to know if she did.

She looked long at him, wishing she could smack him right across the face. If he knew he was returning and he cared for her, he would have offered for her instead of letting her be sold to Balder. It was the second time he betrayed her and she was left stinging from it. "If it makes ye happy then I'm glad for it," she said as she got to her feet. "It matters little to me since I will be relegated to the edge of the world."

She turned on her heel then headed toward Balder who had just made his way into the hall. "If ye'll excuse me, I must attend my husband."

Njord followed her with his gaze while the rip of his heart rang in his ears.

CHAPTER 35

▼

Armagh, Ireland: Church of St. Patrick—Four hours past dawn—14, June 1005 A.D.—Brian's success in Italy left him in good stead with Basil and Pope John. As a result, the Pope offered to bless his reign publicly so his people would know that he had an ally in the church. It was decided that the blessing should be given to him in the church of Saint Patrick located in Armagh north of Lough Neagh. The local bishop would convey the blessing then Brian would be granted the honor of being allowed to sign the church book.

He gathered an army so great that the procession covered a mile of road. As they made their way north they were greeted by villagers and kings alike, offering them food and trinkets to make their journey an easy one. Any doubt that Brian Boru macCennitig was Ireland's one true king was erased by the display.

Through the open tent flap Margreg could see the great oak doors of the church of Saint Patrick. Panels of religious carvings graced the front of the doors while heavy iron hinges attached them to the walls of the church. Soon they would be thrown open to receive her king and behind them the new bishop, Airindach, would recognize Brian as the one true ruler of all Ireland.

She drew air deep into her lungs before turning a scrutinizing gaze toward her cousin's wardrobe. She had convinced him to wear the single lion of his heritage instead of the three that Brian's colors boasted. She wanted Patric to mark his place in the order of the hierarchy and he agreed. She smiled at him then reached out to tuck the wayward strand of hair that escaped its clasp back into the braid plaited at the nape of his neck.

"Am I grand enough for ye?" he asked her with a glint in his eye.

Indeed he was grand. More grand than she ever remembered seeing him. Though his hair had gone light, nearly white at the temples, his skin carried a ruddy hue from their time spent traveling the country. "Ye'll do," she finally offered with her face twisted into a frown, but her eyes didn't agree. Instead they told him how proud she was of him. He regretted not having fought harder to have her join them in church.

"Will ye be alright?" he asked, taking her hand in his then raising it to his lips. "Ye know I want ye to be with us."

"I know," she replied then turned from him, pretending to busy herself with putting away her sewing box. "Just ye make sure that the rot gives ye the blessing. I didn't march all this way with ye to have him renege on the agreement."

The rot she referred to was, Airindach, the church bishop. He was a tough negotiator and a vicious man in general. It would cost them thirty ounces of gold to have him obey Pope John's order to let Brian sign the book. And under no circumstances were there to be any women present.

Patric took Margreg by the shoulders then turned her to face him so he could look into her eyes. She was always beautiful, but somehow her vulnerability made her more so. He brushed the hair out of her eyes then bent to kiss her cheek. He sighed as her arms came up around his neck. "Ye're a bonnie lass, Margreg. If anyone says otherwise I'll strike them down where they stand."

He could feel her tears against his neck and he gave her a moment to compose herself before breaking from her. "Go on now," she scolded as she cocked her chin in the direction of the approaching Ard Ri. "I'll not be standing out here all day waiting for ye."

Patric turned toward Brian. He was bedecked in a white lein and matching coat trimmed in beaver fur. He wore a golden collar and cuffs and his hair, which was usually a riot of waves and curls, was tamed to a ruddy sheen, pulled back from his face with a clasp at the base of his skull. The golden crown, which he so despised wearing, was nestled over his brow in a most regal fashion and his ears were adorned with his finest gold rings.

"He cleans up well, aye," Patric remarked to his cousin who was again busying herself with her sewing box. She was tucking away needles and thread as if they were the most precious things on earth. He took a step closer to her. "I could press him on it if ye wish," he stated as he held out his hand to her.

She took a step back, wiping her eyes and shaking her head. "Nay," she replied in a tone too firm to be true. "The bishop said no women and there'll be no further discussion about it." She lifted her head, letting her eyes go sharp then added, "Are ye after making Airindach change his mind about letting Brian sign the book when ye spent nearly all of yesterday negotiating the price to have him do it?"

"It's just…" Patric began.

Her upheld hand interrupted him. "It's for the best," she retorted, taking a step forward then leveling her gaze at him to underscore her point. "Let the bishop have his foolish edict if he likes. In the end I'll have my satisfaction in the knowledge that I saw ye this far."

He was just about to speak again when the Ard Ri's call forced him to turn. "Do ye come, Ri Ciocid," Brian thrilled, grasping the material at either side of the tent to swing his weight from it. "If we're to do this thing it would be best to do it now, aye."

"Aye, Brian," Patric replied. He was about to make his way from the tent when a thought occurred to him. "I wonder," he cooed, taking a moment to scrutinize Margreg's form. "Do ye think she's about the same size as Munro?"

Brian stuck his head into the tent to follow Patric's gaze then nodded. "Aye," he issued before stepping inside, an odd smile playing on his face. "I should say they were about the same height although Margreg's curves are a bit more inviting."

Margreg narrowed her eyes then looked askance at her cousin. Whatever they were up to it was clear they were of the same mind. "What is it?" she inquired when they circled around her. "What does Munro have to do with anything? Or me for that matter?"

"We could pull back her hair into her hood," Patric offered, ignoring the question but continuing to circle.

"Aye," Brian agreed. "And we could wrap material around her shoulders to square her off."

"Easy there, the two of ye," Margreg snapped back, finally catching on to their plan and not liking it a bit. "As much as I love ye both for worrying over me, I think it best not to tempt fate. Airindach wants no women present and I don't think we should be deceiving him—especially in a church, aye."

"Not to worry," Brian retorted. He grabbed the garment she'd been mending from the stool where she left it then ripped it in half to use it as stuffing. "He has his orders from the Pope. He won't disobey. Besides, he said he didn't want to *see* any women in his church and he won't."

With that he took hold of the neck of her lein to pull it over her head and in no time at all she was transformed into one of his men.

It was Gable who led them into the church. He walked down the center aisle of pews toward the stone altar behind which Airindach and his attendants were seated. He gave a quick glimpse over his shoulder to Brian then looked behind him to where Margreg was marching at the back of the line beside Njord. Though he agreed that she should be with them, it didn't stop his stomach from sinking with the thought of being found out.

He returned his gaze to the bishop whose face was as somber as if they were a funeral procession approaching. He lifted the corner of his mouth slightly in an effort to change the bishop's mood but Airindach continued to stare, unwavering in his humor and clearly eager to have the deed done. When they came to the step leading up to the altar, Airandach rose and Gable stepped aside to allow Brian to pass. There were strict instructions that not even the king's confessor would be allowed to approach the scared altar of Saint Patrick.

Brian nodded at Gable before taking a deep breath then continued on up the steps. Never in his life had his body trembled as it did at the moment when he felt the power of the Lord coursing through his veins. It had been a long hard journey to get to that point and he fought back the instinct to turn and look at his men so they could share in the event.

"Brian Boru macCennitg," Airandach thundered as he looked down his nose toward the approaching Ard Ri, "Are ye prepared to state yer business here?"

Brian looked up at the bishop, taking a moment to assess the type of man he was. Deciding Airandach was someone smitten with his own authority, Brian found his own voice from deep within his chest to reply, "I am, yer eminence."

They looked at each other for a long time without uttering a word and Airindach's eyes narrowed. Though Brian had assisted the church in Italy, it didn't change the fact that he was married to a sorceress and had massacred thousands to claim the throne he now sat upon. If it weren't for Pope John's orders and the gold the Ard Ri offered to repair the church from the raids, Airindach would have denied the request. He chaffed for the subjugation the act he was about to commit would put the diocese under.

He took a step forward, squaring his shoulders and looking down his nose as his free hand came to rest upon the altar. To the right of his hand lay the church book, an ancient archive of information dating back to Saint Patrick himself. It was the most holy relic the church possessed and now the usurper would add his name to the pages, placing him prominently in the annals of history.

He looked to the blank page the book was opened to then to the Ard Ri who was standing a step below the altar but who still managed to tower over him. "Approach," he ordered, letting the last shred of authority he possessed ring clear in his voice.

Brian did as he was bade, taking the last step up to stand before the altar. He cast a quick glance down to the clean page of the book and his heart dipped slightly in his chest. He wasn't sure what he expected to see there but hoped there would be another name, or at least some writing on the page before he lent his own signature to it. Without that it could be a ledger book for all he knew.

"Will ye pay homage to the Lord?" Airindach offered, more of a command than a question.

Brian's head never moved but his eyes darted up to meet the bishop's. He lifted his right hand slowly, touching forehead, heart and either shoulder before he lowered himself to his knees.

The bishop took the pestle from its bucket, walking around to the front of the altar to sprinkle the holy water over Brian's head while the attending priests stepped forward to wave incense around them. The burning reeds soaked the air with a sweet, smoky scent until Brian thought he would choke, but he kept his head bent as the bishop spoke in Latin, "In the name of the Father, the Son and the Holy Ghost—I bless thee, Brian Boru macCennitig and do this day bless thy reign as High King of all Eire. In this covenant thy duties are clear—to protect thy people from scourge—to protect thy country from wrath—and to keep holy the teachings of the Lord thy God in recognizing the Catholic Church as the one true religion to which thy people will pay homage." Then he reached out his hand to allow Brian to kiss his ring.

Brian looked at the red ruby set into the golden band, one of the few items remaining after the last raid against Saint Patrick's. He took Airindach's hand in his then lowered his lips against the ring, moving them in prayer.

"Father, give me the strength and wisdom to guide yer people and to keep holy yer commandments. Give me the courage to protect yer church and the fortitude to cleave its enemies."

Though he couldn't make out the words, Airindach knew it was homage the Ard Ri was offering and in that moment the deed didn't seem so offensive. He waited for Brian to be done before slipping his hand gently from his lips then turned to walk back around the altar.

"Come, great king of Eire," he commanded. "Place thy mark upon this book so all will know that your ascension has been blessed."

Brian rose to the bishop's call, stretching himself to full form then taking the few steps necessary to place him before the book. He watched as Airindach dipped the quill into the pot then handed it to him.

Airindach smoothed the page with his hand, holding it taught at the top to allow the Ard Ri to write more comfortably. But instead of touching the quill to the paper, Brian slipped the bishop's hand from the book to turn back the page. Startled by the action the bishop questioned, "What is it ye seek, lord?"

Brian noticed that both sides of the page he was about to sign were blank, making it easy to remove if someone were so inclined. The facing page was nearly full but there was room enough for him to add his own hand.

He smoothed the page down then leaned forward to emblazon it with a flourish:

On this fourteenth day of June in the year of Our Lord 1005, came Brian Boru macCennitg, Emperor of all Eire, as protector of the Catholic Church and the Church of Saint Patrick.

With that he lifted his head to level his gaze against Airindach's. The bishop let his eyes fall to the ground. Brian turned toward Gable. "Will ye witness it?" he asked of his confessor.

Gable hesitated for a moment and Airindach quickly placed his hand upon the page, opening his mouth as if to object. The steely gaze Brian leveled at him halted any speech.

Brian turned to Gable, cocking his chin toward the book. Gable bent his knee in homage to the crucifix hanging on the wall before climbing the steps. He dipped the quill offered to him into the pot then in tight neat lettering worthy of a scribe he added his own name to the book right below Brian's.

"Very well," Brian offered when it was done. He took the golden collar from around his neck to lay it upon the altar. "Ye shall be looked after," he stated to the bishop before turning to take his leave.

Patric watched as Brian descended the stair then made his way down the aisle. Felim of Munster was the only other king to inscribe his name to the annals of Saint Patrick. His reign was truly blessed. Brian's inscription would mark him as protector of the church and ensure its continuance so long as he held his throne.

"Ye did well, Ard Ri," he whispered when Brian placed a hand on his shoulder.

The Ard Ri twisted the corner of his mouth into a crooked smile then cocked his head toward Margreg who was standing at the back of the church. "Aye, and the old rot never even knew she was among us."

Patric gripped him by the elbow to squeeze his arm. It was those things that kept him loyal to Brian, willing to lay down his life for the man. Soon enough all of Ireland would follow.

∗   ∗   ∗   ∗

The Isle of Man: 24, December 1005 A.D.—Brodir bounced the babe upon his knee while shaking the rattle in front of him. The lad giggled then threw his head back against his father's chest, his red curls falling over his crystal blue eyes. Brodir nuzzled his neck then bounced him again. "Ye're growing like a weed, Olaf," he cooed. "Soon ye'll be a tall as me."

Ospak pinched the lad's cheek before offering him the bread he had dipped in his cup. "Here, son. Have a bit of this. It'll make ye strong."

Olaf took the bread in his mouth without using his hands—those he had tangled securely in his father's long beard. "Mmm," he issued as he chewed it.

"He'll be a warrior for certain, Brodir," Ospak stated. "Ye can see it in his eyes."

"That he will," Brodir replied, turning the child to face him then lifting him in the air until he giggled again. "I'll teach ye well, son. Ye'll be wielding a blade before ye know it."

Olaf grabbed his father's hair as he was lifted into the air again. He squealed in delight, kicking his feet out behind him.

"Shall I take him now, lord?" the nurse asked as she stepped onto the platform. It was late and she knew that if the lad became too excited he would never sleep.

"Nay," Brodir snapped. "I want him with me tonight. I'm planning to hear a complaint. I want him to see how such things are handled."

The woman looked long at the earl, restraining her remark that the lad was still too young to understand such things. It was clear that Brodir wanted his son to be prepared to take the throne once he was gone, but keeping a toddler quiet during court proceedings was a losing battle at best.

"Very well," she stated, taking a few steps back. "I'll be here waiting should ye need me."

Brodir nodded then lifted his son again, rubbing his nose against Olaf's when he lowered him. "Ye'll be a warrior and a chief just like yer father, aye."

The woman looked at them then shook her head. Anyone with eyes could tell that the child's father wasn't even in the room.

*   *   *   *

Caran Balder, Ireland: In the great hall—25 December, 1005 A.D.—
Though he refused his services on the march owing to the danger the harsh
weather of the winter months might cause his village, Balder did agree to lay a
Christmas feast for the Ard Ri and his troops upon their return from Armagh.

The normally treacherous terrain leading to Caran Balder was made even
more so by the driving rains and gale force winds, which were usual so late in the
year. Brian pulled his cloak tightly around his shoulders when they came to a halt
just outside the gates. "Remind me to do something about these roads," he said
to Patric then he rubbed his aching buttocks.

Patric chuckled sympathetically before sparing a glance for the terrain they
had just traversed. "'Tis nay a wonder that they call it the edge of the world, aye."

The gates opened to admit the warriors and slowly the Ard Ri's army entered
the village. Njord's company took up the rear. He sat his horse, letting the wind
play on his face as he gazed upon the raging ocean below.

"'Tis beautiful," Havland sighed when he reined up beside him. "She's a lucky
lass to be surrounded by such nature." Njord's head snapped around and Havland smiled knowingly. "Don't try to hide the fact that ye were thinking about
her. I know ye like the back of my hand, laddie."

"I wasn't trying to hide it," Njord mumbled then returned his gaze to the
ocean, "But I'm nay going to brag about it either. She's a married woman. I've no
right to covet her."

Havland was about to spit on the sentiment then thought better of it. He was
never one to hold fast with fidelity but Njord obviously was. He wouldn't make
light of it. "Ye never know what fate has in store for ye, laddie. Ye just keep yer
eyes open and yer sword sharp. She may be yers yet."

Njord's eyes widened and his mouth gaped. "Ye're not suggesting murder?"

"Och," Havland issued with a wave of his hand. "I most certainly am not. I
was only thinking that Balder is an old man, aye. Near as old as Brian. He doesn't
have many battles left in him. Eilis may soon find herself a widow. Ye'd be wise to
keep yerself ready for her."

All at once hope sprang then died in Njord's heart. He hung his head. "Well,
if he's going to die he would do me a favor by getting it over with. Do ye forget
that I'm betrothed to Saroise? I don't think Patric would look kindly on me setting aside one daughter in deference to the other."

A shiver ran up Havland's spine with the mention of Saroise. There wasn't a nastier woman walking the earth—including Kormlada. He shook his head. "If Brodir taught ye anything at all about how to gain favor with the gods, I would suggest that ye use it to get out of that bargain, laddie. I wouldn't relish the prospect of being strapped with the likes of her for a lifetime."

Njord shot him a look riddled with emotion, not the least of which was annoyance. "Why is it that ye never approve of my choices for a wife?"

"Because ye always choose wrong," Havland said then rode away.

Njord looked around to find that he was quite alone. The army had long since passed through the gates that were beginning to close. He kicked his horse into a trot then entered the village far behind the others wondering what he would say when he finally laid eyes on Eilis.

The army was welcomed with great revelry. Homes were opened to weary soldiers so that they could warm themselves by the fire and share some wine. The tavern was filled to capacity. Camp followers and vendors were given leave to pitch their tents in the southern quarter closest to the gates while Brian's sentries joined Balder's men atop the wall.

Brian and his senior officers were welcomed into the great hall where a grand feast was laid in celebration of yuletide. Eilis dutifully bent a knee for each and every man as they passed through the door, anxiously searching for one in particular. Four hundred and thirty two of them passed, but not one of them was Njord.

"Long life to ye, queen," came Havland's familiar cry, filling her heart with hope as she anxiously spun around to face him. He was alone and her spirits plummeted.

"And to ye, great warrior," she replied through a forced smile then bent her knee.

"Long life to ye, king Balder," Havland stated, reaching an arm out for the man.

"Welcome, Dal Cais," Balder replied. "Make yerself at home." He placed his hand in the small of Eilis' back to lead her away but she squirmed from him. "I'll join ye straight away, husband."

Balder raised an eyebrow but said nothing. Instead he turned to Havland, raking the man from head to toe in obvious scrutiny. Havland still held the charm he possessed in his youth. His hair was golden and his form taught. He flashed Balder an innocent smile revealing his straight teeth but the king didn't trust him. He growled low in his throat then raised his upper lip in warning but Havland smiled still broader forcing the king to bark at Eilis, "Don't be long, aye."

Eilis noticed the tension between the two. It wasn't unusual for Balder to be suspicious of strangers. It was his nature and she accepted it for what it was. "Aye, husband," she replied then rocked herself up on her toes to issue him a kiss on his cheek.

The quick coloring of Balder's skin didn't escape Havland. He smiled again but the king didn't see it. He was well on his way to his table and his cups.

Eilis looked at Havland with desperation in her eyes and suddenly his false smile was traded for one of knowing. "He's here, lassie, never ye worry."

The release of her breath surprised her since she didn't realize she had been holding it. "Where is he then?"

"He's down at the tavern."

Her stomach dropped. Being married, she had come to understand the relationship between men and women. If Njord cared for her in that way he would have come to see her straight away instead of stopping in at the tavern to have a few pints with his men. She felt the blood boil in her veins as she cursed herself for continuing her foolish hope then laced her arm through Havland's so he could lead her to the head table.

Eilis slipped into her seat beside Patric and the Ri Ciocid covered her hand with his. "'Tis good to see ye, lass. Yer mother was beside herself wondering what she would find when we got here. I'm sure she's contented now."

"Aye," Eilis replied. Though she had been anxious to see them all again she couldn't help thinking about the time when they would leave her. It made her sad. "We had a wonderful chat. She's refreshing herself at the moment. She'll be joining us straight away."

"That's fine," Patric replied, squeezing her hand in his. He nodded his chin in Balder's direction. "Yer husband looks well."

"Aye, that he is."

Patric looked around in search of something else to say. "Yer home is beautiful. Quite large, aye."

"Aye."

Something about her was changed and it made the hairs on his neck stand on end. He looked at her but she was staring at the door. "What is it, Eilis? Are ye sad, lass?"

She forced a smile then turned to him. There would be no use in complaining. She had made her choice and now she had to live with it. "Nay, Shaver," she replied, covering their entwined hands with her free one. "I'm just surprised that I didn't realize how much I missed all of ye until ye actually appeared. Do ye understand?"

"Aye, lass. I understand perfectly." And he did. He had spent many years away from his friends and family, living a life that wasn't even his. When he returned to them it was if they were strangers and his old life became the farce.

She dropped her eyes then opened her mouth to ask the question she knew she shouldn't. "How is Torshav?"

"'Tis fine. Yer grandmother has returned there to help Njord with Tyr. The village thrives."

"He must be big now. Tyr, I mean. Such a braw lad."

"Aye, he is. Like his father that one. Smart right down to his very bones. Has three tongues to him already."

"Lara and Saroise? I presume they are well."

"Aye, they are. Happy as hogs living all haughty up in Cashel."

"And Njord?"

He looked at her queerly. "He's with us. Did ye not see him?"

She shook her head sending her hair cascading over her face. Patric stood, searching the tables to find his son among the many men. "I know he's here somewhere. He rode with me most the way."

He was just about to call out to inquire of Havland when she reached out to draw his attention. "Has he remarried, Shaver?"

"Not yet, nay," he replied, giving one more sweep of the room before taking his seat. He looked at her and smiled. "Have ye not heard? He'll be taking Saroise to wife when she comes of age."

As if she had swallowed a stone, Eilis felt her stomach crash to her feet. "Saroise?"

"Aye," he replied. He took a sip from his cup then wiped his mouth with the back of his sleeve. "The whole of it was decided on the day of yer wedding. We're all quite happy about it. I've been waiting a lifetime to bring him into this clan."

She wanted to scream. To tear herself from her chair then beat the walls with her fists. How could that nasty imp possess the man she loved? And how could Njord want her?

There was a rage in her so great that she didn't know how to control it. It was one thing for Njord to marry Ermagh. He was in need of an heir and she was yet too young to provide him one. But to bargain for Saroise's hand on the very day she was being married off to Balder was a testament to the fact that he never loved her—never cared for her.

She felt the beads of sweat break out on her forehead as the room began to spin. She needed air. "Will ye excuse me, Shaver?"

"Are ye unwell, lass?" Patric asked, noticing her sudden pallor.

"Nay. There's just something I need to check on in the kitchens." She passed behind her husband who was as deep in conversation with Brian as he was in his cups. She hoped she might escape him unnoticed but he caught her by the arm. "Where do ye go, wife?"

"In search of my mother. She should have joined us by now. Perhaps she needs my assistance." Balder nodded his assent then held out his hand to her. She dutifully kissed it as she gave him her knee then excused herself to Brian.

She nearly broke into a run when she heard the door slam behind her. The cool breeze on her face was comforting. She headed for the stables—her usual haunt when she needed to be alone with her thoughts—then leveraged all her weight against the heavy door to pull it open. She slipped inside and the door slammed shut with the wind.

The sweet smell of hay filled the air. She breathe deeply, reveling in the scent that could so easily soothe her soul. There was an oil lamp on the sill of the window along with a flint stone and kindling, but she decided not to use them. With so much wind there could be an accident and besides, there was enough moonlight streaming in through the window for what she intended to do.

She moved through the stalls, stroking the noses of the bay mare and chestnut gelding then patting the hindquarter of Balder's prize pony, Gladan. He was lively and he called to her to scratch his back. When she did she could almost swear he was purring.

"That's enough, all of ye," she called to them. "I didn't come here to play, I came to think."

As she looked at them she noticed that the light was beginning to fade. She turned toward the window to see if clouds were covering the moon. She had hoped that the weather would stay fair while her guests were there so they wouldn't be forced to spend all of their time inside of doors. Her breath caught.

"And what is it that ye came to think about, my queen?"

He was nothing but a dark shadow standing before her but there was no denying it was him. She knew his scent, the deep rasp of his voice; the outline of his hair as it cascaded around his shoulders. She had spent a lifetime dreaming of him.

"Ye startled me, Njord."

"I pray ye to forgive me." He sounded sad.

"What is it that ye seek?" she asked, struggling to keep her voice from shaking with the desire she felt for him.

"I too came here to think." He moved from the window so that he could get a better look at her and she took a step back until she was pressed against the stall.

"Is that so?" she asked, clasping her hands behind her so that she wouldn't fidget. "Well then I shall leave ye in peace."

She began to turn but he grabbed her by the shoulders. "Ye look well, Eilis," he sighed, his voice little more than a whisper. She could smell the mead on his breath. "Are ye happy, lass?"

Every nerve in her body shook with her restraint. She wanted to rock up on her toes to kiss him, to taste his lips as she had the day of Brian's coronation. But that was not to be. She thought about the question and the information Patric had given her then replied, "Are ye?"

Her eyes were sharp and narrow and her breaths were coming quickly. Though he wasn't sure for the lack of light, he thought her color was high. He was suddenly reminded of the day that he had returned to Torshav with Ermagh and he shuddered with regret for the pain he had caused her. He wanted to kiss her. To tell her how sorry he was for not waiting for her then and how much he wished that they could be together now but instead he hung his head. "Nay, lass. I'm miserable."

Her eyes narrowed further and a sly smile touched her lips. "Good!" she barked then ripped herself from his grasp to march directly out the door.

CHAPTER 36

▼

Meath, Ireland: The great hall—7, March 1006 A.D.—Malsakin sat in his chair listening intently to his cousin's pleading. When it was done he turned to level his gaze at him. "I want nay part in this," he replied. "I'm content with what I have and I won't do anything to risk it. I advise ye to do the same."

"Ye're a coward, Malsakin," Fladbartoc barked. "Ye always were and I suspect that ye always will be."

"That may be so, but at least I'm living in peace. I've a new wife and a son. I plan on living long enough to enjoy them both."

"So, ye'll just sit by idle as this usurper ruins our country?"

"He's doing well enough," Malsakin replied, raising a brow before offering his next bit. "I dare say that if ye left him in peace there would be nothing to worry over. He has the blessing of the Pope and has allied himself rightly. He's repairing the roads and the monasteries. It seems the only trouble being caused is coming by yer own hand."

Fladbartoc's eyes narrowed and he banged his cup down on the table. "Ye're a traitor is what ye are."

"I'm wise," Malsakin replied, ignoring his cousin's ire. "I'd rather keep what I have rather than risk it for a bit more."

"I'd wager that ye would risk it if it was *ye* who stood to regain the crown."

Malsakin leveled a solemn gaze at him. "Ye would lose that wager."

Fladbartoc looked long at his cousin. He had stood beside him for all those years helping him to rule when the crown should have rightfully been his. Now the man was denying him. The action was unforgivable. "Do I need to remind ye that ye wouldn't have been Ard Ri at all if it wasn't for me?"

Malsakin leered at him, the words he'd been longing to say fast on his lips. "Do I need to remind ye that if I hadn't come to Tara when I did, ye would have been dead?" He leaned forward until his breath warmed his cousin's cheeks. "Heed my advice, Fladbartoc. Give it up. Boru has won and there's nay a thing ye can do about it. Go back to Ailech and be comfortable in what ye have because ye'll not have a bit more."

With that he rose, linking his wife's arm through his as he headed for his chamber.

"Coward," Fladbartoc spit after him. "We shall see if ye feel differently once I claim the throne for myself." He spun on his heel then exited the hall.

✳   ✳   ✳   ✳

Isle of Man, 2 July 1006 A.D.—Olaf giggled then ran from his father, eluding his grasp by ducking between his uncle's thighs. Ospak reached down to grab him beneath his arms then spun him around so his legs swung out behind him.

"Weeeee," Olaf trilled, holding his head back so that the rushing air pushed his red curls back away from his face.

When Ospak ended the spin he handed the lad to Brodir who sat crossed legged on the ground. "Go to yer da. He's a gift for ye, aye."

Olaf stood with his hands out, waiting for the dizziness to pass before taking a step toward Brodir. He stumbled then collapsed into his father's lap.

"Easy there, laddie," Brodir cooed, removing the blade so the child wouldn't get hurt. Though the edges were blunted the point was still sharp. "'Tis yers," he said. He held it by the tip so that Olaf could grab the hilt. "I want ye to learn how to use it, aye."

Olaf took hold of the hilt then watched as the light glinted off the metal of the blade. "Pretty," he sighed then giggled when the ray of light shone in his eye to temporarily blind him. He threw it down then rubbed his eyes, struggling to make out his father's face beyond the white spots. "Da!"

Disappointment marked Brodir's face. He picked up the blade then gathered Olaf to him. He stood. "Come on, laddie. We'll give this another try at the end of the season."

Ospak watched after them as they made their way up the incline. It was clear that his brother was of a mind to shape the lad into a leader. He only hoped he didn't rob him of his childhood while he did it.

*   *   *   *

Caran Balder, Ireland: 7, July 1006 A.D.—The day had been a glorious one. The sky was clear with only tiny wisps of white clouds sailing past the azure. The gentle breeze coming from the sea caught on Eilis' hair to blow it about her face. She pulled back on the mare's reins to slow her into a trot.

She felt the pull low in her stomach and rubbed her hand over it. Soon she would have to stop riding but she wanted to continue for as long as she could before the child in her womb grew too heavy.

She ringed the fort one last time, daydreaming about the life she had conjured in her head. In it she was married to Njord, living in Torshav with a gaggle of children scampering around their feet. In her world he never went to war or that dread Isle of Man, but instead would stay home with her, making love in the moonlight and sowing seeds in the sun.

She sighed when she passed the great hall. They would be receiving guests this evening. A southern Eaghonacht king who was seeking an alliance with her husband. She couldn't remember his name but she was eager to hear the stories he could share. With any luck he would have some news about Njord.

She handed her horse over to the groom then decided it was time for her to dress. Caran Balder was ancient and Balder himself was steeped in old customs. They didn't share a chamber together but instead had separate huts that stood side by side. He would visit her once a month, after her cycle, in his effort to get her with child. Now that he had he didn't visit her at all.

She dressed in a green lien then draped her husband's colors over her shoulders. He insisted that she wear them whenever they had visitors. She swept up her hair with the combs he had given her as a wedding gift then slipped the golden arm ring over her bicep—that was a gift in expectation of her bringing forth his child.

When she was finally dressed she sat on her bed with hands folded in her lap, waiting for him to come for her. They would enter the hall together with much fanfare, presenting themselves to their guests amidst the villager's cheers. Everything Balder did was choreographed down to the last detail. She understood and had come to accept it.

Doncha of Sil Anmachada stood when they entered. He leaned over to whisper something in the ear of the man standing beside him then they both raised their glasses. "Long life to ye, Balder," he called from his place on the platform.

Eilis turned to look at her husband who was smiling for the respect being offered. He nodded silently then swept her around the tables so that they could mount the platform. As they drew closer, Eilis noticed something familiar about the man who stood beside Doncha. He had flowing white hair and a patch over one eye. The hand that held his cup was missing a pinky.

"Turlog," she muttered.

Balder looked down at her. "Aye."

Her stomach sank with the thought that she would be entertaining this man in her own home but Turlog was her husband's guest and she would be forced to give him her hospitality. She swallowed deeply then fell back so that Balder could precede her. As usual, he would exchange pleasantries with the men before presenting her.

She noticed that there was only one ewer of wine on the table and swept her eyes around the hall in search of Resnik, Balder's personal man servant but he was nowhere to be found. When she first arrived in the village she was surprised to know that her husband only kept male servants. Balder had explained that they were more efficient and better suited to the harsh terrain. Indeed, the only unmarried women in all of Caran Balder were the children of soldiers and villagers. Even they were married as soon as they came of age.

She swept the room again then locked eyes with a servant who she didn't recognize. She tried to call him to her with the cock of her head but he turned from her then walked in the opposite direction. She mumbled under her breath before returning her attention to their guests, a forced smile plastered upon her face.

Balder was extending his hand to Doncha. The man took it then pulled him into an embrace. Turlog set down his cup then slid his right hand under his coat.

At first Eilis believed he was cleaning his hand in preparation for shaking Balder's. Then she noticed the sparkle of light from the blade he had withdrawn. He held it back against his forearm as he stepped forward with his other hand extended to Balder.

When Balder accepted the embrace she yelled out her warning. "Nay!" but it was too late. With practiced swiftness, Turlog pulled Balder to him then slit his throat sending blood spraying in every direction. Doncha was stunned when he was splattered by the stuff. He began to whirl on Turlog but Balder's limp body landed directly on him, knocking him from his feet and causing him to bang his head against the table.

Eilis felt her body tremble as chaos broke out in the hall. Men mascarading as servants pulled their short swords from the folds of their leins then began butchering anyone in their path. Warriors being led by Fladbartoc of Ailech, marched through the doors contributing to the carnage. Then all at once the table toppled as the cover of Balder's secret tunnel leading from the sea was thrown open to admit the Viking, Throdier of Orkney.

Eilis slipped into an alcove. Her heartbeat was so loud in her ears that she feared she might not be able to hear an attacker if he came up behind her. There was no doubt that they were after blood because the only people spared were those who looked to be valuable. Her hands shook and beads of sweat rolled down her neck as she pressed herself further into the shadows. She tried to form a plan of escape but deep in her heart she knew her only chance at survival would be to reveal herself as the queen with the hope of being taken as hostage.

Suddenly there was a hand on her shoulder. She whirled, reaching out to claw the cheek of her attacker. His hand flew to his face but he still held her around the waist. "My queen. 'Tis me, Resnik," he whispered as he pressed her against the wall. "I pray ye don't strike again."

Her heart leapt with joy at the sight of the elderly man but there was no time for words as he threw a blanket over her head then whispered, "Trust me."

She could hear the din of clashing swords as Resnick dragged her from the alcove into the long hall leading to the stable area. When they finally stopped he pulled the blanket from her head then shoved a dagger into her hand. He nodded toward the stable doors. "Ye'll need to make a run for it. Keep yerself hidden in the stable with the others. They'll protect ye, aye."

Tears brimmed her eyes causing her vision to blur. "Where are ye going?"

"If we're to survive this thing we'll need to have more then just a few of us safe. I'm doing my best lady."

She wanted to command him to stay with her but she knew he was right. She looked to the stable doors only several yards away then back at him. "Go," he urged. "While there's no one here to see ye."

She looked down at the dagger resting across her palm. It had once belonged to Balder's mother. How fitting that it should be wielded by a woman again. "Come back as soon as ye can," she commanded before making a dash toward the doors.

When she entered the stables and the light fell upon her, more then a dozen women rushed forward to pay her homage. "Thank God that ye're safe, lady," Tressa said as she kissed her hand.

Eilis tried to offer the woman a soothing smile but she was as shaken as the rest of them. The chances of their survival were slim at best.

The expansion of light against the wall in front of her when the stable door opened caught her attention. She could feel the presence of the person who had just entered behind her. Judging from the expression on Tressa's face, whoever it was wasn't there to help them. She whirled around with the dagger in her hand, slashing blindly with the hope of hitting something. She felt the blade pierce flesh then ripped it through for good measure.

The man dropped his sword then raised his hands to his throat in his futile effort to stop the bleeding. She heard the gurgle when he tried to speak then watched as the color drained from his eyes. His knees began to warble and instinctively he reached out before falling atop her, knocking the wind from her as he pinned her against the ground.

She felt the sharp pain in her back then a numbness in her legs as Tressa and the other women failed to lift him off her. There was blood everywhere so it was impossible to get a good grip on him.

Eilis felt the moisture seeping through her lein and suddenly she felt nauseous. She closed her eyes then swallowed hard. "Pull him by the legs," she barked as her stomach heaved then tightened. She didn't think she could stand the pain of being crushed by him much longer. They got him off and she waited for relief to come but it seemed that the pain in her stomach only intensified. She was light headed. All she wanted to do was rest. She fell back then let the darkness engulf her.

*   *   *   *

Cenn Cora, Ireland: 17, July 1006 A.D.—Njord listened as the Ard Ri shared his plans for coordinating the northern Galls but he couldn't help squirming under Kormlada's lecherous gaze. If it hadn't been for the fact that Brian was offering to put him in control of the effort, he would have left the table long ago.

"Do ye think ye can do it, Njord?"

Njord was startled by the call of his name and he pulled his lein away from his chest to cool himself a bit before he responded, "Aye, Ard Ri. I'll bring Harald with me. He's an ancient who carries great sway with those of the north."

Brian's mouth twisted with the use of the term "ancient." Harald was only a few years older than him. Brian's only solace was that *he* looked much younger. "Good," he stated. "Take Thorien with ye, aye. He knows them up there."

"Indeed, Ard Ri," Thorien thundered, puffing out his chest as he accepted the assignment. "We'll bring them into check for ye."

Brian looked long at Thorien who had begun to grow more violent of late. He presumed it had to do with the fact that he was raising four strong lads but in this situation peaceful negotiations were in order. "Try not to make any trouble up there, Viking," he snapped before turning his attention to Patric. "Who else shall we send?"

"Maelmora," Kormlada replied, ripping her attention from Njord long enough to speak up on her brother's behalf. "Send Maelmora with them. He knows a thing or two about the Galls seeing that he was raised with them all his life."

Brian nodded and Murchad rose to his feet. "Then I shall go as well."

Kormlada's lips puckered and her eyes narrowed. Murchad was the most infuriating man she had ever had the misfortune of meeting. "Aye, Brian. Send Murchad with them. While ye're at it, why not send Radec and Madan as well. As a matter of fact, why not send every Ri Tuath in the territory."

"I'm northern Ri Ciocid," Murchad barked at her, remembering Maelmora's secret meeting. "It's my place to accompany them if they are working within my territory. How will it look if the Ri Tuath Ruire is present and I'm not?"

"As it should," she muttered then shrugged her shoulders before inspecting her fingernails.

Murchad opened his mouth to respond but Brian held up his hands. He too remembered Maelmora's secret meeting and his wife's part in it. "Murchad will go. Maelmora will stay behind."

When her gaze shifted to meet his there was fire in her eyes. "Ye make a mistake, Brian," she growled. "Ye should match the man with the task."

He knew what she meant but he turned her words around, "That's what I'm doing, wife. The task is a great one and I am sending my great son."

He was trying to goad her and she knew it. At length they stood in silence, staring each other down like a hunter and his prey. Eventually she blinked. "Very well, husband. Send yer son to the north to deal with the Galls and see if he comes back alive."

The threat unnerved Murchad and all at once he leapt to his feet then lunged at Kormlada. "Easy there, laddie," Patric shouted when he stood to block his path.

Kormlada jumped back with the cry then whirled on Murchad claws extended. "If ye think that ye can defeat me, Murchad ye should think again."

A shiver ran up Murchad's spine when she delivered the words but he shook it off. He didn't believe in mystical powers. Kormlada was nothing more than a woman and an evil one at that.

His chest heaved as he turned toward his father. It was clear by the look on Brian's face that the Ard Ri was dissatisfied by his action. "I pray ye to forgive me, father."

Brian slowly unclenched his fists then released his breath. In truth he didn't blame Murchad for loosing control. Of late Kormlada's taunting had turned vicious. They had gone from dislike for each other to near hatred. "Go home, Murchad," he said as he extended his hand. "Prepare yer Galls for our meeting, aye. We will call it for the fall."

"Aye," Murchad replied then made his way around the table offering parting words to all gathered as he went.

"I'll walk with ye," Njord said when Murchad offered his hand. "I need some air, aye."

Murchad nodded knowingly. It was evident to anyone with eyes that Kormlada had been stalking the Viking. He was glad to see that Njord wasn't giving in. "She's evil, that one," he said, chucking his chin in her direction. "Be careful around her, aye."

"Aye," Njord agreed. They passed through the doors. "What does yer father think of all this?"

"What? Ye mean about me and her or her and ye?"

"Both."

Murchad thought on that. "I would say that if he was thinking to set her aside he would have done so already which leads me to believe that we're all stuck with her."

Njord nodded then hung his head. Murchad clapped his back then laughed. "Don't look so glum. If we stick together perhaps we can defeat her."

"That's easy for ye to say," Njord mumbled. "Ye're on yer way home. I'm stuck here with her."

"Well, if she catches ye alone cut off her head. I hear that's the only way to kill a demon."

Murchad took the reins the groom handed him then swung up into his saddle. "I'll see ye in the fall," he called out with a wave of his hand.

"May the gods deem it so," Njord called back.

He stood in the road watching the contingent leave then turned to make his way back into the hall. When he reached the door he changed his mind. Instead he took a sharp left toward the path leading to the stables.

He was brushing his horse when he heard the door open behind him. The light footfall in the hay told him that the step belonged to a woman. He heaved a great sigh and his nostrils filled with her scent. "I pray ye to leave me in peace, high queen. I'm unworthy of yer attention."

"Are ye now?" she asked, her breath brushing against his ear as she came up behind him.

Though she didn't touch him, he could feel her energy. It was as if a thousand hands were moving over him to ignite his lust. He threw his head back and swallowed hard, the skin over his adam's apple strained. "Please, Kormlada. Don't do this," he whispered.

She closed her eyes then leaned in closer until her breath was heavy on his neck. "I need ye, Njord."

His mind told him to leave—to push her out of the way so that he could be rid of her once and for all. But his body had other ideas. It was as if he were being drawn to her by something deep in the pit of his stomach. He had no free will.

He whirled on her, taking her into his arms so that he could cover her mouth with his. She tasted of wine and smelled of lavender, igniting his senses until he thought he would crack from the desire to be inside her.

She clung to him as if her very life depended on it, kissing him deeply as he lowered her into the hay. She hitched up her lein so he could have access then writhe against him when his hot skin touched hers.

He heard the hoof beats as they made their way up the path. He thought to ignore them but then his good sense kicked in and he got to his feet. "I won't do this!" he shouted as he looked down at her. Her lids were heavy with her lust yet there was fire in her eyes.

"Ye'll regret this, Njord," she threatened as he made his way toward the door. His real regret was in ever having met her.

He ran across the field then into the hall just in time to hear the visitor say, "Caran Balder has been raided. The greatest fortress that ever stood has been reduced to ashes."

Brian looked to Patric then nodded to the servant who had just refilled his cup, silently telling him to offer it to the man. "Have a drink and tell us what happened."

"They came by both land and sea," the man blurted after taking a long draw from the cup. "Caran Balder is gone."

Brian felt his stomach grip. Their march through Ireland was designed to stop these attacks. Now it seemed the action was wasted.

"Is everyone lost then?" he asked, his eyes displaying his concern.

"Balder is dead," the man replied. "They took their pick of women and children to take back across the sea. The rest were slaughtered."

"So, they have claimed the fort."

"Nay," the man replied. Brian raised a quizzical brow. "When it was over they all left by boat. There were a few of us who were left for dead but who managed to stay alive. I don't know what condition we will find them in when we return. This wasn't a land grab. It was done to embarrass ye."

"What makes ye say that?" Brian asked with both brows raised.

"Ye were marching to show yer strength yet ye couldn't protect us." He hung his head to avert the Ard Ri's stare. "I'd say 'twas clear enough."

Brian's anger ignited with the statement but any words he wished to offer were halted when Njord called out, "What about the woman, Eilis!"

The man whirled then jumped to see Njord standing so close behind him. "The queen was in bad shape when I left," he said, meeting Njord's gaze then wishing he hadn't. "Most probably she's dead."

It was then that Kormlada came rushing into the hall. "What's happening?"

"Balder has been slain," Brian replied, motioning for her to take the seat beside him. She might have a thought on how to handle it. "We don't know what's become of Eilis."

Njord balled his fists then followed Kormlada to the table. She took her seat while he leaned over his. A strand of hay slipped from his shoulder. "I pray ye to give me leave to ride to Caran Balder, Brian."

"I'll lead him," Maelmora quickly interjected. Kormlada smiled. "I'll take my men so that we can secure the fort. 'Twould do us nay good to have it fall into hostile hands."

Brian considered the request. With Murchad headed back to Armagh he had no reason to deny him. "Very well, but I expect a full report about what ye find there." He turned back to the man. "Have ye any idea who they were?"

The man nodded eagerly, surprised that the question hadn't been asked sooner. "'Twas Doncha of Sil Anmchada."

"Are ye certain?" Brian asked, his eyes going wide. The Eaghonacht had never acted violently before.

"Aye," the man replied. "He had Throdier of Orkney with him."

For a moment, Brian thought to scold the man for not offering the information sooner but it didn't matter in that he had it now. "Very well," he replied, a smile tugging at his lips. "We'll just have to repay Doncha in kind."

He turned to his wife to see if she had anything to offer. She nodded her agreement then smiled at him. He smiled back but it faded when he reached out to remove the strand of hay tangled in her hair.

*   *   *   *

Caran Balder, Ireland: 31, July 1006 A.D.—They came upon the edge of the world accompanied by four hundred warriors on horseback. Njord rode lead but it was clear that Maelmora was in control. The rise leading to the fort was scattered with a few goats, sheep and chickens in search of food. The cattle had all been taken.

Njord felt his stomach tighten as he glimpsed the charred ring fort. It put him to mind of the raid on Torshav and he hung his head in sympathy for those lost souls who were made to suffer through the annihilation. He prayed that Eilis wasn't among them.

Dotting the fields within the wall were fresh burial mounds marked by uprights and lintels. There were so many of them that it gave the fort the look of a graveyard.

"Those who have survived must have regained their strength," Maelmora said to the man who had come with the news. His name was Tordelbach. He nodded his curly brown head as hope sprang in him.

Njord made his way through the mounds, searching for any mark that would tell who was buried within. He read them carefully, stopping for a time when he found the one bearing Balder's name. If Eilis were dead, she would have shared his grave. That her name didn't mark the stone wasn't unusual. She was a woman—unworthy of such reverence.

"What have ye found, Njord?" Maelmora called out to him.

Njord felt the tear slip from his eye. "'Tis Balder's burial mound."

Maelmora rode to him, surprised by the impact the Ri Tuaths death had on the earl. "Were ye close with him then?"

He shook his head. "His wife was a friend of mine."

"I see," Maelmora replied then hung his head for Njord's loss. "Take yer time, aye," he continued when they observed a sufficient amount of silence in respect for the dead. "We'll just have a look around."

Njord nodded but never took his eyes from the mound. 'Tis a pity such a beautiful woman was wasted so early in life. He hoped she didn't suffer.

He heard the twig snap and turned. In the distance he saw Eilis edging back from the road, slithering between two ruined huts on her way to the stables. Her hair was a tangled mass and a long gash ran down her face. Her lein was bloody and tattered.

Njord urged his horse forward calling her name. She spun on her heel to face him, holding the knife steady in her hand. "Stand back!" she cried, squinting her eyes against the glare of the sun. "I know how to use this thing."

Njord slowed his approach then moved his horse into the shadows so that she could see who he was. "'Tis Njord, Eilis. Drop yer weapon."

He dismounted with a flourish but didn't rush forward. He had been on the defensive enough times to know that it might take a while for realization to set in.

Suddenly her eyes went wide and she took a few steps forward before collapsing to her knees sobbing, "Njord. Thank God ye came."

He ran to her then, his heart tearing for the pain she was in. He scooped her up then brought her to his chest, resting his chin on her head. "It's alright, Eilis. There's nothing to fear."

Maelmora joined them and soon she was leading them to the barn where the rest of the survivors were being kept. She gave them the only information she could recall about the raid. Vikings gained access through the secret tunnel Balder had built leading from the great hall to the sea. She couldn't remember anything else.

"What were they after, Eilis? Do ye know?"

When she looked up at Njord her eyes were filled with terror. "Death," she whispered.

CHAPTER 37

▼

Isle of Man: 3, April 1007 A.D.—Brodir whirled on the nurse, balling his fists in the air as he screamed, "I blame ye for this! Ye must be doing something wrong if the lad continues to shit in his pants."

He looked to Olaf who was crouching in the corner. The smell of human excrement flared his nostrils and he turned his eyes from the child. "Clean him up, now!"

The woman reached out her hand to the lad but he refused to take it. When Brodir screamed like that it usually meant that Olaf would receive a cuff to the ear when he passed him. Her heart went out to the lad.

"Pardon, lord, but I was thinking that if we continued to allow him to wear his kilt, perhaps he would have fewer accidents. The breeches are difficult to handle with all their laces and such. Maybe we can leave him in the kilt until he can learn to undo the breeches more quickly."

Brodir growled at her, issuing her the cuff to the head that should have gone to Olaf. "Now how will he ever learn to undo the breeches if we put him back in the kilt? Think woman! Use that head of yers!"

She pushed Olaf in front of her as they made their way out of the hall. Brodir kicked her in the buttocks. "Clean him up then bring him back here, aye. It's time for his sword lesson."

She nodded her head then hurried Olaf along. "And cut his hair," Brodir yelled after them. "It's so blasted red."

✳   ✳   ✳   ✳

Cashel, Ireland: 3, April 1007 A.D.—Saroise strummed her fingers against the table as her anger built. She was tired of Patric putting Eilis ahead of her and she wanted her mother to do something about it.

"How many more times must I step aside for Eilis?" she huffed, pushing herself from her chair so she could stomp about the room. "She's the daughter of a whore but the way my father dotes on her ye would think that she sprang from his own loins."

Lara's back stiffened. She lifted her gaze to meet her daughter's then lowered her sewing into her lap. "What do ye want with the Viking anyway? With the way he's given to moving around ye could find yerself living in Man instead of here in Eire where yer family is. Now sit down and put it out of yer mind because ye're giving me a headache."

"But Njord was promised to me! So what if he had to wait!"

"Ye're father and Brian have their reasons for wanting him married to Eilis and I won't question them on it. Ye just concentrate on Donchad."

"Donchad?" Saroise blurted, her lips puckering with the thought of him. "He's a child. What good would he do me?"

"He's the Ard Ri's son," Lara replied, lifting her eyebrow as if to say that her daughter ought to know better. "If ye marry him, ye'll be married to someone of importance instead of a Viking who has no real chance of ascending within the clan. Use yer head, Saroise."

There was silence as Saroise considered the statement then her smile turned mischievous. "Och, aye," she blurted. Being married to Donchad would put her in a position higher than her cousin's. "So, do ye think that father will agree?"

"I'll make him agree," Lara replied. She put the last stitch into the hem she was doing then cut the thread with her teeth. "Weddings always put him in a generous mood. I'll convince him of it tonight, after we go to bed."

She handed the lein to Saroise who slipped it over her head then she stood back to admire her handiwork. "Very nice," she said with a nod of her head. "I dare say that ye'll be even more beautiful than the bride."

Saroise smiled then opened her mouth to reply but when she noticed Eilis walking past her chamber she raced outside to speak with her instead. "My mother has sewn me a new lein to wear to the feast. Do ye like it?"

"Very nice," Eilis grumbled without taking the time to look.

"Mother says that it's best for ye to marry Njord so that I can be free for Don-chad."

"See there," Eilis replied, stepping up her pace to be rid of the child. "Now everyone is happy."

"When I do marry Donchad, it will mean that ye will have to bow to me."

Eilis stopped suddenly, knotting her fists before turning to face her cousin. "What is it that ye want from me, Saroise? I've many things to tend."

"Nay a thing, Eilis. I just thought ye should know that ye're getting the short end of the deal is all."

"Should I be surprised?" she replied, lifting a brow awaiting her cousin's response. When none came she continued, "Now if ye've nothing else, I must be on my way."

Saroise waved her hand in dismissal and Eilis continued on through the doors to meet her women on the path leading to the old cave. "What kept ye?" Margreg asked, seeing the distress marking her daughter's face.

"Nay a thing," Eilis replied. "Saroise has a new lein for the wedding and she wanted to show it off for me."

"Dreadful child, that," Hecca mumbled. When she realized that she had said it loud enough for all to hear, her face went immediately red. "I pray ye to forgive me, lady."

"What's to forgive?" Eilis chuckled. "Ye didn't make her that way."

They all nodded knowingly then continued on down the path to the old cave just outside the gates of Cashel. It was a Viking tradition for the bride to bathe with her women before the ceremony. Since Eilis wasn't familiar with any of Njord's customs she was eager to be with them so they could offer their advice.

Hecca poured water on the hot stones in the center of the cave causing a great puff of steam to rise as she spoke. "A Viking husband will expect ye to run his house when he's away. He'll expect an ample field of vegetables and fattened animals for his dinner."

Eilis sat silently, intent on what the older woman was saying. "He'll expect ye to speak kindly of him, both before his comrades and in private. And he'll expect ye to be strong when he leaves ye to go a Viking."

Beside Hecca sat Sedja, a dark haired woman who always spoke her mind without needing to be asked. "Now tell her what she really wants to hear, Hecca. Tell her about her wedding night."

Margreg chuckled and Gertrude slapped her shoulder, fearing that Hecca would take offense if they interfered. "Hush yerself, child!" Hecca barked at Sedja. "She's been married already, aye. She knows what to expect."

"What about the witnesses?" Eilis asked, worrying that she wouldn't be alone with her husband on their wedding night. "Must they be present even on the second marriage?"

"Of course we will, lassie. We will have to put ye to bed and the next morning ye'll have to describe yer dreams so we can tell ye how many babies ye're gonna have."

Eilis rarely dreamed giving her something else to worry about. "What if I don't remember my dream, Hecca?"

"Och, lady! Don't even fool me so. Ye must remember or the marriage will be cursed."

Sedja laughed then waved a hand in dismissal. "If ye don't remember, do as I did and tell them ye saw the great goddess Frigga coming at ye with a babe in both arms. That'll keep them quiet."

Hecca shot Sedja a look but the girl waved it off. "Och, Hecca, ye're trapped in time. No one remembers their dreams, especially if their new husband has a good appetite for the bed. She'll be too tired to remember anything."

"God willing," Eilis mumbled then they all laughed.

Hecca continued, "At the breakfast feast yer husband will offer the Shaver a morning gift. It'll seal yer marriage and let everyone know he intends to keep ye."

Sedja broke in, "Depending on how good ye were to him the night before that's how large the gift will be."

Hecca nodded. "It's for sure too."

Eilis hid her face for the secret that she and Njord shared but Hecca mistook it for worry. "Get on with ye now, child. Njord wouldn't think of offering any less then twenty head of cattle for ye after what he went through to get ye. I've seen many a bride and groom come together in my day but I've never seen so much love as Njord has for ye. Ye're a lucky one alright."

Eilis sat up straight. "Hecca, what are ye saying?"

Hecca laughed, "Even when he was married to Ermagh, I could see how much he loved ye, lassie. Ye were all he could speak about. I think he cursed himself for not waiting for ye."

Goose pimples broke out on Eilis' flesh. She knew that Njord had come to love her but she had no idea that he had loved her from the start. She stood then, eager to get on with the ceremony so that she could see him. "Are we done here?" she asked of Hecca, hoping the question wouldn't offend the woman.

Sedja laughed then poked Hecca in her ribs. "I'd say Njord's the lucky one. Ye barely finished telling her of her marriage bed and she's ready to race off to get into it."

Hecca nodded as she got to her feet. "Good for her, aye. Why shouldn't she have some fun after all she's been through?"

They dressed in silence then Hecca led them out of the cave. She screeched when she ran directly into Njord. "Cover yer eyes, laddie!" she barked at him then turned to Margreg. "Ye tell the lass to cover her eyes as well. 'Tis bad luck for them to see each other before the ceremony."

"Och, Hecca," Njord replied, peeking his head inside to try to get a glimpse of his bride. If luck was with him she might still be naked. "That's nothing but an old wife's tale."

Margreg, Sedja and Gertrude surrounded Eilis to be sure Njord wouldn't see her and Hecca snapped back. "Aye and I'm an old wife. Now cover yer eyes before I swell them shut for ye!"

"Do as she says, Njord," Patric commanded. "If ye don't, we'll be standing out here forever."

Njord did as she asked then shuffled his feet as the women passed him by. He could smell the lavender on their skin and in a moment of weakness, he spread his fingers apart so he could peer through them. He chuckled then dropped his hands when he saw that they had Eilis draped in linen from her head to her toes.

"Did ye think I would trust the likes of ye?" Hecca asked then cuffed him at the back of his head.

Patric sucked his teeth then wriggled past them. "She knows ye too well, son."

"Aye," Njord grumbled then smacked her rump to hurry her along. When they were gone he disrobed then took his seat on the rock closest to the fire. The other men found their spots and Vahn brought the steam with a sprinkle of water on the coals.

"I'm eager to find out who Doncha will call to assist him," Murchad said as he leaned back to stretch himself. His chest glistened from the steam.

"Whoever it is will have been in on it from the beginning," Thorien replied.

"Aye," Brian agreed. "And I wouldn't be a bit surprised to find Malsakin among them."

"I don't know," Patric interjected. "My spies tell me that he's content enough in Meath. Why would he buy trouble by getting into this?"

"I think that Fladbartoc is helping Doncha," Murchad offered. They all looked at him and he continued, "This is his chance to make up for what happened in Tara. Didn't ye always say that if it wasn't for Malsakin getting there first it would have been Fladbartoc ye faced for the high throne, father?"

Brian nodded then smiled. "Ye make a good point, son. If this is a ploy to make Fladbartoc Ard Ri, I highly doubt that Malsakin would be assisting him."

Havland raised an eyebrow. "I heard Fladbartoc nearly cut Malsakin's throat after he handed ye the crown. I doubt they're even on speaking terms."

"Too bad he failed," Njord chuckled before leaning back to stretch the tension out of his muscles.

"We'll know soon enough who'll be in this and who won't aye," Brian replied, "But either way, we need to agree on a time for battle. I'm thinking to do it by the solstice. It'll give us enough time to sew our fields and it'll give our groom here ample time to enjoy his new wife."

The comment sparked a wealth of crude remarks from the other men, Maelmora among them. "I'd say that they'll need more than a moon to cool their lust. Ye should have seen them when they came together in Caran Balder. I thought he would take her right there in front of everyone."

"Get on with ye," Njord barked. "Are ye charging my wife with being a wanton?"

"Ye should be so lucky," Havland mumbled then they all laughed.

Brian looked Njord over. He was beginning to lose face with the spreading rumors of his wife's infatuation with the man. He only hoped this great love professed between Njord and Eilis would ease the situation.

Maelmora turned to him, seriousness doting his face. "I've been keeping Caran Balder for ye lo these months and I was wondering if ye would declare the lands mine? Njord and I have already discussed it and he's agreed that he would rather not have to be bothered with overseeing territory so far away from Torshav."

Brian raised an eyebrow and Njord nodded. "I'll take some lands in Port da Chanoic in exchange. I think it would be best."

Brian began to nod his head but Murchad got to his feet. "Don't I have a say in who gets the lands? After all, they lay in my territory."

"Ye've not cared what's happened to them up until now," Maelmora snapped back. "Why the sudden interest."

"Because they fall under my control," Murchad barked.

Maelmora got to his feet and soon the two men were facing off against each other. They were nearly the same height and build, but while Maelmora was all golden and fair, Murchad was dark and brooding.

Brian rubbed the pain from his forehead as the enmity between the two men was demonstrated once again. "Both of ye sit down!"

They continued to stare at each other until Havland and Thorien rose to tower over them. They took their seats.

"'Twill be Maelmora who takes Caran Balder," Brian said without apology. "Murchad, if ye're so sure that Fladbartoc will stand with Doncha, I want ye to try to get me information about what he's up to. I'd say ye should be more interested in controlling Ailech then the edge of the world."

Murchad opened his mouth to argue but his father's upturned hand put an end to the thought. "Now, getting back to Doncha. I want at least three thousand men with us, aye. That'll show him that he's playing with fire."

"Speaking of fire," Patric broke in. He was looking at Njord. "Didn't Basil give ye instruction on how to make Greek Fire?"

"He did," Njord replied.

Brian became excited. "Do ye think ye can make it, man?"

"He can make it," Vahn replied with a twisted grin. "He tried it in Torshav and nearly burned down the barns."

"It got away from me," Njord admitted with a shrug of his shoulders.

"That's grand," Brian replied then rubbed his hands together before getting to his feet. "Enough of this war talk now. We have a wedding to attend and I for one am planning to enjoy myself."

They left the cave and within an hour, were standing on the rise overlooking the village below. It was Friday, the day sacred to the pagan goddess, Frigga and the one reserved for Viking weddings.

Njord was dressed in a crisp white lien with four purple stripes across his breast. His white cotton cloak was fastened with a gold brooch bearing the mark of a stallion and his hair was bound in a tail at his back.

Patric, on the other hand, looked every bit the warrior, decked out in leather from head to toe with a braid in his hair for good measure. "Are ye expecting trouble?" Njord asked when he came up beside him.

"Just in case she puts up a fight," his father replied with a wink.

They all turned as Eilis made her way up the rise. Her dark hair flowed like gossamer playing in the silken ribbons trailing from her flower halo. She kept her eyes trained on the back of the young lad who was leading the way with the new sword she acquired for Njord tight in his hands. Behind her walked her women, pride beaming in their eyes.

It was Gable's duty to perform the service and he did it with grace and ease, using the Manx tongue he had diligently practiced over the last week.

Eilis offered her husband his new sword. "I give ye this sword to protect and keep ye always."

Njord bowed as he accepted her gift then handed her his old one. "This sword is the sword of my ancestors. Ye are to keep it for our son who will pass it to his so the sword of our family will be kept forever."

They exchanged their rings in similar fashion, she promising fidelity and he promising to keep her and her family safe. When it was done, Gable pronounced them married to the cheering crowd.

To Eilis' surprise, Njord kissed her with the desperation of a man who had been denied then he turned to his guests to shout, "Someone bring me my horse so that the feasting may begin."

It was tradition for the Viking bride and groom to race back to the feasting hall after the wedding blessing was given. The loser of the race would provide the serving duty for the evening. The contest was none at all since the groom was permitted to ride his horse while the bride was forced to race on foot. Eilis thought the custom fun.

Patric looked to Njord who was dancing his horse around anxiously, then to Eilis who hitched up her lien as she stretched her legs in preparation for the race. When he was certain both were ready, he threw down the scarf to set them free.

Njord trotted alongside Eilis for most of the run but when she started to gain on him, he kicked the steed into a gallop. By the time she arrived he had the entrance to the great hall blocked. "And where do ye think ye're going, woman?" he asked, grabbing her by the waist when she tried to skitter around him.

She giggled then let her eyes fall to the ground. "Forgive me, lord, but I must pass. 'Tis my wedding day and I have serving to do."

"Aye," he growled, scooping her into his arms then bending to kiss her. "And the service begins with me."

"Ye set her free, Njord," Hecca scolded when he dipped his head a second time. "We'll put ye to bed when it's nice and proper and not a moment before."

Njord grumbled at the woman then set Eilis down so that he could lead her safely to her seat. He hated the rituals but wouldn't suffer a tongue lashing by breaking them. He turned to Hecca who had been following on his heel then screwed up his face. "Happy now, woman?"

She smiled triumphantly before handing Eilis the goblet. "Do ye remember the words, lass?"

Eilis nodded then offered her husband the cup. "Bless this drink, oh Frigga, so this marriage will be fertile." She spoke in Manx.

Njord smiled before accepting the cup then used it to make the sign of Thor's hammer. "Oh mighty Thor, bless this union so it may be strong. Give me the strength and wisdom to lead and protect my family."

Havland led the crowd in a chant of, "Njord, Njord, Njord," and the new groom drained the cup before slamming it down on the table. He offered Eilis a long, sweet kiss before thrusting his sword into the cross beam above her head. The cut was deep and he howled with delight.

Patric howled with him then laughed. "By the looks of that cut ye'll be blessed with many children, Njord."

Njord puffed out his chest even though he knew better. "Ye best brace that thing before yer roof caves in on my wife's head."

The room erupted in laughter causing Saoirse to squirm under the weight of her own hatred. It should have been her up there instead of that nothing of a woman; that sniveling shadow with no backbone of her own; that whore, Eilis!

Hecca brought forth Frigga's hammer then handed it to Njord saying, "Put it in her lap and don't go dropping it on her."

"This thing weighs heavy, woman," he scolded when he took it in his hands. "If I put it in her lap there might not be a wedding night."

Hecca leered at him. "Do it I say or ye'll have bad luck in this marriage for sure."

He scowled at her before seeking Eilis' approval. She smiled. "It'll be alright, husband."

Njord gingerly placed the hammer into her lap, all the while growling, "What good are these fertility prayers if the woman's too sore to perform the act when the time comes?"

Hecca elbowed him in the ribs before sprinkling the arrowroot dust over the hammer. "Say it," she demanded before letting the last of the dust drop from her hands.

Njord rolled his eyes. "Mighty goddess, Frigga, bless this marriage with fine children," he droned then leaned down to whisper to Eilis, "Ye alright, *m'mil-lish*?"

Eilis smiled slyly as she called him closer with the crook of her finger. "It'll take more than a hammer to keep me from ye tonight." He raised his brows before kissing her but it was cut short when a commotion broke out near the doors.

They both watched as Kormlada and Brian entered, the Ard Ri in a red lein and golden coat and the high queen in a magenta silk lein that caused her hair to shimmer. Eilis swallowed nervously. For all her years, Kormlada was still the greatest beauty Ireland had ever seen, gliding toward the front of the hall as her mere presence parted the sea of people.

"So, Eilis," she cooed once the pleasantries were observed and Njord and Brian were locked in conversation. "Ye have won the heart of the great Njord the Black. I can't believe I was lucky enough to bear witness to it."

Eilis resisted the urge to shrink in her chair. She cleared her throat and willed her voice to be steady, "I think it's me who is lucky to have yer well wishes on my wedding day. Yer presence means a great deal to both me and *my* husband."

"Well, I certainly know what it means to yer husband," Kormlada said, not trying to hide her desire of him.

Eilis took her meaning but before she could reply the high queen had her by the face, turning her head from side to side in scrutiny. "Hmmm. I thought perhaps that some miracle had occurred to make ye beautiful enough to turn the earl's head, but alas I see ye look the same as always. Whatever could ye possess that would make him risk my ire in order to have ye?"

Eilis' knuckles whitened around the hammer in her lap as she struggled with the decision over whether or not to use it to pummel the woman. "That which a woman possesses isn't always obvious to the naked eye," she replied. "It's my good fortune that my husband can see through flesh to things that matter like loyalty, honor and integrity. I believe he married me to show all who cared that he's committed to this union *and* the Ard Ri."

Kormlada smiled slyly, ignoring her implication. She bent closer. "Lend yer ear to a woman who was once married to a Viking. They have no honor, any of them. They're devoted to the sea. They truly love no woman and will take as many as they can to their bed. They live for the battle and even more so for the chase. Today ye sit as a prize won for *his* benefit." She jerked her head toward Njord who spotted her from the corner of his eye. "When this feast is over ye'll be nothing more than a servant carrying the keys to *his* house."

Eilis raised her voice enough to draw both Brian and Njord's attention, hoping they would intercede before she committed violence. "I'll give heed to yer words kind, lady. I'm sure yer advice is sage."

From his place behind the table, Njord spotted Eilis's grip on the hammer. He placed a loving hand on her shoulder to keep her from lifting it. "Kormlada," he trilled, "Aren't ye looking lovely this evening? We're so glad to have ye."

Kormlada flashed her dimples as the Ard Ri slipped his hand around her waist, jerking her against him until she could hardly breathe. "I wouldn't miss this wedding for all the gold in Dublin," she croaked.

Njord traded his gaze between Kormlada and Brian and a shiver ran up his spine when he noticed the anger in the Ard Ri's eyes. He looked away. "Well, we are glad to have ye."

Brian smiled for his victory then started to lead Kormlada away but she stopped and leaned close to Eilis. "By the way," she cooed. "I bid ye sweet dreams tonight."

Eilis' back straightened and her lip began to tremble. Brian noticed and took his wife by the hand to lead her around the table. "What's the matter, woman? Things not hot enough for ye." She leered at him but he ignored her then shoved her ahead of him.

When they were comfortably seated he banged his eating knife against his goblet to call for the great battle of wits and insults that was a Viking tradition. "Give heed, men and women to those who will tell the tale of the great Njord the Black." He looked to Vahn who was immediately on his feet. "Aye, man. Do ye have a tale for us then?"

"I do, Ard Ri," Vahn offered then bowed to the crowd before settling himself on the stool that the servants brought for him.

According to Viking custom, it was the duty of the groom's men to insult him. If his wife didn't take offense at what she heard then he could be certain that she would be true to him. Vahn cleared his throat before regaling them with his version of their trip to Italy.

"The winds were howling over the sea, so much so that it sounded like thousands of babes crying for their mother's milk. I was there beside old Njord while he cowered in the corner like a mouse. I told him there was nothing to be frightened of but still he cowered. He said he missed his ma. I begged him to lay down and rest his head because his fear was giving me the heaves but he refused and instead put his strong thumb in his mouth and began to suck like a babe to a teat."

Njord cried out, "And ye being my man could tell such fabrications?"

Brian banged his goblet with his knife. "Order here. I won't have ye interrupt this most fair account."

There was laughter in the room and when it subsided Vahn began again, "Well, the boat had to be put ashore because Njord's fearful shaking was making it go off course. And when ye thought the man would be glad of it instead he tells us he won't disembark because he's afraid of wild animals lurking on shore. I tell him there's nothing to be worried over because he has his sword with him but still he shrinks to the suggestion that he leave the boat.

"Now we all had our fill of his cowardly ways so we went on ahead without him. We lay upon our shields and settled in for our rest when suddenly Njord comes running from the boat like it was set aflame. I turn to him and said, 'What's yer trouble man?' He said back to me, 'I saw a cross eyed owl and it put me in a state.' I said back, 'Did you hew at it man?' He replies, 'Nay, cause I can't find my sword.' I said to him, 'Yer sword's hanging from yer belt.' And he says again to me, 'I can't find it.'"

Njord got to his feet taking Tyr, who had crawled into his lap, with him. "Foul! It's a mighty foul story ye tell."

Brian chuckled then again banged his goblet. "One more outburst and I'll remove ye to yer chamber." When he noticed the anticipation in Njord's face he added, "Alone!"

Njord sunk back into his chair and Brian turned to Vahn to state, "Go on, man. It's a lovely story ye tell and we're most entertained by it."

Tyr clapped his hands to encourage Vahn and the man continued, "Anyway, now we're on the shore and everyone is asleep save for Njord who's running around helplessly. I says to him, 'What's yer trouble now man?' And he says to me back, 'I think I hear a wolf.' I help him unsheathe his sword and give it to him in his hand. After he dropped it for the fourth time he finally takes hold of it and I said to him, 'Use it if the wolf should come near.' He says to me, 'Aye.' And I return to my rest.

"A little time later, I find him trying to run the wolf through with his short sword. Only trouble is, he has it by the wrong end and is jabbing at the animal with the hilt."

"Falsehood!" Njord got to his feet, holding Tyr in one arm while his other was thrown in the air. "This whole thing is a falsehood!"

"Falsehood!" Tyr mimicked. He too threw up his arm but when he did it hit Njord square in the nose. Eilis covered her mouth to hide her laughter. "Falsehood!" Tyr cried again to make her laugh still harder.

"Oh fine!" Njord cried. He grabbed Tyr's hand to halt further damage then looked to his wife. "Now they got ye believing that I'm a coward and a dolt." He turned to his fellows. "See there! I've not even got her to chamber and already ye got her laughing at me."

"Well she would have laughed at ye anyway once she got a gander at yer wee self," Havland croaked between his spurts of laughter.

"Wee self, father," Tyr called out making hand gestures to demonstrate just how small a *wee self* was. Njord shook his head before slumping into his chair. "Oh grand! Ye're a good bunch of fellows ye are! Got my own son poking fun at me now."

Vahn stood before his stool, his body racked with his convulsing laughter. When he regained his control he spread his arms open to ask, "How many here know this story to be true?" Everyone in the hall raised their hand causing Njord to bang his head against the table while Tyr clapped his hands happily.

The entertainment for the evening included many such stories of cowardice and ineptitude. And though Njord protested he was appreciative of how much his men loved him. Only a man's good friends would treat him to such insulting stories.

There was so much wine and mead that nearly half the hall was intoxicated. At one point, Patric wrapped a cloak around his head and reddened his lips with wine to do his best impersonation of a woman. Brian played his lover and soon the crowd roared, begging them for more. The next bit of entertainment included, Margreg, Gertrude and Havland all taking turns regaling the crowd with the crudest songs Eilis had ever heard.

It was near midnight when Hecca gently rubbed her shoulders to draw her attention. "Are ye ready, lassie?"

Eilis puzzled a moment before realizing what the woman meant. She looked to her lap where the heavy hammer lay. She was eager to be rid of it. Then she cast a glance toward Njord who was engaged in a drinking contest with Brian. She handed the hammer to Hecca then stood, stretching her legs and back before sighing, "I think the question should be, is *he* ready?"

Hecca turned just in time to see Njord guzzle a full horn of ale while his men chanted his name. She smiled wryly. "Not to worry, lass. That one is always ready."

Eilis smiled knowingly then followed Sedja and Hecca to her wedding chamber. She stopped just outside the door. "Must there be witnesses, Hecca? I can tell ye my dreams in the morning."

"Have nay fear," Hecca replied, a slight scowl showing on her face as she stepped into the room. "Njord has already told us that there will be no witnesses."

As if he were summoned by the use of his name, Njord stumbled out of the great hall followed by his men. Hecca pushed Eilis and Sedja inside the hut then threw the bolt. "Let me in, woman," Njord cried as he pounded on the door.

Hecca opened it wide enough to see Njord, Havland, Brian, Eagan, Vahn and Patric swaying against each other. "Ye rots just cool yer heels. She ain't ready yet and I won't have ye rushing her!"

The door closed with a bang leaving Patric pounding on the frame. "Well, hurry up then, woman! It don't take that long to get the lass naked?"

"How would ye know?" Sejda chuckled as she scurried around the chamber plumping up pillows and dabbing fragrance oil on the linens. "Ye got an anxious lot out there, lady. Ye'd think they were coming for their own pleasure by the way they're howling."

Hecca looked to Eilis who was disrobing slowly. "Don't let them get to ye, child. It's just their way." She raised her voice to be certain the men would hear, "They're a bunch of animals is what they are. But ye needn't worry because old Njord will treat ye right."

Eilis chuckled then slipped between the sheets, the heat of her naked body releasing the soothing fragrance of lavender that Sejda had just deposited on them. She arranged her hair on the pillow so she would look attractive to her new husband then looked to Hecca who was standing by the door with her hand on the latch. "Ready."

Hecca yanked the door open and both Patric and Vahn tumbled into the room. "Oh that's grand," she sighed before giving each one a swift kick. "Are ye planning on joining them then?"

Eilis covered her laughter as she watched the two men scramble to get to their feet. Eagan, who was in the worst condition of all, stepped forward to assist them. Soon all three were rolling around on the floor and Hecca, Sejda and Brian failed miserably when they tried to stand them up.

Njord remained in the doorway, watching the display with both hands against the jam to steady himself. The harder they struggled the harder he laughed and Eilis watched him wondering why he hadn't put an end to it by now.

"Shall I lay here and freeze or will ye make way so my husband can join me?" she snapped, drawing Njord's attention.

He took a moment to swat back a strand of hair that was resting on his brow before easing himself into the room. He walked over to Hecca and Sedja, offering each a hand to help them to their feet then did the same for Brian, Eagan and Vahn. But Patric was another story.

The Ri Ciocid was growing increasingly more intoxicated as he continued to refresh himself from the skin he brought with him. Njord offered him a hand up but Patric couldn't focus long enough to grasp it. In the end it took nearly all of them to bring him to his feet. Hecca braced him against the wall as Sejda reached out to take the skin.

"Ye touch it and ye'll be picking yer head up from the floor," Patric teased in good nature then he raised the skin above his head in a toast. "To my children," he slurred. "May their marriage bed be strong enough to withstand the abuse."

He took a deep swig and Hecca used the opportunity to push him through the doorway. "Aye now, lord. Yer guests have been left unattended for long enough. Best get back to the hall before they guzzle all yer wine."

Patric's eyebrows rushed together with the thought. "Och. Ye're right, woman." The mead squirted from the skin as he motioned for Brian and Eagan to follow. "Come on, men. I may need yer help with these drunks."

Eagan stumbled over to Patric then dutifully took his arm so they could sway down the path together. Vahn took his wife by the arm leaving Havland to lead Brian. When they were all out, Hecca beckoned Njord with the crook of her finger.

"Aye," he said as he bent to her.

She screwed up her face before issuing her advice, "Now ye be gentle with her, Njord. Don't go mangling her with those big paws of yers."

"Aye, lady," he agreed then bent to kiss her before closing the door.

She grabbed his ear to keep it close then whispered, "Be sure to give her pleasure before ye take yer own, aye?"

He nodded again but she wasn't finished. "Kiss her on the neck a bit. Women like that. And don't be afraid to tell her what ye want. Give her encouragement when she's doing good, aye."

He straightened himself then pushed the door full open to make way for her. "Maybe ye'd like to stay and join us."

She flushed then gently slapped his cheek. "Nay. Ye could never keep up with me." She spun on her heel and he watched her walk down the path to be sure she was truly gone then he closed the door behind her. She was worried that the marriage would be cursed because he refused to have witnesses but he wouldn't suffer another wedding night like the one he had with Ermagh.

He bolted the door then turned to his wife who was a vision of cream skin and dark hair glowing in the lamplight. "Well," he said as he made his way toward the bed, "I guess we're on our own."

She smiled slyly then stretched beneath the linens. "Do ye think ye can do it without their advice?"

He shrugged his shoulders. "Ye haven't been complaining up until now."

She chuckled then reached out her arms to him. They had been secretly sharing a bed since her return from Caran Balder and since there was no issue from their coupling, she was fairly certain that the miscarriage had left her barren. She picked up the arrowroot dust then sprinkled it on her stomach. "Perhaps these fertility rituals will help us, aye," she stated as she watched him undress.

He knew that she wanted to bare his child. He wanted it too but he tried to play it down. "Have nay worry if they don't. We have Tyr. Ye're his mother now. We need no more than that."

"Aye," she replied, absently stroking her womb to recall the feeling of the babe resting in it. She closed her eyes, trying to conjure the last day of her pregnancy in her mind. She remembered that the day was warm and breezy and that the sky was a brilliant blue. Njord had told her that it was common for people to lose their memory of gruesome events, which was probably why she couldn't recall many of the things that happened that day.

She looked up at him to tell him that she remembered the sky and when she did she glimpsed his hand pulling the dagger from the pocket of his coat. Suddenly it flooded back to her. The dagger—the hand with the missing pinky—the man with one eye. She began to sweat and her breaths came too quickly.

"What is it m'millish?" he asked as he fell to his knees beside her. She backed away when he tried to touch her.

"Turlog," she mumbled. "Turlog! Turlog!"

✻   ✻   ✻   ✻

Thomond, Ireland: The hut of the Ri Tuath—14, June 1007 A.D.—Turlog drank the foul tasting liquid, savoring every bit of the burn as it slid down his throat. It was the only thing that had been working to counteract his illness and he had learned to enjoy it for the healing it brought. Grace sat across from him, eyeing him suspiciously as she poured a cup of ale. He took it then rested back in his chair after taking a sip.

"Yer face is getting some of its color back," she said with a smile.

He looked at her, wondering exactly what she meant by that. "Don't be so eager for my death, woman. Ye may be disappointed. I don't plan on going anywhere just yet."

"Really, Turlog," she gasped, genuinely offended by the comment. Over the past years she learned that if she didn't meet his accusations head on it would put him into a state of paranoia. "I'm not eager for yer death, I'm eager to see ye well again and I'm happy that the concoction seems to be working. Even yer appetite has returned. 'Tis a good sign indeed."

She slid the trencher of salted pork close to him, urging him to take some. He did and she smiled. "Now, why don't ye tell me about yer plans, husband? Ye've been quite busy of late."

He slammed down his cup then leaned forward in his chair until she could feel his breath on her face. "Ye would like that, wouldn't ye? I give ye my plans then ye go running to that fool son of yers to tell him all about them. That would have me dead and buried quick enough for ye, aye? Well, don't hold yer breath because I'll not be sharing my thoughts with ye."

Though she worried he might strike her she reached up to stroke his cheek anyway, hoping that her soothing touch would ease him. He sat still for it and she pushed the fear from her eyes. "Why would ye think that I wanted ye dead. Haven't we waited a lifetime to be together? Now that we are, we hardly act as if we are married at all. I love ye, Turlog. Never doubt that."

She could feel the tremble in his throat as he growled at her then he took her hand in his to turn it palm up. He kissed it then yanked her close. "If ye love me then ye'll swear never to raise yer hand against me."

"I've done that," she replied, her voice calm and even.

"Ye'll promise never again to be giving information regarding this house to yer son, Patric or yer brother."

"Ye know I don't speak with my brother. I wouldn't give him information about ye or anyone else."

"Ah," he cooed, kissing her palm again before leaning his face in until their foreheads touched, "but ye give information to yer son who gives it to the Ard Ri. I want it to stop, Grace. Promise me that ye'll no longer speak to him."

"And what of yer daughter?" she questioned, knowing full well that she couldn't keep the promise if she gave it. "Shall we also cut her off? And Saroise? Is it yer hope to have our family torn asunder?"

"I am yer family now, Grace. I'm yer husband and I should be all that matters to ye. Now, promise me that ye'll keep away from Patric."

"I'll not go to him," she replied, lowering her eyes so he wouldn't see her doubt, "but if they should make their way here, I don't expect that I could put them out."

"If they make their way here, then I'll take care of them," he growled. He pulled her to him from across the table and she could feel his bones protruding out from beneath his skin. He was still weak but some of his strength was coming back and in that moment she offered a silent prayer to the Lord to heal her husband both body and mind.

"Attack!" came the guard's cry as he ran from the gates. "We are under attack! All men to arms."

"Shit," Turlog spit then ran to the window to see what it was all about.

"What is it?" Grace asked, her eyes wide with fear.

"Nay doubt it's yer wretched brother and yer equally wretched son," he grumbled. "Aye, it's them," he issued when he stuck his head out the window to glimpse the yellow tunics in the distance.

"What shall we do?"

"We?" he asked, grabbing her by the arm to pull her against him. His eye was wild and in that moment she feared him. "*We* won't be doing anything."

He uncovered his dagger then pulled it across her throat, watching the change in her eyes as the life drained from her. When she was dead, he cast her to the floor then slipped out the door.

He slid along the wall of his hut until he came to the stables then mounted his steed and headed toward the woods. They might take his village, but they would never take him.

✳   ✳   ✳   ✳

Sil Anmchada, Ireland: 4, September 1007 A.D—The sky was heavy with clouds and the wind blew briskly from the west. The sweet scent of lavender was carried through the air and Eilis lifted her head to it, momentarily forgetting their purpose for being there. She opened her eyes then swept the field, watching as the tents billowed with the breeze then she turned to her mother. "What is it like when the fighting begins?"

Margreg hung her head. She had tried to stop her daughter from accompanying them but the lass was insistent on being present wherever her husband was. "'Tis not good," she replied, closing her eyes as if to recall a particular memory. "There's a lot of screaming and the clanging of metal is so loud that it seems like it's right inside yer head. Ye best keep yer ears covered. That's what I do. It makes it easier to handle that way."

"And the blood?" Eilis persisted. She hated the sight of blood most of all things.

"Och, the blood," Margreg replied. "So much blood that it seems like a river." She shook her head then looked at her daughter whose face had gone white. "Ye shouldn't have come, Eilis. 'Tis no type of life for a woman."

"Och, aye. And I suppose that ye're not a woman."

"Aye, that I am, but I'm used to it by now."

"So, are ye telling me that if ye could chose all over again that ye would do things differently?"

Margreg considered the question then thought about Finn and the lifetime of memories they made together. If she had stayed behind to keep house instead of accompanying him on the march like most wives, she would have been able to count the days they spent together on her two hands. "Nay," she responded at length. "I wouldn't have chosen differently."

"Then neither will I," Eilis replied before putting her arm around her mother's shoulder. "I couldn't bear him being away from me so often. And if he were to be killed I…" Her words hung in the air and a shiver ran up her spine. "I would want to be with him."

Margreg nodded her understanding then stood to get things started. "Very well," she cooed as she clapped her hands together. "If ye want to be a healer then there are things we must prepare for when the fighting starts." She bent to the pile of clothes lying in a heap just inside the tent. She picked up a tattered lein then shredded it from the rip at the side. "Pick them up and start stripping them. We'll need them for bandaging, aye."

Following her mother's example, Eilis did as she was bade. When Margreg was satisfied that it was being done right, she moved further inside the tent to the jars of ointments she had lining a table. "I'll grind the chamomile. Ye check the sulfur. We'll need plenty of mud too, for casting, aye."

Eilis nodded then all at once, jumped when she felt the hot breath on her neck. "M'millish," Njord sighed when he grabbed her around the waist. "Aren't ye looking every bit the healer?"

She giggled when he nibbled her ear then she threw down the material she'd been shredding to turn and offer him her lips. She braced her hands against his shoulder, letting her fingers play in the mail he was wearing. "And ye're looking every bit the warrior."

When she broke from him, her eyes were sad. He raised her chin with his finger so he could look at her. "What is it?"

She shook her head, fearful that if she spoke he would hear the tremble in her voice. "Tell me," he urged, rubbing his cheek against hers until she gave in.

"I worry for ye, is all."

He nodded his head. When she told him that she wanted to accompany him he had thought to deny her. He feared that he might not be able to concentrate on the battle if he knew she was watching and worrying for him. But she was there now and it was best that he address the situation. "Listen to me," he whispered with his lips so close to hers that it was all she could do to keep from kissing him. "On the march, everyone has a job to do. I will fight and ye shall heal, but if either of us takes their mind off their job then both of us will be jeopardized. Do ye understand me?"

She did understand. Her mother had told her about what happened to Finn when she called out to him. She cautioned her to keep her worry to herself.

Eilis blinked back her tears then smiled before looking up at him. "They tell me that ye're pretty good with a blade."

"I've had my share of kills," he replied, his pride for the statement carefully checked.

"Show me," she answered, cocking her head haughtily. He raised a brow and she shrugged her shoulders. "If I know ye can fight then I won't be worrying for ye when ye're out there."

"I see," he cooed. "And what is it that ye'd like me to show ye?"

"Show me how ye use the blade. I've never paid much attention when the soldiers were training. I'd like to see how it works."

Vahn was walking in the distance with Havland and Njord whistled to get their attention. They came to his call, nodding their greetings to both Margreg and Eilis. "Aye, Njord?" Vahn replied, ever the soldier.

Njord raised his brow in a silent message that they should indulge him. "My wife here would like to see if I have the skills necessary for battle."

"Is that so?" Havland asked with a chuckle. "I should think that question was answered at yer wedding feast."

"Aye," Njord agreed. "Perhaps it's the stories ye fellows told her that's got her all worried now, aye."

"We were only having a bit of fun, Eilis," Vahn explained, his expression contrite. "Njord's a grand swordsman."

"The damage has already been done," Njord replied. "Now I'll have to prove it to her. I think it would only be right for ye to be the one to spar with me since ye were the one who heaped the most damage on my reputation."

Vahn nodded his agreement then Njord took the sword from his holster and rounded on the man.

Vahn did the same and Eilis stepped forward. "Ye don't mean to be using those blades, do ye? I thought ye were supposed to spar with blunted ones."

Her eyes were wide with fright but Havland grabbed her by the arm. "Have nay fear, lassie. They do it all the time."

She watched as her husband and his man arced their blades, crashing them against each other until the metal sang out across the field. A crowd gathered around them as they parried then turned then repeated the motions over and again.

Eilis could feel her heart pounding in her chest when Vahn lunged his blade straight at Njord's side. Njord blocked it then spun away.

She had wanted to call out to him but bit her lip as she remembered her mother's warning. It was Njord's turn to lunge. Vahn blocked him then spun away as well but when he came back with his attack Njord had his short sword bared. He pointed it straight at Vahn's neck.

Eilis gulped air but Njord stopped the blade before it touched Vahn's skin. "Ye're dead!" he said, his eyes glowing with what appeared to be hatred.

Vahn nodded then dropped his blade, surrendering to the master. Njord smiled and the gathered crowd cheered for him.

"Ye've nay a thing to worry over, lassie," Havland said as he leaned down close to Eilis' ear. "Yer husband is one of the best."

"How did he learn that?"

"The Shaver taught him," Havland replied then quickly added, "I showed him a move or two myself."

She smiled at the Viking who had been a part of her family for as long as she could remember. They were a good lot and she felt protected when she was in their company. "Will we win this war, Havland?"

Havland nodded. "We'll win it. This war is more for show than for any other reason. The true war will be when we face Turlog."

Just hearing Turlog's name caused goose pimples to rise on her skin. She hated the man thoroughly and hoped that her husband would dispose of him soon. "I just hope ye find him."

"Find who?" Njord asked, the smile on his face fading when he caught sight of Eilis' expression.

"No one," she said as she placed herself in his arms then she cocked her head to the clearing he had just come from. "I think ye could have been a bit quicker out there. He almost had ye for a moment."

"Well then, I'll have to work on that won't I?"

He was just about to press her on who she and Havland had been speaking about when Eagan approached. The captain touched his head for Vahn and Havland then bent a knee for Njord and Eilis. He looked beyond them into the tent where Margreg worked and smiled before stating, "Brian wants ye to join him in his tent, Njord."

Njord nodded then gave his wife over to Havland's care. "Don't let her get into any mischief while I'm gone."

Eilis frowned and he tweaked her nose.

Margreg made her way out to see what was going on and Eagan stepped forward, again bending his knee. "'Tis good to see ye looking so fine, Margreg."

She nodded briskly raising a brow. "And ye, Eagan."

Realizing that he was walking alone, Njord turned to look askance of his wife. She shrugged her shoulders then cocked her head toward Eagan and her mother. Njord called out, "Do ye come, captain?"

"Aye, aye," Eagan replied, taking the time to lift Margreg's hand to his lips before sidling toward Njord. Only when they rounded the corner did he face forward.

"She's a good woman, that," Njord stated as they marched forward.

"She'll do," Eagan replied then he held the tent flap open so that Njord could pass.

The Ard Ri was sitting with Patric and Murchad, going over a map of the field when he entered. "Did ye prepare the Greek Fire?" Brian asked without offering any hospitality.

"Aye. It's ready. My men are assembling the catapults in the north field right now. But are ye certain that ye want to use it Brian? Doncha's army doesn't pose much of a threat."

"All the more reason for us to use it," Brian replied. "Let it be known throughout Eire that a sin against the crown will be revisited twice over on the sinner."

"I agree," Patric offered. "Given the choice between fighting with too many or not enough, I'll take too many any time."

"Speaking of too little," Murchad stated as he picked through the assortment of jerky in the trencher. "Has anyone heard from Maelmora?"

"Not yet," Patric replied. Since he had taken control of Caran Balder there had been little word of Maelmora, a fact that made Patric quite uncomfortable. "Something's amiss with him, Brian. We should keep an eye on him."

Brian nodded his agreement but before he could speak, Sigtrygg called out from his place at the tents entrance. "The coast has been plagued by rain. My army had a hard time getting here. I expect it might be the same for my uncle."

Brian met the man's gaze then smiled before rising from his stool. "Aye, that must be it," he crooned. "I'm glad ye made it, Sigtrygg."

Sigtrygg took the cup offered to him by the servant then rested on the stool beside Njord. "I passed Doncha's army on my way in. He's gathered a large number."

"Aye," Njord agreed. "But we'll handle them easily enough."

"I didn't see Fladbartoc among them."

"Nay," Patric replied. "He's too much of a coward to own what he's done. No doubt that he and Turlog are holed up together somewhere. We'll find them later."

"I heard about yer mother, Shaver," Sigtrygg stated as he lowered his eyes to the ground. "I'm sorry for yer loss."

A shiver ran down Patric's spine with the mention of Grace. After all these years he truly understood Njord's need for vengeance against Turlog. "All the more reason for us to find him," he stated flatly.

"Good," Sigtrygg replied. "So where do ye want me?"

They went over their maps, setting up a battle plan that had Sigtrygg and Njord merging their men in a flanking position. Brian would unleash the Greek Fire at the beginning of the battle, hoping it would cause an immediate surrender. If it didn't, Njord and Sigtrygg would catch Doncha's army in the middle.

At dawn the two armies faced one and other. The catapults released the balls of Greek Fire on Doncha's army even before Brian's men marched in. As predicted, the Eaghonact army fell back, retreating into the forest and surrendering all they had.

The celebration that ensued lasted four days. Maelmora never joined them.

CHAPTER 38

▼

Isle of Man: 5, June 1008—In The Yards—Olaf sat alone by the oak watching as the other lads chased each other with their wooden swords. Ospak approached him, trying not to notice the sadness in his nephew's eyes. "Why don't ye join them?" he asked as he chucked his chin toward the field.

Olaf hung his head, "Father says that I'm not to play with them. He says that if I lose in their pretend battles they may not have respect for me when I have to lead them in war."

Ospak wanted to tell the lad that he thought the edict ridiculous, but he knew his brother well enough to know that if he sent the lad out to play with the others it would be Olaf who paid the price. He lowered himself to the ground. "Perhaps ye and I can have a game then."

Olaf's eyes lit up. "What shall we play?"

Ospak looked around to see what was available and when his eyes alighted on several round stones strewn nearby he got to his feet then began to gather them up. Olaf joined him and soon they had enough. "See those branches there?" he asked the child.

"Aye."

"Go and find me two long straight ones and two short ones."

Olaf did as he was bade. He set the branches down by his uncle's feet. "What now?" he asked, excitement showing in his eyes.

Ospak arranged the branches into a rectangle along an area of ground where no grass grew. Then he placed several of the large stones inside. "Here," he stated as he handed over another stone to Olaf. "I want ye to roll the stone inside the box so that it hits one of the others. The object is to drive them to the edge, aye."

Olaf did as he was told. His stone collided with the other driving it near to the end of the box. "Good," Ospak called. "Ye have a good eye on ye, lad. It'll come in handy when ye go to war." He positioned himself in front of the box then prepared to toss his own stone. "Now it's my turn, aye."

He rolled the stone, purposefully missing all the stones in the box. "Shit," he bellowed. "Alright. It's yer turn again," he said as he positioned Olaf in front of the box. "Try to hit yer same stone again so that it gets to the end. If ye do then ye win."

Again Olaf rolled his stone and as his uncle requested, he hit the first stone sending it to the end of the box until the branch broke free. "I did it," he cried, jumping up and down with excitement. "I win!"

"Aye," Ospak stated. "I hardly had a chance at all."

"What do ye call this game, uncle?"

"It's called, Bocce," Ospak replied as he rubbed the lad's shaved head. "I learned about it when we went to Italy."

"I was born in Italy," Olaf said excitedly then he covered his mouth with his hands when he remembered that he wasn't supposed to speak about it.

"That's right, ye were," Ospak replied. "There's no shame in it, lad."

Olaf looked around the field to see if his father might be near. When he realized he wasn't, he leaned into his uncle. "Father says that people will think less of me if they knew I wasn't born in Man. That's why he makes me keep my hair clipped short, aye. He says I have Italian hair and that no one should see it lest they think me an Italian."

Ospak nodded sadly. His brother's desire to liken his son into a replica of himself was sapping all joy from his life. "What say ye to having another go?" he asked as he began to reset the court.

"That would make me very happy," Olaf replied.

*   *   *   *

Ailech, Ireland: 15, September 1008 A.D.—Fladbartoc wiped his hair back from his face, reminding himself that it took Brian nearly a half century of plotting before he won the high throne. He would have to demonstrate an equal amount of patience if he were to ever have his turn. He looked at Turlog with admiration. The Shaver had been hunting him for all this time yet he still managed to pop up when least expected. The man looked gruesome. His already thin form was that much thinner for his spotty diet and it looked as if pieces of his body could fall right off him. It was evident that the only thing keeping the man going was his hatred of Brian, which was exactly the reason Fladbartoc kept him around.

"We need assistance," Turlog grumbled, laying his tongue upside his loose tooth so his voice wouldn't whistle when he spoke. "We need someone who can get close to Boru."

"Aye," Fladbartoc agreed, passing up the opportunity to remind Turlog that he was supposed to have been that person.

"What about Sigtrygg?" Turlog asked, his eye rolling wildly—it did that whenever he was weary or drunk.

"Sigtrygg will only do what his mother tells him to do. If the woman is loyal to the Ard Ri then so is Sigtrygg."

"And Maelmora?" Turlog asked.

"More of the same," Fladbartoc offered then he began to pace.

"Well, there must be someone," Turlog whined, not ready to give up the fight so easily.

"If there is then I pray ye to point him out to me." Fladbartoc shook his head hopelessly. "I fear that we are in quite a quandary, Ri Tuath, and I don't rightly see how we will get out of it."

Turlog propped his feet onto the table then sucked his teeth as he leaned back in his chair. "Maelmora has a son, does he not?"

The question caused Fladbartoc's back to stiffen. Though he never met Mael-randa there was talk that the lad had no boundaries. He was as dark as a demon and would murder a babe in its bed if it were asked of him just to break his boredom. "I don't think we need go that far, Turlog."

"Well, ye want the crown don't ye?"

"Aye, but not at all costs. I've a limit ye know."

"Well I don't," Turlog stated then he lifted the patch covering his empty eye to scratch inside the socket.

*   *   *   *

Tara, Ireland: 13, May 1009—The fields of Tara were decorated with poles wound with strings of flowers and ribbon. For as far as the eye could see there were colorful tents where vendors offered sweet meats, ale and an assortment of household items guaranteed to make a woman's day easier. There were pens set up toward the rear of the village to house cattle, pigs, geese and chickens and near to the front gates stood the mead vendors directly across from the gaming booths.

Kormlada was dressed in a fine silk lein dyed to match the color of spring leaves. Around her head she wore a crown of flowers with streamers of colorful ribbon flowing down her back. The gold of her hair shimmered in the sun and the blush of youth colored her cheeks. Anyone who looked on her swore that the years hadn't touched her at all.

She walked hand in hand with Donchad, pointing out the fine goods as they made their inspection of booths. "May I have a kite, mother?" the lad asked, pointing to a particularly colorful one hanging on the back wall of the booth.

"That kite is as big as ye, son," she admonished then nodded toward another half it's size. "We'll take that one," she commanded of the vendor, never bothering to put her hand in her purse.

As was the custom, the rotund man working the booth handed over the kite then stated, "There'll be nay charge for ye, high queen."

She bowed her head then flashed her straight white teeth at him before accepting it. "Many thanks, lord," she replied before handing the kite to Donchad.

Donchad's eyes lit up. He'd seen the other lads flying their kites in the meadow earlier and had hoped that his father would purchase one for him. But as always, Brian was being kept busy with people's problems so he wasn't able to take him out into the fair. "Do ye think the wind is strong enough to fly it now, mother," he asked, hoping that he hadn't lost his opportunity.

"Of course it is," the deep voice boomed behind him. "Just look there to the poles. The posies are dancing all on their own. There's wind enough. The question is do ye have the legs to get it up?"

"Murchad," Donchad thrilled. "I can't believe ye came."

"Didn't I tell ye that I would, laddie," Murchad said as he rubbed his younger brother's head. He looked to Kormlada then nodded coolly. "Is my father at the fair?"

"Inside," she replied, jerking her head in the direction of the great hall. She had been having such a lovely time it was a shame he had to come along to spoil it. "He's hearing grievances."

"He's been hearing them all day," Donchad sighed. He kicked a pebble with the tip of his shoe.

"Well, laddie. Our father is an important man. If he doesn't give his people time Eire will fall into shambles."

"But I'm one of his people and he never gives any time to me," Donchad whined.

At first Murchad thought to lecture the lad on the virtue of patience but then he remembered his own childhood. Brian was always off at war. When he was home he spent most his time plotting it. He never had any real time to spend with him leaving him to look for groomsmen and fuidirs to provide his fun.

He looked at the kite Donchad was holding then squatted low so their eyes would be level. "Do ye even know how to fly that thing?" he asked.

Donchad dropped his eyes. "Nay."

"Well then I think we should remedy that. 'Twould be a grand shame to have such a handsome kite turned into kindling because its owner doesn't know how to fly it. What say ye to a lesson?"

"Really?" Donchad gasped. "Will ye show me how to fly it?"

"Don't I look drop dead serious?" Murchad asked as he furrowed his brow to cause tiny creases to form on his forehead. "Let's just see where Tann's gotten off to and then we'll all fly kites together."

"Ye brought Tann?" Donchad asked. He was so excited that Murchad thought he would jump right out of his skin.

"Aye, laddie." Murchad stood up then looked around the field. "He was here just a moment ago. Ah, there he is looking at the birds. Wait here and I'll run and get him."

"Mother," Donchad called. "May I see the birds as well?"

Murchad looked to Kormlada who was doing very little to keep her distaste for the situation from her eyes. "Well, can he, *mother?*"

"I think not," she responded. She lifted her head to look down her nose. "We were having such a grand time together, Donchad. Wouldn't ye like to continue on to see what else the vendors have?"

Donchad knew as well as she did that the vendors would happily offer anything they had to the high queen which meant that he would be laden with packages before they got halfway through the booths. But spending time with Murchad and Tann was the most wonderful way he could think of to pass an afternoon. "I pray ye, mother to let me go with Murchad."

"So ye'd leave me alone to go off with yer brother? That's a fine way to treat yer aging mother." Her eyes had gone soft with the statement and Murchad could almost swear that he saw the hint of a tear in them.

His stomach churned for the way the woman was trying to manipulate the lad. "Ah, *mother*," he sighed. "How could anyone think of ye as aging? Ye're the most beautiful woman here. Now why not let the lad come along with me and Tann to have a bit of fun? Ye'll get him back when we're through."

Donchad's eyes were filled with pleading as he looked up at her. "I pray ye to say aye."

She looked from one to the other hating to concede the competition in Murchad's favor but it was obvious Donchad wanted to go. "Very well," she huffed. "But ye best keep a sharp eye on him, Murchad."

Before her sentence was even finished they had linked hands and were walking up the path. "And what could happen to him?" Murchad called over his shoulder.

They met up with Tann at the exotic bird booth. The vendor was holding a beautiful white cockatoo whose head bobbed up and down as it stated, "Come see the birds!" Donchad took great delight in the bird and the vendor offered it as a gift.

"Did ye see that, father?" Tann asked as he stroked the bird. "He didn't even want anything for it."

Murchad screwed up his face a bit while helping Donchad lash the bird to his hand. "Ye're uncle is a very important little lad. People will offer him gifts in the hope that he will speak well of them to the Ard Ri."

"Nay," Donchad replied. "It's because of my mother that they do it."

Murchad stopped what he was doing long enough to look askance of the lad. "Yer mother?"

"Aye," Donchad replied. "They fear she'll cast a spell on them if they don't please her."

"Nonsense," Murchad bellowed before tying the final knot in the leather binding the bird to Donchad's hand. "She has nay magic. It's all an illusion."

Their eyes went wide. "Don't say such a thing, father," Tann gasped. "If she hears ye she'll turn ye into a toad."

"Or a bat," Donchad added.

Murchad looked them both over then laughed out loud. "Ye can't be serious? I'm especially surprised at ye, Tann. There is nay such a thing as a fairy and the only magic on earth comes at the will of God."

Suddenly both the boys drew back in fear and Murchad noticed a trickle of urine seeping down Tann's leg. "What is it?" he demanded as he took a step closer to them. They backed up and he turned to look behind him. He was startled to see Kormlada standing so close.

"What the fek are ye doing?" he shouted so he could be heard over the pounding of his chest.

She looked at him with eyes so filled with hatred that he thought he would melt right on the spot. "I think it's time for Donchad to come with me," she stated flatly. The lad offered his mother his free hand but before they walked away Kormlada bent to rub Tann's head. "Ye best stick close to yer father, laddie. There are too many people here and ye may get lost."

The trickle of urine quickly turned into a puddle as Tann released the rest of his bladder. Murchad grabbed him close then turned to reprimand the woman but both she and Donchad were gone.

*   *   *   *

Mag Cariann, Ireland: The Ri Tuath's Hut—One Hour to Midnight— 12, June 1009 A.D.—Maelranda had always been an odd child, more given to ripping legs off spiders than to playing games with the other lads. He never had much to say on any subject and though lassies would throw themselves at his feet for his beauty, he much preferred his own company to that of others.

Kormlada looked at him. He had his father's coloring and beautiful features but when it came to his eyes there was something *not right* about them. "Why haven't ye married, Maelranda?" she asked, needing to know exactly what made her nephew tick. "Is it that ye prefer the company of men to women?"

"I'd prefer nay company, queen and I'll prove it to ye if ye continue on so."

"My, my, aren't we touchy," she cooed as she raked him with her eyes once again. "And how do yer people feel about that fact?"

"My people have food, water and protection," he replied while continuing to use his dagger to dig out an imperfection in the wood of the table. "More than that they dare not ask."

"Some do," she stated. "Some people want all that Eire has to give without having done anything to earn it."

Maelranda lifted his eyes from the table. "Why don't ye stop speaking in riddles, aunt and lay it plain? The only time ye come here is when ye want me to perform some mischief for ye. Ye always ask and I always say aye. Why must we go through these theatrics every single time."

He jabbed the dagger into the table until it stood on it's own. "Do ye want me to kill someone? Steal something? What is it?"

She smiled coyly at her nephew, appreciating his bluntness and his willingness to serve. "I want ye to assist me in taking down Murchad."

"Consider it done."

"Just like that?" she asked, thrilling that he would fall so easily under her control.

"What else do I have to do?" he asked with a shrug of his shoulders. "I sit around here all day listening to complaints and handing out justice. Once in a while my father beckons me to the edge of the world where I help him sort out a few things. If ye want me to kill the Ri Ciocid I'll do it."

"Nay," she gasped as she rushed forward to cover his hand with hers. He withdrew fiercely and she backed off. "I don't want ye to kill him as much as scare him."

"And how should I do that?" he asked, his eyes still a bit wild from her touching him a moment ago.

Again she smiled then made her way around the table. She looked to the seat next to him before taking it. "May I?" she asked. He nodded and she lowered herself onto the bench then she withdrew the parchment from her pocket. "I've written a few things down. Next to them are dates. Nothing here is too difficult. Steal a few chickens. Put a few holes in the thatch. Poison a few wells. Childish pranks, really but it's most important that they be done on the dates written beside them. Do ye understand?"

He screwed up his face for her condescending tone. "What am I now, an idiot? Of course I understand. Ye want it to look as if ye put Murchad under a spell."

She sat back in her chair with a start, realizing she had underestimated the man. He wasn't a fool, only strange. "That's exactly what I'm hoping to do," she stated. "Is that good for ye?"

"Why should I care?" Maelranda said. He sounded quite bored with the conversation. "Ye want wells poisoned and chickens stolen then consider it done."

"Very well," she stated then rose to leave.

His hand came down upon hers like a vice. He looked up at her. "I didn't give ye a price," he said, his eyes boring so heavily into her that she felt naked before him.

She felt herself shudder when the vision flashed before her. She knew what he wanted and she would pay. Still she made him ask. "What is yer price?"

"Ye."

She stood silent for a time then at length pulled the brooch from her lein causing the material to fall from her shoulders. He stood to look at her then placed his hand on her exposed skin.

"Earlier ye asked why I wasn't married." She nodded trying not to show her fear. "Perhaps now ye'll know why."

*   *   *   *

Torshav, Ireland: In the Great Hall—24, April 1010 A.D.—Eilis sat beside her husband listening intently to the words Murchad was offering. It seemed incredible that the man could suffer such a string of bad luck for so long a period of time.

"I need yer counsel on this, Njord," Murchad pleaded. "My wife is terrified and Tann continues to wet his bed. Could it be magic?"

Njord rubbed his temples while he contemplated the situation. Unlike Murchad, he knew there was magic in the world. He had witnessed it too many times to deny it. Brodir calling upon his gods to smite his enemies. Kormlada drawing him to her like a fly to honey. Indeed there was magic in the world he just wasn't certain if this was a case of it. "I don't know what to tell ye, Murchad. Brodir certainly had magic."

"But what of Kormlada? Do ye think she has the power?"

"I do," Eilis interjected. They turned to her and she continued, "Whenever I'm around the woman my skin crawls. Her beauty is ageless and she manages to get anything she wants. 'Tis unnatural I tell ye."

Njord nodded his head in agreement. "Aye, there is that about her."

"So, what do I do about it?"

"I wish I could help ye, Murchad," Njord stated in earnest. "But that which I witnessed with Brodir took place when I was younger. After Italy, he swore his allegiance to the church and as far as I know he hasn't practiced sorcery since."

"Is there anyone else who might be able to help me?"

"Maelranda," Eilis stated with confidence. "I've heard tell that he has the help of the gods."

Murchad shivered with the thought of Maelmora's son. "'Twould certainly explain his strange behavior," he replied. "But I could hardly go to the man seeking assistance against his aunt."

"Aye, there is that," Eilis replied. She mulled the situation a bit longer then her head shot up. "Certainly yer father can do something about this."

"Och, aye," Murchad spewed. "That would be grand, me marching in to the Ard Ri to tell him that I think his wife has cast a spell on my household. 'Twould put him in a grand position between his son and his wife."

"As if he's not there already," Njord stated bluntly. Murchad nodded agreement then they all fell silent for a time.

Hecca came to join them. "Ye still seeking a witch?" she asked as if she had been part of the conversation all along.

Njord's eyes grew wide. "Woman, what do ye know about it."

"I know plenty," she stated, patting his hand as if he were the slowest dolt on earth. "Ye just tell me the signs and I'll tell ye what ye're dealing with."

Eilis clapped her hands in excitement and Murchad drew Hecca close to tell her all that had been happening to him. Njord just stared. He'd been with the woman lo these many years and just when he thought he knew her she surprised him again.

✳   ✳   ✳   ✳

Caran Balder, Ireland: 6, February 1011 A.D.—Fladbartoc passed through the gates at the edge of the world with his cloak pulled up tight against his neck. The air was bitter cold and the wind whipping up from the ocean only served to make it more so. He looked around at the village, dotted with huts running off the main road. The tavern stood just at the center and he kicked his horse forward, eager to find some warmth.

Tordelbach was now Maelmora's man. He was average height with muddy dark hair and eyes to match. He was sitting in the corner by the fire pit, sipping from a silver cup. When he spotted Fladbartoc he got to his feet then waved him to the seat beside him.

Fladbartoc offered his hand in greeting then took a moment to survey the premises before lowering himself onto the stool. It was clean enough and the smell of stew filled the air. His mouth watered. "What can I get ye?" Torrdelbach asked.

"I wouldn't mind a bite," Fladbartoc replied, removing his cloak as the heat from the fire began to warm him. "I'm a bit weary of jerky."

"Aye," Torrdelbach agreed, motioning for one of the serving maids to bring the man a dish. "Traveling is hard going at this time of the year."

"But it's worth it when the high crown's at stake."

Torrdelbach lifted a brow. Brian had finally called Maelmora to Tara to explain his absences during their search for Turlog. It was left up to Torrdelbach to find out what Fladbartoc was planning.

"So?" Torrdelbach asked when the maid retreated from depositing the bowl in front of his guest. "What is it that ye ask of us?"

"I have engaged yer master's son in my crusade and I was hoping his father would join us. Brian is old and I hear tell he's ailing. We can beat him this time."

Torrdelbach sat back in his chair. Maelranda had sent word of his plans to Maelmora last month but the father had tried to dissuade him against it.

"Unless ye can show him that ye have the ability to win, I'd say that my master will deny ye. He's quite contented with the way things stand. He's nay a reason to risk what he has."

"Brian will surrender without so much as a battle once we take our hostage. If that isn't enough to convince yer master to join with me then I don't want him requesting my assistance once I've taken the high crown."

Torrdelbach considered the information for a time. He motioned for the serving maid to bring him a fresh cup then leaned back in his chair before looking at Fladbartoc. "Where will ye take this hostage from?"

"Armagh," Fladbartoc replied, his brow lifting slyly.

"Ye can't be thinking to take Murchad," Torrdelbach huffed. "He's much younger than ye are and is quite capable with a sword."

"Not Murchad," Fladbartoc replied. "It's his son, Tann who we are after."

Torrdelbach thought about that for a moment. Many had witnessed the love that the Ard Ri held for his only grandson and many would say that the old man would give his life for the lad.

"And why exactly do ye believe that ye can capture Tann?" he finally asked.

Fladbartoc snorted as he rubbed his hands together. "Because as we speak, Maelranda is removing him from his bed."

*   *   *   *

Isle of Man: The Great Hall—20, February 1011 A.D.—Brodir pushed Olaf again, and again the lad fell to the ground. His face was streaked with tears but he didn't dare wipe them for fear of further abuse. Brodir kicked him hard in the back and the lad rolled away but it wasn't fast enough for Brodir who quickly caught him up to do it again.

"Damn!" the earl bellowed before spitting on the lad. "What is the matter with ye that ye don't defend yerself? Are ye off then, lad?"

Olaf looked to the other lads gathered in a circle. The exercise was supposed to demonstrate his strength to them so that they would fear him but it was clear that the only thing they felt was sympathy for the abuse he was being made to suffer.

"Get up!" Brodir screamed then pulled Olaf up by the arm before he had a chance to find his feet. His ribs ached and his knees were weak causing him to stumble a bit. Brodir noticed then cuffed his ears.

"I pray ye, father, enough," he pleaded.

"Enough! Enough!" Brodir drew the dagger from his belt then began to march forward. He would show the lad what it took to be a man.

"Brodir!" Ospak's voice rang out with force enough to cause an echo in the cavernous hall. He marched forward to place himself between his brother and his nephew. "What are ye doing, man?"

The rage Brodir was feeling was reflected in his brother's eyes. He staggered back, looking around the room as if he didn't know where he was. "Clear out!" he called to the circle of lads. They were immediately gone. Then he looked to Olaf who was being helped to his feet by Ospak.

"What have I done?" he cried out to the heavens.

Olaf and Ospak turned toward him while he continued his rant. "I have turned my back on my gods and now they have turned against me by sending me a coward for a son. Hear me, great Thor and grant me forgiveness. I renounce the Catholic Church and all titles aligned with it. From this day forward I will remain yer humble servant."

He drew the dagger he was holding across the tender meat of his forearm with force enough to open a deep slice then he ran to the fireplace where he let it bleed out.

Ospak shook his head before turning Olaf away from the scene. It would be grave for the lad if he didn't live up to his father's expectations now that his allegiance to his gods was renewed.

*   *   *   *

Tara, Ireland: The great hall—21, February 1011 A.D.—Kormlada sucked her teeth as she looked over the chessboard. Murchad had his finger poised over his bishop but if he moved it Maelmora would come in with his queen to take his rook. She smiled when it seemed he would do it but her attention was drawn when Donchad tugged on her hand. "I'm hungry," the lad whined.

She bent down, pulling on his lein to straighten out the wrinkles. "Then we shall have to remedy that, won't we?" she cooed.

She looked over her shoulder one last time, certain that her brother would put the rot in his place then headed for the table where her husband was sitting with Thorien.

She climbed onto the platform then took her seat beside them, pulling a trencher of ham and potatoes forward to place it before her son. "There ye go, my sweet," she said, patting his cheek tenderly. She turned to Thorien. "What news do ye bring from Limerick?"

9

"All's well, my queen," he replied, turning so his back wouldn't be against her. "The ports are busy and the new abbey is completed. I'd say we are doing well."

"Good," she cooed, picking a piece of ham from Donchad's plate to nibble on. "And what of Torshav?"

Brian straightened in his chair. She hadn't mentioned Njord in quite some time. "Now, why would ye ask about Torshav?" he questioned with a raised brow.

"Just making small talk," she replied, happy to see she could still get a rise from her husband. Things had been better between them since Brian issued the edict naming Donchad as Ri Tuath Ruire of Munster once he came of age but she wanted to remind him that he still had competition in the Viking earl.

Thorien could feel the tension building between them. He wished he could remove himself. "Torshav is well as is Munster. I'm happy to report that the south is peaceful enough."

"As is the north," Brian offered, nodding his head toward Murchad who seemed to be having an animated conversation with Maelmora. The rumors about Murchad's bad luck had been traveling the country like a plague. He wanted to be sure Thorien took back information to the contrary.

Suddenly there was a crash and they all turned in time to see the chessboard topple over. Maelmora got to his feet, hand on his sword hilt and Murchad got to his, leaning forward until he nearly rested against the other man. "Ye're a cheater!" the northern Ri Ciocid proclaimed, backing up enough so that he could clear his blade.

Thorien leapt over the table. He landed on the balls of his feet then took a moment to gain his balance before moving forward. "Easy there, the both of ye," he called as he closed in on them.

Brian moved more slowly. Gone were the days when he could clear the table in a leap, instead he was forced to walk around it. "What's this all about?" he called.

Kormlada was fast on his heels, skirting him to stand beside her brother. "How dare ye call him a cheater? Don't blame him because ye're weak in the game."

"I pray ye to stay out of this, sister," Maelmora crooned, never moving his eyes from Murchad. "We'll settle this ourselves."

Murchad's face glowed hot and he was about to say something further when the doors of the hall burst open to admit one of his men. The messenger had just passed his sixteenth year, wide eyed and golden haired. He searched the hall for his master and when his eyes alighted on Murchad, he rushed forward.

"There's trouble, Ri Ciocid. Tann has been taken hostage."

The color drained from Brian's face and Murchad took a moment to leer at Kormlada before rushing forward. "Who did it?"

"Fladbartoc of Ailech," the messenger stated. "He's sent word that he will kill the lad if king Brian doesn't surrender."

Kormlada stepped forward to take her husband by the arm. "Ye mustn't do it," she whispered in his ear. "Ye can't give in to such tactics."

He looked long at her, trying to assess whether it was her desire to hold onto her position or a vision that caused her to say such a thing. In the end it didn't matter. "Where has he been taken?" he asked the messenger.

"We're nay yet certain. The captain sent a few men north to see what they could learn in Ailech."

Maelmora swallowed hard. He knew where the lad was and when he got his hands on his son he would throttle him for certain.

✳   ✳   ✳   ✳

Torshav, Ireland: 3, March 1011 A.D.—Eilis played with the loops of her husband's mail while he held her around the waist. "Don't look so sad, m'millish. I'll be back before ye know it."

"Are ye certain that nothing can stick ye through this thing?" she asked, needing reassurance that he would be safe.

"Only if they plan on attacking us with needles. I know they do things a bit differently in the north, but I doubt that will be the case."

"When things had gotten better for Murchad, I thought Hecca's spell had worked. Now things are worse then ever. I'm frightened, Njord. Ye said yerself that ye didn't know how to deal with magic."

He took her face in his hands then tenderly kissed her lips. "'Tis nay a spell at work here but greed. Fladbartoc wants the throne and he feels that this will be the way to get it." He shook his head. "Foolish man."

"Will the Shaver be with ye, then?"

"Aye, Havland and Thorien too. Ye have nay a thing to worry over. We'll be in and out before ye know it."

The knock on the door drew their attention. "Are ye ready, earl?" Vahn called. "Aye."

He bent to kiss her again and she held onto him as if her life depended on it. "Promise ye'll come back to me."

"Ye know I will," he replied before rubbing his cheek against hers. "Ye practice yer blade while I'm gone, aye."

He chuckled and she scowled at him. "What's funny about it?"

"Nay a thing," he said chuckling again. She had insisted that she wanted to learn how to wield a blade and he'd been teaching her. Actually, she was quite good. "Eire's history is full of women who led their own army. Perhaps ye can join them, aye."

She swatted her hand at him and he ducked through the door. He mounted his horse then rode out of Torshav with Patric, Havland and Thorien by his side. In all, there were one hundred of them heading to Mag Cariann where it was rumored that Tann was being held by Maelranda.

"What do ye think Brian will do to Maelmora if we find the lad there?" Havland asked of Patric.

"I don't know, but I'd say that the Ard Ri is in a quandary indeed. His wife won't take kindly to him lashing out against her brother."

"That woman doesn't take kindly to anything," Thorien mumbled. "Pure evil that one."

Njord nodded his head in agreement.

They reached Mag Cariann in two days. It was located west of Ferta Nime and just south of Caran Balder in the county of Connacht. Murchad met them upon their arrival and they made camp in the forest just outside the village while they awaited Patric's spy. He came after nightfall.

"He's got him in the keep," the elder man stated. "He's heavily guarded."

"And where is Maelranda?" Patric inquired.

"He's asleep in his bed."

Patric nodded then looked at Njord. "Me and Thorien will go for the lad and ye go for Maelranda. Havland, ye keep the guards busy, aye."

Murchad stepped forward and there was no mistaking the look of hatred in his eyes. "I'll go with, Njord," he growled.

Patric patted his shoulder. "I think ye should stay behind with Havland."

"Ye must be mad," Murchad snapped back. "'Tis my son in there. I'll be going with Njord."

Njord stepped up to draw Murchad's attention. "Listen, brother. Ye're too hot to get into this right now. If ye loose yer temper there'll be more bloodshed than necessary and the lad could get hurt. Why not let me go and take care of things for ye? Stay outside with Havland so that if things go awry yer anger will be a benefit nay a hindrance."

Murchad was about to argue but then he saw the sense of the plan. "'Twill be as ye say, Njord."

Everyone nodded and in the dead of night, the contingent of warriors entered Mag Cariann.

What occurred behind those walls was the stuff sagas were made of. Tales of flying demons swooping down on warriors to blind them, men changing their forms to become animals, women with two heads and snakes for hair biting warriors in half, were all absorbed into the annals of verbal lore to be told by wives and bards alike. The most interesting of these stories was the one of Njord the Black. It was said that after suffering a wound to his shoulder Njord became so enraged that he pinned Maelranda against the wall. Seeing no escape for his life, Maelranda disappeared and was replaced by his aunt, the high queen, Kormlada. Without considering it, Njord charged forward to separate the high queen's head from her neck.

*   *   *   *

Torshav, Ireland: 10, March 1011 A.D.—"Oh my God, ye're hurt," Eilis cried as she rushed to her husband.

He staggered under the influence of the ale. "Och, 'tis nothing, *m'millish*. Just a little scratch."

Yon and Vahn released him to her care but her knees buckled with the weight of him and they took hold of him again. "Why not let us put him to bed, aye?" Vahn offered.

"What happened to him?" she worried. "Will he be all right?"

"I dare say it'll be his head that gives him the trouble in the morning, not his shoulder," Eagan chuckled.

She looked at the dried blood on her husband's forehead and she began to tremble. "Well, it must be a terrible wound if he needed to take the drink for the pain!" she scolded.

Yon followed her eyes to the gash on Njord's head then laughed. "He got that after the raid." She looked askance of him and he chuckled again. "He fell off his horse after he and Havland engaged in a bit of a drinking match on the way home."

She held her hand to her mouth to hide the chuckle. "So I guess he lost then."

Vahn shook his head as he motioned toward the shield being carried by the warriors behind him. "Nay, Njord was the winner. Havland was the loser."

Niamh rushed from the house in time to see her husband being carried on his shield. She burst out crying before checking every inch of his body for the mortal wound. Not a scratch.

Damn the old fool!

With her ire at full throttle and a resolve to make him pay for scaring her so, she marched directly to the well to bring back a bucket of water, which she sloshed over him. He sat up with a howl and she wagged her finger under his nose as she scolded, "So, this is the condition ye come back to me in? I was half out of my mind with worry and ye have the nerve to be carried in here drunk and unwounded."

She began to beat him about the chest forcing him to hold up his hands to defend himself. "I thought we won the battle," he muttered as he swayed a bit. "What goes on here?"

She continued beating him and he continued to block her. "What goes on is that I am too old for this nonsense, Havland. If ye're gonna come home being carried on the shield and stop my heart from beating then the least ye could do is have a wound to show for it."

"If ye don't stop it, woman, I'm gonna give ye my lunch," he belched. He struggled to keep his balance as he swung his legs over the shield but he reeled backwards. His deftness traded for his drunk, he slipped off the shield, solidly rapping his head against a stone. He rubbed at the eagerly forming lump as he sat cross legged on the ground.

"Are ye happy now? I'm wounded." He struggled to get to his knees as he beckoned her with a wave of the arm. "Now come over here and help me to my bed."

She huffed as she brought him to his feet and the warriors watched in silence as she scolded him all the way into the house.

"Och, that was terrible," Njord slurred as he reeled back against the arms that steadied him. "I hope ye're not planning the same for me, *m'millish*. I didn't come in on a shield, I walked in on my own accord." He tried to stand proud but his knees quickly buckled. Vahn and Yon caught him again.

Eilis sucked her teeth in an effort to hide her amusement. "Come in to bed, husband. I'll wait to say my peace until morning."

He smiled as his head rocked on his neck. "Ye're a good wife, Eilis.

*   *   *   *

Tara, Ireland: 16, July 1011 A.D.—Kormlada paced before her husband, wringing her hands in frustration. "Ye can't be meaning to lay this at Maelmora's feet. He can't be responsible for the actions of his son. Maelranda is a grown man—Ri Tuath of his own village. He alone should be responsible for his actions."

Brian stretched himself across the bed, reveling in her discomfort. "Be careful of yerself, wife. Yer loyalty is showing."

"That's not fair. He's my brother. What do ye expect of me?"

His eyes narrowed as he leveled them at her. "I expect ye to stand beside me in all things without question. Lately, that hasn't been the case."

She ran to him, concern clearly dotting her face. "I have always stood beside ye. It's for ye that I do the things that I do."

"Is that so?" he asked, propping himself on one elbow so their eyes would be level. "Why don't ye tell me how it benefits me to have my wife chasing after a young earl in front of everyone in the hall?"

Her stomach gripped and her hands began to shake as she recalled the years Malsakin had her locked away for her similar actions concerning Brian. Her face was desperate. "I pray ye to forgive me my trespass, Brian. It shan't happen again."

"What does he hold for ye that ye would risk my ire to give yerself to him?" Brian asked, much too calmly for her liking.

She hung her head then lied, "Nay a thing."

He was silent for a long while and she looked up at him with desperation in her eyes. "What shall ye do with me?"

He shook his head then rolled over onto his stomach. He hadn't decided that yet.

CHAPTER 39

▼

Isle of Man: 14, November 1012 A.D.—Olaf felt the wind whip his face as he drove the stallion still harder. He leaned low against its neck as they rounded a turn then with practiced swiftness, yanked his blade from its holster to cleave the melon in half.

"Bravo," Brodir called out to him. He turned to the lads who were lining the fence. "Which one of ye can do such a thing? Step up if ye think ye can challenge him."

"Go on with ye now," Ospak called as he shooed them away with his hand. "There's not one among ye that can do it and ye know it."

He reached up to place a hand on his brother's shoulder. "He's doing fine, Brodir. He'll make a great warrior."

Brodir nodded proudly. It had been a long time in coming but Olaf was finally showing his potential. "I knew he had it in him," he lied. "I'm only glad that it didn't take more than renouncing the church to have the gods release their restraint on him."

Ospak nodded his agreement then waved an enthusiastic hand to Olaf who came to rest before them. "That was a grand demonstration, laddie."

Olaf sat his horse, chest heaving, waiting for his father to speak. It took Brodir some time but at last he leveled his gaze at his son. "Ye did fine this time. But I want ye to work a bit harder. Those lads were watching every move ye made hoping ye would fall off. I want ye to show them that 'twill never happen, aye."

"Aye, father," Olaf replied then turned the horse to have another run at it.

Ospak shook his head.

*   *   *   *

Dublin, Ireland: 22, December 1013—The storm of Kormlada could be as devastating as her beauty, leaving things tattered in its wake. The blissful peace of Sigtrygg's lunch turned to immediate indigestion when she burst through the doors.

"He's marching his army to Dublin. They're setting up camp right outside the wall."

The king's golden bob fell forward on his face as he pushed the silver platter away from him. The sweet meat of the pheasant quickly became a memory as her tirade against Brian was laid in his lap.

"I highly doubt that, mother. He would have sent word if he was planning such a thing."

"Look for yerself," she barked, sweeping back the drapery so her son could see what was happening right under his nose.

Sigtrygg took his time moving to the window but when he looked down toward the village his heart dipped. "He can't mean to march on me. I'm married to his daughter."

"Well, he can and he has," she replied, her smugness thick in her voice. "I've already sent for Maelmora. He'll join us here so we can lay a plan on how to deal with this."

"Damn ye!" Sigtrygg barked, whirling on her with hate in his eyes. "Why is it that ye can't leave well enough alone? We were happy enough as we were but ye had to go chasing after the earl like a puppy. Now look where's it's gotten us. Ye lost Donchad, Maelmora has lost Leinster and now I will lose Dublin. Damn ye, woman!"

He had her backed against the table hatred so intense filling his eyes that she could feel it hot against her skin. But instead of shrinking from it, she stood full up so that her head was higher than his. "If it wasn't for me, ye would never have had those things. If ye want them again I would advise ye to heed my counsel now."

Everything in him told him that he should strike at her. If he killed her and removed her from this earth, perhaps he could live in peace. He turned from her, balling his fists against his inclinations then returned to the window to watch as Brian's army moved in to surround the city.

The door opened to admit Sabdah and he turned slightly toward her. "Why does my father bring his army, husband? Are ye planning to march again?"

"Nay," Sigtrygg replied, averting her gaze. He had grown to love the woman. She was every bit as fierce as Brian and it pained him to tell her that they would no longer be welcomed by the Ard Ri.

She moved closer to him and he reached out to put his arm around her shoulder. "It seems that yer father is planning to march on me. I expect that word will come at any moment seeking my surrender."

"But why?" Sabdah asked, her eyes wide with confusion.

Sigtrygg turned to look at his mother and his stomach clenched. "Yer father has set my mother aside and taken Maelmora from Leinster. It only makes sense that he would want me removed from Dublin. It seems he thinks us treacherous."

Sabdah looked long at Kormlada, her hate for the woman quickly rising to the surface. It was common knowledge that she had been lusting for Njord the Black. She was only surprised that it had taken this long for her father to put the woman out.

"Ye're as troublesome as ye are beautiful," Sabdah huffed at her.

Kormlada lunged forward, taking Sabdah's hair in one hand while she used the other to smack her across the face. "Never take that tone with me!" she barked.

It happened so fast that Sigtrygg barely had time to react. He pulled his mother off his wife then shoved her down the step. "And ye never lay hands on my wife again!" He stroked the red welt rising on Sabdah's face. "Ye alright?" he asked, concern showing in his eyes.

She nodded then ran her tongue along the inside of her mouth, tasting the blood left there by Kormlada's battery. She leered at the woman again, then deciding that she wasn't worth her trouble, turned back toward her husband. "Let me speak with him on yer behalf. I'll convince him that ye're not as treacherous as yer mother is."

Kormlada rushed her again but Sigtrygg stopped her with his hand against her chest. "Step back, mother!"

"Sigtrygg," Kormlada huffed. "Ye can't be meaning to have me stand by idle while the woman defames me."

"She only speaks the truth," he barked then returned his attention to his wife. "Ye're father won't listen to ye, Sabdah. If he were willing to hear me out he would have spoken to me already. That he's marched his army all this way can only mean one thing. He wants my surrender."

"But ye don't know him as I do," she pleaded, hoping that there was another way besides surrender. "I beg ye to let me speak with him."

Sigtrygg cupped her face in his hands then pulled her up to kiss him. "Go now and let me speak with my mother about this. Once we know what he wants, perhaps then I will take ye up on yer offer, aye."

She looked long at him, recognizing the fact that he was putting her off but she knew that once his mind was made up there was nothing she could do to change it. She nodded her head then stepped off the platform toward the door, growling low in her throat as she passed Kormlada.

Kormlada opened her mouth to say something but when Maelmora appeared in the doorway she let it go. There was nothing to be gained by arguing with the lass.

Maelmora's face was drawn and his hair had begun to lose its luster. He suddenly looked old. "'Tis a fine mess ye've gotten us into, sister. I only hope ye have a plan to get us out of it."

Sigtrygg looked his uncle over, sickened by the knowledge that it was his son who started this thing. "I would say that Maelranda had as much to do with this as Kormlada has."

Maelmora turned to look at the Dublin earl and a humorless smile split his beard. "If ye believe that, Sigtrygg, than I would advise ye to open yer eyes. Maelranda only did what the high queen told him to do." He turned to Kormlada. "Isn't that right, sister?" She hung her head and Maelmora took her chin in his hand, squeezing so hard that her mouth opened. "Ye were the one to pull him into this. Ye might as well own it because he told me of it. Was it worth it, sister? Was yer competition with Murchad worth the price we are paying now?"

She wrenched herself away from him, stomping around the room indignantly. "I'll admit I sought his help against Murchad. But I wouldn't have needed to do it if the two of ye had taken my part against the little rot instead of bowing to his every whim."

Maelmora wanted to kill her with his bare hands and he would have done it if he knew it would help him regain his crown. He balled his fists then growled low in his throat. "Well, now that we are here tell us if yer gods have given ye a way out of it."

The truth was that long ago her gods had told her that both Brian and Murchad would be killed in battle leaving the high throne open for Njord to take it. It wasn't clear by her visions how the battle would begin but under the circumstances she thought it best to do something to urge it along.

"Let's just say that my gods have foretold a war and now we must make one. Once we do, all will be well."

"When ye say all will be well," Maelmora questioned, "what exactly do ye mean by that?"

"I mean that we will control Eire."

"We or ye?" Sigtrygg questioned as he came to stand beside his uncle.

She looked them over, unwilling to tell either one the rest of her vision. "Let's just say that everyone will get exactly what they deserve."

Sigtrygg and Maelmora exchanged glances. Neither one of them was certain what her answer meant but they didn't have much choice other than to hear her out. "Very well," Maelmora said at length. "So, is this the battle? Shall we meet him now, outnumbered and unprepared?"

She shook her head. Sigtrygg would lead the battle that killed Brian Boru with the assistance of Vikings from across the sea.

"Ye must wait him out, Sigtrygg," she offered, her eyes glazing over as the vision became clear to her. "He will remain until the new moon and then he will depart. When he does, ye must go to Orkney. Once there, ye will find the earl Sigurd. He once confessed to yer father that he would have staked a claim in Eire if it weren't for Boru. As I remember, he was also quite taken with me. He'll lend his assistance if ye offer my hand."

"Ye mean to sell yerself?" Maelmora interrupted, realizing that his sister still believed that the only way a man could be Ard Ri was if she chose him.

"I mean to be certain that we keep the high throne in the family."

"So then it won't be one of us sitting on the throne?" Sigtrygg asked, tired of playing second to her choices for Ard Ri.

"Ye will have Dublin and anything else ye want so long as I'm high queen," she replied.

"Well, that's not good enough," her brother interjected. "If we do this thing it must be one of us sitting on the throne."

"Oh really," she cooed, her challenge clear in her eyes. "Do it then!"

Her words were as good as a knife in his heart. Without a kingdom or an army, he was at her mercy.

When he didn't reply she returned her attention to her son. "Now—if we're clear on the matter, I should like to continue."

Sigtrygg nodded while Maelmora moved to the table to make himself a plate. "After ye meet with Sigurd I want ye to sail to Man and speak with chief, Brodir. He's a great sorcerer and a clever man. He has twenty war ships that can carry thousands. His brother, Ospak, has ten more. Ye must pull them into this battle at any cost, Sigtrygg. If ye do this thing, we'll surely win and Eire will be ours."

Sigtrygg turned to look at his uncle who nodded his acceptance then he returned his attention to his mother. All he had ever wanted was to rule Dublin in peace. He prayed that her plan would allow him to do that.

"'Twill be as ye say, mother."

✳   ✳   ✳   ✳

Isle of Man: The stables—20, February 1014 A.D.—The black coat of the stallion glistened blue as the perspiration of its exertion warmed it to a steamy touch. Olaf rubbed a hand over his own head to release the perspiration clinging to his close cropped hair then took the stiff straw brush in his hand to stroke the beast's mane. It was long and full, and the dust of the road rose up from it, showering the sunlight with its glitter.

"Yer father calls, lord," Jared gasped, winded from his run. "He asks ye to join him in his hall right away."

"Is there trouble?" Olaf questioned, throwing down the brush in exchange for the short blade tucked into his belt.

Jared shook his head. "He's in a state, lord. It seems Sigtrygg of Dublin will pay a visit." He stretched a finger on the wind toward the harbor. "His boat is just now landing."

"Sigtrygg?" Olaf's eyes grew wide. "The earl of Dublin?"

"It seems he's making his rounds," Jared responded. "He's only just left from Orkney."

Olaf looked to the long boat as the anchor was cast. His father had warned him that Ireland was as dreadful as Italy to try and dissuade his interest in it. But as in all things he had spies who told him what was happening there. He was eager to know if their stories about Sigtrygg were true.

He raced up the road toward the massive stone fortress with a practiced swiftness. Jared lagged behind. There were a multitude of servants on every level of the building, scurrying about tending their business and as usual, their eyes turned toward him as he passed, warming his skin with their curiosity. Ever since he could remember, there were hushed mumbles when he passed people by. When he was younger he presumed they were speaking of his awkwardness and how he would never amount to a warrior. Now he hoped it was the opposite.

Cia's blue eyes fell toward the ground as she did also. "Are ye headed for the hall, lord? Shall I lay yer clothing?"

Olaf gave a quick glance to his attire, improper for the chief's hall but Jared said it was urgent. He hadn't time to change. He shook his head gently as he flashed the whitened smile that endeared him to so many. Then with a quick brush of his trousers and leather vest and a moistened palm to head, he raced through the massive doors of his father's hall. "Ye sent for me, Brodir?"

"For all the gods, what took ye so long, lad?" Brodir snapped as he got to his feet, eyes burning.

"I was in the stables. I came as soon as I could. What's the trouble?"

Brodir waved an angry hand to the seat beside him. Olaf again gave a brush to his clothing before taking it.

"Sigtrygg Silken Beard is on his way. The rot means to pull me into a battle."

Olaf raised an eyebrow in confusion. "Sigtrygg challenges ye for Man?"

"Nay." Brodir waved a hand. "It's Brian Boru's head he's after, not mine. I heard he's only just left Sigurd. It seems our Dublin kin means to have Eire for his own. He's offered his mother's hand if that sow of an earl will lend his army."

"Kormlada," Olaf gasped. The mere thought of the woman made him shudder with excitement. He had heard that the king of Leinster married her to Olaf Curran at the tender age of twelve. When their son, Sigtrygg, was born the old king was so pleased to finally have a heir after having fourteen daughters born by six wives, that he directed his druid to provide Kormlada with everlasting youth and beauty.

Brodir chuckled when he noticed his son's reaction. "Get on with ye now. The woman is nearly six times yer age and twice yer size. Whatever would ye do with her?"

Olaf met his father's gaze. Last summer Brodir decided he was ready to experience sex. He spent the first time fumbling and groping causing Brodir to spit on him. Since then he had been practicing the exercise with the same fervor as battle training. "If ye give me a ladder, I'll be happy to show ye what I'd do with her."

Brodir smiled wryly before stroking his long beard. "Well, ye just keep those hands to yerself there, *laddie*. If anyone shall lay with the fair Kormlada, it'll be me."

Olaf agreed easily enough. He only desired Kormlada because it was said that any man she lay with would become the Ard Ri. If his father took the crown first it would eventually come to him. "So then we *will* be traveling to Eire."

Brodir shrugged. "I must hear Sigtrygg out before making a decision, but I should think that ye would want to be in this."

Olaf's excitement caused him to shudder but he dared not let his father notice. Brodir had strict rules about displays of emotion as he did with everything else. "So, ye plan on taking me with ye?"

"Aye. I think it would be a good experience for ye. Besides, there's a particular man that I want ye to meet while we're there."

Olaf lifted his brow. "Who is it, father?"

Brodir turned to look at the lad whose resemblance to his true father was beginning to show most fiercely. "He is known by the name of Patric the Shaver. He's my sworn enemy and I plan to kill him. I want ye there when I do."

Olaf opened his mouth to say something more but Brodir halted him with an elbow to his ribs. "Sit regal now, son. Here he comes."

Sigtrygg hesitated for a moment as he entered the hall. It was opulent in its décor putting his hall to shame. His envy swelled but he dared not show it. He was there to tempt Brodir to Ireland. He'd be hard pressed to make the offer seem attractive if he exposed his awe for Man.

He gave a quick smoothing of his lien before moving forward. "I'm honored ye'd receive me on such short notice, Brodir. Yer kingdom is nearly as glorious as mine."

Brodir raised an eyebrow. "I've been to Dublin, Sigtrygg. Though rich, it carries a foul smell." He waved a hand to the seat beside him. "Now why don't ye take a seat and tell me why ye've come."

The Dublin king eased himself into the roomy seat. Immediately, there was a gleaming blue eyed servant to fill his plate and cup. She spread the linen across his lap before turning away. Sigtrygg cleared his throat then leaned into Brodir. "Boru's hold on Eire has resulted in the near annihilation of my people. He's set my mother aside and I believe he means to have me and my uncle slaughtered only to replace us with Dal Cais who'll stand as adamantly against the Vikings as he does."

Brodir offered a chuckle. "Boru thinks too much of himself if he believes he could rid Eire of our people. That country would still be an uncivilized bunch of animals if we hadn't staked our claim to it centuries ago. I think ye worry over nothing, Sigtrygg."

"But do I, Brodir? To my own ears he confessed he'd kill any of those foreigners who dared tread Eire's soil with looting in their heart. At the time he was only king of Munster." Sigtrygg lifted an eyebrow and spoke low to strike fear. "As Ard Ri he's quite powerful. Once he's secured Eire, he may very well look across the seas to exact his revenge and spread his power. He's already made alliances with Rome—alliances ye once had but reneged on. If we don't stop him now he may one day have Man."

The digestion of the statement was evident in Brodir's face as his lip moved between his teeth. "And what do ye propose to do about this, Sigtrygg?"

"I mean to march on him to stop his encroachment on what's ours. I mean to show him the true power of the Vikings."

Brodir feigned surprise as he offered a clap to Sigtrygg's shoulder. "Good for ye, man! Yer father would be proud."

Sigtrygg's brows knitted. "If we're to be successful, I'll need the support of my kin. I've come to ask ye to stand with me. Eire holds many riches. Ye could have yer share of them if ye agree, Brodir."

"As I recall it, Sigtrygg," Brodir drawled, picking a grape from the bowl then popping it into his mouth, "the last time I was called to Eire it was by yer father. He promised me Limerick but I ended up a slave to Halfden."

"Things will be different this time," Sigtrygg responded, averting the earl's gaze.

"I don't see how," Brodir chuckled. "Ye just asked me to lend my army to take Boru down yet ye offer only a portion of Eire's riches. Sounds like the same deal to me." He popped another grape into his mouth then cut the air with his hand. "Really, Sigtrygg, why would I even consider such a weak offer? I've all I need right here."

Sigtrygg wrung his hands beneath the table as his brain scrambled for the winning plan. If he failed to tempt Brodir into the war, they would lose it. His mother's vision foretold it. "I must warn ye, Brodir. If Boru beats us back he will look to conquer Man in order to expand his power. Ye'd be wise to lend yer assistance."

"I'd be wise to keep my nose out of yer mischief, Sigtrygg!" Brodir snapped back. Threats weren't something he responded kindly to and he meant to have the earl of Dublin know it. "If Brian comes calling here he'll face an army of warriors that will make his look like snot nose children. Don't worry over Man, Sigtrygg—ye just try to keep hold of Dublin."

There was only one move left to play and Sigtrygg offered it cautiously, knowing a wound to Brodir's ego could easily result in the loss of his own head. "I would never have thought that Sigurd of Orkney would pose a more skillful negotiation than the great chief of Man. Indeed, I always thought Sigurd to be dim, but he's managed to bargain for the throne of the Ard Ri as well as my mother's hand for the use of his army."

He shot a glance sideways as he began to rise from his seat but suddenly the steel trap grasp of Brodir's hand clamped down on his arm. "That's what ye promised him?" Brodir screeched. "That blubbering, dithering glutton has been promised all the riches of Eire while ye come to me with nothing left to offer?"

He rose to tower over the Dublin king, placing his hand on his sword hilt as he growled, "Ye should have come to me when ye actually had something to bargain with, Sigtrygg. Maybe then I would have stood with ye. Perhaps now I should just kill ye and let Boru have his precious Eire without yer interference."

Sigtrygg averted Brodir's eyes in an effort to hide his fear but still he spoke. "If ye think that spilling my blood is the best way to handle this, Brodir, then be my guest. It'll only serve to make Sigurd more powerful when he marches on Brian, and that he will. He could hardly contain his excitement when I told him about the plan. If I don't return to lead my army ye can be sure my mother and uncle will do it in my stead."

Brodir growled as he lowered himself into his chair. Sigurd had been his rival since childhood, always manipulating situations to embarrass him. This war might be just the thing to bring the slovenly earl of Orkney to his knees.

"I'll tell ye what I'll do for ye, Sigtrygg," he crooned as he preened his beard. "Because of the affection I hold for yer father, I'll give ye my help."

Sigtrygg drew breath and Brodir continued, "But only if ye promise me the same as ye offered Sigurd. We both know he'll never survive the battle, but his army would be most useful in taking Boru down."

Sigtrygg clapped his hands together as he gushed, "But of course—there's our answer! I'm only embarrassed I didn't think of it myself. But then again, 'twould take someone of much greater talents than mine to see what ye don't Brodir. He offered an eager handshake then drew Brodir close. "Sigurd's awkwardness will find him dead for sure. In the end, ye'll be Ard Ri and we'll all be better for it."

Olaf watched as his father and the Dublin earl celebrated their alliance. There was a question burning in his mind and he sliced a bit of meat from the roasted pheasant before he asked, "Will Malsakin fight with ye?"

Both Sigtrygg and Brodir turned to face the lad and Brodir realized that he hadn't introduced him. "This is my son, Olaf. He has a great interest in Eire and I dare say he keeps up with all the gossip."

Sigtrygg looked at the lad who seemed quite familiar to him. He looked nothing like Brodir so he presumed he had taken his looks from his mother. "Nay, lad," he replied, trying to recall where he had seen those crystal blue eyes before. "Most likely, Malsakin will stay out of it. He's been content enough in Meath since he handed the crown to Boru."

"So, are ye telling me that if we succeed in killing Boru that Malsakin won't be seeking to take the throne back for himself?"

"That's right," Sigtrygg replied. He still couldn't place the lad's resemblance so he decided to give up. "It's his cousin, Fladbartoc who covets the crown. We'll pull him into this of course but when the war is won he won't move against us. My father once thought to kill him. If need be we'll make good on that plan after the war is won."

Satisfied with the earl's answer, Brodir clapped Olaf on the back. "I think ye'll do well in Eire, son. Ye have a good knowledge about what goes on there." He returned his attention to Sigtrygg. "I'll bring my ships. Tell yer mother to prepare for me!"

Sigtrygg smiled slyly. "Don't worry, she'll be ready for ye, Brodir."

Olaf sighed as he sat back in his chair. There was something about this situation that made him uncomfortable.

∗   ∗   ∗   ∗

Cashel, Ireland: 23, March 1014 A.D.—Brian sat at the head table, surrounded by Njord, Thorien, Murchad and Havland. Patric paced before them, feeling uncomfortable about the battle ahead. They had spent the winter outside the Dublin walls, pressing Sigtrygg to forfeit the city. When the earl refused, Brian threw out the challenge that he would meet him in the spring on the battlefield of Clontarf to remove him once and for all. Even at the time of the pronouncement, Patric had been leery of the plan. He would have preferred to march then and be done with it but Brian disagreed. It was the Ard Ri's opinion that the only way they would ever be done with the mischief taking place around the isle was to round up all his enemies in one place at one time. The winner would gain the high crown without question and finally lay to rest the suspicion that Kormlada had anything to do with it.

It was shaping up to be the greatest battle Ireland had ever seen, with unpredictable alliances being made on either side. While Brian had managed to split the O'Neills by drawing Malsakin to his side, Fladbartoc had managed to split the Dal Cais by drawing Turlog. But it was Sigtrygg's alliances that had Patric most worried. Not only had he managed to engage Sigurd of Orkney but he also had the support of Brodir and Ospak of Man.

He looked to the men gathered around the table and when he caught Njord's eye he cocked his head in a request that his son join him privately. Njord slipped from his seat then followed his father through the doors. "What's eating at ye, father? Ye look a fright."

Patric turned to him, exposing the concern in his eyes. "Do ye think Brodir will bring the lad?"

Taken aback by the question, it took Njord a moment to figure out what his father was talking about. When he did he stepped back. "How old would he be now?"

"Ten years," Patric responded, not needing the time to figure it out. Not a day had gone by when he didn't think about the lad, wondering what he looked like and what Brodir was teaching him.

Njord thought about Brodir. For all the years they had spent together he was never truly able to know the man's mind. He thought of Tyr who was several years older than Patric's son. He was a strapping lad who was as capable with a blade as any grown soldier. He shook his head. "I couldn't say for certain, father, but I would expect that if the lad's still too small to wield a blade, Brodir may leave him in Man to ensure he keeps it."

Patric remembered himself at that age. He was a fierce fighter even then, persistent too. If his son were anything like him Brodir would be hard pressed to leave him behind. He bit his lip. "I don't know, son, but I was thinking..." He looked up at Njord, hoping he would assist him, "if he does bring the lad, I want to take him as hostage. It'll be our only chance, aye."

Njord could see that his father was desperate. "Just tell me what ye want me to do and 'twill be done, father."

Patric let out a sigh then smiled before placing his hand on Njord's shoulder. "Though ye're not of my blood, ye will always be my first, aye," he offered, hoping to allay any doubts Njord might have in the pecking order of his heart.

The thought hadn't even crossed Njord's mind, but still he was happy that Patric offered the comment. "I'm grateful for that, father."

For a moment, Patric felt a shudder run up his spine as he stood looking at him. No matter what the outcome, he was certain that he would lose something in this war.

✴   ✴   ✴   ✴

The Irish Sea: On board the ship of Brodir of Man—2, April 1014 A.D.—*She broke through the mist with her long slender fingers then passed the moisture over her black hair as it flowed behind her. The wind lifted the hem of her gauze lien, sending it rippling about her in a most attractive fashion. She reached for him, beckoning with a crooked finger. He went to her. He kissed her supple lips and felt their moisture with his tongue. She pushed him away as the clouds converged behind her, so close he could feel their mist as they swept his cheek.*

The lightening bolted as a warning for him to stand back, but he swallowed his fear, longing to be near her and clinging to her arm as the wind griped her ever backward.

Her eyes glowed yellow as she whispered, "If you battle on a Thursday all your men will die. The Irish king will have their heads and hang them out to dry. But if this battle, you decide, to fight on Frigga's day, success is yours—your men will live to fight another day."

She was gone; slipped through his grasp despite his warrior's hold on her. He bolted.

"Olaf! Come to me, son!"

Olaf crashed through the door, wild eyes sweeping the ship's cabin in search of danger. When he was certain there was none, he tucked his short sword into his belt then rushed to kneel beside his father's bed. "Aye, father. What's the trouble?"

Brodir tugged on the lad's arm as he lifted his head from his pillow. "This battle must be fought on Friday or we'll all die. My gods have foretold it. What say ye?"

Olaf turned a somber face. Since Brodir had renewed his loyalty to his pagan gods there was no rival for the visions they showed him or the extent they would go to support him. He was proof of that. "I say yer gods are indeed powerful so ye must heed their counsel. We'll tell Sigtrygg as soon as we lay anchor."

Brodir sighed relief, "Good, son. Now take yer rest with me. I want ye here in case of trouble."

"Aye, father," Olaf replied then curled upon the wooden floor of the ship.

He lay silent in the darkness for some time but when he didn't hear the deep breathing of sleep coming from his father, he turned his head to find the man staring at him. "What is it?"

"I was just thinking how much like yer mother ye are."

"Am I?" Olaf asked then thought of something else he'd been longing to know. He propped himself on his elbow. "Tell me of Patric the Shaver, father. Why do ye want him dead? Has it something to do with my mother?"

"Ah," Brodir sighed. "Ye're informants do well by ye." He too propped himself on his elbow then looked deep into Olaf's crystal blue eyes. "Ye're mother once belonged to the man but I took her back from him."

"So why do ye want him dead?"

There was a long silence and Olaf struggled to see his father's eyes in the darkness while he awaited the reply. "Because he killed her."

*   *   *   *

Clontarf, Ireland—22, April 1014 A.D.—Abandoned long ago for the more civilized city of Dublin, Clontarf was used as grazing land for Sigtrygg's cattle. It was located just north of the Viking city, adjacent to Dublin Bay. The ships of Ospak, Brodir and Sigurd laid anchor off shore, so closely knit that it was possible for a man to pass between them simply by stepping off one and onto the other. On the shores, a carnival unfurled as children and adults flocked to the clearing just north of the Dublin wall to get a glimpse of those who would be king of all Ireland.

Gaming booths stood in neat rows on either side of the road, their colorful banners waving as their hosts called out, "Dice, swords, spear toss, yancy! Try yer luck right here, mate!"

Just behind them stood the tents of the camp followers, the rows of customers stretching out nearly as far as the road. In front of one stood a rather large woman with sagging breasts and muscular arms. As Patric passed he realized she was a man.

Smells of roasted meats and breads covered the foul odor of the sheer masses and at every turn, vendors called out their wares only to be out cried by the beggars who followed them, awaiting the charity of a customer who might have something to spare.

Patric looked to where Njord and Eilis were sitting beside their fire. He was glad the two would have time together before the battle and for a moment, felt a pang of jealousy grip him that he wasn't similarly blessed in his marriage. As usual, Lara and Saroise were back in Cashel looking over the wares in the market there. Patric laughed to himself that they probably would be quite lonely since it seemed all of Ireland's vendors were in Clontarf.

Margreg was busy in her tent preparing ointments and bandages for wounded warriors but this time Eagan was by her side assisting. Patric walked over to them, taking a moment to offer his greeting to Thorien who was watching his eldest son best a lad in a wrestling match. "He's a warrior for certain."

"That he his," Thorien stated with pride swelling his chest. "Ye just wait and see what he does to those rots when we battle."

Patric nodded then looked over the field. Nearly thirty thousand warriors gathered for Brian's side alone. "Have ye seen Malsakin, yet?"

Thorien's forehead wrinkled. "Not yet. Someone said he would be coming late but I wonder if he'll be arriving at all."

Patric wondered too. He clapped Thorien on the back then continued on toward Margreg and Eagan. "Hail, Shaver," Eagan called when he spotted him "Are ye hungry, man? Margreg has prepared a wonderful stew."

Patric lowered his nose to the simmering kettle then took an empty bowl to fill it. He sat the rock beside Eagan then nodded toward the chessboard that was set up beside him. "Shall we have a game?"

"In the mood to have yer arse whipped?" Eagan mumbled between bites.

"We'll see about that," Patric replied then returned his attention to his bowl.

Ospak's heart pounded as he weaved through the Dal Cais camp wearing the Scottish kilt he'd purchased from the vendor. The whole of it brought a raised eyebrow from the elderly Gall but silver was silver, and a quarter ounce was five times what the kilt was worth. He had offered it in good riddance, taking a moment to show Ospak the many variations in the kilts use. But the foreigner was only interested in one, the simple cloaking wrap that would shroud his face as he moved through enemy lines.

He had offered his lie through a messenger, knowing Brodir's acute senses would alert him if he issued it in person. He couldn't attend the feast because he needed to prepare his warriors for their upcoming battle. It was half true. Indeed they would battle, but not for Brodir, instead he would bring his army to the great Brian Boru—the chosen winner of his gods.

He noticed two men playing chess in front of a healer's tent and decided that they might assist him in finding the Ard Ri. "I'm Ospak, brother of Brodir chief of Man. I've come to serve yer king in this battle. Will ye take me to the Ard Ri?"

Both Patric and Eagan looked to the man, watching as he withdrew the kilt to expose his face. Eagan grasped the hilt of his short sword then rose, tumbling the chessboard as he went. "Back away, man! All here know ye came to stand against Brian."

Ospak had expected as much but he swallowed his fear then continued, "I mean nay harm. I've come in peace. I know that yer king is fair and I've come to fight with him."

"Then where's yer army?" Patric asked as he too gripped his short sword.

Ospak looked to the man whose face was familiar to him. "I pray ye to take me to the Ard Ri. I've news that will assist him. I carry no weapons."

Patric cocked his head in a silent message for Eagan to check him out. He had met Ospak briefly in Italy. The one thing he knew about him was that he was capable with a blade. When they were satisfied that he carried no weapons, Patric stepped closer. "What news do ye bring, man?"

Ospak struggled to place Patric's face. "With respect, brother, my information is for king Brian's ears alone."

The interaction drew Njord's attention and in no time he was standing beside his father, sword drawn and ready for battle. "What is it ye seek, Ospak," he asked, the look in his eyes telling the Viking that there was enmity between them.

"Njord," Ospak stated with relief in his voice. "I've come with news that will assist Boru. Will ye take me to him?

Eilis had taken her place beside her mother inside the tent and Thorien and his sons encircled Ospak. If the Viking came to do Brian harm, it was clear that he would be thwarted. Njord lowered his sword then stepped closer. "Whatever ye have for Brian can be given to this man." He cocked his head toward his father. "He's Patric the Shaver, Boru's second. Either ye speak with him or ye'll be bled out. Do ye understand me, Ospak?"

Again Ospak looked to Patric. This time he remembered him from Italy. But there was something else. Patric the Shaver shared his face with young Olaf of Man—the reason for Ospak's treachery. He fell to his knees. "Forgive my forgetfulness, Shaver. My memory isn't what it once was."

"On yer feet man and tell us what ye know!"

Whether it was the damp evening air or the anxiety of the betrayal he was about to commit that caused it, Ospak wasn't sure, but a shiver began at his shoulders and traveled his spine to his feet. He stood. "Sigtrygg went to my brother to beg his assistance in taking down Brian. He offered his mother, Kormlada, and control of all Eire if he participated in this war."

Patric beat his thighs. "Wherever there's evil ye can be sure Kormlada's behind it."

Ospak continued, "My brother brings twenty ships carrying five hundred men each. Sigurd of Orkney brings the same."

"Ye're giving us information we already have," Havland interrupted as he joined the gathering. Ospak turned to see who had spoken and Havland continued, "Now why don't ye give us something that will help us, Ospak."

The beginning of a smile tugged at Ospak's lips when his one time friend was revealed to him but he held it back. It was a grave matter that they discussed. He didn't want anyone thinking that he wasn't serious. "The gods have foretold of Boru's success."

Havland and Njord exchanged knowing glances. Both Ospak and Brodir were great sorcerers but Ospak always did have a better understanding of the visions than his brother. Njord turned to Patric. "Ye must take him to Brian, father. The Ard Ri must know of this."

Patric looked the three men over. There was no doubt that Njord believed what Ospak had to say, it showed in the way that his eyes widened. Havland looked similarly. Ospak's eyes showed his sincerity.

"Very well," Patric replied then turned on his heel to head for Brian's tent. He held back the crowd with a wave of his hand then called at the tent flap, "May I speak with ye, Brian? I've news that ye should hear."

Brian exchanged glances with Murchad who ripped his attention from the chessboard he'd been perusing then called out, "Aye, Patric. What seems to be the trouble?"

Patric entered then wrung his hands. He never did understand the business of visions and sorcery but he did know that if Ospak stood with them there might be a chance for him to find his son. A shiver of emotion gripped him with the thought. "Ospak of Man is in our camp. He claims to have news of our victory."

Brian squinted then scratched his white beard. "Ospak? Brodir's brother?"

Patric shivered again. "Aye, Brian. He says he's come to serve ye. I think we should hear from him."

Brian nodded. "Aye, bring him in. If Brodir's own brother is willing to stand with us, I would be a fool to turn him away."

"Unless it's a trap," Murchad interrupted.

"Aye, unless it's that," Brian agreed. "But still the same we should hear him."

Patric poked his head through the tent flap and in a moment the tent bulged with the many men standing inside. Ospak stood at the center in front of the seated Ard Ri. He swallowed hard then began, "My brother is a sorcerer with great powers over the elements. His gods are quite faithful to him and have told him of his victory if he fights on Friday. But even though he's a great sorcerer, I have a greater understanding of the gods and their signs. What was shown to him as victory is indeed total annihilation." He fell to his knees to kiss Brian's ring. "I'd be honored to stand with ye against him, lord."

"Tell me why ye believe Brodir's sign to be wrong."

Ospak smiled as he spoke from his place at Brian's feet, "The other night, on board my ship, Brodir boasted that the black angel had come to him telling him of his demise if he fought on Thursday but his utter victory if he fought on Friday, the day holy to our goddess Frigga."

Brian knew a thing or two about pagan worship and Viking rituals. He gave a slight nod of understanding. Ospak continued, "What he doesn't realize is that tomorrow is Good Friday—the holy day of yer Christ. Brodir's gods can't possibly assist him while ye mark His day of sacrifice. Brodir's eagerness keeps him blind to the threat. His gods will surely turn on him for exposing them to failure."

Brian scratched his chin as his yellowing teeth parted the snowy whiteness of his beard. "So then, Ospak, ye've come to the camp of the clear winner. What's yer price for this news?"

Ospak prostrated himself before the great king. "I will bring my warriors to ye at dawn, great king. I only ask that ye allow us to find a home here within yer kingdom once we win this war. My nephew must be protected from my brother. I fear he may kill the lad."

Patric's breath hitched and Njord traded a knowing glance with him. Brian nodded, oblivious to who the nephew was, but still it touched him that Ospak could care so deeply for the lad. "Look around ye, Ospak. Those loyal to me come from many places but what keeps them by my side is their love for Eire. Swear the same and ye shall be welcomed."

"I swear to ye, Brian Boru and I will fight to protect Eire."

Brian patted Ospak's shoulder then got to his feet calling the Viking up with him.

"Very well," he thrilled. "We'll fight tomorrow and receive our victory!"

"Long live, Brian!" came the voice from the tent opening.

They turned to see Tann standing there, his voice cracked as he called out again, "Long live, Brian!"

Murchad went to stand beside him then rubbed his shoulders before exiting the tent. "Aye, son. Long live, Brian."

The smiling teen dutifully held open the tent flap for the other warriors to pass but just as Patric began to make his way out, Brian called to him. "Stay and speak with me, Shaver. There's something I'd like to share with ye."

Patric was anxious to speak with Ospak alone but he turned to look at Brian and his mouth fell open. For the first time since Patric had known him, Brian suddenly looked old. His hair was still a riot of curls but now they were white, tinged with yellow from their formerly ruddy hue. His jowls had begun to sag and his posture was a bit stooped. But the fire in his eyes that intimidated so many still burned. He took the stool the Ard Ri offered. "What is it, Brian?"

"Ye lived as a Viking. Do ye believe Ospak's gods?"

Patric sighed. "I never did understand their religious ways but Havland and Njord seem to believe him. With so many lined up against us, I'm ready to believe him as well."

"'Tis good of him to want to save his nephew. Men have fought with all their heart for less than that."

Patric nodded his agreement, wondering what tortures his son had been suffering to bring Ospak to turn against his brother. Brian continued, "I think I shall have Ospak speak to the troops to give them encouragement. They'll pull strength from his story to ensure our victory where Brodir's gods may fail to assist."

He wiped his face with his hands then kept them there. Patric stood to rub his shoulders. "What else, Brian?"

Brian smiled behind his hands, grateful for his friend's knowing. He turned to look over his shoulder. "I've a feeling that I'm going to lose something in this battle. My stomach turns with a sense of loss but I can't put my finger on why. Our troops are ready and now we have Ospak. I don't think I'll lose the crown but I fear that I'll lose something personal." He sighed as he looked through watery eyes. "I fear I'll lose Murchad."

Patric squeezed Brian's shoulders sympathetically. He too felt that he would face a loss though he couldn't put his finger on what it was. Perhaps they were both getting too old for war. He moved to stand before his king, leveling his gaze to inspire trust. "Don't fear for Murchad, Brian. I'll fight at his back myself."

Brian rose then drew him into an embrace. "Promise me ye'll look after him, Patric. Let no ill befall him."

"I'll look after him as if he were my own son. Ye shouldn't worry for him, Brian."

The Ard Ri forced a smile but his eyes didn't agree. "I feel better for that, Shaver. Ye ease my heart."

Patric embraced his king but when he withdrew, his own eyes were somber. There was still a bit of business unfinished between the two and Patric swallowed hard in preparation for it. "Now I'd like to make a request of ye, Brian."

Brian raised a quizzical eyebrow but Patric turned away—unable to look into the eyes that would draw pain from his words. "I wish to provide ye a shield burg. I've fifteen solid warriors who'll throw up their shields around ye and protect ye from any who'll break through the line."

The Ard Ri's eyes narrowed and his fists clenched as his old friend delivered the blow to his ego. Shield burgs were for the weak or infirm, or worse, for the cowards. More than seventy years on God's earth still found Brian Boru macCennitig tough as steel. Though his eyesight was failing him terribly, he didn't need a shield burg to protect him. His instinct was to lash out at his trusted friend but he didn't. If Patric was the one to bring him the news it must have first come from others who would worry more for him if he fought than for their own safety in the battle at hand.

Brian moved forward with concession bitter on his lips. Before he offered it, he threw a massive embrace around the Shaver's shoulder. "I'll tell ye what we'll do, son. Ye may place a shield burg around me if it will help ye fight clear of mind but when this war is won ye and I will go into the woods to fight hand to hand. I'll show ye that Boru isn't too old to defend himself."

A painful smile broke Patric's face. Offering the shield burg to the great Brian Boru was probably the most difficult thing he ever had to do. "I look forward to having my arse reddened by yer hand, Brian," he croaked.

"Get out of here now and let me think," Brian barked.

Patric exited eager to find Ospak. To his great relief both he and Njord were waiting for him. "Father," Njord called as he rushed him. "Ospak has news of the lad."

Patric didn't need to inquire who the lad was. He led them both to his tent then took a seat in preparation for what he was about to hear. "It is because of Olaf that I have given myself to Brian, Shaver," Ospak began. "He's a good lad. Just as capable with his head as he is with a blade but I fear my brother has tormented him beyond human capacity. I want him to be free of the torture so that he can live life as he should."

"Where is he?" Patric asked.

"He's in Dublin with his fath—with Brodir."

"Does Brodir mean for him to fight?" Njord asked, continuing the line of questions to reduce the tension.

"That he does," Ospak replied. "He'll keep him by his side too. He barely lets the lad out of his sight."

"Very well," Patric replied as he slowly rose from his stool. "If I have to kill Brodir to get at my son then it may as well be done quickly." He turned to Ospak. "On the field tomorrow, I expect ye to mark yer brother's position and tell me of it, aye."

"It will be done, Shaver."

Patric waved a hand to dismiss them but Njord lingered behind. "It will be all right, father. We will win tomorrow."

Patric nodded, but didn't speak. There were too many things riding on this war and he needed to think them over. Njord understood his father's silence. He nodded then left the tent.

Patric's sleep was fitful at best. Moments of his life came back to haunt him. He dreamed of the night that Lorca gathered his men before they marched to Sulcoit. He dreamed of the night Volkren killed his father. He dreamed of the day he found Njord in Torshav. He dreamed of his son, though he couldn't make out his face. And finally, he dreamed of his own death. He woke with a start, sweat pouring from his face as he stared blankly around his tent. There were noises outside—noises of men preparing for battle. The day was finally upon them.

Fladbartoc moved around his tent, his mind dutifully reciting the battle plan laid at the feast the night before. The crown of Ireland had been promised to so many men that it was clear there would be a battle following this battle to see who would claim it. "First things first," he said to himself as he began to dress.

Kormlada looked down from the Dublin wall to see both camps stirring to life. In the distance she saw Sigtrygg walking alone along the shoreline. He was looking to the sea as if he expected to draw strength from it and for a moment she cursed herself for bringing this trouble upon them.

Behind Sigtrygg stood Maelmora and Brodir inspecting the earl's troops. Her brother's face was somber and deep lines creased his forehead. She knew he hated her.

Just north of them stood Sigurd of Orkney. The fat earl was making a display over how he wanted his banner to be held. "Stupid man," she mumbled to herself, certain the man wouldn't live past noon.

To the west she saw the Ard Ri's tent with the banner of three lions dancing atop it. As Brian emerged the wind pushed back his long, white hair exposing his face. He lifted his nose to smell the morning air and a smile split his beard. She knew he loved this time of day most of all.

"Damn ye, Brian," she muttered as the tear escaped her eye. She still loved him.

He turned, looking up at the wall as if he had heard her voice. It was a strange thing, Brian thought to himself, how failing eyesight could sometimes conjure such lovely visions. The rising sun behind the clouds was spreading an array of colors in the east making it seem as though an angel was standing upon the Dublin wall. He laughed at the thought that it was probably a flagpole enchanting him then he thought of Kormlada.

"I would have happily died in yer arms, woman," he mumbled to himself before making his way toward the forest so that he could relieve himself.

Kormlada's watched him go. The sorrow in her heart so heavy she thought it would crack.

In the distance she spotted Murchad speaking with Donchad and suddenly sadness turned to anger. Brian had taken her son from her and given him to that rot to foster. Now the two of them would stand together as her enemy. "I'll have ye back," she whispered in the wind. Brian wouldn't let Donchad fight. He wasn't ready.

She looked up and down the row of tents on either side in search of Malsakin. No sign of him. "Coward," she spit then looked to the sea where a mist was gathering.

The steam rose off the horses as they skittered sideways only to be reined back into compliance by the warriors waiting on the cold field of Clontarf. The lazy fog rolled across in a low, tumbling fashion, leaving a chilled kiss on their faces and their metal implements of war. Patric's bay mare reared, pawing at the air as she called out imagined trouble. He leaned across to place his warm hand upon her chest then offered her a soothing cluck of his tongue but her fear was contagious and soon several of the other horses rose on their hind legs to whinny into the wind.

The sight caused several warriors to invoke the name of Christ as they sank to their knees crossing themselves. Patric cut the haze with his hand, breaking it open to reveal Eagan before him. "Bring them to their feet man! If they continue like that they'll put the shakes into the entire army."

Eagan pressed a firm foot into his horse's ribs then slowly edged forward through the fog in search of a foot captain. Under the cover of his cloak, Patric crossed himself as he mumbled, "Dear, Lord, I pray ye to shroud us with yer protection against these pagans."

His prayers were cut short as Ospak rode up with Brian. He gave the bay mare a gentle kick so that he could join them and together they made their way to a large boulder at the far end of the field. Ospak stood the rock as the warriors gathered before him. He opened his arms and dutifully recited that which he'd told the Ard Ri the day previous.

A slow murmur of confidence began to rise from the crowd, rolling softly like the distant ocean waves then building slowly like galloping horses, then more clearly like thunder until it exploded into a full blown chant that carried on the wind to reach the farthest mountaintops leaving absolutely no doubt of its message:

"Boru!"

"Boru!"

"Boru!"

Brian stood the rock next, his voice shattering the chant, "Have nay fear, warriors of Eire that there are sons of the great Cormac Cas who are not among us. Pray for them for they have lost their way, choosing the side of foreign plunderers against their kin who have vowed to protect Eire from their scourge. They will be put asunder along with their O'Neill cohorts, to loot our homes and raid our monasteries never again. The Almighty God will bless us this day, giving us strength and courage to end forever the Viking tyranny we have been forced to live under lo these many years. Ye will be witness to this great event—the day when the Vikings will be forever forced from the soil of Eire."

He stopped and the low thunder again breached the air to fill his body and soul with the absolute pleasure of knowing that what he'd spent his life fighting for was now in the hearts and on the lips of every warrior who stood before him:

"Boru!"

"Boru!"

"Boru!"

"We'll fight for our God, and our honor, and watch as the pagan gods they worship are thrown forever into the abyss. In Jesus' eyes ye're already victorious for ye fight on the side of humanity. And if ye should happen to fall in this mighty battle know that ye'll live forever in His kingdom of heaven."

His chest heaved as the tears rolled from his eyes, hanging precariously on his nose before dropping to the ground. "Eire belongs to ye!"

Like a song on the wind the crystal clear voice of Brian Boru—Emperor of all Ireland rang in the ears of the mighty army, stirring feelings of strength, love, and a willingness to fight in the heart of each and every warrior. They sang for him,

"Boru!"

"Boru!"

"Boru!"

He bent to rip his banner from the young bearer. It surrounded him, waving freely on the wind for all to see! Njord urged his horse forward, drawing Patric's attention away from the scene. "They are ready, father."

Patric nodded then suddenly a ray of sunlight broke through the mist to fall upon Brian, making him look holy while the banner waved freely behind him. In that moment, Patric knew that they would be victorious. Ireland would finally be free.

Soon the clouds parted and the sun shone down upon the field, drying it out so that the feet of thousands of warriors kicked up enough dust to cloud the spring day. The horn sounded and confusion reigned supreme as Viking allied with Gael, Gael fought beside Viking, and a brother turned traitor brought his pagans to Boru.

Deciphering enemies was virtually impossible without first looking to the banners of the nobles, a daunting task that could find one without a head if their eyes weren't on the battle. It was unfocused; it was chaos; it was every grand thing that ever happened in their world with the most there was to gain or lose as the lines of division blurred and men fell to the blades of their comrades, bleeding the field red beneath the weight of their feet.

The clash of metal deafened them. The cries of the Viking rang in their head, spinning and pressing their brains as they wondered what wrong deed in their life forced them to be a part of this ghastly and gory detail of men who fought for hearth and home and country and for freedom to follow their way as they saw fit, and to have a good king or riches or nothing at all.

The morning sun fell to noon and the shadows loomed more ominous then the mighty golden Vikings standing like trees before them but the Gael wouldn't back down. Sigurd of Orkney's banner fell three times until no one else would lift it. Finally he picked it up himself, making him a target for the Gael riding forward with his spear. It was down a fourth and final time.

Maelmora turned to look as the slovenly earl fell to his death. There would be one less competitor for the high crown. He moved forward in search of Sigtrygg but was cut down when Eagan rode out from the trees to take his life.

O'Kelly was huge, standing half a head taller than Brian, but unlike Brian, he was nearly as wide as he was tall. There was no fear in him, never had been. Long ago, he placed his life in God's hands, an act he never regretted in the years since. He carried no long sword because he claimed the scabbard only added to his girth, instead he fought with the short blade—always had.

With his chunky hand, he flicked the orange curl from his forehead where it insisted it should rest, willing it to stay put until he finished off this lot. They faced him now, all three. One used an ax, the other two the long blade.

O'Kelly circled with his feet spread wide, his fingers dallying and crooking his challengers to come forward but they didn't. Instead, they followed his dance, waiting for the moment that his clear blue eyes would stop their incessant probing to leave them open to strike.

"Come on now, one of you—strike me!" O'Kelly growled. "I'm getting hungry from this dance and I only just finished eating one of yer brothers for lunch."

They continued to circle, unwilling to leave themselves open. Patric shook his head for the man's victims as he marched over to them. "These men giving you trouble O'Kelly."

It was all that was needed. One Viking turned and O'Kelly jabbed him in the eye, sending him screaming into the flailing blade of his comrade. "It appears the Lord still looks favorably on me, Shaver," he chuckled, slitting the throat of the second man. The third fled towards the woods. O'Kelly gave chase. "I'll be back,

Shaver. Now, don't ye go killing all the heathens by yerself without leaving any for me."

"Then ye better hurry it, O'Kelly," Patric yelled after him.

The sun was nearly down, adding blindness to the many plagues the battle offered. Patric squinted against the darkness, slashing out toward the faceless voices hidden in the fog rolling in from the bay. There was still no sign of Ospak or the son he had never met.

Through the last glimmer of sunlight breaking through the clouds, Thorien revealed himself, his head standing far taller than Fladbartoc's. Patric watched as the Limerick earl pierced Fladbartoc through stomach, neck and shoulder in three swift movements. "That's it," he called to Patric when the Ri Tuath fell over lifeless.

Patric lifted Fladbartoc by the scruff of the neck when he heard the call coming from the trees. "Come quick—O'Kelly's down! My master has fallen. There's a massacre in the woods!"

Njord heard it from his place just south of where Patric and Thorien fought. He had sent Margreg and Eilis into the woods hours earlier when the lines began threatening the campsite. He peered through the trees, trying to catch a glimpse of them but the fog was too thick to see anything further than the end of his nose.

He heard a man's voice ahead of him and raised his sword blindly, praying he wasn't about to cut down one of his own. He recognized the Orkney dialect and pressed his blade forward, feeling it enter the flesh of his enemy. There was a gurgle then a cough until finally the man fell dead at his feet. He cut through the fog with his hand to see a golden haired child, no more than seventeen years old, lying on the ground, his eyes blank as his arms reached toward the heavens.

"Eilis—Margreg!" he called as he moved through the trees, aware that his voice might draw the blade of an enemy. He felt a presence just before him then stopped to see if any sound accompanied it. He could hear fighting further into the woods—to the south what sounded like laughter. Ahead of him there was silence.

He moved forward slowly until the presence took shape before him. It was the body of a woman, pinned to the tree by an arrow in her chest. She had long hair and was just about Eilis' height. His heart pounded as he moved forward to lift her head. It was Varna.

"Eilis! Are ye here, wife?" He cocked his ear waiting for a response but the only sound he heard was the whistle of metal as it sailed through the air then the thud as it cut his flesh. With an explosion of heat his right shoulder split to spill hot blood down his arm. He bit his lip as he steadied the blade in both hands then rushed forward, split shoulder first, to knock his attacker to the ground.

The man thrashed and howled beneath him as Njord felt along his body until he found his face. He drew back his left fist to deliver a blow square to the chin then repeated the action until the thrashing stopped. He drew his blade across his neck to make sure it wouldn't start again.

He was winded and his shoulder was bleeding badly. He remained on his knees as he called, "Eilis. Where are ye, wife?"

"Is that ye, Njord?" Vahn called out to him.

Njord squinted to bring the shadow into focus but the fog was too thick. He heard a woman scream in the distance then a clash of metal. He dragged himself forward. "Call out again, Vahn! I can not see ye."

"I'm here, lo…." He strained his ear as Vahn's words were suddenly left hanging in the air. He stepped forward and his foot brushed something that sent an instant shock of dread through his body. He waved away the fog then bent low to see Vahn's head lying at his feet.

Gripped by both grief and pain, he didn't hear the blade coming, only felt it. This one sliced his thigh, opening a wound that exposed the muscle. He looked down at it but instead saw Vahn's blue eyes cooling to white as the blood released from his severed head. An unholy fury built within in him as he swallowed hard and cocked his ear before steadying his sword in his split arm. He charged forward into the mist to pin Vahn's killer against a tree with his sword, kneeing his enemy repeatedly in the groin before forcing his short blade deep into his heart. The sharp smell of blood reached his nostrils then he yanked back his blade to let the dead man slip to the ground.

He took a moment to say a silent prayer for his captain then turned toward what now sounded like a full fledged battle. It came from the north and he made his way there dragging his bad leg behind him. There was so much blood that it dripped from the trees onto his face forcing him to wipe it away with his sleeves. The ground was slippery with human excrement. The air was fetid. He pulled his lein up to cover his nose then limped forward as quietly as he could, struggling to make out the many forms looming ahead of him.

He heard a woman scream and he moved west, deeper into the forest. There was an opening in the trees where sunlight broke the fog. Several warriors were huddled over the woman and she was thrashing against them as she called out for help.

He attacked from the rear, piercing one man through the heart before stumbling forward. The second caught him with his short blade to the cheek. Njord grabbed his arm to flip him over his head. He ripped the blade from the man's hand then used it to cut his throat. The woman screamed then scrambled away leaving Njord facing the last man. It was young Jared, Tyr's companion in Man.

"Ye should have stayed in Man," he growled low in his throat before lunging.

Other than the drops of blood spattered across his face, Jared seemed untouched by the battle. He was fresh and quick and he sidestepped Njord's swipe easily.

Njord tried again. This time Jared spun away but when he returned his sword was bared. "I mean ye no harm, Njord," he said in Manx as he moved his blade between his hands. "Ye're obviously wounded. I do not wish to challenge ye. Let me go and perhaps we shall meet again when this is over."

Njord struggled to steady himself on his feet. Though Jared was once his charge, today he was his enemy. He leveled his gaze against the young man but just as he was about to attack, Jared's eyes went wide and he fell to his knees.

Njord looked behind him to the shadow that stood in the distance. He called out in Manx, "Who are ye, man?" There was silence as the shadow drew closer. It was a small man wearing a hooded cloak. He carried a long sword in his right hand but he wasn't presenting it in battle for the moment.

Another shadow appeared just behind the man and Njord watched it to see what it would do. He lifted his sword and Njord called out in Gaelic, "Behind ye!"

Understanding the words, the man spun on his heel, presenting his sword in time to swipe the enemy at his side. He lunged again and this time his sword pierced his enemy through his neck. The man stood there for a moment, waiting for the body of his enemy to cease its movements before he removed the blade. Then he stepped back.

Njord watched him, wondering what this cloaked one was all about. It was obvious he was Gael—hopefully an ally. He decided to move forward so they could fight at each other's back.

When he stepped between the trees he heard the branch creak above him. He looked up in time to see a man descending upon him. He was large and stunk of onions. It was Throdier.

Njord tried to escape but his leg dragged behind him and before he knew it he was on the ground with Throdier on his back. He struggled to hold off the dagger that was coming toward his throat but Throdier's weight against his shoulder made it nearly impossible. He heard a woman's scream in the distance and thought of Eilis. It may well be her calling out to him but he was certain he would never know. The dagger was coming closer and he was powerless to stop it. He closed his eyes then chanted the words that would prepare him for Valhalla, first silently, then out loud. The enemy stopped his movement.

It took time for Njord to realize that Throdier no longer posed a threat. He threw him from his back then spun around in a striking position. He looked down at him then to the cloaked one who stood above him, blade in hand dripping with Throdier's blood. "Who are ye?" he asked as he wiped his face with his sleeve.

The cloaked one drew breath then all at once collapsed into tears. "Thank God that yer safe."

Confused by the action, Njord cocked his head trying to make out the voice. All at once it dawned on him and he rushed forward blindly, reaching out through the mist to grab his wife to him. "Eilis. I can't believe it's ye, woman."

He threw back her hood to reveal her face marked by the blood of the many enemies she had slain to get to him. Her right eye was swollen and tender and so was her cheek. He rubbed his thumb against it. "M'millish! What did they do to ye?"

She shook her head and sobbed until she had no more breath. She gasped then clawed her way closer to him until he thought that their bodies were nearly one. "Come away from here, now," he said to her. He tried to lift her into his arms but the pain was too much for him. He drew her close around the waist. "Come now."

She looked at him and when she noticed the gashes in his shoulder and in his leg she gasped. "Njord, ye're hurt."

She undid her cape then with quick, fluid movements, stripped the hem of it into bandages. "Come," she whispered, looking over her shoulder to be certain that her voice didn't draw the attention of an enemy. "Let me bandage ye before we go any further."

He wanted to protest that they should be away first but in reality he didn't know where danger would be lurking. They were safe for the moment. He might as well have his wounds tended so that he would be better able to defend her should they come upon another enemy. He moved to the rock she pointed to then silently lowered himself to it. She made quick work of bandaging his shoulder and he watched her face as she did it. "Where's Margreg?"

"Dead," she answered, not bothering to look up at him.

He stroked her face then brushed back her hair to hook it behind her ear. She looked up and he saw the pain in her eyes. "I'm sorry, m'millish. I thought ye would be safe."

She turned her attention to his wounded thigh. Again she stripped the cloth of her cloak, the rip of it echoing through the forest. From what they could hear the fighting had moved further north but still she waited a moment to see if the sound had drawn someone's attention before kneeling down in front of him to apply the bandage.

He kept his eyes roving the trees while she concentrated on her task but darkness was falling quickly and the thick fog continued to roll in. She pulled the material tight around his thigh and he jumped from the pain of it. He looked down at her for a moment and then he heard it—the whistle of metal as it sang through the air. It was coming from the east. He looked up to see the movement in the distance then he caught the flash of metal as it sailed directly for them.

There was a thud and Eilis straightened her back then lifted her head to look askance of him. He could see the tears welling in her eyes and her mouth opening as if she wanted to say something. All at once her eyes closed and she slumped forward against him, resting her head in his lap.

The handle of the short sword protruded from her back. It entered just below her left shoulder blade and was buried up to the hilt. Reflexively, he pulled it from her body then closed his eyes as the blood pumped furiously from the wound. There was no doubt she was dead. He heard the gurgle before she fell against him but still he checked her eyes, pulling her lids up hoping that some miracle would occur and that he would see life in them. There was nothing but white.

He drew her to him, holding her by the neck to kiss her face over and again as his tears moistened her face. They had waited so long to be together and now she was gone.

The snap of the branch drew his attention back to the enemy who was approaching and the blood in his veins boiled with the need to take his revenge. He slipped Eilis from him, resting her head against the rock before drawing his sword in preparation for battle. The tall, thin shadow continued to move closer. When it stepped into the ray of light breaking through the trees, Njord's hatred burned anew.

"Turlog!"

Turlog grinned evilly, his one good eye raking Njord from head to toe. He had been passing the clearing on his way out to the field when he noticed Eilis tending the Viking. It was the fact that Njord was injured that made him stop. The Viking had taken his eye long ago now he meant to take his life.

"So now," Turlog cooed flicking his blade before him. "Ye seek yer vengeance and I seek mine. Who do ye think will win?"

Njord lunged forward but Turlog stepped back forcing Njord's blade to hit the ground. Njord turned then tried again. Though old, Turlog was quite agile and he skittered sideways, catching Njord's blade with the tip of his to angle it away from him.

There was death in Njord's eyes and Turlog saw it. He stepped back a few paces until he was behind a tree but Njord lunged forward with the short sword that had killed his wife firmly in his grasp. He struck out and caught the tree. Turlog rolled against it then withdrew several yards back to the edge of the woods. Njord followed, jumping over bramble and bushes to lunge at the old man again. With no short sword to use, Turlog found it hard to defend himself. The trees were snuggled so closely together that he didn't have enough clearance for his blade. He backed up further, slipping his thin form between the trees and forcing Njord's thick body to go in search of a space wide enough for him to pass.

Turlog stepped out onto the field. He gave a quick glimpse over his shoulder noticing that the Vikings had begun to withdraw toward the sea. When he entered the woods earlier he was certain that victory would go to Sigtrygg but now he didn't feel so sure. There was no more time to think about it, Njord was on him, swinging both long blade and short with impunity. Turlog blocked the first several blows easily enough but suddenly Njord drew back long to come down on his shoulder with a force that nearly severed Turlog's arm.

The old king gasped then looked to the wound that was gaping enough to expose the bone. He watched as the blood pooled into it then all at once turned his head as his hand was separated from his wrist by the next blow. His eyes went wide and Njord laughed, pulling him by the hair to draw him back into the woods. His head began to swim and everything went fuzzy.

Njord pushed him against a tree. Turlog opened his mouth to say something but he didn't have time. Njord drew back again then rammed his long sword through him. Turlog's chest exploded with heat. He tried to breathe but there was no air in his lungs. Suddenly everything went dark.

He gave a final twitch telling Njord he was dead and the Viking withdrew his blade to let the man crumble to the ground. Njord fell to his knees sobbing.

Patric turned to see where the sound was coming from. When he saw Njord kneeling before Turlog's dead body he headed straight for him but suddenly two riders broke through the forest. Brodir was one—the other was a young lad with close cropped red hair who could only be Olaf. He watched as they galloped up the rise toward the tents.

"Come on, son," he called to Njord before spinning on his heel.

Patric ran as fast as his legs would take him, his eyes roving the field in search of Murchad. The northern Ri Ciocid had been fighting just east of him when he turned to look at Njord but now he didn't see his banner anywhere. He jumped onto a rock then scanned the field. The fog was rolling in from the bay like a blanket against the ground, covering men up to their waists. The Vikings were beginning to retreat. In the distance, he could see them jumping into the bay heading for their ships as the Gaelic army pushed them further east. He spotted Havland immediately to his north and waved an arm at him to gain his attention.

Havland's face was grim. He called out, "Murchad is down. The northern Ri Ciocid is dead!"

The blood drained from Patric's face as the words settled on him. Murchad was dead. He failed Brian.

He turned toward the Ard Ri's tent wondering how he would relay the news when he noticed Brodir and Olaf galloping toward it. The shield burg was in motion, one man after the other moved forward against the Vikings only to be struck down by the two blades that seemed far more skilled than theirs. Patric's stomach gripped. He jumped from the rock holding his sword out before him as he yelled out to Havland and Njord. "Follow me! The shield burg is falling!"

He weaved through the many tents until he came upon the one that was Brian's. Olaf sat alone upon his horse, his face splattered with blood. His crystal blue eyes foretold the hatred in his heart as he looked toward Brian's tent.

Patric followed his gaze to see the shadows outlined against the canvass. One carried a sword—the other two were unarmed. He heard Brodir call out, "Now let man tell man that Brodir killed Brian," then all at once his sword lowered and Brian's head was separated from his shoulders.

"Nay!" Patric called before heading for the tent but in a moment he was down, staring up into those crystal blue eyes of hate as Olaf sat astride him. He didn't know what he had expected to find when he looked into his son's eyes. Perhaps some glint of recognition or a blood bond that would draw them together. All he found was utter hatred.

He followed Olaf's hand to see it above him, grasping the dagger firmly. It was moving down toward his throat and he called out, "Nay, son, don't do it," but it was too late. It exploded through his throat like a hot poker. In a moment he was gasping for air.

He watched the lad's eyes as the hatred was exchanged for humor then turned to see Brodir leave the tent. When the tent flap lifted, he caught a glimpse of Brian's headless body sprawled across the ground with Tann lying atop him, one hand missing as he bled out. Then there was darkness.

Njord arrived just in time to see Olaf push the dagger through Patric's throat. Moments later Brodir slipped from Brian's tent. When the earl noticed Olaf's kill he clapped the lad on the back then howled as if he had been vindicated. But when he turned to mount his horse Njord grabbed him.

Njord used his dagger to slice Brodir at wrist, neck and thigh causing blood to flow from the severed arteries. The earl tried to lash out against him but he was bleeding too quickly, weakening him until he was nearly feeble.

Olaf moved in to save his father but Njord disarmed him then pushed him into Havland's arms. "Tie him up but don't kill him," he called.

Havland growled low in his throat. The command went against every one of his instincts but if Njord commanded it there must be a reason for it. He punched the lad square in the chin, rendering him unconscious to make binding him that much easier.

Njord dragged Brodir to the nearest rock then slit his stomach open, pulling out his entrails to wind them around a rock. The earl would die a slow, Viking death.

They watched him die then Njord and Havland both turned as Eagan came barreling up the hill.

"We've won," the captain cried. "They're fleeing to their ships."

He pointed toward the bay where the foreigners were scurrying into the water. Chaotically, ships broke free of their moorings, slamming against each other as they beat a hasty retreat toward the sea. Those Vikings who weren't lucky enough to catch them drowned.

The Gaels lined the shore celebrating their victory. They wouldn't know that their Ard Ri was dead for some time.

"Hold him," Njord said to Havland as he looked south to the Dublin wall. A lone figure stood atop it—the one responsible for his loses. He would make her pay. "I've business to tend."

Eagan looked to the lad Njord was referring to then down to the ground where Patric lay dead. He gasped before throwing himself onto his master's body.

Kormlada turned in time to see Njord's gaze fall upon her. As her gods predicted, Murchad, Brian and Patric were dead. She had known that Brodir and Sigurd would fall as well but was surprised by the loss of her brother. Sigtrygg survived—so did Njord. Now the battle for the high crown would be between them. She was certain Njord would win.

As Njord stood there with the remnants of Brodir's innards in his hands, Kormlada saw the blue haze of power deepen around him. He was looking at her as if he could see her then he began to move forward. He took a moment to exchange a few words with Havland before mounting Brodir's horse. He galloped forward.

She held her breath as he rode toward the Dublin gate. There was no doubt in her mind that he was coming for her. Together they would claim Ireland for their own.

Suddenly riders galloped into his path and her stomach gripped. It was Malsakin and his men. They encircled Njord then stood speaking for some time. This time when Njord looked to the Dublin wall a wry smile adorned his face. He nodded his head before offering Malsakin his hand then together they moved forward.

Kormlada leaned over the edge of the wall trying to see where they had gone. Her visions foretold nothing of Malsakin so therefore he mustn't figure into things. But still her stomach gripped. Moments later she heard footsteps approaching.

She whirled around. Her dread all consuming as she anxiously called upon her gods to assist her. Malsakin appeared before her, bedecked in his finest lein and jewelry—untouched by the war. He moved forward and she took a step back but soon he had her in his arms. He pressed his mouth to hers while he pushed the dagger into her chest. He held her there until she gave up the struggle.

Njord watched as the golden goddess collapsed into Malsakin's arms. She was pure evil and he rued the day he ever laid eyes on her. It was easy for him to give up his claim on Ireland's crown once Malsakin told him what he was going to do. First he reclaimed the woman and now he would reclaim the high throne without her interference.

*   *   *   *

On Good Friday, April 23, in the year of our lord 1014 A.D., Brodir of Man killed Brian Boru macCennitig, Emperor of all Ireland. On that same day, Malsakin the Great reclaimed Ireland's high crown.

*   *   *   *

The funeral procession for the Ard Ri stretched for miles along the road as it headed north to Armagh. Brian's body was carried on a wagon strewn with flowers. Murchad's body followed behind. At the head of the procession rode Malsakin the Great—Ireland's Ard Ri once again.

Donchad, who had been named Ri Tuath Ruire of Munster, led one thousand men ten abreast. Behind them marched the Leinster contingent—equal in amount being led by its new Ri Tuath Ruire, Njord the Black. Havland, Thorien, Falkien, Eagan and Yon marched beside him. Following them was the carriage of the high queen.

"I can't believe she still lives," someone in the crowd mumbled as Kormlada passed with the procession, referring to her age and not the wound she had suffered at Malsakin's hand.

"Aye, and she's as beautiful as ever," came the reply.

Njord looked over his shoulder toward Kormlada's wagon and he felt the shiver run up his spine. She was wearing the white lein and fur-trimmed cloak she liked so well. Her hands were bound to the carriage.

When she miraculously recovered from her wound Malsakin decided that he had no choice other than to keep her close so she couldn't bring about mischief. Though Njord agreed that it was the best plan the man could lay, he wasn't sure there was anything on earth that could keep the woman from mischief.

978-0-595-36512-8
0-595-36512-4

801120007

CPSIA information can be obtained at www.ICGtesting.com
Printed in the USA
LVOW031649051011

249255LV00001B/63/A